ABOUT THE AUTHORS

NELSON DeMILLE is the #1 *New York Times* bestselling author of twenty-one novels, including his most recent #1 *New York Times* bestseller, *The Cuban Affair*. Two of his novels, *Mayday* and *Word of Honor*, were made into TV movies, and *The General's Daughter* was made into a major motion picture starring John Travolta and Madeleine Stowe. He has written short stories, book reviews, and articles for magazines and newspapers. Nelson DeMille is a combat-decorated U.S. Army veteran, a member of Mensa, Poets & Writers, and the Authors Guild, and a member and past president of the Mystery Writers of America. He is also a member of the International Thriller Writers, who honored him as 2015 Thriller Master of the Year. He lives on Long Island with his family.

Learn more at www.nelsondemille.net
twitter: @nelsondemille
instagram: @nelsondemilleauthor
facebook: /NelsonDeMilleAuthor

ALEX DeMILLE is a writer, director, and film editor. He grew up on Long Island and received a BA from Yale University and an MFA in film directing from UCLA. He has won multiple awards and fellowships for his screenplays and films, including *The Absence*, which was named Best Film at Comic-Con. He has edited numerous commercials, shorts, and independent feature films, among them *My Nephew Emmett*, which was nominated for an Academy Award for Best Live Action Short in 2018. He lives in Brooklyn with his wife and daughter. *The Deserter* is his debut novel.

Learn more at www.alexdemille.com
twitter: @alexdemille
instagram: @alexdemille
facebook: /AlexDeMilleAuthor

THE DESERTER

NELSON DEMILLE

AND ALEX DEMILLE

sphere

SPHERE

First published in the United States in 2019 by Simon & Schuster
First published in Great Britain in 2019 by Sphere

13 5 7 9 10 8 6 4 2

Copyright © 2019 by Nelson DeMille and Alex DeMille

The moral right of the author has been asserted.

A CIP catalogue record for this book
is available from the British Library.

Hardback ISBN 978-0-7515-6574-4
Trade Paperback ISBN 978-0-7515-6573-7

Printed and bound in Great Britain by Clays Ltd, Elocgraf S.p.A.

Papers used by Sphere are from well-managed forests
and other responsible sources.

Sphere
An imprint of
Little, Brown Book Group
Carmelite House
50 Victoria Embankment
London EC4Y 0DZ

An Hachette UK Company
www.hachette.co.uk

www.littlebrown.co.uk

To the memory of
Sandy DeMille,
wife, mother, sister

PART I

PART I

PESHAWAR, PAKISTAN
AUGUST 2017

CHAPTER 1

Kyle Mercer walked across the bare room. He had been on his feet for days, hiking across the tribal frontier, into the outskirts of this ancient city, down the canted streets of the old quarter, and into this empty apartment where the walls were covered with peeling paint and splotches of black mold.

A plastic tarp flapped against the third-story window, moved by the warm winds rolling down from the valley. The tarp flashed a sliver of hot sunlight; then the room was dark again. Outside he heard the bustle of the street market, the rapid-fire Pashto tongue that had become familiar to him over the years. But it was different here. Here there were more people, more tongues, the staccato voices overlapping and bouncing off the close mud-brick walls of the old city.

He wanted to walk now, down in the bazaar, past the piles of fruit and nuts and spices. To touch and taste and smell. He wanted to find a woman to fuck.

But instead he was here, in the bare room, in the dark. Here, he had work to do. Here, there was no one to fuck. Just someone to hurt.

The guy was still passed out, slumped in the wooden chair, hands tied behind him. His face was battered. He drooled a line of blood.

Mercer walked over to the man and slapped him across the face. The eyes fluttered open. The mouth moved, but no sound.

Mercer eyed the bloody pliers on the floor. He himself had once been threatened with them, but that felt like a long time ago. He had taken the pliers, and now they were his. But he did not use them to threaten. That wasn't his way. He just acted. You pull out one fingernail and the guy understands that it could happen again, nine more times, and he knows exactly how it's going to feel.

And that's just what he'd done, all ten of them, because this guy was a tough son of a bitch. And that was fine. That was expected. The tougher the nut, the sweeter the meat.

Mercer swung his foot into the guy's shin. The man yelped in pain. It wasn't too loud, because he was spent. Probably no one heard. Probably no one cared.

Mercer leaned in. The man's left eye was swollen shut, so he looked into the right eye, a sliver of hazel surrounded by swollen purple flesh. "Where is he?"

The man's lips trembled. His teeth—he still had all his teeth; he should consider himself lucky—slipped over his chapped lower lip. "F-f-ffff . . ." His lips went slack.

"France? Fiji? Fresno? Where?"

"F-f-ffffu . . . fuck you . . ."

Mercer buried his fist in the man's face and split his nose open. Blood gushed out as the chair toppled backward and crashed to the floor, crushing the man's tied hands beneath the weight of his body. He moaned as the blood streamed from his face and pooled around his head on the concrete floor.

Mercer walked to the far end of the room and sat in a dark corner. He closed his eyes. He was there again. It was so easy to be back there, in that dark, fetid room, chained down like an animal. He didn't care about the beatings, or the taunts. He could handle the captivity, the disorientation and uncertainty, losing track of time. He was trained for that.

The worst thing was watching his body wither away from captivity and malnutrition. His most reliable and powerful tool, becoming this limp and desiccated thing. He touched his left arm beneath the white tunic he was wearing. Already the muscle tone was coming back. It had never fully gone. He had just let them think it had; that his will was spent, that his body had become an impotent object, drained of its lethal venom. They were fooled, and it was the last mistake they ever made.

Mercer stood up, walked over to his captive, and looked down at him. Not long ago he'd been the one down on the floor, looking up. The one who didn't get to decide what happened next.

He hadn't wanted to play this card. He'd thought the pain would be enough. He'd thought it would be the right thing, given the game they were all playing. But he had to go the next step.

He crouched next to the man. The blood had stopped gushing from his nose. He was taking rapid, shallow breaths. "I've seen your house," said Mercer in a low, soft tone. "Near the American Consulate. Nice two-story place, white stone. Tree out front, looked like a eucalyptus. Your wife has short brown hair, a little plain looking but she keeps herself in shape, tight ass. Your son is how old? Five? Six? Nice looking boy."

The man glared at him through his one swollen eye.

"Give me what I want, and nothing will happen to them. Withhold from me, and something will. You have my word on that. This is your last opportunity. Tell me where he is."

The man stared up at him, as though thinking. But not for long. He was going to protect his family. Any decent guy would. The man's lips parted; he was trying to speak. His voice was low and raspy.

Mercer crouched lower so he could hear. "Tell me."

The man told him. He spoke in little more than a whisper, but Mercer heard it. And once he heard it, he understood immediately. Of course that's where the son of a bitch was. Just another turn of the wheel.

He pulled a combat knife from his belt and drew it across the man's throat. Blood spurted from his jugular.

Mercer stood, wiped the blood from the blade on the dying man's pants. He looked at the man's shoes. Leather loafers. He hadn't noticed them before. They were nice, better than the sandals he'd taken off the last guy he killed. He took them off the man's feet and put them on.

The blood coming out of the man's jugular slowed to a trickle, his chest stopped moving. He was dead.

Through the tarp, Mercer could hear the muezzin intone the call to prayer from a nearby mosque. The incantation was low and solemn, almost mournful. All across the city, people would now pause their lives to answer the call, to bow their bodies in a communal act of submission.

Kyle Mercer had once had something like that: common rituals, brotherhood. It had been the Army, and in a broader sense his country. Now all he had was a target. And a destination.

PART II

QUANTICO, VIRGINIA
AUGUST 2018

CHAPTER 2

"Tell me something, Mr. Brodie. Wasn't there some way you could have avoided shooting the mule?"

Chief Warrant Officer Scott Brodie could not believe he had been summoned to the general's office to talk about the f-ing mule. There was nothing left to say about the mule. In fact, everything that could *possibly* be said about the mule had already been said.

Major General Stephen Hackett was the Provost Marshal General of the United States Army—the Army's top cop—and Brodie was a Special Agent in the Army's Criminal Investigation Division, the CID, which was the detective arm of the CIC, the Criminal Investigation Command. The CID was tasked with solving all the Army's law enforcement problems, and on its seal was the motto "Do What Has to Be Done." Brodie took that motto to heart. His critics might say he misinterpreted it to mean . . . well . . . *do what has to be done.*

The office of the Provost Marshal General was located in Quantico, Virginia, about forty miles south of Washington, DC. The Marine Corps had one of its largest bases at Quantico, and also headquartered there was the Naval Criminal Investigative Service—NCIS—of TV fame, and the Air Force Office of Special Investigations. Quantico was also home to the Drug Enforcement Administration Training Academy, the FBI Academy, and the FBI Laboratory. The government might have had synergy and cost savings in mind by co-locating all these law enforcement facilities, but knowing the government, it was probably accidental.

Also sitting in General Hackett's office were Colonel Stanley Dombroski and Warrant Officer Maggie Taylor. Dombroski was the man who normally gave Brodie his assignments. Maggie Taylor was Brodie's recently assigned partner.

Hackett looked like a general from central casting: He was six feet tall and had a full head of short gray hair, and his posture suggested he had a ramrod up his ass. Colonel Dombroski, by comparison, looked like a guy you'd see selling beer at Fenway. He was five foot eight, at least forty pounds overweight, mostly bald, and had a permanent six-o'clock shadow. He also looked as if he might not be the sharpest bayonet in the armory—but there was nothing dull about Stanley Dombroski. Brodie suspected that Dombroski would never rise above the rank of colonel. The Army, often to its own detriment, wants generals who look like generals.

The Army had no problem, however, with Maggie Taylor's appearance, and if Brodie and Taylor weren't frequently required to go undercover, the Army would have plastered Maggie Taylor's photo on recruiting posters. She was five foot nine and had short blonde hair, a perfect nose, full lips, bright brown eyes that radiated intelligence, and a CrossFit body.

Brodie was tall with civilian-cut dark brown hair, and he considered himself a pretty good-looking guy, based on the unbiased testimony of former girlfriends and his mother. Today he was wearing jeans, a black T-shirt, and a counterfeit Armani sports jacket that he had bought in Taiwan for twelve dollars. Army criminal investigators usually wore civilian clothing—unless they were undercover, posing as uniformed personnel. Today, however, Maggie Taylor was in uniform because that was the protocol upon being summoned by a general, as Dombroski—who was always in uniform—had reminded them in an e-mail that Brodie hadn't read. He was sure he'd hear from Dombroski later about how he never checked his e-mail, which was true, because as far as Brodie was concerned most official Army e-mails should be classified as spam.

"Mr. Brodie?"

Male warrant officers are addressed as "Mr." Female WOs are "Ms." Warrant officers are not commissioned officers, as are lieutenants, captains, colonels, and generals, and they exist in a gray area between noncommissioned officers—meaning sergeants—and the commissioned officer corps. It was a nice rank, thought Brodie. You had no command responsibilities and no one called you "sir," but you could still drink at the Officers' Club.

The wall behind Hackett was covered with framed commendations and awards, as well as pictures of him with other generals and the current Secretary of Defense. Among them was a framed photo of Hackett in desert combat fatigues holding an M4 rifle, which Brodie suspected he'd only fired in training. General Hackett certainly had never had one fired at him by a methed-up redneck riding bareback on a charging mule in backwoods Kentucky.

Wasn't there some way you could have avoided shooting the mule? The general's question still hung in the air. And when a two-star general asks you a question, even a stupid one, you are expected to answer.

"I was aiming for the suspect on the mule, sir," said Brodie. "Not the mule itself," he added to be as clear as crystal meth.

Taylor stifled a laugh. They'd only worked this one case together, but Brodie was starting to notice that she found the wrong things funny, and at the wrong times. Also, Taylor was absolutely *golden* when it came to the mule. She'd saved its life.

Two months ago, Brodie and his new partner had been dispatched to Fort Campbell, Kentucky, which was experiencing a major methamphetamine epidemic. Somebody on the base was selling crystal meth to a lot of soldiers, and an M4 rifle that fires seven hundred rounds per minute is not something you want in the hands of a guy flying high on crank. But Army CID agents at Fort Campbell, even with the assistance of the DEA, had had no luck in figuring out who was making and pushing the stuff. So they'd called Chief Warrant Officer Brodie.

Scott Brodie, age thirty-eight, had enlisted when he was twenty-one. He'd been a CID agent for twelve years. In those years he'd apprehended murderers, rapists, Pentagon embezzlers, and people trying to sell military hardware to terrorists. He'd worked hard to establish himself as the guy you send in when the other guys can't solve a case, and the meth case was one of those times.

He and Taylor had gone undercover posing as clerks in the adjutant general's office, and in less than two months they had managed to identify all the members of a small cartel. The ringleader was a master sergeant named Enos Hadley who worked at the base National Guard armory, and his cousin cooked the meth out in some backwoods holler. Sergeant Hadley had a dozen guys on the base, some military, some civilian, who acted as his corner boys.

The day the CID was planning to make all the apprehensions, somebody had tipped Hadley that they were coming for him, so he'd left the base in his pickup, taking with him an M4 and enough ammunition to invade North Korea. Brodie and Taylor went after him in an unmarked car.

They hadn't bothered to notify the Kentucky State Police because the Army likes to solve its own problems. They also hadn't radioed any MPs for backup, over Taylor's protests, because, as Brodie explained to her, he hadn't just spent seven weeks in Deliverance country to let someone else get the glory.

"Brodie," Taylor had cautioned, "these guys are crazy."

And Taylor would know. She was from this part of the world—the strip of rugged country that snaked from southern New York to northern Alabama known as Appalachia. It was full of famously short-tempered Scots-Irish descendants, such as one Enos Hadley, who was currently following the genetic imperative of his ancestors and fleeing to the Highlands—or, in his case, the back hills.

"We can handle it," Brodie had assured her.

And that was the end of it. Brodie outranked her. He was a Chief Warrant Officer Four; Taylor—five years his junior and with only a year in CID under her belt—was a One. He was sure that if she kept at it she'd eventually make Chief Warrant Officer Five, the highest rank. He was less sure about his own prospects. And behavior such as this was a large part of the reason for his uncertainty.

They'd chased Hadley into the hills where he'd been raised, and by the time he got to his backwoods ancestral shack, Brodie and Taylor were less than a quarter mile behind him and saw him run into a barn. Brodie figured he'd barricade himself inside, which would force them to call the local sheriff and tell him to bring a SWAT team and wait the guy out until he either surrendered or blew his tiny brains out.

But that wasn't what happened. Just as they got out of their car with their 9mm Glock pistols drawn, Hadley burst out of the barn on a mule, which they'd learn later was in such fine and fit shape from spending the last fourteen months carting supplies up to the meth lab.

Hadley charged them like a hillbilly Geronimo, M4 firing on full auto, and it was a minor miracle he didn't hit either of them. Their car wasn't so lucky.

Brodie returned fire, trying to kill the guy trying to kill him, which is what they teach you in Basic Combat Training. But it's a challenge to hit a guy bouncing on a mule, firing a submachine gun at you, while you're trying to find cover and shoot at the same time. Brodie missed Hadley and shot the mule in the ass.

The mule bucked and Hadley fell off. He rolled once and came up firing. Taylor shot him, hitting him in the right shoulder. She claimed later that she aimed to wound him, which Brodie knew was complete bullshit since the military does not train you to aim to wound. But as they say in the Army, "Whatever I hit is what I was aiming for."

In the end, both the mule and Hadley survived. Brodie disarmed Hadley and then used a compress bandage to keep him from bleeding to death, while Taylor did her best Dr. Dolittle on the mule, cooing soothingly to the beast while pressing a bandage against its wound. She said, "Jesus, Brodie! Did you have to shoot the mule?" That was the first but obviously not the last time he would hear that question.

The mule shooting made the papers, and it went viral on the Internet. PETA protested, and a lot of people pointed out that a mule happened to be the West Point mascot. Have you no shame, Brodie?

A Pentagon spokeswoman apologized for the mule shooting, the Army paid its veterinary bills, and it made a full recovery. To compensate Hadley's half-wit wife for the mental anguish she claimed to have suffered when she saw the poor animal at the vet hospital, the Army gave her enough money to buy a Kentucky thoroughbred.

The only good news was that Brodie's name and photo were withheld from the media, which was vital, considering the kinds of assignments he was often given. Same with Taylor, though within the CIC she became the hero, the one who'd shot Hadley and therefore saved their lives, and the one who'd saved the mule's life. It was not lost on Brodie that if he had just killed Hadley, no one would have cared and it would have saved everyone a lot of trouble.

Hackett shuffled some papers on his desk. "The mule isn't the reason I called you here today." He looked at Brodie and Taylor, and paused for effect. "This is about Kyle Mercer."

Kyle Mercer. The most famous Army deserter since Private Eddie Slovik, a World War II soldier and the last man executed for desertion.

Brodie suddenly got interested in the meeting.

CHAPTER 3

Brodie tried to recall what he knew about this case. Captain Kyle Mercer had been a member of the 1st Special Forces Operational Detachment—Delta, more famously known as Delta Force. He was the elite of the elite, one of the most potent weapons in the military's arsenal, and the tip of the spear in the counterinsurgency campaign against the Taliban in Afghanistan. One night three years earlier, while stationed with a small team at a remote combat outpost in the rugged Hindu Kush, he walked off. According to his teammates, Captain Mercer must have left sometime after midnight. He took all his field gear with him, along with night vision goggles and his M4 rifle, but no one had actually seen him leave the outpost, and no one noticed he was missing until first light. Conclusion: He'd deserted.

Desertion is rare. Desertion in a war zone like Afghanistan even rarer. And desertion in a war zone by an *officer* in an elite unit, unheard-of. Captain Mercer's desertion was a public relations nightmare that the Army was desperate to get control of.

It was also a major security risk, given Mercer's unique role as a Special Ops officer. He held highly classified Intel that could fall into the hands of the Taliban or al Qaeda if he were captured. If anyone was going to hold the line under torture, it would be an officer in Delta Force. But every man has his limits.

All Brodie knew about Mercer's mission in Afghanistan was what was known to the public through news media reporting, which meant he didn't know much. Delta Force fell under the purview of Joint Special Operations Command—JSOC—which controlled elite special mission units within the Army, Navy, and Air Force. And the full list of what units JSOC controlled, and what those units' duties were, remained classified. The command had been formed in 1980, but it wasn't really taken off the leash until after 9/11, when the Pentagon sought to take a more aggressive counter-terrorism posture, as well as assert control over covert operations that had long been the purview of the CIA. The very existence of JSOC's special mission units had not even been acknowledged until the late Nineties. So Captain Mercer was an enigma even before he walked off in the night into a rugged mountain range in one of the most dangerous and godforsaken corners of the earth.

Whatever Mercer's team's mission was, it was too critical to send his teammates out on patrols to find their missing comrade. Instead, patrols from a Stryker brigade operating in the area were deployed as soon as Mercer was reported missing, and helicopters and spotter aircraft joined in the search.

Mercer's outpost was near the Pakistan border where the Taliban took sanctuary, then crossed back into Afghanistan to engage American and Afghan forces. The rough terrain was thick with IEDs—improvised explosive devices—the ultimate expression of workplace violence.

During the search for Captain Mercer, two soldiers were killed in separate incidents, one by ambush and one by a roadside IED. The media did not make the connection, but Brodie and others within the military were well aware that those soldiers—regular infantry—would never have been patrolling so close to the border of Pakistan's tribal territories had they not been searching for Captain Mercer. The deserter now had blood on his hands.

It was decided, at the highest Pentagon level, to inform Mercer's parents that their son had gone AWOL—absent without leave—which was better than telling the conservative couple from San Diego that their son was a deserter, subject to a long R&R in Leavenworth, or even the death penalty.

War today, thought Brodie, was as much about public relations and spin as it was about war. American soldiers don't surrender. They are captured. And they don't retreat. They redeploy rearward. And they don't desert. They go AWOL.

As a criminal investigator, Brodie was very familiar with this last distinction. The difference between desertion and AWOL is primarily one of *intent*, *duration*, and *duty*. The law, as covered by Article 85 (Desertion) and Article 86 (Absence Without Leave) of the Uniform Code of Military Justice, states that if a soldier *intends* to remain away from the Army *permanently*, and if the reason the soldier abandoned his post was to avoid *important duty*, the soldier could be court-martialed for desertion. Conversely, if the soldier did not intend to stay away permanently and/or didn't leave to avoid an important duty, then he would be considered AWOL.

In one classroom example that Brodie recalled, a soldier working in the motor pool at Fort Sam Houston in Texas decides one day he's tired of fixing broken-down Humvees and would rather be in Arkansas screwing his girlfriend. First, the Army would give him the benefit of the doubt and assume that he was not planning to stay away permanently, that maybe one day soon he'd come to his senses and return to Fort Sam. Also, as essential as draining the crankcase oil out of a Humvee might be, this is not considered *important duty*.

Combat is important duty. Defusing IEDs is important duty. Escorting a convoy through hostile territory occupied by guys who have rocket-propelled grenades is important duty. Basically, any job that is hazardous and that a rational human being would prefer not to do because he might get killed is considered important duty. So when the soldier from the Fort Sam Houston motor pool finally comes back to base, or if he happens to get picked up by the MPs, he'd be disciplined for being AWOL as opposed to being a deserter.

For being AWOL, he might be reduced in rank, forfeit some pay, and spend a few days in the stockade or confined to barracks, but he'd still be allowed to stay in the Army.

For desertion, the maximum penalty still carried on the books is death.

But Brodie knew the death penalty was unlikely unless after you deserted you did something particularly heinous, like help the enemy kill your fellow soldiers, or give aid and comfort to the enemy. A deserter had not been executed since World War II, when Private Eddie Slovik stood in front of a firing squad in 1945. The most likely penalty for desertion today would be a dishonorable discharge from the Army, being stripped of any back pay you were owed, and jail time of no longer than five years.

Mercer's case, however, was different. He wasn't some newly deployed PFC. He was a commissioned officer, and the commanding officer of a team located deep in hostile territory. The disruption in command brought about by his sudden absence could have put his men in greater danger. Also, he possessed valuable Intel about American counterinsurgency operations that could be used against his fellow soldiers. And finally, there were the two guys who'd got killed looking for him. That was a biggie, and the Army was not going to go easy on Captain Kyle Mercer. Especially if he'd deserted to join up with the enemy—which was unlikely, but nevertheless possible.

Three months after Mercer walked off, the Army's worst fears were realized: The Taliban released a hostage video—distributed across jihadist websites and covered by every mainstream media outlet—showing Mercer kneeling in the dirt in front of five Taliban fighters. So obviously Mercer was not there voluntarily—or his offer to become a jihadist had been rejected. He looked bad: sunken cheeks, hollow eyes, a scraggly beard. He wore a white tunic and baggy white pants. His captors all wore black and held AK-47 rifles across their chests. This was in May of 2015, after the public had already been subjected to a grisly parade of ISIS hostage videos that all followed the same tragic script: unrealistic and impossible demands, followed by Western inaction and, ultimately, a beheading. But it was the Taliban, not ISIS, who held Mercer, and they wanted to make a deal. One of the captors read off a list of six Taliban commanders currently held at Guantánamo Bay whom they wanted released in exchange for Captain Mercer. Mercer himself said nothing in the video. He just stared blankly ahead, showing no emotion. No fear. After the Taliban fighter gave his demands, he grabbed Mercer by the nape of his neck and said into the camera, in Pashto: "This is one of your greatest warriors, America. We found him running away like a coward. We would like to shoot him like a dog, but our mujahideen brothers are more important. We are loyal to our soldiers. Are you?" Then the video ended.

It occurred to Brodie at the time that it was strange that Mercer did not speak. It is usually more effective—and demoralizing—to make the hostage deliver the demands. It was possible his captors had tried to get him to deliver the script and he'd refused, even under torture. So they did the talking as Captain Mercer knelt in the dirt on display, defiant in his silence and his fearless gaze.

After the hostage video was released, Mercer's parents went public with their own video addressing their son's captors. Brodie remembered seeing them on TV, looking like they hadn't slept in weeks, shakily reading a prepared script to a band of fundamentalist crazies on the other side of the world.

Betty Mercer looked decidedly worse than her husband, ashen and trembling, and soon she stated why: She had been diagnosed with pancreatic cancer and had only months to live. She pleaded for her son's release, in the hope that she could see him one last time. She even quoted from the Quran, something about God's mercy prevailing over His wrath.

But apparently the Taliban were not interested in mercy. Or maybe they didn't appreciate their own book being read back to them by an Episcopalian from California. At any rate, there was no response. Six months later, Mrs. Mercer died. No one ever heard from Kyle Mercer or his captors again.

General Hackett, however, had some new and classified information. "We learned eight months ago that Captain Mercer escaped his captors, and presumably fled the region. That was all we had to go on until three days ago, when we received a report that an old Army buddy of his spotted him overseas." He looked at Brodie and Taylor. "I want you two to locate and apprehend Captain Mercer and bring him home to face trial by court-martial." Hackett remembered to add, "After an investigation, of course."

Brodie thought about where he'd go if he'd done years of Special Ops duty in one of the most hostile places on earth, then been held captive by a ruthless enemy and subjected to years of physical and psychological torture, and then somehow managed to escape, with the knowledge that he would face a court-martial for desertion if he ever returned home. Mai Tais on the beach in Thailand sounded good. Brodie was ready to pack.

"He's in Caracas, Venezuela," said Hackett. He then added, just for fun: "Murder Capital of the World."

Shit.

CHAPTER 4

While Hackett shuffled through some papers on his desk, Brodie looked over at his partner. She was looking at Hackett, or rather, looking through him with a kind of glazed-over expression that Brodie had come to recognize as a sign of deep concentration. She had gotten that look a couple of times down in Kentucky. Once was right before she made a big break in the case. The other was at the Fort Campbell mess hall, while assessing the edibility of the meat loaf.

Now Brodie wondered if she was thinking what he was thinking—that Venezuela had been in the news a lot lately, and not for anything good. Who in their right mind would escape one shithole for another?

"So here's what we have," Hackett said, looking up from his papers. "A former U.S. Army sergeant named Alfred Simpson saw Mercer in Caracas. Simpson and Mercer knew each other well. They were in basic training and advanced infantry training together before Mercer went to OCS at Fort Benning and Simpson was assigned to the Fourth Brigade Combat Team, Fourth Infantry Division, at Fort Carson.

"Two weeks ago, Simpson was in Caracas on business. He now works as an oil industry consultant. One night, execs from the Venezuelan state oil company, PDVSA, take him to the Marriott hotel lounge, and after a couple drinks he spots a guy sitting alone at the bar. He thinks it looks like his old buddy Kyle Mercer. Simpson, like most of America, knows that Mercer deserted, and he saw the Taliban video on TV. Simpson hesitates, then gets up to take a closer look. He says Mercer's name, Mercer turns around, and they make eye contact. Mercer gets up and quickly walks out of the bar." Hackett added, "Simpson now lives in New Jersey, so I had CID agents from Fort Dix interview him last night. Their interview is in the file."

Brodie asked, "And Simpson was certain it was Mercer?"

"It's all in the file," Hackett repeated.

As much as Brodie relished the opportunity to wander aimlessly through the Murder Capital of the World, he really wished they had more to work with.

Reading his mind, Hackett said, "This is the first tip or clue we've had in three years. It's what we've got."

Right. When you're clueless, you take what comes along.

Taylor asked General Hackett, "Sir, if this happened two weeks ago, why are we just acting on it?"

"Because we just heard about it yesterday. Simpson said he didn't know what to do or who to contact while he was in Caracas."

"How about the U.S. Embassy?" said Brodie. "Is he stupid?"

Hackett ignored that and continued, "Maybe he second-guessed his identification. Or maybe Mr. Simpson didn't want to rat out his old friend, and he struggled with this. In any case, after Simpson returned to the States, he called an old Army friend who was still on active duty, and this individual, a Sergeant Bell, made a few calls and the tip went up the chain, eventually reaching General Mendoza, who called me yesterday. After I was notified, I had the agents from Dix interview Simpson."

General Christopher Mendoza was no less than the highest-ranking officer in the United States Army. He had four stars and he was the Army Chief of Staff, and a member of the Joint Chiefs. In other words, he was God, and God had spoken directly to General Hackett, who was now speaking to them. *Thou shalt not fuck this up, Brodie.*

Hackett continued, "General Mendoza told me he wants Captain Mercer brought back to the United States, but he does not want this turned into a media circus." He added, "While we technically have an extradition treaty with Venezuela, they have not honored it in some time."

Which meant this was going to be a snatch job.

Hackett said, "So your mission is to locate Mercer in Venezuela and get him back home to face court-martial. Your mission is not to interrogate him or attempt to determine guilt, just get him in custody and back to Quantico. Is that understood?"

"Yes, sir," said Taylor with enthusiasm.

Kidnap the asshole if you have to was the subtext, though General Hackett would never say it. Brodie hoped that Taylor understood what she was signing on for. She'd only been a CID agent for a year, and he was certain she'd never dealt with anything like this. This was the kind of job that could land you in a foreign prison if things went wrong—after which your bosses back in the States would say you must have misunderstood your orders. Or maybe they'd say they'd never heard of you.

Over the years, Brodie had been involved in a couple of euphemistically labeled "extraordinary extractions"—a murderer who'd fled to Belgrade, and an embezzler he'd tracked to a Tunisian beach resort. In both cases they were schmucks, in way over their heads, whose one and only bright idea was to get themselves to a country without an extradition treaty. It didn't work out for them. But then, they weren't Delta Force.

Brodie thought back to Kyle Mercer's face in the hostage video. *No fear.*

He still hadn't responded to Hackett's question. The general looked directly at him—he had eyes like stainless steel ball bearings—and said, "Do you understand, Mr. Brodie?"

"Yes, sir. I do." But something was missing from this story, and he added, "You said Mercer escaped his captors eight months ago. How do you know that?"

Hackett and Dombroski exchanged a look, and something told Brodie they had finally reached the heart of the matter.

General Hackett said, "What you are about to see is classified." Brodie was certain the man practiced saying that in front of a mirror every morning.

Hackett took a thumb drive out of his desk drawer and handed it to Dombroski, who plugged it into a flat-screen TV mounted on the wall across from Hackett's desk.

Hackett continued, "Eight months ago, a SEAL team conducting a cross-border operation into the Pakistani tribal territories came across a former Taliban encampment. While they were inspecting the site, they were approached by a local goat herder who presented them with a note, written in English—and, as we discovered later, in Mercer's handwriting—instructing any American military unit to pay the bearer of the note fifty dollars in exchange for valuable information. The SEAL team paid the goat herder and he handed them an SD memory card and then left. The card contained this footage." He added, "It's graphic."

Dombroski pressed play, and they all watched the screen.

A stationary camera showed a burning tent in rugged mountain territory on a moonlit night. A figure was splayed out on the ground in front of the tent. It appeared to be a bearded man in dark clothing. He was sleeping. Or dead.

Another figure was hunched over in the distance, moving in quick repetitive motions. An arm, framed against the sky, raised a long knife and brought it down over and over.

The figure stood. It was a tall, thin man with a beard, his features etched in moonlight. He held the knife in his right hand, and a round object swayed from his clenched left hand.

A human head.

The man walked forward toward the burning tent, and as he got closer to the camera his head disappeared out of frame and his body could be seen approaching a sharp wooden pike staked in the sand. He dropped the knife on the ground and, with both hands, brought the head down onto the pike. A distinctive wet crunch could be heard over the wind and the crackling fire.

"Five men—apparently Taliban—were found like that," said Hackett. "Decapitated, heads mounted on pikes in a circle around the encampment. Three of them, according to the SEAL team report, were killed by bullets. Two had their throats cut."

The figure walked forward and crouched into frame. It was Kyle Mercer. His face looked frightening—gaunt, bloody, illuminated by moonlight and by another fire somewhere off camera. His blue eyes were wide open and alert as he stared into the lens. "I hereby resign my commission as an officer in the United States Army."

He leaned forward and turned off the camera.

The screen went black, and for a moment they all stared at their own dull reflections.

Hackett broke the silence: "For the record, the Army does not accept Captain Mercer's resignation. He is still subject to military justice."

Right, thought Brodie. *You are still one of us, and we will find you.*

Hackett continued, "Captain Mercer was held for over two years by a ruthless and sadistic enemy, undoubtedly subjected to physical and psychological torture. It is remarkable that he was able to escape, and this speaks to his considerable abilities. It goes without saying that this man is dangerous, and unlikely to be taken into custody willingly."

That, thought Brodie, may be an understatement.

Brodie understood something about the stress of war. Before joining the CIC, he'd served as a rifleman in the 2nd Infantry Division in Iraq and taken part in the successful drive to retake Fallujah from the insurgents in Operation Phantom Fury. He fought along dusty alleyways and sunbaked roofs and houses blown open by mortar shells. He saw people ripped apart by bullets and bombs and artillery. Most were the enemy. Some were civilians. A couple were his friends. He'd seen action before that, and he would again, but that battle had changed him.

He wondered what the war had done to Kyle Mercer, not to mention the years of captivity and torture. The Army had turned a kid from San Diego into a trained killer. But what was it that had turned him into a deserter who would abandon his own men? And what had he become when he not only killed his captors, but whacked off their heads and mounted them like trophies? Whatever it was, he must have known he'd crossed a threshold from which he could not come back.

Hackett stood, and they all followed suit. He looked between Brodie, Taylor, and Dombroski and said, "If you have any questions, Colonel Dombroski will answer them." He added, "This meeting never took place."

Brodie wished that were true.

CHAPTER 5

Maggie Taylor was typing on her laptop. "Looks like we can get a cute Airbnb right in downtown Caracas for twelve bucks a night."

Brodie still couldn't tell when his new partner was joking, though he hoped this was a skill he'd pick up over time.

They were sitting in their small shared office on the second floor of an administrative building about a ten-minute walk from Hackett's office. Quantico was their permanent duty station, though they were hardly ever there. Their office walls were bare except for a bulletin board thick with layers of official notices and takeout menus. Brodie's gray metal desk was covered in piles of dusty incident reports that were supposed to be filed somewhere, and the whole place smelled stale. Brodie's last partner, a humorless guy named Spencer from Chicago, was constantly annoyed with the state of Brodie's side of the office. Dave Spencer was a former infantry NCO, but he had spent all of his time stateside, and Brodie suspected he put more care and attention into folding the perfect military corners on his bedsheets than he did into getting his soldiers battle-ready. Scott Brodie had no patience for the finer points of military discipline and etiquette, and he'd noticed that some of the most useless guys in his old infantry battalion had the crispest uniforms, while many of the bravest soldiers he'd ever known couldn't even keep their footlockers organized. So the CID suited him well. He could be an officer without worrying about being a gentleman.

When Dave Spencer was promoted to Warrant Officer Four, he'd jumped at the opportunity to get a new office and find his own lower-ranking partner to boss around, leaving Brodie alone with more room to spread his mess. Then Maggie Taylor came along, fresh off a six-month stint with the CID at Fort Bragg, and as far as Brodie could tell she hadn't even noticed the mess, or the smell. She tended to become manically focused on whatever she was doing, oblivious to everything else. At the moment, her task was making arrangements with the travel office, and Brodie decided he ought to clarify the objective before she found them a room share in the Caracas slums.

"We need a modern hotel. Preferably one that employs private security." He added, "Cost is no object."

Taylor didn't reply, and Brodie took a look at Captain Kyle Mercer's confidential file, which Dombroski had handed him after their meeting with Hackett. Mercer was thirty-three years old, born and raised in San Diego. Mercer's father, Peter, was an accountant, and his late mother, Betty, had managed a clothing store. Kyle Mercer did well in school and earned a scholarship to UCLA. After college he enlisted, and after basic and advanced infantry training he attended Officer Candidate School at Fort Benning, Georgia, where he excelled and graduated at the top of his class. Afterward he received airborne training at Benning, then applied for and was accepted into the Special Forces Qualification Course. He trained at the Special Warfare School at Fort Bragg, where he was ultimately recruited into Delta Force. At this point the specifics of his file became murky, with mission reports full of redactions. What Brodie did see was the impressive pedigree of an elite solider and no red flags prior to his desertion. Among his many listed skills was fluency in Spanish, which he'd studied in high school and college. Kyle Mercer also spoke Pashto, the result of a three-month stint at the Defense Language Institute in Monterey, California. That skill, thought Brodie, must have come in handy during his captivity, and probably kept him alive.

Brodie recalled an old joke: "Join the Army, see the world, meet new people, and kill them."

He returned his attention to the report, which included testimonials from Mercer's Delta teammates. To a man, they described Captain Mercer as a capable, competent, and brave commanding officer. No one remarked on behavior that was out of the ordinary in the days or hours preceding his desertion. The only thing of note about the testimonials was that the names of every man interviewed, and the names of any other person or place they mentioned, were redacted.

Brodie also looked over the report of the Fort Dix CID's interview with Simpson, which was brief and mostly useless. The only new details he learned were that Simpson had had a productive and lucrative meeting with the Venezuelan state oil execs before getting sloshed on rum, and that Simpson was sure it was Mercer because of a distinctive tattoo on Mercer's arm of an ouroboros—the ancient symbol of a snake eating its own tail. Also, according to Simpson, Mercer had a trimmed beard and appeared to have gained about thirty pounds, mostly muscle, since his infamous hostage video seen by most of America on the nightly news.

Brodie asked his partner, "Why does a guy who's in hiding, and whose face has been on TV, sit in a high-traffic hotel bar frequented by Americans who might recognize him?"

"There aren't too many Americans in Caracas these days," replied Taylor.

"Right, but the few that are there, like Simpson, are almost guaranteed to be at a place like the Marriott."

"You think Simpson is lying?"

Brodie opened his laptop and pulled up pictures of the Caracas Marriott's lobby lounge. It was a comfortable-looking, no-frills modern hotel bar with lounge seating located on a mezzanine level above the check-in desks. A wide stairway led up to the lounge, and the bar ran along the left wall as you entered. The bar, notably, had no mirrors along its back wall.

"Simpson said Mercer was sitting at the bar, while he was sitting in the lounge area with his Venezuelan oil company pals. Simpson noticed the tattoo first, which is on Mercer's right biceps, and only positively IDed Mercer when Simpson said his name and Mercer turned around." Brodie spun his laptop around to show Taylor a picture of the bar and lounge.

"No way," said Taylor.

"Right."

"Situational awareness" is a familiar concept to anyone in the military, and second nature to a well-trained officer. In short, it means not having your head up your ass in a given situation—be aware of your physical surroundings, the context in which you are existing in them, and the multitude of potential consequences of your actions or the possible actions of others. No officer—let alone one in Delta Force—who was a fugitive from military justice would sit at that bar with an entire room full of people at his back.

Brodie's cell phone vibrated in his pocket. He checked it and saw a text from Dombroski: *Meet me at the O Club in 15. Alone.*

The Officers' Club at Quantico was Colonel Dombroski's preferred venue for conducting business. It was also his favorite place to drink. These two activities often occurred at the same time.

Brodie got up from his desk. "I need to take care of some personal business; then we'll pay Mr. Simpson another visit. Get us the last flight out of Newark tonight, and adjoining rooms at the Marriott."

Taylor clicked on something, furrowed her brow. "Looks like gunmen shot up the Marriott lobby two days ago. How about the El Dorado?"

"When's the scheduled shoot-out there?"

"Doesn't say."

"Do the best you can."

Brodie left the office.

CHAPTER 6

The Officers' Club at Quantico was a nice enough place. Large windows admitted the morning sun, and it had an elegant bar with high-backed stools and a couple dozen tables with comfortable chairs. Mounted above the bar were plaques for military units stationed at Quantico as well as an old wooden propeller that maybe came off the plane of the guy who shot down the Red Baron.

Brodie and Dombroski sat at the mostly empty bar. Since it was just past ten, they showed restraint and ordered pilsners.

Dombroski looked around. "This place looks like a goddamn Applebee's."

Brodie had heard this complaint before from his superior, and he hoped it wasn't a warm-up to another lengthy diatribe about the changing culture of the military. The O Clubs where Dombroski had caroused and drunk to excess in his misspent youth had been housed in grand buildings containing ballrooms and dining rooms staffed by uniformed stewards. The reason for the decline in these magnificent old facilities was partly economic and partly social. The Army was trying to "deglamorize" alcohol, and didn't want the liability of an officer leaving a club and plowing into a family in a station wagon. But Brodie had seen Dombroski drive, and a couple of beers could only improve his performance.

Dombroski raised his glass to Brodie. "I stopped believing in luck or God, so I'll just say watch your ass and come home safe. That's an order."

"Yes, sir."

They drank.

Dombroski said, "I'm in touch with a Defense Intelligence guy who's posted at our embassy in Caracas, Colonel Brendan Worley. He'll be your logistical support on the ground. He's an Army attaché, been in country a few years so he knows the place well. He's aware of the broad details of your mission, that you're there to track down and apprehend Captain Mercer. You can share additional details with him as necessary, on a need-to-know basis. He'll meet you in your hotel lobby when you check in, and he'll give you your kit."

Brodie nodded. He was glad to hear they'd have some support on the ground. And some tools of the trade they'd never be able to get past Caracas airport security.

Dombroski added, "He'll also supply you with paper currency. It's hard to bring in cash without getting a shakedown at the airport, and your plastic will be no good there. He's sending a car and driver to meet you and take you to your hotel."

"We'll take a taxi. Less conspicuous."

Dombroski shrugged. "That's what I thought too. He said you'll stick out just by virtue of being Americans these days. His driver knows the ropes, he'll be armed and make sure you don't get robbed or kidnapped on the way to the hotel."

"I feel safer already," said Brodie. "What about getting Mercer out?"

"Colonel Worley will be able to help with those arrangements too."

Taylor was booking them round-trip tickets for the sake of appearances, but once Mercer was in custody their flight home would be via private charter. Brodie wasn't too worried about this part of the mission. Over the decades, America's intelligence agencies had gained a lot of relevant experience in how to sneak people in and out of Latin America.

Dombroski pulled an envelope from his jacket and handed it to Brodie. "Your tourist travel visas. They're legit, with your real names and to be used to travel under your regular civilian passports, so if they are entered into a central database at Caracas passport control you'll be fine. Normally takes months to get these and you have to send in your passport book, but it looks like Hackett's people have a guy at the Venezuelan Embassy in their pocket and he expedited them yesterday. On paper, you've been vaccinated for yellow fever, though you'll want to do that for real if you end up needing to head to the interior of the country. Also, although you have different last names, you're married to each other—good luck with that—and you both work as life insurance agents in Alexandria."

"Do we share a room?"

"That's up to you and Ms. Taylor. But you'll book two rooms."

"Right. And why are we visiting Venezuela?"

"Because you're stupid."

Brodie opened the envelope and looked at their visas. They used the same photos that Brodie and Taylor had on their military IDs, but with a combination of cropping and photoshopping to obscure their uniforms. He closed the envelope and slipped it into the pocket of his faux Armani sports coat.

On that subject, Dombroski said, "You're supposed to be in uniform when reporting to a general in his office."

Maybe, Brodie thought, he should have worn his uniform to remind General Hackett—and Dombroski—that he'd been an infantryman before this gig, and that he'd been awarded the Bronze Star for valor, the Purple Heart for too much valor, and the Combat Infantry Badge for being there. Even generals showed you a bit more respect when they saw the CIB on your uniform—which neither Hackett nor Dombroski was authorized to wear.

"Brodie?"

"This is my uniform."

"You make me look bad."

"If I come back with Mercer in cuffs, you'll look fine, Colonel."

Dombroski changed the subject. "You and Taylor worked well together in Kentucky."

Brodie couldn't tell if this was a statement or a question. "We did."

"Except for shooting the mule. But I think we can all agree that was entirely your fault."

"Yes, sir."

"You know Taylor was CA in Afghanistan."

CA meant Civil Affairs, specifically the 95th Civil Affairs Brigade out of Fort Bragg. Civil Affairs was the Army's soft power on the ground, interfacing with the local populace, overseeing public works projects, and, in the case of Afghanistan, navigating the delicate and often messy business of tribal politics. It was tough, dangerous work, and confirmed the old adage that it is harder to build than to destroy.

Brodie, of course, knew Taylor's history. He wished his superior would get to the point.

"Sometimes," said Dombroski, "these Stability Ops people get recruited by the Company."

That was the point. The CIA. That perennial bogeyman of the military and civilian worlds alike. The CIA was everything the Army was not—nebulous and nimble, with a loose command structure and a murky code of ethics. Not to mention a purposely confusing mission statement. This engendered a natural distrust and, in Brodie's opinion, a lot of unhelpful scapegoating.

Brodie asked, "Are you questioning her loyalty?"

"Of course not. But there were rumors going around about her down at Bragg. About certain entanglements."

"Like?"

"Like she was screwing a spook."

Well, thought Brodie, a young unmarried woman ought to be able to screw whoever she wants. But the truth was, while the various military branches and intelligence services were all working toward a common purpose, each of them operated in its own insular world with its own culture, traditions, and prejudices—and when you engaged in extracurricular activities with a member of another tribe, people always noticed, and often judged.

Still, this innuendo was a bit disturbing.

"Colonel, I'm about to fly to a country that might not be a country when I land. I need someone I can count on. You want to assign me a new partner?"

Dombroski shook his head. "She's fluent in Spanish and she'll never sleep with you. We better keep her."

Brodie downed the rest of his beer. "I should be hitting the road. It's a long drive."

"It's less than an hour to Dulles."

"We're going to New Jersey to interview Al Simpson."

"Someone already did that."

"Not very well," said Brodie.

Dombroski gave him a long look. Brodie didn't exactly have a reputation for double-checking his parachute before he jumped.

"This one's going to be a bitch," said Dombroski.

"You picked the right man, Colonel."

"Everybody else turned it down."

"Anything further, Colonel?"

"Stay in touch with me."

"I always do."

"You never do." He reminded Brodie, "Encrypted communication only. And keep in mind this case is a hot potato."

"Right."

"Captain Mercer is a U.S. citizen with constitutional rights, including the right to remain silent and to be represented by legal counsel."

"I'll inform him of that before I kick him in the nuts."

Dombroski smiled, then continued, "Could be that he's left the country after Simpson spotted him. Or he was just passing through."

"Could be."

"Or maybe he feels safe there. Maybe he has a business. Drugs. Arms. Maybe he's a hit man for the government or the opposition."

Brodie had thought about all this, and concluded that speculating without a clue was a waste of time. "I'll let you know."

"My point is, if Mercer has a business there, he's got bodyguards like everyone else in Venezuela who has a few bucks."

Brodie didn't reply.

"Mercer by himself is a one-man army. Mercer with armed hombres is not going to be easy to apprehend."

"I'll figure it out."

"Just so you understand . . . you need to make every effort to take him alive . . . but you are authorized to use deadly force if necessary."

Brodie nodded, wondering if he understood the subtext.

"And don't forget that the Venezuelan government is hostile to U.S. interests."

"Right."

"If you get arrested . . . you got a problem."

"Understood."

"And do you understand that this assignment is voluntary?"

"I do, sir." But Brodie also understood that Hackett's office had secured their visas yesterday. Sometimes in the Army, volunteering was mandatory.

"You good to go?"

"Always good to go."

"And make sure Ms. Taylor understands everything I just told you."

"Will do." He asked again, "Anything further?"

"No. Dismissed."

Brodie walked away from the bar toward the double doors.

Colonel Dombroski called out, "Make me look good, Brodie."

Well, he would find and apprehend Captain Mercer, and he'd let his boss take all the credit he wanted. But there were probably other people in the Army or the government who didn't look forward to a soldier like Captain Kyle Mercer standing before a court-martial on trial for desertion. Bad optics. Bad publicity. Better if he stayed missing. Or turned up dead.

Brodie exited the Officers' Club into the bright summer day.

CHAPTER 7

They drove north along I-95 in Brodie's 2014 Chevy Impala, which was functional and boring enough to be inconspicuous, but handled well at high speeds for the moments when his job got more interesting. The trunk was full of their hastily packed luggage. The drive from Quantico to West Orange, New Jersey, was a little over five hours, and they were already about four hours in.

Taylor had changed out of her uniform into jeans and a blouse, which was a better look when interviewing a voluntary civilian witness. She pulled up the Simpson home phone number that they'd gotten from the Fort Dix CID report and called on speaker.

A woman answered, and Taylor asked, "Is this Mrs. Simpson?"

"Speaking."

"Mrs. Simpson, this is Warrant Officer Maggie Taylor from Fort Dix."

A pause, then, "Yes?"

"May I speak to Mr. Simpson?"

"He's at work."

"I'll be at your home in about an hour, Mrs. Simpson. It would be good if he was there waiting for me."

"Well . . ."

"Or I'll go to his place of work, which may not be convenient for him."

"I'll call him . . . to come home."

"Thank you, ma'am. I won't keep him more than half an hour."

"All right . . ."

"Thank you, ma'am." Taylor hung up.

Brodie said, "You told two lies. We're not from Fort Dix, and we'll keep him as long as we need to." He added, "Also, you forgot to mention me."

"Women are perceived as nonthreatening."

"You threatened to bust into his place of employment."

"Simpson is a voluntary witness, but he could decide to stop talking at any time."

"His personnel file shows he served honorably."

"And now he's a civilian."

"Old soldiers never die, and they do the right thing when the Army calls."

"We'll see."

They rode in silence for a while. Brodie had learned early that Taylor wasn't the sort for idle conversation, which was fine by him. She took out her tablet and started reading through articles about Venezuela that she had bookmarked. At some point she put on a playlist from her smartphone. An old fiddle scratched out an up-tempo folk tune as a man sang in a distant, high-pitched wail. Something about farm hogs and a deal with the devil.

"I discovered this on vinyl while cleaning out my grandpa's basement," said Taylor. "Some of these recordings date back to the Twenties."

Throughout his military career, Brodie had met his share of hillbillies and country kids who had risen far above their station. The Army was good for that. But never had he met anyone like Maggie Taylor. She'd grown up in the hill country of eastern Tennessee, raised by her grandmother after her mother discovered her father with another woman and took care of them both with a double-barreled shotgun.

"Didn't even need to reload," Taylor had boasted during a disturbingly dispassionate recounting at the O Club after not nearly enough drinks. Either Taylor had buried it deep, or she was crazy. Probably both.

Mama went to prison, but Grandma taught her well, kept her away from the drunks and the crooks. Taylor had nurtured her natural intellect into a full ride at Georgetown, where she gained fluency in Arabic and became an Army Civil Affairs Specialist. She, like Brodie, had turned down Officer Candidate School. It was unusual for college grads to reject OCS, but Taylor, like Brodie, did not want the responsibilities or the privileges of commissioned officers; they both wanted to serve in the enlisted ranks, and to work their way up the promotion ladder. They were both promoted to Sergeant E-5, a three-striper, in their respective tours of duty in Afghanistan and Iraq, and now as CID investigators, they were both Warrant Officers. This hybrid rank apparently suited Taylor as much as it suited Brodie: decent pay and a few privileges with none of the stress or command expectations of a commissioned officer. But, as Brodie had quickly learned, there were other stresses on this job.

Taylor had spent two years crisscrossing the tribal lands of Afghanistan in armored convoys, assessing construction projects, negotiating with village elders, and hoping the smiling warlords treating her to tea and kebabs didn't sell her out to the Taliban up the road.

One time, they did. Her convoy got hit by IEDs, followed by an ambush. Her unit fought their way out, and Sergeant Taylor tended to some wounded along the way, all with a leg full of shrapnel. Half of her unit didn't make it. She was awarded the Silver Star for her valor, and the Purple Heart for her bad luck, though Brodie only knew about that because someone else told him. Unlike her mother's hillbilly justice, this was not a subject Maggie Taylor cared much to talk about.

The fiddler picked up the pace. The farmer, it seemed, had traded his wife's soul to the devil in exchange for more hogs, which sounded like a bad deal regardless of what the man thought of his wife.

Brodie was sure this music sounded better while winding through the foothills of the Smoky Mountains than driving along the New Jersey Turnpike. Actually, this music was made for drinking corn likker.

"What do you think?" asked Taylor.

"He should have held out for more hogs."

"The case, Brodie."

Brodie thought on that. They were flying blind if Simpson didn't give them more information. Shoe-leather detective work was fine in some places. But Caracas was probably not one of them.

Brodie hadn't worked a case in South America in years, but he knew that the current situation in Venezuela was bad. While Venezuela was technically a democracy, the current President, Nicolás Maduro, had been taking increasingly authoritarian measures to marginalize political opponents and crack down on civil unrest. He had royally screwed up his nation's economy, following in the fine tradition of his predecessor and mentor, the late Hugo Chávez, but Maduro lacked both Chávez' intellect and his charisma. Most crucially, the price of oil had plummeted soon after Maduro took over, and oil production was the entire basis of Venezuela's shaky economy.

The state treasury emptied, putting an end to government goodies and exposing Chávez' socialist revolution for the house of cards it was. Inflation skyrocketed, basic goods became scarce, and people were starving. In 2017 the Venezuelan people had taken to the streets demanding greater political freedom, but the movement was violently suppressed, and the opposition fractured.

These days, instead of demanding freedom, people were just trying to scrounge for bread and toilet paper. Despite all this, Maduro had recently won a second term in a highly suspect election with record low voter turnout in which he had either jailed or banned from the ballot all viable opposition candidates. The scary thing was that millions of people actually had voted for more of the same shit from this incompetent, autocratic asshole.

"What thrives in chaos?" asked Brodie.

"Crime," replied Taylor. "Criminals and fugitives."

"Is that why Mercer went to Venezuela?"

"That could be one reason. But not a good one."

"Right. Why do most soldiers desert?"

"To avoid the rigors of military service. Including the risk of death."

"Is that why Captain Kyle Mercer deserted?"

"I doubt it."

"Me too."

Someone knows why he deserted, thought Brodie. His Delta Force teammates, maybe. Or some higher-up at JSOC. As CID agents, he and Taylor were able to cross lines of rank and privilege that no one else in the Army could, so long as it was relevant to a criminal case. Justice knows no rank. But they were swimming up to the edge of murky waters here. JSOC. Delta. Black Ops. They couldn't even get the names of Mercer's Delta teammates, let alone interview them. Whatever answers they were going to find, the route of discovery ran through Venezuela. By way of Essex County, New Jersey.

Taylor said, "Here's the exit."

Brodie took the exit and followed a two-lane road bounded by commercial strips. The next song from Grandpa Taylor's dusty basement collection came on, this one a fun little ditty about a prison chain gang.

"You got any Stones on there?"

"No. But I've got some underground Afghani hip-hop I picked up in Kabul."

Brodie laughed, though he was pretty sure she was serious. Her Civil Affairs job had required her to be versed in all aspects of local culture, custom, and tradition. Taylor likely had taken this requirement fifteen steps too far and was now an expert in the ethnomusicology of all of Central Asia.

They drove on, passing gated communities labeled Cherry Ridge and Cedar Grove. Brodie wondered whether these names were the pretentious brain farts of real estate developers or memorials to the natural beauty they had paved over.

Eventually they found Simpson's development—Hidden Springs—and pulled up to a small guard booth where a rent-a-cop was watching TV.

They handed over their driver's licenses and the guard called the Simpsons, read their names, and then punched a button to open an agonizingly slow gate.

Brodie thought back to the many times he'd waited at the entrance gates to Baghdad's heavily fortified Green Zone, where the blast walls grew higher and thicker every time insurgents decided to set off a car bomb. Sometimes the illusion of security was the best you could hope for. Whatever helps you sleep at night.

They drove through rows of densely packed McMansions and pulled into the Simpsons' drive, behind a black Hummer. Maybe the guy missed his Army days, thought Brodie. Or maybe he was an asshole.

They got out and rang the bell. Nora Simpson, a petite, mousy woman, answered the door. She did not look particularly happy to see them. They showed their military IDs and Mrs. Simpson led them into an overly decorated family room with a big flat-screen TV and too many couches.

Al Simpson was deep in a recliner chair that was probably as comfortable as it was ugly, watching a baseball game. A little girl who looked to be about four was playing on the floor. She gave Brodie and Taylor a big gap-toothed grin.

Simpson rose from the chair. He had an average build except for the paunch under his oversize polo shirt. He switched off the TV.

"Just in time," he said with faux nonchalance. "Mets are blowing it."

Simpson's eyes darted to Taylor. His wife's too. Uncommonly beautiful women tend to have that effect, though Taylor was also uncommonly oblivious when it came to her assets.

"Sadie, sweetie," said Nora. "Take Mr. Bickles and Princess Moon to your room, okay?"

"She's a queen now, Mama."

"Well, congratulations to her. Upstairs."

Sadie picked up her toys and walked out of the room, looking up at Brodie and Taylor as she passed. "Are you married?"

"Sadie," chided Nora.

"No," said Brodie, "but I keep asking. Should I try again?"

"Yeah!" Sadie giggled as she ran out of the room.

They all made introductions, shook hands, and took seats around the coffee table. Taylor said, "Thank you for your help."

Simpson nodded and said, "I told the other guys everything. So I'm not sure what you're looking for."

"Something we may have missed," said Brodie, meaning, Something *you* may have missed.

Simpson did not reply, and Brodie thought that the former NCO was not completely comfortable talking to two officers who were also cops. So Brodie reassured him of his civilian status by saying, "Mr. Simpson, just tell us what you told the other two men." He added, "The Army is grateful for your assistance."

Simpson nodded again, and began to recount the same story they'd read in the report, that he was sitting in the Marriott lounge with his American colleague and a group of reps from the state oil company when he spotted Kyle Mercer at the bar.

"How did he look?" asked Brodie.

"A hell of a lot better than the last time I saw him on TV, kneeling in the dirt in front of a line of ragheads. He'd bulked up. Ripped, like how I remembered him from training. He had a beard, but it was trimmed."

"Okay," said Brodie. "So you're sitting with these clients, you look up and see him at the bar. And he sees you."

"Yeah," said Simpson. "I knew it was him, he's staring at me. And I said his name."

"Did you say his name while still sitting with the other guys in the lounge?" asked Brodie. "Or did you get up and approach first?"

Simpson hesitated, realizing that his story wasn't matching up with what he'd told the other CID guys. He glanced at his wife, who put a supportive hand on his shoulder.

"Wait. Sorry. It's been a couple weeks. He didn't see me at first, actually. Because he wasn't facing me. He was facing away, at the bar. I saw his tattoo first. Of the snake."

Brodie had caught him—and importantly, Simpson knew he'd been caught. He proceeded to tell the same story he'd told the other agents, that he saw Mercer from behind, recognized the tattoo, approached the bar, and said his name. Then they made eye contact. Brodie decided to proceed as if nothing had happened, rather than call him out in front of his wife. "So *now* you're looking at each other," said Brodie. "Then what happened?"

"He just kinda stared at me. Cold. Pissed, maybe. My colleague, Pete, and the oil guys were looking at me, and then back at Mercer, and it felt kind of awkward and tense. Then Kyle just gets up and walks out of the bar."

"That's it?" asked Taylor. "You just let him walk off?"

"What was I supposed to do? We'd just closed this big deal, we were celebrating. That's where my head was at."

"Did Pete ask you about who you saw?" asked Taylor.

"No . . . yes, and I said case of mistaken identity, or something."

"Okay," said Brodie. "And what was he wearing?"

Simpson thought a moment. "A dark T-shirt and jeans."

"What was he drinking?" asked Taylor.

"I don't know. I didn't look."

"Where were you before the hotel?" asked Brodie.

"A restaurant in the area."

"What was it called?"

"I don't remember. Spanish name."

"How many drinks did you have before seeing Mercer?" asked Taylor.

Simpson again looked at his wife. This was taking on the tempo of an interrogation, not a friendly and voluntary interview. Brodie needed to pump the brakes.

"Let's step back a minute," he said. "How well did you know Kyle Mercer?"

"We went through basic and advanced infantry training together," replied Simpson. "So, I'd say well, but it's been awhile. Kinda lost touch after he went to OCS and I got assigned to the Fourth Brigade at Fort Carson."

"What kind of man was he?"

Simpson thought on this. "Kyle was intense. Some guys grew up hunting, some came from military families, but he was none of that. I mean, he didn't know shit about how to shoot a rifle or follow orders. But he was *jacked*, you know, really strong and fit, like he'd been training for this. This kid from SoCal who'd lifted weights every day and learned everything he thought he knew about war from watching movies and playing Call of Duty."

"This doesn't sound like the makings of an elite soldier," suggested Brodie.

"You don't understand," said Simpson. "He wanted to be that elite soldier, more than anyone I've ever met before or since. In his mind, he already was. What I'm saying is, he had the *will*. So, Delta Force? No surprise there. No surprise at all."

There was a silence in the room. Brodie thought about the redacted mission details in Mercer's file. Just who was this guy? What had he done, and what was he capable of? Well, he was capable of five decapitations, which meant he was capable of anything. Brodie looked at Simpson and asked, "Why do you think a man with Captain Mercer's survival skills . . . a man who is a wanted fugitive all over the world . . . would be sitting in the bar of a hotel frequented by an international clientele?"

Simpson understood that this was not a rhetorical question. In fact, he understood that Brodie was calling him on his bullshit story.

Simpson stood. He shot Brodie a look. "I think I need a cigarette."

"I'll join you."

Brodie didn't smoke, but that wasn't the point. He got up and followed Simpson to the back deck, which overlooked an artificial lake. Simpson shook out a cigarette from his pack and offered one to Brodie, who took it to share the bond of the addicted.

Simpson lit him up, and Brodie watched him as he lit his, hands unsteady, and took a deep drag.

Simpson said, "I didn't know what to say."

Brodie didn't reply. When a man's about to confess something, it's best to keep quiet.

"I mean, I wasn't going to say anything. But I couldn't stop thinking about the two guys who got killed looking for him. I spoke to my wife . . . she said I had to do the right thing."

Brodie regarded Al Simpson, who'd joined the Army, like Brodie himself, in the aftermath of 9/11. He did his service, did well in the private sector, settled down, and put on twenty pounds. But the war that was now just a memory to Simpson was still going on, and in another year or so they'd be sending soldiers over who weren't even alive on 9/11.

"Al, where did you actually see Kyle Mercer?"

Simpson looked at him, took a deep breath. "My partner, Pete, and I had signed this lucrative contract, everyone was happy, some of the execs took us out, like I said. It started out well enough, they took us to this expensive restaurant. Ate a lot, got drunk, hopped between a few bars and clubs. We did go to the Marriott bar . . . then we got in a car and headed to the outskirts . . ."

Brodie nodded encouragingly.

"We start driving up into the hillside slums, along these narrow, winding roads. We get to this building . . . some piece of shit place like everywhere else around there, but bigger than the rest. I was kinda creeped out, as drunk as I was, I knew something wasn't right. Pete, he's a real dirtbag, nothing's going to stop him. They reassured me, we go in. And . . ."

Simpson trailed off. Brodie was pretty sure he knew where this was going, but he let Simpson take his time.

Simpson continued, "The place was dark, with couches all around, a bar. Naked girls, like, everywhere. Guys too, all locals as far as I could tell, getting grinded on, drinking, some getting led into back rooms. I didn't want to . . . but I mean, these guys were important to our business, and I didn't know what to do."

"Al, look at me."

Simpson looked at him, a tortured look on his face.

"I'm not your priest," said Brodie. "I've got a soldier out there who has a lot to answer for, and I need to find him."

Simpson nodded, swallowed hard. "I should have said something sooner."

"Maybe you held back because you're not sure what you saw."

"No," said Simpson. "I'm sure. It was Kyle. He was alone at this table in the back, just sitting there. Looking nowhere. It seemed like, I don't know, like maybe he ran the place."

This surprised Brodie. "Why would you think that?"

"The way he carried himself. He just seemed comfortable. The girls stayed away from him, and he seemed just fine with that. If he didn't run it, he at least was there for some reason other than to dip his wick, you know?"

"And he saw you?"

"Yeah. He was watching me. It was crazy. I mean, that's the last place you think you're going to run into someone you know."

"I'm sure he thought the same thing."

Simpson forced a smile. "Yeah . . . but I'm not sure he actually recognized me, it's just that me and Pete were the only other gringos there. I don't think Pete even noticed him, he was too busy staring at tits. I stood and moved towards him and said his name, and he's looking at me in this weird way, and, yeah, I saw the snake tattoo on his arm. He got that after we finished basic."

"What did he do?"

"He got up, I thought maybe he was going to walk towards me, but instead he turns and goes through this side door. And this big bouncer gets in my way, makes it clear I shouldn't follow. And then Pete pulls me away."

"To get you safely away from the bouncer."

Another long pause. Simpson took a drag, stubbed his cigarette on the porch railing, and flicked it into the reeds below. The sun was setting, lights flicking on in the houses around the lake. Across the water, a family was setting up for a barbecue.

Simpson took a deep breath, then said, "If I have to testify about this, my marriage is in trouble."

"Only if you admit to getting laid."

Simpson didn't respond to that. He stared out at the lake. "Something else you need to know . . . the girls were young. Some of them."

"How young?"

"Too young."

Brodie nodded. That put this place, and this witness, in a whole new category of sleaze. "Well . . . we'll work out your testimony if the time comes." He asked, "What was the name of this place?"

"Don't know if it even had a name."

"Okay, can you describe the exterior?"

"Just what I told you."

"What color was the building?"

Simpson shrugged. "I think white. Like stucco or something."

"One story? Two stories?"

"One."

"Roof? Windows?"

Simpson thought for a moment. "Flat roof, like most of the buildings up there. I don't think there were windows."

"Interior?"

"Dark as hell. Like I said, there was a bar, couches, tables . . . hard to remember details."

"How long a ride was it from the Marriott to this place?"

"About twenty, thirty minutes."

"What about landmarks on the way from the Marriott?"

Simpson shook his head. "I was drunk, it was dark as shit. The city doesn't even keep the streetlights on any more. The place is fucked."

"Right." Brodie took a drag on his cigarette. "I need to find this place, Al. I need to find Kyle Mercer."

"You going there?"

Brodie didn't reply, and he watched Simpson as he stared out at the water, thinking.

Simpson said, "I do remember there was an airstrip. It was one of the few things that was lit up, the runway lights. I don't think we'd been on the road too long when I saw that. And we passed an old church when we were in the hills—it was tall and it stood out from all the low, shitty buildings."

"What did the church look like?"

"Like it was old. Might have been pink. Like I said, it was dark."

Brodie nodded. "Anything else?"

Simpson thought for a moment. "That's all I've got."

"Okay. I need Pete's last name and contact info."

Simpson shook his head. "He doesn't remember shit. He couldn't even remember if he got laid."

"Okay, but you call Pete, and also see if you can get hold of those Venezuelan oil execs. I'd like to find that whorehouse."

Simpson nodded, but Brodie didn't think he'd be contacting anyone except maybe his lawyer. Nevertheless, Brodie gave him his card. "Leave a voice message if you have any luck."

Simpson glanced at the card and again nodded.

"Thank you, Sergeant."

Simpson forced a smile at the use of his old rank. "I shoulda remembered the first thing I learned in the Army—never volunteer for anything."

"The first thing you learned was duty, honor, country."

Simpson nodded again. "Kyle broke the oath. Kyle deserves to die."

"Captain Mercer will be brought to justice."

Simpson gave Brodie a look of appraisal. "You don't capture a man like that. You kill him. Or he kills you."

Brodie didn't reply.

Simpson added, "The next day, after I sobered up, I realized Kyle could have killed me in a back room."

Brodie nodded. He'd had the same thought. But maybe Kyle Mercer had experienced a moment of human feeling for his old Army buddy. If so, Brodie was sure that Mercer later regretted not eliminating a witness. And if he didn't regret it then, he would when Brodie and Taylor caught up with him.

Simpson said, "That's all I have to say."

Brodie stubbed his cigarette and flicked it into the reeds. "Thank you for your time."

Simpson nodded, lit another cigarette, and stared at the darkening horizon. Apparently he was not ready to face Mrs. Simpson.

Brodie went back into the house, wished Mrs. Simpson a good evening, and motioned to Taylor, and they left.

———

En route to Newark Airport, Brodie gave Taylor the rundown, including that the brothel trafficked in underage girls.

Taylor pointed out, "If Simpson had sex with one of them, that makes him a sex offender as well as an unreliable witness."

"Let's stick to the ID."

"Okay, so he saw a bearded white guy in a dimly lit whorehouse while drunk. Great ID."

"He seemed certain," said Brodie. He reminded her, "The ouroboros tattoo."

"That's not an uncommon tattoo, but I guess that's enough for a trip to Caracas."

"I've gone to other shitholes on less."

"What about this airstrip he saw? Did he pass it on his right or left?"

"I don't know and I doubt he'd remember."

"What did the brothel look like?"

"White, maybe stucco, one story."

"Did he describe the area where the brothel was?"

"It was dark and he was drunk."

"What were the other buildings in the area made out of? Cinder block? Brick? Stucco?"

"I didn't think to ask specifically. Why?"

"In Caracas, according to what I read, different slums are made with different materials depending on when they were built. That could've helped us."

"I think he said the surrounding buildings were made of gingerbread."

Taylor looked out the window, frustrated. Brodie could appreciate why. She'd clearly already begun her obsessive dive into the finer points of Caracas' urban topography, and the only reason she wasn't present for the man-to-man interview with Al Simpson was that she was a woman. Also, Simpson's original false statement threw his whole credibility into question, and maybe Taylor wasn't keen to put so much faith in the rum-soaked memory of a married businessman who was trying to forget what he was asked to remember.

Brodie considered himself a rational man, but over the years he'd gained a certain respect for the value of hunches, gut instincts, and the certainty of a man's sight through the dim, smoky light of a brothel. Sure, there were times when your sole witness was shit and unreliable, and you had to take a step back, reassess. But Kyle Mercer was out there, a fugitive with lethal skills, and he'd already gotten a couple of men killed and killed a few himself. This was the only lead they had, and you had to run down every lead, even if it took you to hell, or New Jersey, or Caracas.

CHAPTER 8

They took the I-78 Expressway east toward Newark Liberty International Airport. It was a little past rush hour, and traffic wasn't bad.

Taylor was scrolling through some articles on her tablet, reading up on their destination. She asked, "Did you pack toothpaste? First aid items? Literally anything and everything you could possibly need?"

Brodie flashed back to his rushed packing job after his meeting with Dombroski, which involved throwing things at an open suitcase and zipping up whatever made it in.

She continued, "We have to assume it will be hard to come by even basic items once we land. Shops are bare. Lines for the few items available can stretch for hours. It looks like a problem even money can't solve."

"Money solves everything."

"Not where we're going," said Taylor. "Let's stop at a pharmacy."

"Let's not."

"We could also get an overnight bag and fill it with extra stuff. Food, first aid supplies. Might pay for a little goodwill on the streets of Caracas."

Brodie thought about that. "Not a bad idea."

"You might even say it's a good idea."

"You might."

Brodie got off the expressway a few miles short of the airport, and their GPS found them a CVS drugstore in a shopping center near the exit. They stocked up on some essentials and found an overnight bag to fill with over-the-counter meds, bandages, batteries, canned goods, and snacks. They each took out four hundred dollars from the ATM in case they needed to bribe their way through passport control or customs when they landed in Caracas.

They paid with Brodie's government credit card and left the drugstore. Brodie threw the overnight bag in the back seat and thought about the contents. Razors. Aspirin. Tissue packets and candy bars. It depressed him, this cheap drugstore haul three minutes off the expressway that would become precious cargo once they landed. He had come face to face with American poverty and misery in the course of his work, from trailer parks in Alabama to the worst housing projects the Bronx had to offer. But going abroad had exposed him to new depths, to places where civilization and human dignity struggled to exist. Places where there was no bottom.

As they got back on the expressway, Brodie thought about the man behind this mission. Kyle Mercer. Middle-class San Diego kid. Wannabe soldier who got to live out his military fantasies in the real world, and excelled. What did it mean, really, that trajectory? Aspiring to something like that, having an idea of the warrior you wanted to be, and then becoming it?

Brodie's relationship with soldiering had been very different. He was raised in Liberty, New York, a historic small town west of the Hudson Valley. He was the only child of Clara and Arthur Brodie, a couple of hippie holdouts who bought an old farmhouse in the early Seventies and fixed it up themselves, then used the land to grow vegetables and raise chickens. They sold some produce to a local grocer and did odd jobs around town for cash or used clothing. "We came up here for Woodstock and never left" was a moldy old joke that Brodie heard from his father too many times throughout his childhood, though it really wasn't far from the truth.

It was a pleasant and idyllic childhood in many ways. Collecting eggs from the chickens, harvesting vegetables in the morning that would find their way into a stew that night, playing on what felt like limitless land. They never had much money, but he didn't know that.

By the time he came of age, he was growing tired of this semi-rural, semi-subsistence existence in a place that missed out on the gentrification of the Hudson Valley towns and that was growing increasingly underpopulated and poor. His parents had left Greenwich Village to reconnect with nature and, he would understand later, unplug from the political and spiritual battles of the 1960s, which they felt had been lost by the end of the decade. He wanted to make that journey in reverse, to engage with a world he felt isolated from.

With his parents' blessing, and a combination of loans and scholarships, he moved to Manhattan and attended NYU, right in the middle of his parents' old bohemian stomping ground of Greenwich Village. It was a world of exciting firsts. First girlfriend. First time trying drugs. First mugging. But there was something surprising and disappointing too, especially about those native to the city and the surrounding upscale suburbs—a kind of urban provincialism shared by many of his classmates, people who did not look beyond themselves because they thought they were the center of the world.

In his senior year, the world came to them. He was just waking up in his tiny fifth-floor walk-up on the Lower East Side when the first plane hit the North Tower. He was down on the street with hundreds of onlookers when the second plane struck, and running from a wall of smoke, dust, and debris when both towers collapsed and blotted out the sun.

He went through the motions for the rest of his senior year and barely graduated. After a restless few months back home, he enlisted in the Army.

His parents were predictably devastated. The specter of Uncle Reggie, his father's older brother who had died in Vietnam and was almost never spoken of, hung in the air. But his enlistment wasn't an act of rebellion against his lefty parents, or even an act of revenge against the people who brought the towers down. He was just trying to make sense of things. And in that moment, the Army was what made sense.

He began basic training on the same day that Secretary of State Colin Powell held up a model vial of anthrax—one of Iraq's supposed weapons of mass destruction—on the floor of the U.N. General Assembly. Four months later he was deployed to Fort Lewis in Washington State as part of the 2nd Infantry's 3rd Stryker Brigade. About six months after that he was on patrols in downtown Baghdad. He recalled very clearly the first time he was shot at. He would never forget the first platoon-mate he saw killed.

They were approaching the exits for the terminals. Overhead, an Airbus roared across the washed-out sky, wheels down, coming in for a steady landing.

"Which airline?" asked Brodie.

"Copa."

"What the hell is that?"

"Panama's national airline. And the only one available to take us from Newark to Caracas on a last-minute red-eye. We've got a three-hour layover in Panama City."

"Next time book a private jet."

"The travel office got us business class."

Right. The Army only splurged on business-class travel when the place you were going to sucked. So that made it official.

Brodie saw the exit for long-term parking. If everything went right with this mission, they wouldn't be coming back through this airport. And if everything went wrong, they wouldn't be coming back at all. Who'd get his Chevy Impala? Probably Newark Airport, to pay for the long-term parking.

He pulled off the expressway.

CHAPTER 9

They took the airport shuttle bus from the long-term parking lot to the terminal, checked in, dropped off their bags, and got through security with over an hour to kill before boarding. Copa Airlines was affiliated with United, so they headed toward the United Club Lounge.

It was a little past 10 P.M., and the terminal was quiet. At one gate a group of backpackers was camped out on the floor, waiting on a delayed flight to Barcelona, where Brodie wished he were going.

They passed a currency exchange booth and Taylor wanted to change some dollars for Venezuela's local currency, the bolívar. An LED screen was updating rates in real time, but the window that was supposed to display the exchange rate for Venezuela was blank.

Taylor said to the middle-aged guy behind the window, "I'd like to buy some Venezuelan bolívars."

"Sorry, miss, we're not dealing in bolívars any more. The market's too unstable. You'll have to take care of it on the other end."

Brodie said to Taylor, "I told you this was a bad idea for our honeymoon." He turned back to the guy. "I said, 'Let's go to Venice'; she says she misheard me."

The man gave him a blank look, and Taylor pulled Brodie away from the window. "I hope you're amusing yourself."

"Someone has to."

They found the United Club Lounge, which was not far from their gate. They showed their passports and business-class tickets to a young female receptionist at the front desk, signed in, and entered the club.

It was a nice space, especially considering it existed inside what is generally ranked as the nation's worst airport after LaGuardia. It featured a well-stocked bar, a buffet table, and deep, comfortable chairs to fall asleep in and miss your flight.

"What are you drinking?" asked Brodie.

"Orange juice," said Taylor as she settled into a chair and pulled out her tablet.

Brodie went to the bar and ordered her an OJ, and a scotch and soda for himself.

When he returned with the drinks, Taylor was reading something on her tablet. She said, "I downloaded some State Department info. The bolívar has become almost worthless in the time since Maduro took power in 2013. They've tried to artificially control the exchange rates, but since they import almost everything it doesn't have much effect. You can spend a month's wages on half a pound of chicken, that kind of thing."

"We'll skip the chicken. Meanwhile, what's the security situation?"

"Precarious, but not chaotic. The opposition is in disarray and there's not much in the way of civil unrest anymore."

Well, that was good to hear. But given the state of affairs, that could change in an instant. Brodie had been to enough screwed-up places to understand the toxic brew of desperation, anger, and fear that runs through unstable societies. If no one's out in the streets protesting, it just means that people woke up that morning more exhausted than angry, or more afraid than brave. But tomorrow might be different. A full civil war might make his and Taylor's job a little tougher.

"Also," said Taylor, "there's a State Department travel warning. But that's no surprise."

The U.S. State Department issues two types of advisories for trouble spots: alerts and warnings. Alerts are short-term in nature, to apprise travelers of natural disasters, disease outbreaks, or upcoming political elections that might bring strikes and protests. Warnings, on the other hand, are for places that the U.S. government considers fucked-up on a more long-term basis. Venezuela fell into the latter category. A State Department warning was not good for tourism.

Brodie took a long drink and thought about their destination. Venezuela wasn't yet a police state like Cuba, or a chaotic failed state like Somalia. But it was a country on the edge, economically desperate, with weak and corrupt institutions and a government openly hostile to American interests. It was a place where you could probably bend a lot of rules, especially with enough dough, but the guys trying to fuck up your day could bend them too.

He reached into his carry-on and pulled out a Venezuela guide book that Taylor had procured from the Quantico travel office. He flipped to the Caracas portion of the book, and to his favorite section: *Dangers and Annoyances.* These types of books usually tried to be a little PC and pull some punches when discussing the questionable locales their readers had chosen to travel to. *Mogadishu has a rich and vibrant cultural heritage, but do your best to never leave your hotel.* But the author did not mince words when it came to Caracas. Many neighborhoods were to be avoided entirely. The "safe" ones were only okay while the sun was shining, and even then, only inside of a vehicle. Murders and kidnappings were rampant, and the cops were no help. In fact, they were often more dangerous than the criminals. Every security apparatus in the country, including customs and passport control at the airport, ought to be considered criminally corrupt, and government officials were often looking to harass and extort foreign travelers. They especially didn't like Americans.

On that subject, Brodie pulled out his laptop, started it up, and changed the settings so it would boot straight into a clean partition on his drive. That would probably be sufficient to protect any of his CID or other Army-related documents and e-mails from a cursory search at the Caracas airport. He advised Taylor to do the same and was not surprised to learn that she already had, and was also planning to wipe clean her tablet before they landed in Venezuela.

"Also," said Brodie, "we're supposed to be married as part of our cover. Send me a picture of you in a bikini so I can make it my desktop wallpaper."

"Is that what married people do?"

"Well, we're newlyweds. We don't know how to be married yet."

"Right," said Taylor, smiling. "This is our honeymoon."

"How do we explain the separate rooms?"

"I'm still a virgin."

"Who's gonna believe that?"

"My grandma."

"Can't wait to meet her."

"You will. She's moving in with us."

"I want a divorce."

Taylor laughed. They made eye contact, and she looked away.

When Brodie first met his new partner, he'd regarded her beauty as a potential occupational hazard. As a matter of principle, he rejected the idea that he would have trouble working with an attractive woman. Also, Taylor had proven herself to be a good partner, and sex was the surest way to mess up a successful working relationship. But buried in even the most well-intentioned modern man is an old pig fighting to get out, and Brodie had to remind himself to keep that porker in check.

He thought about what Dombroski had said about Taylor and her possible romantic entanglement with a CIA guy at Fort Bragg. He'd met more than a few Company men over the years. He liked one or two of them, but in his humble opinion, most of them were arrogant, dead-eyed pricks who would sell out their own mothers. He had a hard time imagining Taylor with someone like that, but then again, how well did he really know her? And even if she had been hitting the sack with a CIA officer, how was that enough to call her loyalty and motives into question? And then he remembered what Dombroski had said about Civil Affairs people in Afghanistan being recruited by the Company.

As with the Kyle Mercer file, Brodie had the feeling there were some things missing from his picture of Maggie Taylor, some black-ink redactions that he would need to find a way to read.

CHAPTER 10

The plane to Panama City was about half-full, and of the sixteen seats in business class only three others were occupied.

Brodie said, "I usually snore on flights."

"Even when you're awake?"

He smiled.

"Just don't drool."

After takeoff Taylor took out her tablet and they both looked over a detailed map of Caracas that she had downloaded. The city ran along an east-west strip nestled in a narrow valley. Beyond the steep mountains to the north was the Caribbean coast, and to the south a vast stretch of hills and forests.

Kyle Mercer had been spotted by an unreliable witness in a sprawling metropolis of almost two million people, surrounded by rugged and sparsely populated terrain. But, as General Hackett said, they had what they had, and Brodie was confident that with some resourcefulness, a little luck, and maybe a lot of cash, they would find their man. Yet, as he looked at the map of the city and the surrounding countryside, the daunting nature of their task was coming into focus.

With Simpson's recollection in mind, they scanned the map for airports and airstrips. Their final destination, Simón Bolívar International Airport, was right on the coast, separated from Caracas by the mountain range, so that couldn't be the airport that Simpson had seen on his ride to the whorehouse. Taylor zoomed the map in to a tighter view of Caracas, and they located the Marriott in a neighborhood called El Rosal, which was east of downtown.

There was a small airport called Base Aérea Generalísimo Francisco de Miranda less than three miles farther east of the hotel, and it appeared to be the only airport or airstrip anywhere within the city proper. Taylor traced her finger along the road that ran past the airport. She tapped an area in the eastern hills.

"Petare," said Taylor. "One of the largest and most dangerous slums in the world. This could be where Simpson saw Mercer."

Brodie took a closer look. The map of Petare consisted of a sprawling network of winding roads snaking along the ridgelines—a complex web with sharp switchbacks and countless dead ends. The vast slum ran from the foothills of the coastal range in the north all the way south to a river called the Guaire, stretching the entire width of the city's north-south axis.

"Could be," Brodie agreed.

"Though it's also the kind of place where an American would stick out like a turkey at a hog show."

Brodie smiled. He liked it when Taylor reverted to her country roots. He said, "If Mercer is hanging around the most dangerous part of one of the most dangerous cities in the world, maybe he's doing something other than hiding. Like working with a gang. Maybe even running a gang." He reminded her, "This is a tough hombre."

Taylor nodded.

Or maybe Mercer was there as briefly as Simpson, and for the same carnal reason. They were starting this case with only one thread of a clue to hang on to, and maybe it wasn't as strong as they wanted it to be.

Hoping that they had at least narrowed down their search, they gave their drink orders to the flight attendant, read a little more on the current situation in Venezuela, then reclined their seats for a couple of hours' sleep in the darkened cabin. Now he could tell Dombroski that he'd slept with her.

The flight to Panama City's Tocumen International Airport took a little over five hours, and they deplaned into a bright and bustling terminal. Their bags were checked through to Caracas and their connecting flight was in the same terminal, so they had a short walk to their connecting gate.

They took a seat at the Caracas departure gate, which was, unsurprisingly, almost empty.

There was a time, only a few years earlier, when the Caracas gate might have been full. Brodie had just read an article about a practice known as "currency tourism." The Venezuelan government was selling U.S. dollars cheaply at their own artificially controlled exchange rate, but the demand was so high that they would only sell to Venezuelans who were traveling abroad and could present an international airline ticket. The farther you were traveling, the more dollars you could buy. So when this practice was at its peak back in 2013, someone could get a ticket to Los Angeles, buy dollars at a rate of about six bolívars to the dollar, have that money credited to their account, and then withdraw it in U.S. currency once they got to California. Then they brought that same money home, sold it back on the black market for an exchange rate of forty-five bolívars to the dollar, and made a nice profit. The clueless government finally caught wind of this scheme and started cracking down, restricting the sale of dollars even further. This, combined with airlines either canceling their flights in and out of Caracas, or refusing to sell airline tickets to anyone paying in bolívars, had led to a dramatic drop in the flow of native Venezuelans into and out of the country. They had become, quite literally, prisoners of their own shattered economy.

The bolívar had been in free fall ever since—by the end of July 2018 the black-market price for a U.S. dollar had ballooned from forty-five bolívars to over three and a half million.

Brodie said to Taylor, "We've been asking ourselves: Why Venezuela? The simplest motive is always money. You said goods are scarce, and it's a problem that not even money can fix. That's because they import everything, right?"

"Right," said Taylor. "Except oil."

Brodie nodded. Venezuela had the largest natural oil reserves in the world, surpassing even Saudi Arabia. "Oil is still cheap, especially with the power of Western currency. Are people smuggling it out of the country? Let's say to Colombia?"

"I'm sure," replied Taylor. "It's a petro-state that's bleeding out, so we have to assume there are enterprising vultures."

"Maybe that's why Mercer is there."

"Here's a simpler explanation: Mercer did something bad, and he is now hiding out in a hard-to-reach place that has no law and order, and that also happens to have great beaches and beautiful women."

Venezuela did have the distinction of producing more international beauty pageant queens than any other nation. And, as Brodie had learned in his brief research, it was also a place obsessed with plastic surgery. Cost wasn't a barrier for entry, either. Plenty of Venezuelan banks offered special high-interest loans for boob jobs.

Brodie thought back to the video they'd watched in Hackett's office. The heads on pikes. The theatrical resignation of his Army commission. Whatever Kyle Mercer was up to, Brodie didn't think he was drinking rum on the beach and chasing señoritas. He said, "Getting rich off political instability and corruption is an angle, and we should keep it in the back of our minds." He advised, "You need to start thinking like a criminal."

"Is that what this job does to you?"

"It's a perk."

The gate agent began the boarding process, starting with business class. Only two other people, a Hispanic man and woman wearing suits, boarded. Brodie and Taylor approached the desk, scanned their boarding passes, and walked through the jet bridge onto a Boeing 737. The flight attendant seemed surprised to see them on the flight to Caracas.

As the plane pulled away from the gate, Brodie and Taylor shared a look. They were a long way from chasing hillbilly drug dealers in Kentucky.

Brodie imagined them days or weeks from now, making this journey in reverse. Hopefully on a private jet under cover of darkness, with Captain Kyle Mercer handcuffed to his seat.

It's good to visualize success. Failure is not an option, as they say in the Army. The joke in Iraq was, "You'll be coming home with a CMH," which didn't mean a Congressional Medal of Honor; it meant a coffin with metal handles. Bad joke.

PART III

CARACAS, VENEZUELA
AUGUST 2018

CHAPTER 11

Brodie looked out the window as they made their approach into Simón Bolívar International Airport.

The Caribbean coast stretched out before them, the cresting waves sparkling orange in the morning light, and the airport's gray asphalt runways cut inland from the shore. Surrounding the airport, the small port city of Maiquetía clung to the coastline and ran up the foothills of the lush green Venezuelan Coastal Range that ascended into the clouds and hid Caracas from view.

As the plane banked to the left and the wheels lowered, they got a closer view of the shore to the west of the airport, which was lined with beachfront homes and a few marinas where rows of glimmering white yachts sat at anchor. Brodie noticed what appeared to be a beach resort with lounge chairs, umbrellas, and thatched huts. Despite the deprivation wracking the country, there seemed to be plenty of sunbathers out on this beautiful morning. He wondered if Kyle Mercer was one of them.

The landing was smooth, and after they deplaned they headed for passport control. A few airport security guards in black fatigues and carrying assault rifles watched them as they passed. One of them made a sound of approval toward the gringo lady, and the others laughed.

Brodie said, "Ask those guys if they'll pose for a picture with you. We can text it to Dombroski."

"No stupid jokes, please. We're operational now. In hostile territory. Stay alert."

"I have eyes in the back of my head."

"But your head is up your ass."

They passed a large photo mural highlighting Venezuela's natural wonders, including a towering waterfall and mountainous plateaus surrounded by rain forest. Beneath the photos it said, <u>VENEZUELA—CONOCERLA</u> <u>ES TU DESTINO</u>.

Taylor translated: "Venezuela. To know her is your destiny."

"I thought it said you have reached your destination."

"Let me do the translating."

The line for nonresidents at passport control was short, and Brodie looked around to see who else was crazy or stupid enough to come here. There was a smattering of euro tourists, a few East Asian and South Asian travelers, and a number of Hispanic-looking men and women, presumably from other Latin American countries.

When it was their turn, Brodie and Taylor approached the booth together. The agent who took their passports wore a scowl along with a uniform a couple of sizes too big for his small frame. He scanned their visas, which didn't seem to raise any alarms, then took his time flipping through their passport pages, paying particular attention to Brodie's. Brodie was used to getting extra attention at passport controls the world over—the various entry stamps and visas from places like Karachi, Amman, and Kabul tended to arouse suspicion. If he'd had a little more notice about this assignment, he would have gotten a clean passport.

The agent asked Brodie something, in Spanish, and Brodie stared back at the guy with a look of honest ignorance. The man repeated it, jabbing a finger on the page of his passport where he had affixed his tourist visa.

Taylor kept her fluent Spanish to herself, and asked, "Habla inglés?"

The agent scowled harder, and said to Brodie, "Why Caracas?"

"Tourists."

"Job?"

"Waste management," said Brodie.

The agent just stared at them, his eyes darting between Brodie and Taylor. Brodie wondered if this was the time for a bribe. He could see at least two security cameras pointed at the passport booths. Though maybe that didn't matter in a country that had been corrupted to the core, and they just needed to pay the gringo admission fee to get moved along. Brodie fingered a few twenty-dollar bills in his pocket, trying to read the situation.

Before he had to make the call, the man slammed his entry stamp on both of their passports, then slid them back to them. He said, without a hint of sincerity, "Welcome to Venezuela."

————

They got their luggage at the baggage carousel, and then approached customs, which consisted of four uniformed agents standing beside long tables in front of a wall of Plexiglas. This was, he hoped, the last wall of security before they found their driver and got on their way to the hotel.

Brodie noticed that all of the agents were staring at them, despite the number of travelers approaching customs. They entered one of the lanes marked <u>NADA QUE DECLARAR</u> and approached an agent, a tall, thin guy with chiseled features whose nametag read "Suárez." They handed over their customs forms, which Señor Suárez looked over, saying, "Hotel El Dorado?"

"Sí," said Brodie.

The customs agent sharply slapped his hand on the table, indicating they should put their baggage on it.

They complied, lifting their carry-ons and their checked luggage. Señor Suárez took his time unzipping and rifling through their belongings, paying close attention to some of Taylor's undergarments. When he opened the overnight bag full of snacks and toiletries, he gave Brodie a questioning look.

"Gifts," said Brodie.

Suárez dug his hands into the bag, feeling around the lining. Then he pulled out a packet of disposable razors, eyed them for a moment, and stuffed them in his pocket without a word. He took a bottle of aspirin too. He didn't look like he needed a shave, but apparently he had a headache.

He looked up at Brodie. "Dólares?"

"Sí," said Brodie.

"Dónde?"

"My wallet."

"Cartera," translated Taylor.

"Cuánto?" asked Suárez.

"Just some drinking money," said Brodie.

Suárez gave him a blank look, and Taylor stepped in and said something in Spanish. They conversed back and forth, and it was clear that Señor Suárez had a problem.

After a few more exchanges with Taylor, he pointed to a door off to the side. "Por ahí," he said curtly.

They gathered their bags and followed Suárez away from the customs check and through a windowless door. Brodie hoped this was just some ritual harassment of Yankee imperialists, and they'd be on their way after some obligatory questioning, possibly followed by the exchange of a few dólares.

They entered a small room with flickering fluorescent bulbs and a flagpole shoved in the corner. Suárez took a seat behind a bare metal desk and gestured at two folding chairs across from him. Brodie and Taylor sat.

Suárez said something in Spanish while looking between them, and Taylor replied.

As they conversed, Brodie noticed a small framed portrait of President Maduro hanging crooked on the wall behind Suárez.

Back in February of 2011, Brodie had found himself in Damascus, on the trail of an Army CENTCOM staffer who was involved in arms smuggling across the Syrian-Jordanian border. While there he had made the acquaintance of a German expat named Marcus, who smoked and drank to excess. One evening over hookah and beers in a café in the Old City, Marcus had gestured at the wall behind Brodie where a portrait of President Bashar al-Assad was hanging. It was crooked.

"That is what this place is, my friend," Marcus had said. "A shabby dictatorship, where everyone fears Assad enough to hang his picture, but does not love him enough to straighten it. You see what has happened in Tunisia? In Egypt? That is nothing compared to what is going to happen to this place. It is going to explode."

And a few weeks later, it did. Was Venezuela also on the brink?

"*Brodie*," whispered Taylor harshly.

He refocused on Señor Suárez, who had clearly asked him a question he did not hear.

"Your passport," said Taylor. "And your wallet."

"Tell him I don't give my wallet to any man who hasn't pulled a gun on me."

"Brodie."

Brodie set his passport and wallet on the desk next to Taylor's, where she had also placed a printout of their hotel reservation and flight itinerary. Suárez opened both passports to their visas and looked at them alongside their customs forms. Then he opened each of their wallets, removing stacks of twenty-dollar bills and rifling through their credit cards and driver's licenses. They'd both left their military IDs in the glove compartment of Brodie's car, and Brodie had also thought to ditch his Army MWR MasterCard, which, aside from having a very low APR, featured a dramatic silhouette of the armored Stryker vehicle in which he'd spent the worst moments of the longest year of his life. It was a good reminder of tougher times while paying for groceries at Trader Joe's. He'd thought he was being overly cautious by leaving it behind, but this prick was going through everything.

Suárez looked up at Brodie and asked him something.

Taylor began to respond, but Suárez raised a hand to silence her, and gestured again at Brodie.

"He wants you to tell him why we are here," said Taylor.

"Why doesn't he ask the person who speaks Spanish?"

"Because you have a dick," replied Taylor.

"We're tourists," said Brodie. "Here to experience your beautiful country." He added, "This is my destiny."

Taylor translated, though Suárez kept his eyes fixed on Brodie. He asked something else in Spanish.

"He wants to know what we are planning to see and do while we are here, since our visas and return flight indicate a monthlong stay and yet our hotel in Caracas is only for a week."

Brodie kept his eyes on Suárez while he said to Taylor, "Good question. Maybe you can answer it."

Taylor rattled off a spiel in Spanish, describing the various sights they were planning to visit outside of Caracas. Brodie picked up the word "Amazonas" and maybe something about a river cruise. Sounded like a nice trip.

All the while, Suárez kept staring at Brodie. This was getting weird. Suárez asked something else.

Taylor said, "He wants to know how much more money we have on us."

Brodie returned Suárez's unblinking stare. "No más."

Suárez said something else, patting the stacks of dollar bills on his desk.

Taylor said to Brodie, "He doesn't believe us. He says Americans staying for a month will have more cash."

Brodie silently cursed Hackett's people for getting them monthlong visas. Clearly they were concerned it would be a lengthy mission and did not want to risk their agents being ejected from the country in the middle of it, but it should have been obvious this would be a red flag. The rear echelon idiots in an infantry division, most of whom had never been in combat, could get you killed quicker than an enemy soldier. The CID was not much different.

Suárez spoke again, and Taylor translated: "He says to show him all of our dollars, otherwise we will be thoroughly searched. Not declaring our cash is a serious crime."

Brodie looked hard at their diligent customs enforcer. Upon closer inspection, the man's features weren't so much chiseled as they were sunken. He, like the man at the passport booth, did not quite fill out his uniform. On the flight over, Taylor had read to him that the food shortages were so bad that the average Venezuelan had lost nineteen pounds. Apparently this was true even of the civil servants who made a side business of shaking down tourists.

Brodie looked up again at the portrait of President Maduro. His thick, well-fed features, hanging askew. *A shabby dictatorship.*

Brodie stared back at Suárez. "No más," he repeated.

Suárez glared at him, then spoke slowly and with emphasis, ensuring that his contempt made it through the language barrier.

Taylor translated, "You are guests in my country. Good guests respect the rules of the host, but Americans are not good guests. Americans think they make the rules everywhere."

Brodie had had about enough of this, and asked, "How much to get the hell out of here? Cuánto?"

Taylor continued to translate as Suárez spoke: "He said that we were supposed to declare our cash on our customs forms, and since we did not there is a two-hundred-dollar fee."

Brodie said, "No. One hundred dollars."

Suárez kept looking at him as Taylor translated; then the man looked down at the cash on his desk, which likely represented well over a year's salary. He counted out one hundred, then took sixty more because he was pissed, stuffed it in his pocket, and stood. He gestured at the remaining cash and paperwork and said something to Taylor in Spanish. She replied, they gathered their things, and Suárez led them out of the room and through the customs check.

"Thank you for the warm welcome," said Brodie as they walked past Suárez, who responded with something in Spanish that Brodie assumed roughly translated to "Go fuck yourself." Contempt was a truly universal language.

Taylor said, "Your macho bullshit is going to get us in trouble."

"Showing fear is what gets you in trouble."

They continued into the arrivals terminal, which was spacious and modern. A number of food counters and restaurants were closed behind metal security gates, including a Wendy's. One of the few establishments that was open, a grab-and-go place with packaged sandwiches and bins of fruit, had mostly bare shelves. One large metal bin, lit up by fluorescent strip lights, contained a single apple.

Brodie said, "I'm going to write a book called The Caracas Diet. How two million people lost a total of forty million pounds."

"That's incredibly insensitive."

"Sorry." He added, "Think about it."

A young man in his early twenties wearing jeans and a T-shirt approached them. "Cambio? Dólares? Good rate."

"No, gracias," said Taylor.

"Best rate. Three million bolívars for your dollar."

They waved him off and continued toward a small cluster of men in suits holding handwritten signs with the names of arriving passengers.

Before they could get close enough to read the signs, a short male cop in a crisp blue uniform stepped in front of them.

"Excuse me, señor, señora. Passport, por favor."

Is this shit ever going to end? thought Brodie.

He and Taylor produced their passports, and the cop gave them a cursory glance, closed them, but did not hand them back. He asked, "Where are you staying?"

"The El Dorado," said Taylor.

The cop rocked back and forth on the thick heels of his black boots, and unsubtly tapped his holstered Beretta. "Very nice. Very nice. But Caracas is very dangerous. You will need a security escort. With this I can help you."

"We've got it covered," said Brodie.

"Yes? And how is this?"

Brodie wasn't sure if he needed to grease this guy to get their passports back, though what he really wanted to do was punch his nuts.

A tall, thick man in a black suit approached, waving a white placard that read <u>BRODIE</u>.

"Señor Brodie? Señora Taylor?"

"Our driver," said Taylor to the cop.

The cop turned and exchanged a few words with the driver. The driver said something to the cop that sounded less than friendly, and the cop spat something back before shoving the passports into Brodie's hand and stomping off.

The driver, a man in his mid-forties with large, friendly features and black slicked-back hair, looked between Brodie and Taylor. "Señor Brodie, Señora Taylor. I am Luis." He extended his hand to Brodie. "I am to take you to your hotel."

He and Brodie shook. "Good timing, Luis."

Luis looked around the terminal warily, as if to indicate they were not out of the woods yet. "The cockroaches no longer scatter in the daylight, Señor Brodie. This way, please." He added, "Quickly."

CHAPTER 12

Brodie and Taylor stepped out of the terminal into a sweltering tropical heat, oppressive even in the shade of the overhang above the terminal's curbside pickup area.

The airport had the illusion of being busy—black cabs waited in a line by a taxi stand operated by a uniformed official, a flow of beat-up old cars and motorbikes slowly chugged through the terminal's roundabout, and a handful of young men stood around, perhaps on the lookout for gullible tourists.

But there were very few actual passengers leaving the terminal, so Brodie felt all eyes on them as they followed Luis toward a crosswalk. A young guy in a white polo shirt and jeans, who couldn't have been older than sixteen, fell into step alongside them, making another pitch to sell them bolívars. While this practice was technically illegal and could land you in jail, the kid didn't even lower his voice as they passed a cop.

Brodie waved the boy off, but he kept trailing them, and Luis shouted something at him. The kid fell back but kept following. Luis looked embarrassed, as if to say, "What has happened to my country?"

Some countries, thought Brodie, were born poor and desperate, and that's all anyone there knew. Venezuela, though, had once been rich, with a large middle class, so this fall into poverty and desperation must be a shock.

They approached a large parking lot that was almost empty. Luis led them to a black Cadillac Escalade SUV, popped open the back, and loaded their bags, while keeping an eye on their surroundings.

As Luis leaned over to pick up a bag, Brodie noticed the pistol grip of a Glock stuck in a holster beneath his jacket.

Brodie asked, "Do you work for the embassy?"

Luis loaded the last bag and looked at Brodie. "Not directly, señor. They call me when they need me."

"What did they tell you when they called?"

Luis looked between Brodie and Taylor. "They told me I was to pick up two American VIPs. They gave me your names and a description of your appearance."

"Who did you speak to?" asked Taylor.

"A man I know as Señor Smith."

"Whose car is this?" asked Brodie.

"The embassy's," replied Luis.

"It doesn't have diplomatic plates."

"It is better that way, señor."

"Did your amigo tell you our destination?"

"No, señor. They do not say. For security reasons."

Brodie and Taylor shared a look. They hadn't gotten their driver's name before arriving.

Luis picked up on what was going on, and said, "I have this to show you."

He reached slowly into his jacket and pulled out his smartphone. He pulled up a photo and handed the phone to Brodie.

"This is me with your Mr. McDermott."

The phone's screen was cracked and the high sun cast a harsh glare, but Brodie could make out a photo of Luis with his arm around a tall, dark-haired man. They stood in what looked like a bar or lounge, and they both held tall drinks topped with cocktail umbrellas.

Brian McDermott had been the U.S. Embassy's Chargé d'Affaires until a few months prior, when Maduro expelled him along with his deputy on charges that they were "conspirators against the government." Until then McDermott had been the top diplomat in the country, as the United States and Venezuela had not had ambassadors in each other's capitals for almost a decade. Brodie had no idea what Brian McDermott looked like, but Luis got a few points for getting the name right.

Luis also told them, "I know your Mr. Worley."

Brodie handed the phone back, looked at Taylor. She nodded.

"All right. Let's go."

Luis rounded the car and opened the rear passenger-side door, and Taylor climbed in. Brodie thought it best to sit next to the two-hundred-fifty-pound guy with the gun, so he got into the front passenger seat. He said to Luis, "Hotel El Dorado."

Luis nodded. "A good choice." He added, "Safe."

On their way out of the lot they stopped at a booth and Luis paid a parking attendant with a couple of bolívar notes that had probably depreciated in the time he'd been parked there. They pulled out, took an airport road for a few minutes, then took the ramp onto the highway toward Caracas. The A/C kicked in, and Brodie felt the sweat cooling on his forehead.

The four-lane highway cut through the western edge of the coastal mountain range, which Luis explained was a national park called El Ávila, and within minutes the vibrant green foothills surrounded them on all sides.

Brodie turned on the radio and flipped through the stations, which was one of his rituals when arriving in a new place. He scanned past some terrible pop and electronic music and a few aggressive-sounding talk stations, and landed on what sounded like traditional folk music. A man sang to a lilting, stamping rhythm of harp strums and maracas.

Luis smiled. "Joropo. Very traditional, Mr. Brodie."

"I am a man of traditional tastes, Luis."

The music seemed to fit the landscape. The sloping, verdant hills. Seabirds circling the brilliant blue sky above. Brodie could almost trick himself into thinking he was on vacation.

He noticed Luis eyeing the rearview mirror with a worried look.

"What do you see?"

"Those cars have followed us since the airport."

Brodie turned and looked through the rear window. Taylor did the same. The highway consisted of two lanes going in each direction, with a concrete divider separating them. Their Escalade was in the left lane, and about two hundred feet behind them, two beat-up old compacts were driving next to each other, rapidly closing the distance.

Taylor asked, "What makes you think they're following us?"

Luis explained, "They were parked on the shoulder when we got on the highway, and then pulled out as we passed."

The car in their lane, a white Toyota, sped up until it was right behind them, close enough for them to see the driver, a twenty-something guy who was staring dead ahead, both hands gripping the wheel.

Brodie glanced out the front windshield. They were approaching the concrete mouth of a tunnel that cut through the hills.

The car in the right lane floored it, speeding past them and into the tunnel. The Toyota behind them veered into the right lane and accelerated until it was next to them.

Brodie looked at the driver, a scrawny guy with a wispy mustache. The driver turned and made eye contact with Brodie. He had that dead-eyed look about him that Brodie recognized from broken young men in trouble spots the world over.

Brodie said to Luis, "Give me your pistol."

"Señor—"

"And speed up."

Luis pulled the 9mm Glock from his holster and handed it to Brodie, who held it out of view.

Luis was pushing on the pedal now, and as they entered the dimly lit tunnel the car in front of them, a blue Honda, swung into their lane and began slowing, while the Toyota to their right kept pace with them.

Brodie glanced back at Taylor. She seemed calm, which was to be expected of someone who had spent two years driving through the badlands of Afghanistan. As for Brodie, this wasn't the worst drive from an airport he'd ever had. In the early years of the Iraq War, the highway to Baghdad Airport had the well-earned nickname RPG Alley, after the rocket-propelled grenades and other munitions the insurgents often prepared for their arrival.

Luis realized he was boxed in by the Honda directly in front and the Toyota crowding them to the right. He said, "They are going to stop us." He added, "I am very sorry."

Brodie rolled down his window, lifted the Glock, and aimed it at the driver next to them. The guy had both hands on the wheel, but if he moved either hand out of view, Brodie was prepared to give his car new red upholstery.

Señor Mustache finally noticed the gun aimed at his head, and he slammed on his brakes, skidding to a stop as they whipped past him.

"*Go,*" said Brodie.

Luis cut into the right-hand lane and floored it. The lead car tried to pull the same trick, veering back into the right lane and slowing down. But this game didn't work with only one car, and Luis cut back into the left lane and sped past him.

The lead guy in the Honda floored it, keeping pace with the Escalade. He started drifting into their lane. This bastard was persistent.

Brodie looked over at the guy. He appeared only a little older than his buddy, and just as scrawny. But he had a nasty and determined look about him, and something told Brodie he wouldn't scare as easily as his accomplice.

The Honda drifted farther into their lane, and Luis, who was obviously not trained in tactical driving, eased off the gas and fell back. Meanwhile, the Toyota was starting to catch up.

Brodie kept his eyes on the driver next to them. He had a clean shot, but he also had an informal rule of trying not to kill anyone within an hour of landing in a new country, so he turned to Luis and said, "Run him off the road."

Luis looked over at Brodie, hesitated, then mumbled what sounded like a prayer and cut the wheel hard to the right. The Escalade's right bumper slammed into the Honda, smashing its left signal light. The car careened toward the tunnel wall.

Their pursuer quickly corrected course and skidded back toward them, slamming back into their car. Luis lost control for a moment, getting perilously close to the tunnel wall. There wasn't much room for error in the narrow lanes, and Luis cut the wheel to the right again and slammed into the Honda, their bumpers grinding against each other as they hurtled through the tunnel.

Luis, who seemed to be gaining some confidence, gave the guy one more good shove, this one hard enough to send the Honda slamming into the right side of the tunnel. The car fishtailed, its rear veering to the left and clipping the back of the Escalade as Luis sped past him.

Brodie turned around in time to catch the Honda spinning out and coming to a stop astride both lanes. The trailing Toyota skidded to a halt, barely avoiding a T-bone collision with his accomplice.

Luis gave a victorious whoop as the Escalade roared out of the tunnel and onto a bridge that crossed over a shallow valley. They were still in the western foothills, but now they had a view of the high-rises of downtown Caracas in the distance.

Brodie kept his eyes on the rearview.

Luis said, "They will not follow."

Brodie handed the pistol to Luis, who slipped it into his holster.

Brodie asked, "This ever happen to you before?"

"I was robbed two times just outside the terminal while picking up passengers. But nothing like this. But the rules are new every day now." He added, "No rules."

"One rule, Luis," said Brodie. "The survival of the fittest."

"Sí."

"You did good."

Taylor, who had said nothing so far, commented, "I think we could have outrun them without the demolition derby."

Brodie replied, "No backseat driving."

They began to see some slapdash structures of painted concrete amid the greenery as they drove toward the western edge of the city. They approached another tunnel that cut through the hills, and above the mouth of the tunnel were vibrantly painted concrete houses that climbed up the hillside like towers of haphazardly stacked shoeboxes. A mural of Hugo Chávez' face was painted on a three-story façade, his thick, grinning features attempting—like all the brightly colored houses—to slap a cheerful patina over this tropical slum.

"Barrios," said Luis. He pointed to the mural. "And there is the slumlord, who is dead now, thanks to God. But they still worship this man like a saint, and who can blame them? He at least pretended to care about the poor."

Brodie said, "Pretending is important if you are a politician."

Luis smiled. "Sí."

The traffic got a little heavier as they entered the next tunnel. Despite the deprivation gripping the country, this was still a place where gasoline was cheaper than clean water. As they exited the tunnel, Luis started to look around nervously. Their late-model luxury SUV stuck out amidst the many Eighties- and Nineties-era cars filling the road, and Brodie noticed that almost every motorist who passed them looked at their car. The embassy should own a beater.

Brodie looked up at the warrens of brick and concrete-block hovels cramming the hillsides on either side of the highway along narrow, winding switchback roads. The tin roofs of the tightly packed slums canted at every angle, shimmering in the bright sun. It seemed as though there was an effort to make almost every inch of the hills habitable as the forests gave way to these great concrete mountains.

Luis said, "You can see the barrios from almost everywhere in the city. They say you see them so much you don't see them anymore."

Brodie informed him, "In America, the rich live in the hills and the poor live in the cities."

"Yes? Why is that?"

"Because shit flows downhill."

Luis seemed to be contemplating that.

They took an exit onto Autopista Francisco Fajardo, a wide elevated highway that ran through downtown and into the affluent suburbs in the east. The barrios gave way to an unremarkable but prosperous-looking skyline of residential tower blocks and shimmering glass office buildings that appeared to be headquarters for various banks and telecom companies. Faded billboards advertised food and consumer products that the average Venezuelan could probably no longer afford or that were no longer available.

Coming up on their right in the distance was a huge, fantastical, cone-shaped building of white concrete, built on a flattened hilltop surrounded by slums. It resembled, thought Brodie, a squashed ziggurat, with a spiral ramp running around the building from the base to the top. "What the hell is that?"

Luis glanced at the building. "It is the Helicoide."

"That explains it."

Luis continued, "It was built maybe in the 1960s. A drive-in shopping mall. But it is another idea that did not work as planned . . . so it was taken over by the Servicio Bolivariano de Inteligencia Nacional—SEBIN, the secret police, who have turned it into a headquarters and prison."

"How's business?"

"Business is good," Luis assured him. "Many people go in, but few come out."

Taylor, who had apparently researched this, added, "It's also where the interrogations are conducted, which often involve torture and sometimes end in summary execution." She added, in a rare display of dark humor, "One-stop shopping."

Brodie added, "Express checkout."

Luis said, "I know many people who have gone in there. Those who come out are not the same."

Well, maybe they shouldn't joke about it.

Brodie looked at the strange building as they drove past it: some 1960s architect's idea of modernity now turned medieval. *SEBIN*. The guys you don't want showing up at your door at midnight. Every police state and wannabe police state had something like it. He glanced at the building again. *Don't want to see the inside.*

The elevated highway followed a river, a natural divider between the east- and westbound lanes. The water looked filthy, and trash was scattered across its sloping concrete banks.

"The Guaire," said Luis. "Caracas' toilet. Chávez promised to clean it up. He said, 'I invite all of you to bathe in the Guaire.'" Luis laughed. "My mother used to say he was the master of bullshit, and every day you see and smell the river of shit that runs through your city."

Brodie could both see and smell what Luis' mother was talking about, and he changed the car's A/C settings so it wasn't pulling in air from outside.

They passed a large billboard for the state oil company—PDVSA—that was newer and more vibrant than the rest. It featured a photo montage of President Maduro in a red beret, his fist raised in the air, amid rippling Venezuelan flags and pictures of muscular men in hard hats turning the wheel of an oil valve. Along the top of the billboard was a slogan that Brodie could decipher without knowing much Spanish: SOLIDARITY: THE WEAPON OF THE REVOLUTION AGAINST CAPITALISM. Oil was Venezuela's lifeblood, and when the price of oil was high, it funded massive social spending as well as the corrupt system of patronage that ensured loyalty to the regime. When the price was low, as it had been for years, people were not so loyal.

On their left, they passed two massive skyscrapers of concrete and glimmering blue glass.

Taylor asked, "What is that?"

"Parque Central," replied Luis. "They were once the tallest buildings in all of Latin America. There are offices, apartments, and some shopping." He added, "But it is dangerous for visitors. Best seen from a distance."

Brodie looked up at the looming towers as they drove past, and recalled the brief history of the city he had read in the guide book on the flight over. Caracas had been a postcolonial backwater for much of the nineteenth century and part of the twentieth. When the first wells started pumping oil in the 1920s, the country was forever changed, and the vast wealth it brought reshaped the landscape of the city through a construction boom that modernized the capital.

Luis informed them that the highway they were on had been shut down by thousands of protestors during the spring and summer of 2017, when Maduro was putting together a Constituent Assembly to rewrite the nation's constitution and subvert the authority of the opposition-controlled legislature. Protests across the country, and the subsequent government crackdown, left more than one hundred fifty dead and thousands injured.

"The people were not afraid," said Luis, "but they lost their heart. Their spirit. They were in the streets to make a change. And the change didn't come. And now people need to worry about where the next meal comes from, about their family's safety." He added, "My nephew was among the dead."

Taylor said, "I'm sorry."

They drove through what appeared to be a museum district that included a large landscaped park and botanical gardens, and after a few minutes they exited the highway into a quiet and affluent tree-lined neighborhood. Brodie noticed a multitude of trendy-looking restaurants, hotels, and upscale clothing stores. There was not much pedestrian activity on the streets, though there were shoppers in the stores, and a number of conspicuously armed private security guards outside the luxury boutiques.

They stopped at a red light in front of the entrance to an upscale shopping mall. A large glass entranceway opened to a wide corridor of polished white marble floors and rows of storefronts. On the curb in the front of the mall, a group of middle-aged men and women wearing T-shirts, jeans, and thick rubber gloves sifted through piles of trash bags. Brodie and Taylor watched them as Luis waited for the light to change.

"What are they doing?" asked Taylor.

Luis replied, "Looking for food."

One of the women found a bag of dinner rolls. She shoved one of them into her mouth, then began stuffing the rest into a plastic bag on her shoulder.

The light changed, and they continued down a winding, leafy street. Brodie knew that their hotel was near the American Embassy, and he said to Luis, "Drive past the embassy."

"Sí, señor." He drove a few more blocks, made a left onto a curving road, and after a few minutes they were driving slowly past the American Embassy compound, which was surrounded by a tall black fence. Inside the compound he could see small concrete structures at the base of the main building, which was a large complex of polished red stone with narrow windows. An American flag rippled above a line of palm trees.

At the main entrance there was a concrete wall where pairs of sneakers were hanging by their shoelaces over the embassy sign.

"What's that about?" asked Brodie.

"A sign of disrespect by the stupid Chavistas," said Luis. "It started when that Iraqi journalist threw his shoe at your Mr. Bush when he visited Baghdad."

Brodie looked at the sneakers dangling from the sign as they drove past it, recalling how on his visits to places like Islamabad and Damascus, the American Embassy had been elevated into a symbol of all that was unjust and malicious about the West, a helpful scapegoat for the host government to divert its people's attention from their real problems, which emanated from their own Presidential Palace.

Luis slowed as they approached two identical twenty-story towers with beige stone cladding and large windows. A ten-foot-high concrete wall, painted a cheery canary yellow and topped with coils of razor wire, separated the towers from the street. Standing in front of the wall, at either end of a sliding metal security gate, were two burly guards in dark blue uniforms who held pump-action shotguns at their waists.

"Hotel El Dorado," said Luis. He felt the need to add, "Very safe."

Brodie said to Taylor, "Reminds me of the post stockade."

She replied, "You wanted a place with good security."

Luis turned toward the gate and slowed as one of the guards held up a hand and approached the driver's-side window, which Luis lowered.

"Tiene reservación?" asked the guard, peering into the car.

"Sí," said Luis. He turned to Brodie and Taylor. "Your IDs?"

They pulled out their passports and passed them to the guard. He looked at them, then spoke into a small walkie clipped to his lapel that was attached to an earpiece. He read off their names, waited a moment as their reservation was confirmed, then handed the passports back and walked to a keypad next to the gate. He punched in a number and gestured them forward as the gate slowly opened.

They entered a circular drive, in the middle of which was a fountain ringed by tropical plants and flowers. Palm trees lined small patches of green lawn on either side of the drive, which led to a high-awning entrance. A smiling bellhop in his mid-fifties wearing a crisp maroon uniform approached the car as Luis pulled up. The bellhop opened the door for Taylor and she climbed out.

"Buenos días, señora. Welcome to El Dorado."

"Gracias."

Brodie and Luis got out, and the bellhop unloaded the bags onto a rolling luggage cart. Brodie checked his watch. Dombroski had given Colonel Worley their flight info, and they had landed on time. They'd lost a little time due to the shakedown at customs, but more than made up for it with the high-speed chase afterward. Worley should be waiting for them in the lobby.

Taylor thanked Luis, then exchanged a look with Brodie, who said, "Go ahead, I'll be right behind you."

Taylor followed the bellhop as he pushed the luggage cart into the lobby.

Brodie said to Luis, "Good driving."

"Thank you, señor." He eyed the dents and scrapes along the side of the Escalade.

"I'll take care of that with the embassy," Brodie assured him.

"Thank you, señor."

"We're going to need a driver later today," said Brodie. "Are you available?"

"I can be."

"What about the rest of the week?"

Luis looked less sure of that. "This might be possible. But the embassy car—"

"We don't want this car. You have your own?"

"I do. But it is not so nice."

"Perfect. What's your day rate?"

Luis thought about this.

Taylor had mentioned that hyperinflation had driven Venezuela's minimum wage down to the equivalent of two U.S. dollars a month—though any Venezuelan who was lucky enough to earn their wage in dollars did significantly better. "What does the embassy pay you?" asked Brodie.

"Ten dollars a day."

"I'll make it twenty. Plus a bonus if we're in a shoot-out."

Luis forced a smile. "Thank you, señor."

"No need for the thanks. You'll earn it."

Luis took a card from his pocket and handed it to Brodie. "My cell and my home number."

"Good. I'll be in touch later. Meanwhile, ditch the suit. But keep the gun."

CHAPTER 13

Brodie caught up with Taylor at the reception desk, and they checked in together, asking the clerk to have their luggage delivered to their suite.

They kept their overnight bags with them and walked into the lobby lounge, a tastefully decorated space with comfortable sofa chairs, glass cocktail tables, and scattered marble pedestals topped with vases of tropical flora. The lounge was mostly empty except for a few tourists speaking French, and a waiter who hovered nearby to take food and drink orders.

They spotted a casually dressed man in his fifties sitting alone in a far corner of the lounge. He held a cigarette in one hand and a drink in the other. He did not look their way.

As they approached, he looked up but did not stand and offer his hand. He just nodded at the two chairs across from him. Brodie and Taylor took a seat.

Military attachés were usually officers and dressed the part, either in uniform or neat civilian attire. But Colonel Brendan Worley had the look and air of a guy who had long ago given up on caring about things like his appearance. He wore a large sweat-stained polo shirt, baggy khaki cargo pants that were blackened around the ankles by the layer of car exhaust and grime that clung to Caracas' streets, and leather loafers that were literally coming apart at the seams. He had an unruly and thinning mop of strawberry-blonde hair and wore a pair of oversize thick-framed glasses. His piercing blue eyes were magnified beneath the large lenses and projected a sharpness and vitality at odds with his schlubby appearance.

"How was your travel?" he asked, in a way that made it clear he couldn't care less about the answer.

"Exciting," said Brodie. "We almost got robbed."

" 'Almost robbed' is a pretty good day in Caracas," Worley informed them.

Brodie briefly recounted their experience on the highway. Worley didn't seem too surprised. "This place is falling fast into chaos and anarchy. Used to be, you had to do something stupid to get into trouble. Now it will find you anywhere."

"Luis was good," said Brodie. "Calm under pressure. We've taken the liberty of hiring him to be our driver for the duration of our assignment." He asked, "Is he reliable?"

Worley nodded. "He's loyal and discreet. And he hates the Maduro government."

Taylor said, "He told us his nephew was killed in a demonstration."

Worley looked at her, took a long drag on his cigarette. "That's true."

The waiter approached. "Buenas tardes, señor, señora. What may I get you?"

Brodie gestured to Worley's glass. "I'll have what he's having."

"Excellent, señor."

"Water," said Taylor.

The waiter left.

Worley raised his glass, a tumbler of rich amber liquid. "Santa Teresa rum. The second best liquid to come out of this country, after oil. People here have been shunning their own great rum in favor of imported whiskey for years, but now that everyone's broke they're rediscovering their heritage. Smooth enough to sip straight." He took more than a sip, then used his foot to slide a leather briefcase toward them. "Courtesy of the Defense Intelligence Agency. Everything in there will get you arrested."

Brodie said, "I assume we don't have to sign for it."

Worley laughed, then said seriously, "You will not reveal, even under torture, where this briefcase came from. We have enough problems in the embassy."

"Sorry to hear that," said Brodie.

Brodie had worked with the DIA before and he knew that the Defense Intelligence Agency was—in addition to its military intelligence–gathering duties—in charge of the Defense Attaché Offices in American embassies around the world. Military attachés like Worley represented the Defense Department's interests in the country where they were posted and liaised with the military of the host country. Sometimes these interests were closely aligned with the host country's and the relationship was friendly, such as with a NATO ally, or mutually beneficial but complicated, as in Pakistan. But in a country like Venezuela, relations were openly hostile and mistrust and suspicion ran high. This was a tough post.

Brodie asked, "So who did you piss off to get this assignment?"

Worley replied, "You want a shit assignment, try Uzbekistan. I served at our embassy in Tashkent for two years. And I was posted in Yemen during the Arab Spring. That was a shit-show. Plus it was hard to find booze, and all the women wore bedsheets. At least here you've got some good scenery." He took a deep drag on his cigarette and added, "We're doing important work here."

Brodie wondered what that important work entailed. It was common for intelligence officers to use the military attaché title as cover for their espionage work. The line between soldiers and spies used to be a distinct one, but they were now in an era of CIA-directed drone strikes and Pentagon spies stationed in embassies around the world. Lines blurred, missions overlapped. This was all done in the interest of a more robust war-fighting posture against a nebulous enemy. But sometimes lines are drawn for a reason.

Taylor asked, "Are you followed?"

"Everyone in the embassy is. Though of course I made sure I wasn't today. In fact, the heat's coming off us a little because the regime has to worry more about its own people. They've got limited resources, which is what you'd expect when your principal patron is Cuba, which is more broke than this place."

Brodie nodded. He'd read in one of the State Department briefings about the close relationship between the Venezuelan government and Cuban intelligence ever since the early years of Chávez' rule. Fidel Castro had long been obsessed with fomenting socialist revolutions among his Caribbean neighbors, and Hugo Chávez' rise to power gave him an ideal proxy on the South American continent. Havana had set up something of a permanent presence in the military and intelligence infrastructure of the Chavista regime. But now both Hugo and Fidel were dead, and their pale imitations— Nicolás Maduro and Raúl Castro—were attempting to carry the flame of la Revolución.

"The embassy is available to you if your cover is blown and you need refuge," continued Worley. "Though the bigger danger here is violent crime, as you saw this morning, so just be smart about where you go and when you go there."

Taylor inquired, "Are the police helpful to foreigners in trouble?"

Worley laughed, which said it all, but he expanded on the subject. "Let me tell you a story. About a month ago, a Venezuelan-American comes into the embassy consulate section looking for a replacement for his U.S. passport that he says was stolen. Stolen by whom? asks the consulate officer. How was it stolen? So the guy says he's a U.S. resident, a musician, and he came back to his home country to record some folk music or whatever, and to see his family. He's driving one night in a borrowed car, and he's pulled over by a police car on a lonely road. To make a long story short, the two policemen take everything he has, including his car and all his clothes, and leave him naked on the side of the road." Worley paused for effect and said, "If he'd been a woman, they'd have also raped him. As it was, he told us he thanked God they didn't kill him."

Brodie and Taylor exchanged glances. Well, that answered the question. Brodie asked, "Did he file a complaint with the Civilian Review Board?"

Worley laughed, then said seriously, "The police are worse than the criminals, if that's possible. Stay away from them."

"Lima Charlie," said Brodie, using the military phonetic alphabet. Loud and clear.

"And then there's SEBIN, the domestic Intel people. In a way they're worse than the police, because they're actually good at their jobs. Don't get on their radar."

Brodie said, "We passed the Helicoide on the way in."

Worley nodded. "That's one of their facilities, mainly a prison. Their main headquarters are in another building closer to the city center. Offices up top, torture chambers in the basement. The locals call the building La Tumba. The Tomb."

"Subtle."

The waiter returned with Brodie's drink, and he sipped it. Smooth and not too sweet. Definitely a more complex and pleasant profile than the Bacardi 151 he used to shoot in college.

Worley reached for a large backpack next to his chair and slid it toward them. "Some local currency. Good for buying an arepa on the street or for wiping your ass when your hotel runs out of toilet paper. Venezuela is not quite at the wheelbarrow full of cash to buy a loaf of bread stage of third world inflation, but they're getting there. That whole bag of bolívars was worth about twenty bucks as of a few hours ago."

"We'll spend it fast," said Brodie.

"Needless to say, don't use the landlines here. This hotel especially is going to be tapped by the government. Your cell phones will probably work in the hotel, but coverage is very limited around the city and getting worse, and also susceptible to eavesdropping if you're relying on the local carriers. There's a satellite phone in the briefcase that will work pretty much anywhere with open sky. There's also a thumb drive with a VPN client you can install on your laptops if you need to connect to the hotel Wi-Fi. Gets around all the government censorship and firewalls, no one can eavesdrop, and if anyone tries to trace your IP address they'll think you're in Miami."

Brodie raised his glass. "Enough of these and I'll think I'm in Miami."

Worley laughed, looked between them. His smile faded. "So what makes you think he's here?"

"We had a tip," said Brodie.

"A sighting?"

Brodie didn't reply.

Worley's piercing eyes shifted between the two of them. "He's a hell of a big fish."

"He is," agreed Brodie.

"But this is also a big pond," said Worley. "I know the city. So if I can help you find this SOB, I will."

Brodie regarded Colonel Worley. The guy was definitely a spook, but a different breed of spook. He was still military, and Mercer's desertion and betrayal probably pissed him off on a personal level. Brodie said, "He was spotted in a brothel."

Taylor added, "We think it's in Petare."

Worley took one last drag on his cigarette and stubbed it out in an ashtray next to him. "That doesn't narrow it down much." He added, "It's a very big slum."

"Maybe you know someone," said Taylor.

"I know a lot of people," said Worley. "But they don't hang around slum whorehouses."

Brodie wasn't sure he bought that. A guy like Worley worked the system, and the system didn't function without the bottomfeeders.

"I'll give you a hypothetical scenario," said Brodie. "I'm a visiting dignitary from someplace where you, Colonel Worley, need a contact or a favor. I'm known to have certain, specific predilections. Let's say underage girls. So I need someone who can direct me to the right place and also keep quiet. Except, of course, the pimp is not keeping quiet because he's reporting to you."

Worley stared at Brodie, unblinking. "You're looking for the CIA. Different acronym."

"With the same bag of dirty tricks," said Brodie.

Worley didn't react to that. This guy was a cool customer. A bit creepy, actually. He downed the rest of his rum. "I might have a guy. If he can help you, he'll call you. You don't want to just start banging on doors in Petare. That will get you killed."

"Right." Brodie gave Worley his cell number. He didn't love handing out his personal number to whatever sketchy underworld character Brendan Worley would pass it on to, but the satellite phone wouldn't work in the hotel room. Taylor also gave Worley her number as backup. Brodie said, "Also, when we find our fugitive, we'll need some help getting him out of the country."

Worley nodded. "I've been apprised of that." He added, unnecessarily, "You can't go through normal diplomatic channels to get him extradited. But there are other ways."

"We assumed there were," said Brodie. "Or we wouldn't be here."

Worley thought a moment, then said, "The less you know, the better. But we usually use a private aircraft which I will arrange to be standing by at a local airport. If and when the time comes, you'll let me know and I will direct you to an abandoned airstrip near Caracas. The aircraft lands, you are there with your prisoner, and off you go."

Brodie nodded. Sounded simple. Except for the details. Such as, this private aircraft would have to be small enough to land at an abandoned airstrip, so it probably didn't have the fuel to get to the U.S.—meaning they'd fly to Guantánamo, or maybe a U.S. military installation in Panama. He asked Worley about that, and Worley replied, "I don't have to know where you're flying to, and neither do you."

"Right. The less we all know, the better."

"You'll know when you get there." He added, "I'll fill you in on the rendezvous details when—if—the time comes."

Taylor asked Worley, "If there's a lag time—like bad weather or something—can the embassy hold our prisoner while we're waiting for the aircraft?"

"No. You'll have to hold your prisoner somewhere else." He added, "The embassy does not get involved with kidnappings."

"Only transportation," said Brodie. He added, for the record, "This is not a kidnapping."

Worley did not respond to that. He stood. "I'm late for a meeting."

Brodie wanted to say, "Those AA meetings never start on time." But he said instead, "It'll look good on your résumé when we bring this bastard to justice."

Worley gave him a long look, and said, "If you need me, my number is programmed on the sat phone."

Taylor said, "Thank you for your help."

Worley looked around the lobby. "There's a great rooftop pool here. Fantastic views. If you face north you won't even see the slums. Enjoy Venezuela."

"It is our destiny to discover her," said Brodie.

"It is," said Worley. "But she can be a real bitch."

CHAPTER 14

Their American taxpayer–funded suite was on the fifth floor and it looked clean and comfortable, with all the modern amenities. A sizable living room separated the bedrooms, and all three rooms had balconies that faced north, where a well-manicured outdoor courtyard and restaurant lay beneath them, and the lush green mountains of the coastal range spread out across the horizon. It was a great view, and Brodie had to lean out over his bedroom balcony to catch a glimpse of the congested hills of Petare, a few miles to the east and a world away.

Brodie and Taylor met in the living room. Brodie set the briefcase from Worley on a coffee table and opened it. Inside were two 9mm Glocks with pancake holsters and four loaded magazines, a Taser, and plastic zip ties.

"Everything we need for a kidnapping," said Taylor.

Or, thought Brodie as he picked up one of the Glocks and slapped in a mag, *a simpler solution to this case.*

There was also the aforementioned satellite phone, stacks of ten- and twenty-dollar bills totaling ten thousand dollars, and two U.S. passports that bore the same photoshopped pictures from their visas but with different names and ID numbers. Brodie had been renamed "Clark Bowman" and Taylor was "Sarah Bowman." Stuck in the passports were new monthlong visas that bore their new names. He couldn't tell if they were legit visas or forgeries, but they'd certainly pass muster with any overzealous cop or soldier trying to shake them down on the street. The passport pages were full of arrival stamps, and the books themselves were made to look worn. Brodie had not yet had the pleasure of visiting the Bahamas, but Clark Bowman had.

Taylor slipped the passport into her pocket and remarked, "I'd never take my husband's last name."

"Clark took *your* name, Ms. Bowman. He's very progressive. His favorite food is quinoa and he loves cats."

"I hate cats."

"Clark is okay with that."

They both clipped their holsters on their belts. Brodie was usually not armed while on overseas undercover assignments, since getting caught with a piece was often more trouble than it was worth. But this was different. Kyle Mercer would not be taken willingly, and asking the local police to detain him was not an option.

They took a few hundred dollars from the stacks of bills and put the rest into a combination-lock safe in a cabinet under the TV. Brodie set the combo to the same numbers he'd used on his wall locker through basic and advanced infantry training, and at Camp Victory outside Baghdad. He did this more out of habit than anything else, though being as he was still alive, maybe he ought to consider those his lucky numbers.

They opened up the backpack from Worley and stuffed their pockets with some bolívar notes of indeterminate value; then Brodie tossed the backpack into the cabinet next to the safe. If the maid felt like helping herself to an extra tip, she was welcome to it.

They had left Mercer's classified file back at Quantico, but Taylor had made a few copies of Captain Mercer's file photo—a posed portrait of him in his dress green uniform and green beret from his time before joining Delta Force—that she had hidden between the pages of a paperback novel in her bag. They each put a copy in their wallet.

Brodie powered up the sat phone. He found a single number listed in the contacts that he assumed was for Worley, and they both programmed the number into their personal cell phones as well. He hoped they wouldn't need Worley's number until it was time to get them out of Venezuela once Mercer was in custody.

"What did you think of Colonel Brendan Worley?" asked Brodie.

"He's not really an Army attaché," replied Taylor.

"No. But it's good cover. He's got diplomatic immunity through the embassy, and an official reason to be in contact with people in the Venezuelan military."

"He's been here too long. You can smell that on people."

"That was the rum."

Taylor took a bottled water from the minibar and sat cross-legged on the couch. She took a sip, looked out the sliding glass doors leading to the balcony. A sheer curtain ran across the doorway, catching dancing patterns of mottled sunlight through the palm leaves. Birds squawked in the distance. "It's actually beautiful here."

Brodie opened a beer and took a seat on the couch across from her. "Is this your first time in South America?"

Taylor nodded. "Until now, my first and only time out of the States was a government-funded trip to Afghanistan. And I guess Landstuhl Medical Center in Germany—to get the shrapnel dug out of me. But I don't really count that. I didn't even get to have a beer."

"I'll make sure our next assignment lands us in Munich in time for Oktoberfest."

Taylor smiled. "You're well-traveled."

"It's always for work, so you're not there in the same way. Last time I tried to take a vacation was to Hawaii two years ago. I couldn't relax. I just felt like I needed to find someone to arrest."

Taylor smiled again. "Solo trip?"

"Ex-girlfriend."

"What happened to the poor girl?"

"She was uptight. Or maybe I was. I dump bad memories once a week on trash day."

"If only it was that easy."

Brodie asked, "So how did a hillbilly from Tennessee learn to speak Spanish so well?"

"If you understood Spanish, you'd know mine isn't that good, but it's enough to get by. I had a TA at Georgetown who was from Madrid. He taught me."

"Did he give you an A?"

"Yeah. But the class was in English literature." She smiled. "The Spanish lessons were a side thing."

Brodie smiled in return.

Taylor finished her water and stood. "I'm going to wash the plane off me."

"Me too. Meet you in the lobby."

They went to their separate rooms. In his bathroom Brodie found a notice from the hotel, in Spanish and English, gently reminding the well-paying guests that there was a water shortage, a paper shortage, and a soap shortage, so please conduct yourselves accordingly. It didn't say you could use bolívars for toilet paper, but that was implied. Brodie doubted that many of the El Dorado's well-heeled guests actually followed the hotel's request, but his years as a soldier had taught him the virtues of austerity and he made his shower brief.

As he was getting dressed, his cell phone rang. The screen read: <u>Unlisted</u>. He answered the phone.

"Hello?"

"Is this Mr. Bowman?" asked a male voice in heavily accented English.

"It is."

"My name is Raúl. I am given this number by our mutual friend. Will you like to meet?"

"Maybe."

"Museum Plaza. Off Avenida Libertador. Nine in the morning tomorrow. I will be wearing a yellow shirt with collar, white baseball cap, and white shoes."

"We need to meet today," said Brodie.

"This is not possible, Mr. Bowman."

"Make it possible, Raúl. And I'll make it worth the trouble."

A long pause. Raúl sounded like the kind of guy who was used to calling the shots.

"Okay, seven o'clock," said Raúl. He added, "You will not approach me. You will follow me."

"To where?"

"The Finance Center. A short walk. This way I see you, you see me, no funny stuff. I go on foot, you follow."

"All right," said Brodie. "Museum Plaza, seven o'clock."

"Okay, señor. I see you later."

Brodie hung up. A finance center seemed like an odd place to discuss brothels, but maybe he was missing something.

He called his office voice mail at Quantico in case Al Simpson had decided to remember something else or had gotten in touch with his Venezuelan oil contacts, but there were no messages from him. No surprise. Brodie was pretty sure that witness had said all he had to say. From now on their clues would come from the streets.

He finished getting dressed and headed downstairs.

CHAPTER 15

Brodie came down to the lobby wearing clean jeans, a collared shirt, and a sports jacket to conceal his holstered piece. He also had on running shoes, in the event they got into more trouble than his fifteen-round Glock could handle.

Taylor, who would never pass up an opportunity to be first at something, was downstairs waiting for him. She looked good in jeans, a T-shirt, and a blue blazer to conceal her holster. She'd removed her makeup, maybe to make herself look plainer, though it didn't work. The pretty, pert blonde was already turning heads among hotel staff and guests. Ms. Taylor had a face—and a body—that once seen was not soon forgotten. This was a problem.

They checked out the ground floor of the hotel, which is always a good tactical move, then got a bite to eat at the hotel's restaurant, called Alto, a pretentious place that served vaguely continental cuisine in small geometric piles. The dishes were portioned appropriately for a country going through a food shortage but priced like a Parisian restaurant. The menu was in Spanish and English and the prices were in bolívars, but the menu came with a daily exchange rate printout for the nose-diving currency. The waiter, an older man with swept-back silver hair whose name tag said "Eduardo," suggested the roasted chicken, promising that it was available, and hinting that it was fresh, which was the clincher. Taylor and Brodie ordered it.

"Excellent," Eduardo assured them, and glided off.

Brodie told Taylor about the phone call with Raúl. "We're following him to the Finance Center. Sounds like a safe enough public place."

Taylor pulled out the guide book, flipped to the map of Caracas, and found Museum Plaza. She cross-referenced the map with a list of points of interest and said, "Maybe not."

"What?"

"It's an unfinished skyscraper, nicknamed the Tower of David after the building's main investor, David Brillembourg. It's not a finance center, and it never was. Construction halted in the Nineties after the Venezuelan banking crisis, and squatters took it over. It was the biggest vertical slum in the world until a few years ago when the government relocated the residents." She closed the book and added, "The guide book says it's a hangout for criminals, and advises that tourists keep their distance."

"We're not tourists. We have guns."

"Brains would be good too."

"I'll go alone."

"Don't tempt me."

Their meals came. The chicken was decent, though Brodie suspected, based on experience, that they'd find tastier food for a hundredth of the price at any local street cart.

They discussed the case as they ate, and kept mulling over the same question: Why would Kyle Mercer come here?

Taylor asked, "What do Afghanistan and Venezuela have in common?"

"Tourism boards with big challenges."

"Drugs."

"Right . . . but this is the land of cocaine, Afghanistan is heroin. And they both export to wealthy consumer markets like America and Europe, not to each other. I see some similarities, but I don't see a connection."

Taylor nodded. "Okay, if you're Mercer, how do you get all the way from the tribal territories to Venezuela?"

"If I'm Delta Force, I figure I'd swim."

Taylor gave him a look like she was questioning this partnership, or maybe her entire career choice.

Brodie said, "He charters a private plane with someone who doesn't ask questions. And if he doesn't have the money, he steals it. Or he just steals the plane. The guy's resourceful."

"He's also crazy. He chopped off those guys' heads."

"In the Army, we call that 'misconduct stress behavior.'"

"In Caracas," said Taylor, "we call it loco."

Eduardo came back to the table. "May I interest you in dessert?"

"We'll take the check," said Brodie. "This will be a room charge."

"Regretfully, we are only accepting cash in the restaurant at this time."

"Give me a good exchange rate," said Brodie.

Eduardo bowed his head and walked off.

———

Luis' car was, as advertised, not so nice.

He crawled up the El Dorado's driveway in a 1980 Dodge Dart, a long, low-riding American boat with a rusted beige exterior and dented chrome bumpers. The side windows and rear windshield had been subjected to a bad homemade tint job.

Luis stopped at the curb, the old V-8 engine chugging away, and smiled at Brodie and Taylor through the rolled-down passenger-side window. He had changed into a pair of plaid cargo shorts, sneakers, and an oversize white polo. Some Joropo music was playing out of fuzzy speakers.

Brodie asked Taylor, "Shotgun?"

"No, sir. That's how I got blown up in Afghanistan. In Tennessee, a lady sits in the rear."

"This is Caracas."

"Then maybe I'll stay here."

Brodie swung open the front passenger door, which emitted a welcoming squeal, and got in. He sank into the sagging seat. Taylor got in the back.

Brodie looked around the car, which smelled like old laundry. On the center console, barely concealed by a rolled-up newspaper, was Luis' Glock. A large bejeweled cross hung from the rearview mirror, just in case the Glock jammed.

"Is okay?" asked Luis.

"It's perfect," said Brodie as he cranked up the Joropo, and they pulled out of the drive.

"Where do you wish to go?"

"Paris," replied Brodie.

Luis laughed. "Me too."

Brodie had asked Luis to pick them up an hour before their meeting with Raúl so that he and Taylor could do a recon of the area—what the Army called "terrain appreciation," and what the CID called "urban immersion." Brodie called it "know your neighborhood beat."

"Señor?"

"Let's see your neighborhood," said Brodie. "We need to be in Museum Plaza in one hour."

"Sí, señor." Luis added, "The museums are wonderful."

"I'm sure they are. So is Paris."

CHAPTER 16

Luis headed south out of the neighborhood of Altamira, and back onto the highway. He commented that the more affluent neighborhoods of Caracas were in the east of the city, and that it grew poorer the farther west you traveled.

This transition was evident as they got onto another highway and took an exit into a decidedly grittier neighborhood. Rows of dilapidated and graffitied concrete buildings lined narrow streets. Rivers of dirty water ran curbside under mountains of trash that no one had come to collect, most of it spilling out into the street, already worked over by scavengers. They passed a covered bus stop that a few people were using for shade from the oppressive sun. They were clearly not waiting for the city bus, which sat with them, empty and idle, its windows broken and its tires long gone.

Luis explained that public transportation had become almost nonexistent, because there was a recent fuel shortage and because it was almost impossible to find spare parts to repair old buses.

Brodie remarked, "I thought this place was swimming in oil."

Luis shook his head. "The refineries don't work, so the crude oil is shipped out and the government has to import most of the gasoline and diesel." He added, "PDVSA is full of morons and thieves."

Brodie thought back to the PDVSA propaganda he'd seen on the drive into the city. It seemed that "the weapon of the revolution against capitalism" was running on empty.

As they drove down the street, Luis pointed out a five-story concrete apartment building. "My apartment is here." He felt the need to add, "It is nicer on the inside."

The building's façade looked pockmarked and grimy, and metal bars covered every window, even on the upper floors. The place was surrounded by a cinder-block wall with a corrugated metal door. All along the top of the wall were cemented shards of broken glass: a low-cost—and perhaps recently added—extra level of security.

They turned onto a wider boulevard and drove past a seemingly endless line of people standing along the shoulder, snaking up a sloping hillside and out of view in both directions.

Taylor asked, "Luis, what are they waiting for?"

"Food." They rounded a curve and saw a slab-concrete building with a red plastic sign above barred windows: <u>SUPERMERCADO</u>. "Every day the government offers different price-controlled items. Today maybe it is cooking oil and bread. Maybe yesterday it was rice and milk. Sometimes people don't know what they are getting until they are inside. You must present your Cédula de Identidad—your national ID card—in order to receive these goods, and the last number on your ID card determines what day you can buy things. Every Tuesday my wife is in this line."

Neither Taylor nor Brodie knew what to say to that.

Their car rolled up the hill and Brodie stared at this unending stream of humanity—young and old, large families with strollers, solitary men and women. A little girl in a yellow dress held on to her mother with one hand, and in the other she dragged a raggedy doll through the roadside overgrowth. A middle-aged man sat on an old motorbike with the engine turned off, slowly inching the bike forward with his feet to keep pace with the glacial movement toward the supermarket. Brodie recalled how annoyed he got when there was a line at the checkout in the post commissary at Quantico, and he was sure Taylor was thinking the same thing.

The people at the supermercado looked mostly patient and orderly, but with a sunken look about them that was partly hunger but partly the humiliation, perhaps, of people who were used to being able to support themselves, now waiting for whatever goods the bureaucrats had decided to offer. All reduced to beggars, to this mass of people who, in their congregation, showed all that was broken about their country.

Taylor said, "I have never seen anything like this . . . not even in Afghanistan."

Luis said, "I did not grow up like this."

As they crested the hill and approached the supermarket, they saw a zigzag walkway that ran from the bottom of a multilevel parking garage up to the supermarket entrance. In more prosperous times, it must have functioned as a ramp for exiting shoppers to roll their grocery carts down to their cars. Now it held crowds of people pressed against the wire-mesh walls lining the walkway, holding on to the walls for support as they waited for a brief respite from hunger.

"How can you put up with this?" asked Taylor.

Luis shrugged. And really, what more was there to say? Protest required energy. And energy required food.

Brodie checked his watch. It was six-twenty. They still had forty minutes to kill before their rendezvous with Raúl. He said, "Let's head downtown."

————

Downtown Caracas maintained some aspects of its colonial flavor, though for every pastel-colored Spanish church or palace, there were ten glass office towers and dull concrete apartment blocks that had sprung up during the building boom of the Seventies when oil was king.

Luis turned into a narrow street and pointed out a single-story stone house. "The birthplace of Simón Bolívar." He added, "Our George Washington."

"He was a great man," said Brodie, leaving it unclear if he was referring to Washington or Bolívar.

Luis smiled and said, "Sí. The Great Liberator."

"Right."

Taylor said, "They were both great men."

A few minutes later, Luis pointed out a handsome white and yellow neoclassical church. "This is where Bolívar was declared the Liberator of Venezuela, in 1813, when the Spanish were driven out."

Brodie remarked, "You could use another Simón Bolívar."

"Sí," agreed Luis.

They drove through an intersection where one of the roads was blocked off by steel security gates, beyond which was a huge pink palatial building.

Luis said, "That is our White House."

"It's pink," Brodie pointed out.

"Sí. Miraflores Palace. The home of our presidents. Now occupied by that murdering son of a whore."

Brodie said, "That's an insult to whores."

Luis laughed hard. "Sí. It is."

The road sloped downhill and Luis gestured toward a white-columned building with long rows of square windows. "Maduro's dogs live there."

"That's a hell of a kennel," said Brodie.

"Kennel? No, it is the barracks for the Presidential Guard. Los Perros. The dogs."

"Right."

"Someday, perhaps, the police and the Army and the National Guard will come to the side of the people. But these dogs will be the last defense of the regime."

"Correct." The geography of the power centers was important in countries with weak institutions. If an angry mob massed outside the President's palace, a rapid and organized display of force was important not only tactically, but psychologically. Considering that Venezuela had experienced four attempted coups in the last quarter century, it was important to have the guards' bedrooms near the President's bedroom.

Luis turned into another side street, and they drove past another grand nineteenth-century building, this one faced with columns and topped by a large gilded dome.

"The Legislative Palace," said Luis, "where the National Assembly meets. And also the Constituent Assembly that our bastard President has created to strip the National Assembly of its power. Both groups say the other is the enemy of the country, and no one knows who is in charge."

"Sounds like Washington," said Brodie.

"We would be lucky to have a government such as yours, señor."

Well, that put things in perspective.

Luis looked up at the gold-domed building as they drove past it. "The National Assembly is the real voice of the people. If there is any hope to get rid of Maduro, it is with them."

Well, there was another way, but it involved tanks in the streets. Luis' version sounded better. Brodie said, quoting Churchill, "Democracy is the worst form of government, except for all the others."

Luis thought about that and nodded.

Brodie said, "We'd like to take a walk around."

"Sí, señor. The area around Plaza Bolívar is good for this." He added, "Safe." He pulled over and pointed out the direction of the plaza.

"We'll meet you back here in twenty minutes," said Brodie.

"Sí, señor."

Brodie and Taylor got out of the car and walked around a corner to enter the old quarter of the city surrounding Plaza Bolívar. The narrow cobblestone streets likely followed the same grid pattern originally laid out by the Spanish settlers four hundred years prior, though many of the buildings here were of shoddy new construction.

"I could use a Coke," said Brodie.

They ducked into a hole-in-the-wall joint called Arepa Planet. It was a long, narrow place with purple-painted walls and bright fluorescent lighting. A printed menu hung above the order counter, and the listed prices next to each item were covered with taped-on handwritten scraps of paper indicating the updated prices. Just keeping up with the plummeting value of the bolívar must have been a part-time job. Another handwritten sign hanging next to the menu read: NO HAY CARNE. No meat.

A dim seating area in the back was full of people watching a baseball game on a mounted flat-screen. Brodie remembered hearing that in Venezuela, unlike the rest of Latin America, baseball, not soccer, was the local obsession. The spectators here were mostly older men, and only a few of them seemed to be eating anything. They were here for the game, and maybe the companionship.

Brodie noticed that a number of patrons were watching them, a few with less than friendly looks. The cook behind the counter, a man in his mid-forties with a shaved head and muscular build, was watching the TV while forming fresh arepa patties out of cornmeal. Brodie noticed the counter waitress, a woman in her twenties who could have been in the running for Miss Venezuela. She wore a tight-fitting T-shirt with an "Arepa Planet" logo stretched taut over her considerable assets.

Brodie commented, "It's a big planet, maybe Jupiter."

Miss Venezuela said something to them in Spanish. Taylor replied, and they conversed briefly.

Taylor translated, "She wants to know where we're from, and what we're doing here. She says tourists don't come here anymore."

"Did they ever?"

"How do I know?"

"Tell her we're stupid Americans. We make bad life choices."

The woman smiled and nodded as if she understood, and Taylor ordered two Cokes.

Miss Venezuela retrieved a couple of Coke bottles from a fridge behind the counter, cracked them open, and put them on the counter. She told Taylor the price and Taylor took a fat stack of bolívars from her pocket, peeled off about twenty or thirty bills of funny money, and handed them to Miss Venezuela. They took their Cokes and left.

Taylor observed, "That woman was beautiful."

"I didn't notice."

"How could you? You never took your eyes off her tits."

"My infantry training. Look for the most prominent terrain feature."

Taylor laughed.

They rounded a corner and entered Plaza Bolívar, a large, leafy square surrounded by colonial-era buildings. Elevated on a high black marble pedestal in the center of the plaza was a large bronze statue of the Great Liberator on horseback. He was decked out in formal military attire including a jacket with epaulettes, a flowing sash, and a long, sheathed sword. He grasped the reins with one hand and in the other held out a feathered cocked hat. He looked out to the distance with a steely gaze, his eyes obscured by slabs of shadow beneath his prominent brow.

Taylor said, "He actually looks like George Washington."

"All statues look the same with bird shit on them."

"Try to be less cool and cynical."

"Okay."

"Luis is proud of his country. Keep your wiseass remarks to yourself."

"I will be more culturally sensitive."

"Please don't. Just zip it."

"Yes, ma'am."

She put her arm through his to show she wasn't angry. Just offering friendly advice.

They walked toward the statue, around which was a crowd of
Chavistas—Chávez supporters—in red T-shirts and baseball caps. A man
held aloft the tricolor Venezuelan flag, occasionally waving it around, and
at the front of the group a tiny woman stood on a plastic stool and spoke
to the crowd through a bullhorn in an angry and urgent tone. She spoke in
short declaratives, jabbing her fist in the air to put an exclamation point on
everything she said, and the crowd cheered or booed as necessary.

"Do you want a translation?" asked Taylor.

"No," said Brodie, though the only words he could make out were the
proper nouns—"Chávez" and "Maduro"—which elicited cheers, of course,
while the names of every recent American president invited hisses and boos.
On this point, the people's vitriol seemed to be commendably bipartisan.

Brodie was more interested in the bystanders on the fringes of this fer-
vent sea of red—the average Caraqueño who passed through or hung around
the square. Couples strolled hand in hand, children terrorized pigeons, pedestrians took a brief respite from the heat in the shade of the flowering
jacarandas and palms that lined the plaza. To the degree that anyone paid
attention to the woman shouting into the bullhorn, it was to shoot a glare
or roll their eyes. The Chavistas tried to draw passersby into their group to
stop and hear what the woman had to say, like desperate cheerleaders at a
pep rally for a team with a few too many losing seasons.

A scrawny middle-aged man strode into the square and started shouting at the Chavistas. He spat at the feet of a dumpy, mustachioed guy in a
red cap and red T-shirt featuring Chávez' face on the back. The two men
started yelling at each other, and the scrawny guy shoved the dumpy guy.
They started throwing punches.

The Chavistas rushed to the aid of their comrade, knocking the scrawny
guy to the ground and repeatedly kicking and stomping him.

On the edge of the square, Brodie noticed a line of cops in light blue
uniforms and black helmets, watching with studied indifference.

Brodie dropped his Coke bottle on the pavement and walked toward the
victim, who was now bleeding.

Taylor grabbed his arm. "Don't."

"They'll kill him."

"We have a job to do, Brodie. And a cover to maintain. Don't do anything that will put us in a jail cell."

Another young guy jumped into the melee, pushing against the surging crowd of Chavistas. A few more young men jumped in too, though it was unclear if they were trying to rescue the guy on the ground or were taking the opportunity to kick some Chavista ass. Either way, it was turning into an ugly brawl, though a few of the older activists, including the woman who was speaking, were able to duck out of the group and safely shout from the sidelines.

The cops finally sprang into action, running toward the crowd with batons drawn. They began beating anyone not wearing red, including a young woman who was taking pictures of the fight. A short, stocky policeman hit her in the midsection with his baton, then grabbed her camera and smashed it against the ground. As she keeled over he hit her again, then cuffed her wrists with a plastic zip tie.

Taylor was still holding on to Brodie's arm, and she gave it a firm squeeze. "Stand down, soldier."

Brodie didn't reply. This wasn't the first time he'd stood on the sidelines witnessing injustice on an overseas assignment, and it always felt like shit. Being an infantry soldier sucked too, but at least there, the moral choices were clearer. Or the adrenaline made it feel like they were clear. But being a CID agent meant you stood on a different part of the stage, in the dark beyond the klieg lights, choosing the right moment to step out of the shadows.

The Chavistas backed away from the brawl as the cops moved further into the crowd, batons flying. A few of the young men knelt and covered their heads for protection, and received hard hits to their backs before being kicked and cuffed. One guy fought back furiously, repeatedly bashing his fist into a cop's helmet visor and kicking at his shins. He got a baton cracked across his jaw in response, and a long rope of blood and spittle splattered against the plaza's black marble. The cop's buddies joined in and they all laid into him.

A few policemen seemed interested in Brodie and Taylor, and Taylor pulled Brodie away from the brutal scene into a building on the square. It wasn't until his eyes adjusted from the bright sunlight that he realized she'd brought him into a church.

It was a tall Romanesque cathedral with a large central nave containing rows of wooden pews and lined with arched colonnades on either side. A few people were sitting in the pews closest to the altar.

Taylor led him toward a side chapel. Behind a metal railing was a statue of the Virgin Mary on a gold-painted throne, with Baby Jesus sitting on her lap. There was a vase of yellow flowers on a table at her feet, and a rack of votive candles stood near the railing. About half of them were lit. Taylor approached the candles and looked for a tinder stick on the rack, but since this was a country with a shortage of everything, there were none, though a resourceful parishioner or priest had made a stack of tiny twigs that had probably been sourced from the plaza. Taylor lit one of them from an existing flame and lit another candle. She offered the burning twig to Brodie.

Brodie had been raised with no formal religious instruction, though he did recall many summer nights lying in the grass stargazing with his parents while Mom and Dad shared a funny-smelling cigarette and debated the existence of God. His grandparents on his father's side were strict Lutherans, though they were also cruel and miserable, so religion didn't seem to be doing much for them. And one time in college he'd gotten serious with a religious Jewish girl and openly entertained converting, but he had no religion to convert from, and he'd dropped the idea and the girl.

"Brodie?"

He took the burning twig and lit a candle, then joined Taylor at the railing. He closed his eyes and tried to quiet his mind, but the muffled sounds of violence outside found their way in.

Whom did he light the candle for? He wasn't sure. Maybe for those people outside—the young guys venting their rage at the fate of their country. Or for the cops springing into action to preserve their dollar-a-day jobs. Maybe even for the people draped in red for their dead idol who, by all indications, was a charismatic con artist who'd promised heaven on earth and delivered hell.

Maybe he lit it for Andy Rucker, a squad-mate from his time in Iraq. Andy had been a reservist from a small town in eastern Pennsylvania. He was doing reserve duty as a part-time gig to help support his family, but he got called to active duty—like so many reservists and guardsmen at that time—as the war that was supposed to be over in six months stretched into years.

Andy wasn't a warrior. He wasn't there for a cause, or a thrill, or to take out his anger issues on some hadjis. He was as brave as he could possibly be, but at the end of the day he was a sensitive soul in the middle of a meat grinder. When they were in the thick of it and a mortar round landed near them, it shook Andy a little extra. And when their unit lost a guy, it took a little more out of him too.

Andy Rucker survived the war, but he brought it home with him. Brodie did too—they all did—but Brodie liked to think he'd left at least some of it behind in the desert. Andy did not.

Andy drank. Andy gambled. Andy called Brodie and other old Army buddies at all hours of the night from bars and bus stops and train stations along the eastern corridor, sometimes asking for money, sometimes for a ride. Sometimes he just needed someone to listen to him. They all tried to help, but Andy didn't want help. Andy wanted to die.

His funeral service had been at a little Presbyterian church in his hometown two years ago, and it was the last time Brodie had set foot in a house of worship. It was a small and modest service, and he saw people from Andy's life that he only knew from stories—his mom and dad, his younger sister, his high school sweetheart he'd once been engaged to. All of them there, all of them diminished by time and grief.

Brodie had bowed his head in prayer then too, eyes closed, listening to a solemn hymn, angry at how things had turned out for Andy Rucker. Angry at a world that had no place for things that were precious and too easily broken.

"Scott?"

He opened his eyes. Taylor was looking at him.

"You okay?"

He looked at his hands gripping the railing, white-knuckled, trembling. He let go and stepped away. "Yeah. Let's get out of here."

CHAPTER 17

They sat in Luis' parked car about a block away from Museum Plaza, which was obscured by a dense ring of trees. The sun was low in the sky, casting long shadows. It was ten minutes before their rendezvous with Raúl, and Brodie had broken it to Luis that they were not here to take in Caracas' fine museum culture.

Luis said, "Torre David is very dangerous. It is a place for thugs."

"Good," said Brodie. "We're meeting a thug."

"I will come with you."

"That's above your pay grade, amigo."

Luis couldn't seem to let this go. "Then you must take my pistol."

Brodie looked at Luis, who had genuine fear in his eyes. "We're both armed," said Brodie.

Luis seemed surprised by that, but he did not look reassured. He must have been starting to wonder who these American VIPs were. He peered out the windshield, then shifted his focus to the bejeweled cross hanging from his rearview mirror. Maybe he was going to ask the Big Guy to look out for these dumb gringos. Couldn't hurt.

The sun dipped lower in the evening sky, and above the downtown sky-line a fiery orange band sat atop the green hills to the north and west. The imposing Parque Central complex was nearby, dwarfing everything in its vicinity, its towering glass façade reflecting the brilliant sky. A warm wind blew past Brodie's arm hanging out the open window. Luis had urged him to keep the tinted window closed, but riding shotgun literally meant you needed to see and hear things clearly—and have a clean shot.

Evening settled in and the street life began to thin out. Storefronts rolled down their metal gates, street vendors wheeled away their carts, and the modest amount of traffic that there was began flowing out of downtown and toward the surrounding neighborhoods. A stream of pedestrians descended into the underground Metro station next to where Luis had parked, and very few people were emerging from it. It was a noticeably early hour for the center of a capital city to begin shutting down, though the reason was clear: Cops and criminals owned the night.

Brodie checked his watch. It was five to seven. He turned to Luis. "Okay, we're walking to the plaza. Find a spot near the Tower of David and wait for us there."

"And how long should I wait before I am to be concerned?"

"Maybe an hour. But we'll call you if there's a problem. If you call us after eight and we don't answer, then you can choose to be concerned."

"Contact the embassy," added Taylor.

As Brodie and Taylor got out of the car, Luis warned them, "The police in this area are the worst in the city. Avoid them."

"Copy that," said Brodie. He turned to Taylor. "Ready for an evening stroll?"

"Locked and loaded," said Taylor.

———

Museum Plaza was accessible from a narrow walking path that cut through a thick line of trees. They entered the path and then veered off into the trees, making their way around the perimeter of the circular plaza, which was bounded by two museums housed in dilapidated neoclassical buildings, as well as the entrance to a heavily wooded city park.

They approached the side of one of the museum buildings and stopped behind a row of palm trees.

They waited. People flowed out of the museums and the park, heading for the walking path that led to the street and the Metro. A vendor hawking miniature busts of Bolívar, Che Guevara T-shirts, and other revolutionary kitsch was packing up his wares and breaking down a vinyl overhang.

Brodie said, "You'd look good in a Che Guevara T-shirt."

She didn't reply to that and kept scanning the plaza. "Look. Over there."

A short, thin man in a yellow polo shirt and white baseball cap ambled out of the park and into the center of the plaza. He checked his cell phone. At 7 P.M., Brodie and Taylor stepped into the plaza.

Raúl saw them. A policeman in a light blue uniform walked between them, heading toward the street. Once he was out of view, Raúl nodded to them, then began walking toward the exit of the plaza.

Brodie and Taylor followed. They caught sight of Raúl's yellow shirt as he turned onto the sidewalk that ran along the wide boulevard in front of the museums. The lack of pedestrians, along with Raúl's bright shirt, made it easy to see him at a distance.

They followed Raúl onto a narrow side street that was dark and empty, lined on either side with nondescript modern tower blocks without any street-level storefronts. None of the streetlights came on. A few motorbikes drove past, but otherwise it was desolate. Up ahead, they spotted a single business with its lights on. As they got closer they saw a lit-up plastic sign bearing the Burger King logo. Just as they reached it, the lights on the sign flicked out. Inside, Brodie saw a manager hastily closing up, racing against the unwritten curfew that was imprinted in the heart and mind of every Caraqueño.

Ahead of them, they saw Raúl pass a tall office building. He turned and looked back at them, then rounded a corner. They followed.

Brodie asked, "Did you ever think about how you'd fare in a zombie apocalypse?"

"Hasn't everyone? Personally, I'd off myself."

"Really?"

"You see these movies where people are running for their lives from these decaying monsters, and then they get away and try to have a normal life for about five minutes before one of those brain-eating bastards pops up out of nowhere. I wouldn't be able to live with that anxiety."

"I thought you were a fighter. Silver Star, right?"

"Yeah, in a real war, with real people who die and stay dead."

"Good point. But—"

Taylor grabbed his arm. "Wait."

A white sedan with a blue seal reading <u>POLICÍA</u> drove slowly through the intersection up ahead. The car rolled to a stop in the middle of the intersection, and Brodie could see the dim silhouette of a cop in the driver's seat, looking around. There was another cop in the passenger seat.

The car turned and drove down the street toward them.

Brodie grabbed Taylor's arm and pulled her behind a column in front of an office building just as the driver flicked on his high beams.

The police car rolled slowly down the street. Brodie ran through their options. If they had been spotted, they would be confronted. The best-case scenario would be a belligerent shakedown. The worst case would be the cops finding the guns on them.

The car inched closer. Given how empty the street was, Brodie figured he and Taylor could light these guys up and beat feet. If they had to. And, recalling Worley's story about the Venezuelan-American visitor, maybe they had to.

He had Taylor pressed against the column, and there wasn't enough space between them to slip a credit card. So while Big Brodie was gaming how to get them out of this situation, Little Brodie was misinterpreting the inputs and stirring awake, which was really unhelpful.

The police car was now almost next to them. They were concealed in shadow as the high beams struck the column in front of them.

The car kept driving, and Brodie and Taylor slid around the column to remain in darkness. Another moment passed . . . then the driver gassed it and continued down the block.

They remained frozen behind the column for another minute as they listened to the car disappear down the street. Little Brodie was continuing to behave in an unprofessional manner, as was his nature, so Brodie took a step back from Taylor and looked down the dark street. No sign of the cop car.

He turned to Taylor, who was looking at him. The hint of something had passed between them, and it could only mean trouble for this mission, not to mention their careers.

Brodie cleared his throat. "That was close."

"Yeah." She looked down the street in the direction they had been walking. "We lost Raúl, but I think I can see the tower from here."

They continued down the dark street, both aware that they were alone in a dangerous and lawless city, on a dangerous and unlawful assignment, with no backup except each other.

CHAPTER 18

The Tower of David, a.k.a. the Finance Center, was actually a complex of buildings, though there was a main tower that loomed above the rest, about forty or fifty stories high. It was an angular structure with a steel and concrete frame, intermittently faced with glass. Whole sections were unfinished, showing exposed floors and ceilings. It resembled a construction site except that the concrete looked old and stained, and much of the glass was shattered. It would not have looked out of place in an urban war zone. Or a zombie movie.

The sun was slipping farther beneath the horizon, casting the tower as a great looming thing against the blue-purple sky. Brodie and Taylor walked slowly toward it.

A concrete wall surrounded the entire complex, and ahead of them was a metal gate. Three figures were in front of the gate, though it was difficult to discern whether they were security, loiterers, or banditos.

As they got closer, they saw that the three men wore dark blue uniforms. One was leaning against a motorbike smoking a cigarette. The other two were standing next to the gate with submachine guns strapped across their chests.

The smoker spotted them across the street and waved them over. "Aquí, aquí."

"Para quién?" asked Taylor.

"Raúl," replied the man with some impatience. "Aquí."

Brodie said to Taylor, "If it comes to it, we hit the two guys with the subs first. I take the right, you the left."

"Copy."

They crossed the empty street, and as they drew closer to the men, they saw that the guy smoking the cigarette was older than the other two, probably mid-forties. He had a pencil-thin mustache, a long gaunt face, and a thick scar that stretched down one of his sunken cheeks. He wore a pistol in a holster at his waist. As they approached he flicked his cigarette toward the curb. The two younger guys, maybe late twenties, stared at them.

Scarface asked something in Spanish, and Taylor responded. They had a brief exchange in which all the men kept shifting their gazes to Brodie, probably wondering what kind of man would let a woman speak for him. He wanted to tell them that he had failed freshman year Spanish before studying French, but that would have required some Spanish.

One of the young guys unlocked the metal gate and pushed it open. Scarface gestured for them to enter.

"After you," said Brodie, gesturing at the gate.

Scarface just stared at him, dead-eyed. "After you," he said back in heavily accented English.

Brodie and Taylor went through the gate, followed by the two submachine-gun-toting guys, while Scarface closed the gate behind them and followed.

They walked abreast of the three men through an area of overgrown grass and slabs of cracked pavement, then passed between two thick columns to enter an open-air circular atrium with multi-tiered wraparound balconies. The place stunk like mold and garbage, and every surface within reach was covered in stratified layers of graffiti, some profane, some artistic. Much of it political. In the gloom, Brodie could make out a large message scrawled across the far wall in big, bold yellow letters: <u>CHÁVEZ VIVE</u>. Chávez lives.

Well, Chávez was dead. As was any hope of Venezuela achieving the lofty financial status imagined by the original designers of this grand ruin.

Evidence of the tower's former squatters was everywhere—jerry-rigged power lines extended across the atrium, brightly painted railings lined the edges of the open balconies, and high walls of stacked brick and cinder block formed makeshift rooms in the upper levels.

"Levanta los brazos," said Scarface.

"Where is Raúl?" asked Brodie.

"Levanta los brazos," the man repeated, mimicking the motion of raising his arms.

"I'll save you the trouble," said Brodie. "We're both armed with pistols, and you're not getting them."

Taylor translated and, judging by the guy's reaction, she did so faithfully. Scarface glared at Brodie and said something.

Taylor translated, "Surrender your weapons or you see no one."

"Then we're leaving," said Brodie. He said to Taylor, "We back out." He stepped back toward the gate. One of the young goons walked quickly toward the gate to outflank him and block his way. Brodie turned to face him. The man had not adjusted his submachine gun, which was still strapped low across his chest, and Brodie was pretty sure he could crack the guy's jaw and own his submachine gun before he could get it into a firing position. These guys were not professionals—more like mall cops with high-caliber toys. The problem was, there were three of them.

"Get out of my way," said Brodie. The guard didn't move, but as Brodie leaned into him he took a step backward.

Brodie saw out of the corner of his eye that Taylor had followed his lead, heading for the exit, but she was blocked by the other submachine gun–toting gentleman.

This looked like it could go bad quickly.

Then again, Raúl was Worley's guy, and if something happened to them, Raúl and Worley would both be in a world of shit. Brodie decided this was likely some customary machismo dick-wagging, and if they stood their ground it would not escalate.

In fact, Brodie decided—based on past experience in situations like this—that it was time for some dick-wagging of his own. He said to Scarface, "Call Raúl. Tell him he does not have to be afraid of our guns. We are here to buy information for the American Embassy, not to rob him. Also tell him he doesn't need three men to protect him, and he needs to get his skinny ass here pronto."

Taylor translated, though Brodie could tell by her tone and cadence that she'd put a little diplomatic spin on his statement.

Still, the guy looked pissed. He pulled out his cell and called. After a brief conversation, he hung up and said something to Taylor.

Taylor said to Brodie, "Raúl wants us to come to him, though by keeping our weapons we are only endangering ourselves."

"I'm not following that logic. Okay, tell this asshole to take us to his leader." He added, "Assholes two and three stay here."

Taylor spoke to Scarface. He nodded, then said something to the two other guys, who headed back toward the gate. He then gestured for Brodie and Taylor to follow. They walked across the atrium toward the main tower, through a doorway and into another lobby-type room with a set of stairs. Brodie spotted a bank of open elevator doors, but no actual elevators. Brodie and Taylor followed Scarface up the wide staircase.

The next level was divided by walls of stacked cinder blocks that rose almost to the high ceilings, creating a sprawling warren of rooms that had obviously been built by the former squatters. They continued up to the next story, which had a similar layout, then followed Scarface down a narrow walkway lined with brick walls and doorways. Some of the doorways had actual doors, but most relied on tattered sheets for privacy.

A line of fluorescent light fixtures hung from chains above the walkway, though the bulbs were all dead, missing, or shattered. Whatever method the former residents here had used to pull power had probably long been cut off.

In the dim light, Brodie could make out some details in the small brick rooms as they passed. Some were interconnected, forming something like apartments, though all that was left now were spoiled relics of home life— broken metal bed frames, shattered plates, old fruit crates and industrial debris creatively reconfigured into tables, chairs, and cooking surfaces. A few of the brick walls were actually painted. In the half-light Brodie could make out dashes of chalk along the edge of a cinder-block wall, each one accompanied by a date. Someone marking the growth of their child.

Scarface gestured toward a doorway. "You go here."

Brodie and Taylor walked into a small brick room lit by a battery-powered fluorescent lamp. There were a couple of ratty couches on either side of a wooden crate coffee table, and a plastic table against one of the walls held a flat-screen TV that someone had put two bullets through. On the far side of the room facing the doorway was a wide opening where a floor-to-ceiling glass window would have been had this tower ever been finished. Instead, there was a low brick wall to protect the former occupants from a thirty-foot drop.

Raúl sat in one of the couches, smoking a cigarette. Brodie looked at him in the fluorescent light. He had large and ugly features—big ears, big nose, big black eyes that darted between the two of them. He took a deep drag and exhaled a stream of smoke. "Who is this pretty lady?"

Taylor replied in Spanish, and Raúl didn't like the reply. He took another drag.

He was slouched in the couch, one arm hanging over the back of it, attempting to look relaxed and in control. But in reality he looked wound up tight. His eyes kept darting from Brodie and Taylor to Scarface behind them. Brodie guessed that Raúl did not own this man's loyalty, but only rented it.

Brodie pulled an American fifty-dollar bill out of his pocket and held it up to Scarface. "Go away. Vamoose."

Scarface looked at Brodie, then at the bill. Without hesitation, he grabbed the cash and headed for the door. Raúl yelled something after him in Spanish, but he kept walking.

Brodie turned back to Raúl. "Now we have some privacy."

Raúl did not look happy. He took a long drag on his cigarette, then stubbed it out on the arm of the couch. "Please sit." He motioned to the couch across from him.

Brodie replied, "I haven't had my tetanus shot. We'll stand."

Raúl remained seated. "What do you want?"

"What did our mutual friend tell you?" asked Brodie.

"He said you wanted women." His eyes flashed to Taylor. "But you already have a good one."

Taylor asked Raúl, "What do you do for him?"

"Mr. Hunt's business is his business."

Mr. Hunt. Naturally, Worley would not use his real name or military rank, though Brodie wondered if this was a deliberate Mission: Impossible reference—which would be consistent with the juvenile humor that afflicted a lot of the Intel guys he'd known.

"Here's the deal," said Brodie. "I've got someone coming to town, and I want you to help me get him into a blackmail situation. Comprende?"

Raúl stared at Brodie for a moment, then nodded. "This is something I can do, yes. I have nice girls for this."

"Hopefully not too nice," said Brodie.

Raúl flashed a crooked grin. "No, señor. Not too nice. And easy to trust."

"And then what?" asked Taylor. "Rooms with hidden cameras?"

He looked at Taylor. "Sí." He seemed a little uncomfortable discussing this topic with a woman, thought Brodie. This pimp was a true gentleman. Raúl assured them, "We have places for this."

"Good," said Brodie. "But a tape of him banging a hooker is not enough. I need something more extreme. Understand?"

Raúl looked at Brodie. "Some of the ladies, they are trained to do this. To push the man into other things. Things maybe he does not ask for, things he does not even know he wants."

Right. One minute you're in bed with a slightly bored hooker, the next you're on all fours wearing a pig mask and getting whipped.

"I'm thinking of younger girls," said Brodie.

Raúl gave him a look. "How young?"

"Very young," said Brodie. "Children."

Raúl's eyes darkened. "This is not something I do."

"But this is something I need," said Brodie. "For the blackmail."

"No, amigo," said Raúl, growing heated. "I tell you on the soul of my mother this is not something I do. I arrange ladies in hotel rooms, clubs, houses, this kind of thing. What you are saying, this is something else." He added, "I cannot help you."

"Raúl," said Taylor softly. "Look at me."

He made eye contact with her.

"We just want information. We want to know where this happens."

Raúl shook his head. "Not my business."

Brodie said, "Five hundred dollars."

Raúl stood, took off his baseball cap, and ran his hand through his stringy hair, then paced over to the open-air window that looked out over the dark city.

Brodie moved close to him. "We're looking for a place, and we think it's in Petare. A place where they have very young girls."

Raúl turned to him. "Do not go to Petare looking for this," he advised.

"Why?" asked Brodie.

"Because . . ." He made his hand into the shape of a pistol and put it against the bridge of his nose. "They will shoot you in the face, and then they will burn your body, and no one will be able to identify you when they dump your pieces on the side of the highway for the dogs to devour."

There was a long silence.

Brodie said, "Just tell us where. A street, a neighborhood." He reminded Raúl, "Five hundred dollars."

Raúl looked at him, then at Taylor. "These days no one cares about a whore in Caracas. We are all whores now, doing what we must to live. But this thing with the children brings attention. This crime must stay in the dark."

"Why is that?" asked Taylor.

Brodie thought the answer was that child prostitution attracted international attention, but Raúl said, "The regime."

"The regime is cracking down on child prostitution?" asked Taylor.

Raúl seemed to think that was funny. "No, señora. People in the regime work with the local gangs. They bring drugs from Colombia, stolen food and medicine from the ports. They sell weapons taken from the military. And the young girls, this is another part of their business. The women and the girls."

Brodie and Taylor exchanged glances. There didn't seem to be any bottom to the pit that this country had fallen into.

Raúl added, "It is mostly the government oilmen. PDVSA. The scum of the scum."

Brodie thought back to Al Simpson. Government oil guys exploiting their power to get rich off the underworld, and taking foreign VIPs on a nocturnal joyride out to a far-flung corner of their criminal empire to engage in illicit carnal pleasures. Then maybe blackmailing them to get a good deal. And maybe that's what they'd done with Al Simpson and his partner, Pete. But what the hell did Kyle Mercer have to do with any of this?

Brodie said to Raúl, "What I need from you, señor, are the names and addresses of the brothels in Petare where child prostitution takes place."

"Why does the American Embassy need to know this?"

Brodie replied, "That's none of your fucking business."

Raúl thought a moment, then said, "Americans are arrogant."

"Tell us something we don't know," suggested Brodie.

Raúl smiled. "Arrogant." He glanced at Brodie. "These places are protected by the regime. If I gave you the names, I would be putting my life at risk."

"We wouldn't rat you out," Brodie assured him. He added, "Six hundred dollars."

"Seven."

"You got a deal."

Raúl lit another cigarette and said, "The colectivos. You know of this?"

"No."

"The colectivos are gangs. But political gangs. Began by Chávez. He armed them. Like a militia—a political militia. They control different neighborhoods in the barrios and sometimes they fight with other gangs, the ones that are not so political. And there is a large colectivo in Petare—MBR-200." He added, "This colectivo is involved with child prostitution."

"Where in Petare?" asked Brodie.

"Barrio Veinticuatro de Julio. July Twenty-Fourth neighborhood. This is where they started. But they have also fought other gangs and expanded to other places."

Taylor reminded Raúl, "We are looking for the names and addresses of the brothels that engage in child prostitution."

Raúl smiled. "Names? You think they have names? With neon signs?"

Taylor said something to him in Spanish that wiped the smile from Raúl's face.

Raúl glanced at her briefly, then said, "I have given you the name of the neighborhood in Petare where you will find these places. There are maybe two, three of them. You will need to find them on your own." He added, "I would advise you to go armed, during the daylight. I would also advise that you, señora, do not go with this gentleman."

Neither Brodie nor Taylor replied.

Raúl, wanting to earn his seven hundred dollars, said to Brodie, "A foreigner is usually brought to these places by someone. Someone connected to the gang or to corrupt regime people. But also a man alone—a sex tourist—can go. And if he is lucky, he will have sex with a child prostitute. If he is not so lucky, he will be robbed and maybe have his throat cut."

"Right," said Brodie. Al Simpson and his partner had been hosted by the PDVSA guys. But how did Kyle Mercer come to be there? Well, Brodie would ask him when he apprehended him. This wasn't much to go on, but it was something. Kyle Mercer had last been seen in a child prostitution whorehouse in a certain neighborhood in Petare. Maybe Mercer was a sex tourist, and was now in Bangkok. Brodie said to Taylor, "This job sucks."

"What was your first clue?"

Raúl seemed confused by the exchange. He stated firmly, "That is all I know."

Brodie nodded. "Okay. Do you take American Express?"

"Señor—"

"Let's do cash." Brodie pulled a wad of twenties out of his pocket and counted seven hundred dollars into Raúl's open palms. "And here's another twenty for the church collection basket."

Raúl didn't think that was funny, but he took the twenty and shoved the cash in his pocket.

Brodie asked, "Is there another way out of here?"

"There is another staircase at the other side of the tower."

"And I don't want to see your three rent-a-cops there."

"I am an honest businessman, señor. You can ask Señor Hunt."

"I think Señor Hunt has been here too long."

Raúl smiled. "Señor Hunt has said so himself."

"You lead the way," said Brodie. "And no funny business—if I see your homeboys, you're the first casualty."

CHAPTER 19

They followed Raúl through a labyrinth of brick and cinder-block rooms. One room was larger than the rest, and amidst the debris and drifts of trash were piles of folding chairs and a rusty metal desk. On one wall was a large spray-painted stencil of Hugo Chávez' face accompanied by painted words that Taylor translated aloud: "'Tower of David Community Council.'" She asked Raúl, "What is that?"

Raúl explained, "Each floor had a representative. They met, they voted. They had their own police. People had shops in here too. Businesses."

Well, thought Brodie, maybe those former squatters could teach the clowns in the Presidential Palace how to run a democracy and an economy. Maybe that's why they were kicked out.

They followed Raúl to a stairwell that had no outer wall and no banister to keep people from falling to their deaths. It was hard to imagine that this place used to house thousands of residents, including children. Brodie said to Raúl, "You first."

From this height, Brodie could see that they were on the opposite side of the tower, out of sight of the entrance gate. The concrete security wall extended around to this end of the complex, though no other gates were visible.

They descended to the base of the stairs and followed Raúl toward the wall. Brodie looked around. It was oddly tranquil here, as they traversed the overgrown weeds, littered with stray chunks of broken concrete and tangles of rusty rebar. The moon hung bright and almost full, and the chirps of nighthawks pierced the soft rustle of palm trees in the wind.

"This way," said Raúl in a whisper. He led them along the outer wall toward a section where someone had broken a hole large enough to crawl through.

Raúl said, "I will leave you here." He added, "You will tell Mr. Hunt I was very helpful to you."

"You will get a good performance review."

Raúl seemed to be processing that.

Taylor said to Raúl, "If this information is good, we'll be seeing you again. If it's not good, we'll be seeing you again."

Raúl looked at her. "Perhaps you should go to Petare with this gentleman."

Brodie thought that was funny, but suppressed his smile. "See ya around, amigo."

"Buenas noches." He walked away.

Brodie said, "Not a bad guy for a pimp." He motioned to the hole. "Ladies first."

Taylor drew her Glock and crawled through the hole in the wall. "Clear."

Brodie followed and emerged into a dead-quiet street. Across the street was a row of dilapidated single-story buildings faced with crumbling stucco. There were steel bars on every window, and coils of razor wire snaked along the edges of Spanish tile roofs.

Brodie pulled out his cell phone and dialed Luis as Taylor scanned the street with her Glock at her side.

Luis answered after half a ring.

"We're ready to go," said Brodie.

"You are okay?"

"We're great. How about you?"

"Yes, but I can see the men with guns—"

"We're on the opposite side of the tower from the entrance." He hung up and said to Taylor, "You want to go to Petare?"

She hesitated, then replied, "I think we should scope it out in the daylight first."

"Mercer could be there right now, in his favorite brothel, playing skip-rope with a twelve-year-old."

"That's disgusting."

"Beyond disgusting."

She thought a moment. "Why's he here, Brodie?"

"Don't know."

"Sex tourist?"

"Bangkok is better and safer."

She glanced at him but didn't respond to that. "He could have just been passing through."

"Simpson said he looked like he ran the place."

She nodded.

"Let's go to Petare. If we get lucky and see him, we'll shove a gun in his ribs, march him out, and stuff him hog-tied in Luis' trunk."

"Then what?"

"Then we'll call Worley, who will arrange our transportation out of here."

"Where would we keep Mercer while we're waiting?"

"In Luis' trunk."

"I think we need a better plan."

"Right. Okay, how about a drink at the hotel?"

"That's what I need."

Luis' Dart turned a corner and crawled down the street toward them, with only his parking lights on. He pulled up to them and they jumped in. Luis turned on his headlights and sped off. He kept looking at Brodie in the passenger seat as if he was surprised to see him alive. "Hotel. Yes?"

Brodie looked down the dark street. Part of him still wanted to make a night run into Petare. But that was the same part of him that had almost got him killed in Baghdad.

Taylor said, "Back to the hotel."

"Sí."

Luis made a U-turn, explaining that they needed to go a little out of their way to take Avenida Boyacá, which ran east-west along the southern foothills of the coastal mountain range, to avoid driving through too much of the city at night.

They drove at high speed through a desolate neighborhood. No one was on the street, and all the streetlights were out. The only light came from the residential tower blocks, where people continued their private lives amidst a city of two million people on lockdown.

They reached Avenida Boyacá, a four-lane highway skirting the base of the pitch-black coastal range. There were no other cars around as they headed east.

Luis seemed to relax. He gestured to the hills. "Very beautiful up there. When I was a boy we would go on long walks on the weekends. My father, he was, how do you say it? Very much into looking at the birds."

"A bird-watcher," said Taylor.

"Yes," said Luis. "So he knew all the different kinds. We would walk for hours through the forest, watching. He had a notebook that was passed down to him by his father, to record all the sightings. My job was to record the different types as we saw them. It was my favorite time with my father." Luis looked wistful as he peered up at the dark mountains.

Taylor asked, "How old are your children?"

"I have a boy who is ten, and a girl who is eight."

"It must be hard for them."

Luis nodded. "Yes, señora. But the worst thing is, this is all they know. They do not remember when there was enough food. They do not understand that it is not normal for no one to trust anybody. For there to be bars on every window, chains and locks on every door." He added, "They have almost never been out at night."

Brodie was getting depressed just listening to this. He asked, "How's the rest of the country?"

"Some parts are the same as here. Some parts . . . maybe better. Maybe safer. Maybe more food . . . Some good people have taken control in the villages and the small towns. But the sickness . . . the evil spreads from here."

Sounded like the zombie apocalypse. The battle between men and monsters who had once been men. Brodie had seen this descent into chaos in Iraq—a postapocalyptic breakdown of society, a quick transition into lawlessness and murder. Every man for himself. Very scary. He asked Luis, "You want to get out of here?"

Luis hesitated, then replied, "This is my country."

"Not anymore, amigo."

"I want my country back. It will happen."

"If you change your mind, let me know and I'll see what I can do with the embassy."

He didn't reply.

"Did Mr. Worley ever mention this to you?"

"He . . . said I was not eligible for an American visa. I would need to be a political refugee. An opponent of the regime." He forced a laugh. "That is half the country."

"Right." Brodie had seen this with Iraqis who worked for the Americans. They were men marked for death, and there had been vague promises made by the U.S. State Department to help them emigrate. But most of these people did not get visas, and many were murdered by one insurgent group or another whose only common cause was a hatred of the American infidels and their Iraqi lackeys.

Iraq was not Venezuela, but the idiots in the State Department sounded the same. And Worley, who actually worked for the Pentagon, sounded like a lying shit. All Worley had to say to get Luis and his family out of here was that Luis, a loyal embassy employee, had been threatened with arrest by the regime.

The world was truly going to hell. Brodie had good job security.

Taylor, who had obviously taken a liking to Luis, said to him, "You should think of your wife and children. Let us know if you decide to leave. We may be able to help."

"Thank you, señora."

"Meanwhile," said Brodie, "do what you can to make Venezuela great again."

Brodie saw headlights in the sideview mirror. He reached for his pistol as the car came up fast in the lane next to them. It was a large SUV, which Luis said was probably armored. It rocketed past them and disappeared down the dark road ahead, and Luis made the sign of the cross.

Brodie flashed back to his night patrols through Sadr City, one of the most dangerous quarters of Baghdad, where no vehicle was on the road without heavy armor. Back then he had the benefit of an armored Stryker with a mounted .50-caliber M2 machine gun in case things got interesting. But now, he and his two-person crew were traversing nighttime Caracas in an old beater, armed with three pistols and a jeweled cross for divine protection.

They arrived back at the El Dorado without incident a little after 8 P.M. Luis went through the security check at the gate, then pulled up to the front entrance.

Brodie gave Luis three American twenties. "Thanks. You did good."

"Too much, señor."

"Hazardous duty pay."

Luis forced a smile. "That is every day here."

"Right. Tomorrow you get combat pay. We're going to Petare."

His smile dropped.

"I'll call you with the pickup time."

"It is better to go in the daylight."

"Right. I'll let you know."

Taylor said, "If you don't want to go, we understand."

"We do," said Brodie, "but we won't be happy."

"Scott—"

Luis said, "I will see you tomorrow."

Taylor asked him, "Will you be okay going home at this hour? I can arrange for you to stay here tonight."

"Thank you, señora, but I do not have far to go."

Brodie said, "Thy Glock and thy cross will comfort you."

"Sí . . ."

A doorman appeared and opened the front and rear passenger doors. Brodie and Taylor wished Luis a good evening and got out. The doorman looked at Luis' low-rider pulling away and inquired, "Are you registered guests, or are you here for dinner?"

"Both," Brodie replied.

"I am sorry to say, the restaurant is closed."

"We're actually registered at the bar."

"Yes . . . ? Good. It is open."

Brodie and Taylor entered the hotel and Taylor said to him, "You're a bully."

"And arrogant. And we have a job to do. Also, I need a drink."

They went to the lobby lounge, which was almost empty, and sat where they'd met Worley.

A waiter appeared immediately and they both ordered the local rum.

They sat in silence awhile; then Taylor asked, "Are you very cool in a dangerous situation, or do you just not understand what's going on around you?"

"Sometimes one, sometimes the other."

"That's very comforting."

Their drinks came and they touched glasses. Brodie said, "You did good today."

"Thank you, but I don't need your affirmation."

"Right. Well, I think we made some progress today."

She nodded.

"Why is Kyle Mercer here?" Brodie asked.

"I think we've been through this."

"Okay." He looked at her in the dim light. "Why did Captain Mercer desert?"

"We've been through this too."

He nodded, then thought a moment and said, "Here's something new. I'm starting to think that there's more to this case than bringing a fugitive to justice." He asked her, "Do you have that feeling?"

"Tell me what you base that feeling on."

"A dozen years of detective work."

"Okay. But maybe you've developed an overactive imagination."

"Maybe."

She sipped her drink. "This is pretty good."

"Better than Tennessee moonshine."

She smiled. "Hardly." She asked, "What more could there be to this?"

"I'm glad you asked." He leaned toward her. "Two things about this case make absolutely no sense. One is that a Delta Force officer deserted his men in a war zone, surrounded by hostile forces. Two, that deserter went through hell in captivity, and then wound up here in the shithole of the Western Hemisphere." He looked at her. "Also, I've been through a hundred case briefings, but I've never been through one like General Hackett gave us."

"Meaning?"

"Meaning I was sure he—and maybe Dombroski—knew more than they were saying, and I was also sure Hackett didn't want us to know anything more." He added, "Hackett specifically told us not to question Mercer."

"I think you need another drink."

Brodie kept looking at her. "Do you know anything I don't know?"

"I should be insulted."

"Sorry."

"Look . . . what you say may . . . be correct. A lot of this doesn't make sense. This case is complex. But our mission is simple: Find and apprehend Captain Kyle Mercer." She added, "Don't complicate it with . . . conspiracy theories."

"I watch too many TV series."

"Apparently."

"You want another drink?"

"No. I'm drained and beat." She stood. "Don't drink too much. And don't knock on my door."

"What if I figure this all out?"

"Tell me in the morning."

"Breakfast at eight?"

"Sounds good."

"Buenas noches."

She smiled. "You too."

Brodie watched her as she walked toward the elevators.

After twelve years on this job, he was good at reading people. Maggie Taylor meant it when she said don't knock on my door. But when she said she was insulted by his question, she was lying.

CHAPTER 20

Brodie had another rum, which put him in the right state of mind to call his boss. He headed up to his suite and entered through the common sitting room, in case Taylor had decided to have a drink and wait up for him. But the sitting room was empty. And the door to her bedroom was closed. *Don't knock on my door.*

That sounded like good advice, even after two drinks. He went to the minibar to fix himself a third.

He found a miniature bottle of local rum and emptied it into a glass, then—noisily—added ice from the bucket and glanced back at her door, which remained closed. *What are you doing, Brodie?*

He went into his room, closed and locked the door, then stepped out to his bedroom balcony.

He set his drink on a table and took out his smartphone. It looked like he had reception and his phone was connected to the local cellular data carrier, so he didn't have to deal with the hotel's unsecure Wi-Fi. He opened Signal, a commercially available end-to-end encryption app that he and Dombroski had started using when he was on sensitive overseas assignments. In the old days you needed specialized equipment to communicate securely, and this equipment was physically located in the U.S. Embassy of whatever country you were in. Now, on any smartphone, you could download a free app that offered encryption that even the National Security Agency couldn't crack. At least, that's what the NSA wanted you to believe.

He called Dombroski, who picked up after two rings.

"Mr. Brodie. How's the Paris of South America?"

"I think that's Buenos Aires."

"Right. Are you alone?"

"I am."

"I received a call from Colonel Worley confirming that you met at the hotel."

"Correct."

"He told me about your drive from the airport."

"No big deal."

"Try not to kill anyone or get yourself killed. You have a job to do."

"Yes, sir." Brodie sat on a deck chair, picked up his glass, and took a swig.

"Worley said you were inquiring about prostitutes."

"Did he also tell you he's an expert on the subject?"

Dombroski laughed. "He didn't. But you're going to tell me why you asked him."

"Well, as it turns out, my and Ms. Taylor's idea to re-interview Al Simpson paid off." *Aren't you proud of me, Colonel?* Brodie continued, "Simpson did not see Mercer in the Marriott hotel bar. He confessed that he saw Mercer in a brothel."

Dombroski stayed silent a moment, then said, "Shoulda figured that."

"Simpson gave me a general description of the brothel, and a possible location. So I asked Worley about hookers and brothels, and he put me on to a guy named Raúl."

"Good detective work. And have you spoken to . . . what's his name?"

"Raúl. Ms. Taylor and I met him, and he suggested that what we were looking for was in an unsavory quarter of Caracas called Petare." Brodie added, "This fits Simpson's description of his drive to the brothel."

"That's good. Do you think Mercer frequents this brothel?"

"Simpson said he looked very at ease there. Like he was . . . maybe more than a customer."

"Okay. How come you're not there now?"

"We're going tomorrow."

"That's not like you, Brodie."

"It's a very . . . dangerous part of the city. Controlled by organized gangs. We decided to recon it in the daylight."

Dombroski stayed silent, then said, "You caught some good breaks. You could have wrapped it up tonight and been home tomorrow."

After seventeen years in the Army, Brodie was used to the military's can-do culture—we do the difficult today, the impossible tomorrow. And he bought into most of it. But not all of it. He'd seen too many men get killed in Iraq who'd be alive today if they and their officers had been a little more cautious, and a little less macho.

"Brodie?"

"Tomorrow." He added, "I'm under the influence tonight."

"Taylor going with you?"

"We'll see."

"That's your call."

"And her call."

"How's she doing?"

"Fine. Let's return to the subject of hookers."

"Okay."

"You should know that this brothel that Simpson was in specializes in underage girls." He added, "Child prostitutes."

Dombroski had no reply.

"So we've got a problem with this witness if we need him on the stand."

"Don't think too far ahead, Brodie. Let the JAG people worry about that. You just need to apprehend Kyle Mercer and get him into this jurisdiction."

"I know that."

"And do *not* interrogate him. If you do, his lawyer will say he was questioned without an attorney—"

"I know that too."

"Don't ask him anything except his name, rank, and service number. Then read him his rights with a witness present—Taylor—and make a note that he understood. Then tape his mouth shut and put a sack over his head."

"When do I kick him in the nuts?"

Dombroski ignored that and continued, "Worley said he gave you a kit."

"Right. No duct tape and no sack."

"Buy what you need, and spend whatever you need to buy information, bribe who's got to be bribed. There's no budget on this case."

"Good. I'm running up a big bar bill." Brodie asked, "Did you speak to Worley about getting transportation out of here?"

"I did. Not a problem."

"So he said. Any details?"

"He'll fill you in when the time comes. How's the weather down there?"

"Hot and humid."

"Nice here. Cooled down."

"Colonel, does it bother you that we don't know why a Delta Force officer deserted?"

"It bothers me that he deserted, and that he disgraced his uniform and
his country."

"Right, but—"

"As for *why* he did that, you can be sure he'll come up with some bullshit
at his court-martial. Meanwhile, I don't care, and neither should you. You
are not his lawyer, his priest, his shrink, or his life coach." He advised Brodie,
"Just find the son of a bitch and get him back here to face charges."

Brodie knew his boss well, and he was sure that Colonel Dombroski did
care about Mercer's reason for desertion—in fact, it was Dombroski himself who always told his investigators to remember the five W's: who, what,
where, when, and why. Clearly Dombroski had been given different marching orders by General Hackett. Brodie was sure of that. But *why*? It always
came down to *why*. To motive.

Brodie changed the subject and asked, "Do you have anything new
for me?"

"As a matter of fact, I do. Do you remember Robert Crenshaw? Guy
from State who got killed in Peshawar last year?"

Brodie did remember. Robert Crenshaw was a State Department analyst stationed with the U.S. Consulate in Peshawar, a northern Pakistani
city within the tribal territories. Since Crenshaw wasn't Army, his murder
wasn't CID's jurisdiction, but the FBI had assisted the Pakistani authorities.
The details of the case were memorable. His body had been found by local
police in a bare apartment, tied to a chair with his throat cut. His body bore
signs of severe torture, including, but not limited to, an extreme manicure.
The perpetrator or perpetrators have never been found, but it was assumed
to be the Taliban or al Qaeda who'd killed the American. Brodie replied, "I
remember."

There was a long silence; then Dombroski said, "I was thinking about
Mercer, how this guy gets from the Afghan-Pakistan frontier to Caracas.
Crenshaw was killed in early August 2017. The video of Mercer, his escape
from the Taliban, is time-stamped July thirteenth, 2017."

Brodie did not reply, but he put his drink down and sat up.

Dombroski continued, "I reached out to an Army contact I have at our embassy in Islamabad. Turns out Crenshaw wasn't State. That was cover. He was a CIA officer, and he'd previously been stationed across the border in Kabul in the years before Mercer's desertion."

Brodie thought about that. Mercer escapes imprisonment in the tribal territories, resigns his commission in anger, and then a few weeks later in a city close to his last known location—the Taliban camp—an American spy is tortured and killed. Could be a coincidence. But maybe not. Brodie said, "We should have been given this information by General Hackett."

"General Hackett might not have known."

"General Mendoza did."

Dombroski didn't respond to that.

There was no world in which Army Chief of Staff Mendoza was kept in the dark on Crenshaw's CIA affiliation after Crenshaw was tortured and murdered—not when one of his most lethal warriors was on the loose in the area. Had General Mendoza briefed General Hackett? Brodie didn't really care if the guy who was withholding information from him had two stars or four. He was trying to put together a puzzle, and someone on their side was hiding some pieces.

Dombroski said, "If Mercer killed Crenshaw, the torture had to do with . . . maybe revenge, or getting something out of him. That's why you torture people."

"Usually. But what—?"

"I'm thinking that if it was Mercer, maybe Crenshaw revealed something under torture that took Mercer to Caracas."

Brodie thought that was a bit of a stretch. But at least it sounded like Dombroski had suddenly recalled a few of the five W's. Stanley Dombroski was not a political animal—he was a cop. But he often found himself caught between the world of Pentagon politics and honest police work—between bullshit and justice. No, Colonel Dombroski would never make general, and his Buddha belly and vertically challenged stature were not the primary reason for that.

"Brodie?"

"Still here."

"This is all off the record."

"Copy."

"This was not part of our mission briefing."

"No, it was not."

Dombroski continued, "If there is a connection between Crenshaw's murder and Captain Mercer, the Intel folks at the embassy in Caracas are aware of this, and they are now wondering what you've been wondering— why is Mercer in Venezuela?"

Brodie didn't respond. Taylor had told him he was being paranoid about this case, but now Dombroski was feeding his suspicions.

Dombroski asked, "Was Worley pumping you for information about your assignment?"

"A little. We told him only what he needed to know. Have you dealt with him before?"

"No. He got in touch with me when I reached out to the military attaché office in the Caracas embassy. But I'd bet money on him being DCS."

DCS stood for Defense Clandestine Service, the human espionage arm of the Defense Intelligence Agency. The Pentagon's spooks. Brodie said, "Could be."

"What was your impression of him?"

"Burned-out. Slovenly. Dumb as a fox."

"Sounds like a DCS guy. Keep an eye on him."

"Right. Let's return to Robert Crenshaw. What was he doing in Peshawar?"

"I don't know. But tracking and killing Taliban is the local sport."

"Right. And that was Mercer's job in Afghanistan."

Dombroski didn't reply. Then he said, "This case may be more complex than it appears."

"It always was."

Again, no reply. Then, "It sounds like you've got a good lead. Follow it where it takes you. Chances are this Crenshaw information won't play a role in that. But I wanted you to be aware that our friends in the Caracas embassy might have more interest in this case than they're letting on."

Brodie thought about everything that Dombroski had said. Nothing pissed him off more than someone else deciding what he did and didn't need to know. But at least Dombroski was giving him something—off the record. Brodie asked, "As long as we're outing spies, any news on my partner?"

"That was just gossip."

Brodie did not reply.

"What do you think?"

Brodie thought back to their drinks in the hotel bar. There was something off. But nothing to go on. He said, "I trust her."

"Good."

"Anything else, Colonel?"

"Just learned my ex-wife remarried."

"Congratulations."

"I found out on Facebook. New guy's fatter than me. I wonder if it'll last."

"Is he rich?"

"He's a retired cop, into local politics."

"Two strikes. Give it a year."

Dombroski laughed. "You've got to take your turn at bat, Brodie. How are the women down there?"

"I'm focused on the case."

"Good. Don't spend government money in a whorehouse unless it's information that you're buying."

"You're welcome to come here and keep an eye on me."

"No, thanks. You get all the glory. Meanwhile, share this new information about Crenshaw on a need-to-know basis."

Meaning, *It's up to you if you want to tell Taylor.* "Yes, sir. Anything further?"

"Negative further."

The protocol was that the superior had the last word, so Brodie hung up and looked out at the view from the balcony. There were very few lights on in the city below and it was hard to tell where Caracas ended and the mountains began.

Every case, from petty theft to murder, is a nexus of people, places, motives, and interests. This case was more complex than most, but it was still made up of the same essential parts. He had a fugitive who was, in addition to being a potential head case, a highly trained member of an elite unit who had been operating for years in a vast Black Ops war without end. The motive for his initial crime—desertion—was a mystery. But he had managed to kill his Taliban captors and escape imprisonment. If he'd then returned to a U.S. military base, that might have been viewed as a heroic act that could mitigate his initial desertion. But instead he had desecrated the bodies of the dead—a crime in both U.S. military and international law—and turned his back on his career and his country. Why?

And now this guy Crenshaw . . . tortured and killed. As a CIA officer in Kabul, Crenshaw would likely have coordinated and worked with JSOC and its special operators on the ground, including Delta Force.

CIA. JSOC. Kabul. Peshawar.

Caracas.

This was the piece that didn't fit, the non sequitur in the unwritten story of Captain Kyle Mercer. Brodie looked out toward the eastern hills and Petare, to the great black wash of mountains and sky. Maybe tomorrow would bring some answers.

He went back into his room, locked his balcony door, and sat at the desk. He then installed the VPN client from Worley on his laptop and wondered if he had just given the DIA access to all of his e-mails and search history. Paranoia fed on itself.

He ran a Google search for "MBR-200," the name of the colectivo gang that Raúl had given them. He found nothing on the gang itself, though he did discover its namesake—the revolutionary movement that Hugo Chávez had founded back in 1982 and that ultimately launched his first failed coup attempt a decade later. The "200" had been added to the name in 1983 to commemorate the two-hundredth birthday of Venezuela's national obsession, Simón Bolívar.

History and memory ran deep here, thought Brodie. These thugs were dealing in child prostitutes and drugs, but they still wore these revolutionary tropes and signifiers like badges of honor. He thought back to the Mahdi Army, a powerful Shi'ite insurgent group in Baghdad formed during the war, which was named for a ninth-century imam who was prophesied to return in the end times. There was a real power to these associations, instilling a sense in these groups' adherents that the fabled battles of old were being refought over and over.

Brodie had told Luis this country needed another Bolívar. But in reality, this place—like the entire world of Islam—needed to move on and find new heroes. Or maybe stop putting men on pedestals altogether.

He finished his rum, stood and pulled his Glock from its holster and placed it on the bedside table, set his alarm, then threw off his clothes and crashed on the bed. It had been a good first day in country. They'd met Worley, hired Luis, reconned the city, and met a pimp, and he had just learned that maybe the fugitive he was hunting had tortured and murdered an undercover CIA officer. And, by the way, his own partner might be a CIA asset as well.

Before he'd left for college, Brodie's father had tried to entice him to stay by pitching a plan to take out a bank loan, buy the vacant acreage next to their house, and make a go at a real family farm. If he'd taken the old man's offer, he'd now be harvesting corn, lettuce, maybe some rhubarb.

Instead he'd gone to college, and then he went to war. Then he joined CID, and that's when life got really complicated. He wasn't sure what he would find tomorrow in Petare, whether it was Kyle Mercer himself or just another breadcrumb along the trail that led to his fugitive. What Brodie did sense was that the scope of this case was widening, the picture slowly growing sharper—and he was sure that when the picture was finally clear, he was not going to like what he saw.

Outside, he heard the wail of a police siren, and what sounded like the distant crack of gunfire. He was suddenly back in Baghdad. He knew he needed to get out of this place before it erupted into civil war.

He turned off the bedside lamp and drifted into an uneasy sleep.

CHAPTER 21

Brodie came downstairs to meet Taylor for breakfast at eight o'clock. She was, as he expected, already at a table with a cup of coffee, reading a Spanish-language newspaper, which she folded as he sat down.

"Buenos días," said Brodie.

"Morning. Did you sleep well?"

"The sound of gunfire always lulls me to sleep."

"I heard that."

Brodie poured himself coffee from a carafe and gestured at the paper. "What's new?"

"Same old. Everything is the United States' fault. They have the *New York Times* if you want something in English."

"I think I'd get the same story."

"I assume you spoke to Dombroski last night."

"Good assumption. He wanted us to go to Petare last night. I'm sure General Hackett is up his ass." Brodie thought about sharing the info about Robert Crenshaw's murder, but decided against it. He told himself this was not because he didn't trust his partner, but because it was not relevant at the moment.

Their waiter, a young man named Mateo, came by and Brodie asked, "What's a traditional Venezuelan breakfast?"

Mateo smiled. "My wife usually makes arepas with eggs, but my wife is not here, so the hotel offers huevos pericos. This is like scrambled eggs, but more . . . exciting."

They both ordered the exciting scrambled eggs, and Mateo bowed and walked off to the kitchen.

Taylor said, "'Perico' means parakeet."

"I was wondering why I didn't hear the birds this morning."

Taylor smiled. Brodie noticed that she had dressed down for their stroll through the slums and had traded her blazer for a windbreaker. Brodie was wearing a monochrome T-shirt and a light cotton bush jacket. It was hot enough that they should not be wearing jackets at all, but when walking around places like Petare, you didn't want people to know you had a gun until they were looking down the barrel.

Taylor informed him, "I didn't want to carry around the drugstore bag but I stuffed a few snacks and medical supplies in my jacket."

"I'm not sure gangbangers around here take bribes in the form of Snickers bars, but it can't hurt."

Taylor replied, "I also brought the Taser and zip ties."

"Good." But if Kyle Mercer was coming at him, it wasn't the Taser he would reach for. In fact, today he'd made sure to pull his extra loaded mag from the room safe, and he had noticed that Taylor had already taken the other one. She, like Brodie, knew that the only thing worse than finding yourself in a gangland shoot-out was being the first one to run out of bullets.

Taylor pulled a map from her jacket pocket and unfolded it. She pointed to a section in the northern end of Petare that she'd circled in pen. "This is the July Twenty-Fourth neighborhood." She moved her finger down to an area toward the center of the slum. "And this is the original historic core of Petare, which actually used to be its own city. There's an old pink cathedral there, which is probably the church Al Simpson described."

Brodie looked at the map. The old quarter was almost a straight shot east from the Marriott, going by way of a road that passed the Francisco de Miranda Airport. "We'll start by following Simpson's route, then work our way north toward July Twenty-Fourth." He added, "We'll do a recon, and also see who responds to our presence, and how."

"And who are we? What's our story?"

"We are Clark and Sarah Bowman, the stupidest fucking tourists that ever lived. Maybe you're looking to snap some poverty porn to punch up your Instagram."

"That's horrible."

"Yeah. Sarah Bowman completely sucks."

"And who is Clark?"

"Clark is looking for a break from his banal life. And maybe he's thinking about getting into some trouble tonight, minus his wife."

Taylor suggested, "Maybe she likes trouble too."

Brodie wasn't sure that would fly. This city might be a hotbed of corruption and murder, but it was still a traditional Catholic, patriarchal country. Would the men who bought and sold women also accept them as . . . voyeurs? Or customers in a ménage, as they did in Bangkok? Brodie said, "We'll see."

Mateo returned with their parakeet omelets, which were, thankfully, just chicken eggs scrambled with tomatoes and scallions. Pretty good. "Get the recipe for the O Club."

They ate quickly, paid the bill, and headed for the door. If Luis had come to his senses, he wouldn't be waiting for them.

"Let's make an arrest today," said Brodie.

"Also, let's try not to get shot or kidnapped today." She added, "And let's not shoot any mules."

"Not funny, Taylor."

———

They walked outside and saw Luis' jalopy idling in the hotel's roundabout. Brodie commented, "My bullying worked."

"Or," said Taylor, "Luis is brave and loyal."

"Or he just needs the money. Or he's reporting to Worley."

"How did you become so cynical?"

"It's an act."

"Had me fooled."

The doorman opened the rear door and Taylor got in. Brodie climbed into the front passenger seat. Luis greeted him with a strained smile. There was no Joropo music playing.

Brodie gave Luis a rundown of their plan to drive by the Marriott and then through the old quarter of Petare before heading into the July 24th neighborhood.

Luis asked, "Are you armed today?"

Brodie replied, "We are. And you?"

"Sí. Always."

They drove out of the security gate and down the leafy streets of Altamira.

Luis informed his passengers, "The National Guard sets up checkpoints around the slums, and sometimes you do not see them until it is too late. They are mostly looking for guns and drugs brought in by locals. But they also stop foreigners, so we must hide our weapons." He assured them, "I have a special compartment for this."

"If we're stopped, we'll bribe them," said Brodie.

Luis shook his head. "They will possibly not be bribed. A few of them are not corrupted, and the ones who are would probably choose to put you in jail until your embassy pays a big fine."

Brodie didn't think Worley had that in his budget. So . . . should they keep their guns on them? Or try to hide them in Luis' special compartment which was probably not so special? He wished Luis had mentioned this last night. In any case, they had to avoid a stop-and-search. "We'll keep our guns, but you need to avoid the checkpoints."

Taylor said, "Scott, we have no right to expose Luis to this."

Brodie asked Luis, "Are you okay with this?"

Luis didn't reply, and clearly he was conflicted.

Taylor said to him, "Pull over."

Luis pulled to the side of the road.

Taylor said, "Thank you, Luis." She asked, "Can we get a taxi to Petare?"

"In the day, yes."

Brodie asked, "Can we get a taxi *out* of Petare?"

"No." He added, "And a car and driver to Petare is difficult."

"Okay," said Brodie, "take us to a car rental agency."

Luis did not reply, but pulled his gun and said to Brodie, "Please open the glove compartment."

Brodie looked at him, then opened the glove compartment.

Luis leaned over, dropped his gun into the black, felt-lined compartment, and closed the door—then reopened it, revealing that the gun was gone. He said, "Just like in a magic show. Yes?"

"You are truly a magician," said Brodie. He unhooked his pancake holster and Glock and took the spare mag out of his pocket, and repeated the trick. Taylor handed Brodie her holster, gun, and mag, along with the Taser and zip ties. "Now you see it . . . ," said Brodie as he put Taylor's stuff in the compartment and closed it, then opened it. "Now you don't."

Luis forced a smile. "A good trick. Yes?"

"The real trick," said Brodie, "is making the guns reappear."

"I will try to remember how to do that." He then assured them, "There is a plastic bag where things go to disappear. I can pull this out later."

Brodie asked, "Why do you have this compartment?"

Luis explained, "I bought this car from my uncle. He sometimes used it to smuggle cigarettes here from Colombia."

Brodie didn't think the hidden compartment could hold that many cartons of cigarettes. Hardly worth the five-hundred-mile drive from the Colombian border. On the other hand, it was probably the perfect size for four or five kilos of Colombian marching powder, which was more likely what Luis' uncle was importing.

Luis pulled back on the road, and within a few minutes they were driving past the Marriott, which did not feature the security fortifications of the El Dorado—there was no gated wall between the street and the front circular drive—but there were five security guards armed with shotguns and rifles flanking the driveway. Probably recent hires to deter another shoot-out in the lobby. Or to join in the fun if it happened again.

They turned onto Avenida Libertador and then merged onto the Francisco Fajardo Highway. Immediately to their right was the Francisco de Miranda Airport, which consisted of several clusters of low buildings and a few hangars. In a break between the buildings Brodie observed a single airstrip, and beyond it a couple of rows of parked twin-engine planes. So far, they seemed to be following Al Simpson's route.

Brodie wondered if Kyle Mercer had landed here in a private plane from Peshawar. Maybe with a refueling stop in a trafficking hub in West Africa like Mali. This airport wasn't as inconspicuous as an airstrip laid down by drug runners deep in the jungle, but it was obviously better than going through an international entry point like Simón Bolívar. And it dropped you right in the middle of Caracas, which was where Kyle Mercer wanted to be for some reason.

The hills of Petare rose up ahead, carpeted with ramshackle structures of mostly red clay block. As the elevated highway crossed over the Guaire River and curved north, Brodie spotted the old historic core of Petare below them on the right. A handsome pink church with a bell tower rose above a central square, and the surrounding streets formed a neat grid of colorful colonial buildings. It was an odd sight, this patch of the old vanished world sandwiched between an elevated highway and modern tower blocks and the crowded and chaotic hillside mosaic of the Petare slums.

Luis took the next exit, which brought them onto a six-lane road that ran between the old quarter and the barrios. Luis explained, "Once you enter the barrios, the roads are crazy—sometimes they go for awhile and then just end, and then you have to be on foot for some time and then maybe there is a road again."

Taylor asked Brodie, "Did our friend mention anything about being on foot for part of his journey?"

Brodie thought about that. Simpson hadn't mentioned walking anywhere, but then again he had been drunk, so anything was possible. Also, Simpson had not mentioned checkpoints, so he either hadn't run into any or the government oil people he was with just got waved through. In any case, Brodie hoped that Luis was being overly concerned about checkpoints, and if not, then he hoped that Luis' jalopy with two clueless gringos would get a wave-through. Brodie said to Taylor, "Let me see your map."

Taylor handed it to him. The roads of Petare appeared like branching arteries creeping along the hillsides and ridgelines, all eventually dead-ending. Vast swaths of the slums showed no roads at all. And it was probably in those blank spaces where they would find some answers.

He looked up at the towering hillside slums to their right. This place made Fallujah look like a prosperous, well-planned city.

Luis turned onto a narrow road and said, "This road will take us into the barrio." As they crested a hill, they spotted an olive green military truck. Four young guys in green fatigues and black body armor sat in plastic chairs, cradling submachine guns. On the side of the truck were the words *GUARDIA NACIONAL*. Brodie said, "Shit."

One of the guardsmen spotted them and stood. It was too late to turn around, so Luis kept going. As he approached the mobile checkpoint, the man did a quick scan of their car. He barely gave Brodie or Luis a second look, and Brodie thought they were getting a pass, but the man's eyes must have landed on the knockout blonde in the back and he held up his hand.

Luis muttered something in Spanish as he slowed to a stop and rolled down his window. He gave the guardsman a wide grin as the man approached. "Buenos días, señor."

The guy leaned over and peered between Brodie and Taylor. He could not have been older than twenty-five and looked to be attempting facial hair. The name badge on his fatigues read "Cordero." He said something in Spanish, then motioned for Luis to get out.

Luis appeared to be making an appeal to reason, gesturing to his two gringo customers and speaking with forced nonchalance.

Whatever he said, Cordero didn't like it. He yelled something at Luis, who turned to Brodie and Taylor. "We must get out for the inspection."

They all climbed out as another of the guardsmen—a short, wiry guy whose badge read "Rojas"—approached the car. He was holding a long pole with an upturned mirror on the end—the kind of tool familiar to Brodie from the many checkpoints set up around Baghdad to look for car bombs. In this context it was ridiculous, and probably just part of the opening theatrics before the shakedown.

Brodie noticed that Cordero was eyeing Taylor. The guardsman asked Luis something in Spanish, and Luis shook his head as he responded. Luis then turned to Taylor. "He asks what a beautiful woman like you is doing here."

"Yeah," said Brodie, "what's a woman like you doing in a nice place like this?"

Taylor smiled at the man. "Tourist." She mimed taking a photograph. "Fotografía."

Cordero said something to Rojas, and Brodie figured it was something lewd since they both looked at Taylor and laughed. Taylor, who understood exactly what they'd said, kept smiling, but Brodie saw she was now tense. He asked her, "What did he say?"

She didn't reply.

Brodie asked Luis, "What did he say?"

Luis hesitated, then replied, "He said to his comrade that maybe they should take the lady into the back of the truck for a search." Luis added, "But . . . I think they are not serious . . . perhaps some money . . ."

Brodie looked at Cordero, then the three other guardsmen. Rojas was still busy pretending to check the underside of their car, his rifle slung over his shoulder, and the other two were leaning against the truck with their rifles at their sides, smoking cigarettes. They had the laziness and over-confidence of unchallenged and corrupt security forces he had seen in too many third world countries.

Brodie said, "Tell him that if he lays a hand on my wife, I'll take his submachine gun and put a bullet up his ass before I blow the balls off his hombres."

Luis said something to Cordero, though Brodie was pretty sure it wasn't that. Luis said to Brodie, "He wants to see your passports."

Taylor took out her forged passport provided by Worley. Brodie did the same.

Cordero looked closely at both passports, then glanced at Mr. and Mrs. Bowman.

It seemed to Brodie that Cordero was trying to decide whether this was a moneymaking moment or an opportunity to see if Mrs. Bowman's blonde hair was her natural color. For sure he wasn't thinking about doing his duty, whatever that was.

Cordero said something to Luis, who translated, "He wants to know why you are in Petare."

Brodie knew that if Cordero did a simple pat-down and pocket search of him and Taylor, he'd find two photographs of Kyle Mercer. So maybe this was the time for a direct and honest answer. He pulled the file photo of Mercer from his jacket and held it up. "We're looking for our friend. Have you seen him?"

Taylor shot him a look. Luis looked confused, but translated to Cordero.

Cordero looked at the picture of Kyle Mercer in uniform, then at Brodie. He had an odd look on his face. "Tu amigo?"

Brodie nodded. "Mi amigo. He has a beard now." He rubbed his hand over his chin.

"Él tiene una barba," translated Luis.

Cordero kept staring at Brodie. "You soldier?"

"No."

"Amigo soldier."

"Sí." And a deserter. Cordero didn't know that, but he apparently knew Kyle Mercer, and Brodie was happy to discover that his instincts were correct—the gringo was well-known in Petare.

Brodie asked, "Where can I find him?"

Cordero didn't reply. He took the photo from Brodie and walked back toward the truck, then whistled to Rojas, who was now examining the Dart's trunk. The four men crowded together in discussion. Brodie noticed that each man barely looked at the photo, though they all stole a number of glances at Brodie and Taylor as they spoke. There was a consensus, and Cordero walked back to Brodie and handed him the photo and their passports.

"You go."

"Where can I find my amigo?"

Cordero gestured toward the road. "Go." He said something to Luis, who translated: "We are very sorry for the inconvenience and wish you a beautiful visit." Cordero turned and walked back to the truck. Brodie eyed the three other guys, who looked back at him with a mix of curiosity and what he thought was a touch of fear. Maybe respect. Apparently Kyle Mercer was one bad hombre. No surprise.

Luis climbed in and started the car. Before Taylor got in, she said to Brodie, "That was reckless."

"Nothing ventured, nothing gained."

"Please consult me before you risk our lives and freedom."

"All's well that ends well."

"Any more clichés?"

"You're beautiful when you get angry."

"Asshole." She got in the car and slammed the door.

Brodie got in the front seat and said to Luis, "Good job." He said to Taylor, "We just learned something. Our man is well-known here, and he's a very important gringo."

Taylor thought about that and said, "I guess they would have found the photos if they searched us."

"Correct." He said to Luis, "Avanti."

They entered the slums of Petare, and Brodie asked Luis, "Will we get stopped by the police for a shakedown? A bribe?"

"No," Luis assured him. "There are few police in the barrios."

"Good."

"It is too dangerous."

"Excuse me?"

"In the barrios, the colectivos are the police." He explained, "The colectivos are armed by the government, which allows them the power and the money from the drugs and the prostitution."

Sounded like The Godfather Part Four with a Latin twist.

Luis continued, "In return, the colectivos help the regime . . . eliminate other gangs and also the political opposition. It is believed that many of the people who died in the protests were actually killed by colectivo members."

Brodie thought of Luis' nephew, and wondered if their driver might have another motivation—beyond money or asylum in America—for risking his ass in Petare.

Luis went on, "The state oil company, too, profits from the prostitution and drugs, and also the military and National Guard are given money and power if they sit and do nothing."

Brodie wasn't sure this was a good business model, but it seemed to work here.

Luis admitted, "It is all a little confusing, and the power shifts sometimes, but those who want the power and the money understand it."

"Right." He and Taylor would sometimes argue about which country was more corrupt, Iraq or Afghanistan. Well, Venezuela wins.

Brodie said to Taylor, "The good news is that the police are afraid of Petare."

"I think that's the bad news, Scott."

"Right. Sorry I asked."

"Me too."

CHAPTER 22

Brodie looked around as they crept along the narrow, winding road. Petare was a study in urban chaos—buildings piled upon buildings, and mountains of trash massed along the roadside. Tangles of jerry-rigged power lines ran up and down the red clay–block façades, and there was graffiti everywhere, much of it political. Along one wall was a mural that offered a cartoonish rendering of Venezuela's pantheon of heroes—Bolívar, Guevara, Chávez, and a couple of other military figures that Brodie didn't recognize. Maduro, El Presidente, was up there too, off to the side and disrupting the intended symmetry of the mural, like an afterthought slapped on out of political necessity.

It was almost ten in the morning, but the streets were quiet. Brodie guessed there wasn't much reason to leave the house when there was no work, no food, and no hope. They passed two old men playing dominoes at a plastic table in front of a garage full of old car parts. The men passed a cigarette back and forth between them.

Taylor said to Brodie, "Let's show them the photo of Mercer."

"Let's not let everyone in Petare know we're looking for Kyle Mercer."

Luis, who hadn't previously offered much in the way of investigative advice, said, "It is perhaps better not to alert the people here that you are looking for someone." He added, "News travels fast in the barrio."

Taylor said to Brodie, "That may be a good thing. If we can't find Mercer, he may find us."

"That may not be a good thing." Brodie reminded her, "We're looking for the whorehouse now." He said to Luis, "Keep going."

Luis continued along the narrow road.

Brodie spotted another piece of graffiti on a building up ahead featuring a collection of raised fists in a full spectrum of skin tones, maybe symbolizing Venezuela's diverse ethnic makeup. On the wrist below each fist was an outline of the Venezuelan flag dripping with blood, as though carved into the bearer's skin. Above the fists was the familiar face of Hugo Chávez in his signature military fatigues and red beret. And above Chávez, in big, bold letters: <u>MBR-200</u>.

Brodie asked Luis, "Are we in the July Twenty-Fourth neighborhood?"

"It is just ahead."

"We need our guns."

"Sí." Luis squeezed to the side of the road, put the car in park, leaned over, and opened the glove compartment. He pulled on the open door and the entire glove compartment slid out, followed by a black plastic bag.

Luis ripped the bag free and handed it to Brodie, who asked, "Was your uncle's name David Copperfield?"

"Señor?"

"Never mind." Brodie distributed the munitions as Luis slid the glove compartment back into the dashboard.

Brodie pulled the Taser and zip ties out of the plastic bag—which probably had enough white powder residue on it to constitute a felony—and handed the bag to Luis, who shoved it under his seat. He said to Luis, "We'll walk. You stay with the car."

Luis looked around apprehensively. "It is daytime, so it is maybe okay, but it is much safer to stay in the car."

Brodie looked at Luis. He was nervous, which was understandable. The guy had a family, and he was risking his culo on an assignment he hadn't signed up for and knew nothing about. Time to brief and motivate the useful local.

Brodie took the photo of Mercer out of his jacket and showed it to Luis. "We are looking for this man, as you know. He has committed a very serious crime and we must bring him back to the United States to answer for it. He was last seen in a bordello somewhere around here, and we need to find it."

Luis nodded, processing this.

Brodie continued, "The brothel we are looking for has child prostitutes."

Luis' face dropped. "Oh, señor . . ."

"I know, Luis. But this is the shit world we live in." He added, "The guy we are looking for is a piece of shit."

Taylor added, "He is also very dangerous. And also dangerous to Vene-zuela."

Well, thought Brodie, that might be a stretch. But maybe not.

Brodie said to Luis, "We'll call you if there's a problem."

"There is no cell service, señor."

Brodie remembered a line from an old country song: "If the phone don't ring, it's me."

"Señor?"

"If we're not back in an hour, go directly to the embassy and report to Señor Worley."

Luis nodded.

Brodie asked, "Which way is July Twenty-Fourth?"

Luis pointed to a steep staircase between two buildings. "By foot, that way is the quickest." He added, "That neighborhood is more dangerous than this one."

"Right." From Shithole A to Super Shithole B. "Are there signs that say 'Welcome to July Twenty-Fourth'?"

"No. But you will know." He added, "The colectivo of MBR-200 is the government in July Twenty-Fourth."

"Okay. See you later." He got out of Luis' Dodge Dart, followed by Tay-lor, who wished Luis good luck.

Luis replied, "Vaya con Dios."

Brodie and Taylor headed for the staircase.

———

They worked their way up the steep, crumbling staircase, which had twists and turns along the way and crossed through several narrow alleyways lined with densely packed buildings. Brodie heard voices up ahead, and in a few minutes they reached a flat space full of men, women, and children. At the head of the crowd was a young man standing on a platform of wooden crates, calling out numbers from a list in his hands. As the numbers were called, people yelled out and pressed forward through the throng, holding slips of paper aloft. It was like the slum's answer to the floor of the New York Stock Exchange. But what was the commodity?

Brodie took a closer look at the crowd and saw that many of the people were visibly ill or in need of care. An older man coughed violently. A young pregnant woman sat on a chair in the shade holding her belly while a group of women stood over her. A young man near them clutched his forearm wrapped in a blood-soaked rag.

Taylor said, "Looks like the med clinics we set up in Afghanistan."

"Right."

Up ahead was a low, aquamarine-painted building covered in a mural of tropical birds. Above the entryway was a red cross, and flanking the building's entrance were four muscular men in black T-shirts, jeans, red berets, and matching red bandanas tied around their thick biceps. Each man held an AK-47 rifle across his chest as they all scanned the crowd. Unlike the clowns down at the National Guard post, these hombres looked like they meant business.

Taylor added, "These clinics were set up in the barrios by Chávez. But most have closed because of the shortages. And because the doctors have left."

"I'll never again complain about an Army hospital."

"This is very sad," said Taylor.

Brodie spotted a few more men with berets and AK-47s patrolling through the crowd. "I think these guys are MBR-200. The gang is running the clinic."

"And the regime is running the gang," said Taylor. "They use access to health care and food as leverage. If you cross the gang or the regime, you do not get what you need." She added, "Winning hearts and minds."

Brodie nodded. Winning "hearts and minds" was a counterinsurgency concept with a long and mostly dismal track record, employed most recently by the U.S. in Vietnam and then Iraq and Afghanistan. The U.S. military blew a lot of hot air about making "emotional and intellectual appeals" to the target population, building roads, schools, and hospitals, offering promises of security—though in practice it generally amounted to organized bribery.

But there was a flip side to the hearts-and-minds concept. What Uncle Sam—or Uncle Nicolás—giveth, he may also taketh away. There was always a hierarchy to who received the government's largesse, and how quickly.

And in places on the edge like Afghanistan—and now Venezuela—those decisions sometimes meant the difference between life and death.

Brodie eyed the young man calling out names and numbers from atop the wooden crates. He wondered what it took to get your name on that list. Or struck from it.

Taylor said, "Three o'clock."

Brodie turned to his right and saw one of the MBR-200 guys heading toward them.

The man stopped a few feet away and looked at them as though they'd arrived on a spaceship. He was tall, square-jawed, with dark deep-set eyes that darted between the two of them, eventually landing on Brodie. He said something in Spanish.

"No habla español," replied Brodie. He wondered if Taylor was going to decide that she too couldn't habla, though he didn't feel this was the time to play dumb.

She said something to the man in Spanish before translating for Brodie: "He wants to know what we are doing here."

"We are the Bowmans. The dumbest fucking tourists since the Griswolds. Ask him what *he's* doing here."

"Scott—"

"We're Americans, interested in socialism. Try that."

She nodded and spoke to the man in Spanish.

He seemed pleased at the response, though perhaps, thought Brodie, not quite buying it. Taylor and the MBR guy exchanged a few more words; then Taylor translated: "He says we are lucky that MBR-200 are in charge now. This neighborhood—July Twenty-Fourth—used to be run by criminals. They would have kidnapped us." Taylor paused, then said: "He says MBR-200 killed all the criminals."

"Lucky us."

Brodie glanced at the man's AK-47. The Russian-made automatic rifle was one of the most popular weapons in the world among gangs and militias. It was relatively cheap, durable, reliable, and easy to use. Brodie had seen many AKs in the hands of all sorts of dangerous assholes in the course of his work, and they were almost always beat-to-shit knockoffs, made in somebody's back room. This one, however, looked like the real thing. So did the ones held by his friends at the clinic entrance. These people had access to money and a good weapons supplier. Brodie also noticed a coiled rubber cord extending down from the guy's ear. He was wearing a com. This was one teched-out colectivo.

The man said something, and once again Taylor translated: "He says we need to leave July Twenty-Fourth. If he sees us here again, he will turn us over to the revolutionary justice committee."

"Well, that sucks. Ask him where we can get a Chávez T-shirt."

"Scott—"

"All right. Let's quit while we're ahead."

Taylor spoke to the man, and he seemed satisfied with her response.

Brodie suggested, "Give him a Snickers bar."

Taylor looked as if she was about to tell her partner to shut the fuck up. But then she reached into her pocket and pulled out a big bottle of aspirin; she handed it to the MBR guy with a smile and said, "Por la clínica."

The MBR guy took the aspirin and barely managed a gracias.

Brodie said, "Viva la Revolución."

Taylor took Brodie by the arm and steered him back toward the stairs. She said, "That could have gone either way, and you don't make it easy with your smart mouth."

"I say stupid things when I'm nervous."

"You make *me* nervous." She added, "Thank God you don't know Spanish and they don't know much English."

"Right. Well, we just got banned from the July Twenty-Fourth neighborhood."

They began descending the staircase. Taylor asked, "What are we going to do?"

"We're going to find another way in."

Taylor didn't respond.

They descended the stairs, leaving Shithole B and reentering Shithole A.

They found Luis standing next to his car and looking nervous. He eyed them as they walked toward him. "It's okay?"

"It's okay," said Brodie. He told Luis, "We need another way into July Twenty-Fourth."

They climbed back into the car, with Brodie riding shotgun, and pulled onto the road. They continued up the hill, and after a few minutes approached a T intersection where a narrow, winding road off to their right snaked farther up the hill.

Luis informed them, "We are in July Twenty-Fourth now."

Brodie looked up the hillside road. Even in a place like this, the whorehouses would probably be set back from the main drag. He said to Luis, "Turn here."

Luis made a right and they drove up the narrow, unpaved road, which was lined with houses made of clay blocks and corrugated tin roofs that stacked up the hillside. Between every few houses there was another stairway or alley that led deeper into the maze. Everything looked precarious, and Brodie wondered how these denuded hills survived heavy tropical rains and the accompanying mudslides. As he was wondering, he saw a swath of dried mud and brick that had once been houses.

Taylor said, "My God . . . Luis, do you think anyone was killed?"

Luis shrugged. "Perhaps." He added, "They know when to leave the houses."

"Right," said Brodie. You leave when the house starts to change addresses. Meanwhile, they were reconning for a whorehouse while trying to avoid MBR-200.

Luis' air-conditioning didn't work, so they had the windows down, and they heard loud voices ahead, then saw a young woman step out into the dirt road while angrily yelling back at wherever she came from between drags on a cigarette. She was dark-skinned and pretty, with bright-red lipstick, platform shoes, a miniskirt, and a tight-fitting tank top that showed off the goods. She did not seem to notice them as she turned in the same direction they were headed and walked up the hillside.

Brodie said to Luis, "Follow that hooker."

Luis' car crept up the hill behind the woman. After a few minutes she turned, and they followed her onto a road that was lined with beat-up parked cars and featured a small gated-up bodega.

The woman stopped at the door of a gray, two-story concrete-block building and spoke to someone on an intercom, then entered. A painted sign above the door read EL CLUB DE LOS MALDITOS.

Luis translated, "The Club of the Damned."

This was obviously a brothel, though it didn't fit Simpson's description of a one-story building. But assuming that all whorehouses knew their competition, this would be a good place to start. Brodie said to Luis, "Pull over."

Luis complied, and Brodie said to him, "Let's see if they're open for business." He said to Taylor, "Stay with the car and cover us."

"I'm coming with you."

"Women don't belong in whorehouses unless they're working."

"I am working."

"Then get behind the wheel and be ready to get us out of here." He added, "That's an order."

"Yes, sir."

Luis grabbed his gun and they all got out of the car. Taylor slid behind the wheel.

Brodie unholstered his Glock and slipped it in his waistband under his jacket, then motioned Luis to follow him.

Luis, who had by now come to realize that he'd scored the worst job in Caracas, dutifully followed Brodie toward the bordello of the damned.

Brodie did a quick case of the building as they approached. It was about forty feet square, and there were no windows on the second floor, which Brodie assumed was where the girls did their tricks. Toward the back of the building was a concrete enclosure, and Brodie recognized the sound of an electric generator. The bordello's clients might not mind screwing in the dark, but they wanted their cerveza cold and the hellhole air-conditioned.

There was one steel-barred window on the side of the building, and Brodie looked into the dim interior, where he could see bar lights and a neon beer sign.

They approached the front entrance and Brodie noticed a security camera above the metal door. He pushed the intercom buzzer and waited. A voice came through the speaker in Spanish and Luis responded. Brodie didn't know what Luis said, but he recognized the words "cerveza" and "turista." Beer for thirsty tourists was not the primary business of the Club of the Damned, but the door buzzed open. A tall guy with a big nose and shifty eyes looked at them.

Luis, playing the part of a driver or guide with an Americano client, said a few words to the man, who gestured them inside.

The place was cool and dark, and smelled of cigarette smoke and stale beer. There was a bar along one wall, and mounted on the other wall were some colorful spinning club lights. Two large speakers sat silently on the concrete floor. The only other patron they could see was a heavyset guy in a T-shirt and jeans who was sitting on a stool at the bar sucking down a beer. The young lady they had followed was sitting at a table near the speakers, smoking. She shifted in her seat and smiled at Brodie.

Brodie said to the guy who had let them in, "I'm looking for something special."

Luis translated, and the guy smiled. He replied, and Luis translated: "We have very special girls. Monica here will give you a good time. We have other girls too, upstairs. I can bring them down for you to see."

"I want younger than her," said Brodie.

The man replied, and Luis said, "He has an extra-special girl, Lucia, she just turned eighteen last week and is still a virgin. Very beautiful. He can call her to come in. This will cost you extra, of course."

Brodie took five twenties from his pocket. "Younger."

Luis translated: "Una niña." The man stared at the money, then looked Brodie in the eyes and said in English, "Not here."

"Where?"

The man hesitated, then said, "El Gallinero."

Luis said, "A gallinero is like a . . . a place for lady chickens."

"A hen house," said Brodie.

"Sí," said Luis. "The Hen House."

Brodie looked at the guy. "Where's the Hen House? Dónde?"

The man looked between Brodie and Luis, sizing them up. He said something to Luis, who said to Brodie, "He says El Gallinero is a place you are brought to, not a place you seek out."

"What's this guy's name?"

Luis asked, and the guy replied, "Pepe."

"Okay," said Brodie. "Pepe from the Club of the Damned recommended the Hen House to us."

Luis communicated that, and Pepe nodded, then said something else to Luis while gesturing as if he was explaining directions.

Luis said to Brodie, "The barrio roads have local names, but no signs.

But he has given me directions that I think will make it possible to find. It is farther up the hill, a big white building, one story, no windows."

That matched the description Brodie had gotten from Al Simpson. It was pretty general, but then again, how many child prostitute whorehouses could there be?

Pepe spoke again, and Luis translated: "It's open only at night. At seven."

Brodie looked at the shifty-eyed man and wondered what Pepe's relationship was to MBR-200. Would he report this to the colectivo? Brodie would soon find out. He gave the guy the money.

Pepe didn't say thank you, but he looked happy with his unexpected score of greenbacks, the equivalent, thought Brodie, of maybe eighty billion bolívars.

Brodie and Luis walked out onto the street toward the car.

Taylor got out and Luis slid behind the wheel as Taylor and Brodie both got in the back seat as though they were tourists with a driver.

Taylor asked, "Any luck?"

"Sí," replied Brodie. "There's a place called . . ."

"El Gallinero," Luis said as he pulled out and began driving up the hill.

"Right. The Hen House. Very young chickens."

"You think this is the place?"

"Let's check out the location and exterior to see if it fits our friend's description, and if it does, I'll come back tonight."

"I'm coming with you tonight."

"We will discuss."

They rode in silence as Luis navigated the narrow, unpaved streets of the July 24th neighborhood.

Well, thought Brodie, if El Gallinero was the place where Simpson had seen Mercer, it had been easy to find. Trouble was always easy to find. Sin and corruption and human depravity were easy to find. He'd found those things all over the world. Even in the hills of Kentucky and the barracks of Army posts. He always had to remind himself that virtue and goodness were also easy to find. But that wasn't what he was looking for on this job.

Taylor said, "I hope our guy is there tonight."

"We will see." And Brodie hoped there weren't guys from MBR-200 there waiting for him.

CHAPTER 23

Brodie sat in the rear seat next to Taylor as they drove through the narrow passages that made up the streets of this neighborhood of jerry-built hovels. Through the window Brodie could feel the day growing hotter, and the smell of garbage and human waste hung in the stagnant air. The slums of twenty-first-century Caracas were a regression to the Dark Ages.

They passed another piece of MBR-200 graffiti. This one was simpler and to the point: the gang's name painted above an image of an AK-47 firing a hail of bullets.

They came to another narrow road that snaked north up the hillside, and Luis pointed out the windshield. "Pepe says turn left at the Jesus."

On a building up ahead was a large graffito of a Latino Jesus in a dazzling white robe holding a Venezuelan flag. Piles of flowers lay in the road beneath his sandaled feet.

Luis hooked a left onto the narrow road, then narrated the next step of the directions—"right at the blue house"—and slowed the car as they approached a cinder-block hovel painted in bright blue. He turned right onto a wider road that ran along the edge of a ridgeline, offering a panoramic view of the slums and Caracas below. A red and blue macaw glided over the barrio and toward the towering green mountain range to the north. Up ahead was a large flat-roofed one-story structure, windowless and faced with white stucco.

Luis said, "This is the place."

The building had a large footprint, built on a natural plateau in the hillside. A rusty green low-rider was parked out front. As they got closer, Brodie spotted a security camera mounted above the doorway. There was a concrete enclosure to the side that probably housed a generator. He said, "Well, if Pepe wasn't lying, then this is the Hen House."

"Or," said Taylor, "it's MBR-200 headquarters." She added, "I don't see a sign."

Luis interjected, "There would be no sign for such a place, señora . . . and if this was a place for MBR-200, there would be a very big sign."

Brodie said, "We'll come back tonight and see what goes on inside."

Taylor reminded him, "I'm coming with you."

"But you'll stay outside." He said to Luis, "You'll just make the introduction for me at the door, and you and Ms. Taylor will wait in the car with the engine running and your Glocks ready to rock and roll." He looked at Luis. "Okay?"

Luis nodded.

They continued on past the white building. Brodie had made some difficult arrests in some dicey places, but if Kyle Mercer was in that bordello tonight, this would be one for the books. Dombroski, as always, would criticize Brodie's recklessness while patting him on the back.

Taylor said to Brodie, "Our fugitive might not be there tonight. Or this might be the wrong bordello, or not a bordello at all."

Luis said, "It is a bordello."

"Trust Luis," said Brodie.

Taylor said to Luis, "Stop the car." She got out of the car, and Brodie followed. They both looked back at the white building and checked out the surroundings.

Taylor said, "You know it's possible that the National Guardsmen got the word to Mercer that two gringos are looking for him."

"That's entirely possible."

"Would he run? Or be waiting for us?"

Brodie replied, "If I were Kyle Mercer, I'd guess that the two gringos were CID, tipped off to the bordello by his Army buddy Al Simpson—who he knew he should have killed. Captain Mercer would also know that eventually we'd locate the bordello and come looking for him." Brodie continued, "And he'd also know that we have very few resources or allies here, and that we're coming for him without backup. Therefore, he won't run. He'll be there waiting for me—or us, if you want to come in—and even though he's a one-man army, he'll arrange all the help he needs to drag us into a back room and cut little pieces off us until we tell him who we are and what we know."

Taylor had no reply, but Brodie thought she looked a bit worried. He continued, "That would make an arrest difficult. But if he hasn't been tipped off by the barrio grapevine, and if he's in that bordello tonight, I will make the arrest."

Taylor thought about that, then said, "This is crazy. We can't—*you* can't go in that place alone."

"If I get in trouble, I'll call the police."

"Not funny." She looked at the white building and the surroundings. "Scott . . . maybe we should stake out the place and see if he enters, then wait for him to leave and take him on the street."

"You mean follow standard procedure? That's boring." He added, "I want to drag his ass out of there."

She looked at him.

"I want him to remember how he was taken down."

She kept looking at him. "If you go in there, I go in there."

Brodie made eye contact with her. Maggie Taylor was not into macho bullshit as he was; she said what she meant and meant what she said. "We'll play it by ear."

She reminded him, "The mission comes first. The mission is to apprehend Kyle Mercer. We don't need a barroom shoot-out to satisfy your ego."

"You take the fun out of everything."

"You're an asshole."

"Who squealed?" He assured her, "We'll consider all scenarios and methods tonight."

They got back into the car, and Brodie again took the back seat with Taylor. Luis, without comment, hit the gas and headed out of Petare.

Taylor said to Luis, "Tonight is optional."

Luis did not reply, but nodded.

She told him, "You did a good job today."

"Gracias."

Brodie said to him, "If all goes well tonight, you and your family will get tourist visas from the embassy and tickets to anyplace in the U.S. Once you are there, you can request political asylum." He added, "The embassy will back you on that."

Again, Luis nodded.

The flip side of all going well was probably not worth mentioning.

Taylor leaned toward Brodie and whispered in his ear, "It's not fair to ask him to risk his life for the promise of a new life."

"Sure it is. We are offering salvation." He reminded her, "Do what has to be done."

She nodded. "You're the officer in charge."

"Indeed I am."

How many times had he heard the standard Army lecture on responsibility, authority, and power? If you are given the responsibility, you must be given the authority to match the responsibility. Power was something else. Power came out of the muzzle of a gun. Power was what Kyle Mercer had in the bordello, and Brodie's authority to make an arrest wasn't worth shit there. Therefore Brodie needed the power to enforce his authority and to fulfill his responsibility to bring Captain Mercer to justice. And that power came from his gun and his guts.

"What are you thinking about?"

"A cold beer."

"That's easy." She put her hand on his, which surprised him. She said, "I trust you."

"Good." He added, "But don't hesitate to tell me when you don't."

She squeezed his hand.

They rode in silence, down from the once-pristine hills of Petare, through the man-made squalor that scarred the breast of the New World, now grown old and ugly. *Poverty sucks*, thought Brodie. But it was more than financial poverty here; it was a poverty of the soul, a culture that had gone terribly wrong. He suddenly thought of Kyle Mercer as a maggot, living off the rotting carcass of a dying nation. "Why is he here?"

"Ask him."

Brodie nodded. He thought about Worley, and what Dombroski had said, and what General Hackett had not said, and he knew instinctively that he wasn't going to like Captain Mercer's answer.

CHAPTER 24

Luis continued along the winding roads leading out of Petare, and in fifteen minutes they were out of the barrio and back on Autopista Francisco Fajardo, heading west toward Altamira and the El Dorado Hotel.

Brodie looked in the side mirror as Petare receded in the distance. It was striking how prominent a part of the cityscape these slums which ringed the Caracas Valley were. Luis had said, *You see them so much you don't see them anymore.*

Well, they'd seen them from the belly of the beast itself. And they would see them again, after sundown, which definitely went against the advice of Brodie's guide book.

Taylor said, "When we get back to the hotel, we need to update the boss."

"There's nothing to report," said Brodie.

"We found the brothel."

Well, they *thought* they had found the brothel. Brodie liked to hold off on his sit-reps until he had something of substance to share, like, for instance, "Kyle Mercer is hog-tied in the trunk." Dombroski was consistently annoyed by Brodie's infrequent updates while on assignment, but Brodie saw no reason to change his MO. "Let's see how tonight goes."

"You have an unhealthy disrespect for authority. I really can't picture you as a soldier taking orders."

"I couldn't either. That's why I transferred to CID."

Luis, who was apparently listening to the conversation, asked, "You were a soldier, señor?"

"I was. Iraq. Ms. Taylor was too. She served in Afghanistan."

"Those are dangerous places."

"Not as dangerous as this place."

Luis laughed, then said, "Señor Worley was also in Afghanistan."

Brodie and Taylor shared a look. Brodie asked Luis, "How do you know that?"

Luis hesitated, realizing he was perhaps sharing privileged information. "I just hear things." He added, "Señor Worley mentioned it once in the car."

Brodie asked, "To you?"

Another hesitation, then: "To a gentleman we picked up at the airport . . . they spoke of their time together in Kabul."

"And this man was an American?"

"Sí . . ."

They passed the Francisco de Miranda Airport and Luis took the next exit into the neighborhood near their hotel.

Brodie processed this new information. There was nothing inherently suspicious about Worley failing to mention that he'd worked in Afghanistan when he was complaining to them about his other armpit assignments. If Worley was a DCS spook, his work in Afghanistan would have been classified. On the other hand, Worley undoubtedly had looked at the files of his two visiting CID agents and learned that Maggie Taylor had served in Afghanistan—yet he didn't say, as soldiers always say, "I was there too." Brodie was already suspicious of Colonel Brendan Worley. He added this to the list of reasons why.

Taylor asked Luis, "When was this?"

"Perhaps . . . three weeks ago."

She asked, "Do you recall this visitor's name?"

"Señor Worley does not make introductions."

"Did you drive this man back to the airport?"

"No."

Clearly Luis was not comfortable discussing embassy business with his new clients, charming though they might be. Brodie was sure that Luis heard and saw all sorts of things while driving embassy people and important visitors. No one ever thinks about the driver while they're talking in the rear seat of his car—except maybe Intel people, who are trained to be paranoid. Also, Brodie was certain that Luis had been told never to repeat a word of anything he heard. But Luis could be coaxed, or hoaxed, so Brodie asked, "How did Señor Worley address this man?"

"I . . . I am not—"

"Jim? Bill? Bob?"

"I . . . I think Ted."

Brodie said to Taylor, "That must be Ted Mallory. Our old friend from Washington."

Taylor agreed. "Must be." She asked Luis, "What did he look like?"

"He was . . . Anglo, gray hair. Perhaps sixty years of age. A tall man." He added, "Very thin."

"I think that's our Ted," said Brodie. "Glasses and a mustache?"

"No."

"Definitely our Ted."

Brodie and Taylor exchanged glances and a smile. Bullshit was their stock in trade. And if Luis realized he'd been bullshitted, he also realized he'd been bullshitted by pros.

Brodie had no idea who Ted was, and he was fairly sure Ted had no relevance to the case, but it was the Afghan connection that interested him. Brendan Worley had been in Afghanistan, as had Kyle Mercer, and yet Worley had never mentioned that. Odd? Or just tight-lipped tradecraft?

Brodie asked Luis, "Did they mention anyone else we may know?"

"Señor?"

"Any *names*, Luis?"

"Señor . . . I do not listen to conversations . . . and when they speak in English I do not always comprehend . . . I must concentrate on my driving."

"Right."

Brodie was ready to let this go, but then Luis said, "One name jumped out to me. Tomás de Heres." He asked, "You know this man?"

Brodie replied, "I think he was Ted's frat brother. Sigma Chi."

Luis seemed confused, then said, "Tomás de Heres was a military hero during the war for independence." He added, "Very loyal to Bolívar."

"Why were they talking about him?"

"This I do not know. I just heard the name."

Local history buffs? Maybe. Probably not. Researching the relevance of nineteenth-century Venezuelan military figures and explaining to Brodie why he should give a shit sounded like a job for Taylor.

Taylor asked Luis, "Any other names?"

"No, señora."

"Any names of places? Cities? Countries? Like Kabul?"

"No . . . but—yes, one I remember. Flagstaff."

Brodie asked Luis, "Flagstaff, Arizona?"

Luis shrugged. "I have heard of this place in America but . . . I did not understand the meaning."

Taylor and Brodie looked at each other. Brodie asked Luis, "Who said Flagstaff?"

"Both gentlemen."

Well, thought Brodie, Flagstaff was a nice place, and maybe Worley and Ted were planning a visit. But Luis said he did not understand the meaning, which could mean he didn't understand the context, and that could mean Flagstaff was the code name of something, or someone, as was often the case in this business. Or that he, Brodie, had been in this business too long and he was starting to see secret messages in the entrails, which were actually full of shit. Time for a beer.

They arrived at the El Dorado Hotel, and the doorman opened the back door for Brodie and Taylor as Luis let himself out of the car.

Taylor said to Luis, "You are an excellent driver and a very knowledgeable guide."

Luis smiled. "Gracias, señora."

She asked him, "Have you made a decision about tonight?"

"Sí. What time tonight?"

Brodie replied, "Seven."

Taylor said to Luis, "If you change your mind, leave a message for us no later than three P.M."

"I will see you at seven."

Brodie wanted to tell Taylor to stop giving Luis options. Luis had made his decision and he was picturing himself in a supermarket in Miami or San Diego with his family safe and sound, filling their shopping cart with frozen TV dinners and two-liter bottles of RC Cola. The American Dream.

Brodie looked at Luis. Luis was important to the mission—but bottom line, he was a civilian with a wife and two kids, and just because he owned a gun didn't mean he knew how to use it. So Brodie, in a weak moment, said, "It's okay if you change your mind."

"Seven."

Brodie nodded and made eye contact with Luis. "Whatever you heard or saw today is not to be discussed with anyone."

Luis nodded.

"And we will all forget what you said to us in the car about Señor Worley and his visitor."

Again Luis nodded.

Brodie said to him, "Go to a car rental place and get a nice sedan. Black, tinted windows if possible, and a big engine. And a big trunk." Brodie gave him six hundred American dollars. "Keep the change."

"Gracias."

"And don't forget your pistola—or the cross."

Luis smiled, got in his car, and drove off.

Taylor said, "He's either very brave or very desperate."

"I'll take either."

As they walked toward the front doors of the luxurious hotel, Taylor said, "Those slums, Scott . . . I can't believe what we saw . . ."

"You're just a clean-living country girl at heart."

"The hills I grew up in were poor, but . . . not like that."

"Right. On another subject: Brendan Worley, Afghanistan, Ted, Tomás de Heres, and Flagstaff. What was that about?"

"It wasn't about Kyle Mercer." She reminded him, "Focus."

"Right."

They entered the lobby of the air-conditioned hotel and Taylor said, "I'm going to stop at the gift shop."

"Get me an AK-47."

"Then I'm going to wash the grime off and take a dip in the rooftop pool. Meet me there in an hour and I'll buy you a beer."

"You can wash the slums off your body, señora, but not from your heart or your mind."

"That's what the beer is for. See you later."

He watched her as she walked toward the gift shop, then got in the elevator and rode up to his room.

There were three possible outcomes of this mission: getting Mercer, getting killed, or getting laid. Or some combination thereof. Meanwhile, a dip in the pool before a plunge into the abyss sounded good.

CHAPTER 25

Brodie entered the suite, got a cold beer from the living room bar, and went into his bedroom. He rehydrated as he stripped off his sweat-soaked clothes, then hit the shower, wrapping his Glock in a shower cap—a trick that a young lady in his business had shown him some years ago. You're always vulnerable in hostile territory, but you're most vulnerable naked, in the shower or in bed, which was why you should have company in both places.

He scrubbed the day off his skin, as he'd done in Iraq on the occasions when they'd gotten to base camp and headed straight for the quartermaster showers. Rub-a-dub-dub, doomed men in a tub.

Brodie dried himself, then slipped into a pair of shorts, hotel slippers, and a bathrobe. He put his sat phone and smartphone in the robe pockets, then went back into the living room, where he locked his Glock and extra magazine in the safe. He saw no sign that Taylor had returned from her shopping trip, and he exited the room and rode the elevator up to the pool.

The expansive rooftop terrace held a sixty-foot swimming pool ringed by lounge chairs and a few cabana tents. Potted palms and bursts of tropical flowers decorated the terrace. The surrounding slums looked pleasant from up here.

There were a few guests enjoying drinks or floating in the pool, and he wondered who these people were, and why, if they had the money to be here, they weren't someplace else. He suspected that many of them were wealthy locals who found this place to be a safe oasis, a way to remain in Caracas without really being in Caracas.

He was early for his rendezvous with Taylor, and he found an empty cabana, signaled to a waiter, and sat in a wicker chair in the open-sided tent.

The waiter inquired, "What may I get for you, señor?"

"A very cold beer."

"Sí, señor. Will anyone be joining you?"

"A very hot blonde. Keep an eye out for her."

The waiter smiled and moved off.

The thought of alcohol was intimately tied to thoughts of Dombroski, so he decided maybe he should take Taylor's advice and call the boss. He made sure no one was within earshot, took out his smartphone, opened Signal, and dialed.

Dombroski picked up and said, "Señor Brodie. Working hard or hardly working?"

Brodie watched as a brunette with bronze skin and a skimpy pink bikini did a dive off the board.

"Brodie?"

"Yes, sir . . . Well, we're fairly sure we found the brothel."

"Good work. And?"

"And we're going back tonight when it's open."

"I'm glad to hear you're respecting the posted hours of a whorehouse that specializes in child prostitution. Where are you now?"

"At the rooftop pool." He added, "Waiting for Ms. Taylor."

"That should be interesting. But shouldn't you be doing something productive?"

"I should be, but I decided to call you instead."

"Good one, Scott. When's your efficiency report due?"

"Next month."

"I'll start on it today."

"Yes, sir."

"Shouldn't you be staking out this suspected brothel?"

"That's not easy, Colonel. Bad neighborhood, gringo-free zone, controlled by a colectivo—a political gang with ties to the regime." He added, "Taylor and I were run off and told not to come back."

"Okay . . . but you're going back."

"Correct. We've hired the embassy driver who picked us up at the airport. He's armed and reliable, and he and Taylor will wait outside while I go in. I have a description of the interior from Simpson, and if it's the right place, I'll see if Captain Mercer is there, and if he is, I will make the arrest."

Dombroski did not respond for a few seconds, then said, "The brothel will have security and they will probably kill you if Mercer doesn't kill you first."

"Do you think I need another plan?"

"I think you need another brain." Dombroski suggested, "Okay, go in, verify it's the right place, and see if you spot Mercer. If you do, exit quickly and take him down when he leaves. If you don't see him, stake it out and wait to see if he shows up. If you have no luck, repeat all that for the next . . . let's say four or five days and nights. If no luck, think about bribing people in the brothel. You may get a tip. If not, it's over. Come home."

And that was the reason he rarely called Colonel Dombroski. He should have trusted his instinct, but Taylor liked to call home. "Colonel—"

"That's an order."

"Ten days."

"Six."

"Okay . . . but—"

"The trail is already cold, Scott. Mercer is not so stupid as to return to a place where he was spotted by an old Army buddy."

"Then why am I here?"

"Just in case Mercer is stupid. Or arrogant. You'll see tonight."

"Right." Brodie thought about telling Dombroski about their encounter with the National Guard, and the possibility that word had reached Mercer that two gringos were looking for him, which would lead Dombroski to conclude that Captain Kyle Mercer might be planning an ambush or a kidnapping at the whorehouse. And he might be right. Dombroski, for all his pushing and prodding of his agents, was at heart a cautious man. One might say a man who was concerned about the safety of his agents. Dombroski was caught in that age-old military bind of producing results while also producing as few casualties as possible. A good commander knows when to order an attack, when to dig in, and when to retreat. It's not an easy job.

"Brodie?"

The waiter appeared with a beer on a tray, which he put on a side table, and Brodie said to Dombroski, "Hold on—I'm getting a tip." He signed for the beer and added a nice tip to the bill. "Gracias."

"What tip?"

"I just tipped the waiter."

"I hope you're not drinking alcohol on duty."

"Roger that." Brodie poured the beer into an iced glass and stared at the effervescence.

Dombroski inquired, "How are you and Ms. Taylor getting along?"

"Her fluency in Spanish has proved invaluable."

"I'm sure. Meanwhile, don't complicate your professional relationship."

"Good advice."

"Did you fill her in about the murder of Robert Crenshaw in Peshawar?"

"Not yet."

Dombroski had no comment on that and changed the subject. "I checked with JAG, and they stress that there is to be no field interrogation of the suspect."

"I've already made a note of that."

"Good." He asked, "Anything further?"

"Yes . . . Look, we know that Mercer was in a brothel, probably this one called El Gallinero—the Hen House—so I'm assuming he's known in this barrio called Petare, in the neighborhood called July Twenty-Fourth—"

"You're losing me."

"So if I don't find him tonight, Taylor and I will do a standard canvass of the neighborhood, using Mercer's photo—"

"This gang will kill you. Or Mercer will find *you*."

"I'm hoping for the latter."

Dombroski didn't reply.

"Anyway, that's Plan B."

"Does Ms. Taylor know about Plan B?"

"She suggested it."

Again, Dombroski didn't reply; then he informed Brodie, "The two most common elements in the universe are hydrogen and stupidity."

"Really?"

Brodie could hear Dombroski take a deep breath. Then his boss said, "Do what has to be done."

"Right."

"Six days."

"Copy."

"Don't get your partner killed." Dombroski paused. "You're responsible for yourself."

"As always." He added, "I'm going to bring this son of a bitch back, dead or alive."

Dombroski didn't reply, leading Brodie to conclude that "dead" was okay.

Brodie said, "General Hackett will put another letter of commendation in your file." He wanted to add, "And maybe you'll make general," but that was a touchy subject for Colonel Dombroski.

Dombroski said, "I always give credit where credit is due, Scott."

"You do."

"And criticism when it's appropriate."

And advice when it's not asked for, but Brodie said, "I appreciate your input."

"Good. Here's some more. Think about asking Colonel Worley if there's any way he can provide you some backup tonight—some margin of safety."

"All I want from Worley is transportation out of here for me, Taylor, and my prisoner."

"All right . . . but—"

"Hold on. Civilian in the vicinity." Brodie picked up his beer glass and chugged it. What's better than a cold beer on a hot day?

"Brodie? You there?"

Brodie suppressed a belch and replied, "All clear."

"Are we done?"

"One more question. Does Flagstaff mean anything to you?"

"Flagstaff? Like, Arizona?"

"Just the word. Like the name of an operation? A program? A weapons system? Maybe a code name for a military base? Something like that."

Dombroski stayed silent, then said, "Never heard the word in that context. Why?"

"Someone just sat next to me. Insecure."

"Next time call me from your room."

"Right. FYI, I'm calling Señor Whiskey later about my plane transportation." He added, "With luck, we might see you tomorrow."

"Let's hope . . . Okay, good luck tonight, Scott, and pass on the same to Ms. Taylor."

"Will do."

"Sit-rep ASAP."

"Of course."

"Negative further."

Brodie hung up and stared out toward the hills of Petare. Somewhere in that vast slum was his quarry—or his fate.

He looked toward the rooftop café and saw Taylor speaking to his waiter—who knew a hot blonde when he saw one—and the waiter was pointing toward him.

Taylor headed toward his cabana, and Brodie saw that she was wearing a diaphanous wrap that she'd probably bought in the gift shop.

Brodie stood, as an officer and gentleman should, and met her halfway. She checked out his slippers and bathrobe and said, "You look like a patient in a mental ward."

"I'll take that as a compliment."

She smiled, then looked out at the view of the green mountains and the encircling slums. "It's too nice up here. I feel guilty after what we saw today."

"Guilt helps no one."

"You're all heart, Scott."

"Drink?"

"I ordered for both of us."

He led her back to the open-sided cabana and she sat upright in a chaise longue as he sat in his wicker chair and finished his beer.

They watched the sunbathers and swimmers for awhile, and Brodie wondered how many more days, weeks, or months this idyllic scene would play out before Caracas and Venezuela descended into chaos. Someday, maybe soon, those poor bastards in the slums would all decide to head downhill into the city and take what they didn't have. It would be interesting to see that, but a revolution would put an abrupt end to his mission. In any case, the regime, through the colectivos, seemed to have the slums under control.

Taylor said, "Let's call the boss."

"I did."

She looked at him. "Why didn't you wait for me?"

"I was overcome with a desire to hear Dombroski's voice." He added, "You can make the next call. Tonight."

She nodded.

The waiter appeared with two drinks that he set on the table between them; Brodie signed, and the waiter moved off. Brodie eyed the drinks, which had mint sprigs in them. "This is not beer."

"They're Mojitos." She swiveled her legs off the chaise, faced him, picked up her glass, and said, "To a successful operation tonight."

They touched glasses and he said, "Amen." He sipped the drink. Awful.

She looked at him. "That's the second time you called Colonel Dombroski without me being there."

"You make the mistake of making an assumption. How do you know I didn't call him ten times?"

"Scott, cut the shit."

"All right. When I was briefed by him in Quantico, he passed on to me privileged information. Need-to-know stuff. And you don't have a need to know, so he and I need to speak in private."

"What do you need to know that I don't need to know?"

"If I told you, then I'd be disobeying orders."

"I am your partner."

"This is standard procedure." He put down his drink and asked, "Are you in contact with anyone I don't know about?"

"No."

"Do you know something I don't know? Other than how to speak Spanish?"

"I don't like this conversation."

"Then let it go."

She stood and took off her wrap, revealing a white bikini that looked like it was made from dental floss. In fact, she was nearly naked. Did she know what she was doing to him? Of course she did.

"I'm going for a swim."

"Don't get dragged down by your bathing suit."

She walked to the edge of the pool and dived in.

Brodie watched her as she swam the length of the pool. She seemed to be a strong swimmer, which might come in handy if they wound up swimming to Aruba, which reminded him to call Worley about transportation.

He took out the sat phone and dialed Worley, who answered and said, "Mr. Brodie. Enjoying Caracas?"

"Not even slightly."

"It grows on you."

"So does toe fungus."

Worley chuckled, then asked, "Was Raúl helpful?"

"What did he tell you?"

"We haven't spoken."

Brodie didn't reply.

"So what can I do for you?"

"There's a chance that we will have our suspect in custody tonight."

"Excellent."

"If we do, I need to know where I'm taking him."

"That's not a phone conversation."

"I thought this line was secure."

"It is. Until it isn't."

"Okay, then we need to meet. Are you at the embassy?"

"Actually, I'm at the Marina Grande Yacht Club. You can meet me here. I'll give the Bowmans' names to security."

Brodie was happy to discover that Brendan Worley was working hard on behalf of the American taxpayer at a yacht club. Although, given the breakdown in relations between the two countries, the new directive from Washington might have been: Put your feet up, have a drink, and watch Caracas burn.

Worley asked, "Where are you now?"

"We're at the El Dorado rooftop pool."

"Good for you. And is Ms. Taylor with you now?"

"No. She's signed up for tango lessons."

Again, Worley chuckled, then said, "I understand that Luis was moonlighting for you today."

"Correct. And you need to inform your consulate people that he and his family need tourist visas."

"We can discuss."

"Nothing to discuss."

"All right . . . See if you can be here in an hour." He added, "I have another meeting at five."

Probably with Señor Martini. "See you later." Brodie hung up, stood, and watched Taylor as she did a backstroke down the length of the pool, aided by her God-given flotation devices.

He signaled the waiter and ordered another beer, then looked at the city. Tall palms swayed in the breeze, and from up here Caracas looked good. He could see how Venezuela used to be a major international tourist destination in decades past, competing with the Caribbean islands, and calling itself "The Country in the Caribbean." Those days were over and he didn't think they would return in his lifetime—which actually might be shorter than that shown in a life-expectancy chart.

Taylor climbed out of the pool and ran her hand through her slicked-back blonde hair. The sun was behind her and cast her in a gold-hued glow. Brodie suddenly felt that he was in a James Bond movie and that Maggie Taylor, like all of Bond's femmes fatales, was going to be his downfall. But first, he had to sleep with her.

A pool boy handed her a towel and she dried herself as she walked toward the cabana. She stood in the sunlight, soaking up the rays on her perfect body. Brodie, remembering a Bond film, said to her, "Something big has come up."

She toweled her hair. "What?"

"I called Dick Worley—"

"Brendan Worley."

"Right. We have a meeting with him. To discuss our transportation out of here."

"Okay. Good. Where and when?"

"He's at a yacht club. We need to cut short our R&R."

"So I don't get to see you in your Speedo?"

Brodie smiled.

The waiter returned with Brodie's beer and Taylor sat at the edge of her lounge chair and finished her Mojito. "Can I have yours?"

"Sure." He drank his beer out of the bottle. They sat in silence, enjoying the moment. A big blue heron landed on the terrace and began strutting between the lounge chairs, maybe looking for food, like those trash scavengers they'd seen yesterday. He said, "What's the difference between a tropical paradise and hell on earth?"

"Not much, apparently."

"Right. Every society comes to a Y in the road . . . the road to hell is downhill and looks easier than the uphill road. Until you get to the end."

She looked at him. "Is that you talking? Or the beer?"

"It's me talking to the beer."

"Old bad joke."

They exchanged smiles and she looked at the blue heron, giving Brodie an opportunity to look at her, sitting a few feet from him, nearly naked—and maybe still pissed off at him for excluding her from the two Dombroski calls.

He now noticed pockmarked shrapnel scars running along the right side of her waist and hip and down the length of her right quad. Taylor, he reminded himself, was more than his subordinate officer in the CID. They shared the bond of surviving combat. And of having friends who didn't.

So he—or the beer—decided to share some information with her. Not the info about her being involved with a CIA guy, but the info about Crenshaw. He said, "Do you remember the murder of Robert Crenshaw in Peshawar?"

She looked at him. "I do. Why?"

"Well, in my first phone call to Dombroski, he told me that Crenshaw was not a diplomat—he was actually a CIA officer—and that he had been stationed in Kabul before Peshawar."

Taylor kept looking at him, but didn't respond.

Brodie related his conversation with Dombroski regarding the timeline and geographic connection between Captain Mercer's escape from the Taliban and Crenshaw's torture and murder.

Taylor listened, then said, "That's a stretch. But even if it were true, we don't know why Mercer would want to torture and murder a CIA officer. Or what that has to do with why Mercer deserted. Or why he came to Caracas."

"Correct. But now we also know that Colonel Worley was in Kabul."

"We don't know *when* he was there."

"Correct. But maybe we'll ask him later."

"Okay . . . but Afghanistan is a seventeen-year-old war, and thousands of Intel officers have served there."

"Right. But it would be interesting if Worley was there at the same time as Mercer and Crenshaw." He reminded her, "Ted was there at the same time Worley was."

"We don't know who Ted is." She chided, "You're getting off base, Scott. We're here to find and apprehend Kyle Mercer, not to develop conspiracy theories. Focus on the mission."

She was right, of course, but her disinterest in all of this seemed somewhat out of character for Maggie Taylor, who was so diligent, manic, and detail-oriented. He said, "We are CID Special Agents, not a couple of MPs sent to go out and fetch."

"We are *investigators*—cops—not Intel officers."

"Okay . . . but also consider this: Robert Crenshaw's murder was big news at the time, so Worley knew about it, and Worley—who's an Intel officer—must have heard that Crenshaw was actually a CIA officer. And if Brendan Worley is half as smart as he thinks he is, then he's pondered the possible connection between Robert Crenshaw's murder and Kyle Mercer's geographic proximity to Peshawar at that time—just as Colonel Dombroski thought about that connection."

"Talk about making assumptions."

"All right. But we do know that Worley was in Afghanistan and he never mentioned it to us—and when someone withholds information, you have to wonder why, and also wonder what else he's withholding."

"Scott, he may not have mentioned it because of security issues." She added, "CIA officers, for instance, don't tell you where they've been."

And she would know about that.

She said, "If you ask Worley if he was in Afghanistan, do it in a friendly way."

"I always ask questions as though I don't already know the answer." He added, "It will be interesting to see if he lies."

She nodded.

"Stick with me, Maggie. You'll learn something."

"I already have."

Brodie changed the subject. "Did you look up Tomás de Heres?"

"I did. He was an officer in Bolívar's army and he helped lead the liberation of Peru. He was assassinated when someone set off a bomb in his house. The killer was never found."

"An Army cold case. Let's look into it after we find Mercer."

"Wrong army." She asked, "Did you mention Tomás de Heres to Dombroski?"

"I didn't. But I did mention Flagstaff."

"And?"

"Didn't ring a bell with him."

"Did you mention that Worley didn't tell us he was in Afghanistan?"

"I decided to withhold that information."

"Why?"

"I'm protecting my source. Luis."

"Why?"

"Colonel Dombroski has no need to know."

"He's our boss."

"General Hackett is *his* boss."

"So General Hackett is on your list of co-conspirators?"

"General Hackett has not been straight with us."

Taylor finished her drink, looked at her partner, and said, "Here's what I've learned—you're either a very smart detective or you're a paranoid asshole."

"There's not much difference."

"We should get moving."

He stood, and she did the same. As she was putting on her pool wrap, he asked, "How much did you pay for your bikini?"

"About twelve dollars."

"That's a lot for a little."

She smiled. "Sometimes a little goes a long way."

They walked into the rooftop café and took the elevator down to their floor. As they went to their respective bedroom doors, Brodie asked, "Can you meet me in the lobby in twenty minutes?"

"Can do." She opened her door, looked at him, and said, "The pool's open all night. So if we're back here tonight without our prisoner, that's our consolation prize."

A midnight dip in the pool with Maggie Taylor sounded good. "It's a date."

She smiled and disappeared into her room.

He entered his room and, rather than try to analyze that interaction, thought about what to wear to a Venezuelan yacht club. He also thought about Brendan Worley, and about bringing Kyle Mercer to justice, and about how to survive the night.

If he could do all that, then he could always ruin his professional relationship with Maggie Taylor back home. As in Iraq, the mission came first, but the ultimate goal was to go home—standing up, as they used to say.

CHAPTER 26

Brodie and Taylor met in the lobby, and he noticed that Taylor was appropriately dressed in white slacks and sandals and wore a blue boater top that hid the bulge of her gun. She also had a small handbag for her lipstick and extra mag. Brodie had rescued his khaki slacks from the laundry bag and wore an untucked green shirt, beneath which was his pancake holster and his Glock to accessorize his Venezuelan yacht club attire.

Brodie asked the front desk to call them a taxi, and a few minutes later a black Ford Explorer pulled into the hotel drive. The car had a yellow seal on the door that said <u>TELETAXI</u>, and their driver—a graying man in his fifties—was running a meter and had his cab license displayed, so Brodie figured the odds were good that this was not a kidnapping. The doorman told the driver their destination and they set out.

The cabbie, whose license said "Ramón Sanchez," spoke English and asked them, "You are Americans?"

"No," Brodie replied reflexively, "we are Canadians."

"Good. The Americans threaten my country. They are planning an attack." He added, "They want to control our oil."

"They're imperialists," Brodie agreed. "They just took over Tim Hortons, our national donut chain."

Ramón processed that, then asked, "Why do you go to the Grande Yacht Club?"

"We're interviewing for a job," Brodie replied.

"You want to work for the rich? They are parasites."

"They suck," Brodie agreed.

"Yes, like parasites. They suck the blood of the people. Someday we will free Venezuela of the rich."

Taylor chimed in, "You've already done a good job of freeing Venezuela of the middle class."

Brodie smiled and gave her a wink.

Ramón continued as he navigated out of the city, "There should be no private clubs."

Brodie and Taylor sat in silence and let him talk, interrupting only to say they agreed with him. The Americans suck.

They followed their original route back toward the airport and over the mountains, then cut west onto a two-lane road that ran along the coast and offered a nice view of the ocean. The sun shone in a cloudless sky, and the blue water was speckled with yachts and sailboats.

They turned off the coastal road and approached the entrance to the Marina Grande Yacht Club, which consisted of a guard booth and a sliding metal gate topped with razor wire. Like the entrance to the El Dorado, this bubble of luxury did its best to look welcoming despite the prison-like fortifications. A sign in gilded paint advertised the name of the club, and the smiling booth attendant wore a crisp white suit. To the side, next to a line of palm trees, stood an armed guard in black fatigues, holding an AK-47.

Brodie and Taylor gave the booth attendant their fake passports, which he checked against a guest list. The attendant instructed the cabbie in Spanish as to where Señor Worley could be found, then pushed a button to open the gate, and they drove through.

The cab dropped them off in the parking lot near the beach, and Brodie paid the driver in bolívars, but didn't insult him with a tip.

They walked onto a wide, flat beach surrounding a cove. At the far end of the cove was the marina, where rows of gleaming pleasure boats of all sizes sat at anchor.

It was a hot day, but the air was significantly cooler here by the water than in the city. Brodie observed the beachgoers who were sipping drinks on recliners under palm-thatched huts or wading in the cove's shallow waters. A handsome couple walked past them, hand in hand, toward an outdoor café on an elevated deck overlooking the water. Maybe money couldn't buy happiness, but it could buy this, and this looked pretty good.

They found Worley sitting in a beach chair in the shade of a thatched hut, sipping a dark drink out of a tall glass, watching the ocean. He'd swapped his dirty slacks and beat-up loafers for a pair of wrinkled shorts and plastic flip-flops. He wore a Tommy Bahama T-shirt.

Worley looked at them through a pair of aviator sunglasses as they sat down in adjacent chairs. "How's married life?"

"Unconsummated," replied Brodie.

Worley laughed.

Taylor ignored that as she looked around and asked, "Is this place secure?"

Worley assured them, "The employees are paid to hear only what you want them to hear, and to remember only your drink order."

Brodie asked, "What about the guests?"

"All anti-government. Regime people are not welcome here."

A young female club attendant in a white collared shirt and short white skirt came by to take drink orders. Worley ordered three Venezuela Libres—whatever that was—before downing the rest of the drink he was working on and handing her the empty glass. She smiled and walked away.

Brodie got down to business. "We're fairly sure we found the brothel."

"I'm glad Raúl was helpful."

"We're planning to make the arrest tonight."

"I'm sure Captain Mercer will have other plans." He added, "I don't think a fugitive would hang around a place where he was spotted."

"We'll see."

"Actually, he may be waiting for you."

"I hope so."

Worley looked at him. "Be careful what you wish for."

Brodie asked, "Do you know anything about MBR-200?"

"What is that? A new workout plan? Breakthrough boner pill?"

Brodie had a feeling that Brendan Worley was feigning ignorance, which was probably his specialty. "It's a gang in Petare. They run the brothel."

Worley shook his head. "Gangs rise and fall by the hour up there. I don't keep track."

"Right. What we need from you—"

"I hope you're not going to ask for backup. The embassy can't get involved in extrajudicial—"

"I need a plane, Colonel. Ms. Taylor and I will take care of the rest."

Worley nodded. "All right . . . There is an abandoned airstrip we use ten kilometers southwest of Caracas. A chartered aircraft will take off from Francisco de Miranda Airport and fly a holding pattern over the airstrip. I will give you the sat phone number of the pilot, and when you are at the airstrip with your prize, you will call him with your sat phone and he will swoop down and pick you up."

Brodie and Taylor exchanged glances; then Taylor asked, "What kind of aircraft? And where are we being flown to?"

Worley replied, "The aircraft we use is a single-engine Otter, good for short takeoffs and landing on shit airstrips. It has an external sat phone antenna, so the pilot is able to receive your call. The Otter seats seven or eight if you want to kidnap anyone else."

Brodie had the impression that Worley had used that line before.

Worley continued, "As for your destination, that is not for me to know, but we can assume it is an American military installation in Panama or Gitmo. And then home."

Brodie nodded, and it occurred to him that he and Taylor might be relieved of their suspect in Panama or Guantánamo. In fact, that was probably the plan, and that didn't give him much time to interrogate the hog-tied Captain Mercer.

Taylor asked, "How do we find the airstrip, and what is the pilot's sat phone number?"

Worley looked at her. "When or if you make the arrest, you'll call me and I will give you that information, then I will call the pilot who will be on standby at Francisco de Miranda Airport, and all the moving pieces will come together at the airstrip."

Brodie pointed out, "The only reason we're sitting here with you is because you didn't want to talk over the phone."

"It's not the only reason. I enjoy your company."

Taylor said, "Please give us the pilot's number and the location of the airstrip." She added, "Now."

"Will you have a driver tonight?"

Taylor nodded.

"Luis?"

Taylor replied, "Doesn't matter."

"Just tell your driver to take Route Nine off Francisco Fajardo, south until it becomes Route One. Then you will call me. I will give you the rest of the directions to the airstrip and the pilot's sat phone number at that time."

Brodie said, to him, "We need this info *now*, Colonel. Just in case you don't hear your phone ring in a noisy nightclub."

"I will be waiting for your call tonight in a quiet place, where I will have phone service, and you will tell me if you have Captain Mercer in custody. If I don't hear from you, I will assume you are both in someone else's custody, or dead." He added, "The location of this airstrip and the pilot's number are both need-to-know, and you don't need to know until you have Mercer."

Brodie understood that, but he was concerned that the operation could hit a wall at the goal line. He pictured himself and Taylor in Luis' car with Mercer tied up in the trunk, speeding out of Petare, maybe with the National Guard or MBR-200 on their tail, trying to find Route 9 in the dark while listening to Worley's phone message: *The party you have reached is screwing a señorita and can't take your call now.*

Brodie thought about calling Dombroski to have him contact the embassy attaché office, but when it came to the subject of covert airfields and flying Otters, Brendan Worley might be the top authority.

Brodie looked at Worley. "Okay. But with all due respect, Colonel, if you screw this up tonight, I will see that you are held responsible. In fact, I will personally deliver to you some non-judicial punishment."

Worley lifted his aviators and stared at Brodie for a long time, then said, "This is all moot. You know why? Because you have close to zero chance of arresting Mercer tonight, and a much better chance of getting yourself and Ms. Taylor killed." He added, "I would advise you to file a report with your superior congratulating yourselves on finding the brothel, but also stating that Captain Mercer has apparently fled to an unknown location. Then go home." He looked at both of them. "I give you this advice because I like you. Also, if you get killed, the embassy will have a ton of paperwork to fill out."

Brodie replied, "We will call you tonight for the information you are withholding."

Worley did not reply.

The waitress returned with their Venezuela Libres. Worley took his and said, "It's a Cuba Libre, plus gin and bitters." He continued, "The Cuba Libre was first mixed during the Spanish-American War to commemorate Cuban independence. Cuba is no longer free, but it will be again, and so will Venezuela." He raised his glass. "To a free Cuba and a free Venezuela."

Brodie was happy he could agree with Worley on something. He took a sip. Not bad. But it might be better if he arrived at the Hen House sober, so he put the drink down on a side table, as did Taylor.

Worley gestured toward the ocean, where the late afternoon sun was glinting over the placid waters of the Caribbean. "I came here to see a Venezuelan friend off on his journey. He's in one of those yachts out there. He's a top petroleum engineer, worked all over the world but came back to his mother country to help modernize the oil refineries. A couple of days ago, someone shot through his daughter's bedroom window, and that was the last straw. He's taking the family to Argentina." He took a long drink, watched the water. "People focus on the runaway inflation, the crime and corruption. A country can bounce back from those things. But losing its best people, that outflow of human capital, can take generations to recover from. You've got thousands of Venezuelans fleeing across the Colombian and Brazilian borders every day. This is not just a brain drain. It's a diaspora."

Well, that was bleak. Brodie thought of their cabdriver, Ramón, who totally bought the regime's bullshit. Or maybe he just found it easier to hate the rich and the Americans than to hate the assholes he'd voted for who had taken away his freedom and his dignity.

Brodie glanced at his watch: 4:50 P.M. Time to get back to the hotel and get ready for Luis at 7 P.M. He glanced at Taylor, who seemed in no hurry to leave. In fact, she said to Worley, "What was the worst posting you've ever had?"

He looked at her, and Brodie could see the wheels turning in his head.

He replied, "I am assigned to all the shitholes in the world." He added, "Not because I have screwed up, but because I am very good at what I do."

"And what do you do?" Taylor asked.

"I clean up the shit."

"I'm surprised you've never been to Afghanistan."

He looked at her again. "I have been there."

"I'm surprised you didn't mention it to us."

"I don't like to brag."

"Neither do I. But it's nice to meet a fellow veteran who's seen the same shit you have. I spent two years over there with the Ninety-Sixth Civil Affairs Battalion."

Brodie, who did like to brag, added, "She earned a Silver Star and a Purple Heart." Colonel Worley needed to know he wasn't dealing with a couple of lightweights. But probably he already knew that.

Worley looked at Taylor. "Thank you for your service."

"When were you there?"

"About the same time that Kyle Mercer was there." He added, "I remember when we all heard about his desertion."

Well, thought Brodie, Worley couldn't lie about something that could be checked, so now that his original lie of omission had been outed, he had to be truthful. Brodie asked, "Were you there when Robert Crenshaw was murdered in Peshawar?"

Worley looked at him. "No. I was here by that time."

Worley's next question should have been: "Why do you ask?" But he didn't ask, so Brodie said, "Did it ever occur to you that Kyle Mercer may have killed Crenshaw?"

"Why would Kyle Mercer want to kill a State Department analyst?"

"We've been briefed about Mr. Crenshaw," said Brodie. "So let's cut the shit."

Worley stared at Brodie for a moment, no doubt wondering who'd briefed these CID agents about an undercover CIA officer in Pakistan, and why. Eventually he said, "Yes, it did occur to me that Mercer may have killed him."

"And when did that occur to you?"

"When I was fully briefed about Mercer's escape from the Taliban camp, which apparently was near Peshawar."

Brodie asked, "Did you ever work with Robert Crenshaw?"

Worley stared out at the water.

By now, Brodie thought, Colonel Worley had realized that the conversation was a CID interrogation.

Worley finally replied, "That is privileged information."

"Can I take that as a yes?" asked Brodie.

Worley did not answer the question, but said to Brodie and Taylor,

"Your orders are to find and apprehend Captain Mercer, which you may do tonight. You should stick to your orders."

Brodie replied, "I'm a big fan of mission creep."

"You're a cop. Not an Intel officer. That's my world, Mr. Brodie, not yours." He dropped his aviators back over his eyes, sat back, and watched two señoritas coming out of the water.

Brodie knew that Intel guys like Worley got high off their own mystique—which was to say, their own bullshit—and they always needed to feel like they were playing four-dimensional chess, even when they were just day drinking on the beach.

"In matters of criminal investigation, my authority knows no bounds." Brodie informed him, "I have arrested Intel officers, but to the best of my knowledge no Intel officer has ever arrested a CID investigator."

Worley kept staring at the girls. He took a long drink and said, "I think we're done here."

Brodie remained seated. He said, "Here are the questions that are running through my military mind and my criminal investigator mind: Why did a decorated war hero desert his unit? And did he kill Robert Crenshaw? And why? And why did he come to Venezuela?"

"Ask him if you actually sit next to him at the whorehouse bar. He'd be happy to answer your questions before he kills you."

"Let's be optimistic. Let's say I do get to ask him those questions, and I live to tell about it. Do you think his answers will reveal something more than Captain Mercer making some bad career choices?"

Worley replied, "Obviously there is more to this than meets the eye. Any idiot—even a cop—can figure that out. What you also have to figure out, Mr. Brodie—and Ms. Taylor—is if you really want to know more than you're supposed to know."

More secret agent posturing and bullshit, thought Brodie. But Worley had a point. Also, maybe Brodie shouldn't be sharing his thoughts and concerns with Brendan Worley, but sometimes you have to shake the tree to see what falls out. In any case, Colonel Worley didn't believe that his two CID guests would have Kyle Mercer in custody tonight, or any night. So this was just Worley doing what these people did best—warning mere mortals not to tread on their sacred ground.

Brodie stood. "I'll call you tonight." He added, "And don't forget Luis' family tourist visa."

Taylor rose too, and said to their host, "The arrest of Captain Mercer is not the end of our mission. It is just the beginning of the investigation into the questions we've raised here."

Worley replied, "You disappoint me, Ms. Taylor. I thought you were the rational member of the team."

She continued, as per textbook, "You may be called upon in future investigations or judicial proceedings to provide truthful testimony in this case."

Brodie couldn't help but say, "Now he's definitely not answering the phone tonight."

Worley laughed, and so did Brodie. Taylor looked at both of them as if to say, "*Men.* The brotherhood of assholes." She began walking across the sand toward the parking lot.

Brodie followed and caught up with her. "I thought we were going to do a group hug."

She ignored that. "You shouldn't have raised any of those questions with him. We need him tonight, and you antagonized him."

"Me? You just told him he'd be called on to provide truthful testimony."

"If he had a truthful thought in his head, it would die of loneliness." She looked at him. "Scott . . . we need to leave this alone. We have enough to do here."

"Then why did you bring up Afghanistan?"

"You were going to ask him anyway, so I did it in an indirect way. As we were taught to do."

"I missed that class."

They reached the parking lot and headed for what looked like the clubhouse where they could call a taxi.

Taylor said, "He gives me the creeps."

"That's what he wants to do. Look, I've worked cases where I butted heads with CIA guys, Army Intel, and spooks from other agencies. They go out of their way to make you think they're doing you a favor by keeping information from you that could be dangerous for you to know. They invented the phrase 'If I tell you, then I have to kill you.' It's ninety percent bullshit."

"How about the other ten percent?"

"That's the part that *could* get you killed. And on that subject, Brendan Worley thinks we're the walking dead, so I wonder if there really is an aircraft waiting to take us out of here."

She glanced at him. "You're scaring me, Scott."

"Hey, I scare myself sometimes." He added, "As they say in the infantry, the best-thought-out battle plans fall apart as soon as the first shot is fired. Then you improvise."

"Unless that first shot went through your head."

"Never thought of that."

They reached the clubhouse and Brodie said, "Ask for a taxi driven by a free-market capitalist."

She went into the building and Brodie stood in the sunlight, watching the gulls over the water. Well, they'd stirred the shit a bit, and he could picture Worley on the phone with the appropriate people, saying something like, "This guy has made some connections. He and the lady need to be spoken to when they get back to the States." Or Worley might say, "But don't worry about them. They'll probably get themselves killed tonight."

Well, given the choice between being read the National Security Act by some assholes in a basement in Washington or getting into a shoot-out in a Caracas whorehouse, he'd pick the shoot-out. It was quicker and less boring.

Taylor came out of the clubhouse. "Taxi in five minutes." She added, "I asked for Ramón from Teletaxi."

"You're a pain in the ass, Maggie."

"Life's a pain in the ass, Scott."

Especially if you don't get laid, don't get your man, and get killed in a whorehouse. Could be worse, though. He could be raising rhubarb.

CHAPTER 27

Teletaxi arrived, but Ramón was not driving.

Brodie said to the driver, "El Dorado Hotel."

The driver, Gustavo, like his colleague Ramón spoke English and commented, "One night in that place would cost a working man a year's salary."

Brodie said to Taylor, "This is going to be a long ride."

Gustavo asked, "Are you Americans?"

"Canadians."

"I do not see many Americans in Caracas."

"They don't know what they're missing."

"Do you enjoy my country?"

Brodie replied, "What can I say about Venezuela that hasn't already been said about Cuba or Nicaragua?"

Gustavo thought about that, then asked, "You are here for business or pleasure?"

"A little of both."

"Good. You must go out of Caracas and go to the south where are the jungles."

"It's on our itinerary," Brodie assured him. "Venezuela—to know her is my destiny."

"Sí." Gustavo, who obviously got his news from the same source that Ramón did, said, "If the Americans invade us, we will go to the jungles. Venezuela will be like their Bay of Pigs, their Vietnam, their Iraq and Afghanistan."

Brodie said to Taylor, "You should rejoin the Ninety-Sixth Civil Affairs Battalion. I see a career opportunity here."

Taylor said something to Gustavo in Spanish, then told Brodie, "I told him I'm tired and want to sleep."

Well, that was a nice way of shutting him up. Brodie had considered pulling his Glock. But Taylor took a softer approach. Good cop, bad cop. They made a great team.

He looked at Taylor, who was already feigning sleep, then gazed out the window as they drove along the coastal road, then cut south through the mountains. The sun sat low, casting long shadows over the dense trees carpeting the mountainside, and in the distance Brodie could see the shimmering glass and steel towers of the Caracas skyline.

Venezuela sucked. But it hadn't always sucked. Not so long ago this had been a functioning democracy, a church- and family-oriented society. He thought of Luis, and of the pleasant staff in the hotel, and he remembered Miss Venezuela, of course, and the citizens on the streets who looked normal, though frightened. He also recalled the dumpster divers, the queue at the supermarket, and the downtrodden denizens of Petare who were one meal away from starvation. He also thought of the Chavistas in Plaza Bolívar, the predatory police, the thug at airport customs, the National Guardsmen, and the sick people at the health clinic controlled by MBR-200.

It seemed to him that Venezuela was a place where the worst elements of humanity had defeated civilization. He'd seen this in other countries, and it was as depressing as it was frightening. And what was even more depressing were the useful idiots like Gustavo and Ramón, who were not evil—they were true believers, deaf, dumb, and blind to the evil around them. Or maybe they were cowed.

Fear. This was a country that was gripped by fear.

If Kyle Mercer, who spoke some Spanish, was looking for a Spanish-speaking country to settle in, Brodie could think of a dozen other not quite so fucked-up places in South and Central America to make money and disappear. Therefore . . . Mercer had come here for another reason. Criminals on the run usually go where they know someone who can help them—a friend or relative. Or they go someplace to settle a score. But once the score is settled, they leave.

The car descended into the Caracas Valley. A haze hung over the city, making the surrounding hillside slums seem spectral in the fading light.

As the taxi approached the El Dorado, Gustavo said, "If I go through the security, the guards want a tip from me." He added, "What you call a shakedown."

Taylor sat up and said, "Pull over. We'll get out here."

Gustavo pulled over. Brodie paid the fare in bolívars, *sin* tip, and said to Gustavo, "You need to tell the guards to go fuck themselves."

"Señor?"

"This whole country needs to stop putting up with this shit."

Gustavo had no response.

Taylor took Brodie's arm and led him toward the gate, saying, "Sometimes you surprise me when you get angry at social injustice."

"I surprise myself." He added, "My parents were hippies. Peace, love, and justice. Must have rubbed off."

"I won't tell."

———

Back in their suite, they sat in the living room across from each other, eating junk from the minibar and drinking the local high-octane cola, which might have been made with the real thing.

Brodie asked, "Okay, what's your take on Colonel Worley?"

Taylor thought a moment. "He's a drunk. But we need him, and I believe in the end he'll come through, despite his posturing."

Brodie nodded. Cases involving Intel or Special Operations tended to get complicated because in those worlds there were lots of valid reasons to keep secrets. So when Brodie ran into deceptions and obstruction—which would normally hint at criminal wrongdoing—he knew these lies and refusals to provide answers were just a part of doing business. As Brendan Worley made clear. Brodie said to Taylor, "He advised us to go home."

"He's the one who should go home. He's burned-out."

"I think he's concerned about what we could discover if we had Captain Mercer in our custody. In fact, I wouldn't be surprised if Colonel Worley's military Intel people were also looking for Mercer now that they know he's here."

Taylor thought about that but didn't reply.

It often happened that the spooks and the cops were looking for the same suspect, but for different reasons—and to deliver different methods of justice. Intel guys generally didn't have the power to arrest, as Brodie had reminded Worley, and that left the Intel people with two choices: turn the suspect over to the CID or FBI, or kill him. Actually, there was a third choice: Intel people were infamous for offering deals to scumbags who belonged in jail. They called it "turning a guy around," "making him a double agent," and all that crap. It sometimes worked in that world of smoke and mirrors, but Brodie found it distasteful. Criminals, spies, and traitors belonged in jail. Not on the payroll. In any case, if Worley and his friends *were* actually looking for Kyle Mercer, they probably weren't looking to recruit him—they were possibly looking to shut him up permanently. But why? The answer to that question was the answer to why Captain Mercer had deserted.

Taylor finished her cola and a handful of nuts and suggested, "Let's go over the plan for tonight."

"You want a plan?"

"Just for laughs, Scott."

"Okay . . . I'll be entering the whorehouse with the assumption that Kyle Mercer is probably not going to be there. So I need to find the opportunity to question people who are there regularly, but who are not motivated to protect Señor Mercer."

"You mean the girls who work there."

"Correct." He explained, "I'm going in as a john, and I want an English-speaking hooker with whom I can discuss Venezuelan culture." He added, "A girl of legal age."

She looked at him. "Okay . . . sounds . . ."

"Somebody has to do this, Maggie."

"Is Luis going in with you?"

"Yes, I need a translator. Just in case they don't have an English-speaking hooker."

"I see you've thought this out."

"I'm thinking out loud."

"Are you thinking you'll go into a room with this girl?"

"I'll try the front lounge area first."

"Are you going in armed?"

"Gringos would not be armed. But Luis, like everyone else in that place, will have a gun, and even if they check for iron at the door, they won't ask for Luis' weapon if it means they lose a customer." He added, "It's like the Wild West here, Maggie. A man and his gun are not parted at the door of a whorehouse. That would be like asking him to leave his dick outside. Once we're inside, Luis will slip the Glock to me."

She nodded, then asked, "Does Luis know about this?"

"He's figured it out." He reminded her, "He lives here."

"Okay, but . . . I don't know how you can ask a civilian to risk his life for something that has nothing to do with him."

"We did it all the time in Iraq. You hire the locals when you need them. They can say no." He asked her, "Didn't you do that in Afghanistan?"

"Yes, we hired locals, but not for dangerous assignments."

"Just by hiring them, you put their lives in danger." He pointed out, "The Taliban kill American lackeys."

"All right, but—"

"Look, if Luis gets cold feet, I'll leave him at the door, and I'll go in myself, unarmed." He added, "I know you'll worry about me, Maggie, but at least Luis will be safe."

"Don't be sarcastic. I'm saying I'll go in with you."

"That doesn't work. But thank you for the offer. Okay, so Luis has come in with me, but then he leaves and I take this girl into a room. I can't have Mercer's photo with me in case I'm frisked at the door. But it's easy to describe a bearded gringo with a snake tattoo on his arm. I offer her a lot of American dollars, and with any luck, she'll know him and maybe tell me when he usually shows up, or the last time she saw him, who he hangs with, maybe where he lives, and so forth." He added, "Standard police procedure."

Taylor nodded, then said, "At that point, you've gotten what you paid for and you get out of there."

Brodie smiled. "When you go deep undercover, you've got to play the part all the way."

"I'm inspired by your professional commitment."

"Thank you. Okay, another possibility is that Kyle Mercer is there, and he's there just out of chance, or he's there waiting for the gringo he heard about. If it's just a chance appearance, I leave, and we take him down when he leaves." He went on, "If he's there waiting for me, with backup, then I've got a problem."

"Actually, you'll be dead."

"I should be so lucky."

Taylor looked at him. "Why don't we just stake out the place tonight?"

"I'm impatient. And Dombroski has put a time limit on us." He lied, "Four days."

"Why four days?"

"I think he doesn't want us to get killed in Caracas."

"That makes two of us. I'm not sure about you."

"I'd like to arrest this son of a bitch and fly out of here tonight. I'm going right for the golden egg in the Hen House."

"How did you survive combat?"

"I knew when to duck."

"Is that it for the plan?"

"I think so. Basically, we'll all play it by ear tonight. Be ready for anything, be able to adapt to the situation, and, as always, show initiative and good judgment—and remember the mission."

"Thank you for the pre-battle pep talk."

He let her know, "I'm not crazy. I know when something looks and smells wrong. I know when to retreat. That's why I'm still alive."

"I'll remind you of that."

"Also, I had another thought about the Hen House. According to Raúl, it's run by MBR-200, which is connected to the regime. So this raises the question of why Mercer would be in a place that he must know has connections to the mob who have connections to the government—a place where he'd be likely to run into MBR-200 guys, police, and even government officials." He reminded Taylor, "Simpson said Mercer looked comfortable there. Like he ran the place, or maybe he was there for some reason other than to dip his wick."

She nodded. "We've established that Al Simpson uses colorful language in his eyewitness account."

"Point is, if I were a gringo on the run, I'd pick someplace else in Caracas to hang out and have a beer. Unless . . ."

"Unless he's somehow involved with the colectivo and/or the regime."

"Right. Though that may also be a stretch. But . . . why the hell would he be in a whorehouse that's dangerous to him on many levels?"

"He could be into child prostitutes."

"Somehow, I don't think so . . . and if he was, he'd have one delivered to his place of residence." He added, "It's the Hen House, not the girls, that he finds comfortable."

"Ask him when you arrest him. Or ask the girl who you pay for information."

"I will ask the girl. Or several girls. We are not allowed to interrogate Captain Mercer."

"And you always follow orders."

"If I can remember them, I follow them." He glanced at his watch. "We should change into evening wear and get moving."

Taylor looked at him. "One more thing, Scott. We're about to embark on a mission that may end badly. So I want to know what Colonel Dombroski told you that I had no need to know."

Brodie had seen that coming and replied, "I told you. Robert Crenshaw."

"No. It's something else. Something that has to do with me."

"Good deductive reasoning." He added, "We can discuss this back in the States."

"No, we can discuss it now."

"All right . . . As you have already guessed, Dombroski told me you were once involved with a CIA guy."

"And I am forever tainted."

"No, you are forever under suspicion."

"That's total bullshit."

"Be that as it may."

"I slept with the guy, Scott. I didn't get recruited by him."

"Good. End of discussion."

"Is this going to follow me for the rest of my Army career?"

"I hope not."

"If I slept with a Mafia guy, does that make me a suspected member of the Mafia?"

"Actually, yes, and the police would like to speak to you." He pointed out, "If nothing else, it shows bad judgment."

"That's ridiculous. Who have *you* slept with?"

"Not you. Despite your bad taste in men."

"This is not funny." She looked at him. "Dombroski had no right to impugn my loyalty or to suggest that I might have ties to the CIA, or—"

"He just mentioned it in passing. Cool off."

"Do you think I'm passing on information to the CIA? Is that why you were questioning me at the pool?"

"I was just showing you what it felt like to be grilled."

"Bullshit."

"This is not the way to set out on a mission."

"Do you trust me?"

"With my life."

She didn't respond and seemed to be deep in thought, then said, "His name was Trent."

"I think every CIA officer's name is Trent."

She forced a smile, then continued, "He was a PSYOPs guy. He taught at the Special Warfare School at Bragg. I was in a class he ran for Civil Affairs." She stared off into the past. "He tried to impress me with war stories from his time as a paramilitary—he was part of the initial assault on Tora Bora to get bin Laden—back in the beginning of the war that everyone thought was going to be over in a year."

Brodie had no idea why he needed to know any of this, but Taylor seemed to want to reminisce—or explain how she got involved with a spook.

"We dated for almost a year, then I was deployed to Afghanistan. When I came back, he tried to get things going again, but . . . I was all grown up and not so easily impressed."

Right. A student-teacher relationship that went cold after the student went out and saw more of the world. And saw dead people, and heard gunfire, and got hit. Nothing remarkable there. Young Maggie Taylor, a few years out of Georgetown, could be forgiven for falling for an older spy guy who regaled her with tales of combat in the wilds of Afghanistan. Conclusion: Just because Maggie Taylor got in bed with a guy in the CIA didn't mean she was in bed with the CIA.

She said, "I seem to be paying a high price for a shitty relationship."

"This is the Army, Ms. Taylor. Shit follows you from duty station to duty station."

"It's the part I don't like about the Army. The gossip and the petty and provincial attitudes."

"The CIA is more sophisticated. I'm sure Trent's career took off after he dated you."

She smiled, then said, "Well, I won't make that mistake again. My next boyfriend will be a moonshiner from Appalachia."

Brodie couldn't picture that. On the other hand, it was possible. People return to their roots. He said to her, "I will advise Colonel Dombroski that we had this conversation and that I am confident that your past relationship was personal and not professional." He added, for fun, "The opposite of ours."

She smiled again. "Thank you."

They both stood, and while Brodie was trying to determine whether this conversation increased or decreased his chances of having sex with Maggie Taylor, she said, "I'm still not sure what I'm supposed to do tonight."

"You're driving the getaway car. You'll have your Glock, all the extra mags, and the Taser and ties in case we can take Mercer on the street."

"How long do I wait for you and Luis to come out of the Hen House?"

"Luis should be out after he gets me in and asks to use the baño." He added, "I may take a bit longer. Let's say an hour."

"And then what? Our cell phones are no good up there."

"You should use the sat phone to call Worley."

"What can he do?"

"Nothing. But he'd enjoy telling you that on the phone."

"Scott, I can't just wait outside, worrying—"

"You can't come in."

She looked at him. "I remember one of the first things I learned in the Army—a soldier is a person who runs *toward* gunfire, not away from it."

"Let's not keep Luis waiting. Lobby, ten minutes."

They went through the doors of their separate rooms.

Well, thought Brodie, what had started in General Hackett's office could end tonight. He'd had a bad feeling about this case in Quantico, and a couple days in Caracas hadn't made him feel any better. But now he'd come to the conclusion that Captain Mercer's bizarre desertion was just the proverbial tip of a big iceberg that stretched across the chain of command. An interesting case had become more interesting.

As for Maggie Taylor, he was glad he'd cleared the air on that. And yet . . . there were still a few things that seemed off—including her deductive reasoning, based on nothing. Except maybe a guilty conscience. Could be she'd worked for the CIA in Afghanistan, as some Civil Affairs people did. But why the involved story about Trent? As Brodie had learned on this job, only people who lie go into unnecessary detail.

Colonel Dombroski didn't spread rumors; he gave reliable information. Then it was up to his agents to analyze and come to conclusions. To come to the truth.

CHAPTER 28

Brodie and Taylor waited at the front entrance to their hotel. It was 7:10 P.M. and there was no sign of Luis in the rental car.

Taylor said, "Maybe he's stuck in traffic."

Brodie pointed out, "There is no traffic in Caracas after dark."

"Maybe he got robbed by the police."

"That's more likely." Or, Brodie thought, Luis had reconsidered tonight's job. But he'd have called or texted. *Sorry, Señor Brodie, you're crazy and I'm not.*

Brodie rolled back his shirt cuffs. He had been on dozens of undercover assignments and he could usually match his attire to the part he was playing. But he hadn't known he was going to be a scumbag sex tourist when he packed, so he'd had to improvise from his limited travel wardrobe, and he wore black slacks, loafers, and an untucked baby blue dress shirt, half-buttoned to show his chest hair. His Glock, which he would give to Luis before they entered the Hen House, was stuck in his waistband. He had no holster and no wallet—only a wad of cash and his fake passport in case anyone at the Hen House demanded ID. He'd considered wearing his twelve-dollar Armani sports jacket, but someone might kill him for it.

Taylor was wearing cargo pants into which she'd stuffed the zip ties, Taser, extra mags, and Brodie's photo of Kyle Mercer, which he didn't want found if he was frisked at the door of the Hen House. Taylor also had the one sat phone Worley had given them. The sat phone was good commo, but it couldn't send or receive unless it had clear sky—like his annoying car satellite radio, which cut out under a bridge or in a tunnel—so it was useless in the Hen House. And in any case, if it was discovered in a frisk at the door, it would arouse suspicion. So Taylor had it now, and later, if they were on the run, she could hang out the car window, sat phone in one hand, Glock in the other, shooting at their pursuers while trying to call Worley or the Otter pilot. She was good at multitasking. He asked her, "Did you stuff any Snickers in your pockets?"

She didn't reply, and he thought she looked tense.

Brodie did have his smartphone, in which he'd saved some offline maps of Petare that he could access in the hills where there was no reception and no street signs. Also no street lighting, which was good, but also bad. Luis was a competent driver, and so was Taylor, but whoever was behind the wheel for a quick getaway would have some challenges in the dark, mountainous slums.

He'd been in shitholes like this before, and in similar situations—he recalled his extraordinary extraction of the Army embezzler in Tunisia—and he took comfort in the fact that pursuers were always at a disadvantage, since the pursued were running for their lives and were thus more motivated.

In any case, he had no idea how this was going to go down tonight. But if, by extraordinary luck, they had Kyle Mercer in the trunk, all they needed was a little more luck and some smarts to get to that airstrip to rendezvous with the Otter. Next stop, U.S. soil in Panama or Gitmo. If that successful scenario transpired, he and Taylor would not be coming back to the El Dorado tonight, or ever. So they'd left everything in their rooms as though they'd gone out on the town and never returned—not an unusual occurrence in Caracas. In fact, that was another scenario: dead in the Hen House.

"What are you thinking, Scott?"

"I'm wondering if the Army will reimburse us for the personal possessions we left behind."

"I think that's the least of our worries."

"I think I should go up and get my Armani sports jacket." He added, "I'll grab your new bikini for you."

"Is this an example of GI humor before battle?"

"Sort of."

She nodded. "Whatever works for you. Meanwhile, I think we've been stood up."

"He'll be here."

The doorman, whose tag said "Tito," asked them for the third time if they needed a taxi, and Brodie replied again, "We're waiting for our driver."

"Sí." The doorman gave Taylor a quick once-over, noticing her informal attire—black T-shirt, dark cargo pants with stuffed pockets, and hiking boots, with her hair tucked under a baseball cap—and Brodie thought Tito was probably wondering why the gentleman was better dressed for the evening. Brodie considered explaining to Tito that he was going to a whorehouse with their tardy driver, and the lady was going to wait outside while he got laid. That might have been TMI for the doorman, but it would explain why the Americanos never returned.

Again he thought back to his Tunisian abduction at the beach resort. His idiot partner at the time, a guy named Nick Peterson, couldn't find the keys to their rental car that he was supposed to drive onto the beach where Brodie had chloroformed the suspect in his lounge chair. Brodie clearly recalled the frantic cell phone conversation with Peterson as the suspect began to regain consciousness—a comedy of errors that Brodie had retold many times to laughing colleagues in too many Quantico bars. But as he always said, all's well that ends well. The Army embezzler was doing ten to twenty at Leavenworth. Captain Kyle Mercer would be lucky if he didn't get the death penalty, reduced, of course, to life without parole. All Brodie had to do was find him, kidnap him, and get him home. And all he needed was a car and Luis. For want of a nail . . .

Taylor said, "I'm getting worried."

Brodie said to the doorman, "Get us a taxi to take us to a brothel in Petare."

The doorman looked at him, maybe unsure of his own fluency in English. He replied, "This is . . . not possible."

Brodie said to Taylor, "See? Just like in the States. Can't get a taxi to the slums."

She had no reply, but pulled out her cell phone, presumably to call or text Luis.

Just then the gate slid open and a silver midsize Mitsubishi sedan with a dented passenger door pulled into the circular drive and stopped in front of them. Brodie barely gave the vehicle a glance as he looked toward the open gate, watching for the big black sedan he'd instructed Luis to rent. The driver of the beat-up Mitsubishi got out—and unfortunately, it was Luis. "I am sorry for my lateness," he said, and explained, "There is some police activity . . ."

The doorman looked at the vehicle as if to say, "You waited for this piece of shit?" He shrugged to himself and opened the rear door to let Taylor in as Brodie went around to the other side, followed by the doorman, who seemed happy to get rid of them. Brodie gave Tito an American five and said, "Wish me luck tonight," and winked at him.

The doorman said something to Luis, and the only word Brodie could understand was "loco."

Luis got in the car, and Brodie noted that Luis had changed back into the dark suit he'd worn when he first met them at the airport. Luis said, "The doorman asked if the gentleman was crazy for going to Petare with this lady."

"He should have asked the lady." He asked Luis, "What happened to the big black sedan I asked for?"

Luis pulled through the open gate and got onto the road. "Unfortunately, there are no more luxury cars to rent in Caracas. They tell me these cars were all sent to Bogotá or Panama, where they will not be stolen from the car lot or hijacked on the road."

Brodie recalled what Taylor had said before they left, that this had become a place where sometimes no amount of money could get you what you wanted or needed. A real nightmare for any spoiled American—especially if you needed a dark car with a big trunk and a big engine.

Brodie watched out the window as they drove through the dark streets of Altamira. The streetlights were dead, and even a few of the signal lights they passed were out. The occasional café or club offered stray islands of light in the darkness. He wondered what went on in these places, and he remembered phoning his friend Marcus, who had been crazy enough to stick around Damascus after the civil war began. What had happened to all of Marcus' old clubs and drinking holes? "They're packed!" he'd said. "What else are you supposed to do when the rebels are lobbing mortars into your neighborhood every night? May as well die with a drink in your hand."

Venezuela was a country dissolving in slow motion, and that too was something to escape, if only for a night. It occurred to Brodie that the Hen House might be crowded with roosters tonight.

Brodie noticed that Luis had transferred the plastic jeweled cross from his car to the rearview mirror of this rental. He asked, "Does your wife know where you're going tonight?"

"I just say an embassy client. She knows not to ask more."

Right. Luis could do the worrying for both of them. Brodie wondered what it would be like to be married.

They followed the same route as that morning, taking the Francisco Fajardo Highway east toward the hills of Petare, now shrouded in darkness. Traffic was light to nonexistent. As they passed the Francisco de Miranda Airport, Brodie saw how it must have stood out to a very inebriated Al Simpson as a memorable landmark, because the runway was the only thing lit up for miles around. Brodie spotted a twin-engine plane taking off into the night. He thought back to Worley's spiel at the yacht club this afternoon and wondered how many of these departures were one-way flights.

The highway curved north, and they passed the old quarter of Petare on their right. Again, Al Simpson's recollection made sense—the church's spire was the only thing around that was illuminated. It was nice to know that even in Caracas, God kept the lights on for you.

Brodie took out his smartphone and pulled up the satellite image of Petare, along with the GPS pin he had saved earlier. He thought he could see a more direct route to the brothel, and he instructed Luis to drive past the turnoff they had taken earlier into the barrios, and to take another road farther north. This time, Luis made no mention of hiding their weapons before entering the slums. They all understood that once the sun was down, the rules changed.

They passed their original turn, then took the next uphill road and entered the slums. No sign of National Guard soldiers, police, or anyone else on the desolate streets. Brodie made out a couple of silhouettes in a dark alley, and somewhere in the distance he heard the whine of a police siren followed by the unmistakable sound of an AK-47 doing business. Through the windows of many of the barrio houses, he noticed flickering candlelight. The slums looked better in the dark, but they felt worse.

Brodie referenced the satellite map, then instructed Luis to turn onto a narrower road that snaked up the hillside. After about ten minutes of following the twisting roads, they turned onto the road that ran along the ridgeline. Brodie looked out the window, down at the darkened city below. There were a few pockets of light, mostly clustered in the more affluent eastern districts they had come from. Farther west, toward downtown and the government center, he saw the lit-up gilded dome of the Legislative Palace, and the pink façade of Miraflores Palace, which was bathed in floodlights that were probably illuminating security barricades.

Luis continued along the road, and up ahead the Mitsubishi's headlights revealed the white stucco brothel on the right. Brodie noted that there were about a dozen cars and SUVs parked haphazardly on the dark street near the Hen House, and there were a number of drivers standing around, smoking and joking while their passengers were inside getting laid.

Brodie had witnessed scenes like this around the globe—businessmen and tourists out slumming and fucking the poor, just as Al Simpson and his partner had done. Brodie had not indulged in this activity himself, but he didn't begrudge a hardworking man an opportunity to relax and to put some money into a poor working girl's G-string. What bothered him about the Hen House was the child prostitutes. And on a practical level, the "by introduction only" policy—which was necessary in a place that was beyond the pale even in Caracas—could be a problem at the door.

Taylor said, "This is disgusting."

"Men are animals," he agreed. He told Luis, "Go past the place," then said to Taylor, "Get down," which she did.

Luis continued, squeezing his car through the randomly parked vehicles, and up the ridgeline road.

Brodie pictured himself running out of the whorehouse and up the hill to the car with a posse on his tail. That was going to be difficult—especially if Captain Mercer was leading the posse. Also, he didn't see how he could take Mercer on the street with all those cars and drivers around. On the other hand, he'd made arrests in public places in third world cities, and most citizens looked the other way, figuring it was just another criminal or lawful activity—or something in between—that had nothing to do with them. And they were always right.

Taylor said, "This is not going to work."

"We'll make it work."

"Scott, we can't stake out the place, and we can't take him on the street with all those cars and people—"

"You overestimate the willingness of people in front of a whorehouse to get involved in a public kidnapping." He added, "What could possibly go wrong?"

"Are you crazy?"

Before Brodie could think of an answer, Luis said, "Señor Brodie is correct. In Caracas, no one sees anything, no one hears anything, and no one does anything." He added, "Unless this man who you are looking for has a driver who is also his security man."

"Thanks for that," said Brodie.

They continued up the hill on the dark road and Brodie said to Luis, "Make a U-turn, turn off your lights, and stop."

Luis did as he was told, and Brodie said to Taylor, "Make yourself small on the floor here." He told Luis, "Get a little closer to the Hen House, but not too close."

Luis nodded and began driving slowly down the hill toward the Hen House, while Taylor reluctantly sat on the floor with her back to the door.

Luis stopped about fifty feet from the brothel, and about thirty feet from the closest parked car. Brodie swapped Glocks with Luis and gave Luis' Glock to Taylor. "Okay," Brodie said, "Luis will walk me to the door to make the intro. If we're turned away, we'll be right back and we'll hang here and do a stakeout. If we get inside, Luis and I go to the baño, where I get my gun, and he leaves. You'll both wait for me, engine running and ready to roll."

"Scott, you have no commo and no backup, and this breaks with every CID procedure—"

"This is infantry procedure. A recon in hostile territory. End of discussion."

"All right. And what if you're not out in an hour?"

"Call Worley, report me missing in action, and get out of here." He added, "Look, Maggie, this is standard undercover work. Let's not get paranoid. I'm just a dumb gringo looking for action. The worst that can happen is that I get robbed and thrown out in my underwear. They know I'm not going to the police, so they don't need to put me through the wood chipper." He looked at Luis, who was sitting quietly behind the wheel. "Right, Luis?"

Luis did not reply immediately, then said, "True, the brothels sometimes rob, but do not kill."

"Right. That's bad for return business." Brodie had a final thought and said, "If you feel threatened by anyone approaching this car, get out of here."

"Scott, we're not leaving you—"

"Or if you see our suspect entering the Hen House, do not attempt to take him down. I'll deal with him inside."

Taylor replied, "If I see him, I'll take him."

He looked at her sitting on the floor. "No, you will follow orders."

Taylor didn't respond to that, but said, "This is what happens when you have no commo."

"As they told us in Iraq, you go into battle with the equipment you have, not the equipment you'd like to have." Brodie concluded, "Also, if you see him exit, I'll be right behind him."

Taylor looked at him. "Unless you're going through the wood chipper."

"Don't be negative." He looked out the window at the Hen House. "Okay, Luis, let's take a walk."

Luis got out of the car.

Taylor reminded Brodie, "Kyle Mercer may be waiting for you."

"If he is, he'll have more questions than I have. He may want to talk, maybe make a deal, maybe give me a message to carry back to the States." He added, "I'd rather take my chances with a fellow officer and combat vet than with the management of the Hen House."

Taylor nodded, evidently remembering that Captain Mercer had not killed Sergeant Simpson when he could have, and probably should have. She cautioned, however, "We don't know where his head is at now."

"I know who he was. That's the man I'm going to talk to if he's waiting for me."

Again she nodded. "Good luck."

Brodie got out of the car, and he and Luis started down the hill toward the Hen House.

CHAPTER 29

Brodie and Luis walked past the parked cars and SUVs. A few of the drivers looked them over, and a few called out to Luis, who replied, and they all got a laugh about something—probably about the gringo with a wad of cash bigger than his pene.

Brodie had played many parts in undercover assignments, and he had a sense of how to look, walk, and act for every role. Tonight, he was Clark Bowman, an insurance salesman from East Wheatfield, Kansas. Clark was nervous but excited, following his dick to a real brothel that his driver had recommended. Clark would try to dress the part of a cool guy going to a whorehouse, but he was still recognizable as a dork.

Deeper inside Clark Bowman was Scott Brodie, a man who had killed other men and would do so again if he had to.

They approached the black steel door of the Hen House and Brodie glanced up at the red eye of the security camera, which stared back at him.

Luis pushed the button on the doorjamb, which Brodie knew would cause a light to flash inside. They waited.

Brodie reminded Luis, "You need to use the baño."

"Sí. I do." He added, "But most drivers use the street."

"You want to wash your hands."

Luis nodded.

"And don't forget—Pepe from the Club of the Damned sent us here."

"Sí."

Brodie also reminded him, "Soon you'll be in the U.S. with your family."

Luis didn't reply.

Finally the door opened, and a big man in a tight black T-shirt and black chinos looked at Brodie, then at Luis. "Qué?"

Luis introduced his client, and gave Pepe's name and whorehouse as reference, but the man didn't reply and looked again at Brodie.

Brodie now noticed that the man wore a leather holster and was packing what looked like a six-shooter with an ivory handle. He made contact with the man's dark eyes, and for a moment Brodie thought he saw something dawning in the man's tiny brain—like, *Ah, you're the gringo we've been waiting for.* But maybe that was just his imagination.

The man stepped aside and motioned them into a small foyer.

He said something to Luis, who replied and tapped his hip where he carried his—or now Brodie's—Glock. The man nodded, and as Brodie had guessed, he didn't ask for Luis' gun.

The man then reached out and frisked Brodie, exhibiting a passable degree of expertise matching that of a TSA guy in an airport, except he didn't go for the crotch.

The man plucked Brodie's passport out of his pants pocket and flipped through it while glancing at Brodie's face. "Bow-man."

"Sí," said Brodie. "Call me Clark."

The man held on to the passport, then pulled the wad of greenbacks out of Brodie's hip pocket, took a twenty for himself, and handed the money back to Brodie along with his passport. Brodie hoped the cover charge included a drink.

The man said something to Luis—maybe directing him to the baño— then motioned them to a door which Luis opened, stepping aside to let his customer in first.

Brodie walked into a dimly lit, smoke-filled room, and as his eyes adjusted he saw that it was a large lounge with a long L-shaped bar to the left. A few men sat at the bar with their backs to him, except for the men at the short arm of the L who had a view of the door, and were looking at him.

Luis stood beside Brodie and said, "We should sit."

They found a small plastic table and sat in plastic chairs. Brodie looked around. There were tables scattered here and there, along with couches, which Simpson had mentioned, but that didn't mean they were actually in the same brothel where Simpson had seen his old Army buddy—who did not appear to be among the customers at the bar or at the tables.

On the concrete floor was a low-pile leopard-print rug that probably did a good job of hiding stains, and in the middle of the room a topless twenty-something of average appearance danced lethargically on a pole as mounted speakers piped in a bad Spanish-language Katy Perry rip-off. Red rope-lights lined the underside of the bar and ran up and down the walls, casting the whole room in a crimson hue. The walls themselves were cement block, painted dark red, and the ceiling was unfinished, revealing electrical conduits and air-conditioning ducts with grates, through which a small amount of cool air seeped into the warm room. The place didn't smell too bad, all things considered.

Brodie also noticed that the walls were adorned with neon beer signs, pinups of Venezuelan beauty queens, and lots of grimy mirrors. The waitresses were all naked or wearing G-strings, which saved on uniforms.

A naked waitress, modestly covered with glitter, came to the table and checked Brodie out before asking Luis in Spanish what she could do for them.

Luis ordered two cervezas and the lady moved to the bar.

Brodie noticed that Luis was sweating. He said to him, "Go to the baño. I'll follow."

Luis nodded, but didn't move.

The waitress returned with two bottles of beer in her hands—no tray—and put them on the table. "Ten dollar."

Brodie gave her a twenty and said, "Keep the change," wondering where she'd put it. He asked, "Do you have souvenir mugs?"

Luis did not translate, and their waitress smiled and moved off to another table where the beer was probably a buck.

As in places like this all over the world, the beer bottles were delivered unopened and there was an opener on the table for paranoid customers who didn't want to be drugged or poisoned. Brodie opened both bottles, and he and Luis clinked and sipped.

Brodie glanced around again, upping his situational awareness. An elderly man sat alone at a table near the pole dancer, an audience of one, and the pole dancer smiled at him a few times. Naked waitresses worked the few occupied tables, and Brodie thought they were all of legal age. The kids were obviously kept out of sight.

No one was on the couches except one young guy and a naked lady who was sitting on his lap, wearing his cowboy hat. Brodie said to Luis, "I don't think Miss Taylor would have appreciated this place."

Luis forced a smile. He was still sweating.

As Brodie's eyes adjusted to the dim light, he noticed two burly guys at a table at the far end of the room. They wore dark T-shirts, and each wore the distinctive red beret and arm bandana of MBR-200. They seemed to be looking at him and Luis, but then went back to their conversation. Before Brodie turned away, he spotted an AK-47 propped against the couch near their table. There were probably more handguns in this place than there were people, but the AK fully automatic assault rifle was the equalizer.

Brodie also noticed four men in suits. Their ties were loosened and their jackets hung on the backs of their chairs. They were smoking cigars and sharing a bottle of rum. One of them patted the bare ass of a passing waitress and they all laughed.

Luis said, "Regime men."

Right. They looked the same all over the world. The assholes at the top of the food chain. In fact, these four were a bit too plump for a country that was on short rations. More interestingly, they seemed at home in the Hen House, like they were silent partners—maybe along with the MBR-200 guys. Well, Brodie thought, at least this place wasn't going to get raided by the police tonight.

Brodie sat back and sipped his beer. He pictured Kyle Mercer suddenly showing up, and he ran a few scenarios through his mind: Go talk to him as he'd done a few times with other fugitives in public places? Ask him to come along peacefully and assure him he'd get a fair hearing? That worked well in the States, but not so well overseas. And probably not well with a rogue Delta Force guy anywhere.

The best thing to do if he saw Mercer was what Dombroski had suggested—get out of there quickly and quietly and wait for Mercer to exit, hopefully drunk. Or at least depleted of some of his precious bodily fluids, which reminded Brodie to remind Luis, "You have to take a pee, amigo."

Luis nodded and stood, looked around, and began heading toward a curtained doorway near the bar at the far end of the lounge. The two MBR-200 guys watched him as he approached. Luis hesitated, then disappeared through the curtain.

Given the size of the lounge area and based on the exterior of the building, Brodie figured there was another thirty or forty more feet of space on the other side of the curtain, and since the Hen House didn't seem to serve dinner or provide quiet places for meditation, Brodie guessed that the unseen space was divided into a number of fuckie rooms. In fact, the cowboy on the couch was now making his way toward the curtain with his lap lady, who must have aroused his interest, though for Brodie the big thrill was watching the clothes come off. These girls didn't leave much to the imagination.

Brodie tried to picture Al Simpson here—if this was the place—along with Pete, his partner, and the Venezuelans from the state oil company. Simpson might have been shocked by what he saw, and he was nervous, but excited. And just as he was getting over his shock and thinking about what to do with his whiskey dick, he was shocked again to see Kyle Mercer sitting at a table. And then Mercer stood and disappeared through what Simpson described as a side door. But Brodie couldn't see a side door.

Then he spotted the door, painted red like the walls, and nearly invisible in the dim, smoky room. The door—a steel exit door—would lead outside about where the generator was, and also where the garbage was tossed—which probably included customers. It was good to know where that door was.

To the left of the exit door was a curtain on the rear wall that matched the one that led to the baño, so it appeared there were two entrances from the lounge to the back rooms.

Brodie stood to join Luis in the baño, get his gun, and release Luis from the Hen House.

As he started for the curtained doorway, a tall, thin man of about his age came over to him and said, in good English, "Do you see a girl you like, señor?"

Brodie looked at the guy. He wore tight pants and a loose black silk shirt, beneath which would be his gun. He was obviously management, and his title was pimp. Brodie replied, "They all look good."

"Pick one."

"Later. I'm enjoying the show."

The man smiled, revealing gold-capped teeth. "We have special girls in the back. Is that what you are looking for?"

"Maybe."

"Are you not the American who was asking my colleague Pepe for a young girl?"

"Yeah . . . but I don't want to do anything illegal."

The man smiled again. "My name is Carlo. You please come with me." He motioned to the curtain. "I have several to choose from."

Well, thought Brodie, this was part of the plan—to pay one of the girls and ask her about an American amigo with a snake tattoo and see if in fact this American was a customer, and to learn whatever else she knew about the gringo—like he arrives every night at ten, has a beer, and goes into a back room to be spanked or something. But the timing was not good. Luis was still in the baño, holding his pene at the urinal, waiting for Señor Brodie to relieve him of his gun so he could get out of here.

Brodie said, "I have to take a piss. Excuse me."

He started to go around the pimp, who took hold of his arm and said, "Allow me, Señor Bow-man, to show the way. Then we go see the girls."

"Let go of my arm."

Carlo released his arm, then nodded to someone behind Brodie. Brodie glanced over his shoulder and saw the guy who'd met them at the door, crowding him from behind.

Carlo said, "Please, señor. Come with me. I know what you want. They cannot come to you, so you must go to them. You understand."

Brodie took stock of the situation and decided to go along with Carlo, duck into the baño, get his Glock, then let Carlo show him the Hen House's selection of virgins. He asked, as any customer would, "How much?"

Carlo replied, "Whatever you have left in your pocket that my friend Lupe here did not take from you."

They both laughed, and Brodie wanted to punch Carlo in the balls, pivot, and drive his foot into Lupe's groin. That would be instant gratification, but not a good long-range plan. He said, "I want a girl who speaks English."

Before Carlo could reply, Lupe said something in Spanish. Carlo laughed and explained, "He says he is happy to stay in the room with you and translate."

Even Brodie thought that was funny, but he didn't smile and insisted, "English-speaking. Maybe an older girl."

"Sí. I have Pia who watches CNN all day to learn her English. You can argue politics." He added, "She also has nice tits."

Again, this got a laugh from both men, and Brodie felt Lupe's breath on his neck. He glanced at the curtain to see if Luis had been worried enough to come look for him, but Luis was not there. He glanced around the dim room and saw that a few customers, including the MBR guys, had become interested in the conversation between the gringo, the bouncer, and the pimp.

"Come with me, señor. Por favor."

Brodie followed Carlo through the curtain; Lupe did not follow. They stepped into a small anteroom with two metal doors. The one to Brodie's left was marked <u>HOMBRES</u>, and the one directly ahead featured an orange diamond-shaped construction sign that read in English: <u>WOMEN AT WORK</u>. Funny.

Without saying anything to Carlo, Brodie opened the bathroom door. A hanging lightbulb revealed a small, single-toilet room. Luis was not there. *What the . . . ?*

Carlo said, "It is the policy of El Gallinero to reward the drivers and guides who bring us good customers. Your amigo is enjoying himself." He added, "On the house."

Brodie wasn't buying that, but he nodded. Clearly Carlo was up to something, and it didn't take a lot of CID training to figure out it wasn't something good. Brodie had no doubt he could drop-kick Carlo's bolas into his throat and own his gun, then shoot his way out of there if he had to. But he couldn't leave Luis behind, and he had no idea where Luis was.

"Señor? Perhaps you pee later?"

Brodie nodded.

Carlo insisted he go first, and he walked through the <u>WOMEN AT WORK</u> door and down a long, narrow corridor lined with wooden doors, which were numbered with a grease pencil. From behind a few of the doors Brodie heard the rhythmic squeaking of cheap spring mattresses and the occasional unconvincing moan of female pleasure. Just when you think your job sucks, you discover a worse way to make a living.

Carlo said, "Stop here."

Brodie turned to see Carlo opening a door and motioning him inside.

Brodie walked into a small, windowless room lit by a single bedside table lamp, which cast a weak glow over the pink carpet and yellow-painted cement-block walls. Rounding out the décor were a wooden chair, a sagging bed, and an assortment of frilly pillows, dolls, and stuffed animals. Creepy.

Carlo stayed in the corridor. "Have a seat, señor. Pia will be here shortly."

Brodie remained standing.

Carlo looked at him, smiled. "You will get what you came for." He closed the door, and Brodie heard a bolt slide shut.

This was not going according to plan, but it was still possible that he'd get his time in the room with an English-speaking hooker who knew Kyle Mercer. Possible, but not probable. In fact, he was actually locked in a room, deep in the bowels of a mob-controlled whorehouse, with no gun and no commo, and Luis was missing in action. On the brighter side, he was fairly sure now that this was the place where Al Simpson had seen Kyle Mercer. So this was where he'd get some answers, either from Pia or from whoever walked through that door.

He looked around the small room, remembering that even the most unlikely object could make a good weapon. Stuffed animals don't count.

There was a single drawer in the bedside table; he opened it, revealing a scattering of cosmetics and a metal nail file, which he slid into his pocket.

The only loose object in the room was the wooden chair, which he lifted and found heavy enough to crack a skull or two. As he put the chair down on the pink carpet, he noticed the electrical cord that led from the lamp to the wall socket, and he wrapped the cord around the chair leg.

Before he could do any further exploring, he heard the bolt slide and the door opened, revealing not Pia but one of the MBR-200 guys he'd seen in the lounge, complete with red beret and bandana.

The man, who was in his late twenties and muscular, shut the door and stared at Brodie. "Sit."

Brodie sat in the wooden chair and made eye contact with the man, whose face was not friendly.

The man remained standing near the door and asked, "Who are you?"

"Clark Bowman. I didn't get your name."

"What is your business here?"

"I want a woman."

"You have a woman." He let Brodie know, "You were seen with your woman at the clínica."

"We're just friends."

"You were told to leave this barrio and not return."

"Sorry. I thought this was a different barrio."

"We control this barrio and we decide who is welcome here."

"Right. I'll leave."

"I will decide that."

"Right again. Look, amigo, I just came here to have a woman, and I have money, which I can give to you if you go get Pia for me."

"There is no Pia."

"I didn't think so."

"But you may call me Pío, which means 'pious,' which I am not."

"Clark means 'clerk,' which—"

"I am going to ask you some questions, and if the answers you give me are not the same as the answers we are getting from your driver, then someone is lying, and one of you will pay for your lies. Perhaps both of you."

"My driver knows nothing about me."

The man reached behind his back and produced a gun, which Brodie recognized as a Beretta M9 with a silencer screwed into the barrel. Not good.

The man raised the gun and Brodie saw a flash, followed by the muffled sound of the bullet exiting the muzzle, then the thud of the round hitting the cement wall above his head. He felt a chip of concrete or bullet hit the back of his neck.

The man said, "The next one goes into your kneecap. The next . . . who knows? Maybe your cojones."

Brodie had no doubt that the guy meant what he said. Brodie also didn't think the Clark Bowman persona was coming through, so he tried pleading: "Please, señor, take my money and accept my apology—"

"Shut up!" The MBR guy raised the Beretta and took a two-hand aim at Brodie's right knee. "Now I will ask you an important question and you will answer in truth—or lose your knee. Comprende?"

"Sí."

"Good. Now you tell me why you look for Señor Kyle."

That was the question Brodie did not want to hear. Playing dumb would get him a bullet in the knee, and answering truthfully would probably get him a bullet in the head.

"I am waiting. I am getting angry."

"Okay . . ." So obviously the National Guard guys had dutifully reported to MBR-200, who were the real power around here. Brodie regretted his impulsive decision to flash Mercer's photo, but it had seemed like a good idea at the time. On the positive side, it had apparently shaken some apples from the tree. And here he was in the right place—though at the wrong time—looking down the barrel of a gun, answering questions about his undercover mission.

"You now piss me off." The man steadied his aim.

"Hold on, Pío. I'm looking for Captain Kyle Mercer to question him about why he deserted from the American Army."

Pío seemed to be processing that, then said, "Who say he desert?"

"The American Army says."

"He was a brave soldier."

"He was. Then he deserted. Ran away."

"He was a prisoner of the Taliban."

"Right. After he ran away."

Pío relaxed his aim a bit and asked again, "Who are you?"

Clark Bowman, insurance salesman? Not anymore. "I am an American Army investigator. I need to speak to Captain Mercer." Brodie asked, "Do you know where he is?"

"He is gone, man." Pío reminded Brodie, "It is me who asks the questions."

"Right. Fire away. No—I mean—"

"Shut up." Pío looked at Brodie, and Brodie could tell that Pío was trying to decide if he needed to kill Brodie or take him somewhere else for further questioning, or maybe turn him over to someone else for revolutionary justice.

Brodie was concerned about Luis, but to show concern would give the MBR guy another card to play. He was also concerned about Maggie Taylor sitting alone in the car not far from here. But Taylor could take care of herself, and by now she realized that Luis was overdue and that something had gone wrong in the Hen House. He hoped she had followed orders and driven off.

Brodie asked, "Can you get a message to Captain Mercer for me?"

Pío smiled for the first time. "Sí. The message will be that you are dead."

"That will not make Señor Kyle happy. He will want to talk to me."

Pío nodded. "Sí. He will want to kill you himself."

"Probably. So—"

"Shut up, man." Pío got into a firing stance again and aimed the barrel of the gun at Brodie's crotch. "Now you tell me where your lady is, or I take off your cojones."

"If I tell you, I have to kill you."

"Qué?"

Brodie rolled off the chair, pulling it with him, and thank God the lamp plug pulled out of the socket, throwing the room into pitch darkness. He saw the flash of the Beretta and heard the sound of the bullet buzz over his head as he pulled the nail file out of his pocket, shoulder-rolled toward the second flash of the barrel, and thrust the file upward into what he hoped were Pío's balls. He connected with something and heard Pío scream, then heard him crash into the wooden door behind him. Brodie stayed low and delivered left and right blows to the guy's gut and crotch until he heard and felt Pío slide down onto the floor; then he followed up with a roundhouse punch toward Pío's head that missed in the dark, then a pile driver left that hit its mark somewhere on Pío's face. He heard Pío grunt, then silence.

The gun was still in play, either in Pío's hand or on the floor, and since he didn't know, he had to kill Pío the old-fashioned way with his hands. He found Pío's head with his left hand, pulled back on his hair, and delivered a powerful punch to the man's throat, crushing his windpipe.

Brodie scrambled across the carpet and found the electrical cord, then located the socket with his hand and pushed the plug in. The lamp, which was now lying on the pink carpet, lit up, and Brodie spun toward the door.

Pío was still sitting on the floor with his back to the door, and the gun was in his hand. Pío's face was a mess but his eyes were open, staring off into space, his chest heaving as he fought for air.

Brodie stood and moved toward him, keeping his eye on the gun. He reached down to pull it out of Pío's hand, but Pío saw him and moved the gun away, then tried to raise it.

Brodie said, "Here, let me help you." He pulled the Beretta out of Pío's hand, put the silencer to the side of his head, and fired a bullet into Pío's brain.

Brodie picked the lamp up off the floor and put it back on the night-stand, then went back to the dead man and dragged him across the rug and rolled him under the bed, noticing that the nail file was embedded in his abdomen. Brodie pulled the bedsheets down to hide the body, then threw a few pillows and stuffed animals on the rug to cover the blood trail.

"Good job, Mr. Brodie," he said to himself. "Now what?"

CHAPTER 30

Brodie shut off the lamp, moved to the door, and listened. The walls of the rooms were thick concrete block, but the wooden doors were thin, and he could hear Carlo's voice in the corridor. A room door shut, then footsteps, then the sound of the heavy metal door shutting at the end of the corridor.

He considered his next move.

The mission comes first. Which meant he needed to find an English-speaking hooker who knew Señor Kyle. In fact, Señor Kyle could be in one of the rooms right now, riding the pony.

Leave no man behind. Which meant he needed to find Luis.

The safety and welfare of the troops under your command is of paramount importance. Meaning he needed to make sure Taylor was safe.

And finally, according to the Code of Conduct, it was his duty to avoid capture at all costs. Meaning he should get his ass out of there, pronto. Especially after wasting an MBR-200 guy.

Could he do all that? Worth a try.

Brodie kept the Beretta at his side as he opened the door and scanned the long, dimly lit corridor. No one there.

He slipped out of the room, closed the door behind him, and walked toward the rear of the building, past the closely spaced wooden doors, behind which were the working girls, and maybe Luis.

Brodie noticed that a few of the doors had hallway bolts—as his had—and he guessed that these were the rooms where the underage girls were locked away so they couldn't wander around.

Brodie continued his recon, and at the end of the building the corridor turned right along the back wall, then right again to form a horseshoe shape. The second long corridor was a copy of the first with about six doors on either side, for a total of about twenty-four rooms. This was quite an operation if every room had a double-occupancy turnover every half hour or so. More to the point, that was a lot of doors to open if he was going to find Luis—assuming Luis was still alive and on the premises. *Shit.*

Also, he had to find a hooker who knew Mercer. Then he had to get out of there.

He saw a metal door at the end of the corridor that was a copy of the one in the first corridor near the baño. If his mental image of this place was correct, this door would also lead back to the lounge, concealed by the curtain he'd seen.

Brodie walked quickly toward the door, which had a push bar on it. He could hear music and some voices from the lounge.

This door would be about fifteen feet from the outside exit door that he had noticed—the door through which Captain Mercer had departed upon seeing his old buddy Al Simpson. Brodie had no doubt that he could open this inner door and be through the outside door in three seconds, then put some distance between himself and the Hen House, circling around to see if Taylor was still parked up the hill. This was called a tactical retreat—as opposed to running for your life. It was the smart thing to do, but not the right thing. He had to find Luis, and maybe find a talkative hooker. If she didn't speak English, Luis could translate. If Luis was alive. Or Taylor could translate. If she was alive.

Brodie turned and retraced his steps along the corridor. He could open a door at random, or he could eavesdrop and try to determine which door might lead to Luis or to a room with a hooker on a break. The odds of finding either on the first try were about two dozen to one—not counting the room where he'd left a dead body. On that subject, it was only a matter of time before Carlo, Lupe, or maybe the other MBR guy checked out that room.

He continued slowly down the dark corridor, listening at each door. Some rooms were quiet, some not so quiet.

He heard a door open behind him and spun around. A fat, sweaty man, whom he recognized as one of the four regime guys, exited a room. He was holding his suit jacket in one hand, and he was wearing a shoulder holster. He looked at Brodie, who kept his own gun out of sight, then said something in Spanish; it seemed to Brodie that it was a question that needed a response, so he replied, "Sí," ready to paint the guy red if that was the wrong answer.

The man laughed, then turned and walked unsteadily toward the metal door. He pushed the bar and the door opened, letting in the sound of thumping dance music. As the man parted the curtain, Brodie could see the pole dancer, who had a larger audience now. The place was filling up.

He also caught a glimpse of the table where the two MBR guys had sat. It was empty. One guy was confirmed dead, but where was the other guy? Probably with Luis. The regime guy disappeared into the smoky lounge as the automatic door swung shut by itself.

Sometimes the best solution to a problem is the most direct, and sometimes it's the most unexpected. With that in mind, Brodie went to the end of the corridor and put his back to the rear wall of the building. He raised his silenced Beretta and yelled out, "Luis! Dónde estás?"

He listened, but there was no reply.

Brodie moved quickly along the rear wall to the corridor he'd first entered, and again called out, "Luis! Dónde estás?"

No reply.

But a door opened right in front of him, and the second MBR-200 guy stepped into the corridor, holding a gun. He and Brodie looked at each other for a half second before they both realized that the other guy needed to be dead. The MBR guy raised his pistol, but Brodie was already in firing position and he shot first, hitting the guy in the chest, which sent him back into the open doorway. Brodie followed up with a kick to the guy's groin, causing him to drop his gun and slump to the floor.

Brodie quickly entered the room, kicked the gun aside, and closed the door behind him.

The MBR guy was on his back, frothy blood gushing from a sucking chest wound.

Brodie stayed in a firing stance and quickly scanned the dimly lit room.

Luis was sitting on a chair in the far corner, his head resting on his chest, and Brodie thought he was dead, but then saw his chest heave.

He moved quickly to Luis, whose hands were tied to the arms of the chair with multicolored bondage scarves. Brodie lifted Luis' head by his chin and saw that he had a bruised cheek and puffy eye. "Luis!"

Luis opened his eyes and stared at Brodie.

Brodie asked, "You okay?"

Luis nodded.

The MBR guy had a sheathed knife on his belt, and Brodie took it and cut through the ties on Luis' wrists. "Okay, amigo. Can you stand?"

Again Luis nodded, then stood unsteadily.

"You okay?"

"Sí . . ."

"Can you run like hell?"

Luis took a deep breath. "Sí . . ." He looked at Brodie. "Thank you."

"Hey, I got you into this, I'll get you out."

Brodie retrieved the MBR guy's gun, which was another Beretta with a silencer, and gave it to Luis.

He took Luis' arm and led him toward the door. The MBR guy was now fighting for air and a pool of blood spread from under his back where the bullet had exited. The Rules of Land Warfare stressed that you never shot a wounded enemy combatant—you offered aid where possible. But this guy could conceivably crawl into the hallway and cause a problem. As Brodie looked at the guy, trying to decide if he should tie and gag him, he heard a soft pop, and the guy sprouted a third eye on his forehead.

Brodie looked at Luis, who kept the Beretta trained on the MBR guy to see if he needed another bullet in the head. Luis was obviously looking for payback for his battered face. Or maybe for his dead nephew, or for everyone he knew who'd been victimized by the unholy alliance of the regime, the military, and the colectivos.

Brodie said softly, "Okay. It's done. Let's go."

Luis seemed not to hear and walked over to the bed to retrieve Brodie's Glock, which he handed to him. Brodie stuck it in his waistband, but Luis was not finished collecting armaments, and he went to the foot of the bed where the MBR guy's AK-47 was propped against the footboard. He looked at the automatic rifle as though trying to decide who should get it, then handed it to Brodie.

Brodie noted that the rifle had two thirty-round banana clips duct-taped together. One was upright and loaded in the magazine well and the other was upside down, allowing for an easy flip and reload. He'd seen this makeshift configuration among militia guys before—double the fun without the hassle. Brodie pulled back the charging handle to see if a round was chambered, which it was. The rifle was on safety and Brodie moved the selector switch to full automatic. He now had the power.

Brodie stuck the silenced Beretta in his pants pocket, then motioned to Luis to stand behind him with his Beretta at the ready. Brodie opened the door and quickly scanned both ends of the corridor. A customer was exiting through the steel door near the baño, and Brodie stood motionless as the man left and the door swung shut.

He stepped into the corridor and motioned Luis to follow and to watch the rear as they headed toward the back of the building.

They turned the corner and entered the second corridor. Brodie looked at the steel door leading to the lounge and to the outside door and to escape.

Luis, who'd also figured out where that door led, whispered to Brodie, "There is a door in the lounge to the outside."

Brodie nodded. But so far the only thing he'd accomplished in the Hen House was getting himself and Luis captured, and escaping by killing two guys who had nothing to do with his mission. A civilian would beat feet and call it a night. But the mission comes before avoiding capture. He needed to find a witness—a hooker—who could tell him about Kyle Mercer.

Luis was glancing between the steel door and Brodie, as if to say, "Let's vamoose. Pronto, señor."

Brodie said to him in a whisper, "I need to find a girl who could know about the man I'm looking for."

Luis processed that, then reluctantly nodded. He hesitated, then went to a door, knocked, and said something in Spanish. An angry male voice—somewhat out of breath—came through the door.

Luis crossed the corridor and knocked on the opposite door, and again said something. No reply. This door had a closed bolt, which he quietly slid open. He then opened the door slowly, looked inside the room, and said softly, "Dios mío," then made the sign of the cross.

Luis walked into the dimly lit room and Brodie followed, closing the door behind them. The room looked similar to the first one Brodie had been taken to—yellow cement-block walls, creepy kiddie décor.

A young girl, no older than twelve, sat on the bed with her back pressed against the wall, alone. She was balled up, gripping her legs tight. She wore a pink tank top and denim shorts and her face was speckled with glitter. She eyed Brodie and the AK-47 rifle, terrified.

Brodie propped the rifle against the wall and said to Luis, "Tell her we're not here to hurt her."

Luis communicated that. The girl nodded. Luis asked, "Cuál es tu nombre?"

The girl hesitated, then said in a quiet voice, "Julieta."

Brodie said, "Ask Julieta if she knows Kyle Mercer. An American. He spends time here." He added, "Snake tattoo on his arm."

Luis asked, and she responded. Luis said to Brodie, "The American soldier. He was here."

"Cuándo?" asked Brodie.

Julieta replied and Luis translated, "About three weeks ago." Luis added, "She says he liked the older girls, so she only saw him one time in person."

Brodie asked, "Dónde?"

Julieta pointed down at the bed. "Aquí." Here.

Julieta kept speaking, and Luis translated: "He paid for her, for six hours. When he came in the room he brought her food and some money. He sat near the bed while she ate . . . just staring at the wall. He told her to rest. She fell asleep and when she woke up he was gone."

Brodie processed that. It sounded like Señor Kyle had decided to give Julieta a break from her bleak profession. Brodie had known some truly vicious men who got moralistic and self-righteous when it came to protecting children and animals. It was a bright and easy moral line to draw, and guys who were otherwise up to their eyeballs in other people's blood could at least hold something up as sacred. Maybe it kept them feeling human.

Brodie asked, "Did Señor Kyle have a favorite woman here?"

Luis asked, and then translated as she responded: "Sí. Carmen. She speaks good English and so she was one of his favorites. She is in Room Twenty-One."

"Gracias," said Brodie. He took five American twenties out of his wallet and placed them on the table next to the bed. He said to Luis, "Tell her to hide that."

Luis translated, and she took the money and looked at it before shoving it in the pocket of her shorts.

Luis said, "Maybe we can take her with us."

Brodie considered that, but rescuing Julieta was not part of the mission. "If we have to shoot our way out of here, she's likely to get hurt or killed."

Luis nodded reluctantly. Being the father of a young daughter probably made this particularly painful, but he seemed to come to terms with the fact that there was not much they could do for Julieta—or the other girls like her behind every bolted door in this godforsaken place. Calling the police was not an option in a country where the vice squad ran the vice.

Brodie retrieved the AK-47 and looked at the girl. "Gracias, Julieta."

She stared up at him and did not reply.

They left the room and closed the door, and Brodie slid back the bolt. He noted the door number marked in grease pencil—17. They continued down the hallway in the direction of the steel door leading to the lounge, and stopped at the door marked 21.

Brodie gestured to Luis, who knocked on the door and said, "Carmen, estás ahí?"

There was no response at first, then a female voice shouted, "Estoy ocupado!"

Luis turned to Brodie. "She's busy."

"Let's interrupt." He turned the knob, swung open the door, and quickly entered the room. Luis followed and closed it behind him.

The room was the same size as the others, but with a décor that skewed more adult—bondage gear hanging from hooks on the red-painted walls, a leopard-print rug, and a table draped in purple satin with some lit candles for a touch of romance.

"Hey! Qué mierda!"

An attractive, well-endowed, stark-naked brunette in her mid-twenties was standing over a full-size bed, leather paddle in hand. A middle-aged guy was bent over the bed, wearing only fuzzy pink handcuffs.

Carmen shouted again at them, gestured with the paddle. She did not seem very intimidated by two strange men bursting in with weapons. Maybe not an uncommon occurrence at the Hen House. The john, on the other hand, was looking back over his shoulder at them, wide-eyed, probably wondering if this was part of the role play as he tried to remember the safe word.

Brodie looked at the man. "Get up." Luis translated. Carmen started to protest, but the man managed to stand up and almost lost his balance as he turned to face them, hands cuffed behind his back and his pene at full attention. He blubbered something in Spanish, and Carmen told him to shut up, which he probably liked.

Luis said to Brodie, "He says his wallet is in his pants, which is on that chair."

Carmen, who was beginning to figure out that her visitors were not with the management, started to look a little more concerned. She asked in English, "What do you want?"

Brodie gestured to her client. "Tell him to get on the ground."

Carmen hesitated, then communicated that to the guy, who lay face down on the leopard-print rug.

Brodie said to Carmen, "Tie his ankles."

Carmen looked to the door. "Where is Carlo?"

"Getting an enema. Move."

Carmen walked to the wall with the hooks and took down a piece of bondage rope, then crouched next to the guy and tied his ankles together.

Brodie said, "Roll him under the bed. And tell him if he makes a sound, I'll kill him." Carmen said something to the man in Spanish and then rolled him under the bed.

Brodie spotted a pink robe hanging on a nearby chair and tossed it to Carmen. She glared at him for a moment, then put it on and sat on the edge of the bed.

She asked, "Who are you with?"

Brodie thought that was an interesting question that told him something about Petare, and maybe the whole country. Not who are you, but who do you represent? What is your tribe? Brodie replied, "The United States Army."

She didn't respond to that.

"I'm looking for an old Army friend," said Brodie. "Kyle Mercer. Someone told me that he is your friend also."

"Who told you this?"

"Doesn't matter."

Carmen shook her head. "I do not know this man."

"Five hundred dollars to help you remember."

She looked at him, then at his pockets. *Show me.*

He pulled out his wad of cash and peeled off ten fifty-dollar bills and held them up.

She looked at the cash, then said, "Maybe I do know this man."

Brodie nodded, put the money back in his pocket. She furrowed her brow.

"Information first," said Brodie.

"Money first," she insisted. "What if you cheat me?"

"What are you going to do about it? Spank me?"

She smiled. "No, man. That's extra."

Brodie gestured toward the floor under the bed. "How long are you supposed to be with this stud?"

Carmen looked at the wall clock, trying to remember, then leaned over and asked the john under the bed. Brodie heard a muffled reply, then Carmen looked up and said, "He paid for a full hour. So . . . another twenty."

"Good," said Brodie. "We may need it."

He leaned the AK against the wall and sat in a nearby chair. Luis stayed standing with his Beretta in hand and his eye on the door. The man had good instincts. And he had just killed a man. Luis had found his inner warrior.

Carmen reached over to a side table near the bed for a pack of cigarettes, shook one out, and lit it.

Brodie asked, "Is Kyle Mercer here?"

She took a drag and blew out a long trail. "No. He hasn't been here for, like, two weeks."

Two weeks. That would have been right after Al Simpson spotted him. Maybe he did get spooked.

"How long have you known him?"

Carmen thought a moment, then replied, "Maybe four months. I was dancing in the lounge, see this big gringo at a table, watching me. He was handsome. Because of my English these men usually are sent to me, and he was. So we come here, spend some time, he pays me and leaves. Next night, I'm dancing in the lounge, he's there again. But this time he's talking to the colectivo guys. You see them out there? Gang guys?"

Brodie nodded. Best not to go into detail on that subject.

"Yeah, you don't fuck with them. So he's talking to them, and I ask Carlo about it. It was weird for a yanqui to be talking to them, but . . . Carlo told me to mind my own business. So I did. And then Señor Kyle pays to see me again, and he starts to see me, like, two or three times a week. At first he never says much. Seems like . . . his head is somewhere else. Always thinking. Then he starts to talk a little—"

A man started shouting in the hallway just outside their door. Luis walked over to the door and put his body against it and listened. A second voice could be heard. It was Lupe. They were having an argument.

Carmen stared at the door, worried.

Luis turned to Brodie and whispered, "Customer is unhappy with his girl. Says she is sick."

There was a scuffle in the hallway; then the voices died down as a door slammed shut.

Carmen shook her head, muttered something in Spanish, took another drag. She said, "They shouldn't make the sick girls work."

Brodie thought that sounded reasonable. He also thought this place and this country had truly descended into hell. There was no mercy here, and life—like the national currency—had no value.

Brodie checked the wall clock. There was a lot of activity in this place, there was no way to lock the doors, and now two of the twenty-four rooms had corpses in them. This was like a battlefield interrogation of a civilian— you wanted to cut through the bullshit quickly and get to the information that will save your life or serve your mission before the bad guys find you and try to kill you.

Brodie focused on Carmen. "What did Señor Kyle talk about?"

Carmen watched the closed door for a moment, and then turned back to Brodie. She looked nervous, took a drag. "I told you, not too much . . . but after a couple weeks he tells me he was in the American Army, and he was taken prisoner in Afghanistan. And now he is somehow working with the colectivo, but he does not give me details. And out in the lounge I see him sometimes talking to the colectivo guys, and one time even with the regime guys, those pigs in the suits. I hear one or two of them call him 'camarada.' Comrade. I don't know, just seemed weird, this yanqui soldier just shows up out of nowhere and now he's a regular of this place and maybe an amigo of the Chavistas?"

Was Comrade Kyle a commie? Brodie doubted it. Mercer was doing what he had to do to get in with these people, for whatever reason. At least, that was Brodie's assumption. Then again, who knew what two years in Taliban captivity could do to fuck up your head and your allegiances?

Carmen was looking at him. "So you're an Army guy too?"

"Yes."

"You with Señor Kyle in the war?"

"Different war. Same shit."

Carmen gave him a look. She finished her cigarette, stubbed it in an ashtray on the table, and lit up another.

Brodie asked, "Did you ever overhear a conversation between Señor Kyle and any of these colectivo or regime people?"

"No . . . but one night, he's with me and we do what we do, and after, he tells me he needs the room and I need to leave. I say okay. This is not something we are supposed to do with clients, but Señor Kyle is different and I understand this. I get dressed, leave to go to the lounge. And on my way down the hall, I pass this old guy I been seeing around lately. Dark-skinned guy. Last few weeks I notice him, sits at the bar alone sometimes, doesn't say much, never had him as a customer but a couple of the other girls did. So I pass him in the hall and he just glare at me and then I turn and I see him go into my room. I go to the lounge, I ask Carlo, who the fuck is that guy anyway? Carlo tells me to shut the fuck up and mind my own business. But I am curious, so I sit at the bar and ask Amando, the bartender, and he says this guy is an officer in the army, a general. Amando recognizes him from the TV and newspapers. General Gomez."

That sort of surprised Brodie. A general. But as Brodie had suspected, Mercer was a regular here and used this place as a kind of hideout and hangout. Rick's Café with hookers. But more than that, it was a base of operations of some kind for Captain Mercer, and he had apparently insinuated himself with the local power. What the hell was he up to?

Brodie asked, "Did you ask Señor Kyle about his visitor?"

She shook her head. "He wouldn't tell me if I did."

More footsteps in the hallway. Carmen stared at the door to the room, then at Brodie's AK leaning against the wall. She asked, "Where you get that?"

"Dick's Sporting Goods."

Carmen seemed confused by that. She was now looking at Luis' battered face as he started pacing nervously between the door and the far wall, and she was putting together the fact that these two guys had already raided the Hen House before coming into this room.

She said, "If Carlo find out I'm talking to a yanqui about Señor Kyle, he's gonna kill me."

"I won't tell if you won't." His witness was getting jumpy. Time to cut to the chase. "Do you know where Señor Kyle is now?"

She nodded. "Sí. I went with him."

Brodie leaned forward in his chair. *Jackpot.* Witnesses often bury the lede. "Where did you go with him?"

"The jungle."

"What jungle?"

Carmen shrugged, took another drag. "I don't know, the fucking jungle."

"When was this?"

"Same night as General Gomez, who leave thirty minutes after he comes. Then Señor Kyle comes out and tells me he paid Carlo to take me on a trip for a week. Sometimes I have clients, you know, like, rich guys, who pay extra to take me to a hotel or wherever overnight. But he says a week, we're leaving Caracas. Won't tell me where."

"And what did you say?"

"It's not for me to say. Guy wants to pay for seven days, twenty-four hours, and you say no? Then I'd be fucked. Also, you know, I liked him."

She said that last part as if her opinion of Señor Kyle had since changed. Brodie asked, "So you went to the jungle?"

"Sí. We fly. I collect my things, we get in a car with a driver and go to La Carlota Airport."

"Where's that?"

"It's, like, in Caracas. Not far, small airport. The official name is Francisco de Miranda."

Brodie nodded. That was at least one hunch confirmed.

She continued, "We got to the airport. I'm excited, I never leave Caracas before. We get on a little plane with a pilot and he takes off. I don't know where the fuck we're going and Señor Kyle is very quiet."

Señor Kyle was sounding like the strong, silent type. "What kind of plane was it?"

Carmen shrugged. "Like a plane. A little plane."

"Jet? Propeller? One engine? Two?"

Carmen thought for a moment. "Two propellers."

"How many seats?"

"Six, I think."

"Make of the plane? An airline name?"

She shrugged. "Why would I give a shit about that?"

"Good point. Continue, por favor."

"Okay. So we are flying for maybe an hour and a half, and we land in Ciudad Bolívar."

Brodie turned to Luis. "You know this place?"

Luis stopped pacing and nodded. "It is a city in the south."

Carmen continued, "And then we go to the airport building, and there are no people there at night. Then some airport worker comes and gets us, and we get on another plane. Smaller than the first one. And we take off again. Fly for maybe an hour. And we land in this little village."

"Did you land at an airport? Landing strip?"

"There was a strip of dirt to land. There was some little huts or something, dirt roads. And in the village was all these native people. It was fucking weird."

"Did you get the name of the village?"

Carmen looked at him. "Why you want to know?"

"I want to find my friend." Brodie repeated, "Did you get the name of this village?"

"No."

"If you can give me a good description of the village, I can give you another hundred."

Carmen thought for a moment. "It was near a small river. And we stayed the night in a guesthouse. The next day I see it better. Like a bunch of huts with straw roofs, in this grassland that was on the edge of the jungle. And I saw this big fucking mountain. Bigger than the hills around Caracas, and this mountain has just a big flat top. Fucking weird. And the side was flat too, like a big rock wall. And one of the native guys who speak Spanish, he sees me looking at it and tells me on the other side of the mountain is Salto Ángel."

"What's that?"

"Angel Falls," said Carmen. "This is a famous sight, the highest waterfall in the whole world. And I realize this village must be a place that visitors come to see the waterfall, because there was a wooden sign that says 'Bienvenido' in Spanish and also in English says 'Welcome.'"

Well, this was something. Señor Kyle had taken his favorite hooker to a well-known spot in the south of the country, and now she was back here in Caracas to tell all about it. This was the kind of break that cops pray for— then say it was just great detective work. Which in this case it was.

Brodie asked, "How long did you stay there?"

"Just the morning. Señor Kyle gets me from the hut, we walk to the little river. Then we get on a skinny boat with a motor. Two native guys get in the boat, one got a rifle. Señor Kyle tells me he's going to blindfold me. I ask him what's going on, he says not to worry. I am going to be doing what I do in Caracas, just somewhere else. So I'm thinking, I guess I gotta fuck these weird little native guys? Okay." She laughed. "So he blindfolds me and we go."

"How long were you on the river?"

She thought about it, shrugged. "I don't know, man. Hard to say. It felt like a long time. Maybe one hour. But then we stop and he takes off the blindfold. We are deep in the jungle now, just trees everywhere. We get off the boat and walk through the jungle, maybe fifteen minutes, and we get to this place with wood and straw huts under the trees." She chain-lit another cigarette, stared thoughtfully into space, then continued, "There is more of the natives around, but now I'm seeing a few Venezuelan dudes too. Rough-looking guys. They got guns. Señor Kyle takes me to a big hut with maybe ten beds, tells me to rest. I can see there are other women sleeping in there. I take a nap, but I wake up to shooting noise, I jump out of bed and run out of the hut and I run into some guy, young Venezuelan guy with a big gun. I ask about the shooting, he laughs. He says the boys are training, go back inside. So I go, and I see the other women in the hut now are awake, six others. I talk to them. One is from Caracas, four are from Ciudad Bolívar, and one from a village. They tell me we are in a military training camp, and that the men will come in and pick a girl whenever they want and take her back to their hut. The girls say they supposed to get paid by their pimps when they go back to where they came from, but they been there for weeks and so they don't even know if they will get paid."

Or, thought Brodie, ever get out of there.

Carmen continued, "Later Señor Kyle takes me to his hut and tells me to stay there, I am only for him. I felt bad for the other girls, a couple of nights a group of the guys did a bunch of blow and they kept the girls busy all night." Carmen laughed bitterly.

Brodie heard voices coming down the hallway again. It sounded like Carlo, with another client. Carmen was supposed to be with her guy for another ten minutes, but there was no lock on the door, and if Carlo or anyone else decided to open it Brodie had a problem that only Señor Beretta could solve. More likely, Carlo might decide to check in on how Pío's interrogation was going. Time to wrap this up.

"How many men were there in the camp?"

She shrugged. "Twenty? Thirty? Guys would come in and out. They did everything in shifts, including fucking." She laughed again. "People were always on guard around the camp."

"Venezuelans? Or natives?"

"The natives come just to bring food and to cook and do other shit, but all the guys there with guns were Venezuelans or Colombians."

"What kind of weapons did they have?"

"Big guns." She eyed the AK-47 propped against the wall. "Like that."

"What were they wearing?" Aside from big smiles when they were getting laid.

She replied, "What do you call these . . . like soldier clothes?"

"Camouflage?"

Carmen nodded.

"Did you see trucks? Jeeps?"

She shook her head, finished her cigarette, and stubbed it out. "Couldn't get a truck through there, unless there was some road I don't see."

"And they were training?"

She nodded. "Someplace away from the huts, I didn't see it but I hear it. Shooting, people giving orders, a few times I hear an explosion."

Captain Mercer's Summer Camp for Psychos. Get high, get laid, and blow shit up. Sounded fun. Brodie said, "So you stayed there a week."

Carmen's face darkened. "He wants me to stay longer." She hesitated, then said, "One night I go out of the hut to take a piss, and this Colombian guy who's high as fuck just attacks me, gets me against a tree and . . . it's over quick, he leaves. And I . . . I tell Señor Kyle because it felt wrong and I thought . . ." She trailed off, looked down at the floor. "You don't get made to feel special in this job, señor. So when someone does that, it's nice. And I thought maybe he would . . . protect me."

"Did he?"

"He told me not to worry about it. So I go to sleep. And the next morning, Señor Kyle is not in the bed. I go outside, to the clearing . . . He's there, the Colombian guy. Hanging from a tree. His body beat to shit, his . . ." Carmen touched her stomach. "Things were just hanging out of him."

Kyle Mercer was an officer and a gentleman with a soft spot for old Army buddies and child prostitutes. And this was the same man who cut off heads, maybe tortured a CIA officer to death, and, as per Carmen, defended her honor by disemboweling her rapist. Or more likely Mercer was defending his own honor and his position as alpha male. Brodie thought that an insanity plea at court-martial would work well.

Carmen continued, "I tell him I wanna leave. He don't understand, says he was just making sure it don't happen again. He thinks I'm gonna be fuckin' grateful or something." She shook her head. "He tries to convince me, he tells me it's bad in Caracas, here I can live in peace. I say, what kind of peace is this? This is when I know that the one-week thing was bullshit, he wanted to keep me there, and I am afraid he won't let me leave. But the next day he tells me he is going back to Caracas and I can come. So I fly back. The other girls stay. He brings me here. And that is the last I seen him."

Brodie asked, "And you think he went back to the jungle?"

"I think . . . yes, he seem happy there."

Right. Happy to be where the law of the jungle is his law. Captain Mercer had probably read Heart of Darkness twice, and seen Apocalypse Now ten times. Brodie wondered just how much of the well-trained career Army officer was left in him.

Beyond that, it was a major security breach to let Carmen return to Caracas, even if she had been blindfolded for the critical last leg of the journey. Brodie thought back to how Mercer had spared Al Simpson, and how that act of mercy led directly to the CID being on his tail. And now this, letting a witness who spoke perfect English return to the Hen House where he'd already been spotted, instead of keeping her prisoner—or killing her. Señor

Kyle must have really liked her. Which was too bad for him, because this señorita was going to lead Brodie and Taylor right to him. *You fucked up, Captain.* They all do in the end.

Brodie said, "I need more description of the village you flew into."

She seemed annoyed or impatient, but replied, "It was just this little place with huts . . . but it had this tourist guesthouse. Only a few people. I think the village is just for tourists, but there was no tourists so it was just us and the natives."

"What were the huts made out of?"

Carmen thought a moment. "Stone or mud or some shit."

"Color?"

Carmen thought. "Yellow, I think. Maybe like they were painted."

"Any churches? Stores?"

She shook her head, then lit another cigarette and glanced again at the door. "We done?"

"Almost. Tell me about the trip down the river."

"I was blindfolded."

"Try harder."

Carmen shot him a look, then thought for a moment. "There was a lot of turns in the river. It took maybe an hour? Maybe longer."

"Were you going upriver or downriver? With the flow or against it?"

"Fuck, man, I don't know."

"You said the boat had a motor. Was the motor running the whole time?"

Carmen considered this. "Sí. Almost the whole time."

Brodie nodded. They were probably going against the current. "When the boat stopped, did you get out on the left bank or the right bank?"

Carmen thought. "Right."

"And how long was the walk from the river to the camp?"

"I told you, maybe fifteen minutes."

"Was there a path?"

"There was fucking trees."

"Palms? Flowering plants?"

"There was palm trees in the grassland, but when we go in the jungle I don't see them. I see lot of big trees, a lot of . . . like, vines and some nice flowers, all different colors."

"What else did you see?"

"Nothing."

"Think."

She thought for a minute. "Okay, yeah. So there was, like, a little stream close by where there was no trees, and I could see there was another one of those flat mountains."

"Maybe it was the same mountain."

She shook her head. "This one was different. It was more green, trees up the side. Was hard to tell how far away it was because it was so big."

"Did anyone say why these men were in this camp? What they were training for?"

Carmen looked at him. "They were training to kill people."

It sounded like Carmen needed an education in the five W's. Brodie asked, "Who were they training to kill, and why? Did Señor Kyle talk about it?"

She shook her head. "He don't talk to me about the camp."

"Did you ask him? Or ask anyone?"

"I don't want to know."

Right. The less you know, the better. But Carmen had asked Carlo and the bartender questions about Señor Kyle, and about Señor Kyle's guest at the Hen House. So Carmen was the curious type, and Brodie was sure she knew more than she was telling. He was also sure that Carmen had been honest with him so far, and she wasn't making stuff up for the money. If he had ten more minutes with her, he could get the last piece of the puzzle: What was Kyle Mercer training for in that camp? But time had run out. So he'd have to answer that question himself when he found the camp, and found Captain Mercer.

Meanwhile, he now had some Intel—a city, Ciudad Bolívar, a tourist village, a boat trip upriver, and some distinct topographical features—and that might be enough to get Kyle Mercer's general location.

Brodie stood. "Gracias, señorita. You've been very helpful." He handed her the five hundred dollars and added another hundred to it. "For your retirement fund."

Carmen looked at the bills, stood, then shoved the cash in the drawer of the night table. She stubbed her cigarette in the ashtray and turned to Brodie. "I think Señor Kyle is not really your amigo."

"Correct," said Brodie. "He is not."

"You gonna kill him? That why the Army sent you?"

"I'm just going to talk to him."

Carmen thought that was funny. "Good luck. He's a crazy guy. But maybe all you American soldiers are crazy."

"Maybe." Brodie walked over to the wall and took a couple more lengths of bondage rope from the hook. He said to Carmen, "Put your hands out."

"I do the tying, papi."

"Not today."

Carmen looked at him, and then at Luis, who held the Beretta at his side. She looked back at Brodie. "No."

He explained, "This will look better for you when Lupe or Carlo finds you."

Carmen got that and brought her hands out in front of her. Brodie tied a secure knot around both her wrists. He said, "On the ground."

She lay down on her back, and Brodie used the other piece of rope to tie her ankles. He looked down at her. "You've got five minutes left with your guy. Talk dirty to him."

Carmen said something in Spanish that sounded colorful and not very nice as Brodie rolled her under the bed next to the john. The poor guy definitely wasn't getting his money's worth, but maybe they'd comp him a drink at the bar.

Brodie nodded to Luis, then picked up the AK and looked at the door. Well, he'd freed himself, rescued Luis, and gotten good Intel about the location of Kyle Mercer. All that was left to make this a perfect night was to get out of there alive.

CHAPTER 31

Brodie and Luis left Room 21 and turned right toward the steel door at the end of the corridor that would put them in the lounge—about fifteen feet from the side door that led out of the brothel.

Brodie handed Luis the other Beretta. "Keep them concealed but accessible."

Luis stuck one of the Berettas in his belt, under his suit jacket, and the other in his pants pocket. Brodie had his Glock stuck in his waistband beneath his untucked shirt. Trying to exit with stealth was the best option, but he wasn't willing to part with the AK-47. He checked that the selector was on full automatic, then held the rifle along his left side, keeping it out of view of most of the customers in the lounge. If the wrong person didn't look up at the wrong time—maybe if all eyes were on the pole dancer, and if these guys' brains were clouded by alcohol, and their dicks were doing their thinking—this could work.

They reached the steel door. Brodie said to Luis, "We will walk quickly, but not too quickly, to that side door exit. Don't look at anyone, but be aware of your surroundings. If someone yells anything, pull your gun. We're not talking our way out of this one."

Luis nodded.

"Ready?"

"Sí."

Brodie pushed open the door, and a blast of loud music and talking filled the quiet corridor. Brodie parted the curtain and walked into the dim, smoky lounge.

A different pole dancer was now onstage directly in front of them, surrounded by a small audience. Out of the corner of his eye Brodie could see some activity at the bar, but he turned toward the side door and headed directly for it. Luis followed.

Brodie was less than ten feet from the door when he heard someone shout over the music, "Hey! Where the fuck you going?"

It sounded like Carlo. Brodie quickly turned his head toward the bar. Carlo was standing with his back against the bar, a cigarette in his hand. He looked confused. A few customers were sitting on stools on either side of him, and they now turned to see what was bothering Carlo. The regime men were still at their table, smoking cigars and knocking back rum. They too looked over at Brodie and Luis.

The bouncer, Lupe, was standing near the front door and must have spotted the AK. He suddenly pulled his six-shooter from its holster.

Brodie pivoted toward Lupe and raised the AK, bracing the butt of the rifle against his left shoulder as he wrapped his fingers around the grip and squeezed the trigger. The rifle had a powerful recoil and pulsed against his body as he fired a line of bullets across the lounge at Lupe, raking him across his chest and putting a few rounds in the wall behind him as the man went down.

The pole dancer screamed, then jumped down from the stage and ran toward the back. Customers—most of whom were no strangers to gunfire—dived for cover beneath the tables, and a few guys at the bar jumped off their stools and dashed to the front door, or dived over the bar, while a few ran for the door that led to the baño.

Luis had drawn his Beretta as the four regime men drunkenly fumbled with their shoulder holsters. Luis, without hesitation, started squeezing off rounds, hitting one man in the gut who toppled backward over his plastic chair and onto the floor. Another guy jumped to his feet and managed to get his gun out of its holster before Luis put two rounds through his chest. The man collapsed and took the table with him, sending bottles and glasses shattering across the floor. The two remaining guys hit the deck.

Luis stopped firing but kept his Beretta raised as Brodie aimed high over the bar and squeezed off another burst, just to make sure everyone who wasn't already on the floor got the message. He ruined a few Miss Venezuela pinups, exploded a neon beer sign, and put a good dent in the Hen House's liquor supply. The AK's distinctive pop-pop-pop brought back bad memories of Fallujah.

The dance music suddenly stopped and the lounge was quiet except for the beat of the AK. Brodie eased off on the trigger and quickly scanned the room for Carlo, but no one was left standing, and in the dim light he couldn't make out who was who among the people crouched for cover near the bar. He kept the AK raised as he backed toward the side door and shouted to Luis, "Go!" Luis pushed open the door and exited. Brodie fired a burst into the ceiling for fun, then ducked out.

They ran along the side of the Hen House toward the road. There were no streetlights, but the parked cars were starting their engines as their customers fled from the bordello. Just another night at the Hen House.

As they cleared the side of the brothel Brodie heard a nearby gunshot, and he dropped to his knee and aimed his AK at the open front door, but the shooter took cover behind the door. Brodie held for a moment, took aim. Carlo popped out with his pistol raised and Brodie fired a three-round burst into his chest. The man's body jerked violently and crumpled in a heap in the open doorway.

Brodie's mag was empty so he ejected it, flipped it, and slapped in the other one that was duct-taped to it, then chambered a round.

He heard the pop of silencer shots behind him and glanced at Luis, who had just nailed a man coming out the side door. The door swung back on the body now lying in the doorway.

Brodie motioned Luis forward and they ran toward the street. Brodie glanced at the front door of the Hen House as they moved but couldn't see any activity.

By now all the drivers who were parked haphazardly in front of the brothel had either taken off or taken cover in their cars. Brodie and Luis ran through the maze of cars along the road, headed uphill toward where he hoped Taylor was still parked, though he couldn't see the Mitsubishi in the dark.

Just ahead of them a car window exploded in a hail of gunfire, and Brodie and Luis hit the ground. Brodie heard pistol fire coming from up the road, and he hoped it was Taylor. The car with the shattered window, a big black sedan, peeled off down the road, and another car took off behind it. Now they were exposed.

Brodie got to his feet and ran in the direction of the Mitsubishi, which was now just visible up the hill. Luis, apparently not used to physical activity, lagged behind. To cover him, Brodie pivoted with the AK as they ran, firing short bursts at the Hen House, keying off his white tracer rounds to zero in on the dark building. He pegged one guy, and saw another duck back inside.

As they got closer to the Mitsubishi, Brodie saw Taylor taking cover behind the open driver's-side door. She fired a few rounds past them as they approached the car.

"Get in!" shouted Brodie.

Taylor squeezed off another two rounds, then jumped in the driver's seat. Brodie heard the soft pop of Luis' Beretta behind him; then it sounded like the mag was empty, and Luis tossed the pistol in the road and drew his other gun.

From the bottom of the slope, a white pickup truck roared uphill past the Hen House, its high beams on. Apparently the colectivo had been alerted and the posse was arriving. Brodie dropped to one knee and took a firing stance.

Luis was running past him, out of breath, and Brodie called out, "Take the back seat and tell Taylor to turn the car around!"

He heard the rat-a-tat of automatic fire as the oncoming truck weaved between the remaining parked cars in front of the brothel and sped toward them. A few tracer rounds streaked uphill and hit the road just short of Brodie's position.

Brodie aimed the AK a foot above the headlights and fired a burst. The pickup lurched to its left and almost drove off the edge of the ridgeline before correcting. The vehicle kept coming. He fired again, then turned and ran toward the Mitsubishi just as Taylor had swung it around to face uphill. He jumped in the passenger seat and Taylor gunned it.

The road bent along the curve of the hill, and Taylor rocketed along the bumpy road at full speed. They were heading east, which was basically the opposite direction from where they wanted to go. But they needed to lose the pickup truck, which was still on their tail.

Taylor kept her headlights off, relying on the few points of light below to see where the edge of the road was in order to avoid taking the express route down the hill.

Brodie checked the rearview as another burst of automatic fire came at them from a guy riding in the truck's flatbed. Brodie heard a shot ding off their rear bumper, and another went through the rear windshield and then out through the roof just above Brodie's head.

It was a tight curve along the ridgeline; as Taylor sped up they lost sight of their pursuer, and the road began to flatten out toward the top of the hill.

Suddenly a motorbike shot out of an alley and into the road just ahead of them. Taylor instinctively swerved to avoid hitting the biker, who then swung toward them, drew a pistol, and fired two shots at their windshield. The first missed and the second punched through the top of the windshield between Brodie and Taylor.

Taylor kept her speed up and they whipped past the biker as he swung around and took after them.

Taylor made a sharp left turn at full speed onto a smaller road running downhill, and the car skidded perilously close to the wall of a building, but she cut the wheel and corrected. Brodie reminded himself that when it came to outrunning armed crazies, this wasn't Taylor's first rodeo. He also remembered that too many of these barrio roads dead-ended.

Brodie rolled down his window, turned in his seat, and leaned out with his AK-47. On the rear driver's side, Luis too was leaning out with his Beretta.

The biker was maybe twenty yards behind them, his single head-beam lighting up the narrow road. Brodie saw three flashes from the biker's pistol, and thought he heard one impact on the car.

Brodie took aim with his AK and squeezed off a short burst. He was firing uphill at a small moving target, and the AK tended to ride up on automatic, so he aimed low, and his second burst connected. The bike spun out in the narrow road and smashed into the side of a building, sending the biker airborne. Brodie was about to relax when he spotted the pickup roaring down the road after them, but it had to swerve around the bike in the road, which allowed them to get more distance as Taylor took a few more tight turns in the maze-like barrio roads. The Mitsubishi handled better than it looked.

Brodie sat back down in the passenger seat and kept his eyes on the sideview mirror. He couldn't see the pickup, but he heard the roar of its diesel engine behind them, reverberating off the dense buildings as they navigated the winding barrio streets. He checked the AK's mag and saw three rounds left.

They hit another straightaway and Taylor gassed it, then looked over at Brodie. "Everybody okay?"

Luis said from the back, "Sí, señora."

Brodie said, "No Purple Hearts today."

She asked, "What happened?"

"We were being chased by armed men."

"I mean in the bordello, asshole."

"Mission accomplished."

"You got Mercer?"

"No, but I know where he is."

"Where?"

"I'll tell you later." He added, "Good driving."

Taylor made a few more random turns, and Brodie could no longer see or hear the truck behind them.

He said to Taylor, "Try to avoid dead-end streets."

"What the fuck do you think I've been doing?"

"Right."

Taylor approached a wide road that looked like it would take them out of the barrio. She turned onto the four-lane road, put on her headlights, and sped downhill. The shanty barrio houses began to thin out, giving way to abandoned industrial buildings and long stretches of dense forest that climbed up the hills on either side of the road.

Brodie asked Luis, "Do you know where we are?"

"Sí. The other side of the hills. East of Caracas. If we head north toward the mountains, we will hit a highway that will take us back to the city."

Brodie looked in the rearview. No sign of the pickup, or any other vehicle in pursuit. He wondered how territorial these gangs were, and if they would cross into a rival gang's turf to pursue them. But no matter how much distance they put between themselves and Petare, they still might have to contend with the police, the National Guard, the Venezuelan Army, or SEBIN. A gangland shooting was no big thing, but Luis had plugged two regime guys.

Taylor looked at Brodie as she sped down the road. "Did you satisfy your ego and your macho male fantasy?"

"I did."

"We almost died."

"Still might."

Brodie took out his smartphone and checked his GPS. There was no cell service, and they were approaching the edge of the offline maps he'd downloaded at the hotel, but it looked like they were coming to a turnoff that would snake north through the hills and link up with the east-west highway that ran along the base of the coastal mountains and back toward Caracas. "There's a turnoff coming up. Take it."

She nodded.

Brodie noticed Luis' bejeweled cross swinging from the rearview mirror in front of the bullet hole in the windshield.

Luis saw where Brodie was looking and said, "Jesus protected us tonight."

Should he put that in his report? Probably not.

Brodie took the cross from the mirror and turned to hand it to Luis, who kissed it, made the sign of the cross, and put it in his pocket.

Brodie saw that Luis held the Beretta in his lap, and was now staring off into space. The man had just killed at least four men in the span of twenty minutes, and chances were they were his first kills. Brodie remembered the first time he'd killed a man, an insurgent during a firefight in a small town outside of Baghdad. He saw the body afterward—a young guy, not older than seventeen, his organs punched out of fist-sized holes in his back from Brodie's M4. It rattled him. Then the next time it got a little easier. After a while, it just became a good day's work.

But that was a war he'd volunteered for. Luis hadn't asked for any of this. Luis had just picked up the wrong people at the airport.

Brodie said to him, "This is almost over, amigo."

Luis made eye contact with him. "Sí."

Brodie looked ahead at the dark road, and the black wall of trees around them. They were really in the middle of nowhere now, in a car pocked with bullet holes and with shattered windshields. This battle-scarred wreck was going to attract attention, even in Caracas, so they would need to ditch it at some point before arriving back at the hotel.

As they drove, Taylor asked again, "What happened in there?"

"I think they were waiting for us." Brodie added, "Maybe I shouldn't have shown Mercer's photo to the National Guard guys."

"Your first mistake."

"Right. Then the a-hole I spoke to in the Club of the Damned probably called the Hen House."

"Second mistake."

"Then I show up there with Luis—"

"Third mistake."

"Then I see two colectivo guys and four regime guys, and everyone's packing heat except me, so—"

"You decided to stay." She added, "You're an idiot."

Luis came to Brodie's defense. "He is very brave, señora."

"He's fucking crazy." She admonished, "Don't encourage him."

"Sí, señora."

Brodie continued, "So, as per plan, Luis goes to the baño . . . You remember that scene in The Godfather? Well, it doesn't always work out."

"Apparently not."

"On the other hand, I got hold of an AK-47—"

"How?"

"The usual way. I killed the owner."

Taylor stayed quiet for a while, then said, "Give me the details later. Just tell me about mission accomplished."

"Right. So Luis and I secure a cooperating witness. Carmen, nice girl, speaks idiomatic English with lots of F-bombs, and we hit the jackpot. Carmen is Señor Kyle's special lady and she once accompanied him to his hideout in the jungle."

Taylor glanced at Brodie as she drove, but said nothing.

Brodie related his conversation with Carmen, and Taylor did not interrupt or critique his interrogation methods, understanding that Brodie's time had been limited and that Carmen, like Al Simpson, was not expecting that anyone would ever be asking her for a detailed recounting of her journey and surroundings.

When Brodie finished his briefing, Taylor nodded and said, "That should be enough info for someone—a team—to go find him."

"Right." He added, "We are the team."

She looked at him. "No. We are not."

Brodie motioned toward Luis in the rear seat. "We will discuss later."

Luis, who was listening, said, "Señora, I never did get to use the baño. Perhaps you could pull over?"

"Of course." She found an area with a dirt shoulder and pulled off the road. She kept the car running but turned off the headlights.

As Luis climbed out of the car, Brodie said to him, "Take your time."

"Sí, señor." He shut the door and walked toward some bushes behind the car.

Brodie and Taylor sat in silence for a moment. Then Taylor said, "This is no longer about us apprehending a fugitive. This is now a paramilitary operation, and it is out of our hands."

"We just need to locate the fugitive. If we do that, and if we assess it's going to take more resources than we have at our disposal to successfully apprehend him, we'll get help."

Taylor didn't ask him to define what kind of help he was referring to, and if she had he wouldn't have had an answer. This was a hostile nation without any security arrangement with the United States. But Brodie thought that Worley might have some assets at his disposal. And if not, Brodie would do what he'd always done—wing it.

But Taylor had a better idea. "We have Special Ops units in Colombia."

Right. Chasing Marxist guerrillas and drug cartels for the Colombian government.

"JSOC could insert a team—a Delta team—into the Venezuelan jungle to apprehend Mercer."

Taylor was coming perilously close to a logical solution.

She continued, "That would be a very fitting type of justice."

"Right." But Brodie wanted to be the one—with Maggie Taylor's help—to bring Kyle Mercer to justice. He didn't need or want an already over-hyped, star-studded Delta team to get the credit. This was a CID operation. His own ego, he assured himself, had nothing to do with it. He was going to do this for the CID and for Colonel Dombroski who could take the credit. He wouldn't object, however, to a letter of commendation, maybe even some public recognition for finding and arresting the famous deserter Kyle Mercer—Brodie's face and voice disguised, of course.

"Brodie?"

"Right. Good thinking." He added, "But we—you and I—need to locate that camp before a team is inserted into Venezuela. I'm not going to file a report based on my interview with a prostitute and expect the Pentagon to act on it." He reiterated, "We need to get down there and get a fix on this camp."

Taylor thought about that and nodded reluctantly. "All right . . . I see your point."

"Good." He thought about Mercer's armed camp, whatever it was. It was interesting but not altogether surprising that Captain Mercer would recreate some version of the rugged combat training and maybe even the camaraderie he had left behind on the Afghan frontier. But the question was, why? Captain Mercer could tell him, and also tell him why he'd deserted. That remained the big question.

Taylor said, "Our chances of actually finding the camp are not good. The forests and jungles in the south of Venezuela are massive."

"We have Carmen's travel itinerary to go by."

"For a man who doesn't believe his superior officers are being straight with him, you put a lot of credence in the paid testimony of a prostitute."

"She seemed sincere."

"I guess we'll find out." She asked, "Should we call the boss now?"

"I need at least two drinks to talk to him."

"Brodie—"

"Later. I have to think about how to make Dombroski think it's his idea that we go into the jungle to find Mercer."

"You're a manipulator."

"I manipulate the brass, but I'm straight with my peers and subordinates."

She looked at him. "I believe that. But it's still not right to withhold information from your superior officer."

"That works both ways."

She didn't reply to that. After a moment she said, "We do need to call Worley since he's got his pilot on standby." She opened the glove box and handed him the sat phone.

"Right." He leaned out the window to get clear sky and dialed Worley.

As promised, the man picked up immediately. "Worley."

"Brodie."

"Still alive?"

"Sorry to disappoint."

"You need a plane?"

"Not tonight."

There was a pause, then Worley said, "I'm sure he skipped town. And you should do the same."

"I'll take that up with Quantico."

"You should. So did you stake out this brothel? Go inside? What happened?"

"After I make my report to Quantico, I'll brief you."

"All right . . . but—"

"Meanwhile, Luis is looking forward to his trip to America." He added, "I need visas for him and his family tomorrow. This is not negotiable."

"Everything is negotiable. When you brief me, we'll negotiate." He asked, "Where are you? And when can we meet?"

Brodie replied, "I'm lost in the woods. We can meet tomorrow."

"Tonight."

Brodie ignored that and said, "Look, there might be some heat on us. So we're lying low for a while."

"What kind of heat?"

"Well . . . unfortunately, when we got to the brothel, a shoot-out started, and—"

"A *shoot-out*?"

"Right. And two or three regime guys got hit, and some other people, and, you know, everyone blames everything on the Americans, so—"

"What the hell happened? Did you kill anyone? What the—?"

"Just giving you a heads-up, Brendan, in case you hear about this from an unreliable source."

"For God's sake, man, did you kill anyone?"

"'Kill' is an ugly word."

Brodie listened to Worley taking a deep breath; then Worley said in a controlled voice, "Destroy your fake passports, and put the sat phone, the Glocks, and everything else I gave you in the briefcase and leave it in a safe deposit box at your hotel. Someone will retrieve everything tonight or tomorrow." He added, "We have an understanding with the hotel."

"Okay." But Brodie had no intention of leaving anything at the hotel for Worley to reclaim. Especially the Glocks.

"I strongly suggest that you and your colleague take the first available flight out of Caracas tonight. Tomorrow morning latest."

Brodie didn't think anyone at the Hen House could possibly ID him or Taylor—and anyone who could was dead. There was, however, the security camera. Also, the colectivo guy who'd roughed up Luis had probably checked out his ID and maybe taken it or passed it on to someone before Brodie clipped him. And maybe somebody'd got the license plate of Luis' rental car. The police might not be quite up to U.S. standards, but SEBIN might be competent, and it was possible that they would be motivated to find whoever whacked the regime guys. All the other corpses were just collateral damage.

"Brodie?"

"I'll call Quantico and get back to you."

"I am the power and the authority here on matters—"

"We've already been through this. Do not impede a criminal investigation."

"*You* have become the criminals."

"Interesting point. Okay, see you tomorrow. Bring the family visas."

"Tonight. Meet me at the embassy."

"You're breaking up. Hello? Brendan?"

"I'm here."

"I think our satellite is over China. Call later." He hung up and tossed the sat phone back in the glove compartment. "Can't rely on these things." He said to Taylor, "He wants us to leave the country, ASAP."

"I got that."

"He also wants us to meet him tonight at the embassy."

"I got that too." She asked, "Why not?"

"I'll think about it."

"We might still need him for something."

"We'll cross that bridge when we get to it."

"Unless you've already burned the bridge." She added, "You should call him back. Or I can."

"He's recording everything, and I've said enough."

"Maybe he can help us get to this area where Mercer is."

"We can make our own travel arrangements."

"Two questions, Brodie. Do you trust the hooker who gave you this information? And do you trust Brendan Worley?"

"I've gotten fucked more times by Intel guys than by hookers."

Taylor had no reply to that, and said, "We should get moving."

"Right."

Luis had finished his business and was lingering behind the car, and Brodie indicated to Luis he could return. Luis climbed into the back seat, and Taylor started the car and pulled back onto the road. Brodie directed her to the turnoff, which she took north through the winding hillside roads toward the mountains.

Brodie asked Luis, "Did the colectivo guy get your ID?"

"Sí. My driver license."

Which would be found on the guy's dead body. Luis should have retrieved it, but Luis was not thinking about that. Brodie told him, "Go first thing tomorrow to the embassy with your family and with your passports, and ask the consulate for Mr. Worley, who will expedite your visas and put you into an embassy car to the airport. You will fly to Washington, DC, and call a number that I will give you and ask for Colonel Dombroski, who will take care of you and your family."

Luis stayed silent for a while, then said, "Gracias."

Taylor added, "This is thanks for all you've done for us."

And, thought Brodie, *to keep you out of a SEBIN interrogation cell where they'll torture you for info about what happened at the Hen House.* When you leave corpses behind, you leave a blood trail that even idiots can follow. In that respect, Worley was right—he and Taylor should also get out of Venezuela. But . . . well, they'd come this far, and they had picked up Mercer's scent. Bloodhounds stick to the scent.

They rode in silence for a few minutes; then Taylor took a ramp onto the highway that would take them west back to the city. On the highway they got a few looks from passing drivers, but there weren't any police or National Guard units in sight.

Brodie looked out the window at the black mountains on one side and the darkened city on the other. They had arrived here with a very flimsy lead, but as often happens with a criminal investigation, one lead leads to another. That's why they're called leads. There is a truth out there, a reality that exists and that can be revealed if you persist, and if you show some smarts and some balls. A little luck helps too, and Brodie believed that the more you broke the rules, the more luck you had. Now and then, though, if you broke too many rules, your luck ran out. Had almost happened in the Hen House. And if he and Taylor went looking for Kyle Mercer in the jungle, they would definitely be testing Brodie's theory that good luck was a product of breaking bad rules.

But that's where Kyle Mercer was—the jungle. That's where a guy like Captain Mercer would end up: at the frontier of nowhere, deep in the heart of a darkness that matched the darkness of his heart and his soul. Brodie and Taylor needed to drag Kyle Mercer into the light, and before a jury of his peers to answer to the law for his crimes. But first, they had to meet him in the dark.

CHAPTER 32

The highway was nearly deserted, and as much fun as Brodie'd had with the AK-47, he decided this would be a good place to ditch it. He wiped it clean with his handkerchief, then pulled the magazine out, extracted the three remaining cartridges, and tossed them out the window, followed by the duct-taped mags. Taylor glanced at him as he quickly broke down the AK-47 into its component parts and threw each part out the window. He asked Luis for his Beretta and similarly disposed of it. "We're clean," he said. "But I worry that a kid will find a piece, then find the other pieces, put them all together, and go join a colectivo."

Neither Luis nor Taylor thought that was funny. Brodie preferred working with people who shared his dark, post-battle humor, but his team had shown good balls tonight, so he gave them a pass.

Luis said, "This exit, señora."

Taylor took the exit for Altamira. "We need to dump this car within walking distance of the hotel."

"Right," Brodie agreed. "It could be hot."

"It's also shot to shit," Taylor reminded him.

"It looks like every other car in Caracas."

Luis thought *that* was funny and added, "The hotel doorman will not even notice."

"Good one," said Brodie. He said to Taylor, "Are you rolling your eyes?"

"You know I am."

They cruised slowly through the darkened streets of Altamira, looking for a place to dump the Mitsubishi. Luis suggested, "There is a no longer used petrol station . . . if you turn here."

Taylor turned onto a side street, and ahead was an abandoned gas station. She pulled in and drove behind the deserted service building, shut off the engine and the lights, and pulled out the key. Then she leaned over and took the rental papers and the satellite phone out of the glove compartment.

They all exited the car and Brodie examined the damage, which included holes in the windshield and rear window, and maybe six or seven holes in the car's skin. He said to Taylor, "In Iraq we used to circle the bullet holes in the shot-up vehicles and choppers with yellow chalk, then connect the dots to spell out something, like 'Holy Shit.'" He asked, "You do that in Afghanistan?"

Taylor looked at him, but said nothing.

"Time to get serious." Brodie said to Taylor, "Put the key back in the ignition. Someone will steal this car before the sun rises, they'll take it to a body shop, and it'll be on the road with a new paint job before lunch."

Taylor hesitated, but Luis said, "This is true, señora."

She nodded and put the key back in the ignition.

"And last but not least," said Brodie, "we need to get the plates off." He opened the trunk and took out the lug wrench, which he used to pry off the front and rear plates. He took the rental papers from Taylor and said, "Wait here." He went around to the front of the building, found a storm drain in the road, and dropped the plates into the drain, then shredded the rental papers and did the same. In CID training they didn't teach you how to cover your tracks, but after ten years of seeing how criminals did it—or tried to do it—he'd learned most of the tricks.

As he walked back toward the service building, he passed beneath a tall, darkened pylon sign featuring the PDVSA logo, indicating that this had once been a state-run fueling station. The gas pumps were gone, and the service building and attached convenience store looked like they'd been stripped of anything worth stealing.

Taylor had told Brodie on the flight over that Maduro had recently turned over control of PDVSA to military officials in order to cement their loyalty. But according to Luis, Venezuela couldn't even pump and refine enough crude to meet domestic demand, so maybe having a piece of PDVSA wasn't worth as much as it used to be—and maybe the generals were getting restless. This place was so bankrupt and fucked-up that even the corruption wasn't working.

He thought about General Gomez, who was hanging out in a brothel in the slums run by a colectivo gang with strong ties to the regime, and about Gomez meeting with an American Army deserter who had renounced his loyalty to his country. What was that all about? Was Gomez looking for help in staging a coup? Or help in trying to prevent one? Or something else? And how did this relate to Kyle Mercer's motive for being in this country? That was one of the questions Brodie had been told to avoid but was determined to answer.

He returned to the car behind the service building, and they set off on the four-block walk to the El Dorado, just three people with guns strolling the dead streets on a hot summer night.

They kept their eyes open and their ears tuned to potential dangers as they walked. It would look pretty dumb, Brodie thought, to get mugged in Altamira after surviving a firefight in Petare. They passed an empty city park with a playground, and then what looked like an expensive restaurant protected by a guard with a pump-action shotgun. Brodie had been in a lot of dangerous cities around the world, but Caracas scared him. He actually looked forward to a trip to the jungle.

They reached the El Dorado, and the security guards both became alert as the three figures approached on foot.

As they got closer, Taylor said, "Buenas noches." The guards must have recognized them, because one of them punched a code into the keypad and the security gate swung open. The guards looked at them quizzically, especially at Luis and his bruised face, but gave polite nods as the three of them walked through the gates.

They walked up the roundabout to the front entrance where Tito was still working the door. He smiled at them, probably surprised to see them alive. "Good evening, señora, señores."

"Good evening," replied Taylor. She said to Brodie, "I'll run up to the room and get something for Luis." She went into the hotel.

Brodie turned to Tito. "We need a taxi to take our driver home."

Tito looked at Luis, probably wondering what had happened to the man's crappy car, not to mention his face. "Certainly . . . and how was your evening?"

"Exciting," said Brodie. "We were carjacked."

Tito did his best to look shocked. "I am so very sorry, señor. May I have the hotel contact the police?"

"The police are the ones who carjacked us."

Tito didn't know if the American was joking or just reporting, so he didn't reply. He blew his whistle and waved over a cab.

As the cab pulled up Brodie and Luis walked out of earshot of the English-speaking doorman. Brodie said to Luis, "You did well tonight, amigo."

"Gracias."

"Thank *you*." He told Luis, "When you get to Dulles Airport, you'll make an asylum claim to the immigration officer, then you call Colonel Dombroski."

Luis hesitated, then said, "I will discuss with my wife tonight."

"There's nothing to discuss, Luis." He reminded him, "Your driver's license is on a dead body."

Luis stared off at the trees beyond the security wall, then said, "My wife's parents have friends living in Miami."

"Good. Lots of Venezuelans in Miami." He reminded Luis, "You have my personal cell number. Call if there's any problem at the embassy."

Luis looked at him. "Sí."

Brodie recited Dombroski's personal cell phone number and told Luis to memorize it, and not to write it down or put it in his cell phone. He further advised, "Address him as General. He'll buy you a beer."

Luis forced a smile, no doubt thinking about leaving his country and heading into the unknown.

Brodie assured him, "Someday you can return."

"Sí. Someday."

Taylor returned with a plastic bag, which she handed to Luis. "Traveling money."

Luis hesitated, then took the bag. "Gracias."

Brodie said, "Don't get robbed."

Luis tapped the Glock under his jacket. "I am okay."

Right. Luis had undergone his baptism of fire and he wasn't afraid anymore. He was scared, which was normal and healthy, but he wasn't afraid. Brodie recalled when he'd made that subtle transition himself.

Taylor gave Luis a hug and Brodie shook his hand, but neither man said anything. Taylor said, "Vaya con Dios."

Luis got in the waiting taxi, and Brodie and Taylor watched as the cab went through the open security gate and disappeared on the dark street.

Taylor said, "We really had no right to drag him into this."

"He volunteered." He added, "When you're out there someday, Maggie, in some fucked-up country—without me—you won't hesitate to recruit a trustworthy local. Kids, pregnant women, Christian missionaries, Buddhist monks . . . anyone who can help you accomplish the mission."

"The only part about that I liked was 'without me.'"

Brodie smiled. "I think this is our last assignment together."

"You can bet money on it."

"Which reminds me—how much did you give him?"

"Three thousand."

"Bolívars?"

"Dollars, Brodie."

"That's more than I made tonight."

"You didn't get beat up."

"I got shot at," he reminded her.

"Me too. Thanks to you."

"Right. Ready for a drink?"

"Been ready since the first bullet went through my windshield."

"Any excuse for a drink."

Taylor went into the hotel and Brodie followed. He said, "If we have a drink in the bar, we might run into Worley, which I don't want. Let's raid the minibar in the room."

"Okay, and we can call the boss and report."

"Right. After two drinks."

They rode up the elevator in silence. The doors opened on their floor and Brodie said, "Meet you in the living room for a post-op. Twenty minutes."

"Thirty." She opened her door and went into her room.

Brodie entered his bedroom and walked to the balcony. The night air was warm and thick with humidity, and the sky was cloaked in a dense cloud cover. He stared out at the city and the dark hills of Petare. One day, he knew, he would meet his fate in some godforsaken shithole. But until that day arrived, he was happy doing what he did. Tempting fate. Giving the cosmos another shot at him. Sometimes he wondered why he did this. Maybe it had to do with Iraq, and survivor's guilt. Maybe it had to do with nothing more than the thrill of looking death in the eye, spitting in his face, and getting away with it.

Brodie had a feeling, a sense that Kyle Mercer was a kindred spirit, fucked up by war, maybe afraid of peace, and definitely high on danger.

Why did he desert? Why did he come to Venezuela? Why was he in the jungle?
Brodie looked forward to asking him.

CHAPTER 33

Brodie took off his shirt and went into the bathroom to wash up. He noticed a few small cuts on his face, maybe from the glass shards flying around the Mitsubishi. Better than a bullet hole through the head.

He had Pío's blood on his hands, and noticed his knuckles were swollen from battering the guy's face.

Brodie washed his hands and face with soap and hot water, and again looked at himself in the mirror, seeing Sergeant Brodie a dozen years ago in Iraq.

The Army had given him the Combat Infantry Badge, a Purple Heart, and a Bronze Star, which sort of summarized and memorialized his time in hell. These uniform adornments meant something to the Army, and to him, and maybe someday his service would mean something to a future civilian employer—or a future wife and children. But only those who'd been to hell could know that every medal and every scar recalled a memory of death, blood, and brutality.

But there was also the brotherhood. The bravery and sacrifice. The extraordinary concept of trusting your life to the man next to you, and discovering that your trust was reciprocated, with no questions asked.

He'd known men who'd gone wrong after a combat tour—drugs, alcohol, crime—and men who'd found God and lost God, and men who'd blotted it all out, and men like himself who tried to find some meaning in their experience, or tried to do something that would balance the great scales of life that had tipped the wrong way. For him, it was the CID. The law. Due process versus a well-aimed bullet. This was working for him most of the time, but not all of the time.

Then there were men—like Kyle Mercer—who embraced war the way some men embrace a woman who they know has killed her past lovers. It's an incredible high if you survive.

Brodie thought he understood a little of what made Kyle Mercer tick, and it was no surprise to discover that Captain Mercer had gone to the jungle and recruited his own Fuerza Delta.

There was something out there—a missing piece—that would tie this case together. Mercer. Crenshaw. Caracas. And there were other missing pieces to this puzzle, and those pieces were probably in the pockets of people like General Hackett, General Mendoza, Colonel Worley, and maybe even Colonel Dombroski. But he, Scott Brodie, was not going to be given those pieces, and he couldn't demand them. He could, however, go to the source: the puzzle-maker, Kyle Mercer. As in all criminal investigations, the answers lay with the perpetrator. All you had to do was find him and make him talk. And finding Mercer had just become a little easier, and making people talk was something Brodie was good at.

Brodie recalled the video of Kyle Mercer as a captive of the Taliban—unbroken and defiant. And he recalled the video of Mercer lopping off Taliban heads—crazy-eyed and angry. Angry at the Army. Which told Brodie something: You don't resign your commission because you deserted and got captured by the enemy. Captain Mercer had lived up to his responsibility under the Code of Conduct to escape. So, if you're Kyle Mercer, you go find an American unit, turn yourself in, and beg for forgiveness, which you could reasonably expect under the circumstances. But that's not what Captain Mercer did. He was pissed off about something. And Brodie had no doubt that Kyle Mercer would be happy and eager to tell him about it if they met—especially if it was Mercer who had the gun pointed at Brodie rather than vice versa. In either case, Brodie would have his answer and Mercer would have his moment of truth. Everyone would be happy and satisfied. But probably only one of them would walk away alive.

Brodie found his mouthwash, rinsed, and spit. Maybe Maggie Taylor wanted to give him a big kiss on the mouth for his bravery. Maybe not.

He went to his bedroom, found a clean polo shirt in his luggage, and pulled it on, then went into the living room.

He found Taylor sitting cross-legged on the couch, barefoot, wearing a T-shirt and shorts that revealed the scars on her leg. She had her tablet in her lap, and spread out on the coffee table was a large map which Brodie assumed was of Venezuela. She referenced something on her tablet, then took a Sharpie and circled a location on the map. Obviously she was planning their journey into the heart of darkness.

He walked to the bar, made two rum and colas, and took them over to the couch. He put her drink next to the map and sat, noticing that she'd circled a few places in the south of the country, and that, based on the color coding, a lot of southern Venezuela was covered with forest and jungle. Finding a whorehouse in a city of two million people had been tough enough. Finding a hidden camp in a jungle was going to be a challenge. This was where his infantry training and map-reading skills would come in handy. He asked, "Where'd you get the map?"

Taylor took a break from her tablet and picked up her drink. "Gift shop. Free with the bathing suit."

Brodie smiled and raised his glass. "To you. You did good tonight." Give me a big kiss.

She touched her glass to his and said, "If you ever put me in a situation like that again, I'm bailing and you'll be flying solo."

He glanced at the scars on her leg. "You know you don't mean that."

"Try me."

"I'd be there for you, Maggie."

"If I did something as crazy as you did, I wouldn't expect you to be there."

"I didn't actually *plan* it that way."

"You didn't plan it. Period."

"Seemed like a good idea at the time." He suggested, "Let's move on." He looked at the map. "You find Mercer's secret camp yet?"

She didn't reply to that, but pointed to a circle she'd drawn on the map. "This is Ciudad Bolívar. Where your prostitute said she flew to with Mercer."

"Her name is Carmen."

"Look at the map, please."

He looked. Ciudad Bolívar, which was on the southern bank of a river called the Orinoco, looked like a decent-size city. South of the Orinoco River was a vast stretch of national parks and nature preserves that ran to the border of Brazil and the Amazon rain forest. There seemed to be very few towns south of the river.

In fact, Taylor said, "The southern half of the country, south of the Orinoco, is sparsely populated. This is an area about the size of California—like, one hundred fifty thousand square miles of very rough country."

"Captain Mercer has chosen well."

"Luckily, you've gotten some directions from your witness."

"Good luck is the result of hard work."

She ignored that and continued, "According to my research, all these national parks were formed when tourism was big. Now tourism is almost dead, and there are also travel restrictions in place for these parks and nature preserves."

"Why?"

"The government says it's for your safety because of the extreme terrain. But there are probably other issues. This region is notorious for drug trafficking and cocaine labs."

"Maybe Mercer is providing muscle for a drug cartel. Or maybe he's hired himself out to anti-regime forces. Mercer the Mercenary."

"All possible."

And maybe General Gomez was plotting a military coup against the regime, and that was why Gomez and Mercer met in the Hen House. That made sense. But it could also make sense that Gomez was loyal to the regime and he'd hired the crazy American Delta Force renegade and his mercenaries to hunt down the anti-regime guerrillas. Both theories were equally valid. Bottom line, Venezuela was so fucked up that anything was possible.

Taylor continued, "You need a permit and a local guide to go into most of these areas."

"Carmen never mentioned that." He added, "I'm sure we can get around that."

"I'm sure you think you can. The point is, if we go down to this area, we will stick out."

"We stick out in Caracas. I stuck out in the Hen House. You stick out anywhere because you're too good-looking."

She didn't reply.

"Also, Kyle Mercer must make this trip regularly, and he would stick out. If he can do it, we can do it."

"Scott, I'm sure Mercer has figured out how to travel to and from this restricted area."

"Apparently he has. And we're CID. This is what we do."

"Let's move on." She pointed to another circle on the map. "About three hundred miles south of Ciudad Bolívar is Angel Falls, which your witness mentioned."

Brodie looked more closely at a large patch of green, labeled *Canaima National Park*. Angel Falls appeared to be on the edge of a large flat-topped topographical feature named Auyán Tepui, which must have been the flat-topped mountain that Carmen had seen when she landed at the airstrip in the village. So far, everything—flight times and place names—seemed to check out.

Taylor continued, "This area is famous for these flat-topped mountains called tepuis, which were formed billions of years ago."

"Really?"

She also informed Brodie, "Auyán Tepui is where Angel Falls originates. 'Tepui' means 'house of the gods' in the language of the native Pemón people."

Brodie wasn't sure that was information he needed to find Kyle Mercer, but Maggie Taylor, as he'd discovered, overresearched everything. "We'll get that into our report. Maybe as a footnote."

She handed Brodie her tablet, which showed an aerial shot of the massive plateau-like formation surrounded by dense jungle. The summit of the flat mountain reached above the clouds. This looked like the travel posters they'd seen at the airport. If he had Carmen in the room, he could have asked her if this was what she'd seen. But how many flat-topped mountains with a waterfall could there be? Still, a meticulous investigator would show the witness three or four photographs and ask her to ID what she'd seen. His mind drifted back to Carmen with the paddle in her hand, before he'd handed her the robe . . .

"Brodie? Are you listening to me?"

"I am. Yes."

She continued, "I looked up tours of Angel Falls to see where tourists might stop in this area. There are three villages that seem to have lodging—guesthouses—and also an airstrip."

"Good thinking."

She pointed at the map to a place she'd circled. "This is a village called Kavak . . ." She pointed to another circled town. "And this is Uruyén. And here is a larger town called Canaima. All three have airstrips, all three are on a river, and all have a view of the tepui." She added, "There's no way we can know which, if any, of these villages your witness landed in."

Maybe he should have gotten Carmen's cell phone number.

"Unless," said Taylor, "you thought to get a description of the village."

She was obviously reminding him that he had not asked Simpson for a description of the barrio houses around the brothel. Well, Scott Brodie never made the same mistake twice, and he told her, "Actually, I did ask."

"And?"

"Let's take a look." Brodie ran a search on the tablet for shots of Canaima, and saw that it was a substantial town of stone and white stucco buildings with a church, which was not what Carmen had described. He then pulled up shots of Uruyén and Kavak, which looked similar to each other—thatched huts in open grassland with the massive tepui in the background. The two villages were only a few miles apart, but there was a difference in the color of the huts—those in Uruyén appeared to be painted a deep umber, and the huts in Kavak were a mustard yellow. Carmen had said yellow.

"Brodie?"

"Well . . . I'll bet Carmen could tell us."

"I thought you asked her."

"I did . . . You know, standard operating procedure is to take the witness to the scene—"

"Are you serious?"

No. Horny.

"What did she say to you?"

"Yellow. Yellow huts."

Taylor looked at the photos on the tablet. "That's Kavak." She asked, "Are you sure?"

"She was sure."

"All right . . . So Kavak fits all the parameters. Airstrip, view of the tepui, yellow huts, and on a small river. She took a boat upriver. Correct?"

"Correct."

"Did Luis hear all this?"

"He did."

"Should we call him?"

"I'm sure he wasn't paying attention."

"Were you?"

"I resent the implications of that question." He added, "Let me remind you that you're addressing a superior officer."

She started to reply, then said, "I apologize."

"Accepted." Brodie took a swig of his drink. "Kavak. Doesn't sound Spanish. Sounds Polish."

"It's an indigenous name."

"Carmen said there were Indians down there."

"We say 'indigenous people.'"

"Right." Brodie thought about his hippie mother, who'd populated a whole room of their farmhouse with questionable "indigenous art" she picked up from local thrift shops. She'd probably owned more Native American buckskin dresses than any other white lady in the tristate area, back when Native Americans were still Indians and no one had yet coined the term "cultural appropriation."

"I need a drink." He stood and went to the bar.

As he was pouring another rum, Taylor asked, "Did you check your room messages?"

"I did not."

"Well, I checked mine. Brendan Worley wants you to call him."

"Can I freshen your drink?"

"No. And I also have a voice mail and text message from him."

"Persistent little shit, isn't he?"

"I'm sure he also called your cell."

"It's off."

"You want me to call him?"

"I told him I'd call him after I speak to Dombroski. Brendan doesn't listen well."

"He may come to the hotel."

"We are not accepting visitors." Brodie picked up the phone on the bar, dialed the front desk, and told them that he and Ms. Taylor were not in for visitors or phone calls. He added, "We're indisposed," hinting that they were in the sack.

When he hung up, Taylor reminded Brodie, "We may need Worley later."

"At this point, the only thing he will help us with is leaving the country."

"He has to offer assistance if we ask."

"We're not asking. And you can be sure he's been on the phone with Dombroski or someone higher up, making the case that you and I have become a danger to ourselves and others, and that we need to exit quickly for our own safety and for the good of the mission, and so forth."

Taylor thought about that and asked, "Do you think we'll get pulled?"

Brodie brought his drink back to the couch, sat, and stared at the map.

"Scott?"

"It's a possibility."

She nodded. "Maybe Worley is right. Maybe after what you . . . what just happened, we have become a liability."

"Maybe. And that's why we need to become an invaluable asset. We have information no one else has, and we need to leverage that."

"All right. But you need to assure me that if we go down to this jungle"— she tapped the map—"we're only doing it to verify your witness' story. We're not looking to apprehend Kyle Mercer. We are gathering information and evidence about this camp, and we will turn our findings over to Colonel Dombroski, who will take appropriate action."

"Right."

"Can I have a more affirmative response?"

"Right you are." He took a swig of rum. "Okay, so Carmen spent the night in this village that we think is Kavak, and next morning she got on a boat and went upriver—against the current—for about an hour. So if my map reading is good, this small river—which is not named on this map—is a tributary of the Orinoco, so it would flow northwest and therefore the boat was traveling southeast . . . and let's say the boat made seven knots, maybe eight . . . and if Carmen was correct about the trip being one hour—"

"If she was blindfolded, time seems to pass more slowly."

"How do you know that?"

"From my last date. More importantly, I don't think we need to get on a boat and actually go up this river. We'll go as far as Kavak, check it out, maybe talk to some locals—"

"If we talk to some locals about a gringo who regularly lands on the airstrip and takes a boat upriver, we will probably have the same experience we had in Petare, and that was not good."

"Okay, but—"

"We are ecotourists. Clark and Sarah Bowman, the stupidest fucking adventure travelers since Michael Rockefeller, who got eaten by cannibals in New Guinea."

She nodded. "We can be ornithologists. Bird-watchers. Like Luis' father."

"Good thinking. Download a bird-watching book in your tablet, and let's see if we can get hold of a pair of binoculars before we set out."

"All right, but we're not going upriver looking for this camp."

"We'll do—as our motto says—what has to be done."

"What has to be done is to get out of there alive and report back to headquarters."

"All recon missions present that problem. How much is enough? When do you push on, and when do you turn back? You don't know until you get there."

"Thank you for that acquired wisdom."

"You can turn back now if you want."

"You can stop questioning my dedication to the mission."

"You, Ms. Taylor, have previously indicated that you'd bail out and—"

"I reserve the right to use my brains when you're thinking with your balls."

Brodie thought about that. Sounded reasonable. "Okay . . . let's move on." He looked at the map. "Carmen said they came to shore on the right bank, so let's say they'd traveled about seven or eight miles on the river . . . then walked inland for about fifteen minutes . . ." He took the Sharpie and drew a large oval on the right bank that encompassed about forty square miles of dense forest. "Somewhere in here is Mercer's camp."

Taylor looked at the map. "Maybe. But your variables are the speed of the boat and the travel time upriver—if it *was* upriver and not downriver."

"You seem to have a prejudice against my star witness."

"She probably doesn't know her ass from her elbow. How much did you pay her?"

"Six hundred."

"For that kind of money, she'd tell you you were hung like a donkey."

Brodie smiled, then looked back at the map. "Carmen also said she could see another flat mountain when she got to Mercer's camp." He studied the map. "Here is a big cluster of tepuis called Chimantá Massif . . . and here are some smaller, unnamed tepuis. So if my guess about the general location of Mercer's camp is correct, then that matches up with these tepuis, which I'm sure could be seen from Mercer's camp."

Taylor focused on the map, computing the variables of speed and time from the probable starting point of Kavak, along with the terrain features. "Okay . . . if Kavak is correct, and if she went upriver for about an hour, and if you're correct about the speed of a boat going against the current, then we've got a general idea of where this camp is."

He assured her, "I took the land navigation course at Benning."

"Did you pass?"

"I did. More importantly, I passed the real test in Iraq."

She looked at him. "I have a lot of confidence in your skills. It's your judgment that worries me."

"Me too."

She looked back at the map. "All right . . . A recon drone from Colombia or from a U.S. naval vessel could pinpoint the camp in a few hours." She looked at Brodie. "Then a Delta team goes in and takes him."

"Right."

"That's what we need to tell Colonel Dombroski." She reminded him, "I will be present for this call."

"As promised."

"Good. So call him and let's see if Worley has spoken to him, and if we're being pulled from this case."

"Okay, but to argue against that, we need to present Dombroski with our operational plan going forward." He added, "We need to book a flight to the airstrip in Kavak."

Taylor nodded, picked up her tablet, and ran a search, finding an international air charter company called Apex that claimed to run planes out of Caracas' Francisco de Miranda Airport.

Brodie thought it would be better security to use the sat phone to call the U.S. toll-free number listed on the Apex website and he went out on the balcony to get clear sky. Taylor followed.

Brodie dialed, and a woman who sounded American and efficient answered. "Apex International Air Charter Service. This is Ann Muller speaking. How may I help you?"

"My name is Clark Bowman, Ms. Muller, and I am currently in Caracas. That's Venezuela. I need to charter a flight from Francisco de Miranda Airport to a place called Kavak, also in Venezuela, and I need to leave as soon as possible."

"Yes, sir. And what type of aircraft will you need?"

"Well . . . a teeny-tiny aircraft."

"Okay . . . how teeny-tiny?"

"Kavak has a teeny-tiny airstrip, so the aircraft has to be teeny enough to land on the tiny airstrip."

"Yes it does . . . Let me go into my program and find Kavak. Can you spell—?"

Brodie spelled it for her, adding, "This is not the Kavak in Poland."

"Yes, sir. You said Venezuela . . . here it is. Yes, this is very tiny. Sixteen-hundred-foot grass runway . . . no control tower . . . no runway lights . . . no refueling—"

"It's just an airstrip, Ms. Muller. Hopefully with a wind sock. If it was an international airport, I wouldn't be calling you to charter a puddle jumper."

"Yes, sir. I'm looking at what we have in Caracas . . . It appears that we have only one pilot operating out of Francisco de Miranda Airport, and he flies a single-engine, six-seat Cessna Stationair, but he also has access to other aircraft that may be more suitable for this landing and takeoff. He'll know." She asked, "How many passengers will there be?"

Brodie glanced at Taylor, who was staring out at the city but undoubtedly listening to his conversation. "Two." Unless they could take Carmen along. "Me and my wife, who is light as a feather. Speaking of which, we're bird-watchers."

"All right, that's . . . interesting . . . Will you need a return or ongoing flight?"

"We will, but I don't know when." Or where, for that matter.

Taylor had obviously figured out the question and said to Brodie, "We are leaving the same day we get there."

"Hold on, Ms. Muller." He covered the mouthpiece and said to Taylor, "I want to spend the night in Kavak like Carmen did. I want to reconstruct her trip, take some photos, see how you get a boat, see how fast the river flows—"

"I think we can do that in one day. But . . . all right. *One* night. Then we leave in the morning. No boat trip on the river."

He nodded, and said to Ms. Muller, "The next morning. Returning to Caracas." But probably Bogotá, Colombia, though that was not information Brodie wanted to share with Ms. Muller or anyone.

"Then the pilot should stay overnight." She explained, "Even with you paying for the pilot's overnight accommodations, that will be less expensive for you."

"The pilot can sleep with my wife."

"Sir?"

"Just a bird-watcher joke. Okay, so can do?"

"I need to contact the pilot to check his and the aircraft's availability before confirming any booking."

Brodie wondered if this was the same pilot that Kyle Mercer used to fly to Ciudad Bolívar, or from there down to Kavak. That would be interesting. He said, "A friend of mine went from Caracas to Kavak by first flying to Ciudad Bolívar, then he took a smaller plane to Kavak. Why would he do that?"

Ms. Muller replied, "He may have taken a scheduled commercial flight to Ciudad Bolívar, then gone on to Kavak by private charter because there are no commercial flights to Kavak."

"Why would he do that instead of flying a charter directly from Caracas to Kavak as I want to do?"

"I don't know."

"Well, I do. He was trying to cover his tracks."

"Sir?"

"Just thinking out loud." He asked, "Is your pilot a local guy?"

"No, sir. He's an American. Captain John F. Collins. FAA certified, very experienced—"

"Good. Down here taxi drivers are allowed to fly a plane."

"Really?"

Brodie wondered what John F. Collins was doing in Caracas. Probably running drugs or guns. The world of private aviation, especially in third world countries, was a world of no questions asked. He thought about Worley's pilot and the Otter. "Does Captain Collins have access to an Otter?"

"I'm not familiar with that aircraft. Are you requesting an Otter?"

"No. I'm just asking dumb questions. Okay, so can you get hold of Captain Collins and get us out of Caracas tonight?"

"When I contact Captain Collins, I'll get back to you. But you won't be able to make a night landing in Kavak." She reminded him, "There are no runway lights."

"Okay . . . then let's plan the flight to land at dawn. I need to be in Kavak early to catch the yellow-bellied Worleys." He added, "They hide during the day."

Taylor said to him, "You're cuckoo."

Ms. Muller said, "All right . . . let me see if I can contact Captain Collins, and see if we can accommodate you."

"Do what has to be done, Ms. Muller."

"Yes, sir." She recapped: "You will want the pilot to stay overnight and return to Caracas the next day with the same two passengers. Correct?"

"As far as I know."

"I ask about the number of passengers because of the short airstrip and the takeoff weight."

Should he mention that they might have a two-hundred-pound former Delta Force soldier stuffed in the luggage hold in cuffs? Probably not. "Okay."

"Depending on the aircraft and the weight onboard, and other factors, the captain will have to decide if and when he needs to refuel in order to meet required fuel reserves."

"Whatever."

"I can give you an estimate of the cost, but there are some variables, including fuel cost, actual flight time—which is dependent on wind and weather—and the cost of the overnight lodging for the pilot, and—"

"What's the bottom line?"

"About three thousand to thirty-five hundred dollars."

"You take cash?"

"No, sir. I need a credit card number to secure the booking."

"This sounds like a legitimate operation."

"Sir?"

"Let me give you my wife's credit card." He motioned to Taylor, who pulled her card out of her wallet and gave it to him. He said to Ms. Muller, "She uses her maiden name. Taylor." He spelled it. "First name— what . . . ?" He looked at her. "*Magnolia?* What the hell kind of cracker name is that?"

Taylor looked embarrassed, then recovered and gave him the finger.

"Sir?"

"First name Magnolia. It's an Amex." Brodie recited the card number and expiration date.

"Thank you, sir. And may I have a phone number to contact you?"

Brodie gave her his and Taylor's cell phone numbers so that they didn't have to stand on the balcony waiting for a call on their sat phone.

"Thank you, Mr. Bowman. I'll call you as soon as I reach Captain Collins."

"Call me within the hour either way."

"Yes, sir."

"We really need to get out of here. This is the mating season."

"Sir . . . ? Oh, the birds."

"Yes, the birds, Ms. Muller."

"I will do my best." She added, "Also, I should have mentioned that fuel and other fees at Tomás de Heres will be put on that card."

Brodie stood motionless, then said, "Say that name again."

"Tomás de Heres. That's the airport in Ciudad Bolívar. Where you will probably land to refuel."

Brodie stayed silent.

"Sir? Is that—?"

"That's fine, Ms. Muller. Thank you for your assistance."

"Thank you for choosing Apex."

Brodie hung up and looked at Taylor.

She asked, "Everything okay?"

He nodded. "We just got the answer to a question."

"What's the question?"

"Who is Tomás de Heres?"

"I told you who he was."

"Well, your research was interesting, but not pertinent." He wanted to add, "As with most of your research," but he said, "Tomás de Heres is the name of the airport in Ciudad Bolívar."

She looked at him. "Okay . . . so Worley and his friend Ted may have been talking about the airport."

"You think?" There are coincidences, thought Brodie, and there are signs. To Brodie, this was a sign that his paranoia and suspicions were not unfounded—that Brendan Worley might be a little more knowledgeable about Kyle Mercer's whereabouts than he'd let on. And maybe all the Intel they had just risked their lives getting was already known by Worley and his friends, who were supposed to be on their side. He shared these thoughts with his partner and asked, "What do you think?"

She thought about that and replied, "It's a stretch."

"According to Luis, Worley's car ride with Ted was about three weeks ago. That was a week before Al Simpson's sighting, and more than two weeks before the Army even knew that Kyle Mercer was in Venezuela."

Taylor replied, "You're engaging in leaps of logic. Even if Worley and Ted were talking about the airport in Ciudad Bolívar, that does not mean they were on the trail of Kyle Mercer." She added, "You're trying to make a fact fit your suspicion—whatever it is."

"My suspicion is that the spooks are running their own manhunt for Kyle Mercer, and I think the spooks are a few steps ahead of the cops."

"Scott . . . focus on the mission. Not on Brendan Worley."

"Brendan Worley has become part of my mission."

"Not mine." She went back into the living room and Brodie followed.

They sat on the couch, and Taylor swiped her tablet for a minute, then said, "There's a Venezuelan army base southeast of Ciudad Bolívar, not too far from Tomás de Heres Airport. So if Worley and his friend Ted were doing actual military attaché work for the embassy, they would have legitimate business down there." She added, "They were not going from the Tomás de Heres Airport to someplace in the south to look for Kyle Mercer."

He reminded her, "The U.S. and Venezuela are not allies, and not even on speaking terms. So I doubt that our military attachés would be welcome at a Venezuelan military base."

"Scott, we don't know that world. For all we know, Worley and others are meeting secretly with the Venezuelan military to plot a coup against the regime." She added, "That would be a good reason for Worley and Ted to be flying to this military base."

"You're messing up my conspiracy theory. Worley and Ted flew to Tomás de Heres Airport, then on to the south because they had a lead on Mercer's whereabouts."

"We don't even know that they actually flew to Tomás de Heres Airport."

"Right. Maybe they were just talking about what a great name that is for an airport."

"Can we move on?"

Brodie took her tablet and typed and swiped. "Okay . . . Ciudad Bolívar is the capital of Bolívar State . . . considered the gateway to southern Venezuela, and the way station for tourists going to visit the national parks . . ." He looked up. "Now this all makes sense. Ted was in Venezuela to look at the waterfalls and the wild monkeys."

"Let's put Tomás de Heres in the clue bag and look at it later. Okay?"

"Okay." Mercer was the mission and the rest was noise. They had a very good lead on Kyle Mercer's whereabouts, and they had to stay on track.

It occurred to Brodie that Kyle Mercer's fatal flaw might not be his soft spot for old Army buddies or his fondness for English-speaking prostitutes, but his arrogance. Mercer must have known that after he'd literally turned his back on his old buddy, Al Simpson would have done the right thing and contacted the Army. Mercer also knew, as a soldier, that it would be the CID who would be coming for him. But a guy like Mercer, with his elite military pedigree, would look down his nose at—and underestimate—an organization like the CID. When you spend your career operating outside the rules, the people who dedicate their lives to enforcing the rules look like schmucks.

And Kyle Mercer didn't just break the rules, he broke the law, and he also broke his sworn oath of allegiance to his country, and he literally walked away from his duty to the men under his command. And two soldiers died as a result. Captain Mercer would pay for that. CID Special Agent Scott Brodie, himself a combat veteran and a rule-breaker, would see that he did. In fact, it almost didn't matter *why* Captain Mercer had deserted. Brodie could not think of anything that Kyle Mercer could say during the extenuation and mitigation phase of his court-martial that would in any way justify his actions. And quite possibly Mercer, in his arrogance, would offer no extenuating or mitigating circumstances. Which was why Brodie had to look Kyle Mercer in the eye and ask, "Why the fuck did you desert, Captain?"

"Scott? Where did you go?"

"I'm thinking about Kyle Mercer. About why he deserted. But I'm also wondering why he's training men in the jungle."

"What I'm wondering is, where does the money come from? Guerrilla forces have to be fed, clothed, and armed."

"Right. As we say in the Army, 'Beans, bandages, and bullets.' And as the spooks say, 'It's not important to know who fired the bullet—it's important to know who paid for it.'"

"So who is paying for the beans, bandages, and bullets?"

Maybe General Gomez. Were Gomez and Mercer involved in a coup against the regime? Or had Gomez hired Mercer to hunt down anti-regime insurgents? Brodie hadn't briefed Taylor on Carmen's mention of General Gomez, so he replied, "In my experience with paramilitary and insurgent groups in Iraq, I learned that many of these groups are self-funded. They deal drugs, rob banks, raid military armories, steal oil, and even impose taxes. Sort of like politicians. So, given what we know about Kyle Mercer, I have no doubt that he takes what he needs." He added, "And/or, he's being backed by General Gomez."

"Who is General Gomez?"

"Well, according to my witness, he's a Venezuelan general who visited Kyle Mercer in the Hen House."

"All right . . . let's see what we get on him." Taylor began typing on her tablet while Brodie went to the bar.

Taylor called out to him, "You're on duty, Mr. Brodie."

"*You're* on duty. I'm celebrating."

"You need to call Dombroski."

"Right. I'll make it a double." He poured one mini bottle of rum into his glass, added the local high-test cola, and took a seat on the couch opposite Taylor.

She glanced up from her tablet. "I found a General Ricardo Gomez. Did you get his first name?"

"No."

"Well . . . how many General Gomezes can there be in the Venezuelan Army?"

"Probably twenty, and they're all related. What does it say?"

"Not much—just his CV. Born in Caracas, fifty-six years old . . ."

"Photo? For Carmen to ID?"

"No. And you'll never see Carmen again, Brodie."

"Right. Okay, political affiliation? Chavista?"

"Doesn't say . . . but here's something: He took a junior officer leadership course at Fort Benning . . . back in 1986 . . . looks like we trained this guy."

"Interesting." The American Army trained a lot of foreign officers at Benning, Carlisle Barracks, and other installations, at U.S. taxpayer expense. The concept was sound: to instill in these officers—most of whom were from underdeveloped allied countries—U.S. Army discipline, values, and leadership skills, which they could take home and hopefully remember. Also hopefully, these officers would be grateful and think kindly of America and the U.S. Army, and they'd somehow show their gratitude if and when America needed the help of their pisspot military for something. And maybe one of these guys would become El Presidente. It sort of worked, now and then. But often it didn't—especially when the country whose officers were being trained went from ally to enemy, as Venezuela had. Then the U.S. Army had created little Frankenstein monsters that could be a problem in a future conflict. Unless, of course, these American-trained officers still harbored a secret affection for the United States.

So, who and what was General Gomez? A gringo-loving, anti-regime plotter? Or just another Venezuelan general whose loyalty was bought and paid for by the regime? And what did this general have to do with Kyle Mercer? That was the question. He asked Taylor, "Anything else?"

"Not much. You can read it yourself." She handed the tablet to him.

Brodie glanced at the short bio. As with most public figures in troubled countries, there wasn't much info online—no home address where he could be found and assassinated, no mention of a wife or children who could be kidnapped. Brodie said, "No mention of the Hen House." He handed the tablet back to Taylor.

"I'm sure military Intel has good info on him." She suggested, "We'll ask Dombroski to run a search on him."

Brodie didn't reply.

She looked at him. "Is this something else you're going to keep from our superior officer?"

"Maybe."

"Scott—"

"When you ask questions, you alert people that you know something. And maybe this is something we are not supposed to know."

"Scott . . . look at me."

"That's easy."

"You're becoming increasingly paranoid. You know that. Right?"

"You never told me your name was Magnolia."

"That's irrelevant."

"But it shows that you keep secrets from your superior officer."

"Call Dombroski. On speakerphone."

"Okay . . ." He pulled out his cell phone and turned it on. As he waited for service, he said to her, "We'll see if Dombroski and Worley have spoken, and if Worley has convinced our boss to call us home."

She didn't reply.

"The thing about information is that you have to guard it carefully when you're in the field, because if you share it with people and it somehow falls into the wrong hands, it can get you killed."

Taylor nodded, but Brodie wasn't sure if she was agreeing with him or just humoring the paranoid schizophrenic she'd found herself working with.

He added, "You can appreciate that after your tour of duty in Afghanistan."

Again she nodded, then said, "I understand." She suggested, "Sit next to me so we can both talk to Dombroski."

Brodie stood, sat next to her on the couch, accessed Signal, and dialed, except for the last digit. He said, "You have my permission to say what you want. But protect your sources. And protect yourself. Assume everyone talks too much. Also, we don't know what Dombroski tells Worley, or vice versa. I will tell Dombroski about Mercer's possible whereabouts, but we will not mention the name of Kavak. That's our secret. Know what you need to redact, and what you need to report. Okay?"

She nodded.

He hit the last number, and the phone rang as he put it on the coffee table and turned it on speaker. He said to her, "Remember, I did mention Flagstaff to Dombroski, so let's see if he brings it up, or knows anything."

She stared at the ringing phone and said, "If Dombroski can't tell you about Flagstaff, I can."

He looked at her. *What?*

Dombroski answered, "I've been waiting for your call."

Neither Taylor nor Brodie replied.

"Hello? You there?"

Brodie said, "Here . . . I have Ms. Taylor on speaker."

"Good evening, Ms. Taylor."

"Good evening, Colonel."

Dombroski said, "I would have called you sooner, Brodie, to see if you were both still alive, but Brendan Worley called me and assured me you were."

Brodie replied, "Alive and well."

"But not on your way to Quantico with our fugitive."

"No, sir. We're in our hotel."

"Have you spoken to Colonel Worley since you called him earlier?"

"No, sir. We needed to speak to you first. That is the protocol."

"Indeed it is. So why has it taken you so long to call?"

Brodie replied, "Ms. Taylor and I were preparing a clear and concise briefing for you." He added, "I hope we didn't cause you any anxiety."

"I'm used to waiting for your calls, Brodie. The anxiety comes from your call."

"Yes, sir. I hope I don't disappoint you."

"You never do. All right, tell me about the shoot-out in the whorehouse."

"The—? Oh, right . . . Well, maybe it was more of a shout-out. Worley may have misunderstood—"

"Did you kill anybody?"

"There was some gunfire."

"Okay . . . I guess I don't need to know the details at this time."

"Correct." So you don't have to report to General Hackett what you don't know.

Dombroski reminded him, "I gave you some instructions on how to handle this tonight. I advised caution."

"Yes, sir. You are on record for that."

"Your problem, Scott, is that you revert to your aggressive combat training and forget what you learned as a criminal investigator."

"You're absolutely right, Colonel. Ms. Taylor would agree with that."

Ms. Taylor said, "I agree, Colonel. But Mr. Brodie, from what he told me and what I observed, handled the situation with . . ."

"Bravery and courage," suggested Brodie. "Resourcefulness, and the minimal use of force." Except for the AK-47.

"All right," said Dombroski. "I just hope you haven't created an international incident."

"It was a whorehouse," Brodie reminded him. "It's not like I shot some government officials or anything."

"God forbid."

"Right. So—"

"You're coming home. Worley is nervous. You need to book the next flight out of Caracas. To anywhere. You have to leave the country. Tonight."

"Colonel—"

"Do not check out of your hotel. But leave nothing behind that could be compromising. Do as Worley instructed you to do with your guns and your—"

"Colonel—"

"Do not interrupt me, Mr. Brodie. This is not a suggestion—it is an order."

"Yes, sir."

"You can be sure that our fugitive has heard about the brothel incident, so you have managed to alert him, but not apprehend him."

"Yes, sir, but I have—"

"That was the worst possible outcome. You will not get a second chance to find him."

"Actually—"

"The mission is blown, Mr. Brodie, and you blew it."

Taylor said, "Colonel, if I may speak—"

"You may and you will. When I'm finished with Mr. Brodie."

"Yes, sir."

Dombroski continued, "The average police officer in Venezuela might be no better than a street thug, but Worley informs me that they have a very sophisticated and smart intelligence service, SEBIN, trained by the Cubans. And they will be investigating this incident because it involved a man—you—who I'm sure someone in the brothel will identify as an American." He asked, "Did you ID yourself as an American?"

"Yes, sir. I was Clark Bowman—looking for a lady."

"They knew who you were looking for. Mission blown. Cover blown. You need to get out of Venezuela before the police or SEBIN find you and Ms. Taylor." He added, "If you're lucky, you're two steps ahead of them. Get to the airport. Now."

"Actually, we've booked a private charter—"

"Good. Don't let me keep you."

"Colonel, if I may, I think you have been influenced by Brendan Worley's abundance of caution. Meaning he's a weenie and he doesn't know shit. Also, he wanted to meet us tonight—"

"I don't take orders from Brendan Worley, Mr. Brodie, and neither do you, but if he advised caution, it was with good reason. You and Ms. Taylor are in danger. Kyle Mercer is in Mongolia by now. There is not a single reason for you to stay there." He added, "I will not have two CID agents arrested in a hostile country. We have enough problems in Venezuela. And I have enough problems."

Obviously, Worley had spooked Colonel Dombroski. Brodie didn't mind being called home from a foreign mission. It had happened before—but always under circumstances that were not his fault. Dombroski, however, was calling him and Taylor home for possible official reprimand. And Dombroski didn't even know the bad news that his special agent, Warrant Officer Brodie, and his agent's local recruit, Luis, had killed two Venezuelan government officials, two members of a colectivo, two whorehouse employees, and probably a few other people during his and Luis' escape. All in self-defense, of course. But Worley would find out about the body count and tell Dombroski, who would have to tell General Hackett. The only way Brodie could save his and Taylor's asses and careers would be to find Kyle Mercer.

"Mr. Brodie? I hope you are now hailing a cab for the airport."

"Still here, Colonel." He turned the map over, took the Sharpie, and wrote, *You're on. Save the mission.*

Taylor looked at his note, then said into the phone, "Colonel, may I speak?"

"Only if it's something I need to know immediately. Otherwise, you can both speak to me in Quantico, before we see General Hackett."

"Yes, sir. This is immediate Intel that needs immediate action."

"Speak."

"All right . . ." She looked again at Brodie, then said to Dombroski, "Scott has developed a good lead on the whereabouts of our fugitive."

There was no response from Dombroski, so Taylor continued, "He interviewed a witness . . . in the brothel . . . a woman who had recently accompanied Captain Mercer on a trip to what sounds like his hideout—a jungle camp in the south of the country."

Again there was a silence, and Brodie wrote on the map, *Don't give any details.*

She nodded and continued, "Scott's witness gave us enough information to make this trip and to verify what she said. We have booked a charter flight—"

"Don't tell me this was a hooker."

Brodie broke in, "A waitress. Spoke perfect English. I told her I was Captain Kyle Mercer's amigo. He broke her heart, and I told her I'd take her to him and play cupid. She's hot to trot." He added, "She trusts me."

Taylor looked at Brodie, obviously in awe of his bullshit.

Colonel Dombroski stayed silent again, then said, "All right . . . give me the details of her trip, and I'll fly two agents down there to follow up." He added, "You need to come home."

Brodie replied, "We're going to lose this guy, Colonel. This is a hot lead. You know what happens when we don't follow up immediately." He added, "I've gotten this lady to trust me. Won't work with someone else."

"The police may be looking for you."

"Ms. Taylor and I are willing to take the risk."

Taylor said, "What you should also know is that according to the witness, Captain Mercer is apparently training insurgents of some sort in this jungle camp."

"Are you serious?"

Brodie replied, "That's what my witness said."

"You believe her?"

"Why would she lie?"

"Could be a trap."

"That would be an elaborate trap, Colonel."

Taylor said, "We don't intend to try to apprehend him. We just need to verify what the witness said—to follow the trail, get a fix on this camp, and report to you, and you can turn this information over to the proper command for follow-up." She added, "We have military assets in Colombia, and in the waters off the coast here."

"All right . . . this is tempting . . . but—"

Brodie jumped in: "Colonel, let me be blunt. This will be a huge feather in all our caps."

"This is about justice, Mr. Brodie."

"Goes without saying. But if we let this slip through our fingers, we'll all be speaking to General Hackett." He added, "And Mercer will be making another video telling us to go fuck ourselves."

No reply.

Brodie continued, "We agree that we need to get out of Caracas, so we'll head south with our witness, get a fix on this camp, then take our charter plane to Colombia and call you from Bogotá with our findings, which you can pass on to the appropriate people." He added, "Now that you have this new information, I'm sure that's the course of action you would suggest."

"Well . . ."

Taylor pointed out, "This is safer than us trying to board a commercial flight out of here." She reminded him, "They may be looking for us at Simón Bolívar Airport. We're flying charter out of a smaller airport, where we can use our alternate passports."

"I understand. But . . . a side trip to—where are you going?"

"Not sure yet," replied Brodie. "Our witness will fill us in at the airport."

Dombroski asked, "What are you going to do with this lady when you get down there?"

As Brodie tried to think of more bullshit, Dombroski said, "You will not use her for bait to try to apprehend Kyle Mercer."

That wasn't a bad idea, but Brodie replied, "Of course not. We just need her to get a fix on this camp. We'll make sure she gets safely back to Caracas.

Then, if I may make a suggestion, it would be very fitting if a Delta Force team finished this business."

There was silence on the line; then Dombroski said, "That would be fitting."

Brodie offered, "I would be happy and honored to accompany the team. To represent the CID and make the actual arrest." He added, "Ms. Taylor would also like to join the operation."

Taylor wrote on the map, *Ms. Taylor would not.*

Dombroski said, "I doubt if that's possible. But your offer is noted." He added, "If a Special Ops mission is successful in finding Mercer, he will be taken to you and Ms. Taylor—in Colombia, or aboard a U.S. naval vessel—and you will be the arresting officers."

Brodie had a different plan, but he said, "Thank you, Colonel. I think you and I and Ms. Taylor have worked out a good plan going forward."

Dombroski didn't respond to that, but asked, "When does your flight leave?"

"Soon," Brodie replied.

"Call me from the airport."

"We will." Not.

"And call me when you get to your destination."

"If we have cell service—"

"Colonel Worley gave you a sat phone."

"He wants it back," Brodie reminded his boss.

"You will keep what you need."

"Yes, sir. Also, it goes without saying that Brendan Worley should not be privy to anything we've discussed."

Dombroski thought about that. "He wants you to call him."

"Colonel, let me be blunt—Ms. Taylor and I do not trust this man."

"I think the feeling is mutual."

"Good. We have different agendas. And I'm sure he'd like to hear from you that you have taken his suggestion and relieved your agents of this assignment and ordered us home."

"I'll call him."

"And I'd like to ask a favor. Our driver, Luis, who was with us tonight. He and his family will present themselves at the U.S. Consulate tomorrow morning seeking visas. Brendan Worley needs to be there and attest that Luis has aided the embassy in furthering U.S. interests in Venezuela and has thereby put himself and his family in danger. Mr. Worley needs to request expedited visas, which the consulate will issue on the spot." He added, "Their bags are already packed."

"Have you discussed this with Worley?"

"We have. It's not one of his priorities."

"Not one of mine either."

"It could be. I've told Luis to book a flight to Dulles, and to make a claim for political asylum on landing. I've given him your personal cell number to call."

"Thanks."

"When you meet with him, ask him to tell you about conversations he's overheard while driving embassy people and guests. Specifically ask him about Worley's conversation with an American named Ted."

"What does this have to do with our fugitive?"

"I'm still developing this lead."

"You're going a little cryptic on me, Brodie. I do not like cryptic."

"Do me and yourself a favor, Colonel. Twist Worley's arm to get Luis and his family a visa. This will pay off."

"It better. Okay . . . so I'll twist Worley's arm, then lie to him about you and Ms. Taylor leaving the country. Anything else I can do for you?"

"Yes, sir. Just trust us to do what has to be done."

"If I didn't trust you, Brodie, you wouldn't even have been given this case."

"Yes, sir. I know that."

"Is Ms. Taylor still there?"

She replied, "Yes, sir."

"You may want to leave the room."

She hesitated, then replied, "Whatever you have to say to Scott, Colonel, you can say to me."

"One of the benefits of your junior rank, Ms. Taylor, is that you're spared the reprimands. But, okay—you can listen to me chew on his ass." Dombroski paused, then said, "Scott, what you did tonight was beyond reckless. You endangered not only your life, but also Ms. Taylor's. This is the CID,

Mr. Brodie; not the fucking infantry. But if you want to go back to a combat unit, I can arrange that, and your ass will be in Afghanistan before you can spell it."

"Yes, sir."

"And you are not in military intelligence, Mr. Brodie. If there is more to this case than a violation of the Uniform Code of Military Justice, that is not your business. You are a criminal investigator. You are not James Bond, and you are not Rambo. Do you agree, Mr. Brodie?"

"Yes, sir." He wanted to remind Colonel Dombroski that it was the colonel himself who had brought up the subject of CIA agent Robert Crenshaw's death in Peshawar. But Dombroski had obviously gotten spooked by Worley, so Brodie didn't mention it. Nor would he ask again about Flagstaff—he might have the answer to that very soon. Nor would Brodie ask Colonel Dombroski to run a background check on General Gomez. And finally, Brodie would not mention his suspicion that Worley and Ted had flown to Tomás de Heres Airport, then on to the jungles of southern Venezuela in search of Kyle Mercer. In fact, as Colonel Dombroski was chewing him out, Brodie felt there was a lot that he wasn't obligated to share with his boss, and most probably his boss did not want to hear any of it. Colonel Dombroski had understood from the beginning—either instinctually or from General Hackett—that this was more than a criminal case, and Dombroski had been handling it like the hot potato it was. And now that Brodie had informed his boss that Captain Mercer was not just a fugitive, but some kind of jungle warlord, Dombroski saw a way out of this troublesome case. But he also wanted it to be the CID who apprehended the most infamous Army deserter since Benedict Arnold. Or at least assist in the apprehension. Colonel Dombroski wanted justice, of course, but he also wanted to retire with a general's pension. And his most reckless agent might make this possible.

Poor Colonel Dombroski, Brodie thought. Caught between caution and a big gamble. Between pressure from General Hackett, and pressure from Brendan Worley and Worley's colleagues in the Intel establishment. And also caught up in some shit he could only guess at. Well, that made two of them. He glanced at Taylor, who seemed to be enjoying hearing Dombroski chewing on Brodie's ass.

"Are you listening to me, Brodie?"

"Yes, sir."

"You have put yourself in a world of shit, Mr. Brodie. And only you can dig yourself out of it. And make sure you don't dig yourself and Ms. Taylor deeper into the shit."

"Yes, sir."

Dombroski seemed to have satisfied his appetite for Brodie's ass, and asked, "Do you have anything you'd like to say?"

"Well . . . can I speak off the record?"

"Everything we've said is off the record."

"All right . . . I believe that Brendan Worley is running his own operation to find Captain Mercer. I also believe that there are people in Washington who don't want Captain Mercer arrested. They want him dead. And I think you know that. And the only reason for this that I can think of is that Captain Mercer knows too much about something."

Colonel Dombroski didn't reply, and Brodie didn't expect him to. He pictured Dombroski at home in his crappy post-divorce bachelor pad, contemplating another drink, and thinking about two possible futures—forced retirement on a colonel's pay, or a general's star, and maybe a less stressful job in the bowels of the Pentagon.

Brodie, too, was at a crossroads in his career, but maybe he had civilian options—assuming he returned alive from the jungle.

Most of the time in the Army, there is no easy way out—like when you're ordered to attack. Now and then, however, you're ordered to stand down. But something in your training and in your gut says to push on; to ignore the order and the odds and go for the big win. This is how heroes and legends are made. It's part of the Army culture. It's also how dead soldiers are made.

He glanced at Maggie Taylor, whose career and life span were tied to his. Maybe, to be fair to her, they should take that charter flight to Curaçao, instead of Kavak, and lie on the beach for a week.

"Are you finished, Mr. Brodie?"

"No. You mentioned justice, Colonel. Brendan Worley and his friends deliver a kind of justice that isn't due process, but is the kind of justice that the American government and American people have become comfortable with in the years since 9/11. Think Predator drones armed with Hellfire missiles. That solution might be attractive to a lot of people in Washington because it has the beneficial effect of vaporizing Kyle Mercer, and with him the answers to a lot of uncomfortable questions. We, Colonel—you and I and Ms. Taylor—are after the truth. When we have that, we can have justice."

Colonel Dombroski stayed silent for awhile, then said, "The truth, Mr. Brodie, can not only be uncomfortable. It can be fatal."

"We all know that."

"Be very careful, Mr. Brodie. And Ms. Taylor. And be aware that you are entering into a dangerous area."

Brodie didn't think he meant the jungle. "Copy."

"Ms. Taylor? Anything further?"

"Nothing further, Colonel, except thank you for your confidence in us."

"I have confidence in your common sense, Ms. Taylor. I'm not so sure about your partner."

Brodie said, "Magnolia will keep me in line."

"Who . . . ?"

"Maggie. Magnolia. That's her full name."

"Really . . . ? All right, Scott . . . Mag—Maggie . . . good luck. Call home."

They replied in unison, "Yes, sir."

Brodie hit the end button.

They both sat in silence; then Brodie stood and moved to the couch across from her. He said, "Tell me about Flagstaff."

CHAPTER 34

Maggie Taylor finished her rum and asked Brodie to make her another.

Brodie rarely refused a drink request from a young lady, but whatever Maggie Taylor was offering while sober needed to be given the same way. "Later."

She nodded. "Okay . . . Well, Flagstaff. It's the name of a CIA program in Afghanistan. Once you know that, you know that the code name is obviously a sort of in-joke takeoff on the Phoenix Program."

He nodded. But there was nothing funny about the notorious Phoenix Program—the CIA Black Ops initiative in Vietnam that had been tasked with wiping out the Viet Cong infrastructure through infiltration, kidnappings, torture, and of course assassination. Literally thousands of Viet Cong—or suspected Viet Cong—had been executed without due process and often without much evidence. As Brodie understood it, CIA officers, in partnership with Army intelligence, did the Intel work and also a little of the wet stuff, but most of the dirty work was done by the South Vietnamese National Police, and even by U.S. Army Special Forces personnel who'd been recruited by the Agency. The program was always controversial because ICs—innocent civilians—had been killed by mistake, and it had been shut down after a congressional investigation. But history showed that Phoenix was very effective in accomplishing its mission. Therefore it would not surprise Brodie if, like the mythical phoenix that rose to life from its own ashes, the spooks at Langley thought that Phoenix—reborn as Flagstaff—would work well in Afghanistan.

He looked at Maggie Taylor, who he assumed had some knowledge of this from her CIA boyfriend. "Go on."

She nodded. "When I was deployed to Afghanistan, I stayed in touch with Trent." She glanced at Brodie and continued, "He told me he was working on something very important. With Special Ops units in Afghanistan."

And Special Ops often became Black Ops when the CIA got involved—as happened in Vietnam. Some things never change—except for the name. Brodie said, "And this was the Flagstaff program."

"Trent didn't give me a name for this program, but later he slipped up and used the name. He hinted that people in Civil Affairs . . . people I knew . . . were also helping the Agency with this program, and maybe I'd like to help." She stared off into space, then continued, "That should have set off alarm bells, but . . . I was naïve, stupid, and eager to assist in the war effort."

Brodie had heard enough confessions to know not to interrupt when the suspect was crossing the threshold, and to ask questions only when the person began to dissemble or contradicted an earlier statement. Or when they started to justify what they'd done. He wasn't so sure Maggie Taylor was that stupid and naïve not to understand that her old boyfriend was recruiting her, but he let it pass. He was tempted, however, to point out that she showed poor judgment in that relationship. Brodie had been there himself, so he could be sympathetic, but he had never let the personal cross over into the professional. Apparently she had. Getting involved with the spooks was messy, and it didn't easily wash off.

Taylor continued, "I was working mostly in Helmand Province, west of Kandahar. Taliban country and opium country. The peasants were making good money from the opium, but so was the Taliban. So the Afghan government, at the urging of the Americans, was ordering the peasants to burn the poppy fields, and Civil Affairs was working with an NGO that was helping to convert the fields and the farmers to raising food." She forced a smile. "Doing God's work."

Actually, thought Brodie, it was an exercise in futility, courtesy of the policy geniuses in the Pentagon. Last he heard, Afghanistan was now producing more opium than it had before the war. Veggies are good for you, but opium pays better. His father should have been growing marijuana instead of smoking it.

Taylor continued, "Trent called me on my sat phone about once a week while I was deployed. He seemed interested in what I was doing, and asked a lot of questions about the villagers and the Afghan officials that I dealt with." She paused, then admitted, "I understood that Trent was gathering

Intel, but I didn't have any classified information, and even if I did . . . I didn't think there was any law against sharing information with someone who had a high security clearance."

Especially if you'd slept with him. Brodie said, "There are actually rules and procedures relating to sharing information with other government agencies."

She nodded. "I understand that now."

"You understood it then. Instinctively, if nothing else."

Again she nodded, but insisted, "I had no classified information."

"Everything you see and hear in a war zone is classified."

"I know that. Army Intel also asked us a lot of questions about what we saw and heard. Everyone wanted to exploit the Civil Affairs teams. We were supposed to be helping the Afghans, and winning their trust—hearts and minds—but we wound up being the eyes and ears for Army intelligence, and we were under orders to cooperate with them."

"Right. But not with the CIA."

She stared at him for a few seconds. "You're not making this easy."

"The truth," said Brodie, quoting the CIA motto, "shall make you free."

She thought for a moment. "The truth is I let a personal relationship cloud my judgment, and I was partly aware of that, and I knew it was wrong. But another part of me figured I was helping anyway, and that was more important. We're all on the same side, right?"

Well, the CIA was on its own side, and played well with others only when it suited the Agency's interests. If Taylor didn't know that then, she certainly understood it now through some hard experience.

She sat back on the couch and looked out the glass doors to the balcony. A tropical storm was on the way, and heat lightning flashed across the dark sky, followed by the sharp clap of thunder, which reminded both of them of artillery. She said, as if to herself, "The job sucked. We accomplished almost nothing. The Afghans were duplicitous. The only reason we were able to operate in Taliban territory is because the Taliban took half of what we gave the peasants. But now and then, the Taliban would decide to engage a Civil Affairs team—just to show us who ran the show and whose country it was—and the Afghans, who we were trying to help, would set us up for an ambush. On top of all this, Army Intel would debrief us, asking the same kinds of questions that Trent asked me. And whenever a villager in a place where we'd been working got arrested by the Afghan National Police or picked up by an American Army unit, the locals assumed it was because Civil Affairs had fingered them, which didn't do much for our mission of establishing trust—which actually didn't matter because there was no trust on either side." She took a deep breath. "So I got the Silver Star, a Purple Heart, and a bad case of the blues."

And, thought Brodie, you got out of there on a medevac chopper, leaving behind a little blood and a lot of innocence. War will do that. It did something to Kyle Mercer, the patriotic kid from San Diego. It did something to Scott Brodie.

She poured herself some cola and continued, "Trent told me they were trying to gather Intel on peasants who would slip out of their villages after the spring planting to go fight with the Taliban."

Brodie nodded. *Where have all the young men gone? Gone to soldiers, every one.* Afghanistan had been at war so long that they actually had a "fighting season" that came every spring and lasted until the part-time jihadists returned to their villages to harvest the wheat and/or the poppies. There were a lot of downsides to perpetual war, but it did drive a year-round economy.

Taylor went on, "So after a month of me answering Trent's questions came the big ask." She paused, then continued, "He wanted me to start documenting my info more closely . . . like who these young guys were, their names, and how many there were, the names and the layouts of the villages, did I ever see any guys who had apparently been wounded, did I see anyone who didn't seem to belong in the village, did I have any suspicions about the village elders . . . that kind of thing."

Brodie wondered when Taylor had realized that the guys she was reporting on were being marked for death. Or at least arrest, torture, and—if they were lucky—imprisonment. Sounded a lot like Phoenix reborn.

Generals liked to use the same tactics that had worked in past wars, which, unfortunately, didn't often work in new wars. The Intel establishment, including the CIA, did the same, but with somewhat better results. And nothing succeeds like success.

The combat units, like the one he'd served with in Iraq, weren't completely innocent of ignoring the Geneva Conventions from time to time, but the CIA didn't consider themselves bound by the military rules of war. Kidnapping, torture, murder—whatever it takes. And Brodie was not overly judgmental about these tactics. If you're fighting a brutal, unconventional enemy, you use brutal, unconventional methods. But there is a line that should not be crossed. Unfortunately, different people saw the line in different places. Phoenix had crossed the line. And no doubt, so did Flagstaff. He looked at Taylor. Did she know this? And when did she know it?

She seemed to be thinking about the same questions and said, "It felt wrong. Even though Trent told me I was doing important work that would save the lives of American soldiers." She looked at Brodie. "And maybe it did."

"Maybe." Actually, you could save even more American lives if the Pentagon ever figured out how to end the wars it started. Baghdad fell in three weeks. Kabul in a month. A testament to American fighting capability. The problems came in sticking the landing, in not letting these things grind on for years and years until morally dubious programs like Phoenix and Flagstaff became almost inevitable.

Taylor continued, "I put my written reports in a designated locker back on base. A report a week. Someone retrieved these reports, but I never saw who it was."

"Not Trent. He was back in the States, where being out in the field meant mowing his lawn."

She shot him an angry look. "I've known a lot of combat veterans, and if you think Intel guys can be arrogant and cynical, you should listen to yourself."

Brodie did not reply.

"And moody. When they're not drinking too much."

"We're all trying to work our way home, Maggie."

She took a breath, looked at him, and said, "I know."

Well, he'd thought that it was going to be sex that screwed up their professional relationship, but it might be the baggage they both carried—the PTSD thing, which he didn't totally believe in, but which like other things he didn't believe in—ghosts, Santa Claus, and God—must be real if everyone kept talking about it.

Meanwhile, he was violating his own rules about interrogations, which is what happens when you're emotionally or personally involved with the subject. "I interrupted you."

She seemed to be collecting her thoughts, then continued, "About four months into my tour, our convoy headed into a village called Mirabad. A collection of mud huts in a river valley between the highlands, which were infested with Taliban. This area had gone back and forth between government and Taliban control. Our Civil Affairs unit hadn't been making much progress there, and Mirabad was particularly resistant to converting all its opium fields to crops." She added, "We'd been in Mirabad about five times, and the village elders were sometimes hostile and sometimes hospitable— it was a game to see how much they could get out of us. Also, they were trying to walk a thin line between the Americans and the Taliban." She paused, then continued, "A few weeks before, three American helicopters had taken ground fire from the vicinity of Mirabad, and one of the crew got hit and died later of his wounds, so we were cautious as we approached. Our platoon of about thirty personnel rode in five vehicles. For security purposes, these visits were never preannounced to the village or to Afghan authorities. In fact, we'd just gotten our orders that morning to go to Mirabad, so they didn't know we were coming. The purpose of our visit that day was to speak to the village elders about burning the remaining poppy fields. We had Afghan currency to pay for the burned poppies and we had wheat and barley seed with us. Our orders, as usual, were to be polite but firm, to offer the carrots and show the stick, and all that . . . but when we got there . . . the village was empty . . ." She looked at Brodie.

Nothing like an empty village, recalled Brodie, to get the adrenaline pumping. Usually you were about to get ambushed.

"At first," she said, "we thought the villagers had fled when the hard-core Taliban fighters came out of the hills and saw that half their poppy fields were gone."

Where have all the flowers gone?

"Then we noticed bullet holes in the mud huts, and blood spatters . . ."

Where have all the soldiers gone?

"We couldn't make sense of it. We were tense . . . ready for a fight . . . then this old man comes out of the wheat field and he's crying . . . and he's screaming at us . . ." She took a breath and continued, "Our translator told us that four helicopters landed in the middle of the night, on each side of the village . . . American soldiers came into the village and went from house to house, pulling out all the men and the young boys . . . anyone who looked old enough to be a Taliban fighter, boys as young as twelve or thirteen . . . those who resisted were shot on the spot . . . including some women who tried to intervene . . . the rest of the men were taken to a drainage ditch at the edge of the village . . . about fifty or sixty young men, boys, and all the village elders, except this one who had hid, and they . . . shot them."

Gone to graveyards, every one.

Operation Phoenix had been more surgical, targeting only the Viet Cong infrastructure in the villages. Operation Flagstaff sounded like Phoenix with a meat cleaver.

Maggie Taylor was composing herself, and Brodie listened to the torrential rain beating on the balcony.

Taylor continued in a flat, distant tone of voice: "We had dealt with complaints of U.S. soldiers killing civilians, and it was usually accidental—collateral damage. Or these complaints were made-up—a story to get compensation from the Americans. That was part of what we did in Civil Affairs. Pay for dead people, dead livestock, bomb-damaged houses . . . but what this old guy was saying . . . this was something else."

Indeed it was. It was, in fact, a hard lesson delivered to the villagers, and by extension to all the surrounding villages, that there was a price to pay for providing a cash crop and part-time fighters to the Taliban. They certainly wouldn't do that again.

Taylor gulped some of her cola, and continued, "This elder is crying . . . he says he lost four sons . . . and he shows us a big mound of freshly dug dirt and tells us it's a mass grave of all the men and boys the Americans killed . . . the women dug the grave . . . with the help of some men from nearby villages. We still weren't believing this and we wanted to see the bodies, but the elder says no, Islamic tradition prohibits digging up the dead, but he shows us all the shell casings that the women had gathered . . . from American M5 rifles . . . and he shows us a pile of blood-soaked clothing . . . he says men from the surrounding villages had stripped the bodies and wrapped them in burial shrouds . . . and then he takes us to the drainage ditch and we can see the water, red with blood . . ." She closed her eyes. "Our translator, a schoolteacher from Kandahar, was very upset, and he's looking at us like we owed him and the elder some explanation." She added, "It was awful."

Brodie looked at her, wondering how long it took her to see the connection between that massacre and her reports to her erstwhile boyfriend.

Taylor stayed silent awhile, then continued, "We told the elder that we'd report this to our superiors and that military investigators would be coming to speak to him and to the women who'd survived, and we left. Quickly." She added, "We were all pretty shaken by this, and most of us still didn't believe we'd seen evidence of a civilian massacre by American soldiers . . ." She looked at Brodie. "I mean, the Afghans were notorious for lying to get compensation. They'd blame the Americans for Taliban killings and even for natural deaths."

And then came the denial. *The Americans couldn't have done that. I couldn't have done that.* It's what you have to say to yourself.

Brodie made eye contact with her. "Maggie, it seems obvious from what you've told me that what you saw, and what you heard from the witness, was strong evidence of a mass murder perpetrated by American troops."

She nodded, but didn't reply.

Brodie looked at his partner. She appeared more vulnerable than he'd ever seen her. Her professional polish made him forget sometimes that at the end of the day, Maggie Taylor was Magnolia Taylor, a country girl from the hills who had clawed her way out of a hardscrabble existence in a place that, like much of rural America, celebrated a kind of bold, unsophisticated, and unequivocal patriotism. She had answered the call without questions, and she'd worn the uniform with pride. But nothing had prepared her for a man like Trent, who probably paid lip service to the things that Maggie Taylor held most dear.

He asked her, "How did you follow up?"

She held his gaze. "We followed procedure. Our platoon leader, a newbie lieutenant, and the three squad leaders, including me, reported in person to our immediate superior, Captain Evers. He seemed . . . a little distraught and a little unbelieving. He told us he'd pass this on to the colonel. A few days later, he told us that a task force, comprised of military Intel people, CID, and a forensic team, was going to visit Mirabad, take statements, look at physical evidence, and get at the truth."

Brodie nodded. "Good." He asked, "And did anyone take a written statement from you or anyone in your unit?"

"No."

"Did anyone get back to you about the results of the investigation?"

"No."

"And when you didn't hear anything, did you or anyone inquire further?"

"I asked Captain Evers what was happening. He said the investigation was ongoing, and that it was up to the CID to contact us if and when they needed any further statements from me or anyone in my unit." She added, "I'm still waiting."

"Right." If the first casualty of war is the truth, then the second casualty is justice. He informed her, "You could have bucked the chain of command and gone right to the commanding officer of your Civil Affairs battalion. Or even higher." He reminded her, "You can do that in extraordinary circumstances."

She nodded. "I could have . . . but I was told by Captain Evers, in no uncertain terms, that because of the sensitive nature of this incident—he called it an 'alleged incident'—that I was to say nothing to anyone—including senior officers. I was to speak only to CID or JAG, and only if asked for a statement."

"And you did as you were told."

"I did. We all did." She added, "Now . . . if something like that happened, I would act differently."

"I'm sure you would." And that probably included writing a negative report on Chief Warrant Officer Brodie, who was breaking a few rules and procedures of his own in the Mercer case. Maggie Taylor had learned a few things over the years, and there was a lot more to be learned. Like when to open your mouth, and when to keep it shut. Every soldier is schooled on the subject of obeying a lawful order, no matter how crazy or dangerous it sounds, and disobeying an unlawful order—if you're sure it's unlawful. Clearly Captain Evers had given her an unlawful order not to speak to superior officers in her chain of command about a crime that she had direct knowledge of. It was a tough position for a young soldier like Maggie Taylor, and she could only guess at what would happen to her if she went over Captain Evers' head. Also, she half believed that the system would work and that justice would be done. As for the truth, the truth was that four helicopters full of men did not take it on themselves to wipe out a village. The order had come from a high place. In fact, what Maggie Taylor had seen was no doubt a small peek into Operation Flagstaff.

He asked her, "Anything else you'd like to say about the alleged incident?"

"Just that I've had to live with this for all these years."

"It's not about you. But do you feel better now?"

"No."

"Would you feel better if we could find evidence connecting our criminal investigation of Kyle Mercer to Flagstaff?"

"I would . . . and that's why I told you about this."

Brodie nodded. "Also, you know that if I actually get my hands on Mercer, he might tell me something similar to what you just told me."

"You heard it here first, Scott. Give me some credit for honesty." She added, "I didn't have to tell you any of this."

"Actually, after Luis told us that Worley and Ted used the word 'Flagstaff,' you did. And if you had told me earlier, I would have had a better understanding of the bigger picture." He added, "Also, let me remind you that you told me, quote, I slept with the guy, Scott. I didn't get recruited by him. End quote."

She had no response to that, but said, "You need to focus on this mission. Find and apprehend Kyle Mercer."

"Right. But now it appears that Brendan Worley is trying to make sure that he finds Kyle Mercer first." He added, "And I don't think Worley intends to apprehend him. He could leave that to the CID. Worley intends to shut Mercer up. Permanently."

She nodded. "That was another reason I told you what I knew."

"Good. So you unburdened your soul, shed some light on this case, and trusted me with a dark secret. All within"—he looked at his watch—"ten minutes. That's a good night's work."

"The night is not over."

Did that mean she was ready to sleep with him? Probably not.

"And let me remind *you*," she said, "that what we've agreed to do here—kidnapping—is also pushing the limits of the law."

"I don't need reminding. But kidnapping—extraordinary extradition— is not murder." He added, "I'm sure Kyle Mercer would rather be kidnapped by us than murdered by Worley and his friends."

She looked at him but didn't reply. She finished her cola.

Brodie listened to the torrential downpour and the crack of thunder that shook the glass doors. "What else should I know about the aftermath of Mirabad?"

She thought a moment, then replied, "Our Afghan translator disappeared without notice, and my Civil Affairs unit was transferred to Paktia Province a week later. Then a few people from my unit were assigned to other units. Also, a few people got orders to return to the States before their tour ended." She added, "We got scattered."

"Right." Obviously, the Army was worried. And more obviously, Operation Cover-Up was in full swing. "At what point did you call Trent? Or did he call you?"

"I called him."

"To tell him about Mirabad."

She nodded.

"After Captain Evers told you to keep quiet."

"The day after."

"And?"

"And . . . I told him what I'd seen, and he says it could have been an elaborate hoax to get money out of us . . . or if this massacre actually happened, why did I believe it involved American troops. It could have been the Taliban. Also, he said, the Afghan Army has helicopters and we supply their uniforms and weapons, and the Afghan Army has committed similar atrocities on their own people . . . to punish them for giving aid to the Taliban." She looked at Brodie to see if he found this plausible, which he would have before he'd heard about Flagstaff.

Taylor continued, "It wasn't clear to me if this elder said these soldiers were speaking English—or if they spoke at all—and if they had any uniform insignia—"

"They did not."

She nodded, then forced a smile. "I wasn't CID then, so I never thought to ask probing questions."

"Even if you had, Trent already had the answers for you."

Again she nodded. "I did push him a little, and I asked if what I had been reporting to him had anything to do with what happened in Mirabad. And he gets angry and hangs up."

He was probably angry at his bad luck—that the very village that had been marked for death was the village that his former lover—and recently recruited asset—had arrived in to carry out a Civil Affairs assignment. Shit happens. Maybe there is a God. Brodie looked at Taylor. "I'm sure he called you back."

"If you know so much, why don't you tell me what he said?"

"It makes no difference what he said. But he probably told you what Captain Evers told you—keep your mouth shut."

"I'm ready for a drink."

"You're close. Okay, you said that Trent, in one of his sat phone conversations with you, used the word 'Flagstaff'?"

She nodded. "But as soon as he said it, I could tell he regretted it. A slip of the tongue."

"It happens. And now we can connect Trent to Flagstaff. But can we connect Kyle Mercer and his Special Ops team to Flagstaff? And how are Brendan Worley and Ted connected to Flagstaff? And was Mirabad a Flagstaff operation? And does the death of CIA agent Robert Crenshaw in Peshawar have anything to do with this? And why are Mercer and Worley both in Venezuela?" He looked at his partner. "We have a lot of pieces to the puzzle, and we know now that they somehow fit, but we don't know how to put them together."

She stood. "We may never know."

"We will know when we question Captain Mercer."

She didn't reply to that and went to the bar and made herself a rum and cola. Standing behind him, she said, "So I was assigned to Paktia Province, and six months into my time there, our convoy got hit. I was medevaced to the Bagram Airfield hospital, then on to Landstuhl, and then back to Bragg. End of story."

Brodie didn't think so. This story should end with Maggie meeting Trent back at Fort Bragg, but apparently she wasn't ready for the epilogue.

She sat on the couch across from him and downed half her drink. She asked, almost rhetorically, "How could they do that?" She looked at Brodie. "How can American soldiers do that?"

Apparently he was the only expert on that subject in the room, so he replied, "Most atrocities happen in the heat of the moment. Battle fatigue, combat psychosis—what we now call misconduct stress behavior . . . revenge and retribution for your dead comrades. But what happened in Mirabad sounds premeditated and cold-blooded. That's harder to explain. Especially if the troops involved were an elite force, like Delta. They're trained to kill, but they would consider it a dishonor to kill unarmed civilians. It would be beneath them." He thought a moment and added, "On the other hand . . . they are also trained not to question orders. Even orders that could be illegal. And they are also notorious for secrecy. They know when to keep their mouths shut—which is all the time. So . . . I can see how Delta Force teams, such as the one Captain Mercer commanded, would be the best force behind Operation Flagstaff." Brodie wondered what toxic brew of JSOC, CIA, military Intel, and Pentagon planners had led to Flagstaff, and to using Delta Force teams—if that's who got off those helicopters—to teach the peasants and the Taliban a lesson in terror tactics.

These things sometimes worked, and sometimes they made things worse. In any case, terror tactics were a sign of desperation—unimaginative thinking disguised as a bold new tactic. Actually, it was a war crime. And, as with the Phoenix Program, sometimes people went to jail. Most perpetrators, however, did not. These crimes, when they were conceived of at the highest levels, and when they had a nice code name, were no longer crimes; they were unconventional war-winning strategies.

And finally, to answer Maggie Taylor's question, soldiers in combat do what they're told to do if a higher command tells them it will save American lives, shorten the war, crush an inhuman enemy, and keep the war from coming to America.

Sometimes, however, what you are ordered to do and what you have to do to carry out those orders does cross the line. Soldiers begin to feel guilt and become conscience-stricken, and they start to think about what they're actually doing. The military is its own world, but every soldier comes from a family.

"What are you thinking?"

He looked at his partner. "I'm thinking that Kyle Mercer, if he was involved with the Flagstaff Program, had somehow run afoul of his superiors. Maybe he had a crisis of conscience. Maybe he was going to make waves—"

"You always tell me not to speculate."

Brodie nodded. "But sometimes the maybes fit what you know. We know that Mercer deserted his post, and we know that he was captured by the Taliban. But what if he hadn't been captured? No one has asked the question of where he was going. Hard to get to Paris or Tahiti from the tribal territories. So maybe he was going to the nearest large American base to see a high-ranking commander. Or talk to the CID or a JAG officer." He looked at her. "Make sense?"

"Maybe."

"Consider the videotape of Captain Mercer separating Taliban heads from Taliban necks. Then Mercer, very angry, looking into the camera and resigning his commission." Brodie asked, "Why would an officer who just escaped captivity do that? I'll tell you. He was pissed off about something, and it wasn't the Taliban." Brodie finished his drink and said, "Maybe Captain Mercer didn't betray his country. Maybe his country betrayed him."

They both listened to the rain awhile; then Taylor said, "I've thought about that."

"Good thinking." Of course, she'd had the advantage of knowing things that he didn't. And she might know even more. He looked at her. "Can I assume you heard from Trent when you were at Landstuhl?"

She nodded. "He called me."

"No flowers?"

She shot him an annoyed look. "Lay off, Scott."

"Sorry. Did he bring up the subject of Mirabad?"

"No. And neither did I."

"Right. And if I may get personal, what was the content of his communication with you?"

"Just to see how I was doing. Looking forward to seeing me at Bragg. Congratulated me on my Silver Star."

Brodie wanted to ask her if she had the feeling that Trent was not as delighted as he was disappointed that she'd survived the ambush. Maybe that had crossed her mind at some point, but maybe not. He couldn't get a clear picture of that relationship, and maybe Trent wasn't as big an ass-hole as Brodie had made him out to be. Hard to know from the slim testi-mony of Maggie Taylor. But in his experience, all ex-boyfriends of women he was interested in were monumental assholes. More importantly, Trent was involved in something murderous. Maggie Taylor understood that, but . . . something kept her from telling her ex to stop communicating with her. This was not the first time he'd seen this in his personal and professional life. He called it the Bonnie and Clyde Syndrome. "Please continue."

She looked at him. "Why do I think you're being judgmental?"

"Comes with the job."

"You're not supposed to show it during an interview."

"Right. But . . . well, I'm concerned."

"It almost sounds like you care about me."

"I almost do. Please continue."

"All right . . . So, when I got back to Bragg, he came to my apartment to welcome me home . . . He had a bottle of champagne."

Brodie wished he had a CIA expense account, but he kept that to him-self.

"We talked about what I was going to do next, and I said I was thinking about applying to the CID."

"Did he take that as a veiled threat?"

"He didn't seem happy with my new career choice." She thought a mo-ment and continued, "He seemed to be trying to decide if he needed to be charming or not so charming. I mean, I could see right through him. Then he wanted to . . . be intimate. I said no, I was still recovering—I wore shorts so I could show him my scars, which were still purple and gross . . . I wanted him to see this, and I wanted him to understand that I was not the impres-sionable girl he'd known." She looked at Brodie.

"I understand. What I don't understand is the purpose of you inviting him to your apartment."

"He invited himself."

"All right, but a public place might have been better."

"I wanted to show him I wasn't afraid to be alone with him."

Brodie nodded.

"After Afghanistan, there's nothing I can't handle."

"Right. But I hope you had a gun handy."

"I did."

"Good. So . . . who broached the subject of Mirabad?"

"I did. I told him I thought he'd used me, and that the information I'd given him about Mirabad led to what happened. I thought he was going to tell me I was crazy, or that he found out that it was the Taliban that did it, but he dropped the charm and told me if I ever said anything about this to anyone, I would be jeopardizing an important wartime strategy, and that if there was an investigation, the Agency would prove from my written reports that I knew exactly what I was doing, and that if people were indicted, I would be one of them. And not only would he not protect me, he would testify that I was an active participant in Operation Flagstaff, and that I was not the dumb, clueless girlfriend I was claiming to be." She seemed to be getting angry at this recollection and continued, "He said if he was going down, then I was going down with him. And that I was looking at five to ten years in a federal prison."

Brodie nodded. The old CIA would have just thrown her out a high window. They'd really gone soft. He asked, "How did you respond?"

"I told him to leave."

He was happy to hear that Trent didn't get laid. "And did he?"

"When I say leave, I mean leave."

"I'll remember that." Her mommy should have given her daddy the same choice instead of blowing him away. Maggie Taylor, however, was an officer and a lady, though she was also probably only one hillbilly gene away from pulling a gun on her cheatin', lyin' skunk of an ex-lover.

"What are you smiling at?"

"Was I? Must be the rum. So he left. Did you hear from him again?"

"No."

He wanted to re-ask the question, to get the right answer, but his cell phone rang and he saw it was the Apex number, so he took it. "Bowman."

Ms. Muller said, "I can confirm your flight, Mr. Bowman."

"Wonderful. I was afraid my wife's credit card was maxed out again."

"Please be at Francisco de Miranda Airport no later than two forty-five A.M. for a three-fifteen departure. Captain Collins will meet you and your wife at Hangar One. He has both your cell phone numbers if there is a problem." She gave Brodie Captain Collins' cell phone number and also advised him that he could call the Apex eight hundred number if he couldn't reach Captain Collins on his cell.

"You are most efficient, Ms. Muller."

"Thank you." She further advised him, "Captain Collins will be flying a Cessna Turbo Stationair HD, and he will file a flight plan to Kavak with a fueling stop at Ciudad Bolívar, so you should be landing at Kavak at dawn— about six-fifteen A.M."

"If you were a bird-watcher, you'd know how exciting this is."

"Yes, sir." She continued, "May I confirm that Captain Collins is staying overnight in Kavak, and that you will take care of his lodging and meals?"

"And I'll buy him a drink."

"May I also confirm that you and your wife will return to Caracas, before noon on the next morning?"

There was no way he and Taylor were going back to Caracas, but he replied, "Correct." He'd have to persuade Captain Collins to fly them across the border into Colombia. Money was a good persuader. So was a Glock.

"Have a good flight, Mr. Bowman, and thank you for choosing Apex. If you need a charter flight in the future, Apex would be happy to assist you."

Not after he hijacked the plane and pilot to Colombia. "Thank you."

"I hope you see that yellow-bellied Worley."

He hoped not. "I'll e-mail you a photo of them mating."

"That won't be necessary." She added, "Bon voyage."

"Buenas noches." He hung up and said to Taylor, "Two forty-five A.M. airport arrival for a three-fifteen flight to Kavak, stopping at Ciudad Bolívar for fuel." He added, "So hopefully we'll have enough gas to get us from Kavak to Colombia."

She nodded.

"Well," said Brodie, "we have a few hours to kill."

She suggested, "We should get some sleep."

"Right." Or they could do something else.

She stood and went over to the balcony doors, and he followed. She said, "I hope this storm passes so we can take off on time."

"It seems to be moving out to sea."

She watched the rain and lightning, then asked, "Are you going to call Dombroski?"

"We've done that."

"You know what I mean."

"This may be one of those times when you agree with me that he doesn't need to know everything."

She nodded. "Thanks."

Brodie had the feeling, based on instinct and experience, that Trent and the CIA had kept in touch with Maggie Taylor after she'd kicked Mr. Wonderful out of her apartment. He would have pushed her on that, but a good interrogator knows when to stop asking questions. Especially if the interrogator is thinking about getting laid.

A huge sheet of lightning lit up the sky and illuminated the distant hills of Petare in an incandescent glare. Seconds later an earth-shaking thunder rolled across the dark city and rattled the glass doors.

Taylor asked, "Did you ever see an arclight?"

Meaning a flight of B-52s, dropping two-thousand-pound bombs. "No."

"I did. Once." She stared off at the hills, silhouetted by the distant lightning. "It was like the world was coming to an end . . . The mountains and the night sky were lit up, and the earth shook, and the explosions were like eruptions from far-off volcanoes. It was apocalyptic. It was the most awesome . . . beautiful thing I'd ever seen."

Brodie was sure that the people in the strike zone had a different perspective, but he said, "One day, when you realize you love the sound of outgoing artillery, the sight of air strikes, the smell of gunpowder . . . you are then changed forever."

She nodded, then turned to him, and they looked at each other. She said, "I'm sorry I didn't tell you about Flagstaff sooner."

"Better late than never."

"I don't want you to jeopardize your career by not reporting this conversation."

"Let me worry about that."

Taylor looked away, like she had something more to say and was trying to figure out how to say it.

Maggie Taylor was not combat infantry like Brodie, but she'd gone through the same fire anyway, and she had the scars to prove it. But she had other scars too, apparently, the kind unseen. It must have been a shock to join an outfit supposedly built on optimism like Civil Affairs, where one day you're helping plant crops and build schools, and the next you're painting civilian targets for a Black Ops death squad.

You lose your innocence in war, but Maggie Taylor had also lost faith.

And just as Sergeant Scott Brodie had responded to the mind-fuck of the Iraq War by swapping his M4 rifle for a CID badge, Maggie Taylor was trying to balance the scales once again toward justice. If she sometimes came across as a little too obedient to the rules, it was maybe because she saw the darkness that was possible in their absence.

She looked back at him as a flash of lightning lit up the room. They stood in silence, looking into each other's eyes as the tropical storm raged outside, two people a little buzzed and a lot horny and a thousand miles from home. Secrets had been shared. Walls had come down. And they were a few hours from takeoff on a dangerous recon they might not come back from.

"Scott . . . I . . ."

He took her in his arms and they kissed.

He put his hand under her T-shirt and ran it along her back. His fingers did a recon, reporting back that her bra had a front clasp. He hiked her T-shirt up and unclasped her bra, then hiked his polo shirt up, and they pressed their bare skin against one another as they kissed.

A loud crash of thunder startled both of them, and Brodie could feel her skin getting sweaty.

She backed away from him. "Scott . . . I can't." She pulled her shirt down.

He looked at her. "You okay?"

She nodded, looked at him. "I just . . . I can't make the same mistake twice."

Well, he was her superior officer and partner, not a manipulative spy, so technically it was a different mistake. "Okay."

She moved quickly back to the couch, grabbed her tablet, and said, "Call me when you're ready to leave."

"Right."

She went into her bedroom and closed the door.

Brodie stood there, wondering how he had gone from rounding third base to striking out. Well . . . no use wondering. Game over.

He went into his bedroom, shut the door, and got out of his clothes.

Maggie Taylor was thinking about her career, and trying to reestablish a wall between her personal and professional lives. But Brodie's instincts and experience told him there was more to her inner conflicts.

He got into the shower and let it run cold to sober himself up and cool himself down. He imagined she was doing the same thing.

He got out of the shower, dried off, and started packing his bug-out bag.

As his head cleared, he tried to put the best spin on what had just happened. Sex on the job had too many pitfalls. He was her superior officer, and sex would have changed the balance of power, thereby compromising and complicating the short chain of command. How could he give orders to someone who'd just given him a blow job? She'd be giving *him* orders.

The Army wasn't just a job; it was a life—and Army life had rules about sex, and somewhat archaic laws about sexual conduct and morality. You could get laid all you wanted, but don't fuck the colonel's wife, or anyone's wife, because adultery is still a crime, and don't fuck anyone who takes orders from you. There were other commandments, and Brodie knew them all, and in fact he'd investigated a good number of sexual misconduct cases. Consensual sex was no defense if it violated the Uniform Code of Military Justice. So he was very happy that he hadn't gotten laid tonight. He couldn't wait to tell Dombroski that he hadn't had sex with Maggie Taylor. The colonel would be proud of him. And probably call him a loser for not scoring.

On the other subject—Trent—Brodie was sure there was more to that. It would be a stunning coincidence if Warrant Officer Maggie Taylor had been randomly assigned to a case that might involve the Flagstaff Program. If Brodie was paranoid, he might suspect that the CIA had had a hand in Ms. Taylor's assignment. If that was true, then Chief Warrant Officer Brodie had not been chosen for this assignment because he was the best of the best; he'd been chosen because his partner was Maggie Taylor. Was that possible? And if so, what was the purpose of getting her sent to Venezuela? Was she still a CIA asset with orders to report back? Or did the dark forces behind Flagstaff want her—along with Mercer—dead? When the Agency wanted someone dead, they made sure that person was first on foreign soil.

Brodie walked to the window and watched the rain falling on the dark city. And if they wanted *her* dead, and Mercer dead, then . . . Chief Warrant Officer Brodie could become collateral damage.

The fog of war had rolled out of the hills of Afghanistan, and into the

Pentagon, Quantico, and Langley. And now it had followed them to Caracas, and it was waiting for them in the jungle.

A sane person would get himself back to Quantico and dump all this in the lap of his commanding officer. But as Maggie Taylor had discovered in Afghanistan, that was no guarantee that the information of a crime would make its way to the top—or if it did, the information might reach the wrong people, meaning the people who were complicit.

Paranoia was a fun brain exercise. Until it wasn't.

Well, there were no more answers in Caracas, and no more questions to be asked here. The questions, the answers, and the truth were waiting for them in the dark green expanses of that map.

If he didn't get on that plane to Kavak, he would never know the truth—not about Mercer, or Flagstaff, or Worley . . . or Maggie Taylor. And in the end, the only work product that Warrant Officer Brodie produced was the truth. And truth was the critical component of justice.

He turned from the window and continued packing.

The truth will set you free. John 8:32. *The truth can get you killed.* Scott 1:1.

CHAPTER 35

Brodie lay on his bed, wearing cargo pants and a black T-shirt, unable to sleep, waiting for his 2 A.M. wakeup call.

Starting your day at zero dark thirty was a time-honored tradition in the U.S. Army, but if you lived off base, as he did, at least you weren't awakened by the bugle sound of reveille blasting out of pole-mounted speakers. But even off base, or on assignment, you still had to get up with the birds to get a jump on the worms.

But to put things into perspective, what sucked even more was being in a combat unit in hostile territory in the dead of night, unable to sleep because there were people out there who wanted to kill you.

Even worse was when you'd gotten the word that your unit was going to mount a dawn attack—the two worst words in the English language for an infantryman. *Dawn attack.* Bad enough that you slept on the ground with your boots on in scorpion-infested dirt, and breathed desert dust all night. But to add insult to injury, some officer or NCO was going to come around and wake you up at zero dark so you wouldn't be late for your dawn attack. Which, by the way, you'd been thinking about all night: You were going to attack an enemy position, assault rifles and machine guns blazing, grenade launchers firing, mortar and artillery exploding while the infantry moved forward, trying to keep up with the armored vehicles that were firing everything they had at some poor bastards who a few seconds before had been jerking off, dreaming about their seventy-two virgins in paradise whom they were about to meet.

We attack at dawn, men. Before breakfast, for God's sake. You were going to kill someone before you even had coffee. Or it was you who was going to get killed. And the last thing you'd see was the rising sun. *Shoulda gone to grad school.*

Well, if he could handle that, there was little he couldn't handle. The shoot-out at the whorehouse would barely make the Battle Update Brief in Iraq.

Brodie canceled his wake-up call and got out of bed. He put on his running shoes, took his overnight bag, and went into the sitting room, hoping to find Maggie Taylor there.

Over the years he'd become adept at navigating any morning-after awkwardness with the women he'd slept with. It was situations like this—a swing and a miss—that were awkward. And annoying. As the boys used to say at NYU, "Getting laid is no big deal, but not getting laid is a very big deal."

Taylor wasn't there, so Brodie sat on the couch and looked closely at the map by the light of the table lamp. What the hell was Kyle Mercer doing in the jungle? And why hadn't the asshole gone someplace nice, like Barcelona, where he could practice his Spanish in a tapas bar? It occurred to Brodie that most of his world travels had taken him to shitholes. It also occurred to him that his mood might be better if he was now in a postcoital sleep in Maggie Taylor's bed. He deserved a thirty-day leave after this assignment. He pictured himself on a nude beach in the Caribbean, walking hand in hand with someone who looked like Maggie Taylor.

———

"Scott. Time to go."

Dawn attack?

Maggie Taylor had her hand on his shoulder and shook him gently. "You ready?"

He looked at her, hoping she was naked, but she was wearing cargo pants and a T-shirt, same as him, except her shirt said: "Georgetown."

She said, "I've called for a taxi."

He stood, yawned, and stretched.

The overnight bag they'd bought at the CVS was on the coffee table, and she said, "I emptied the safe. Cash, ID, Glock, mags, Taser, zip ties, and sat phone. I also took the map, and I downloaded a bird-watcher guide onto my tablet."

He wondered if she'd also made a pair of binoculars out of toilet paper rolls.

He walked to the bar, opened two bottles of orange juice, and handed one to her.

They sipped the OJ in silence; then she said, "I'm sorry."

Sorry for what? For lying to him about her knowledge of the Flagstaff Program? Or for not giving in to his reasonable carnal desires?

"I'm sorry if I led you on."

Brodie had that feeling that he'd gotten fucked without getting laid. "Okay. Drop it."

But she didn't. "Let's get this assignment behind us, then . . . I'll have you over for a nice dinner at my place."

He'd never been invited to her apartment, and he hadn't invited her to his—even when he had friends over for drinks. In fact, they'd kept their distance when off-duty, which was a bit odd considering how much time they spent together in the office and on assignment. Or maybe not so odd. Maybe it was smart.

"Scott?"

"No catfish, no rabbits, no possum, and no grits."

She smiled. "Promise." She asked, "Ready?"

"Did you leave anything behind that could be compromising?"

"Just my new bikini." She said seriously, "I've shredded and flushed our photos of Kyle Mercer. We won't need them where we're going."

"Right." They were not going to be showing Mercer's photo around Kavak, and they wouldn't want to have it on them if they were stopped and searched somewhere along their travels. Maggie Taylor thought of everything. He hoped she hadn't forgotten whatever contraception she used.

Brodie scanned the room for anything else and spotted the briefcase that Worley had given them, sitting on the desk. He opened it.

She assured him, "I checked it. It's empty."

"Worley wanted this left at the front desk."

"I think he expected things to be in it."

"Right." Brodie retrieved a foil-wrapped condom from his overnight bag and threw it in the briefcase. "Do you think he'll understand that means 'fuck you'?"

"Don't provoke him, Scott."

"It's lubricated." He closed the briefcase and spun the combination wheels to lock it.

He saw that the TV was on, though it was muted. "Anything interesting on 'Good Morning Venezuela'?"

"I was flipping through the news shows to see if there was anything about last night."

He didn't think that his failure to get laid last night was that newsworthy.

She said, "Nothing about the shooting in Petare."

"Good."

"How could that not make the news?"

"The Hen House is under the protection of the regime and the colectivos, and dead customers are bad for business."

She nodded.

"But you can be sure Kyle Mercer knows about it."

Again, she nodded. "I hope Carmen keeps her mouth shut about what she told you."

"Me too."

"All right . . . ready?"

Brodie took the briefcase and his overnight bag and Taylor grabbed her bag, then they exited the suite, checking that the No Molestar tags were hanging on all three doors. Brodie checked his watch: 2:25 A.M.

On the ride down, Brodie said, "Keep an eye out for Worley or his minions. Also, don't forget we may be the subject of a police manhunt."

She nodded.

"Where's your Glock?"

She patted the pocket of her cargo pants.

"Follow my lead if we're stopped by anyone."

"Does that mean you have no plan?"

"I plan to be on that plane."

The elevator doors opened and they stepped into the deserted lobby, checked it out, then walked quickly to the front desk.

Brodie put the briefcase on the counter and said to the clerk, "This is for Señor Brendan Worley, who will send someone from the American Embassy to pick it up."

"Sí, señor." He gave Brodie a piece of hotel stationery and a pen, and Brodie wrote Worley's name and his own name and room number, then wrote, *Foxtrot Uniform*, which in the military phonetic alphabet was *FU*, which, if carefully decoded, meant "Fuck you."

Taylor had no comment, but Brodie felt her eyes rolling. The clerk gave Brodie a receipt for the briefcase, and Taylor said to the clerk, "We should be back around seven tonight. Could you ask the concierge to make us a dinner reservation for eight P.M. at a restaurant of his choice?"

Brodie added, "We don't eat rabbits."

"Sí, señor . . . señora."

Brodie gave him an American five and headed for the door with Taylor. He said to her, "We're really good at this bullshit, aren't we?"

"Speak for yourself. I have trouble being duplicitous."

"Really?"

She didn't reply.

They exited the hotel. The rain had stopped, but it left an oppressive humidity behind. The deserted roundabout was under a foot of water and the air smelled as though the sewers had overflowed. More importantly, the police and SEBIN might be closing in on them. Or Worley's people might be lying in wait. "I won't miss this place."

"You will when we're in the jungle."

"Thanks."

The doorman noticed them and hurried over. "Taxi?"

"I think we need a boat."

The doorman smiled. "Sí. Big pour-down."

"Right. We've ordered a taxi."

"Sí, señor. He waits your coming." The doorman blew his whistle and signaled to a black Honda SUV, which moved slowly toward them, leaving a wake of water behind.

The doorman looked at them curiously and asked, "Do you go where?"

Taylor replied, "The Marina Grande Yacht Club." She added, "Fishing."

"Ah, good fishing."

Brodie said to her, "It's always good to create a few witnesses to your bullshit."

She had no reply.

The SUV, a Teletaxi, stopped at the curb, and Brodie gave the doorman a dollar as Taylor climbed in and slid over so he wouldn't have to walk through the water.

The doorman called out to the driver, "Los Marina Grande." He said to his guests, "Have a good fish," and closed the door.

Brodie said, "That guy should come with subtitles."

"Relax."

They exchanged greetings with the driver, who introduced himself as Gabriel, and who seemed to speak better English than the doorman.

As they passed through the security gates and onto the street, Gabriel asked, "Why you go Marina Grande?"

Why is everyone so fucking nosy? "Fishing," said Brodie. "But first we have to pick someone up at Francisco de Miranda Airport."

Gabriel nodded.

Taylor said to Brodie, "You're the expert at impromptu bullshit."

"I've had a lot of experience."

They drove through the dark, flooded streets, and Brodie glanced out the back window a few times.

Gabriel noticed and said, "We okay. Nobody bother Gabriel." He raised his right hand, which held what looked to Brodie like an old U.S. Army Colt .45.

Brodie said to him, "If this was Uber, I'd give you five stars."

"Señor?"

Taylor said, "My husband will give you a big tip."

"Gracias."

They got onto the Francisco Fajardo Highway and Gabriel gassed it.

Brodie tried to imagine living in a city where you were equally likely to get robbed by the police or by the criminals, or even by your pistol-packing taxi driver. On the other hand, if everyone had a gun—including the potential victims—it could get funny: a Venezuelan standoff with everyone waving pistols at one another, demanding money. He said to Taylor, "The jungle is probably safer."

"Get back to me on that tonight."

Brodie took the satellite phone out of the CVS bag, and Taylor said, "Scott, you can't call . . . the boss here." She nodded toward the driver. "And it won't work inside the taxi."

"Right."

"He wants us to call him from the airport."

"Right." Brodie removed the battery from the back of the phone, then took out the SIM card that was underneath it.

"What are you doing?"

"I'm making sure the wild Worley bird can't track us."

She didn't reply, but nodded.

Brodie put the battery and SIM card in his pocket, and the sat phone back in the overnight bag. He then took out his smartphone and used the toothpick from his Swiss Army knife to pop out his own SIM. If Worley was motivated enough, he had both the authority and the capability to use their cell phone numbers to track them.

Taylor seemed to get this and reached out for the toothpick, then did the same with her phone.

At some point, deep in the jungle, they might need the satellite phone—to call Dombroski, or even Worley if they needed to arrange an extraction. But in the meantime, they had gone electronically silent—off the grid and under the radar, location unknown. Worley would have a shit fit when the commo people at the embassy reported the lost signal. Two shit fits, actually, when the briefcase was delivered to him. Well, Worley deserved it for trying to get Dombroski to pull them off the case. The man was up to something, and it might be just the usual—a turf war, coupled with diplomatic worries about the Hen House incident. But there was growing evidence that Brendan Worley had his own agenda. Brodie hoped that Dombroski had a good colonel-to-colonel talk with Worley. Meanwhile neither of them needed to know where he and Taylor were.

They drove in silence, and Brodie saw the lit-up airport on their right, reminding him of their ride to Petare. If the news did report the whorehouse shoot-out and the body count, they'd toe the party line and blame it on the Americans—and in this case, they'd be right.

Brodie asked the driver, "You been to this airport before?"

"Sí. Sometimes I drive important people. Sometimes turistas. They fly on the private planes."

"Where do they fly to?"

Gabriel shrugged. "Not my business." He added, however, "Turistas to the south. Beautiful country." He also revealed, "The rich, they go some-place, never return."

"Long vacation."

Gabriel laughed. "Sí, very long."

Taylor asked, "Have you driven any Americans to this airport?"

"No." He asked, "Who you meet here?"

Brodie replied, "Another fisherman."

Gabriel did not respond.

Gabriel took the first exit and doubled back along a service road to the airport's entrance, which was marked by an illuminated sign that identified it as a military airport, though Brodie understood it was used by anyone who could help pay for the upkeep.

And in keeping with the banana republic theme, there was a dilapidated shed at the entrance where an armed guard sat half-asleep in a plastic chair. The guard stood and ambled over to the taxi.

Gabriel and the young man exchanged a few words, and Gabriel lowered the rear passenger window so the guard could get a look at his passengers. The guard said something, and Gabriel translated: "He requires a parking fee. Five million bolívars, or one dollar." He added, "I tell him we don't park, so then he say it is an entrance fee." Gabriel laughed. "Gringo tax. You pay him, por favor."

Brodie thought a dollar sounded reasonable, considering the guard didn't ask for their IDs or inquire about Gabriel's pistol on the passenger seat. He would actually have given him two if he'd just admitted it was a shakedown. Brodie gave him a dollar and rolled up his window, and Gabriel drove off.

Brodie inquired, "How much to get out of here?"

"Three dollar." Gabriel laughed again.

Well, at least they could laugh about it. What else could you do?

They continued along a flooded and potholed airport road and Brodie said, "Hangar One," wondering if there was a Hangar Two.

"Sí."

A military vehicle passed them going the opposite direction, and up ahead on the grass Brodie could see two military helicopters that looked to be Russian-made. Farther away, on the tarmac, he saw two jet fighters that looked like Russian MiGs. This seemed to be the extent of the Venezuelan Air Force here, and he suspected that the choppers and the MiGs were grounded for parts, service, or fuel. This military airport had become a no-questions-asked port of embarkation for the rich and nervous, and probably for drug runners and others who would prefer no record of their air travel. Like Kyle Mercer.

Gabriel turned toward a row of three hangars and headed to the one on the left, marked number one by a badly lit sign above the open doors. As they got closer, the taxi's headlights picked out a tall man standing beside a single-engine high-wing aircraft, smoking a cigarette or cigar which, in the States, was not allowed on the flight line. If this was their pilot, he was a rule-breaker, maybe a risk-taker.

Gabriel slowed as they approached the aircraft, and the man motioned them forward, then held up his hand, and Gabriel stopped. "This is your amigo?"

"Looks like him." He said to Taylor, "Wait here. I'll check this out."

He got out of the SUV, and as he walked toward the tall man he saw by the taxi headlights that he was a broad-shouldered guy of about forty with a ruddy complexion and close-cropped brown hair. He wore an open-collared white short-sleeved shirt with striped epaulettes, and black slacks. To offset the Apex-required uniform, he wore flip-flops, which Brodie always associated with jerk-offs.

The man stomped out his cigarette and extended his hand, and Brodie took it, receiving a firm handshake. "Captain John F. Collins."

"Clark T. Bowman."

Captain Collins glanced at the idling taxi. "Your wife coming?"

"She's petrified of flying in small planes."

"Me too."

Brodie smiled. He liked Captain Collins. "I'll let her know." He said to Collins, "If I asked you to take us to someplace else, like Curaçao or Aruba, for instance, is that a problem?"

Collins replied without much thought, "Not really. Apex has your credit card, and if you have your passports, I can file another flight plan." He added, "This is not an official port of entry or exit—no customs or immigration—and the jokers here don't care where you go if you give them a few bucks."

"Okay . . ." Well, he felt he should give Taylor that option. He walked back to the taxi and motioned Taylor to get out, which she did, carrying both overnight bags.

Gabriel asked, "Why you take bags?"

"Change of plans." He gave Gabriel a ten and said, "Wait here in case we have another change of plans."

"Sí. Gracias."

Brodie took his bag, and he and Taylor walked toward the aircraft. He said to her, "Collins looks like an okay guy."

"Good."

"He says he can file a new flight plan and take us to Curaçao or Aruba." He added, "Right off the coast."

She glanced at him. "Is that what you want to do?"

"I'm asking you."

She didn't reply.

"No one would fault us if we decided to get out of this country. In fact, that's what Worley and Dombroski wanted us to do."

"Thanks for the option. I'm all in for Kavak."

"Okay." *Just remember you said that.* He added, "I think he'd also be game to take us from Kavak to Bogotá."

She nodded, then said, "You need to call Colonel Dombroski, as per orders."

"It would take the embassy commo people less than three minutes to pinpoint our signal."

"Call from a landline."

"I don't see a phone booth."

"Scott—"

"Let's just get the hell out of here. We'll call from Tomás de Heres."

"Promise?"

"No. Look, Maggie, we are like ballistic missiles on a mission—unguided, and not able to be controlled, called back, or aborted by an electronic signal. We are on our own, flying toward our target. And that's the way it's got to be."

She thought about that, not looking totally convinced, but said, "Okay."

"I could learn to love you."

"Don't bother."

They continued toward the aircraft, where Collins was checking out Mrs. Bowman in the dim light. He extended his hand to her. "Pleased to meet you, Mrs. Bowman."

"Same here."

"The bad weather has moved out to sea. This will be a very safe and smooth flight."

"Good."

"Is this all your luggage?"

Brodie replied, "We wanted to keep the plane light."

"Okay . . . Weight shouldn't be a problem at Kavak."

"Have you flown there?"

"A few times." He looked at Taylor. "Nothing to worry about."

"I'm not worried."

"Good. You just relax and enjoy the flight."

Taylor glanced at Brodie, suspecting that he'd indulged his sick humor at her expense.

Collins motioned to the aircraft and assured her, "This is a Cessna Turbo Stationair HD, new model, one of the best and safest aircraft—"

"Let's get moving," Taylor suggested.

"Yes, ma'am. Just a formality, but I need to see your IDs."

Brodie and Taylor handed him their fake passports, and Collins gave them a cursory glance in the dim light and handed them back, saying, "I'm supposed to check your luggage, but if you assure me you're not carrying explosives, guns, drugs, or smelly cheese, I'll take your word for it."

"You have our word," Brodie assured him.

"Good." He continued, "I'm also supposed to be sure you have special travel permits to go into this protected region."

Brodie tapped his cargo pants where he had his Glock. "Right here."

"Okay . . . somebody might ask you for them. Also, you were supposed to get yellow fever shots a week before you go to the jungle."

Taylor replied, "We're good to go."

"Great." He looked at the idling taxi. "Why's he waiting?"

Brodie replied, "Because I told him to. How long before we lift off?"

Collins glanced at the nearby control tower. "Let's see if these jokers will clear us for takeoff a little early." He added, "We should be off the ground in ten minutes. Or less."

"Less is good."

"Right. Anybody need to use the head? Last chance. Okay, come aboard."

Brodie waved Gabriel off and followed Collins and Taylor to the right side of the Cessna where a set of rolling stairs led into the passenger cabin.

Brodie and Taylor climbed into the small, comfortable-looking cabin, featuring two leather chairs facing forward and a two-person bench seat behind them, which Brodie thought looked big enough to hold a hog-tied Captain Mercer. For now he tossed his bag on it, and so did Taylor. Collins pulled the stairs away, shut and latched the door, then rounded the plane to the left side, where he climbed through the cockpit door into his seat.

Collins latched his door, saying to his passengers, "Welcome aboard Apex Flight One, nonstop to Ciudad Bolívar's Tomás de Heres Airport where we refuel, then on to Kavak." He added, "Please fasten your seat belts." He put on his headphones, then fired up the engine and did a quick instrument check. He contacted the control tower and requested permission for takeoff, and since he seemed to be the only aircraft going anywhere at this hour, Collins got the go-ahead.

He taxied across the tarmac onto the illuminated runway, then throttled up the Cessna to takeoff power. He said to his passengers, "And away we go," and began racing down the concrete runway.

The Cessna lifted off into the black night.

Brodie looked out the window as the aircraft gained altitude, watching the dark city slowly shrink beneath them, a dense slash of human habitation in a narrow valley, its tendrils climbing into the surrounding hills. He hoped he never saw this city again—not even on the nightly news.

Taylor was looking out her window and Brodie asked her, "Can you see Curaçao?"

"I can see Simón Bolívar Airport. I hope Luis and his family are on a flight out of there."

"Me too." Maggie Taylor sometimes showed too much empathy. Not a bad trait, but sometimes it got in the way of the mission. Which always came first. Except, of course, when he, Scott Brodie, wanted to get laid. He wished she'd shown such concern for the happiness of others back in the hotel.

"What are you thinking about?"

"I'm thinking about Luis and his family in an American supermarket."

"That's nice."

The Cessna banked right, heading south. In the moonlight Brodie could see the endless expanse of hills, fields, and forests below, blanketing the countryside. Venezuela—to know her is your destiny.

Taylor tilted her seat back, yawned, and closed her eyes.

They reached cruising altitude and Collins' voice came over the PA: "You can unbuckle if you want, but I suggest you stay strapped in. There's water, cola, and juice in a cooler behind your seats." He added, "Should be a smooth flight, but there are barf bags in your side seat pockets. We're bucking some headwinds, so we should be landing at Tomás de Heres in about an hour and fifteen, hour thirty."

Brodie asked Taylor, "You want something to drink?"

"Only if there's a baño onboard."

Collins overheard and said, "I have pee-pee tubes under your seats. Male and female." He added, "I won't look."

"An officer and a gentleman," said Brodie. He asked, "Mind if I come into the cockpit?"

"Not at all."

Brodie unbuckled and squeezed between the front seats and into the cockpit.

Collins' flight bag was on the co-pilot seat, and he said, "You can stow that behind you."

Brodie picked up the flight bag, which was open, and saw flight charts, a pair of boxer shorts, and what looked like a .357 Magnum revolver.

Collins glanced over and noticed. "Never leave home without it."

"Right." Especially if your home is in Caracas. As Brodie placed the bag behind the seat, he also noticed a pair of binoculars that Captain Collins was going to loan him, though Collins didn't know that yet. As for the .357 Magnum, that would have to be dealt with when Brodie gave Collins a choice of incentives for an unscheduled flight to Bogotá—Glock or dollars.

Brodie sat in the co-pilot seat and buckled in. Collins said, "I'm told you folks are bird-watchers."

Brodie thought Collins said that as though he didn't believe it for some reason. The man, despite his flip-flops, was not stupid. "Correct."

"Most people I fly to the jungle area are hikers. Like, naturalists and adventure travelers. Big-time into photography. I never flew bird-watchers before."

"Lots of people don't like to admit they're bird-watchers."

"Really?"

"People think we're weird."

"I don't think that."

"Good."

Collins stayed quiet, then asked, "Are those bulges in your and your wife's pockets cameras?"

"No. They're actually nine-millimeter semi-automatic pistols."

Collins nodded. "Good that you have them. Bad country where you're going."

"Caracas was no treat either."

"It's got its charms, Mr. Bowman. You just have to give it a chance."

Every shithole in the world had its defenders, Brodie thought. Usually white guys with enough money and privilege to avoid the unpleasantness endured by the locals. "You live in Caracas?"

"I was based in Rio, but I met a Venezuelan woman and moved here to be with her."

"Must be some woman."

Collins laughed. "She is." He lowered his voice and said, man-to-man, "You're doing okay yourself."

"Thanks."

"She okay? I got tranquilizers if you need them."

"She's fine." Brodie asked, "Do you have an external satellite phone antenna?"

Collins glanced at him. "I do." He pointed to a receptacle with a coiled cord on the instrument panel. "You need to make a call?"

"Maybe later. I assume you have a sat phone."

"I do." He added, "Sometimes better than the radio to keep in touch with the Company."

"Right. And to keep in touch with your girlfriend."

Collins laughed. "Yeah."

Well, thought Brodie, it was good to know he had an alternative sat phone if he needed it. With luck, his first and last call to Colonel Dombroski would be: "Mission accomplished. Meet us in Bogotá." And maybe a side call to Worley: "Foxtrot uniform."

The Cessna flew on into the dark night, a speck of metal and electronics alone in the cold, endless void of time and space.

Collins asked, "Are you with a tour group?"

"No."

"People usually travel down there with tour groups. In fact, it's almost mandatory."

"No one mentioned that."

"Do you at least have a tour guide?"

"No. But I'm sure we can find one in Kavak."

"Yeah . . . you should be able to." He advised, "You shouldn't go into the jungle alone."

"Really?"

"It's, like, dangerous. People get lost, and there's no rescue units to find you."

"I'm pretty good at land navigation." He added, "Moss grows on the north side of the tree."

"Yeah, but . . . the biggest danger is people. Like, drug runners, banditos. Then you have the indigenous people, who are usually okay, but sometimes they're not."

"We have Señor Glock to protect us."

Collins didn't reply to that, but said, "I wouldn't take"—he cocked his head toward the rear—"a beautiful woman into that jungle."

"Would you like to come with us?"

"Hell, no." He added, "To be honest, I don't even want to stay in Kavak overnight."

"We'll all sleep together."

Again, Captain Collins had no reply, but he was probably hoping his passenger wasn't joking, and also wondering who Mr. and Mrs. Bowman actually were. In fact, he asked, "How long have you been bird-watching?"

"Not too long."

"I don't get the thrill of that."

"Me neither. I do it for my wife."

Collins nodded. "Yeah. The things we do."

"Tell me about it."

Brodie wanted to feel Collins out about doing something good for his country—like flying from Kavak to Bogotá with a hog-tied criminal in the cabin—but they needed to bond more. So after they refueled in Ciudad Bolívar and were close to landing in Kavak, Brodie would make his pitch. Recruiting the locals was a matter of money; recruiting American expats, as he'd discovered, was usually a matter of flag-waving.

Ironically, no one was more patriotic than an expat. But the timing had to be right. Or the caliber of the gun you pulled had to be big. Money helped too.

The important thing was that Captain Collins—who by now was thinking that he didn't have bird-watchers aboard—knew that Mr. and Mrs. Bowman were not engaged in criminal activity. Brodie asked, "You ex-military?"

"No. Thought about it, though."

"My wife and I served. Iraq and Afghanistan."

"Thank you for your service."

"We live in the DC area. Where you from?"

"All over. Originally from Montana. Big Sky country."

"Right. That would inspire you to become a pilot."

"Yeah."

"I'm from upstate New York. Farm family. My wife is from Tennessee. Moonshine family."

Collins chuckled.

"Bird-watching is our hobby. Back in the States, we work for the federal government." He added, "Nothing interesting. Department of the Interior. We're geologists."

Collins thought about that, maybe coming to the logical conclusion that Mr. and Mrs. Bowman were scoping out the terrain for possible oil deposits.

Brodie said to him, "That's not for public consumption. We're just bird-watchers."

Collins nodded.

Brodie said, "I'm going to get some sleep. Unless you want me to take the controls so you can get some shut-eye."

"You fly?"

"No. But I've been watching how you do it."

Collins thought that was funny.

Brodie squeezed back into the cabin and took his seat next to Taylor.

He watched her as she slept, her breasts rising and falling, a look of perfect peacefulness on her face. He hoped she was dreaming about waking up in bed next to Scott Brodie.

As he started to buckle in, her arm extended toward him, zombie-like, and in her hand was a scrap of notepaper. He took it and read, *First Place for Bullshit goes to Scott Brodie.* Then, *P.S. Never made moonshine.*

He smiled, tilted his seat back, and closed his eyes. His body needed sleep, but, as in Iraq, his mind was in survival mode and his thoughts were racing toward what lay ahead.

And what lay ahead would be partly determined by what lay behind. Meaning the shoot-out at the Hen House. And Carmen. If Carmen was grilled by the police or SEBIN, she might crack. And if she did, and if Mercer did in fact have contacts in the regime and the military, then Mercer could be waiting for them at the Kavak airstrip.

Brodie could have killed Carmen, of course, and also Luis, who had heard too much. And Carmen's john, too, though he didn't understand English. But you had to draw that line somewhere. Or, as Nietzsche said in Philo 101, "Whoever fights monsters should see to it that in the process he does not become a monster."

Good advice for whoever dreamed up Flagstaff. And good advice for Captain Mercer, who had apparently looked deep into the abyss and saw it was looking back at him. And good advice, too, for Scott Brodie, who had come too close to that abyss a few times. And this might become one of those times.

PART IV

CANAIMA NATIONAL PARK, VENEZUELA
AUGUST 2018

CHAPTER 36

The Marines hit the beach before dawn, and eleven-year-old Kyle Mercer was there to see it.

The sky was a deep purple, the water an inky black, and the sunlight was just beginning to bloom on the horizon. He saw the dark shapes breach the water, big, boxy amphibious assault vehicles on tank treads that rolled up the shore. Men with rifles and heavy gear poured out, sloshing through the breaking waves, running onto the beach, barking orders and fanning out along the shoreline, establishing a beachhead.

It was all a drill, but it was real to those men down on the beach, and so it was real to their small audience, too, watching from a distance through the chain-link fence at the freeway rest stop somewhere between Anaheim and San Diego.

Kyle Mercer remembered standing pressed against the fence, just off the I-5 freeway that ran along a stretch of off-limits coastline belonging to Camp Pendleton. It was by chance that he was there, on the way home from a family trip to Disneyland that was cut short by the sudden death of Kyle's grandfather. Kyle barely knew the old man, who was estranged from the family, and he couldn't even remember how the old bastard died.

But he did remember the fence, and the beach, and that they stopped because his mom had to use the restroom. His dad had bought him a Coke from the vending machine and they walked over to the fence where a group of mostly men and boys were hanging out watching.

A few of the spectators looked like they could have been Vietnam vets, maybe former Marines, who'd made a point of being there to see the Pendleton boys in action and be reminded of their own glory days. The rest of the observers were the kinds of guys you might expect at a rest stop at 6 A.M.—truckers headed down to Mexico, workers returning home from a graveyard shift, and a few burnouts who were doing whatever they do at rest stops.

Kyle Mercer remembered being in awe of what he was seeing. Those men on the other side of the fence were of another world and another breed. An elite warrior class. He wanted to be like them, and that day he promised himself he would.

He sat up in bed—a pungent foam mattress on a bamboo platform—in his jungle hut. He looked at the woman next to him. Rosalita. She was sleeping, naked, the bedsheet pushed down below her pubis. She had a boyish body, not much in the way of tits or ass. But she had a certain appeal. Perfect facial bone structure. Big brown eyes. Long, slender limbs and luxuriant black hair. She could have been a runway model in New York or LA in another life. But in this life she was a whore in Caracas.

She hadn't been a very happy hooker in the Hen House. It's hard to really enjoy it when you're living in fear of your next client, or of your boss if you don't get a next client.

Mercer had taken her out of that cesspool, out into the wild. He made her free, and it turned out she was a tiger. That's the thing about freedom. It shows you who you are.

Someone knocked on the door of the hut. He picked up the Desert Eagle pistol from the crate that served as his nightstand and got out of bed. "Quién es?"

A voice from behind the door said, "Es Franco, señor. El hombre está aquí."

"Un momento." Mercer looped his belt and holster around his camo pants and slipped on a white tank top, then pulled the bedsheet over Rosalita's naked body. He held the Desert Eagle at his side as he walked to the door and looked through a crack in the wood slats. Franco stood in front of the hut, alone.

Mercer holstered the pistol, then opened the door and stepped outside.

Franco flashed a gap-toothed smile. He was a weird-looking guy—short, head too big for his body. He was the kind of man other men underestimated, until they looked into his eyes. You don't fight for the FARC in the Colombian jungle for ten years and live to tell about it unless you've got some big cojones and serious skills.

Franco told him, in Spanish, that the man was waiting for Señor Kyle in the Situation Room. La Sala de Situación. That was the name he'd given to the hut where he held his meetings. It was kind of a joke, but no one else got it.

They walked through the encampment, past a cluster of small thatched huts set among the trees. The jungle was thick here, and even though the late afternoon sun was blasting overhead, it was dim on the forest floor.

Camp Tombstone. Every camp needed a name, and that's what Kyle Mercer had picked for this place. Another inside joke that was only for him. Franco had politely asked about this choice when he'd learned the meaning of the word: "Is this not a morbid thing, señor?" Mercer had explained that it was named in honor of a town in the American state of Arizona where some famous banditos made a stand. That seemed to satisfy Franco.

They reached a small clearing, where a Pemón man was building a campfire while another was cleaning a fresh catch of catfish from the river. They looked at Señor Kyle, but did not say anything to him. No one spoke to Señor Kyle unless they were spoken to.

Mercer looked up at the small patch of unbroken blue sky. From the air this would look like any other indigenous village. He'd thought about suspending camouflage netting to cover the opening, but a drone's thermal imagery would pick up their heat signatures regardless. No different than Afghanistan, really. Nowhere to hide so long as the Predators knew where to look. But Mercer didn't think they did.

In the distance, he heard the crack of gunfire. His men were keeping busy on the rifle range. Some of them were real sharpshooters. Others were liable to blow their own dicks off. But the training was helping.

Franco and Mercer approached a large open-sided hut on the far end of the clearing. In the middle of the hut was a bamboo table surrounded by log stumps that served as chairs. A man sat on one of the logs, smoking a cigarette.

Mercer dismissed Franco and walked into the hut. The two men looked at each other. Mercer did not sit, so his visitor reluctantly stood.

General Ricardo Gomez was a stocky guy in his sixties with a dark complexion and tightly curled salt-and-pepper hair. A lot of African and indigenous blood, like his hero Hugo Chávez. And proud of it too, just like

Chávez. To men like him, looking the way he did and wearing a military uniform with two stars on his epaulettes was itself a revolutionary act. Except he wasn't wearing his uniform today—just a sweaty white dress shirt and jeans. No one who was headed to this camp wanted to draw attention to themselves.

Gomez took a drag and blew a trail of smoke. His eyes were deep-brown slits beneath heavy eyelids, which made him hard to read. "Good afternoon, Comrade Kyle." He spoke heavily accented but otherwise perfect English.

Comrade. He'd first got called that by one of those Chavista thugs in the barrio, and it seemed to stick, at least among the true believers. He preferred Señor Kyle, but maybe comrade was better than captain, a rank he'd renounced and would never go by again.

"Buenas tardes, General," Mercer replied. He would use the general's military title, of course, but would never salute him. He got the feeling this irked General Gomez, but he didn't really give a shit.

"I have this for you. From SEBIN." Gomez took an envelope from the pocket of his jeans and tossed it on the table.

Mercer picked up the envelope and removed a long, typed list of names, locations, and job titles. *Manuel Gutiérrez, Caracas, Student Activist. Tomas Palacios, Maracaibo, Journalist. Alberto Fernandez, Ciudad Bolívar, Lieutenant Colonel, National Guard.* Each name also included an address.

"What is this?" asked Mercer, knowing the answer.

Gomez looked at him with his narrow, inscrutable eyes. "A list of people who need to die."

Mercer tossed the document back on the table. "A lot of these are civilians. You don't need me for this shit."

"Some of them are not civilians. More importantly, all of them are working with your government."

"It's not my government."

"Sí. You are a man without a country."

Mercer stared at Gomez. He thought he sensed a hint of sarcasm in the man's tone and expression, but he could never tell.

What Mercer did know about General Gomez was that he'd once been trained by the U.S. Army, which was the only reason Mercer would work with him. In an odd way, they spoke the same language, and had once worn the same uniform. Mercer had no idea why Gomez had developed an animosity toward the U.S.—maybe his U.S. Army trainers had made fun of him, or the chow in the officers' mess gave him diarrhoea—but Gomez was now a full-fledged anti-American Chavista, dedicated to wiping out the last vestiges of protest and democracy in Venezuela. Kyle Mercer's goal was more complex, more personal, and far less ideological. But, as often happens in life and in war, you make alliances with people whose motivations are different than yours but whose goals are the same. It works until it doesn't.

The American government knew that lesson well, from decades of ratfucking elections and sponsoring insurgencies and counterinsurgencies in almost every country south of the Rio Grande. Now Uncle Sam had turned his eyes toward Venezuela, a country with an incompetent and corrupt socialist government, a weak military, and more oil reserves than Saudi Arabia. A target too tempting to resist.

And oil wasn't the United States' only motivation. According to a briefing Mercer had received from General Gomez in the Hen House, China and Russia were loaning the bankrupt Maduro government billions of dollars, and when the bill came due and the Venezuelans didn't have the cash or oil to repay it, they would give away political influence instead. Russian mercenaries were already in country to protect Maduro, and more were on the way. Venezuela, like Cuba before it, was becoming a toehold in the Western Hemisphere for America's enemies, and the U.S. was determined to change the equation. Kyle Mercer had learned in grade school that the Cold War was over, but as he'd learned firsthand in Afghanistan, one war just morphs into another.

And now Kyle Mercer was here, doing some ratfucking of his own. He was working with the Chavistas, but not for them. An important distinction.

So far Mercer and his men had killed a pro-American Air Force colonel in Caracas, an anti-Chavista National Police captain in Ciudad Bolívar, and an outspoken pro-democracy mayor in a nearby small town. But that was all warm-up for the big show—a counterinsurgency operation against armed groups currently being trained by the Americans across the border in Colombia.

Kyle Mercer had arrived here suspecting the Americans were up to something, but it was General Gomez who gave him the Intel on Operation

Boyacá, an ambitious American plot to destabilize and ultimately overthrow the Maduro government. Mercer had assumed Boyacá was something along the lines of a traditional Latin American coup—recruit some disgruntled officers, have a plan to seize the Presidential Palace and maybe a media outlet, make some high-profile arrests. The kind of plan whose success relied on a swift, psychological blow. But, as Gomez had explained to him, coups had not been working in Venezuela for some time. Not for Chávez' two coup attempts in 1992, or in 2002 for the people who tried to depose him—or just this past May, when a group of military officers were hatching a plot to arrest Maduro in the run-up to the presidential elections. The plot was exposed by SEBIN, and the conspirators were jailed and awaiting punishment.

So now there was Operation Boyacá—named after the victorious battle waged by Simón Bolívar that marked the beginning of the end of Spain's rule in the north of their New World empire. Like Bolívar's army, these U.S.-trained insurgents would sweep down out of the Andes to liberate Venezuela in the name of the people. No more top-down coups. This would look like a genuine people's revolution, and the illusion needed to last just long enough for a group of pro-American Venezuelan Army officers to take command, promise elections at a future date, and kick out the Russians.

General Gomez had seemed particularly offended by the Americans co-opting the name of his beloved Bolívar's military victory over the Spanish Empire for their own imperial project. But Kyle Mercer thought it was smart branding. Besides, whether you're promising freedom or vengeance, revolution or restoration, the only constants in war are that a lot of people will die and nothing will turn out how you planned.

He looked again at Gomez' list—a grab bag of assassinations to soften up the opposition on the home front before the battles to come. Maybe Gomez and his fellow Chavistas believed that if they killed enough collaborators now, they could starve Boyacá of vital support on the ground in Venezuela and stop the operation in its tracks. And maybe they were right.

At any rate, SEBIN could deal with all these people, but Mercer suspected that the regime was getting international heat for eliminating its opposition, and they wanted to outsource the killings to make them appear to be the work of patriotic Venezuelans who had risen up to defend the duly elected government of Nicolás Maduro. There were no such people, so Señor Kyle got the job.

Mercer looked at Gomez. "We'll make it happen."

Gomez nodded and took a long drag on his cigarette. "There is something else. Disturbing news from Caracas that I received just before boarding my plane. There were two Americans going around Petare this morning asking about you, Comrade. Their names are Clark and Sarah Bowman, and they claim to be your friends."

"Never heard of them."

"I am sure these are not their real names."

"Good deduction. Who did they speak to, and what were they told?"

Gomez took a long drag on his cigarette. "They were stopped at a National Guard checkpoint, where they said they were looking for you. They even had your military portrait. The guards tell them nothing and wave them through. Then two Americans, a man and a woman of the same description, were sighted at a health clinic by the colectivo. And finally, an American man matching the same description as Mr. Bowman, along with a Venezuelan driver or maybe bodyguard, went into a bordello called El Club de los Malditos to inquire about underage girls. The man at this bordello directed them to El Gallinero."

The Hen House had been a good spot—a no-go zone for foreigners and police, where he could get laid when he wanted to, and be left alone when he didn't. Also, he'd recruited a few colectivo gangbangers there, and they were here with him now. More importantly, the Hen House was a place where powerful men came to not be seen.

But now, someone had tracked him right to it. But who? And how?

A rat in the National Guard or the colectivo could have been bought off by American Intel, but if that were the case, the Bowmans would have known to go directly to the Hen House instead of parading around the slums drawing attention to themselves . . .

"Comrade?"

Mercer looked at Gomez. "The Americans will return to Petare tonight. Either the man will attempt to enter El Gallinero, or they will stake out the place. Get word to your barrio thugs to be ready for them."

Gomez appeared to bristle at being given orders by a man he outranked.

He said, "This was already done before I boarded the plane to come see you, Comrade. The Americans will be taken care of."

"Good. Then it's nothing to worry about."

"Is this so?" asked Gomez. "This sounds like something yanquis say. No worries. But I do worry, Comrade." He added, "The Americans are making connections. They know of you and El Gallinero, and perhaps of me and you."

Mercer stared at Gomez, who looked back at him stone-faced. General Gomez was no doubt pissed off that the Americans had learned of Kyle Mercer's Caracas hideout. Gomez was the only direct link between Mercer and the regime, and Gomez was the regime's bagman, carrying money to the renegade yanqui and his men. But Mercer had already made a contingency plan in the event this relationship soured.

There was a cocaine lab in the vicinity, and his men were more than equipped to hit it and take what they needed to fund themselves for a while.

Mercer said, "I can handle anything that comes, General."

Gomez stared at him a moment, nodded, and then threw his cigarette in the dirt. He walked around the table toward Mercer and extended his hand. "My government is grateful to you."

Mercer took his hand, looked in his eyes. "I'm not doing it for your government."

Gomez let go of his hand. "I understand this. Nonetheless, the people of Venezuela will owe you a debt when the last of the imperialist elements in our society have been eliminated."

Actually, thought Mercer, as soon as the regime felt it didn't need him or his men, they'd be happy to send an army battalion to his camp and kill all of them. That's what his Special Ops friends had tried to do to him in Afghanistan. It hadn't worked there, and it wouldn't work here. When your masters teach you how to kill, and tell you who to kill, they forget that killers owe no loyalty to anyone, and trust no one.

Mercer said, "I will collect that debt."

"Yes. Good." He looked at Mercer. "Perhaps someday you will tell me why you are helping us."

"I believe in the Revolution."

Gomez smiled. "I think not."

"Perhaps, General, you will someday tell me how you went from American lackey to American hater."

Gomez' smile dropped. "I was never an American lackey. I took their hospitality and their training and I use it to fight them."

Mercer was sure that General Gomez had made that decision after the fact—when Chávez took power, and when career choices needed to be made. If the wind started blowing the other way, General Gomez would present himself at the American Embassy with his U.S. Army training certificate in hand, asking for a job. Mercer had seen this in Afghanistan, where local loyalties shifted like the sand dunes. The world was corrupt, and the only loyalty that lasted was to one's self.

Mercer recalled a time when he thought differently. He thought of the day at the induction center in San Diego when he'd raised his right hand and sworn allegiance to the Constitution of the United States, then took the literal and figurative step forward and shook the hand of the officer who'd sworn him in. *Congratulations, son.*

Kyle Mercer had come a long way since then . . . like a man whose lover and soul mate had cheated on him, made him into an angry and untrusting mutation of his former self. And there was no going back. No forgiveness. No road home.

He looked at Gomez, who was staring at him.

Gomez asked, "What is on your mind?"

"Nada."

Gomez knew not to press Comrade Kyle on any issue, so he asked, "When can you begin your work?"

"You'll know when the first corpse shows up."

"The journalist is particularly troublesome."

"I'll send you his eyeballs in a box of chocolates."

Gomez didn't know if the American was joking or serious. "That won't be necessary." He pulled a thick envelope out of his pocket and put it on the table. "The eagle flies today," he said, using the GI slang for payday.

Mercer pocketed the envelope without acknowledging Gomez' attempt at humor or bonding or whatever. The envelope would contain about two thousand American dollars in small bills—the monthly costs of keeping his forty men paid, at ten dollars a month, and the Pemón at two dollars, with the remainder of the money going toward food, supplies, medicine, and incidentals—beans, bandages, and bullets, as they used to say. Anything left over paid for the whores, the occasional airfare to Ciudad Bolívar or Caracas, and Señor Kyle's R&Rs at the Hen House—though there would be no further R&Rs. Also, Mercer had no doubt that General Gomez pocketed some of the American dollars for himself.

Camp Tombstone was on a shoestring budget, even by the standards of the bankrupt Venezuelan government. But when Mercer's men started fighting the American-backed insurgents, their budget would increase, and so would their ranks. Mercer looked forward to the coming battles.

"Thank you for making the trip, General. Safe journey to Caracas."

Gomez was not used to being dismissed, but he turned to leave, then asked, "Is there anything you need here?"

"One less general."

Gomez forced a smile, to show he shared the Yankee humor and was not offended. He said, "I leave you with one piece of advice, señor—the Americans have always hated their traitors more than they've hated their enemies. They will treat a defeated enemy well. They will never forgive a traitor." He added, "They are coming for you."

Mercer nodded—but he had not betrayed his country; he was a man without a country to betray. In fact, he had become an enemy combatant and should be classified as such under the Geneva Conventions. His real crime was that he, Captain Mercer, had walked away from his men and his duty. He had deserted. And for that, the Army would put him in prison for the rest of his life—or if the Intel people got to him first, they would end things a different way.

Gomez said, "The more enemies of the state that you kill, the stronger the regime becomes. The regime can protect you."

"Bad motivational talk. You learned nothing from the Americans. Good day."

Gomez needed to have the last word. "Arrogant. You mistake that for machismo."

Mercer didn't reply, and Gomez turned and left the hut.

Mercer watched him as he walked through the clearing, toward the river and the boat that would take him to the Kavak airstrip and a plane back to Caracas—back to the squalor and the misery of his revolution.

They are coming for you. But who?

He thought back to his chance encounter in the whorehouse two weeks ago. He couldn't believe his eyes at first. Seeing a couple of doughy Americans in a place like that was already strange, but when one of them started staring at him and Mercer realized it was that fuckup Al Simpson he'd befriended in basic training a lifetime ago . . . He should have killed him, but . . . then he'd have had to kill the other American with him, and also the locals who'd brought them there. And that might be too many corpses for the Hen House to dispose of.

In any case, Mercer had figured that Simpson was too drunk, too scared, or too embarrassed by his own presence in a brothel to report it to anyone. But apparently he had. And that changed the equation. That meant CID might be in Venezuela.

Whoever these two Americans were, they'd likely meet their end tonight in Petare. But whether they were Intel or CID, they were part of a larger machine, and once that machine's gears start turning they don't stop.

He also thought of that whore Carmen, who would sell him out for a pack of cigarettes. She would have no clue where the camp was, but if anyone managed to find her and speak with her, she'd help them make a few more connections . . . It occurred to Mercer that he was leaving too many witnesses alive.

Mercer glanced again at SEBIN's list of the soon to be dead. There were women on the list. Also a priest. They were probably all good people—Venezuelan patriots. And probably some of them were backed by the Americans. The CIA. And also the Defense Intelligence Agency.

Which meant they were working for Brendan Worley, and therefore, they had to die.

CHAPTER 37

Mercer walked out of the hut and turned onto a path that led deeper into Camp Tombstone. The camp had grown darker as the sun sank beneath the towering trees, and the Pemón were lighting torches on the paths. Mercer's men were starting to return from the obstacle course and the rifle range, hungry for dinner. The changing of the perimeter guard would take place at exactly 8 P.M. Kyle Mercer ran a tight ship, and the men hated the discipline. They were by nature anarchists. But he, Kyle Mercer, by the sheer power of his will and his command presence had transformed these men into a coherent fighting machine. He treated them with dignity and respect—something most of them were not used to. And in return he demanded—and earned— their loyalty. They weren't exactly Delta Force, but they followed orders, and they would follow Señor Kyle to hell if he led the way.

Mercer continued along the dark trail. The tree canopy rustled with birds and monkeys. Insects buzzed and chirped; lizards skittered through the underbrush. This jungle was bursting with life, with sounds and smells, unlike the craggy brown wastes of the Afghan frontier, a dead place where all you could hear was the mournful wind and the sound of your own breathing.

The trail ended at a small bamboo hut where a tall, muscular man stood, wearing jungle boots, camo pants, a tight black T-shirt, and a holstered pistol. This was Emilio, who, like Franco, was a veteran of the brutal and unending drug wars. Emilio had once been a hit man for the Sinaloa Cartel in Mexico until the Zetas killed his family and Emilio got out of the drug business. This part of the world produced an abundance of cocaine, corpses, and dead souls.

Emilio stood straight as Mercer approached. "Buenas tardes, Señor Kyle."

"Hola. Cómo está el prisionero?" How is the prisoner?

"Alive. Wishing he was dead."

Mercer knew that feeling. "If he dies on your watch, you will take his place."

Emilio nodded.

Mercer opened the bamboo door and entered the windowless hut, which his men had nicknamed la Capilla—the Chapel. Light and air filtered through the bamboo walls, so this wasn't the worst prison cell Mercer had ever seen—that honor went to his own stone hut where he'd spent more than two years lying on a dirt floor, baking in the summer heat and freezing in the winter cold. This jungle hut also had a dirt floor, but it was covered with palm fronds, a bit of luxury for the important prisoner.

In the middle of the floor lay a huge log, and embedded in the log were two eyebolts, anchoring chains connected to manacles that were clamped onto the prisoner's ankles.

There was a waste bucket on the floor, and Mercer could smell it. Also on the floor were an empty plastic water bucket and a wooden bowl of ground yucca root, uneaten.

Mercer looked at his prisoner in the dim light, lying on the palm fronds. He was either sleeping or feigning sleep, which Mercer recollected doing when he'd had a visitor who'd come to beat him or torment him. This prisoner had been beaten only once, when he first arrived, just to show him how it felt, and to make him live in fear of another beating—or something worse.

The prisoner wore only boxer shorts, and his body was covered with sweat, insect bites, heat sores, and dirt. He hadn't been allowed to bathe or shave and he'd grown a weeks-old beard, gray and matted, as was his long hair.

Mercer crouched beside the man. "Hello, Ted."

The man lay motionless, eyes closed.

"Don't make me punch you in the balls."

The man opened his eyes, but said nothing.

Mercer looked at the man's face in the dim light. Ted Haggerty was in his early sixties, and Mercer recalled that he'd been good-looking a few weeks ago, before he'd had his nose broken. Also, he stunk.

"You're looking a little thin, Ted. Are you on a hunger strike?"

Haggerty did not reply.

"I can tell you from firsthand experience that it takes over a month to die from starvation. You can speed that up if you don't drink water. But it's hard to go thirsty. Would you like some water?"

Again, Haggerty did not reply.

"Here's the deal, Ted. It's me, not you, who gets to decide if you live or die. So you will eat and drink, or I will do what I've seen the Taliban do— cut off your face. And shove it down your throat, piece by piece." He added, "Please believe me."

Haggerty gave a slight nod.

"Good. Sit up."

Haggerty strained to lift his body, and Mercer helped him by grabbing his hair, pulling him into a sitting position. "Look at me."

Haggerty looked at Mercer crouched in front of him. They made eye contact and Mercer could see that the man's blue eyes were cloudy, but still alert. The eyes were indeed the window to the soul, and Ted Haggerty still had enough spark in him to care whether he lived or died.

Mercer picked up the bowl of yucca root and shoved it at Haggerty. "Eat."

Haggerty took the bowl in both hands and lowered his face into it.

Mercer sat on the log and watched him. Ted Haggerty, who Mercer was sure was an Intel guy, probably a CIA officer, had been poking around Tomás de Heres Airport, asking too many questions of too many people. Haggerty had obviously been following a lead—inquiring about his compatriot, Kyle Mercer, who was known to fly out of Tomás de Heres to someplace in the south. Haggerty had with him a photograph—Mercer's official Army file photo—which had been altered to replace his uniform with a plain white shirt. Mercer had the photograph now, along with Haggerty's passport, travel visa, and an interesting collection of phony business cards that identified Ted Haggerty as everything from a freelance journalist to a travel agent, with no mention of the Central Intelligence Agency. Haggerty had explained to people at Tomás de Heres that Señor Mercer was his amigo, and Mercer's father was dying, and Señor Mercer needed to be found and informed.

Mercer could picture Ted Haggerty, full of CIA arrogance and swagger—and twenty-dollar bills—asking about Kyle Mercer. Eventually, Haggerty had hit pay dirt and chartered a flight to Kavak, where the agents

of SEBIN—who had been alerted by an informant at Tomás de Heres—
were waiting for him.

SEBIN would normally take a prisoner back to the Helicoide in Caracas
for interrogation. But in this case, the SEBIN agents—undoubtedly on the
orders of the regime or the military—had assisted Señor Haggerty in his
quest, and turned him over to the Pemón in Kavak, who kindly transported
the tied and blindfolded American by boat to Señor Kyle's jungle camp.

Haggerty finished the mashed yucca root and raised his head, still holding the wooden bowl, which Mercer knew he was evaluating as a weapon.
Haggerty was well-trained, but training and reality were not the same. Mercer, still sitting on the log, kicked his foot out and sent the bowl flying across
the hut. "Look at me."

Haggerty turned his head toward Mercer.

"I've been patient with you, Ted, because there was no particular ur-
gency to my questions. But now there have been some new developments
in Caracas which you, as a trained CIA officer—"

"I am a freelance journalist, and I wanted to do a story on you—"

"All right. That's a good legend. And your story at Tomás de Heres Airport that you were trying to find me to tell me my father was dying is also
good. People respond to that. And I might have even believed you were a
journalist, except that you were carrying my Army photograph. Which you
could only have gotten from the Department of Defense."

"That photograph is available—"

"And it was altered to erase the uniform. Why?"

Haggerty did not reply.

"The real question is, how did you know I was in Venezuela?"

Haggerty took a deep breath and replied, "I told you . . . I was already
here doing a story on the food shortages and riots in Caracas, had some
contacts in the National Guard, and there were rumors going around about
an American soldier—"

"So you said. But your story doesn't explain how you knew that I flew in
and out of Tomás de Heres."

"I acted on a hunch."

"You're a hell of a journalist, Ted. Or the CIA has paid informants in
SEBIN, or in the Venezuelan military."

"I got a lead on your whereabouts from a private pilot at Francisco de Miranda Airport . . ."

"And SEBIN got a lead on you because you asked too many questions about me to the wrong person at Tomás de Heres. And SEBIN IDed you as possible CIA. Are they lying to me? Or are you lying to me?"

"They are incompetent, paranoid, and stupid. I am a journalist—"

"That's your story and you're trained to stick to it. Okay. Let's try a different approach. I'm not fond of torture, but I have a dozen men here who are. One guy, Mercado, likes to cut people's tendons with a razor until they can't move a muscle. Emilio out there has a pair of pliers he uses to extract teeth and fingernails. But the best one I've ever seen is locking a guy in a bamboo cage filled with monkeys. Sounds funny, but you can't imagine what those hungry monkeys could do to you in an hour." Mercer looked at Ted Haggerty, who, he guessed, was trying not to imagine any of those things. Mercer said, "Do you want to talk to me? Or should I call Emilio in?"

Haggerty did not reply, but Mercer sensed he was ready.

"Okay, let's begin. If your answers are truthful, I promise you no torture. If your answers are useful, I promise you your freedom."

Haggerty looked at Mercer.

Mercer assured him, "Someone has to die, Ted. But it doesn't have to be you." He added, "You know who has to die."

Haggerty had no response.

"Okay. Are you a journalist?"

Haggerty shook his head.

"Good. CIA?"

Haggerty nodded.

"How did the CIA know I was in Venezuela?"

"You know."

Mercer nodded. It didn't take much Intel training to figure out that it was Captain Mercer who had tortured and killed Robert Crenshaw in Peshawar, and that what Captain Mercer wanted from Crenshaw was the location of Brendan Worley. And it didn't take too much psychological profiling to figure out that Kyle Mercer would follow Brendan Worley to the ends of the earth to exact revenge. Mercer asked, "How did you know I flew out of Tomás de Heres?"

"I . . . started with the assumption that you were traveling with a false passport . . ."

"Good assumption, Ted, since the only thing I carried out of that Taliban prison was the rotting clothes on my back." He snapped, "Continue."

Haggerty continued, "I also assumed you wouldn't try to fly into Venezuela by way of Simón Bolívar . . . so that led me to assume you somehow chartered a private plane and arrived in Venezuela via Francisco de Miranda Airport."

"Correct. Which is not an official port of entry, and where no questions are asked on arrival or departure." He looked at Haggerty. "Good work. Not inspired, but good. So as you were poking around Francisco de Miranda Airport, flashing my photograph and some cash, asking if anyone remembered this yanqui arriving there from overseas, you also discovered that this gringo had actually been flying in and out of Francisco on private charters to and from Tomás de Heres."

Haggerty nodded.

"You got lucky."

Haggerty actually seemed to take offense at this and replied, "Not luck. I knew who to ask . . . the military people at Francisco de Miranda. They sold you out for twenty bucks."

Mercer nodded. His unholy alliance with the military was necessary, but it was also a security risk. American Intel could buy anything from anyone in this country if they knew what to ask for. And Haggerty had followed up on his lead at Francisco de Miranda and flown to Tomás de Heres, where he'd again flashed the cash and showed the photograph and got a hit. Mercer asked, "Did you report to Worley before you flew to Kavak?"

"I . . . said I had a lead."

"Okay. Can Kavak expect a visit from Mr. Worley?"

"I don't know."

Mercer looked at Haggerty. "Now that you've disappeared, I'm sure he's more worried about himself than he is about you."

Haggerty thought about that and said, "I understand why you . . . want to kill him . . ."

"No, Ted, you can never understand that. Only he and I can fully understand that. And I understand why he hasn't left Venezuela and fled to safety.

You know why? Because there is not a place on this earth where he is safe from me. He understands that one of us has to die, and it might as well be here and now. Do you understand that?"

Haggerty nodded.

"And do you also understand that me killing Brendan Worley is only part of my payback?"

"I . . . think I understand . . ."

Mercer pulled the list of names out of his pocket and pushed it close to Haggerty's face. "These are anti-regime men and women who work for you or Worley—for the CIA or for Defense Intelligence. Do you recognize any of these names?"

"I . . . can't see . . ."

Mercer pulled the list away. "Doesn't matter, Ted. What matters is that everyone on this list will be dead within the month. Also dead will be the American government's mission to topple the Venezuelan government." Mercer leaned in toward Haggerty. "I will fuck up your mission here. I will do to you and Worley what your colleagues ordered me to do in Afghanistan— to kill all opponents of the government. And if the Venezuelan government decides that a whole village needs to be taught a lesson, I will use my learned skills from Afghanistan to kill every man, woman, and child in that village." Mercer put his face close to Haggerty's. "Are you understanding this, Ted? Does Worley understand that what he ordered me to do in Afghanistan is what I am doing to him and his mission here?"

"Everyone understands why you're here."

"That's good. I hope he sees the irony."

"We all accept our responsibility. We'd like to help you."

Mercer laughed.

Haggerty took a deep breath. "Captain . . . Kyle . . ."

The two men made eye contact. Mercer said, "We are all beyond help, Ted. You, me, Worley, the bastards in JSOC who made my warriors into murderers—we, like my new comrades here, are beyond help . . . beyond salvation . . . We are killers. So we kill." Mercer looked at Haggerty. "Isn't that why you're here? To kill me?"

"I'm here to find you." He added, "Worley will kill you."

"I appreciate your honesty, Ted. No more bullshit about helping me. No bullshit about turning myself in for a fair trial. Because if I go on trial, everyone goes on trial. So thank me for keeping this a private affair. Just between us killers. We'll work it out."

Haggerty didn't respond to that.

Mercer asked, "What was your role in Flagstaff?"

"I . . . knew about it. But I had no role."

"Of course you did. That's why you were sent here. To tidy up the loose ends. You and Worley—unindicted co-conspirators, on a mission to silence a witness."

Haggerty looked at Mercer and said in a surprisingly strong voice, "You should more closely examine your own role in Flagstaff. Accept your responsibility, Captain."

"Captain Mercer is dead. You and your friends killed him."

Haggerty did not reply.

Mercer looked at Ted Haggerty. This conversation could go on for hours, days, but there was nothing left to say, and nothing more Kyle Mercer needed or wanted to know. Ted Haggerty would make a good hostage, or a valuable bargaining chip, or good bait to draw Worley out. But sometimes the best strategy in war and in life was to burn your bridges behind you, to signal to your friends and enemies—and to yourself—that there was no going back. He said, "Your colleague Robert Crenshaw was very brave. I had to torture him for hours before he told me where Worley was."

Haggerty had no reply.

"I'm glad I didn't have to torture you. And now, as promised, I give you your freedom."

Haggerty closed his eyes and nodded. He understood.

Mercer stood, drew his knife from his belt, and moved behind Haggerty, quickly so that the man didn't have to wait for death. Mercer cupped Haggerty's chin in his left hand and with his right hand he drew the blade across Haggerty's throat.

Mercer didn't bother to look at the dying man as he walked out of the hut, his knife still dripping blood. He said to Emilio, "You are relieved. Go to dinner."

Emilio glanced at Señor Kyle's knife, and replied, "Gracias," and moved off down the trail.

Mercer stood there a moment and listened to the night sounds of the jungle.

They were coming for him, as he knew they would. He understood and never underestimated the long arm of American power. He was one of them, and had been part of that power. What had started in Afghanistan was coming to an end here, and it was coming soon.

CHAPTER 38

Kyle Mercer entered the long, open-sided structure draped in mosquito netting. Coleman lanterns hung from the bamboo rafters illuminating four long tables, at which sat about thirty of his men, eating and talking. There was a lull in the conversations as he entered, and, if he'd still been in the U.S. Army, he'd have shouted, "Carry on!" but there were no such protocols in his own army, and the men would carry on with their talk as soon as they were sure he had nothing to say to them, which he didn't.

One protocol he did observe was having his own table—the officers' table—and since he was the only officer at Camp Tombstone, he sat alone, though usually he invited one or two of his team leaders to join him. Sometimes he would also invite one of the men he wanted to congratulate for something he had accomplished or learned. Tonight, however, he wanted to dine alone. Tonight he had just killed a man—an American—and by now, everyone in the camp knew about it from Emilio. They also knew that Señor Kyle had spoken to a man from the outside, whom they had seen before. They didn't know that this man was an army general, but they knew he was an important man. So to avoid any questions on these subjects, Señor Kyle sat by himself. The women in the camp—the prostitutes, including Rosalita—ate in the women's hut.

A Pemón man hurried over with a bowl of beans and rice, and a freshly caught and fried catfish. Also on the menu was a piece of cassava root flat-bread, brought in by Pemón women from the nearby native village.

As in the U.S. Army, where officers ate only what their men ate—and sometimes less, because officers in the field were served last—Kyle Mercer made sure that the orderlies, the Pemón men, did not give him anything special. His men noted this and, coming as most of them did from societies where rank had extravagant privileges, were impressed by Señor Kyle's show of shared hardships and brotherhood.

The beverage of the day was bottled water, which the Pemón brought from Kavak. Dysentery and other waterborne diseases had destroyed more armies than artillery. The men wanted cerveza, of course, or more potent beverages, but alcohol—and drugs—were available at Camp Tombstone only when Señor Kyle distributed one or the other. Anyone caught using drugs or alcohol at other times spent a week in the Chapel—the hut where Ted Haggerty now lay.

Mercer picked at his food. It was good, but he wasn't particularly hungry. And that wasn't because he'd just killed Ted Haggerty, or because General Gomez annoyed him; it was because he had a lot to think about. Specifically about the gringos poking around the barrio, who at this very moment might either be staking out or attempting to enter the Hen House. He had no doubt that the colectivo and the management at the Hen House could handle them, and get whatever information they possessed before disposing of them.

If the two Americans were Intel officers or otherwise working with Brendan Worley, then that meant the little shit was getting more proactive about locating him, which was a development that Kyle Mercer welcomed. The two men had been playing a distant and psychological game of cat and mouse ever since Worley became aware that Kyle Mercer was in Venezuela. But it was well past time to engage the enemy.

Most men would flee from a person who wanted to kill them. But Brendan Worley was a soldier, and he knew that his job was to kill Kyle Mercer. In any case, sooner or later the men were fated to meet, and it might as well be sooner—though Mercer enjoyed the game, and took pleasure in undoing the work that Worley had been sent here to do. For every anti-regime person that Kyle Mercer killed, Brendan Worley's reputation in Washington as a man who could clean up the shit and advance American interests was diminished. And that was Kyle Mercer's mission—to diminish the man, to destroy his mystique, and to kill his spirit before killing the man himself. In fact, a simple killing was too good for Brendan Worley—it would be better if Mercer put him in the Chapel, and watched him die slowly.

Mercer was aware that several of his men were stealing glances at him in the dimly lit mess hall, so he resumed eating. If it wasn't Worley who'd sent the two Americans to Petare, then who was it? He had to assume that Simpson had reported his Kyle Mercer sighting in the Hen House. Therefore the Army's Criminal Investigation Division would have sent agents to Caracas to investigate and make an arrest. Mercer was sure that the CID would have made contact with the American Embassy as a matter of protocol, and for logistics and backup—it was the only way they could operate in a hostile country. And if that was the case, the CID agents would by now have made the acquaintance of Colonel Brendan Worley, an Army man working for Defense Intelligence, and also the resident expert on Captain Mercer. But would the CID or its agents know that? Maybe not. And maybe Worley would not tell them. But Brendan Worley would make it his business to host the CID agents who'd arrived in Caracas, and he would definitely want to be looking over their shoulders, because Brendan Worley was as guilty as Kyle Mercer. Actually, more guilty. As was the late Ted Haggerty. Like the people on the SEBIN kill list, if you worked with or for Brendan Worley, you paid with your life. And that would include any CID agents who were looking for him.

His thoughts turned back to Ted Haggerty. If Haggerty had gotten a message to Worley about his Kavak trip, why hadn't Worley acted on it? Two possibilities: Haggerty had *not* gotten a message to Worley, and had impulsively chartered a flight to Kavak, intending to report when he got there. Had SEBIN found a sat phone on Haggerty and taken it before turning him over to the Pemón? Mercer should have pressed Haggerty on this, but as he'd learned in Afghanistan, information gotten under duress was unreliable and often led you astray. It was best to just assume the worst, which in this case was that Haggerty *had* reported to Worley—or to his own CIA station chief at the U.S. Embassy—and that the Intel people at the embassy were waiting for another report—and still waiting. Or maybe Worley was taking his time planning his mission to Kavak. Or . . . the mission was now underway, and Worley was close. Mercer thought about what kind of mission it would be. An air strike from a carrier in the Caribbean? A Predator drone strike? Or maybe a ground operation launched by U.S. forces in Colombia? Maybe they'd send a Delta Force team to kill him. That was the only thing Kyle Mercer really worried about, because there was no one else on the face of the earth who could kill or capture Kyle Mercer.

Mercer drank from his water bottle and stared out through the mosquito netting at the dense rain forest. He felt safe here, though he could move his camp easily enough. That's what soldiers did. Don't get too comfortable. Home moves around, and you move with it. On the other hand . . . if you stay put, the enemy you're trying to find will save you the trouble by finding you.

And finally, how did Haggerty know to begin his search for Kyle Mercer at Tomás de Heres, and then fly to Kavak? Probably it was just as Haggerty said—good Intel work coupled with the usual sobornos, bribes. This was how Captain Mercer himself had accomplished his missions in Afghanistan. Intuition helped, and so did a little luck. It was both of these things that had saved his life in the 'Stan—saved him from being killed by the Taliban, and at the last minute, saved him from being killed by his friends.

Mercer finished his water and looked at his men through the haze of cigarette smoke. They were what the Army called a motley crew. Men from different cultures and countries and different walks of life who had taken different paths to Camp Tombstone.

There were, first, the conflict junkies like Franco and Emilio, who had never known a day of peace and never would, jumping from war zone to war zone until their luck ran out. Then there were the true believers, the Venezuelan Chavistas like the two guys on loan from MBR-200, Alejandro and Iván, who always sat together at meals and still wore their berets and bandanas even though they were five hundred miles from anyone who gave a shit.

Mercer looked at a skinny young guy named David who was in animated conversation. David lived in one of the barrios of Petare, and had been a janitor at an office building in downtown Caracas before losing his job like so many of the service workers who inhabited the slums. He got involved with the black market trade, linked up with a gang, and eventually found his way to the Hen House once word got out that Mercer was looking for young men seeking work that was high-risk and well-paying. Guys like David reminded him of the best kind of Army privates, the ones who were eager to please and grateful for the opportunity. The ideologues and the conflict vets came with their own baggage and arrogance. But the Davids, the former janitors and trash collectors whose livelihoods had been destroyed along with the Venezuelan economy, and who would do anything to earn and send money back to their starving families, they made good soldiers. About a third of Mercer's men were like David, in various stages of training to become professional fighters.

A lanky guy with dark hair and fair skin sat at the table nearest Mercer, chewing on a piece of flatbread. This was Nico, the only true technician in this crew. He looked like a criollo—a Venezuelan of mostly Spanish ancestry—and he had been a specialist in the National Guard's bomb squad in Caracas before he got laid off. He was an expert in detecting and defusing explosive devices, and he now used those skills to build them.

Earlier in the day, Nico had told him, "Está listo." It's ready.

He and Nico had gone over the logistics of transporting the bomb to Caracas, where it would be wired onto the car of a former Venezuelan Army colonel who'd been dismissed and was now working for the Americans. The official government line was that the colonel had been fired for corruption, but probably the opposite was true. In a broken country like this, the regime wanted everyone on the government dole to ensure their loyalty. It was the men—and women—with principles who were the problem.

Nico had wanted to do his work closer to the site of the attack, but Mercer had insisted that all operations originate at Camp Tombstone. The run from here to Caracas—or wherever an operation needed to happen—was relatively low-risk, while the population centers themselves were a hive of backstabbing government officials, dirty cops, and violent criminals. This whole country was teetering on the edge, and the safest place to be was far away from the chaos until it was time to strike. That's what he'd learned from the Taliban in Afghanistan.

Mercer stared at the bony remnants of the catfish—alive this morning, a pile of shit tomorrow. It was good to be at the top of the food chain. And he intended to stay there.

He stood, left the mess hall and took a path through the trees that led to the river and a view of the sky.

Kyle Mercer took in the world around him: the river's trembling waters, the dark leaves of the forest, cast silver in the moonlight. And looming above it all, Chimatá Tepui, that great ancient monolith rising into the black, starry night.

He thought back to his years of imprisonment in that filthy stone hut somewhere in Afghanistan's mountainous borderlands. He remembered the small window, a one-foot-by-six-inch rectangle. In the daytime it was a patch of bright blue, and at night it was starlit sky. The infinite universe reduced to a sliver by the confines of his prison.

Most nights he was chained to a wooden yoke, enveloped in darkness except for his view of the stars. He would stare up at them as he heard his captors outside perform the final prayer ritual of the night as they bowed to Mecca.

One day he asked for a Quran. They gave him one, in Arabic with a side-by-side Pashto translation he could read. He began performing the prayer rituals inside his hut, five times a day. One of the Talibs who had come in to empty his latrine bucket saw him praying, and laughed at him. He was doing it wrong by praying in Pashto instead of Arabic. "Teach me," said Mercer. The man refused.

The headman, Farzaad, thought the American was trying either to trick them or to mock them. In response, they made his conditions worse. His midday meal was cut, his thin blanket taken away. Once in the middle of the night one of them came in and beat him with a wooden rod, breaking his rib.

He kept praying. He began listening to his jailors' Arabic prayers through the walls and memorizing them. A week later, a different Talib, Mateen, saw him trying to recite the Arabic prayer, and showed him the proper way, when to stand and when to bow. Mateen brought him a bucket of water and a cloth so he could wash himself before prayer. He performed the Fajr at dawn, the Zuhr and Asr during the day, the Maghrib at sunset and the Isha after nightfall.

His conditions did not improve, but he kept up the prayers, five times a day, every day for months. One day Mateen gave him a prayer mat. Weeks later they began giving him regular meals again. They stopped beating him. Months after that, they invited him to perform the Isha outside along with them. It was one of the few times he'd been out of the hut in almost twenty months. He joined his jailors under the stars, bowing to the west. And every night thereafter he did the same. He made sure not to look around too much, to focus on the prayer and on the act of prostrating himself before God.

Each night, he gave himself one small thing to observe. He noted there were always five men, though not always the same five. There was a pickup truck parked in the camp, and he noticed the tire marks in the dirt that told him the direction of their village. There were two torches staked into the ground, one near his hut and one where the pickup truck was parked. One night he focused on counting the weapons—five AK-47s, piled in the flat-bed of the pickup truck during prayers, and two knives, which their wearers removed and set beside them as they prayed. One night he observed the physicality of the men—who seemed the strongest, who the weakest. Who carried himself with assurance, who averted his eyes when Mercer looked at him.

He sometimes asked them questions about their faith after the completion of the prayer. They were, not surprisingly, somewhat ignorant of their own religion. But he listened to their stupid ramblings. He didn't flatter them personally—that would be too obvious. It was always about their faith. About growing closer to God and saving his infidel soul.

One night, he decided it was time. He had built up enough strength, gone enough weeks without beatings, without being denied a meal. They led him outside for the Isha. This time he laid his prayer mat down next to Akram, one of the men who wore a knife. Akram removed the knife and sheath, and made sure to set them down on the opposite side from where Mercer had placed his mat. They, of course, still didn't trust him. But the months of his charade had bred something else in them—an indifference to him. He had bowed and bowed until they had forgotten who—and what—he was.

The six men—five Afghans and one American—began the prayer, standing under the stars, turning their palms to the heavens. They dropped to their knees and bowed down—and closed their eyes. Mercer bowed too, then rose back to his knees as they continued to recite the prayer. He reached over the back of Akram, unsheathed his knife, then grabbed him by his hair and drew the blade across his throat. Blood spurted onto the man's prayer mat.

It happened so quickly and so silently that the other men did not notice for a moment. Mercer turned to the man on his other side and cut his throat. The man cried out before his windpipe was severed, and the other three sprang to their feet.

Farzaad drew a pistol from beneath his tunic. It was a weapon Mercer had not counted on and had never seen. Mercer dropped his knife, grabbed the pistol with both hands as he'd been trained to do, twisted it free, and pressed the muzzle under the headman's chin and blew his brains out. He shot the two other Talibs in the back as they ran for the AKs.

It was all over in a matter of seconds. Mercer stood over the bodies, under the stars, his heart pounding. Two years in chains and then suddenly he was free. And freedom meant making choices—something he had not been able to do for almost two years, but something he'd thought about for most of those years. Virtually every soldier would now do what they were trained to do and sworn to do under the Code of Conduct—escape and evasion, making every effort to link up with friendly forces. And this was something that Captain Mercer, Delta Force, would do. The difficult part would come when he had to explain to the American Army why he'd left his post—why he'd deserted—but even that wasn't so difficult, and if they believed him, he, Captain Kyle Mercer, would be truly free: free to go home, free to remain in the Army, and free to testify about Operation Flagstaff. The deserter would become a hero. And he would get his revenge in a court of law.

But that wasn't the kind of revenge Kyle Mercer wanted. And it wasn't the kind of revenge he trusted. So he'd walked to the pickup truck and found the camcorder that his captors had used over the years to record his beatings and his interrogations, and to record their own stupid posturing as they played with their guns, or the time they'd recorded the torture and mutilation of a captured Afghan soldier.

Mercer felt the sweat forming on his face as he recalled all of this—his moment of freedom and his moment of truth. At some point during his captivity he knew he would not take the easy path to revenge if he escaped. He would take the difficult and unexpected path—the path an ancient warrior would take. The path to personal revenge and retribution that would lead him to Brendan Worley's throat.

No, he wasn't going home. His mother was dead, and his captors had taunted him with that information when they'd heard the news. His father, he hoped, would understand why his son had chosen not to come home. And if he didn't, it didn't matter.

Mercer stood in the Taliban camp, knife in hand, looking at his kill, illuminated in the moonlight and by the flickering fire of the torches. The two men whose throats he had cut were still face down, bleeding out onto their prayer mats, forever facing their holy city.

He filled with rage—rage at these sadistic and stupid half-wits and their miserable cult. And rage, also, at the bastards in Washington and Kabul who didn't understand war, and didn't understand the warriors they'd created. And Kyle Mercer raged at himself—his former self—the boy peering through the chain-link fence at Camp Pendleton, mistaking theater for truth.

That boy was dead, and so was the man he'd become—Captain Mercer was dead. And all that remained was the killing machine they'd created. But killing wasn't enough—so he took the camcorder and began taking heads. And when he'd finished, he delivered his final verbal message to the Army: I quit. I am no longer one of you. I am now your worst nightmare.

Kyle Mercer looked up at the tepui, the dwelling place of the gods. Someday—on the day he killed Brendan Worley—he would climb up there and look down on the world. And he would step into the fast-flowing stream and be carried to the edge of the waterfall, and he would be one with the water and the air and the earth—he would be free. He would be home.

PART V

BOLÍVAR STATE, VENEZUELA
AUGUST 2018

CHAPTER 39

Captain Collins' voice came over the PA: "All right, folks, we're cleared to land and we are beginning our initial descent into Ciudad Bolívar's Tommy-Can-You-Hear-Us Airport." Collins thought that was funny, and he pretended to radio, "Tommy, can you hear us?"

Brodie smiled. The captain was a little crazy. And crazy was what they needed today.

Collins said, "Might be a little bumpy. Buckle up."

Taylor roused herself from a half-sleep on the back bench seat, and sat next to Brodie and buckled in.

Brodie asked her, "Do you think a six-foot, two-hundred-pound man can fit back there?"

"Do you mean you?"

"You know who I mean."

"We're on a recon mission, Mr. Brodie."

"Right."

As the Cessna descended, Brodie looked out the side window. In the clear predawn he could see vast fields of patchwork farmland, and directly below he spotted acres of oil storage tanks. Up ahead were oil wells scattered throughout the farms and cattle ranches.

Collins spoke over the PA: "I guess you folks know this because you're geologists, but this area north of the river is known as the Orinoco Petroleum Belt where all of this country's heavy crude is located." He added, "The largest reserves of petroleum on the planet."

Brodie called out over the sound of the engine, "I sometimes dream about the Orinoco Petroleum Belt." He said to Taylor, "Don't we, dear?"

She had no reply.

Brodie looked down at the oil fields scattered among the rich agricultural land, finding it hard to believe that this country was an economic basket case. Venezuela, like much of South America, was blessed by nature and cursed by men. *Totally fucked up.*

Brodie continued to peer out the window, and he could now see the muddy waters of the Orinoco River snaking through the countryside, and up ahead he got a glimpse of Ciudad Bolívar clinging to its southern bank. It was a small city laid out in a grid, and as they got lower and closer he could see the buildings, a mix of picturesque colonial and slapdash modern. Beyond the city to the south, there was less farmland and more forest, and he recalled that Ciudad Bolívar was called the Gateway to the South—a frontier town, beyond which were vast tracts of sparsely populated land, indigenous people, jungle, and Kyle Mercer.

Sunlight was filling the cabin now, and he looked at Taylor, who was staring out her side window. He wondered what was going on inside her head. Possibly she regretted telling him about her complicity in Operation Flagstaff—unwitting complicity, according to her version of the story. It occurred to him that only actors stuck to the script. But maybe he shouldn't be so cynical and untrusting. Her admission had the ring of truth—though not the whole truth. Maybe she'd truly been in love with Trent, and maybe she still was. And now she was on a CID assignment to track down Kyle Mercer, America's most infamous deserter and a possible participant in Flagstaff. So maybe this assignment was calling up the ghosts that Maggie Taylor thought she'd left in Afghanistan.

Empathy was not one of Brodie's many strong points, but he'd seen those ghosts himself, at unexpected times and in unexpected places, so maybe he and Taylor had an unspoken bond—the brotherhood of war. She certainly had balls. He knew lots of men who would not have agreed to this mission into the heart of darkness. He made a mental note to write a glowing letter of commendation for her file. But then Dombroski and everyone else would think he'd had sex with her. So he should preface the letter by stating that he hadn't. And on that subject, he wondered if she had regrets that she'd let that moment pass. Since the beginning of time, men had said to women, "I'm going into battle. I could be dead tomorrow. Let's fuck." That approach had a good success rate. But in this case, they were going into battle together—at his suggestion—so maybe she reasoned that if she'd agreed to the dangerous mission, she didn't have to agree to the sex. His father had once told him, "If you can learn how to think like a woman, you'll get laid more." Good advice. Better than the old man's advice on how to roll a joint.

Collins contacted the control tower and was cleared for the low approach toward Tomás de Heres—a.k.a. Tommy Can You Hear Us?—which Brodie saw was a small airport with a single runway, maybe a mile long, suitable for large aircraft, probably built when tourism to the south was big. But now there was only one large aircraft on the tarmac—a military transport. He also noticed a few smaller aircraft parked near the small terminal, probably carrying government oil people or adventure tourists, or maybe cartel kingpins.

Collins lined the Cessna up with the runway and communicated with the control tower. He passed over the outer marker, and within seconds he made a smooth touchdown. Brodie said to him, "Those people down there look like ants."

Collins knew the old joke and said, "They are ants. We're on the ground."

They both laughed. Brodie knew how to bond with men. Women were more of a challenge.

Collins contacted ground control, then turned the plane onto a taxiway and headed toward a row of hangars where other small craft were parked. He steered toward a tanker truck and the propeller spun down as he stopped and cut the engine. "Welcome to nowhere." He added, "They say they have fuel. Let's see." He said something in Spanish into his headset, then told his passengers, "I'm gonna hop out and monitor the refuel. You can get out and stretch, use the baño in that hangar, but stay together. I'll stay with the plane to make sure nobody steals it."

Brodie asked, "How long is this layover?"

"Maybe fifteen or twenty minutes—unless the fuel crew is on siesta break."

"Okay. Are you topping off?"

"No." He explained, "That might make us too heavy for a takeoff at Kavak. The plan is to refuel again here on the way back to Caracas." He added, "It's all about weight, runway length—just enough fuel for a margin of safety if we run into weather."

"Right." Brodie didn't want to tell Captain Collins yet that they weren't going back to Caracas, so he said, "We're going to want to fly around Kavak before we land. A little sightseeing, maybe a little terrain recon. You know? Oil and birds. So why don't you top off?" He reminded Collins, "I'm paying for the fuel."

Collins thought about that. "Okay . . . shouldn't be a problem if we burn off enough fuel."

"Good. And with a fill-up you get your windshield washed and they'll check your oil and tires."

Collins smiled.

Brodie asked, "Are there security cameras here?"

"Yeah. There's lots of stealing here."

Plus, thought Brodie, the police would want to know who's arriving and departing. He said, "We'll stay here."

"Okay." Collins climbed out and shut the door behind him.

Taylor said, "We could call Dombroski from a landline."

"The last pay phone here was stolen two years ago."

"Scott—"

"When you lived at home and were out on a hot date, did you call home?"

"Actually, I did."

"Really? And when you came home with a Gideon Bible in your purse, did your grandma think you spent the night in church?"

She smiled. "I never stole a Bible from the motel."

"You're a good girl. Meanwhile, we are traveling dark. For security reasons. End of discussion."

"Yes, sir." She added, "But I do have to pee."

"You'll have to do it here."

"I'll wait."

If they'd had sex, she wouldn't have been so modest. Should he say that? Probably not.

Brodie watched Collins speaking to a guy in a green jumpsuit who was speaking into a walkie. They were probably negotiating the gringo price of the aviation fuel. The only thing you could be sure of here was that you couldn't be sure of anything. Finally someone unhooked the long hose from the tanker, which reminded Brodie that he, too, had to pee.

He found the urine tube under the seat—he didn't think that Taylor, who'd peed behind rocks and in drainage ditches for a couple of years in mixed company, would mind if they shared a pee together. Good bonding. But she suggested he go into the cockpit, and he agreed. "I guess that's why it's called a cockpit."

Brodie squeezed into the cockpit and Taylor used the female tube, and as they were tinkling, a guy appeared outside the left-hand windows on a rolling ladder with the fuel hose in his hand to fill the wing tank. The guy waved at them through the windows.

They finished, and Brodie returned to the cabin and stowed the tube under the seat. "That felt good." He asked her, "You want something to drink?"

"OJ. Thanks."

Brodie stood and reached behind the bench seat and opened the cooler. "You didn't put your pee tube in here, did you?"

"You want the small bottle with the label."

"Right." He retrieved two bottles of orange juice.

They sat side by side, sipping their juice. The refuel guy was at the right wing now, topping off the tank. Brodie pulled Taylor's map out of the overnight bag and studied it. The Colombian border was about four hundred miles west of Kavak. Maybe beyond the range of the Cessna, which would be burning fuel just to get to Kavak, then more fuel for their recon. He'd have to speak to Collins about that, after Collins agreed to the change of plans.

Taylor asked, "What are you looking at?"

"Distances."

She glanced at the map. "If we can't make it to Colombia, we can easily make it to Brazil or Guyana."

"Right. But we have military and Intel assets in Colombia, and we're supposed to get debriefed at our embassy in Bogotá."

"We won't have Mercer onboard, so it doesn't matter where we fly to first, as long as we're out of Venezuela."

Brodie did not reply.

She said, "We are about to fly into what could be hostile territory."

"We've been in hostile territory since we landed in Caracas."

She continued, "So I just want to be clear about the mission before we get there."

"Right. Well, this is a recon mission. Intel gathering."

"All right. So if we do take that boat trip up the river, there will come a point when we hit the one-hour mark, and I know you'll want to go just a little farther—"

"We stop when we see the first shrunken head." He assured her, "We will go to the edge of danger, but no further."

"You know as well as I do that you don't know where that edge is until you're over it."

Brodie finished his OJ and held up the bottle. "Is this bottle half-full, or half-empty?"

"It's completely empty, like your brain."

"Right. Can you get me another?"

"Another brain?"

"Juice, please."

She stood, reached behind the bench seat, got another OJ from the cooler, and handed it to him.

They sat in silence for a minute; then Brodie said, "We told Dombroski we were going to get a fix on Mercer's camp. And that's what we're going to do. And you suggested having a Delta team go in to take Mercer out. And Dombroski liked that idea. But without actionable intelligence for such an operation, we may as well have gone to Aruba."

Taylor didn't reply for a moment, then said, "In Afghanistan, I wasn't afraid to die. I just didn't want to die for a stupid reason."

"In war, that's not usually your choice."

"True. But now it is."

"Right. We'll play it by ear."

"And I get to call the tune."

"You get to hum along." He reminded her, "Our original assignment was to find and arrest a fugitive—"

"That has changed."

"Okay, but—"

"I hope you learned something from that shit-show at the Hen House."

"I did, which is never go into a whorehouse without a gun."

"I think you missed the bigger lesson, Scott, which is don't walk into an armed enemy camp without a battalion behind you."

"Right. Look, I'd like nothing better than to see Kyle Mercer hog-tied in that back seat with a mango stuffed in his mouth. But I'll settle for a fix on his camp."

"Good. So we're clear on the mission."

"We are."

"No fantasies about capturing Kyle Mercer."

"I have a new fantasy."

Taylor looked at him but didn't reply. Then she said, "If we get out of here alive . . . I'll make you a nice dinner."

"Looking forward to that." So all he had to do to fulfill his fantasy of sleeping with Maggie Taylor was to get them home alive. She knew how to cement a deal.

He watched Collins peeling off money from a wad of cash, paying for the fuel. He also noticed that Collins had a cigarette in his mouth—standing right next to the <u>NO FUMAR</u> sign. That idiot was going to get them killed before they got a chance to get themselves killed.

Brodie sat back and finished his juice. It was quite possible that Kyle Mercer had been briefed by now about the Hen House—by radio, sat phone, or messenger—and that Mercer and his armed thugs might be staking out the Kavak landing strip, waiting for unwelcome company. Well, that would put a quick end to this assignment.

Taylor asked, "What are you thinking about?"

"I'm just thinking that Kyle Mercer could be waiting at the Kavak airstrip to see who arrives on the next plane from Ciudad Bolívar or Caracas."

"Mr. and Mrs. Bowman are arriving for bird-watching."

"Will that turkey fly?"

"We will see."

"Yes, we will."

CHAPTER 40

They were about an hour and a half out of Tomás de Heres, and for most of that time Taylor had had her eyes closed, leaving Brodie to read the Helm Field Guides *Birds of Venezuela* on Taylor's tablet. Most birds, he discovered, were not monogamous. He must have been a bird in his previous life. Maggie Taylor must have been a scarlet macaw who mated only once a year.

The refuel at TDH had taken longer than expected—like most things in Venezuela, except death—and it was now almost 8 A.M. The sky was cloudless and the sun was well over the horizon, lighting up the terrain, which was heavily forested now with not much evidence of human habitation.

Collins announced, "Kavak is about fifteen minutes." He asked, "You still want to do some aerial sightseeing?"

Brodie called out, "We do."

Taylor opened her eyes. "What's happening?"

"Kavak, fifteen minutes."

She nodded.

Collins said, "We'll reach Auyán Tepui and Angel Falls first, and we can do a flyby. Kavak is on the far side of the tepui."

"Sounds like a plan," said Brodie. He leaned toward Taylor and said softly, "We'll do an aerial recon of the Kavak airstrip to see if we have a hot LZ."

Again, she nodded, and noticed her tablet in Brodie's lap. "What are you reading?"

"Bird porn."

"Can you sound knowledgeable about birds?"

"I'm CID. I can sound knowledgeable on any subject when I'm playing the part."

"Give me an example."

"Okay . . . If you're watching a pheasant in full flight at about fifty yards, you lead him by about five feet before you fire."

Taylor smiled. "What if it's a guy on a mule who's firing back? Do you aim for the mule's ass?"

"As a matter of fact, Ms. Smartass, if cavalry is attacking infantry, the infantry would aim for the horses. The bigger target."

"You should have used that defense at the inquiry."

"I just thought of it."

So, with the pre-mission banter out of the way, he said, "If the airstrip looks hot, we'll just do an aerial recon of the area, take a few photos to spice up our debrief, then tell Collins to fly us to Bogotá."

She nodded. Brodie handed her the tablet and she plugged it into an outlet next to the seat to charge it.

Collins announced, "Auyán Tepui, right ahead. Can't miss it."

Brodie and Taylor looked out the windshield at the massive tabletop mountain, its east-facing escarpment lit yellow by the rising sun. Its peak reached at least a couple hundred feet above their altitude, and clouds ringed the upper edges of the tepui, obscuring its summit. Stretching in all directions from the foot of the mountain was endless, dense jungle, threaded by small tributaries of the Orinoco Basin.

Taylor said, "This is breathtaking."

Brodie agreed, "They don't make them like that any more."

Taylor took a few pictures with her smartphone, and Brodie hoped he didn't have to see a slideshow in her apartment.

Collins continued his guided tour. "There's a valley cutting into the north side of the tepui called Devil's Canyon, and the falls drop from the canyon's western wall, which will be on our right. So Angel Falls drops into Devil's Canyon." He thought that was funny—right up there with Tommy Can You Hear Us?

Brodie stared at the tepui and thought about Carmen, who maybe flew to Kavak, maybe went upriver for an hour, maybe got off on the right bank, and maybe walked fifteen minutes to Mercer's camp.

What had felt like solid information in Caracas was starting to feel a little sketchy in the presence of Venezuela's enormous hinterlands.

Collins continued his climb as they approached the tepui to make sure the Cessna and the mountain did not meet.

Taylor asked, "Can you land a plane up there?"

"You can, but it's prohibited now." He added, "Back in Jimmie Angel's day, back in the Thirties, you could do whatever you wanted."

"Those were the days," said Brodie. "Who's Jimmie Angel?"

"American aviator and explorer. He flew here looking for gold."

"How'd he make out?"

"He landed on Auyán Tepui with his wife, and his plane got stuck in the mud. He and his wife had to climb down and find the nearest settlement."

"How long did that marriage last?"

Collins chuckled and continued his tour spiel. "The plane stayed up there for over thirty years before it was brought down and put on display in front of Tomás de Heres Airport."

"So did he find gold?"

"No. But he got the falls named after him. Angel Falls." Collins added, "Better than gold. That's immortality."

More like a consolation prize. Well, thought Brodie, that might be the story of human exploration—looking for one thing and finding another. Looking for gold and finding a waterfall. Looking for the fountain of youth and immortality and finding death. The great cosmic joke.

Collins said, "The indigenous people say the gods live on top of the tepuis."

Well, thought Brodie, they damn sure didn't live in the mountains surrounding Caracas.

They flew in silence for a few minutes, and Brodie could see Devil's Canyon, which was a few miles wide and mostly in shadow at this early hour. Thick jungle filled the valley and climbed up the base of the tepui's sheer rock walls.

As they descended into the canyon, they saw the towering waterfall on their right, its source obscured by clouds, making the water appear to be tumbling out of the sky as it cascaded down the steep face of the tepui, plunging thousands of feet into a river below that cut through the valley's jungle floor.

Brodie thought about Kyle Mercer, who was down there somewhere.

Captain Mercer's journey had taken him from the dead mountains of Afghanistan to here, the dwelling place of the gods. Could this place heal him? It didn't sound like it had.

Collins continued his tour: "These tepuis are so old and so isolated that they have their own unique species of flora and fauna that don't exist anywhere else."

"That's why we're here," said Brodie. "To find a rare bird."

Collins made a tight one-hundred-eighty-degree turn in the canyon, then exited and rounded the eastern side of the massive tabletop mountain. To the south they could see a break in the jungle where miles of grassland fanned out from the tepui's southern base.

Collins asked, "Ready to land?"

Brodie called out, "No—but fly around Kavak before we go on."

"Okay . . . Any reason for that?"

"My wife wants to take pictures."

"Okay."

"Mind if I borrow your binocs?"

"Not at all." Collins retrieved his binoculars from his flight bag, which he'd returned to the co-pilot seat, and handed them back to Brodie.

Brodie looked out his side window and adjusted the binoculars as Collins rounded the south side of the tepui and began his descent toward Kavak.

After a few minutes of flying over the expansive savanna, Collins said, "Kavak coming up on your side, Mr. Bowman. One o'clock."

Brodie looked out at the grassland and spotted a small, winding river, then to its east a group of about twenty thatched-roof huts—a mixture of round, square, and oval—about half a mile away. On the south side of the village was the airstrip, which was actually just a swath of cut grass with a wind sock and some markers, about six hundred yards long.

Collins said, "Kavak is not really an indigenous village. It's more like a tourist place. Seven or eight guesthouses, a storage hut for stuff that people order and have flown in, and a few transient huts for the Pemón natives who are either guides or caretakers for the guesthouses, boat landing, and airstrip."

Brodie asked, "What's the best bar and restaurant in town?"

"There's one communal dining hall."

"How's the food?"

"Fresh. There's no refrigeration. No electricity." He added, "There's rum and beer for sale. Sometimes other stuff." Collins began a right bank over the village.

"Get a little lower over the airstrip so my wife can take some pictures. Mind if I come forward?"

"Okay."

Brodie squeezed into the cockpit, moved Collins' flight bag behind the seat, and sat in the right-hand seat while Collins began a corkscrew descent over the airstrip. Brodie peered through the binoculars out his side window, focusing on the tall grass around the airstrip, then on the scattering of huts, which appeared to be painted yellow, as per Carmen. There didn't seem to be any unusual activity down there. In fact, no activity except a few people down by the river, fishing. He spotted a mudflat, on which sat about ten small watercraft. "Can I rent a boat?"

Collins leveled the Cessna at about five hundred feet and continued his banking turn over the airstrip and village. "Yeah. The Pemón guides will take you up- or downriver. Buck an hour."

"I just want the boat."

"I don't know . . . you can ask."

Taylor was kneeling now between the two cockpit seats, and she asked Brodie, "See anything interesting?"

"Looks green," he replied, using the radio code word for a safe LZ. Yellow meant caution, and red was hot, but you usually didn't know that until you were on the ground.

Taylor said, "I would call yellow. Too quiet."

"Maybe."

Collins did a few glances at his passengers. "Folks?"

Brodie explained, "I think the huts are green. My wife says a quiet yellow." He peered down at the airstrip. "I see the wind sock. Wind coming from the east, Captain."

Collins glanced out his windshield. "Thank you."

"No problem." He remarked, "I don't see any birds."

"They're probably in the jungle, Mr. Bowman."

"Right. They hang out there." He asked, "Anything down there that can eat you?"

"Yeah. Cougars and jaguars."

"Sorry I asked."

"Also piranhas in the river. Maybe some crocs."

Brodie said to Taylor, "There goes our midnight skinny-dip."

Collins agreed, "I wouldn't go in that river."

"Good advice." He thought they'd circled enough—maybe too much if anyone was watching—and he said, "Okay, let's continue our sightseeing."

Collins glanced at his fuel range. "Yeah, we can fly maybe another hour and still have plenty of fuel to get to TDH." He put the Cessna into a climb. "What do you want to see?"

Taylor replied, "We'd like to see an area along that river, maybe six or seven miles southeast from Kavak." She added, "That's where we're going later to see birds."

"Okay." He banked left and took a new heading.

Taylor said, "Lower, and slower please."

Brodie recalled that Carmen had mentioned seeing another tepui from Mercer's camp, so he asked, "Any other tepuis around here?"

Collins nodded. "If we keep heading in this direction about twenty miles, we'll reach Chimantá Massif—a huge complex of about a dozen tepuis. Together about the same size as Auyán."

Brodie nodded. So far the terrain was checking out with Carmen's testimony.

They flew low and slow over the small muddy river as it snaked its way through the grassland and then entered the jungle, which stretched to the south and east as far as the eye could see. When Brodie thought they'd gone about six or seven miles he said to Collins, "Let's do a tight circle over this area."

"Okay." Collins put the Cessna into a steep right bank and began circling.

Brodie raised his binoculars and looked down at the carpet of jungle below.

Taylor moved to Brodie's passenger seat and also peered down into the jungle canopy. "Let me take a look."

Brodie handed her the binoculars and they both looked out through the side windows at the right bank of the unnamed river as Collins kept the Cessna in a tight turn. He asked, "You folks looking for something in particular?"

Brodie replied, "Wouldn't mind seeing a real native village."

"Well, they'd be hard to spot from up here."

"Right." So would Mercer's camp. "Maybe we'll come across a village while we're bird-watching. Are the natives friendly?"

"Well . . . it's situational."

"Give me a situation."

"Okay. They used to depend a lot on tourism for a living, but tourism is way down, so they're a little stressed, and some of them have taken to crime."

"Sounds like Caracas."

"Yeah . . . like the whole country. So if you're in the wilds with a tour group with Pemón guides, you're okay. But if you're alone—like you and Mrs. Bowman—and you run into some Pemón in the jungle, they can be a little intimidating."

"So can I and Mrs. Bowman."

Captain Collins glanced at his passengers.

Brodie smiled to show he was not really intimidating, and asked, "Do they eat people?"

"They prefer fish."

"Good. They got blowguns? Poison darts?"

"I don't know. But I know they have rifles." He added, "For hunting. Look, the Pemón are nice people, and I don't want to—"

"Got it. Okay, if we run into Pemón while we're bird-watching, I'll let you make the introductions."

"I'm staying with my aircraft."

"Don't say you weren't invited."

Taylor called out from the back, "I see what looks like a village along the bank of the river. Three o'clock, low."

Brodie peered out the side window and saw a long, thatched-roof structure close to the riverbank.

Collins banked the Cessna and took a look through Brodie's window. He said, "That's a native fishing platform. It's on, like, stilts—poles. They store their nets there, hang out, sleep, fish, and maybe have a beer and chew the fat."

"Sounds like Tennessee."

Collins laughed, but Magnolia didn't.

Brodie was waiting for the right moment to tell Captain Collins about their change of plans—but first, a little prep. He asked Collins, "You ever miss the States?"

"Sure. But I enjoy the pilot's life. Flying to new places."

"But always returning to Caracas."

"Yeah . . . she doesn't want to leave."

"It's got its charms," Brodie reminded him.

"Actually, it sucks."

"Right. I saw that." He added, "You're a good guy to stay with her in Caracas."

Collins didn't reply for a few seconds, then said, "She's a former beauty queen."

More likely a cocktail waitress, thought Brodie. "No offense, Captain, but the world is full of beautiful women who live in nicer places."

Collins didn't respond to that, but said, "I own a place in Pensacola. That's my plan—and it will become her plan too."

"Good plan." A better plan would be not to let a woman fuck up your life, and he would have said that to Captain Collins, but Maggie Taylor was in the back seat, probably thinking about how she could fuck up Scott Brodie's life.

Collins asked, "Still want to circle?"

Brodie called out to Taylor. "What do you think?"

She lowered the binoculars. "I don't think so . . ." She snapped a few pictures with her smartphone. "Can't really see anything through the canopy. But maybe go upriver another mile or so."

Collins again glanced at his fuel gauge. "These maneuvers burn a lot of fuel. But . . . okay. Then we need to put it down."

"You're the captain."

Collins came out of his turn and took an easterly heading, farther up the river.

Brodie looked out the front windshield as the unbroken expanse of rain forest passed under their aircraft. He was convinced now that Kyle Mercer was down there—somewhere. Or Mercer was in Kavak, waiting to see who flew in.

Taylor shot pictures of the riverbank and the adjacent jungle, then called out, "Do you see those boats?"

Brodie looked at the narrow river and spotted three small boats headed downriver, toward Kavak. He wondered if that was their welcoming committee.

Collins said, "Could be Pemón. Or tourists with Pemón guides." He advised, "The best way to travel in this terrain is by boat. Unless you're real jungle experts." He expanded on that: "You got venomous snakes down there. Howler monkeys, who can be aggressive, plus the big cats. Then you got bugs and slugs and all kinds of things that bite." He added, "The mosquitoes can drive you crazy. And give you malaria."

Brodie called out to Taylor, "Screw the bird-watching. We're going to Aruba."

Collins laughed. "That's a layover I wouldn't mind sharing with you. I could pick up my girlfriend in Caracas."

Or find a new one in Aruba. Brodie was about to tell Captain Collins that they weren't going back to Caracas, when Taylor called out, "Two o'clock."

Brodie and Collins looked out the windshield. Up ahead, Brodie saw a break in the jungle canopy—a long gash that was obviously man-made.

Collins said, "A jungle airstrip." He added, "You see them now and then. And nearby, you usually see where a patch of trees has been thinned out. That's where they grow the coca, and close by is the lab where they make the white stuff." He added, "You don't want to land at those airstrips."

Brodie asked, "Anyone ever ask you to do that?"

"I make an honest living, Mr. Bowman."

"So do we. You want to hear about it?"

Collins stayed silent, then replied, "I think it's time to turn for Kavak. We can talk on the ground."

"You can turn, but we need to talk up here."

Collins didn't respond, but put the Cessna into a one-hundred-eighty-degree right turn.

Brodie said, "Mrs. Bowman and I are not actually with the Department of the Interior, and all I know about geology is what I learned in the eighth grade. Got a C in the course. But Mrs. Bowman and I did actually serve in the Army, me in Iraq, her in Afghanistan. I got a star in that course. Bronze. She got a silver. We both have Purple Hearts."

"Thank you for your service."

"You're welcome. Now we're working in an official capacity for our government. Yours and mine. We're not looking for any more Purple Hearts, but we have a job to do here."

Collins nodded as he stared out the windshield.

Taylor said, "We may—or may not—need your help."

Brodie wanted to add, "And if you agree, she'll show you her scars." But that might be promising more than he could deliver.

"What are we talking about?" Collins asked.

"A few things," Brodie replied. "The first is that we can't go back to Caracas." He explained, "We are hot there. So after we leave Kavak, we need to fly to Bogotá."

Collins nodded. "Okay . . ." He looked at his fuel gauge. "We should have enough fuel to make it to the border . . . then I'd need to check my charts to see where we can refuel in Colombia to get to Bogotá."

Brodie said, "I don't want you to humor us just because we're carrying Glocks. I want you to do this voluntarily." He added, "For your country."

"Okay . . . Can I see some government ID?"

"You did. Our passports. You can see more ID if you ever get to Washington. But for now, the less you know, the better."

"Okay . . ."

"And this flight to Colombia cannot be logged with Venezuela's aviation authorities or with Apex. Comprende?"

"Yeah . . . but I will need to file a flight plan with Colombian air traffic control and request clearance."

"All right. Once you've gotten us to Bogotá, you can fly back to Caracas and say whatever you need to say. You can say we skyjacked you. Whatever."

"Okay . . . I can think of something."

"I'm sure you can. And when you get back to Caracas, you can buy something nice for your girlfriend, and you'll have five thousand dollars to do that." Brodie added, "And you can put the extra fuel on my credit card."

Collins nodded.

Brodie called out to Taylor, "Let's pay Captain Collins up front."

Collins seemed to have no objection to that, but asked, "What . . . I mean, are we staying here overnight?"

"Let's stay flexible."

"Okay . . . so . . . you meeting somebody here?"

"We may be picking someone up. You okay with that?"

Before Collins could reply, Taylor said from the back, "We are not picking anyone up."

"Right. That was the last mission."

Taylor said, "There is five thousand dollars in American currency in your flight bag, Captain."

"Thank you."

Brodie said to him, "And thank you for your service to your country, Captain."

He nodded.

Taylor added, "When the story of what this is about can be told, you'll receive the public thanks of our government."

Brodie interjected, "Then you'll really have to leave Venezuela."

Collins forced a smile. Clearly he was not a hundred percent good to go.

Taylor leaned forward and put her hand on his shoulder, which Brodie thought was a smart move. Maybe she should sit in his lap. She said, "When we land, Clark and I may take a boat on the river. You'll stay in Kavak and we'll leave our bags with you. There's more money in those bags. But we trust you to be there when we get back."

Brodie wanted to whisper to Taylor, "Pinch his cheek," but she slid her hand off his shoulder and sat back in her seat.

Well, they now had a quick and secure way out of Venezuela—with or without Kyle Mercer. There were a couple of other ways out, like a walk through the jungle to the Brazilian border, which would be a challenge, but not impossible, if they didn't get their heads shrunk by the natives. Another way out was an air extraction, which had the unpleasant quality of having to rely on Brendan Worley and his flying Otter. The third way out was getting caught and killed by Kyle Mercer, but death was never a good way to end a mission.

Brodie said to Collins, "We can stay in touch on the ground via sat phone. Where's yours?"

"In my flight bag."

"Okay, Sarah, can you take Captain Collins' number and put our number in his flight bag?"

"Ready to copy."

Collins rattled off his sat phone number and Taylor wrote it somewhere—or committed it to memory. She said, "Our number is written on your notepad in your bag."

Collins had no comment, but he was probably happy to have Mrs. Bowman's number. Brodie advised him, "Don't let your girlfriend find that phone number in your bag."

Collins again forced a smile, then banked the Cessna as they crossed the northern edge of the jungle and flew back over the savanna south of Auyán Tepui. Up ahead they could see Kavak, and Collins began his descent.

Brodie asked him, "You know what a hot LZ is?"

Collins glanced at him. "Yeah . . . ?"

"Well, hate to mention this, but Kavak could be hot."

Collins had no reply, but he did continue his descent.

"I will make that call," said Brodie. "You and Mrs. Bowman—Sarah—will keep your eyes glued to the ground. And if you see anything that does not look right, you let me know, and if I say 'red' at any point in the landing, even on the runway, you will give it full throttle and get us out of there. Comprende?"

Collins looked at Brodie, then glanced over his shoulder at Mrs. Bowman, now Sarah.

She said to him, "This is just standard procedure when flying into a rural airstrip in a foreign country. Just a heads-up." She added, "We don't expect any problems."

Collins nodded.

Brodie suggested, "Just concentrate on your landing." He asked Taylor for the binoculars, which she handed to him, and focused on the approaching airstrip. "Wind's still coming from the east." He added, "I love wind socks. Simple, cheap, and reliable. Wind blows, sock fills with air, and it swivels." He asked, "How you doin', Captain?"

"Okay."

"We'll be on the ground soon. I'll buy you a warm beer."

Collins said, "Buckle up."

Brodie and Taylor fastened their seat belts, and Brodie continued to look through the binoculars at Kavak and the approaching airstrip. He'd always taken calculated risks when he was looking for a criminal, but this assignment had changed the calculations. And the reason for that was Kyle Mercer—a unique and dangerous variant of *Homo sapiens*, who'd been spotted here, and who could disappear and never be seen again. And he, Scott Brodie, would live the rest of his life regretting having let Kyle Mercer slip away, without answering for his crimes and without answering the question of *why*. That was not the way Chief Warrant Officer Scott Brodie was going to end this mission.

CHAPTER 41

As they got lower and closer, Brodie saw that the people who'd been fishing at the river were gone. The village of thatched-roof huts sitting on the open savanna seemed as deserted as when they'd made their earlier pass, but he now noticed hammocks strung between the clusters of palm trees. At least two of the hammocks were occupied by loafers—or by plane spotters.

Collins asked, "See anything?"

"No." And they probably wouldn't until they were on the ground. He tried to put himself inside Mercer's head; assuming Mercer had heard about the Hen House shoot-out, what would he do? Brodie didn't think Mercer would come to Kavak in person—unless he actually ran the village. More likely Mercer would send a few trusted men with some smarts, who would question anyone landing in Kavak to see if they were tourists—or if they were people who needed to be killed or kidnapped. Well, at least he and Taylor had some cover, but when your cover is thin and your bullshit doesn't pass the smell test, you go right for the guns. Or they could skip Kavak and go on to Bogotá.

Taylor asked, "Should we circle again?"

"We've done that."

Collins glanced at Brodie sitting next to him.

Brodie didn't want to spook the guy—actually, he was already spooked, and he might abort the landing. Brodie could pull his gun, but threatening to shoot the only pilot in midair was counterproductive. He said, "This is an unannounced arrival, so there's no way that anyone could know we're coming." Which was not so much a lie as it was a shared hope. "But to put your mind at ease, Captain, you just have to land, we'll get out, and you stay with the plane while we check out the situation."

Collins did not reply, but Brodie thought the captain might be regretting taking that call from Apex.

They were a few minutes from touchdown and Brodie continued to scan the village and the taller grass around the landing strip with his binoculars. He said to Collins, "When we get to a bar in Bogotá, I'll get a cocktail named after you. A John Collins—like a Tom Collins, but with big nuts."

Captain Collins did not laugh, but he seemed less tense when Brodie was making stupid jokes. He eased back on the throttle, adjusted his flaps, and kept the Cessna lined up with the short, narrow runway.

Brodie asked Taylor to put the SIM card and battery in the satellite phone and give it to him, which she did. He plugged the phone into the cord on the instrument panel, but didn't turn it on. If things went south, he owed it to the mission to call Dombroski, telling him the name of the village and the approximate location of Mercer's camp, as per Carmen. The mission comes first.

And if he had time for a second call, it would be to Worley, who was actually the last person on earth he wanted to talk to, but Brodie would make a final sit-rep as to their location and the nature of their distress call—like, "We're surrounded by Indians." Duty first, as they reminded you often.

And finally, he said to Taylor, "Put the boss' number in Captain Collins' flight bag." He said to Collins, "If you leave here and we don't, you will call that number."

"Okay . . . and . . . ?"

"And you just tell Colonel Stanley Dombroski that you flew the Bowmans to Kavak, but they missed the return flight. Then answer all his questions."

"Okay . . ."

Brodie assured him, "I'm sure you won't have to make that call," but Collins didn't seem so sure. Neither did Brodie.

The Cessna seemed to float over the dry, brown grassland, then settled onto the runway and began bouncing over the turf, the prop and landing gear kicking up clouds of dust. Collins applied the brakes and the Cessna came to a bumpy halt a few hundred feet short of the end of the grass strip.

"Did we land, or were we shot down?"

Collins replied, "The ground is uneven."

"Right. Okay, Sarah and I will get out here. Mind if we borrow your binoculars?"

"No. But hold on." Collins taxied to the end of the strip and turned the Cessna around so he could make a quick takeoff. He left the engine running.

Brodie unplugged his sat phone, squeezed into the cabin, and grabbed his overnight bag as Taylor took her bag and opened the cabin door. Brodie found Collins' sat phone in his flight bag—between the money and his boxer shorts—and handed it to him. "I'll call you with the all clear." Meaning, *If you don't hear from me, it's not.* He also handed Collins his Magnum revolver, without comment.

Taylor stood at the doorway and again put her hand on Collins' shoulder. "I'll buy you that drink in Bogotá."

In fact, maybe two. Brodie was impressed with Maggie Taylor's use of her feminine charm.

Taylor jumped to the ground, and Brodie said to Collins, "See you shortly."

Collins nodded.

Brodie jumped, and he and Taylor began walking down the airstrip with their overnight bags in their left hands and their right hands free to draw their guns from their cargo pants pockets. The air was hot and humid, and it was quiet except for the buzzing of flying insects.

Taylor asked, "Do you think our ride will wait?"

Brodie glanced back at the Cessna, still idling at the end of the runway. "I think he's conflicted—one hand on the engine throttle and the other on his joystick."

"That's crude."

"I meant it as a compliment to you, Mrs. Bowman."

"I do what has to be done." Taylor stopped, then walked to the edge of the airstrip. "What's this?"

Brodie looked. Embedded in the short grass was a metal tube, about two feet high. "I think . . . you put a pole, like a tiki torch, in the tube."

"So the airstrip can be lit at night."

"Or they have calypso dances on the airstrip. Okay, so Ms. Muller said you can't land here in the dark, but Carmen said she did. And this is how they landed."

Taylor nodded and continued Brodie's deductive reasoning: "Mercer's pilot must radio ahead, or it's prearranged that someone in Kavak sets out the torches."

"Right. So that means Mercer has help in Kavak, which is no surprise. But we can't question anyone here, or we'll wind up swimming with the piranha."

Taylor thought a moment, then said, "Didn't you tell me that Carmen said there were Pemón who accompanied her and Mercer on the boat to his camp?"

"Right. And also Pemón in the camp."

"So there is definitely some level of cooperation—complicity—between Kavak and the camp."

"That's good deductive reasoning."

"So . . . ?"

"We are tourists. Bird-watchers. However, I think we need to get out of here as quickly as possible, before someone in Kavak gets word to Mercer that unscheduled tourists have landed."

"Okay . . . you mean get back on the plane?"

"No. I mean get a boat."

"That's what I was afraid you meant."

"It may all be moot. They could already be waiting for us in the village."

Taylor stayed silent, then said, "All right. Let's see if your impersonation of a married man and a bird-watcher is better than your impersonation of a john in a whorehouse."

"Collins bought it."

"He did not."

"I'll work on it. Bird-watcher is easy. Married man, not so easy."

"Really."

They continued along the edge of the airstrip, and about a hundred yards farther on they saw another tube in the ground, confirming Brodie's guess that torches marked the runway at night.

Brodie raised his binoculars. The tall grass thinned out up ahead, and on the left he could see the village of thatched-roof huts with mustard-yellow walls, sitting in the grassland amidst a scattering of trees. On the western edge of the village the terrain sloped down toward the narrow river they'd seen from the air, which flowed north out of the distant jungle. Rising up beyond the village was the massive tepui. Brodie said, "This looks like the village that Carmen described."

"There would be no doubt if she knew the name of the place she landed."

"Right." They continued on toward the end of the airstrip, where they saw a crudely built ladder in the grass, which was obviously Kavak's answer to a jetway. They turned toward the village and approached a column of wooden signs including one that said <u>BIENVENIDOS</u>, and another that said <u>WELCOME</u>. But nothing from the Chamber of Commerce that said: <u>KAVAK—THE SMALL TOWN WITH A BIG HEART</u>. There was, how-ever, an arrow that pointed the way toward a <u>PEMÓN EXCURSION</u>.

Brodie and Taylor stopped and looked around at the apparently deserted village. "Well," said Brodie, "it appears we were not expected."

"I don't like quiet villages."

"I hear you."

They continued into the village, which was a collection of well-built and well-maintained huts of different shapes and sizes sitting apart from each other in the short grass. The thatched roofs were picturesque, as were the earthen walls, but all the huts had modern doors and windows, giving the village the appearance of a Disney theme park. Pemón World.

Brodie stopped and so did Taylor. Up ahead, he saw a man lying in a hammock, apparently asleep. In a nearby hut, he saw another man looking at them through a window. Brodie put his hand in his gun pocket.

Taylor said, "It's either low tourist season, or this village was cleared out in anticipation of a hostile encounter."

"Right. Meanwhile, we have no cover or concealment." He glanced at a round hut. "Those walls are thick. Let's move inside and see if anyone comes to greet us."

She nodded.

As they walked toward the hut, they saw a man come out of another hut about fifty yards away. They stopped and watched him approach.

The man was short and dark-skinned, maybe a Pemón, with a mop of black hair.

He appeared to be in his mid-forties, but it was hard to tell. He wore cargo shorts, sandals, and a white T-shirt. More importantly, he didn't seem to be armed, except for a clipboard. He waved to them.

Brodie said, "Beware of men carrying clipboards."

"Better than you-know-what."

Brodie walked toward the man and Taylor followed.

The man stopped under the shade of a flowering jacaranda tree, and motioned them to join him.

Brodie and Taylor stopped a few feet from the man, who was now partly obscured by shade. He smiled and said, "Bienvenidos."

"Same to you," said Brodie.

The man replied in English, "Welcome. I am César."

"Then I'm Mark Antony," said Brodie. "And this is Cleo."

"I am pleased to meet you. I am Pemón chief tour guide." He added, unnecessarily, "I see you plane land."

"Right." Brodie now noticed that César's T-shirt sported the word "Leones"—lions—in faded blue script. Probably the local blowgun team.

César glanced at his clipboard, maybe looking for Mark Antony and Cleopatra. He asked, "You have reservation?"

This encounter had a surreal feel. "Reservation?" He said to Taylor, "I thought only Indians had reservations."

"Scott—"

"Clark. No . . . Mark."

Taylor said to César, "We are Sarah and Clark Bowman. We have no reservations. My husband and I just decided to come here." She added, "We are bird-watchers."

Brodie raised the binoculars hanging from his neck to reinforce that. "You got room at the inn?"

César looked at his unexpected visitors. "How long stay?"

"One night. Maybe two."

"Tour group, German people, they come tomorrow." He tapped his clipboard, and Brodie noticed that the sheet of paper had the heading *Canaima Adventures.*

"They come, you go."

"Okay. We also need a room for our pilot."

"Pilot stay here?"

Brodie glanced at the sky. "I hope so."

"Yes, okay. Two room. Fifty dollar."

"Each?"

"Sí."

"I can get a Motel Six for that price."

"Clark—"

"Call Trivago."

Taylor said something to César in Spanish, and he seemed happy to speak to the lady in a more familiar language.

They chatted; then Taylor said to Brodie, "Meals are included."

"Who's for dinner?"

She continued, "There is a five-dollar entrance fee for the park."

"What park?"

"This is a national park."

"Right. Okay—"

"And he wants to see our travel permit."

Brodie looked at César. "Travel permits are in our aircraft."

"Yes? Okay. Pilot bring."

"Right. Okay, let's see our rooms."

"Okay. You follow."

The check-in completed under the tree, they carried their own bags and followed César, who led them toward an oval hut.

Taylor and Brodie exchanged glances. She said, "Seems okay."

"Ask him if they have express checkout."

"No more stupid jokes, please."

"I told you, I get nervous in dangerous situations and say stupid things."

"The stupid things you say make *me* nervous." She mimicked him: "Who's for dinner?" She added, "A-hole."

"Sorry."

As they walked, Brodie wondered how Kyle Mercer had wound up here. At first glance, Kavak was an odd choice of a way station if you were setting up a clandestine camp in the jungle. True, it was off the beaten path, but it was also accessible by air, and it was a tourist stop. But maybe Kavak checked off some boxes: Foreigners and strangers coming and going didn't attract too much attention, the natives seemed to be friendly and probably looking to make a buck, and Mercer's camp could be resupplied by air— including fresh supplies of hookers—then by boat from the nearby river.

Also, Mercer could commute to Ciudad Bolívar or Caracas—or disappear into the jungle if things got hot. So maybe Captain Mercer had chosen well. He might be crazy, but he wasn't stupid. In fact, he was experienced and well-trained. And so were Brodie and Taylor.

As for César, he was either straight out of central casting or he was a major player making a cameo appearance. The clipboard was a good prop, but it could also be legitimate. Was it possible that the Pemón who worked in Kavak as cast members, but lived elsewhere, didn't know about Mercer's camp? Not according to what Carmen said. So they were complicit. But to what extent? Money buys anything, including silence.

Brodie said to Taylor, "Don't relax."

"Goes without saying."

César stopped at the oval hut and opened the door, which as Brodie had noted was of modern construction, including a doorknob and a keyhole. The large open windows were also factory-made and they had screens. A real, but not *too* real, Pemón experience for the tourists.

César entered first, and Brodie followed. Taylor brought up the rear and closed the door behind them.

César asked, "Okay?"

Brodie dropped his bag on the tile floor and looked around the small oval room lit only by sunlight. The walls were whitewashed, and at either end of the oval was a bunk bed. On the wall opposite the door hung two stowed hammocks, which could be opened and stretched across the room and fastened to the opposite wall.

César explained, "Hammock is how Pemón sleep. Maybe you sleep in hammock, maybe you sleep in bed."

Maybe they wouldn't sleep at all. Brodie asked, "Baño?"

"Outside. Nice."

"Right. Shower?"

"Outside. I show you later."

"Snakes?"

"Outside." He pointed at the ceiling. "For walk in night."

Brodie looked up at the thatched roof and saw four battery-operated lanterns hanging from the ceiling rafters on pulleys, which might be safer than an open flame close to the thatched roof. He pictured himself trying to find the outhouse at three in the morning, carrying a lantern and a Glock.

Well, thought Brodie, if a Caracas hooker could stay here for a night without complaint, then surely a former infantryman could do the same. He wondered if this was the Carmen suite. In any case, this hut could hold six European tourists with low expectations, and in fact César suggested, "You pilot sleep with you here. You save money."

Brodie and Taylor exchanged glances. Three guns were better than two, so the smart, tactical thing to do would be to stay together through the night. On the other hand, there was no bedroom door in this hut for Ms. Taylor to shut on Collins. So . . . safety in numbers? Or three's a crowd? This was not a call he wanted his dick to make, so he said to Taylor, "Your call."

She said to César, "The pilot will want his own room."

"Sí, señora."

"Good call," said Brodie.

Taylor looked at him. "I might want my own room too."

"It's not in the budget."

César gestured around. "Okay?"

Taylor assured him, "Perfecto."

César smiled. "Good. You leave bag, you come with me. Breakfast for you."

Brodie replied, "We'll unpack and meet you outside."

"You come."

Taylor said something to him in Spanish, and César left.

Taylor said to Brodie, "He understands English, so please watch what you say."

"He probably learned his English from Kyle Mercer."

She nodded. "Will César report our presence here?"

"I'm sure that's part of his standing orders."

"All right . . . so . . . ?"

"We're bird-watchers."

"That might not fly, pardon the pun."

"I think we're okay for now."

"I told you we shouldn't stay overnight."

"But we should give the appearance we're staying overnight."

She nodded.

"We'll take a boat upriver, and if we're satisfied with our Intel, we can fly out of here before nightfall."

"Good."

He looked at her. "If we do stay overnight, I thought you'd want another gun in the room."

"I do. But César doesn't have to know that."

"Okay . . . smart."

"I'm thinking with my brain."

"I resent the implication."

"Scott—"

"Clark. We're married."

"César is waiting for us."

"Right. We'll take our bags to breakfast."

She picked up her overnight bag. "Should we call John?"

"Oh, so it's John now, is it?"

"Scott—please—should we call our pilot and give him the all clear?"

"He's probably halfway to Caracas by now."

"No he's not."

"The best place for him right now is in the Cessna. We'll call him when we know it's all clear."

"All right. But we should call Dombroski. Maybe Worley."

"We'll call Dombroski as soon as we're alone with open sky."

She nodded but said, "I hope the sat phone works here."

"Me too. Let's have breakfast."

They left the hut, and César glanced at the overnight bags in their hands. Taylor said something to him in Spanish, and he nodded and led the way.

Brodie did an eye-recon as he walked, and he noticed that Taylor was doing the same as she chatted in Spanish to César.

About fifty yards from their guesthouse, César motioned them into a large open-sided pavilion, draped in mosquito netting. Inside the pavilion were long wooden tables with benches, and César invited them to sit.

Brodie and Taylor sat across from each other, and César sat next to Brodie, apparently staying for breakfast.

Brodie asked him, "Do you recommend we order off the menu, or do the buffet?"

"My wife bring good breakfast."

"Wonderful."

César asked to see their passports, so this was a working breakfast.

Brodie and Taylor handed him their passports, and he looked through them, glancing at his guests to be sure their photos matched their faces. He then took a pen and very carefully wrote their names and passport numbers on his clipboard roster, under the names of people named Rolf, Fritz, Magda, and Gerda.

The Europeans, Brodie knew, were more adventurous travelers than Americans, which didn't mean they were braver—they just had a higher tolerance for shitholes, or maybe they just expected to die and were happy when they didn't.

César handed them their passports, then looked at Taylor's T-shirt. "What say . . . ?"

"Georgetown," Taylor replied. "My university. Universidad."

"Ah . . . César collect T-shirts."

Better than collecting heads, thought Brodie. He suggested, "Swap T-shirts."

Taylor said to César, "I'll give this to you later."

He smiled. "Gracias."

Well, thought Brodie, César seemed to be what he said he was: the chief tour guide. And probably any connection he had with Mercer and the camp was one of mutual convenience. César owed no allegiance to Kyle Mercer or to the government in Caracas, or to anyone except his own people. And most probably César had no idea why the American had set up an armed camp nearby, nor did he care, so long as they didn't bother him or his people. In fact, Mercer's camp probably provided some sort of employment for the Pemón who had been left adrift by the central government. And maybe Mercer paid for use of their land, as the American military did in Iraq and Afghanistan. Kyle Mercer knew how to live in tribal territories, and rule one is: Be a good neighbor to the locals. Rule two is: Buy whatever you need from them—food, manual labor, and silence. Rule three: Pay the locals to report what they see and hear. And that's what César would do. Nothing personal. Just business.

César looked at Taylor and asked his new friend, "You stay in Caracas?"

Taylor replied, "Yes, and we will return tomorrow."

César had no response, and Brodie wondered what the indigenous people thought about Caracas and civilization in general. Probably not much.

César suggested, "You pay now. American dollar or euro. Okay?"

"Okay." Brodie took out his wallet and gave César a hundred dollars. "Two deluxe rooms for one night, outdoor shower, meals included, and a view of the tepui."

"Sí." César put the money in his pocket and said, "Park fee. Five dollar."

"Right. Here's a ten. Keep the change."

"Gracias." César also informed them, "You go jungle or tepui, you need guide."

"Let me get back to you on that." He asked, "What is the name of this river?"

César replied, "It has name in Spanish. Pemón people call it River."

"That's very clever." Not unlike Brodie calling his dick, Dick. In Spanish, it would be Ricardo.

Taylor asked César for the Spanish name, but he seemed to have forgotten it. He did remember, however, to tell them, "Pilot bring permit."

"No problemo."

"Okay."

Taylor spoke to him in Spanish as she took her tablet from her overnight bag. She pulled up the Helm book, which had photographs, and turned it toward César as she scrolled and narrated.

He stared at the screen, but he didn't seem to think it was magic or witchcraft, and Brodie guessed that he'd seen a few of these before, and maybe wanted one for himself, though he'd need a very long extension cord to charge the batteries.

Brodie said to César, "We're especially anxious to see a scarlet macaw."

"Señor?"

"They mate once a year. Like American wives."

Taylor actually laughed, though César seemed confused. So, they'd established a little rapport with César and reinforced their cover, and César said, "I see one time bird-watcher here. American."

Brodie took the opening to inquire, "Do you see many Americans here?"

César hesitated for a fraction of a second. "No. Long time. No come here."

"They don't know what they're missing."

"Sí." César stood. "Breakfast. You wait." He left the dining pavilion and walked off.

Brodie said, "He'll be sending smoke signals to Mercer."

"Or sending someone in a boat. Or they have radio or sat phone contact."

Brodie nodded. "Let's be confident in our ability to pass as innocent tourists." He added, "Two men traveling alone arouse suspicion. A man and a woman look harmless. That's why Dombroski wanted you to accompany me."

She looked at him. "First of all, I'm not harmless. Secondly, I was picked because I'm good at what I do."

"No argument there." But there could be another reason that Maggie Taylor had been assigned to this case, though Brodie was hoping he was wrong about that.

She glanced around and asked, "Should we call Collins?"

"We should if we think it's safe. And if we don't, we should walk to the plane and leave."

"That's your call."

"Could use some breakfast."

She stood, fished the sat phone out of her overnight bag, and walked out of the pavilion to get open sky.

Brodie called out, "Tell him we're sharing a room." He added, "Keep it short and turn the phone off when you're done." Brodie dug into Taylor's overnight bag and retrieved a Snickers bar, which he unwrapped and bit into.

Taylor returned. "Sat phone works. He's on the way."

"Good. Want a bite?"

She sat and said to him, "Please don't go into my overnight bag again."

He looked at her. "My apologies."

"That's all right . . . We're operational, so . . . whatever you need."

He didn't reply.

They sat in silence; then Taylor said, "Collins says he has never stayed overnight in Kavak, and he's concerned about his plane. He says he's slept in his plane in places like this, and he may do that tonight."

"We'll see."

"Now that Collins is joining us, we don't have a cut-out guy to call Dombroski. So we need to call the boss now."

"I'd rather wait until we're actually on a boat going upriver."

"Why?"

"So I have more to report. Also, I don't want to keep using the sat phone if Worley's people are looking for our signal."

"Worley is not the enemy."

"No, but he is our competitor. And he has his own agenda." He added, "I'm not giving him our location unless he needs it."

"It's us who may need him."

"Maybe. But in this game you have to know what bridges to cross, and what bridges to burn."

"How can I argue with your eloquence?"

"You can't," he assured her.

"We will call Dombroski five minutes after we get on that river."

"We will."

A petite woman wearing a yellow sundress and nothing on her feet appeared carrying a large tray, which she set down on the table.

Brodie said, "Good morning, Mrs. César."

She smiled and Brodie was glad to see her teeth weren't filed to a point. Maybe he'd read too many *National Geographic*s when he was a kid.

She put three mugs of what looked like steaming coffee on the table, and three wooden bowls of steaming hot mush, each topped with a fried egg. She said something to Taylor in Spanish and Taylor replied, then said to Brodie, "César will return to see our travel permits when the pilot gets here."

Hopefully César didn't give a rat's ass about the travel permits and would take twenty bucks instead, but if he was reporting to Mercer's camp, he would mention that the bird-watchers had no permits. Brodie said, "Ask her what this stuff is."

Taylor exchanged a few words with César's wife and said to Brodie, "It's ground manioc root, with an egg and coffee." She added, "All locally sourced."

"Obviously."

Taylor thanked the lady, who turned and left.

Sitting on the tray were three wooden spoons to highlight the authentic experience. "Where are the napkins?"

"In Caracas."

Brodie took a spoon and tapped the egg. He'd eaten bowls of shit in third

world countries on three continents, and invariably the shit was topped with
a fried egg for some reason. Sometimes the eggs even had embryos in them.
Sometimes salmonella. He sipped the coffee, which was bitter and made
with suspect water. Cream and sugar would have helped. He wondered what
they ate and drank in Mercer's camp. And who paid for it. He had lots of
questions for Kyle Mercer if he should actually find him.

Taylor said, "Be polite and eat that."

"I'll ask Mrs. César to wrap it for later."

"Don't insult her. I'm sure food is scarce here." She spotted Collins and
called out to him. He smiled and waved as he made his way toward the pavilion, carrying his flight bag, which meant he planned to stay, or he didn't
want to leave it in the Cessna. By now, Brodie thought, Captain Collins—
John—had concluded that his passengers were not using their real names,
so maybe Sarah was single. Brodie sometimes wondered if his job would be
easier if he was a beautiful woman. Probably not.

Collins came into the pavilion, took a seat opposite Taylor, and looked
at the food.

Brodie encouraged him to dig in.

He admitted, "I ate. I always bring a sandwich when I fly to these native
villages."

"Thanks for sharing." Brodie asked, "So you've been to Kavak?"

"Yeah. I think three times."

"Do you know César, the chief tour guide?"

"I think I met him once."

"You know anyone else here?"

Collins shook his head. "I just fly in with a few people who are part of a
tour group, I get out, stretch, use the baño, maybe have my sandwich, then
leave." He added, "I don't stay longer than I have to."

"Why is that?"

Collins shrugged. "Not much to do here if you're not in a tour group."

"You could hire a guide and take a boat on the river."

"I need to have the aircraft in sight." He reminded Brodie, "I'm not on
vacation."

"Right. Do the Pemón make you feel comfortable?"

Collins replied, "If you mean do they make me nervous, the answer is no. But . . . twice I spotted some tough-looking hombres who were not natives. They gave me the once-over."

Brodie and Taylor exchanged glances. Brodie asked, "You ever carry any cargo for Kavak?"

"Once. Like ten cases of bottled water."

Well, thought Brodie, they weren't using it in the coffee.

Collins asked, "What are you getting at?"

"You never know until you get there." He looked at Collins' breakfast bowl. "Mind if I have that?"

"Help yourself."

Brodie slid his and Collins' bowls in front of Taylor. "All for you."

Collins sipped his coffee and made a face, then said, "I taxied to this end of the runway, so the plane is closer." He added, "In case we need to make a quick exit."

Taylor said, "Good thinking, John."

Collins smiled.

It always amazed Brodie how fast a local hire—after some jitters—got into the game. Every guy wants to be James Bond. Brodie informed him, "We'll be sharing a room tonight if we stay."

"Mrs. Bowman said . . . but . . . company policy is that at unattended airfields, I stay with the aircraft." He explained, "It's not my plane. It belongs to a rich Venezuelan who has it in a rental pool to make some American dollars. But . . . we'll see . . ." He looked at Taylor.

So Captain Collins was torn between his duty and his desire to maybe see Mrs. Bowman in a short nightshirt. Brodie could relate. He said to Collins, "Okay, we'd actually rather have you as the cut-out guy. Here's the plan, John: Sarah and I are going to take a boat on the river to do some bird-watching in about fifteen minutes. We will be gone maybe three hours, four max. You stay here with our bags, and if we don't return in four hours, or you don't get a sat phone call from us, you call us, and if we don't answer, you take off and call the number we gave you for Colonel Dombroski."

Collins had no reply, and Brodie couldn't tell if he was excited to be part of this adventure or if he was scared shitless.

Taylor said to him, "You should actually put our bags onboard, and maybe wait in or near the plane like you're doing some maintenance, and be ready for a quick takeoff."

Again no reply, but he nodded.

Brodie said to him, "Play it by ear. Use your judgment. Don't fall asleep. Keep your gun and phone on you, and act natural around any Pemón you see." He reminded Collins, "You're just a pilot working for Apex."

Again, Collins nodded.

Taylor made eye contact with him. "This is important to our country, John, and we trust you. Any questions?"

Collins seemed to be thinking; then, remembering something Brodie had said, he asked, "Are you looking for somebody?"

Brodie replied, "We are looking for birds. We may return with a bird. If curiosity gets the best of you and you look in our bags, you'll see zip ties. And you'll also see our real passports." He informed Collins, "We are not married."

Collins nodded as though he'd figured that out.

Taylor added, "You'll see money too. It belongs to the government." She smiled. "But the candy bars are mine. Take what you want."

Collins forced a smile.

Brodie asked, "Anything else on your mind?" Aside from wondering if you're going to die here, or if you're going to get lucky in Bogotá?

Collins took a deep breath, then said, "I'll follow your instructions." He again forced a smile. "You're the customers."

"And you're a good pilot," said Taylor.

He looked at her. "Maybe this is what I needed to wake up and get out of this country."

Taylor assured him, "We may be able to help get your girlfriend out."

If Taylor was in charge of immigration, thought Brodie, half of Caracas would be in Miami.

Collins said, "Thanks, but . . . she'll want to stay here."

More likely she wouldn't be asked. Sounded like the captain was signaling to the ex–Mrs. Bowman that he'd drop his beauty queen for her. Maggie Taylor's good looks were not always a liability to the mission.

Well, thought Brodie, it seemed that the deal was done, and they could rely on Captain Collins. And if not—if he got cold feet and took off—there was always Brendan Worley to call on for an air extraction. Or a jungle hike to the Brazilian border, which might be a more reliable extraction than dealing with Worley.

Brodie noticed that Taylor had actually eaten all three fried eggs, along with her bowl of mush. "Leave the rest for the Pemón. They dip their darts in it."

She looked at Collins and rolled her eyes.

César suddenly appeared and, without invitation, sat next to Collins. "See passport."

Collins reached into his bag and produced his American passport, which César flipped through, then copied Collins' name and passport number onto his growing roster. He looked at the pilot. "I see you one time."

"I have been here before."

"Sí. This time you stay."

Collins nodded.

"I have good room for you." He tapped Collins' epaulettes. "You important man." He laughed.

Collins smiled. "I am a pilot."

"Sí, you have travel permits?"

Collins looked at Brodie, who said, "I think I left them in my other plane."

Taylor said to César, "We just decided at the last minute to come here." She then spoke to him in Spanish, and César listened, then responded. Taylor said to Brodie, "We were not allowed to fly here without a permit, so we must leave—or pay a fifty-dollar fine." She added, "Per person, per day. Pilot included."

"If we leave, do we get our money back for the room?"

"Clark, darling, just pay the fine."

"Okay." He looked at César. "We'll pay for one day."

"Pay now."

Brodie pulled out his wallet and counted out a hundred and fifty dollars. Obviously César had learned how to make a few extra bucks on his government-regulated national park job. Therefore it shouldn't be a problem for Brodie and Taylor to rent a boat without a guide. This was César's World, and he made the rules.

César pocketed the money, then eyed the bowls of mush. "You no like?"

Brodie said to him, "My wife and I would like to rent a boat, and we'll take that with us."

César nodded. "Boat and guide. Five dollar."

Collins had said it was a dollar, but César was on a roll and he knew suckers when he saw them. He also knew he wasn't going to get an extra euro from the German tourists, so today was payday. Brodie said to him, "We don't need a guide."

"Need guide." César said something to Taylor, who translated, "It's the law."

"So is the permit." He said to César, "Twenty dollars. No guide."

But César seemed adamant on this point. "No guide, no boat."

"Sounds like the Pemón guides have a strong union."

César spoke to Taylor, who translated: "It's a safety issue." She added, "He would be responsible if we got lost or hurt."

"How could we possibly get hurt in the jungle?"

César did not reply.

Well, they could steal the boat, or up the offer to a hundred bucks, but either solution would arouse suspicion. Or they could take the guide upriver and feed him to the piranha. He hadn't come this far to run into bureaucratic bullshit. He said to César, "We are bird-watchers. We need silence."

César shook his head.

Well, they'd come to an impasse, so Brodie said, "We'll think about it. Meanwhile, Captain Collins would like to see his room."

César stood, as did Collins, who took all three bags, as per instructions, with no help from César.

Taylor smiled at Collins. "We'll see you for lunch, John."

He returned the smile, and he and César walked off toward the guest-houses.

Brodie looked at Taylor. "Do you think we'll see Collins or those bags again?"

"We will very shortly if we can't get a boat." She added, "And if we do get a boat, we will not be returning here with a bird."

"Right." Brodie suggested, "Let's go down to the river. I need to walk off that breakfast."

"All right . . ." She stood and they began walking through the village toward the river.

Taylor said, "We are not stealing a boat."

"No, but maybe we can buy a boat from a local who doesn't care about the rules."

They continued down the slope, and they could now see the small, murky river. The tepui rose up on their right.

Taylor asked, "Can I make a suggestion?"

"Of course."

"I think the gods who live on that tepui are telling us to get the fuck out of here."

Brodie smiled. "You may be right."

"We've gone above and beyond the call of duty, Scott, and we have been very lucky so far. We've seen and learned enough here and in Caracas to make a convincing case that Kyle Mercer's camp is about ten miles up that river. I will take a few photos of you standing on the riverbank, pointing upriver. Okay? Then we go back to the village, find Captain Collins, get on his plane, and get the hell out of here before people from that camp come to Kavak." She asked, "Sound rational?"

"It does."

They reached the bank, and Brodie stopped and looked at the river, which was about a hundred feet wide. He said, "The water is flowing at maybe four or five knots. It's a little deeper than I thought, but no more than chest-high. We could actually wade upriver."

"The piranha would enjoy that."

"Right . . . well . . ." He looked to his left, where he saw the mudflat that he'd glimpsed from the air. There was a scattering of wooden canoes in the mud, all about fifteen feet long with square sterns and small outboard motors. "So near, and yet so far."

"Ready for your picture?"

"Let's get the boats in the shot." He walked down to the mudflat and stood by the canoes, which he noted had wooden plank seats every few feet, and were wide enough to hold two Pemón or one hog-tied Captain Mercer, stretched across the seats. The canoes had nylon bow lines, and that should do the trick. Then all they had to do was call Collins with a heads-up, get Mercer ashore away from the village, cut through the grass to the landing strip, and board the plane. It's all about planning and logistics.

"Scott? Hello? Smile for the camera."

He smiled, and pointed upriver. Taylor took three shots and said, "Okay, let's go."

"Hold on." He noticed a bamboo platform on which was a pile of wooden oars and also yellow life vests, which weren't needed in this chest-high water unless the piranha and crocs had made off with your legs.

He walked over to one of the canoes. The small, gas-powered engine had a recoil starter that Brodie was familiar with. He guessed it was about two horsepower, and given the speed of the current they'd be going against, he thought his initial estimate of seven or eight knots was about right.

"What are you doing?"

"I'm verifying Carmen's testimony. It all fits."

"Good. We'll mention that in our debrief. Let's go."

"I have an idea."

"Like the one you had when you walked into the whorehouse?"

"Even better. Why don't we get into one of these canoes, paddle out to the middle of the river, and take a few pictures?"

"Why?"

"So we can say we did a river recon." He added, "No one has to know we were fifty feet from the boat landing."

"That's deceptive."

"Right. It's our turn to be deceptive."

"Don't justify—"

"Come on. This will take ten minutes." He added, "We need to make a convincing case for what we believe."

She looked around. "All right . . ." She walked to the canoe where Brodie was standing and he handed her the nylon bow line.

"You pull, I'll push. But first I'll get some paddles." He grabbed two oars and two life vests and threw them into the canoe, then rounded the back of the canoe to push. Taylor remained standing, holding the bow line.

He asked, "What is it?"

She kept looking at him, then asked, "How far are we actually going, Scott?"

"About an hour." He looked at her. "Okay?"

"I don't like being bullshitted."

"No one does." He added, "You knew where we were going since we left Caracas."

"Right. I should have known to just apply the Brodie Rule."

"What's that?"

"In any given scenario, do the thing most likely to get you killed."

"I'm offended."

"No, you're not." She pulled on the line as Brodie began pushing the canoe through the mud.

They got the canoe into the shallow water and both scrambled aboard. Brodie grabbed an oar and pushed against the river bottom until they were clear of the shore. The canoe began floating downriver, and Brodie moved to the stern, tilted the propeller into the water, then started the engine and gave it some throttle until the canoe began moving upriver. He steered it into the middle of the river and twisted the throttle. The canoe gained speed, cutting through the tea-colored water, moving along the grassland toward the jungle.

The morning sun felt good, and Brodie felt good. They were close to their fugitive now, under the same sky and sun, breathing the same air, and heading up a river that Kyle Mercer had traveled. The detective work was behind them and this was now a reconnaissance mission into hostile territory, and the success of this mission depended on the skill and instincts that Scott Brodie and Maggie Taylor had honed in war zones on the other side of the world.

He and Maggie Taylor had been sent here with fairly simple and straightforward orders: Find and apprehend Captain Kyle Mercer, and return him to face American military justice. Or, if they couldn't bring Captain Mercer to justice, they—or a drone or a Delta team—would bring justice to Captain Mercer. Either way, Captain Mercer was going to pay for the blood on his hands.

CHAPTER 42

Taylor sat on a life jacket in the bow, facing Brodie, who was on the bench beside the outboard, his hand on the tiller and throttle. The small engine didn't make much noise, which was good for a river recon. He said to Taylor, who was about to call Colonel Dombroski, "Call his message line," which was the number that anyone within the command could call to leave sit-reps and other messages that didn't need a response or conversation. Sort of like calling your girlfriend's answering machine to tell her you accidentally ran over her cat. In the case of the CID, the recorded messages were accessed by the intended recipient using a unique four-digit code number. This was Brodie's preferred method of communication with the boss.

Taylor looked up from the sat phone. "Why?"

"Because you're going to file an oral report—not have a conversation." He advised, "Keep it short and concise, and end it by saying that you are shutting off your sat phone to save battery." He added, "Promise to call his cell later."

"Scott—"

"I do not want him telling me—us—what to do. Or what not to do." He explained, "I would never disobey a direct order, and I don't have time to argue with him. So this is the way to avoid all that." He confessed, "I do this all the time. You should too."

"Thanks for sharing, but—"

"Here's another piece of advice: You can be half as obedient as the next guy if you're twice as competent."

"Not to mention arrogant."

"And I deliver what I'm asked to deliver. Also, don't forget that Worley has gotten Dombroski's ear, and Worley is looking for our signal. Make the call—or give me the phone."

She hesitated, then dialed the message line number and entered the four-digit code for Colonel Dombroski's private mailbox.

Brodie reduced the throttle and listened as Taylor had a one-way conversation with the mailbox. She began by identifying herself; then, as per training, she gave their present location—in a boat, on an unnamed river, heading southeast from the village of Kavak. She remembered that place names needed to be spelled phonetically—Kilo, Alpha, Victor, Alpha, Kilo, which was correct even if she spelled it backward. She also read off their lat long from the satellite phone. She then backtracked to Francisco de Miranda Airport in Caracas, Apex, Captain John F. Collins, Ciudad Bolívar and Tomás de Heres Airport, and the aerial recon over Kavak.

Military reports were notorious for burying the lede, which in this case was the possible nearby location of Captain Mercer's jungle camp, and Taylor finally got to that, citing the testimony of Mercer's girlfriend, the cocktail waitress in the whorehouse, who, Taylor reported, had not actually accompanied them to Kavak.

Brodie was impressed with his partner's reporting skills, but she'd been on the phone about three minutes, and he pictured the commo wonks at the embassy trying to pinpoint the signal.

Taylor relayed their intention to recon by boat, gather actionable Intel, then fly to Bogotá with Captain Collins—ETA, late afternoon or early evening.

Brodie would also like to have Captain Mercer onboard, but the odds of that happening were slim to none. The odds of Captain Mercer apprehending them, however, were better, which was why Dombroski had to know all this for his missing agents report.

Brodie said to Taylor, "Tell him to text our cells with the name and cell number of our embassy contact in Bogotá, and we'll retrieve the text when we get there."

Taylor relayed Brodie's message, then advised, "We are shutting off the sat phone to save battery, but we will—"

"Ask him not to share any of these details with Worley."

Taylor also relayed that to the voice mailbox, then concluded, "We will call you by sat phone from the plane when we're in the air—in about three or four hours." She ended the call and shut off the phone.

Brodie glanced at his watch. About five minutes. Enough time for Worley to fix their latitude and longitude if the embassy commo people were actively searching for their loaned—now stolen—satellite phone. Well, if he had called Dombroski directly, they'd still be talking—or it would have been a very short conversation, ending with Dombroski ordering him to turn around and get out of there. He said to Taylor, "That was very good."

She didn't reply, and he recalled that she took compliments as patronizing. He'd have to remember that if they ever made it to bed.

She said, "I forgot to tell him this boat trip was your idea."

She'd also forgotten to tell him that his agents almost had sex last night. Dombroski would want to know. He said, "What you forgot was our personal threat assessment—Kyle Mercer's connection to Kavak, and possible SEBIN interest in us via the Hen House incident. Maybe even Worley's meddling in this CID case."

"He already knows that. Also, threat assessments can sound . . . like you feel threatened."

"Don't you?"

"I'm not stupid. But there's nothing Dombroski can do for us at this time." She reminded him, "This was your idea. Not his."

"Correct." He looked at his watch. "We've been on the river fifteen minutes and I haven't seen a shrunken head yet."

"I'm looking at one."

"That's just the swelling going down. Okay, let's do a reality check in fifteen minutes."

"You're calling the tune, Mr. Brodie. I'm just humming along."

He smiled at her. Well, he'd played chicken with lots of guys in Iraq, and a few men in CID, but never with a woman. She had cojones. Plus she was probably a little pissed at him, which was good motivation. If things went south, she'd enjoy saying "I told you so." They all do. More importantly, they both needed to focus on the mission. The problem was, the mission had become as murky as the river.

He watched her as she shot a few pictures of the riverbanks, then one of him piloting the boat, which he hoped showed his steely-eyed determination. They could use that photo in the debrief in Bogotá. Also in General Hackett's office.

She said, "We should call Collins to tell him where we are."

"More importantly, where is he?"

"Let's do a commo check and find out."

"He's probably figured out that we stole a boat. So ask him if César has realized that." He reminded her, "Quick call."

She dialed Collins' sat phone number from memory.

"Ask him to find out how much the boat-stealing fine is and pay César from our stash."

Taylor held the phone to her ear and listened to the ring, then ended the call and turned off the sat phone. "No answer."

Which could mean anything your imagination wanted it to mean—sleeping, showering, flying off with all the money, or dead.

Taylor said, "I'll try again later."

"Okay." Brodie looked at the landscape passing by. There was still open grassland on the left bank, which gave him a clear view of the terrain. But on the right bank, the savanna was giving way to thick jungle which he, as a half-evolved *Homo sapiens*, instinctively equated with danger.

He looked back toward Kavak and stared at the massive tepui that dominated the terrain for miles around. The towering gray escarpment looked like a wall built by giants, and the flat peak was still shrouded in white, rolling clouds in an otherwise cloudless sky. This place, he thought, was primeval—Jurassic Park on steroids. Pemón World. Kyle Land.

He thought back to that travel poster at the airport. It was prescient. *This is my destiny.*

He looked at Taylor, who was playing with her cell phone. "If you have service, I want the name of your carrier."

She glanced up from her phone. "I'm looking at the aerial photos I took. I think I see where we are, and where we're going."

"That's always good to know."

"I took a basic course in aerial recon. How about you?"

"I was just a lowly infantryman. All I needed to know was what I could see, hear, touch, and smell at ground level."

"I . . . when I was in Afghanistan, I was called into Bagram a few times . . . to look at aerial photographs of towns and villages that I was working in . . . to try to ID residences of suspected Taliban collaborators and sympathizers."

Brodie had no comment, but apparently Operation Flagstaff was still weighing on her mind—and her conscience.

She said, "They told me these people would be turned over to the Afghan security forces for interrogation."

Also known as torture. Followed by the usual bullet in the back of the head.

Maggie Taylor must have known this on some level. He asked, "Who was asking this favor of you?"

"Army Intel . . . and other people who were . . . not identified."

"Friends of Trent."

"Probably."

They continued upriver. Walls of tropical trees towered on both sides now, and the riverbank was choked with vegetation. Brodie kept the canoe in the center of the river, away from both banks. Every few minutes he cut the throttle and listened to the sounds of the jungle—lots of squawking birds, and now and then a crazy shriek that he guessed was a howler monkey. It was getting hotter, and the flying insects were becoming annoying. He thought of his uncle Reggie, who'd served in the Mekong Delta on a river patrol boat. Reggie got killed a few months after arriving in country, ambushed by bad guys who opened fire from the riverbank. His dad had a photo of Reggie on his boat, young and dumb, smiling and shirtless with his dog tags hanging around his neck, and in the background was a thick jungle wall that came right up to the river. Brodie remembered thinking that he'd never want to be in a place like that.

Reggie had never come home from the war, and in a way Captain Mercer had never come home either. And in never coming home, Kyle Mercer never took off his armor, never hung up his sword and shield. He was still a soldier, untempered by peacetime, fighting his own endless war.

Brodie raised his binoculars and scanned the riverbanks, but the growth was so dense that he couldn't see more than ten feet into the dark jungle. But somewhere along here, farther upriver, would be a place where a boat could come ashore.

Taylor, who was still looking at her aerial photos, said, "We should be coming to a sharp right bend in the river."

"Okay."

"What do we do if we see indigenous people in boats coming toward us?"

"Wave."

"What if they have rifles?"

"They hunt."

"Can I make a suggestion?"

"I'm all ears."

"We should hug the riverbank, and if we see anyone coming toward us, we can beach the boat and get into the jungle."

"I sort of like it here—out of blowgun range of the shore."

"Scott, the Pemón have rifles, not blowguns, and Mercer's people have rifles. We're sitting ducks here."

He reminded her, "No, we're bird-watchers."

"Forget the cover story. Think armed confrontation."

"Okay . . . you make a good point."

"I've made several."

He steered the boat toward the right bank and got within ten feet of the shore. The water was shallower here, and there were banyan roots threading into the river, so he slowed the boat and kept an eye on the water. He saw some fish that he thought might be piranha. No skinny-dipping here.

It was also buggier here, and the heat was oppressive.

Taylor, who was sweating and swatting insects, reminded him, "We never got vaxed for yellow fever."

"That's the least of our problems." He suggested, "If you want to cool off, you can go over the side and hang on."

"You go first. I'll steer."

He smiled.

She looked at her watch. "Thirty minutes."

"We're halfway there."

"Time for a reality check."

"I think that time has come and gone."

She didn't reply, but took the sat phone and dialed. "I'm calling Collins."

Brodie could hear the faint ringing of the sat phone. Or was that the mosquitoes?

She let it ring for a long time, then ended the call and shut the phone off. "Why is he not answering?"

Brodie did not reply.

They came to the sharp bend in the river, and as they rounded the curve Brodie saw that the river was starting to narrow, the opposing walls of trees closing in and the blue sky above hemmed in by the thickening jungle.

Brodie was getting thirsty, and he was sure Taylor was too, but she didn't mention it. Also, his stomach was growling and his memory of that bowl of mush was getting better. Also left behind was Taylor's tablet, on which was the stupid bird-watcher guide, which along with the binoculars and their bullshit was their cover story in case they ran into Pemón or Mercer's men. Seemed like a good cover story back in Caracas. They'd sort of gone off half-cocked and run into the reality of the jungle, just as he'd run into the reality of the Iraqi desert. But they did have their Glocks and extra mags in their cargo pockets, and most importantly they had their wits, their nerve, and their experience in worse places than this.

He looked at Taylor, who was now flushed and covered with sweat. As long as she was still sweating, he didn't have to worry that she was going into heatstroke. He looked at his watch. "Almost forty-five minutes." He assured her, "We'll turn around in another fifteen minutes. The return going down-river will be faster."

She nodded.

He asked, "You ever see African Queen? Bogie and Hepburn?"

She forced a smile. "They had a bigger boat." She added, "And you're not Bogart."

He smiled. "You're cruel, Maggie." He asked, "You okay?"

"Happy to be here."

"Can I make a suggestion?"

"You've made a few too many."

"Soak your T-shirt in the river."

She thought about that, then peeled off her T-shirt and dangled it over the side.

"Watch out for the crocs."

She pulled her T-shirt from the river and squeezed the muddy water over her head, then draped the wet shirt over her head and shoulders.

Other than the heat, humidity, bugs, piranha, crocs, and a psychotic renegade in the vicinity, this was a pleasant river cruise.

Taylor repeated her shirt dunking, but this time she pulled it back on.

She could easily win a wet T-shirt contest. Should he say that? Probably not.

"You should get yourself wet, Scott."

"I was thinking of going in for a quick dunk."

"Don't let the piranha get your worm."

"It's actually an anaconda."

She smiled. "Favorite croc food." She glanced at the water. "Do you think there are poisonous snakes in there?"

"Probably. And snakes in the jungle."

She nodded. "How can he live here?"

"We'll never know. Because he's going to die here. One way or the other."

She thought about that, then said, "That would not be a satisfying end to this case."

"No. But it would be the kind of rough justice he deserves."

"We don't really know that." She reminded him, "You were looking forward to talking to him."

"I'd like nothing better. He knows what we don't know, and what other people don't want us to know. And I'd also like to see what makes him tick. But we'll have to settle for reporting map coordinates for a drone recon, followed by . . . whatever someone else decides." He added, "Worley and his colleagues want Mercer dead."

She nodded, then looked at her watch. "Almost an hour."

"I still haven't seen a place that matches the description of where Carmen said she and Mercer got off the boat."

"For all we know, we've passed it. Sorry, Scott, but I'm not putting that much faith in the jungle descriptions of a Caracas call girl who's probably seen more dicks than trees in her life."

"Well, if you put it that way . . ."

"I'm thinking it's time to turn around."

So, yet another moment of decision.

He had a vision of himself and Taylor, back in General Hackett's office, trying to explain why he went into the Hen House against Colonel Dombroski's advice, and then the subsequent shoot-out that not only left dead bodies behind, but also probably alerted their fugitive that people were looking for him. Even harder to explain was Brodie cutting off Worley, their embassy contact, without providing convincing evidence to General Hackett that Worley was part of the problem. Hardest to explain would be his withholding of some key information from Colonel Dombroski, who would be there in the general's office. So far, Brodie had taken a lot of big risks with not enough rewards to ensure his continued employment.

"Scott?"

"Well . . . I say push on."

Taylor went back to her cell phone and pulled up a few more photos. "Okay, I see a place . . . a few hundred meters farther, where the trees recede from the riverbank . . . sort of a mudflat."

"Good. Let's check it out."

"All right . . . Before we get to the mudflat, I see that thatched roof that Collins said was a Pemón fishing platform."

"Okay. That's a good landmark for the drones." He added, "We'll get the coordinates of the mudflat from the sat phone. Mission accomplished."

She looked at him. "You've lowered your mission goals."

"Close enough for government work. Now that I'm actually here, I see there is no way we can snatch our fugitive and get him on the plane."

"I'm not even sure we can get ourselves on that plane."

"Collins is still there. But I'm not sure who else is in Kavak with him. Maybe waiting for us."

She thought about that, then said, "There's always Worley."

"That may be our next and last play. Meanwhile, call our pilot."

Taylor called again, but again there was no answer. That would be a long shower, but maybe not a long nap. Or Collins had gone out to take a crap and a cougar ate him. Brodie said, "Most likely he's sitting someplace—or sleeping—where he doesn't have clear sky. That's what happens when you hire an amateur."

She nodded. "The cute ones are always stupid."

Brodie smiled. He said, "When shit happens, you turn it into fertilizer for your tree of knowledge."

"I'll pass that on to my next partner."

"Tell him where it came from."

Brodie raised his binoculars and looked up the river. A gray and white bird plunged into the water and took off with a large silver fish in its beak. A snatch job should be that easy.

His mind returned to Uncle Reggie in the Mekong Delta. The Vietnam War had been an abstraction to Brodie—a tropical Hollywood tableau of jungle and napalm. To his parents, it was a cautionary tale about American militarism and hubris, and Reginald Brodie himself was reduced to nothing more than a check mark on the ledger of wasted lives.

Brodie had often wondered what his death in Iraq would do to his parents. When a platoon-mate took Brodie's picture with his cell phone, he'd sometimes wondered if it was the image his parents would look at to remember him, to frame on the wall, maybe send to the local paper with his obit. Or maybe they would try to forget, the way his father had with his brother Reggie, whose memories were stuffed away in a shoebox in the basement.

Scott Brodie had survived the war and come home. But there were no war stories, and no questions asked around the farmhouse table. Which was just as well.

His parents, however, were elated when he transferred to the CID. Good old-fashioned detective work. No more killing, no more danger.

Taylor broke into his reverie. "It's one hour." She looked at her cell phone. "That thatched structure should be around the next bend, then the mudflat."

"Good. Take a few pictures. We'll end our debrief with those shots. Then you'll say, 'We believe, based on the testimony of a reliable hooker, that Captain Mercer's camp is a fifteen-minute walk into that jungle.'"

She forced a smile. "I'll let you have the last word."

"You take the first question."

He followed the curving bend in the river, staying close to the shore. He said, "Can I ask you a question?"

"All right . . ."

"Now that we're at the end of this recon, and now that our safe return is in some doubt, I'd like to know what was in your overnight bag, aside from your knickers and your Snickers."

They made eye contact, and Taylor said, "I could lie to you and if we don't make it back to Kavak, you'd never know."

"That's why I need you to tell me."

"All right . . . Well, I was given something to take with me."

"By whom?"

"By . . . friends of Trent."

"Not a complete surprise. When?"

"The day before we met with General Hackett."

"Apparently they knew you were going on a trip."

She nodded. "They knew before we did."

This was getting interesting, and maybe complicated, so Brodie steered toward the shore, killed the engine, and tilted the prop out of the water as their momentum put the bow into the thick growth along the bank. "Tie it up."

Taylor wrapped the bow line around an overhanging branch, and the boat swung starboard in the current and held fast against the shore.

Brodie looked at her in the shadows. "What did they give you?"

"A . . . it's called a Garmin inReach." She looked at him. "Do you know what that is?"

"I can guess."

"It allows two-way texting via satellite to sat phones or cell phones, independent of any cell network."

"That was a nice going-away present."

She continued, "It can also transmit lat long."

"Photos?"

"No. But exceptional battery life."

"Where can I get one of these?"

"In my overnight bag. I left it there."

"We could have used it here. But—oh, you didn't know you were going on a river cruise with me."

"I wouldn't have taken it anyway."

"Really?"

"I've never used it . . . never even turned it on."

"Not even a commo check?"

"Scott . . . look at me. I never used it."

"Then why did you take it?"

"If I didn't take it, I'd still be back in Quantico."

"And that's where you should be."

"No. I want to be here."

"No, *they* wanted you to be here."

She didn't respond.

Well, this seemed to be the conclusion of her coerced multi-part confession. Unless she was about to confess that she'd been instructed to whack him, and was seriously considering it. At this point, he could inform her that she was in violation of several articles of the Uniform Code of Military Justice, and he could also ask for her weapon. But considering they were heading up shit's creek with two paddles and a small motor, her gun would be better off in her pocket than his.

"Scott . . . say something."

"You'll need to answer for this when we get back."

"I will. If we get back."

He was glad now that he hadn't slept with her. That would complicate his report to Dombroski. He looked at her. "Do you understand what you did?"

"I do. But . . . I didn't *do* anything."

"You agreed to conspire with another government agency. Same as you did in Afghanistan."

"I agreed to take the tracking device with me. I never used it. Never sent a text, never—"

"And you understood the criminal conspiracy that Trent and his colleagues were trying to cover up, and you aided and abetted it. You understood what Flagstaff was about."

She nodded.

"And you know they want to kill—to murder—Kyle Mercer, to keep him quiet."

"I'm not sure about—"

"We work for the Criminal Investigation Division, Maggie, not Murder Incorporated."

"Don't lecture me." She looked at him. "You'd put a bullet in him if you couldn't kidnap him."

"I would not."

"We'll never know. But what do you think the Army is going to do with the map coordinates we give them of Mercer's camp? Drop a copy of the Code of Conduct on him?"

He ignored that, and continued, "Do you also understand that Trent and his friends must have known before we did that Kyle Mercer was not in Caracas? They gave you that device because they wanted to see if we left Caracas, and where we went."

"I guess I did wonder why I needed the Garmin in Caracas, where I could text and make a cell phone call to . . . anywhere."

"Well, now you know. Trent's colleagues suspect or know that Mercer is somewhere out of Caracas, and if you and I were lucky enough or smart enough to get a lead—which I did—you and your Garmin would tell them where we were, in real time, right down to the grid coordinates."

"I . . . understand that."

"And did it also occur to you that you, like Kyle Mercer, know too much?"

"I was never threatened with harm. I was threatened with exposure." She added, "I've kept their secret, but if we ever get back, I'm ready to tell CID everything I told you."

"You're not paying attention. You and Captain Mercer could be sharing the same fate."

"That's . . . I don't believe that."

"That is why you're here. The wet stuff is done on foreign soil."

"You're trying to frighten me. I'm frightened enough."

"I'm a little worried too, Maggie, being so close to you."

"Scott—"

"You should never have gotten involved with Black Ops people."

"I got involved with Trent."

"And he played you like a harp."

"I don't want to hear that."

"You stepped in quicksand, Ms. Taylor, and every move you make gets you deeper. How many times have you seen this in criminal cases?"

"I've said all I have to say. I confessed to you. You can do what you want with the information. I'll even give you the Garmin device for evidence."

"If you'd given it to me back in Caracas, I could be more sympathetic—"

"We were in Caracas when you gave me a pass on this instead of reporting it to Dombroski. And if I'd slept with you, we wouldn't be having this conversation. In fact, you're angry, but I want you to forgive me—and trust me—for the right reasons, *not* because we were having a business trip romance."

He thought about that and concluded she had some valid points, but she was also distracting him from the central issue of her betrayal and lying. If he had duct tape, he would have used it on her.

"Don't get angry, Scott. Get even. Help me make this right."

"You'll need to resign."

"All right . . ."

"And give testimony."

"I'm ready to do that."

"What is your current relationship with Trent?"

"Mutual blackmail. Same as our relationship."

"Meaning?"

"Meaning you failed in your duty to report me to Dombroski in a timely manner. Do you want me to include that in my report?"

"No good deed goes unpunished."

"Look, Scott . . . you didn't do anything wrong—you tempered justice with mercy. I owe you for that. And I never really did anything wrong—I just didn't do the right thing. I stayed silent, when I should have blown the top off Operation Flagstaff. Innocent civilians were killed, and even the guilty deserved better justice. My grandma dragged me to church every Sunday, and I paid attention in church and CID training, and I know right from wrong, and lawful from unlawful. And I'm not going to blow smoke up your butt, soldier, and tell you I like you, because I don't. You're an asshole. But . . . I *could* like you . . . well, maybe I'm attracted to you—in a physical way. Which is probably mutual. So . . . let's continue the mission. Do the best we can, try to see that justice is done, and not hurt each other." She added, "We could have a future."

Well, who'd disarmed who? He tapped the gun in his pocket to make sure it was still there. "You done?"

"I am."

"Let's finish this and get out of here. Unless you want my Swiss Army knife to carve our initials in a heart on this tree."

"Total asshole." She unwrapped the line from the tree and used a paddle to push off.

Brodie started the engine, and they continued along the riverbank. Up ahead, he could see the thatched-roof platform, which sat on stilts, overhanging the river, about five feet above the water—looked like a nice place to have a cocktail.

Brodie tried to replay that three-minute conversation, to figure out who'd got the best of it. And more importantly, figure out the future implications—legal, professional, and personal. But for now, the future was on hold, and the present needed his attention.

He focused his binoculars on the platform and thought he saw movement up there, but it could have been a moving shadow made by sunlight coming through the trees.

Taylor used her cell phone to take a long shot of the platform, then said to him, "Maybe we've reached that edge of danger."

The platform was still about a hundred meters ahead, and the mudflat where Carmen might have disembarked was maybe another hundred meters, according to Taylor's aerial recon shot.

"Scott?"

"I'd like to get one ground shot of the mudflat to verify your aerial shot."

"Not necessary for a drone recon of this area."

"I'm thinking more of a White House press conference with visuals."

"Scott . . . there will be no—"

"After the mission is successfully completed, of course, and Captain Mercer has eaten a Hellfire missile, or has been taken into rough custody by a Delta Force team."

She looked at the wall of jungle. "His camp is somewhere right in there."

"Carmen said a fifteen-minute walk. Assume a trail, but also assume the lady is not used to much walking, so that could be between two hundred and fifty and five hundred meters of dense jungle." He assured her, "They can't see or hear the river from the camp."

"I know, but . . . they could have lookout posts."

"Captain Mercer would do that."

"Correct. So—"

"This isn't the first motorized canoe to sail up this river from Kavak with pale faces onboard."

"It might be the first without a Pemón guide."

"In retrospect, we should have taken César with us for five bucks. For another five, he'd have pointed out the gringo's camp."

"I agree. But there are no redo's today, so time to turn around."

"I need to verify with my own eyes what Carmen said to me and what you saw from the air." He added, "Perfect triangulation of Intel. That wows them back in the Pentagon."

"We're CID, Scott, not a recon team, and this is a criminal case, not a combat mission."

"It's sort of morphed and overlapped. But, okay . . ."

The elevated platform was less than fifty meters away now, and he checked it out with his binoculars—no one there—then steered the boat to the opposite shore where he had a longer view of the river, which was bending to the right.

After they passed the fishing platform, Brodie raised his binoculars again and focused on the right bank while he steered. "Okay . . . I see it . . . definitely a mudflat, and definitely a partially cleared area . . . Take a look."

Taylor moved quickly toward the stern, took the binoculars, knelt on the bench seat, and focused on the opposite riverbank as they continued upriver. "I see it . . ."

"Good. We agree that we saw the same thing."

"I agree." She handed the binoculars back to him, took out the sat phone, and pulled up their grid coordinates, then called Dombroski's message line and left a brief message with the coordinates. "All right . . . we can turn around."

"Take a picture."

"It's a hundred meters away."

"I'll get closer."

"No. I'll take the picture." She pulled her cell phone out of her pocket, shot three photos, and said, "I'll even do a video."

"Good idea."

She did a ten-second video, then put the cell back in her pocket. "Mission accomplished."

"Agreed." He added, "I'm not totally crazy." He brought the boat around and they began gliding downriver, making, he thought, about ten knots. "Kavak in less than an hour." Which sounded better than "From the frying pan into the fire."

Just when he thought it was safe to be on the water, he heard the unmistakable sound of automatic rifle fire.

Taylor, who was scrambling back toward the bow, froze and turned toward him. They made eye contact, but neither of them had to say, "AK-47s," whose sound they both knew well.

The firing was distant, about five hundred meters, the hollow popping echoing through the rain forest. Brodie said, "Training."

Taylor nodded, but didn't move.

He twisted the throttle to full open, and the boat picked up a little speed. He should have checked the fuel before they left, but the worst-case scenario would be paddling downriver with the current. He recalled the Army's famous advice: "Lack of prior planning makes for a piss-poor performance." Good advice for next time. But for this time, so far, so good.

"Scott . . ."

"What?"

She pointed at the elevated platform, about twenty meters ahead.

He looked, and he didn't need his binoculars to see two men—not Pemón, but bearded, bad-looking hombres in jungle fatigues—standing at the edge of the platform, pointing AK-47s at them.

One of the men yelled something; then the AK-47 spoke and a stream of red tracer rounds streaked into the water less than a meter in front of their bow.

One of the men again yelled something, and Brodie didn't need much Spanish to understand "Stop or I'll shoot!"

They were totally exposed, in an open boat without cover or concealment, armed with two pistols that didn't have the firepower or accuracy of an AK-47, and jumping into the piranha- and croc-infested river was not a good option.

He looked at Taylor, who was looking at him.

They were abreast of the platform now, and he glanced up into the muzzles of the two automatic rifles.

"Alto!"

Well . . . there is a time to fight and a time to run. There is never a time to surrender—but there is a time to bluff. This was that time. He put the motor in idle and said to Taylor, "Talk to them."

"What should I say?"

"Maggie. We're *bird-watchers.*"

She nodded, but didn't say anything, and he saw she was staring past him. He looked over his shoulder at two boats, similar to theirs, coming toward them from the direction of the mudflat.

Taylor said, "This does not look good."

"No." He looked at her. "Sorry, Maggie."

"Not your fault. I'll do my best with the cover story."

"Okay." He glanced up at the two men still aiming their rifles at them, then looked through his binoculars at the approaching boats and saw that each boat had three armed men aboard. He said to Taylor, "I think we're going to meet Captain Mercer."

CHAPTER 43

They drifted downriver past the fishing platform where the two men stood with the AKs trained on them. One of the men shouted something and motioned them to get closer.

Taylor replied in Spanish, then said to Brodie, "We should drop our guns overboard."

Brodie twisted the throttle and moved the boat slowly toward the platform. "We're close enough now to use them." He unsnapped the lower right pocket of his cargo pants where he kept the Glock. "You take the guy on the left. On the count of three . . ."

"Scott, there are two boats filled with armed men coming at us, less than a hundred meters away."

Brodie moved the boat to within ten meters of the platform and stared up at the two men, who looked like tempting targets.

One of them shouted and Taylor replied, then said to Brodie, "He asked if we have an anchor, and we don't." She looked at him. "Scott?"

He glanced at the approaching boats. Sixty meters. He looked again at his two targets, working out the math. The first shot is a big surprise to everyone except the guy who fired it. The second target has a split second to react before the second shot surprises him when it punches through his chest. Then the AKs are just heavy metal objects on the battlefield, waiting for new owners. Guns don't kill people—people with guns kill people.

One of the men shouted at them and motioned them closer.

"Scott—"

"I think I can take both of them. Get ready to jump on the platform and grab an AK."

Taylor glanced up at the two men, then at the approaching boats. "Won't work, Scott."

"It's either this, or something you don't want to think about."

She took a deep breath, then said, "We're bird-watchers, Mr. Bowman. That has a better chance of getting us out of here than a zero-odds firefight."

He didn't reply, but he moved his right hand along his leg toward the open pocket and his fingers felt the butt of the Glock. In five seconds or less he could be pulling an AK out of a dying man's hands—just like in the Hen House.

Taylor said to him in a calm, controlled voice, "Scott . . . no. You wanted to meet Kyle Mercer. Mr. and Mrs. Bowman will do that."

He looked at her.

One of the men threw a nylon line into their boat and shouted something.

Taylor looked at the line, then at Brodie, who nodded, and she tied the line around the bow cleat. Brodie shut off the engine.

The two other boats were approaching the platform, and Brodie could see that each held three men—one piloting, and two with AK-47s, which were aimed at them.

The moment to fight, if it had ever existed, had passed, and with no more options to consider, Brodie found himself in a strangely calm state of mind.

The two boats pulled alongside theirs and Brodie thought that he and Taylor were going for a boat ride, but one of the men in the boats motioned them to climb onto the platform. Taylor grabbed the line with both hands and pulled herself onto the bamboo deck. Brodie followed, and they both stood facing the two men with the AKs as two men from each boat also scrambled onto the platform. So now there were six men with AKs around them, with two men left in the boats, and Brodie didn't even bother to compute the odds.

One of the men from the boats, a tall, muscular guy with a black T-shirt and a bad face, who seemed to be el jefe, was shouting something, and Taylor put her hands on her head, so Brodie did the same.

Brodie heard the two boats rev up, and saw them making their way back upriver, toward the mudflat. The good news, if there was any, was that their boat was still tied to the platform. So if this was just a stop-and-search—or a stop-strip-search-and-steal—Mr. and Mrs. Bowman, the stupidest tourists on the planet, could be back to Kavak in an hour or so. Not likely, but still possible.

Brodie glanced around and noticed a green plastic table and four matching chairs on the bamboo deck, which seemed oddly out of place in the middle of the jungle. He recalled what Collins had said about the Pemón gathering on these fishing platforms to socialize, but he had no doubt that this platform, which lay between Kavak and the mudflat, doubled as Captain Mercer's observation post. In fact, he saw a pair of binoculars on one of the chairs.

El jefe handed his AK to one of the other men and came over to Brodie and glared at him, then pulled the binoculars from around his neck, examined them, and handed them to one of his men. El jefe then went through Brodie's cargo pockets, pulling out cash, his cell phone, and his Swiss Army knife, all of which he pocketed. He looked through Brodie's fake passport, then handed it to another man. He then reached into Brodie's lower cargo pocket and found the Glock, which he pulled out and exhibited to his men as though he was really good at finding stuff. They all began talking and looking at Brodie with renewed interest. El jefe stuck the Glock in his waistband, then continued his search and found the extra magazine, which he held up in front of Brodie's face as if to say, "Take a last look, gringo, you'll never see this again."

Brodie glanced at his Glock in el jefe's waistband. The asshole was putting options back on the table.

El jefe now turned his attention to Taylor, but he patted her down first, enjoying himself, before he then went through her pockets. He pulled out the Glock and magazine first, then her cash, cell phone, and passport, which he looked at, then glanced at Brodie, realizing that Sarah and Clark Bowman were husband and wife. He handed Taylor's Glock and extra mag to one of his guys and then pulled out the final item, the sat phone; he stared at it as though it was more interesting than the Glock, then showed it around to his men. He said something to Taylor, who replied, and el jefe didn't seem satisfied with the answer.

He spoke again to Taylor and she hesitated, then pulled off her T-shirt and dropped her pants, which Brodie knew was eventually going to happen.

Taylor stood there in her bra and panties and kept eye contact with the man, who then turned from her and said something to the other men, who laughed. One of them whistled, and another yelled, "Bella!" El jefe turned back to her and noticed the scars on her thigh and leg. He pointed: "Qué es esto?"

She replied, "Accidente . . . vehículo."

He looked at the heat and shrapnel scars as though he recognized them for what they were. He glanced at her, then said something in a commanding tone of voice.

Taylor shook her head firmly and replied, then nodded toward Brodie, who understood that she was refusing to take off her bra and panties in front of all these men with her husband standing there.

El jefe looked at Brodie, then smiled and motioned for Taylor to get dressed. She pulled up her pants and put on her T-shirt.

The men made exaggerated sounds of disappointment—though maybe not so exaggerated.

Brodie wondered if Maggie Taylor was now thinking that a firefight would have been a better option than this.

Taylor said something to el jefe, which apparently surprised, then amused, him, and he replied, "Emilio."

Brodie didn't know if Taylor was in Sarah Bowman mode or Civil Affairs mode, but it was a good move to get the guy's name.

Taylor looked at Emilio and addressed him by name, then lowered her arms and began speaking to him in a respectful but firm tone of voice, interjecting the honorific "señor" a few times. Brodie could make out the words "turistas," "Kavak," and even "César," who Brodie was sure Emilio was acquainted with. Brodie didn't know the Spanish word for "bird-watcher," but he hoped Sarah Bowman did.

Emilio listened impassively, then said something to her, and Brodie could make out the word "Pemón," so Emilio was asking why they didn't have a guide.

Taylor replied, probably pleading ignorance, and Emilio nodded.

This seemed to be going well, despite Taylor's explanations smelling faintly of bullshit.

Emilio didn't look like the sharpest machete in the jungle, but he seemed to be listening and trying to think of his next move. Brodie suspected that

Emilio had someone higher to answer to, and Brodie hoped that higher authority was Señor Kyle. Because if these guys were working for a drug cartel, or were jungle versions of mountain men from Deliverance, then Maggie Taylor was in worse danger than Brodie, whom they'd just shoot and throw in the river. At least with Kyle Mercer, Brodie and Taylor would have a civilized conversation in English before he decided if they were the Bowmans or someone else.

Emilio was now saying something to Taylor about the sat phone he was holding, and about the Glock in his waistband.

Taylor seemed calm as she replied, and Brodie knew that having a gun in Venezuela was not prima facie evidence of anything. In fact, it was a fashion accessory.

The sat phone was a bit of an outlier, but not an unusual thing for a tourist to have in a place where the closest cell tower was two provinces away.

Again, Emilio nodded, but Brodie was beginning to recognize this tail-wagging as an interrogation technique that he, Brodie, was very familiar with. Maybe Emilio wasn't as stupid as he looked.

Brodie noticed that the five other men were listening to Emilio and the gringo lady who spoke passable Spanish. Three of the guys were smoking, and they'd all lowered or shouldered their AKs, which neither Sergeant Brodie nor Captain Mercer would approve of.

Brodie thought it was time for him to speak up, so he said to Taylor, "Tell them they can keep everything except our passports. We need to get the boat back to César."

Taylor translated, and Emilio smiled and said something to Brodie as he theatrically motioned him to get into the moored boat, saying, "Adiós, señor."

Brodie didn't think Emilio was serious, and in fact the other men laughed, so Brodie smiled to show he was a good sport, but kept his hands on his head in case someone was looking for an excuse to shoot him. This was definitely starting to go sideways, so he again did the math. If Emilio got within arm's reach of him, he could easily snatch the Glock, blow off Emilio's balls and get off five more shots, left to right, and nail the smoking and joking jerk-offs in less than four seconds. Except maybe they weren't the complete jerk-offs that they appeared to be. One way to find out.

Brodie said to Emilio, "Please, señor, take what you want, take my watch—"

"Cállate!"

Brodie figured that meant "Shut up," so he did, but he began unstrapping his watchband, and Emilio nodded, probably reprimanding himself for missing it.

Brodie kept his left hand in the air and offered Emilio his watch with his right. Emilio stepped toward Brodie, then made eye contact with him and stopped. They looked at each other, and Brodie saw Emilio figure out he wasn't looking at a scared-shitless tourist. Emilio gestured for Brodie to drop the watch.

Brodie hesitated, then dropped it on the bamboo deck, and Emilio motioned him back before he picked up the watch and said something to his men, who laughed. He then spoke to Taylor, and she gave him her watch. He said, "Gracias, señora," then added something else that he apparently told her to translate.

She said to Brodie, "He says we don't need to know the time where we're going."

Brodie didn't know where they were going, or where this was going, but he could imagine a gang rape and a double murder if Emilio was not under the control of Kyle Mercer. Or even if Emilio was, he might decide that he had first dibs on Mrs. Bowman.

Brodie realized that when your last best hope is a psychotic killer, you've really hit bottom. So . . . it was time to throw the dice, as he'd done in Petare. He said, "We are here—"

"Cállate!"

"—to speak to Señor Kyle."

Emilio looked at him, then at the five other men. Then he snapped something at Taylor, who refused to respond except to say, "Señor Kyle. Ahora." Now.

Well, the bird-watcher bullshit was now down the toilet, but that got them to the next level, away from these guys. Maybe.

Emilio didn't seem to know what to do next, but like every soldier he knew how to cover his ass, so he pulled a walkie out of his pocket, said something, listened, and shoved the walkie back in his pocket. He said something to his men, who got their rifles at the ready, then gestured to Brodie and Taylor to follow him.

Emilio walked to the end of the platform and descended a narrow ramp made of tightly-woven bamboo that creaked with each step he took—a sort of primitive early warning that someone was coming. Brodie wondered if this was Pemón technology, or Delta Force training. He was sure that everyone here was learning from everyone else in Captain Mercer's camp. Most importantly, Brodie was sure now that Emilio and his men were not freelance crazies; they were organized crazies, commanded by a psychotic. And that was the good news, which showed how fast you could lower your expectations.

Emilio led the way onto a narrow jungle path, followed by his prisoners, who were followed by his five men with AK-47s.

Brodie recalled that the Code of Conduct stressed a soldier's duty to escape from captivity, and every escape and evasion course strongly advised that you do so in the very early stages of your captivity—while you were still psychologically and physically fit, and before you were starved, beaten, or restrained in a POW camp. Captain Mercer knew that too, but apparently had not acted on that advice, which resulted in two years in a Taliban hell. The E&E course also pointed out that your place of capture would probably be close to a place where you could reach the safety of friendly forces or the relative safety of no-man's-land. And finally, you were reminded that the frontline soldiers who captured you were not trained to deal with prisoners—which all sounded good in theory, and which was actually true in the case of these six jokers, who hadn't even bound their wrists or blindfolded them.

And on the subject of blindfolds, as Carmen and everyone knew, if you were blindfolded, that could mean your captors were going to let you live—or at least consider it. But if you saw everything you weren't supposed to see, that would be the last thing you saw.

All things considered, maybe Mr. and Mrs. Bowman didn't want to meet Kyle Mercer. Maybe this was Warrant Officers Brodie and Taylor's last opportunity to make a break for freedom, before they got into the bowels of Mercer's camp.

The jungle here was thick and offered good concealment, but not much cover from AK-47 fire. Also, the jungle wasn't made for sprinting. Still . . .

He said to Taylor in a low whisper, "When I say break, you break right and I break left, and we run a zigzag. We can lose these guys."

"We can't outrun a bullet."

"We're betting they want live prisoners and will hold their fire and pursue."

"Bad bet."

Emilio looked over his shoulder. "Silencio."

Taylor ignored him and said to Brodie, "Whatever we do, we are not splitting up."

"Doubles our chances—"

"Cállate!" Emilio looked very pissed and drew Brodie's Glock and pointed it at him.

Taylor said something to Emilio and he seemed to calm down.

They pressed on, then turned left on another path, which, if Brodie's internal compass was correct, was taking them in the direction of the mudflat, but farther from the river—the fifteen-minute walk that Carmen had made to the camp. So they were going to the same place, but the difference was that Carmen was ready to fuck every man in the camp, and Brodie didn't think Maggie Taylor was ready for that.

An escape attempt was still an option, but maybe there'd be a better time and place to try it. Like at night, if they lived that long. Or . . . they could do what they'd come here to do—what he would have done in the Hen House if Mercer had been there: talk to the man and see if he had a shred of Captain Mercer left in him, or a memory of the soldier that Al Simpson had seen in basic training. Or better yet, maybe there was something left of the kid from San Diego. If none of that was true, then Brodie and Taylor had one card left—the good cop card that almost always worked with a criminal. *Tell us, Kyle, what happened to make you do that?* Or, *Who made you do that? Was it Brendan Worley? Tell us about that.*

Or Brodie was putting too much faith in his powers of persuasion and bullshit.

They kept walking, and Brodie could see that Taylor was starting to drag.

They came to a small clearing where an open-sided hut stood, and in the hut were three Pemón men sitting on logs around a long table, cleaning fish and tossing the guts into plastic pails. The Pemón stopped what they were doing and stared at Brodie and Taylor as they approached.

Brodie saw bottled water on the table and called out, "Agua! Por favor!"

One of the Pemón took a bottle of water, stood, and came toward Brodie and Taylor.

Emilio barked something at the man, and he stopped and looked at the two prisoners, then back at Emilio, who repeated his command. The man went back to his fish-gutting.

Brodie whispered to Taylor, "Faint."

Taylor shook her head. "You faint."

Well, tough is good. But heatstroke, as he and Taylor recalled from their respective deserts, could kill you. Maybe that's what she wanted.

Emilio continued on the path and one of the men behind them shouted, "Caminad!"

The jungle path wound through tall trees that blocked the sunlight, and the air was thick with the smell of decomposing vegetation.

Brodie could hear the crack of single-round shots, so Mercer's men were now practicing marksmanship instead of having fun mowing down targets on full automatic. So what was this camp all about? They were close to an answer.

They approached a clearing with a few huts around the perimeter, and also a fire pit in the middle where Pemón women were burning what appeared to be food scraps and other garbage, and what smelled like raw shit. Another Pemón woman was sweeping out one of the huts. So apparently Captain Mercer taught and practiced good field sanitation, meaning he hadn't gone completely off the rails, so hopefully they wouldn't meet Mercer in a dark room filled with human skulls.

The Pemón women, who probably also worked in Kavak, glanced at the two outsiders, who were obviously prisoners. One of them looked closely at Taylor, and if Brodie could read minds as well as he could read faces, then the woman was thinking, *Oh, that poor pretty girl. What they will do to her.*

Brodie felt his gut tighten.

Ahead, Brodie saw more huts and what looked like a long, open-sided mess hall, and he had the sense that they were reaching the center of camp, and thus whatever it was that passed for a headquarters building. He pictured

Kyle Mercer, el comandante, standing in front of the HQ building, waiting for them. He wondered if Mercer had his own flag flying on a pole—a large nut would be appropriate.

Emilio turned off the path and onto a much narrower trail that was hemmed in by thick growth. Brodie and Taylor exchanged glances, and kept walking, with Brodie taking the lead.

At the end of the trail was a small bamboo hut with no visible windows, and Brodie guessed it was the one building that every military facility needed—the stockade.

Emilio opened the small door, motioning for his prisoners to enter.

Brodie went first, ducking his head as he entered, followed by Taylor. They found themselves in a dark, fetid room that smelled faintly of urine, sweat, feces, and fear. The floor was covered with dried palm fronds and in the middle of the room was a thick log, about six feet long, stretching nearly wall to wall.

Emilio entered and pointed. "Sentad." Sit.

Brodie and Taylor stepped over the log and sat with their backs to the wall, and Brodie noticed now in the dim light that two chains were bolted to the log, and at the ends of the chains were leg shackles and open padlocks.

Brodie, more out of habit and training than out of any plan of action, assessed the situation. Emilio was standing in the doorway, and one of his men was inside, pointing his AK-47 at the prisoners. The other four guys were outside, so Brodie couldn't put them into the equation. Taylor was weak from dehydration, and Brodie too was feeling the effects of a few very long days without enough sleep, hydration, or food, unless you counted the Snickers bar. So if escape was the goal, maybe what they needed now was to be left alone to scope out the jail, which didn't look impressive, and also to see what kind of guard was posted.

Emilio said something to them, and Taylor reached out and put a shackle around her left ankle, then put the padlock hasp through the shackle holes and snapped it shut.

Emilio shouted at Brodie, who was learning Spanish the hard way, and he did the same.

Emilio seemed happy that these two were about to become not his problem, though Brodie suspected that Emilio still had visions of Taylor in her bra and panties. In fact, Emilio looked at her and said something that made him and his man smile.

Emilio then became abrupt, and pointed out a plastic pail for urine and feces, and a plastic jug that held agua. He took a last look at his prisoners, then spoke briefly to Taylor, and Brodie heard "Señor Kyle." Emilio turned and left, followed by his man.

The door closed, and the small, windowless room got darker, lit only by sunlight filtering through the bamboo walls.

Brodie listened to hear if a lock snapped on the door, but all he heard were the voices of Emilio and his men as they walked away.

Brodie and Taylor sat in silence awhile; then Brodie asked, "What did he say?"

"He said he was sure Señor Kyle would want to see us."

"That's good."

"The last gringo who was in this room had his throat cut by Señor Kyle."

"Not good."

"I need water." She reached out and pulled the plastic jug toward her, then tipped it to her mouth and drank. She finished and passed the jug to Brodie, who saw that there was only a few inches of water left, so he passed it back to her, but she insisted he drink, so he drank the foul-smelling water, which was going to cause them both problems if they lived that long.

He asked her, "What did he say when he was smiling and leering at you?"

"It doesn't matter."

"Tell me."

She took a deep breath and said, "He told me that I was too beautiful to kill, and that I would join the other women here who service the men."

Brodie figured that was what Emilio had said, so he told Taylor, "If you get that kind of freedom, you need to take it, and figure out a way out of here and—"

"Don't tell me what I have to do. I'll figure it out if the time comes."

"Sorry."

She sat back against the bamboo wall and said, "I'm sure Kyle Mercer misses the companionship of a woman he can . . . talk to . . . so I'll do what I can to keep us both alive."

"Let's change the subject to escape and evasion."

She didn't reply, and Brodie saw she'd closed her eyes.

He bent forward and examined the eyebolts in the log. They looked to be about half an inch in diameter, which meant they were at least five or six inches long and embedded into the log, which was nearly a foot in diameter. He put his feet on the log and pressed against it, discovering that it was very heavy—probably mahogany. And at six feet long, it would weigh maybe two or three hundred pounds. He could lift that weight himself—he'd carried a two-hundred-pound squad-mate who'd been hit—and with Taylor helping they could easily bust open the bamboo door, locked or not, or maybe drive the log through a wall—though bamboo was stronger than most people understood, which was why it was used to make cages for animals and people.

So busting out in the middle of the night was possible, but he had to factor in an armed guard near the door, not to mention the padlocked shackles. And if there was a guard, and if it was three in the morning, the guard would not be ready for a battering ram crushing his skull. But if the guard didn't have the keys, how long could he and Taylor carry a three-hundred-pound log through the jungle? Actually, they only had to get to the river—about a fifteen-minute walk downslope—and then they'd be floating downstream toward Kavak, and hopefully get there before anyone here knew they were gone—and hopefully before the crocs and piranhas knew they were there.

They would have more options if they were unshackled. So who had the keys to the padlocks? Maybe the guard, if there was one. Or whoever came to unlock the shackles and escort them to Mercer—or to someplace else.

Every problem has a solution, but some solutions cause more problems than the problem. Meaning, in this case, escape attempts could lead to a beating or a cut throat or worse if you killed someone during the attempt.

He said to Taylor, "Are you willing to try to escape, and are you ready to die trying?"

"Scott . . . let it go. Sleep on it." She informed him, "You're impulsive and you take too many unnecessary risks."

"That's not true."

"Then how did we get here?"

"Bad luck."

"No, we got here because you wanted to raid the Hen House, then you bullshitted Dombroski, then you chartered a plane to this fucked-up place, then you stole a boat—"

"All right. I've made a few bad decisions, but I followed the trail, and I discovered in a few days what Worley and his pal Ted and all their people haven't found in a year of trying. I found Kyle Mercer."

"Congratulations."

"Thanks. Look, if we can keep alive long enough, we could possibly be rescued. Collins will call Dombroski—"

"Collins is missing in action."

"You gave Dombroski our last grid coordinates, and if he doesn't hear from us, he knows what to do." He added, "I've backed us up, so now it's only a matter of buying time."

"All right. We'll try to do that. I'll . . . do what I can . . . what has to be done."

"Stay alive, Maggie."

She didn't reply.

There remained the possibility that Worley and his friends—which probably included Taylor's friend Trent—were also looking for them. He would have mentioned this, but she already knew that, and didn't want to hear any more from him on the subject.

He said, "By sundown tomorrow, there'll be a Delta team rappelling from helicopters into this camp."

"The chances of that happening would be better if I'd brought the Garmin tracking device."

Brodie didn't know if she was reprimanding herself or him. "Think positive."

"Here's another thought for you, Scott—a few dozen Hellfire missiles landing in this camp."

"The Army wants Mercer alive, so they'll do a bin Laden–type raid."

"If I was running the operation, I'd start with the Hellfire missiles, then send the Delta team in to put the blood and guts in pails and bring it back for DNA analysis."

That was also what Brodie would do, though he hadn't mentioned it. Taylor had seen enough in Afghanistan to understand how the military took out bad guys on their most wanted list: high explosives, followed by a mop-up operation when and where possible. They didn't need Kyle Mercer's body; they just needed his nose or his dick for a DNA match. Brodie hoped they'd also find some of him and Taylor after the Hellfires. Better yet, he hoped they wouldn't blow up the camp if they suspected friendlies were alive there.

Well, there was no use speculating about what could happen tomorrow; they just needed to get through today. And escape was still an option. In fact, rescue fantasies aside, and reasoning with Kyle Mercer not being a very sure path to freedom, escape was the last option. And escape, which had the crucial element of surprise, was often easy. He'd done it in POW training six times. It was the evasion part where people got fucked up.

A shaft of sunlight came in through the bamboo and illuminated what looked like dried blood on the log. Brodie wondered who the unlucky gringo was—which made him think about Robert Crenshaw, who'd been tortured before having his throat cut. He didn't know if it was Mercer who'd done that, but Brodie was sure that Mercer, who'd decapitated five Taliban on video, was capable of it. Brodie also thought about Carmen's rapist who'd had his guts ripped out by Mercer. And then there was Operation Flagstaff and the dead of Mirabad and other Afghan villages, and it occurred to Brodie that Kyle Mercer had gone very wrong even before he deserted, and before he'd spent two years as a prisoner of the Taliban, who themselves indulged in psychotic behavior.

Taylor put her hand on his shoulder. "You okay?"

"I've been better."

"We need more water."

"Right." He thought a moment, then said, "I'm not sure there's a guard out there."

"I'll call—"

"But if there is, and he pokes his head in the door, you and I are going to ram this log in his face."

She didn't reply, then said, "What if there are two guards?"

"There won't be."

"Scott . . . we're actually chained to this log."

"He'll have the keys."

"Please. Let it rest. Think about what to say to Kyle Mercer." She added, "We could be seeing him in ten minutes."

"Right." He stood, then crouched and looked at the chains, which were long enough for them to get the log up to waist level and still have freedom of movement with their legs. "Stand up."

She hesitated, then stood.

"Okay, crouch, and on three, lift."

"Scott—"

"We need to see if we can do this before we get too weak from hunger." He asked, "Do you remember what you were taught about escaping early?"

"I do, and I also remember that you forget everything you've learned except what suits you."

"Right. Okay. Ready?"

She took a deep breath and crouched, and they both dug their hands into the palm fronds and under the log.

"One, two, lift—"

They lifted, and the log rose from the floor; they were able to get it up to hip level. It was heavy, but not as heavy as Brodie had anticipated. "Okay?"

She nodded.

"I'll swing it around. You just hold." He took small steps, swinging the log so it was pointed at the door. "Let's step forward. Ready?"

"Okay . . ."

"Step." He took a step toward the door, which was less than four feet away. "Okay, if I charged that door—or someone standing in the door—could you keep your end up and follow?"

"I think . . . it's getting heavy."

"Okay. Good practice run."

Brodie moved his end of the log back to where it had been, and Taylor held on as he positioned it. "On three, we drop it. One, two, three—"

They let go of the log and it dropped to the ground, making a dull thud, and the chains rattled.

"Sit."

They both sat with their backs against the wall and their shackled feet up on the log.

They waited to see if a guard had heard the noise and came in. But there was no sound outside the door.

Brodie drew a deep breath. "Okay . . . that is a weapon in our arsenal."

She didn't respond.

"We'll use it at the right moment."

"When is that?"

"Always after dark." He reminded her, "Dark is the great equalizer. The friend of the fugitive."

"You're impressing me with your sudden textbook recall."

"It all comes back to you when you need it."

"True. All right, now that we've done that your way, can we talk about Kyle Mercer before we see him?"

"Okay."

"Can you tell me why Mr. and Mrs. Bowman would ask for Señor Kyle by name?"

"Because Scott Brodie didn't want Maggie Taylor raped or himself murdered."

"Okay . . . so we can drop the Bowmans."

"I didn't like them anyway."

"So we are Warrant Officers Taylor and Brodie, CID."

"Correct."

"All right. You and I need to be on the same page. We need to present ourselves as the tip of a great iceberg that is coming toward him. He can kill us, but he can't kill what we represent."

"He knows that. And by the way, he doesn't like what we represent," Brodie pointed out.

"We represent justice. That's what we can offer him."

"It's hard to reason with a man who has crossed every line there is."

"We have to convince him that he can cross back. We have to offer him a way to redemption. To salvation."

"Is that from Sunday school?"

"It is."

"Well, then you should ask yourself how you crossed those lines before you ask Kyle Mercer."

"I know what I did. I lost my way. And I know that confession is good for the soul. And Kyle Mercer is no different from any human being in that regard."

"I don't know about that, Maggie."

"Ask yourself why he didn't kill Al Simpson. Or why he didn't kill Carmen."

"He should have. And by now he knows or suspects he should have."

"But *why* didn't he kill them?"

"He didn't think he needed to. He's arrogant."

"I believe there is still a spark of humanity in him."

Brodie thought about Mercer in the Hen House, buying a night of freedom for Julieta. What was that about?

"And if we find that spark, we'll know what we can offer him."

"Maggie, the only thing we can offer him is a long stretch in Leavenworth. He knows that, and if we try to bullshit him, he'll get pissed, and if we try to save his soul, he'll laugh. Either way, he's not buying what you're selling."

"All right, how would you handle this interview with the suspect?"

"First, I'd make it clear that we are here to arrest him. Then I would make him aware that before we were cops, we were real soldiers, like he was, and we saw the same shit, like he did."

She nodded. "Good."

"I would then invite him to tell us his story about what happened over there—as little or as much as he wants to tell. Then I might dangle a deal in front of him. Assuming he was involved in Flagstaff, I'd assure him that he would have an opportunity to testify about that in a public venue. This would mitigate his own guilt if, in fact, he killed civilians. I'd also give him a pass on the charge of desecrating enemy bodies. That's a nonstarter in the court of American public opinion anyway. I would also not mention the name of Robert Crenshaw. That's a capital offense if he did it, and it's a hard charge to prove. So we're down to desertion, which can be reduced to dereliction of duty and some other non-hanging offenses." He added, "He's got to pay for his crimes, but the Army defines the crimes and hints at the penalty if the accused agrees to plead guilty, and to pay the price. That saves time and money on a court-martial." He reminded her, "No one wants this to become a public spectacle."

She stayed silent awhile, then said, "I think it's important to him that he tells his story, and tries to find peace—in his heart, mind, and soul. I don't think he cares about making a deal or getting a reduced sentence.

I don't think he cares if he faces a firing squad, which he'd probably prefer to life behind bars."

"Maybe you and I can offer him both. Justice and salvation. Like, good cop, good cop."

"Like honest cops."

"All right . . . But more likely this is all moot, because Kyle Mercer is happy where he is. And not happy to see us."

"It's worth a try."

"Right. We'll talk to him like our lives depend on it."

She didn't reply.

"I take the lead."

"Don't antagonize him."

"Captain Mercer will respond well to military authority, and to a call to do his sworn duty as an officer."

"He resigned his commission."

"Not accepted."

"All right . . . but get a sense of him before you go Army on him. If he's talking, let him talk."

"I always do."

"Except when you get pissed off."

"That never happens."

"It happened when I was telling you about Flagstaff. Specifically about Trent."

"Okay . . . let me make a confession. I'm a little jealous."

"I never would have guessed."

He didn't respond to that, but said, "We'll get out of this, Maggie. I promise you."

She took his hand and squeezed it.

"And remember this—no matter what happens, we are not Captain Mercer's captives. We are his arresting officers. And he knows that."

"All right . . ." She took a long breath and squeezed his hand tighter. "I've never been so frightened in my life."

"Neither have I. And neither has Kyle Mercer. This is the end of the line for him, one way or the other, and he knows that, and he has to decide how this is going to end for him."

"And for us. Okay . . . I understand all that."

"I know you do." Brodie leaned back against the wall and looked at the door.

Eventually it would open. And someone would come in. Maybe Mercer, to talk. Or Mercer with a knife. Or Emilio with an invitation to see the boss. Or Emilio with an invitation for Señora Bowman to come with him.

No use speculating. Just be prepared.

CHAPTER 44

Brodie sat with his back against the wall. The heat and dehydration were sapping him, but he needed to be awake to think and act when the time came.

Taylor was sleeping soundly, and he let her sleep. As a woman in the military, she probably always felt she had to prove herself. As his partner . . . who knew what she felt? Brodie suspected it was complex, ranging from gratitude for his mentoring, to a sure certainty that Scott Brodie was a loose cannon and an asshole. Now, however, she was just a woman, fresh meat for the camp. And there wasn't much he could do for her, except talk her into an escape attempt. Or let her know it was okay to do what she had to do to survive, and not worry about him.

Chivalry was dead, especially in the civilian world, but in the military traditions take longer to die. There was an old Army saying: "All the brothers are brave, and all the sisters are virtuous." The update would be: "Call the JAG office if you have a question about appropriate behavior."

Or, look inside yourself.

He glanced at Taylor, whose peaceful sleep was actually heat exhaustion. She'd be herself with a little food and water.

On the question of whose fault this was, he took full responsibility for his actions—though maybe the gods who lived on the tepui had screwed him up. Or maybe he had engaged in some unconscious macho posturing for Maggie Taylor. Whom the gods wish to destroy, they first make horny. None of this would have happened if he'd been partnered with that dork Taylor had replaced.

And on the subject of partners and assignments, had he got this case because Colonel Dombroski and General Hackett had faith in him—or because of the CIA's faith in Maggie Taylor?

This would seem to be an unimportant question under the present circumstances, but it bugged him. He might discover the answers to all the questions he had about Kyle Mercer from Kyle Mercer, but he'd never know what had gone on behind the scenes in Quantico and the Pentagon unless he got back.

He thought about Mercer again—about appealing to the thing that Kyle Mercer, Scott Brodie, and Maggie Taylor had in common: They had all been there.

There. The bullet-scarred alleyways of Fallujah, the IED-riddled back roads of Taliban country, and a lonely outpost in the Hindu Kush— fucked-up war zones that seep into your soul and stay there.

And now, for all three of them, it meant this jungle, the terminus of their separate journeys. He wondered what Kyle Mercer was thinking right now.

Brodie heard voices and he shook Taylor awake.

She woke quickly. "What?"

"They're back."

She listened to the voices outside the door. "Emilio." She kept listening. "Someone said, 'Take them to the river . . .'" She looked at Brodie.

Well, that could mean they were going to swim with the crocs and the piranhas. Or, more optimistically, they were being taken to their boat and sent on their way—on orders from the boss. Except Kyle Mercer would certainly want to know why Mr. and Mrs. Bowman had asked for him by name.

The door opened and Emilio entered alone, though Brodie could see men outside. Emilio looked at them, then drew Brodie's Glock with one hand and tossed something toward him with the other.

Brodie looked at what landed on the palm fronds: two keys on a chain. He picked them up and tried the first key on his padlock, which worked. He opened Taylor's lock with the second key.

Emilio shouted, "Levántense!"

Brodie and Taylor slipped the shackles off and stood.

Brodie thought they were going to be marched out, but Emilio had something else in mind and he shut the door, then said something to Taylor.

She didn't reply.

"What did he say?"

"He said . . . now that we are alone, he wants to see me naked . . . then we go someplace nice."

Brodie didn't know what to say, but Taylor knew what to do, and she pulled off her T-shirt, unclasped her bra, and kicked off her shoes.

Brodie turned away as Taylor removed her pants and panties, but he glanced at Emilio, who was smiling.

Brodie stood with his back to Taylor as Emilio satisfied two of his desires—seeing the pretty woman naked, and humiliating her and her husband at the same time. But Brodie wasn't humiliated; he was enraged—though he wasn't going to do anything stupid. Maybe later.

Emilio spoke to Taylor and she bent down, retrieved the keys, and walked the few feet to Emilio and handed them to him, giving him a closer look at her body, and a view of her rear as she walked back to the log.

Emilio said something, and Taylor translated: "He wants you to know he likes my body. You are a lucky man."

"Fuck him."

He felt Taylor's hand on his shoulder. "It's okay."

Brodie looked at Emilio, who was now looking at his watch—Brodie's watch—and Emilio barked two words at Taylor that Brodie assumed were "Get dressed."

Obviously they were on a schedule, which could mean the boss was waiting.

Taylor quickly put her clothes and shoes back on. Brodie was sure that if they'd come into a different kind of camp—a narco camp—Emilio wouldn't have stopped at just having Taylor strip. But this place was run by a former Army officer who, apparently, at least half remembered what he'd been taught about the treatment of prisoners, and maintaining discipline, and keeping to a schedule.

Which didn't mean Emilio wouldn't have his way with Ms. Taylor later. He just had to wait until the boss man gave the green light. Brodie was sure that the worst shit that happened at this camp happened by Señor Kyle's hand, or on Señor Kyle's order.

Emilio walked toward the door and motioned for them to follow.

They exited the hut into the glaring sun, and as Brodie's eyes adjusted to the light he recognized the same five men from the platform who'd brought them to the prison hut.

Brodie expected that he and Taylor would have their hands bound, because hands were the most dangerous weapons, but Emilio seemed to think that his five men with AKs were all he needed for these turistas, one of whom was a woman, and therefore not in his equation.

Emilio motioned for them to follow and he led the way, single-file down the narrow trail, then past the clearing where the Pemón women were still at work tidying up the huts—the barracks—while the men were shooting up the jungle. Brodie pictured these ladies making beds in Kavak. Maybe he'd run into them later when he and Taylor were saying good-bye to César on their way to the airstrip. Maybe not.

Emilio was taking a slightly different route through the maze of jungle paths, but still heading in the downslope direction of the river. Maybe they were going to Mercer's quarters, and Brodie wondered how Kyle Mercer treated himself here.

As they walked, the path widened and Taylor came next to Brodie and held his arm. He didn't know if it was a gesture of affection or if she was getting wobbly. "You okay?"

"I'm okay."

Brodie yelled out to Emilio. "Agua!"

Emilio turned his head and nodded. "Sí, agua." He pointed to a large hut ahead that Brodie could see through the trees. Apparently Emilio thought he owed the lady something for his three minutes of fun. In fact, if they weren't getting out of here—and Brodie didn't think they were—Maggie Taylor had something to barter. She understood that, and he hoped she used it to survive, then to break out.

They reached the small clearing in front of the hut, and Brodie saw a few green tables and chairs, the same as those on the fishing platform. To the right side of the hut was a small bamboo structure that looked like a two-seater outhouse. To the left was an outdoor shower—four canvas buckets with showerheads suspended from a long pole, and surrounded by half-walls of bamboo for privacy—if anyone cared.

In the clearing were also three hammocks strung between trees, and in one of these lay a woman in a short dress and white tank top. The woman glanced at them, then sat up and called into the hut.

Emilio stopped and lit a cigarette.

From the open door of the hut came six young women in short skirts, tank tops, and shower clogs.

They weren't Pemón, and it didn't take Brodie long to figure out that the ladies were not camp nurses.

Emilio shouted at them, and one of the women went back in the hut and returned with two plastic water bottles that she offered to Emilio's guests, looking curiously at Brodie, then sizing up Taylor as a possible roommate.

Taylor, an officer and a lady, thanked the woman for the agua. Brodie, too, said, "Gracias."

Emilio said something to Brodie, and motioned toward the ladies.

Taylor started to translate, but Brodie, who understood "Take your pick" in any language, said, "I got it."

Emilio laughed.

Taylor finished her water in one long swallow, and Brodie drank half and pocketed the bottle in case there weren't any more hooker huts along the way.

Emilio was speaking to the women, motioning toward Taylor now and then, and they were nodding and smiling, happy, it seemed, to be welcoming a new hire who would take some of the workload off their backs . . . or wherever.

On that subject, the ladies were well acquainted with all five of Emilio's men, obviously, and the seven ladies and six men chatted a bit and joked about something. This all seemed frighteningly normal, and Brodie saw that the women didn't seem intimidated by Emilio, nor did they seem zombie-like. In fact, they were spirited and looked relatively healthy and happy. If they were from Caracas, this was R&R.

Brodie understood Emilio's purpose in bringing them here—for Taylor to see her future, and for Brodie to see her fate. As for his own fate, that seemed either sealed or in the balance. He couldn't get a reading on all this.

Emilio had apparently told the ladies that the American woman spoke Spanish, and he invited them to speak with her, so Warrant Officer Taylor found herself in conversation with seven Venezuelan hookers who were probably filling her in on the job requirements.

Brodie watched Emilio listening and smiling; then Emilio said something about Señora Bowman, and the ladies looked at Brodie, so Emilio must have told them that the gentleman was the señora's husband. Or maybe her pimp. Emilio then motioned to Taylor, and Brodie heard the word "desnuda," which made the women laugh. Brodie guessed that the asshole had told them that he'd seen Señora Bowman in the nude, and that they had some competition. Or something equally funny.

By now it was clear to Brodie that Emilio was at best a sociopath who enjoyed tormenting people, and at worst he was a smiling psychopath, and anything might set him off—which was good to know. The icy cold guys were hard to kill. The psychos were subconsciously suicidal. The true psychotic, however, was a dangerous combination of both—cold, calculating, fearless, and cunning. Like Kyle Mercer.

Brodie was concerned about Taylor's physical condition. He didn't know how far they'd be walking, and she needed to cool down, so he called to Emilio and motioned to the shower and to Taylor. Emilio seemed to be considering this—another eye-fucking opportunity—but he glanced at his stolen watch again, and shook his head. He shooed the ladies away, then motioned to Brodie and Taylor to follow.

Brodie wondered which of these trees Mercer had used to gut Carmen's rapist. If they'd brought Carmen with them, she could have pointed it out. Also, the girls could have a reunion.

The path was wide enough for Brodie and Taylor to walk side by side, and Taylor put her arm through his. The five chaperones behind them didn't seem to care.

Taylor said in a low voice, "Those girls seem . . . taken care of. They said the men were under orders from Señor Kyle to be good to them."

Brodie had no reply.

"So maybe . . . I can tough this out . . ."

He hoped so. But those girls were pros, and they were there more or less voluntarily. She was being conscripted. But Maggie Taylor had enough on her mind, so he said, "I think this was just Emilio having fun with us."

"Silencio!"

"Ask this asshole where we're going."

Taylor hesitated, then called out to Emilio. She translated his reply: "We asked to see Señor Kyle, and Señor Kyle wants to see us, so we should be happy."

"This is what we came to Venezuela for."

Taylor had no response.

They turned onto a path that Brodie recognized as the one they'd taken from the fishing platform, and within a few minutes he saw the river through the trees, then the platform ahead. As they got closer, he saw a man sitting at the green table, his back to them.

Emilio again checked his watch and picked up his pace, urging them to keep up.

Apparently Señor Kyle was on a tight schedule and ran a tight ship.

They approached the narrow bamboo ramp that led to the fishing platform, and Brodie could see the man at the table more clearly, though he still hadn't turned around. The man was wearing a tight olive-drab T-shirt, and he had dirty blonde hair, so—racial profiling aside—he was probably a gringo. And it was most probably Kyle Mercer. In fact, the man raised a pair of binoculars to his eyes, and Brodie saw the ouroboros tattoo on his muscled biceps. With his other hand, he was drinking a bottled water. Mercer seemed relaxed, and hopefully he was having a good day. But not for long.

Emilio held up his hand to Taylor and Brodie, and they stopped about twenty feet short of the platform and exchanged looks. Taylor whispered, "Our boat is still there."

"Good. We'll get Mercer onboard and go."

Emilio stepped onto the ramp, which made a sharp squeak, and Kyle Mercer glanced over his shoulder and motioned Emilio onto the platform. Emilio did the quickstep and positioned himself in front of Señor Kyle, like a general's adjutant about to announce a scheduled visitor.

Brodie noticed that Emilio didn't salute, so apparently el comandante didn't require it. They spoke for a few seconds; then Emilio motioned for Brodie and Taylor to come up on the platform.

Again they exchanged glances, then moved up the path to the narrow ramp.

Brodie said, "Rank before beauty," and walked with long, deliberate strides, followed by Taylor.

Apparently Mercer was going to speak to them together, which was not the way any cop interrogated multiple suspects. Or even how you interrogated POWs. Divide and conquer. But Kyle Mercer either was pressed for time, or he actually thought the Bowmans were dumb tourists—or more likely he was just going to tell them to talk quickly or die slowly.

Emilio directed them to a spot near two plastic chairs about ten feet— five is correct protocol—in front of Señor Kyle, who was again looking through his binoculars—which Brodie recognized as Captain Collins'.

Brodie didn't expect Mercer to stand, or to offer them a chair, but he had expected Mercer to show a bit more interest in the meeting. *Hello? Captain Mercer, I presume?*

Brodie now noticed that on the green table were two American passports. Also their sat phone and two cell phones. Emilio was now standing behind his boss, and the five other men were positioned on the riverbank, their AK-47s ready to rock and roll if he or Taylor made a sudden move. Brodie glanced over the side of the platform just to see the boat and imagine himself and Taylor in it, heading downriver, chatting on the sat phone with Collins, then Dombroski. He tried to imagine Kyle Mercer coming along voluntarily, but that was too far a stretch for his imagination. But you never know.

Brodie focused on Kyle Mercer, his face still partially hidden by the binoculars.

His blonde hair was buzz-cut, military style, and he was clean-shaven. He looked muscular and healthy, though his skin had that tropical jungle pallor that comes from excessive humidity, bug spray, and too little sun. Still, this was a far cry from the gaunt specter in the hostage video or the decapitation video they had seen in Hackett's office.

Mercer lowered the binoculars and stared off across the river.

Brodie now saw his watery blue eyes, and he noticed the crow's feet edging his eyes and age lines in parentheses around his mouth. The two years in Taliban captivity had caught up with him, and the jungle wasn't helping his boyish good looks.

Mercer glanced at Brodie and Taylor as though he had just become aware of their presence. He motioned for Brodie to come forward, and as he did, Mercer handed him the binoculars and said, in a conversational tone, "Here. Take a look at that white bird on the riverbank over there."

Brodie hesitated, then focused the binoculars on the opposite bank, where he saw a big white bird with long legs and a long beak.

"See it?"

"Yeah."

"What is it?"

"Uh . . . a pigeon?"

"No, Mr. Bowman. Not a pigeon."

"Right." Brodie lowered the binoculars. "Could be a heron."

"Could be. And you could be a dead duck."

Brodie put the binoculars on the table. "We need to talk, Captain."

Mercer looked at him, then at Taylor. "Maybe."

"Will you invite the lady to sit?"

Mercer looked at Brodie, then back at Taylor, and motioned to the plastic chairs. Emilio stood a respectable distance behind his boss, his hand on Brodie's Glock, which was still in his waistband.

Taylor and Brodie sat, and Mercer flipped through their passports, glancing at the photos, then at them as though he were an immigration officer. "Emilio tells me you are bird-watchers."

Brodie replied, "Obviously we're not."

Mercer nodded. "So?"

Brodie said, "I'm Chief Warrant Officer Scott Brodie, CID, and this is Warrant Officer Maggie Taylor, also CID, based at Quantico."

Mercer didn't seem to react to that. "CID."

"Correct."

"Not CIA?"

"CID."

"Maybe military Intel. Or FBI."

"Still CID."

"What brings you here?"

"You."

Brodie thought he saw a trace of a smile on Mercer's face, but not a nice smile. Mercer said, "I assume you're here to place me under arrest."

"Correct. The charge is desertion."

"Do you have a warrant?"

"We have written orders. Back in Quantico. Couldn't get that past customs."

"But you got two Glocks past customs."

"They were given to us here."

Mercer nodded and asked, "So have you seen my old friend Brendan Worley?"

"We have." Brodie added, "How do you know him?"

"Didn't he tell you?"

"No."

"Then you don't need to know." Mercer asked, "How is he doing?"

"Enjoying Caracas."

"He should enjoy it while he can."

"Right. So—"

"Does he know where you are right now?"

"Of course."

"Then why isn't he here?"

"This is a criminal investigation."

Mercer nodded as though trying to recall Army protocols and areas of responsibility. "So you're here to arrest me."

"That's the plan."

"But you have no warrant, no identification, and actually no authority to make an arrest on foreign soil."

"You'll have to take our word that we're CID investigators. Not sure about our authority here, but I can show you our written orders when we get back to Quantico."

"All right. So should I just come along peacefully?"

"That would be good."

Mercer pretended to think that over, clearly enjoying himself. It probably wasn't that often he got to spar in English.

He took a sip of water, then looked at Brodie and Taylor. "Correct me if I'm wrong, but it seems to me that you are my prisoners. So how can I become your prisoner?"

"I'm glad you asked. You need to accept our authority, Captain, return our weapons, and fulfill your duty as an officer by turning yourself over to our custody for transportation back to CONUS," meaning, in military acronym, the continental United States.

Mercer seemed to be considering that, then asked, "Aren't you supposed to read me my rights?"

Brodie confessed, "I don't have the cheat card with me, and to be honest, I can never remember the wording." He turned to Taylor. "Maggie?"

She nodded and looked at Mercer. "First, are you Kyle Mercer, a captain in the United States Army?"

"I am Kyle Mercer. I have resigned my commission—so I don't think the Army has any authority over me."

"For the record, Captain, the Army has not accepted your resignation."

Mercer stared at her, then looked at Brodie. "How does the Army know I resigned?"

Brodie replied, "We saw the tape you made."

Mercer seemed genuinely happy about that. "I was afraid it wouldn't make it to Bagram."

"It did. And to the Pentagon. Maybe even the White House."

"That's good. And you both saw it?"

"We did."

Mercer leaned forward in his chair. "Do you want me to tell you how I turned the tables on those bastards and cut off their fucking heads?"

Taylor replied, "We do. But we can't continue this conversation until I read you your rights."

Brodie thought she should let Mercer talk about a subject that obviously excited him—decapitation—but Taylor played it by the book.

Mercer seemed bemused and motioned for her to continue.

Taylor informed him, "You have the right to remain silent, and anything you say can and will be used against you in a court of law. You have the right to an attorney. If you cannot afford an attorney, one will be provided for you." She asked, "Do you understand the rights I have just said to you?"

"I do."

"With these rights in mind, do you wish to speak to us?"

"Actually, I want you to speak to me."

"All right," said Brodie, "let me speak to you about your thug standing behind you, Emilio. He sexually abused Ms. Taylor by making her strip naked in front of him."

Taylor said, "Scott—"

"Let Captain Mercer respond."

Mercer nodded as though he had a good response. "A strip search is not abuse, it is standard procedure when a suspect—or a POW—is apprehended, especially if a weapon is found on them. I'm sure you know that, and I'm sure the CID engages in this practice." He continued, "I'm sorry there's no matron here—only whores—but if Mr. Brodie was present at the strip search, then there's your required chaperone." He looked at Brodie. "Were you present?"

Brodie didn't reply.

"Knowing Emilio's predilections, I'm sure you were." He smiled, then looked at Taylor. "Did Emilio touch you in any way?"

Taylor did not reply, so Mercer looked over his shoulder and said something in Spanish to Emilio, who managed to shake his head while alternately glaring at Taylor and Brodie.

Mercer turned back to Taylor. "It seems everything was done properly except he should have given you a body cavity search." He added nonchalantly, "That is the least of your problems today."

Which, Brodie knew, was true. But he had gotten Mercer to react to a complaint like a commanding officer. Mercer was doing it to amuse himself, for sure, but if Brodie spoke to him as an officer and a gentleman—instead of a homicidal renegade—Brodie hoped he would respond accordingly, even if Mercer seriously didn't give a shit.

"For the record, Captain, I was not strip-searched, so your defense of Emilio's behavior is bullshit."

"Scott—"

"Here's a tip, Captain—if you let your troops get out of control, you lose their respect."

"I don't need advice from you or anyone on how to command troops." He suggested, "You shouldn't antagonize Emilio—he'll be your warden for the time you're here—short as it may be."

Captain Mercer and Señor Kyle seemed to be inhabiting the same body, and it was hard to know who was in control, so Brodie had to be careful not to push the wrong button, and not to push any button too hard. He kept thinking of that video of Mercer dangling a Taliban head in front of the camera.

Mercer asked, "Are you actually married?"

Brodie replied, "Ms. Taylor and I have only a professional relationship."

"I see . . . so . . . ?"

So we have no emotional attachment, Kyle, and you can't use that to your advantage. Brodie said, "We are not intimate." But almost.

Mercer nodded. "So your concern for Ms. Taylor is only professional."

"I would call it human."

"I would call it chivalry. Ms. Taylor might call it male chauvinism."

Taylor suggested, "Can we move on?"

He looked at her. "All right." He eyed her T-shirt. "Georgetown."

She nodded.

"Raised in an upper-middle-class DC suburb, poli-sci major, daddy's a diplomat or upper echelon bureaucrat, and you joined the Army to go slumming for awhile, and you went CID because you thought it was safe and would look good on your law school application."

Taylor replied, "My daddy was an auto mechanic when he was sober enough to work. I went to Georgetown on a scholarship, and the Army is my career path out of poverty." She added, "Profiling isn't your strong suit."

"Maybe not. But I can usually tell who's lying to me." He looked at Brodie. "Where'd you go?"

"NYU."

Mercer nodded. "I hear the East Coast accent."

"Upstate New York farm boy."

He looked at Taylor, who said, "Tennessee."

"I don't catch that in your accent."

"You will if I get really pissed."

Mercer smiled. "I'm from San Diego. But you know all about me from my file. Except what was redacted."

Brodie had a growing sense that none of this was real. The jungle was real, but no one in it was real. He looked at Kyle Mercer, and they made eye contact. The man was still smiling, but his eyes were . . . empty.

Kyle Mercer was crazy. Not pleasantly crazy—just crazy. But highly functional. And highly aware that he was off the rails. Or else he enjoyed acting the part. Maybe a combination of both. In any case, if Captain Mercer ever did go home, an Army shrink would take one look at him and one look at that decapitation video, and pronounce him mentally unfit to stand trial. Which was actually a moot point, because Brodie didn't think anyone on this fishing platform was going home.

But Kyle Mercer seemed to be enjoying the conversation, and maybe he was homesick—if a psycho can be homesick. So Brodie said, "Sorry about your mother."

Mercer didn't react to that.

Brodie said, "I'm sure your father misses you." He told him, "It's time to come home, soldier."

"I am home."

"No you're not."

"Then I'd rather be here than in Leavenworth." He asked, "Wouldn't you?"

"Well, tell you the truth, Captain, this place sucks." He added, "No offense."

Mercer didn't respond to that, but said, "Do not call me Captain."

"You are a captain in the United States Army."

"I won't make that point again."

"How should we address you?"

"Señor Kyle."

"How about Scott, Maggie, and Kyle?"

Mercer looked at Brodie, then at Taylor. "I think you both need more time in the stockade." He glanced at his watch. "Maybe twenty-four hours on bread and water—without the bread. And maybe we'll do those strip searches to your satisfaction." He glanced over his shoulder at Emilio.

Apparently Mercer was no longer enjoying the conversation. Brodie said, "I don't think any of us has twenty-four hours, Kyle."

He turned back to Brodie, thought awhile, then asked, "How did you find me?"

"Al Simpson."

Mercer stared off into space, probably replaying the chance meeting in the Hen House and reprimanding himself for not strangling Simpson with a bondage rope. He looked at Brodie. "That could only get you as far as looking for a random whorehouse in Caracas."

"We're good detectives."

"Are you? Half of Petare was aware of your presence by noon yesterday." He added, "And you, Mr. Bowman, were expected at the Hen House last night. I assume you thought better of it, or else your bloated body would have washed up on the banks of the Guaire this morning."

Brodie didn't respond. As he suspected, the National Guard, and MBR-200, and probably Pepe the pimp, all shared Intel on the two gringos who were asking around about Señor Kyle and underage girls. Word traveled quickly in the slums, but apparently took a little longer to reach the jungle, and Kyle Mercer didn't know about last night's excitement at the Hen House.

Mercer sat forward in his chair. "How did you find me? Who did you speak to?"

"We don't disclose our confidential sources to our suspects."

Mercer's cool was heating up. "I hold all the high cards, and whatever low cards you hold I will get now or later. Now is better. For everyone."

Brodie didn't want to rat out Carmen, but . . . she was probably being grilled by SEBIN anyway. Still . . . He said, "You can come to your own conclusions."

Mercer looked at Taylor. "I'll ask you the question. How did you get from the Hen House to here?"

She didn't reply.

"You can make this easy on yourself . . . Maggie . . . or you can entertain the troops tonight."

Taylor glanced at Brodie, then looked at Mercer and nodded. "All right . . . Your friend . . . General Gomez. He works for American Intel." She looked at Brodie. "Sorry, Scott . . ."

The Master Bullshitter Award goes to . . . Warrant Officer Maggie Taylor. Congratulations.

Brodie gave his partner a look that he hoped conveyed to Mercer that he was disappointed in her—though, of course, he understood that ratting out Gomez as an American agent was preferable to a night with the troops.

Mercer stayed silent, then said, "I don't believe that." Of course he did. This was Venezuela.

Mercer looked at Taylor, but he apparently decided not to pursue that line of questioning. He did say, however, "If I find out you're lying to me about anything, Ms. Taylor, you'll wish you'd spent the night pleasuring my men—which would be less painful than me dangling you over the side of this platform in a fishnet so the piranha can eat you alive. Do you understand?"

"I'm telling you the truth."

"I'll find out if you are."

"You'll also find out that Gomez was trained by the U.S. Army."

Mercer probably already knew that, and he might already have some suspicions about General Gomez, who might wind up as fish food. And he probably deserved it.

Mercer addressed Brodie. "If you hold back information again, you'll be sharing a cage with howler monkeys, who like to bite dicks and balls."

Sounded like a staff meeting at Quantico. "I'm here to be honest with you."

"Good."

Well, Señor Kyle had taken over Captain Mercer's head, and it was a little scary. But Captain Mercer—man on the run—needed more information from them than they needed from him. And as long as that was true, they wouldn't be part of the food chain. But eventually this game had to end. A happy ending would be Kyle Mercer being persuaded to come home with them and face the consequences of his actions. But that didn't seem likely at this point. Another happy ending would be the sound of helicopters and the sight of Delta Force guys rappelling into the camp. Hellfire missiles could be a happy ending, but only if they hit everything except him and Taylor. He wondered if the Pentagon planners would use high explosives if they suspected that friendlies—he and Taylor—were in the camp. Maybe they would if Brendan Worley had any input into that decision. Meanwhile, they had to buy time.

Mercer finished his water, and Brodie said, "We need water, Kyle."

Mercer didn't seem to hear, and he looked as though the info on General Gomez had put him off his game.

Brodie pulled his half-full bottle of water from his pocket and gave it to Taylor, who drank and passed it back to him. He finished it and held up the empty bottle. "Agua?"

Mercer came out of his dark thoughts and looked at Brodie. "What?"

"Clean water. We need it. Minimum standards of detention as defined by the Geneva Conventions. Speaking of which, your camp's field sanitation seems good overall, but the stockade could use some work."

Mercer turned to him. "What the hell do you know about living in the field?"

Glad you asked. Brodie informed him, "Before CID, I was a grunt. Second Infantry Division, Iraq. Maggie was Civil Affairs. Two years in the 'Stan."

Mercer looked at both of them, but didn't respond.

Brodie continued, "I was at Fallujah. Got a purple and bronze. Maggie got a purple and silver."

Mercer seemed unsure if he should believe any of that.

Brodie said, "Your thug saw her wounds."

Mercer looked at Taylor. "How'd you get hit?"

"IED. Maybe a piece of an RPG."

"Show me."

She stood, walked to Mercer's table, turned, and pulled her pants down to reveal her thigh.

Mercer stared at the white and purple scars. "You lose people?"

"Six."

"How many did they lose?"

"Hard to say. More than six."

Mercer nodded, seeming to approve of that. Brodie watched the man as he stared at Taylor's scars, and he looked like he was about to reach out and touch them. Instead he sat back and motioned her to sit.

Taylor hiked up her pants and took her seat.

Mercer didn't seem interested in seeing Brodie's wounds, which, all things considered, were not interesting—a half-dozen pockmarks on his back from an RPG round that missed him, but hit a wall behind him. It wasn't his time that day. Today, however, could be the day.

Mercer looked at Taylor. "When were you there?"

"About the same time you were. I deployed in spring of 2013 with the Ninety-Sixth Civil Affairs Battalion. I was in country for almost two years."

Mercer seemed to go distant, as though he was back there.

Taylor said something to him in what Brodie figured was Pashto, and Mercer looked at her, then replied in Pashto.

Brodie hoped the Pashto didn't send him off the deep end.

Mercer said something, and Taylor nodded and replied in what Brodie recognized as Arabic.

She said to Brodie, "Kyle also learned Arabic from a Quran written in both languages." She added, "While he was a captive."

Brodie wanted to tell him he could learn ten more languages by the time he got out of Leavenworth. Brodie knew a few words of Arabic, like, "Stop, or I'll shoot," but he didn't think that would be useful here.

More importantly, there were now three combat veterans having a conversation. That didn't mean Mercer was going to tell them they were free to go—in Pashto or Arabic—but they were engaging with their captor in a way that held his interest, and that meant they were momentarily safe from the piranha and the monkeys. Brodie had the sense that he and Taylor were playing with a cougar that had once been trained, but had reverted to the wild. As long as they amused the animal and fed him scraps of information, the cougar would let them rub his tummy. Sometimes the cougar purred, sometimes the cougar snarled. And you never knew when the cougar was going to bite.

Mercer asked, "Why did you transfer to CID?"

Brodie replied, "It's interesting work. You get to ask questions instead of answering them. Can I ask you a question?"

"No." He looked at Taylor, who said, "I believe in justice and the law."

"They're not the same."

"They need to be."

"They will never be," he said.

"They can be."

"You could be right. I am the law here, and I dispense justice."

"You dispense punishment."

"Not every time."

But often enough to be familiar with disembowelment, cutting throats, severing heads, and feeding people to the wildlife.

Mercer was looking at Taylor. "Civil Affairs. Did you do good things for the Afghan people?"

"I tried."

"Me too. I sent a lot of them to paradise." He looked at Brodie. "How about you?"

"I did what I got paid to do."

"I did more than I was paid to do."

Taylor said, "Tell us."

"I think you might already know." He looked at Brodie. "How'd you get hit?"

"Standing in the wrong place at the wrong time. Same as everyone else who got hit."

"I never got hit."

"Right. We read your file, Kyle."

He nodded.

"You served honorably," said Taylor.

"I did. Then I didn't."

"Tell us."

He ignored that and asked Brodie, "What was your rank?"

"E-Five," meaning a three-stripe sergeant.

"Ms. Taylor?"

"Same."

"Good soldiers. Good schools. Surprised you didn't go to OCS."

Brodie explained, "I don't like officers."

Mercer smiled. "I don't like wiseasses. But I liked my sergeants. They were good men."

"And," said Brodie, "by all accounts you were a good officer. So what made you desert?"

Mercer again ignored the question and asked, "Are you working with Worley?"

Taylor replied, "We are in contact with Colonel Worley, but we are here with CID orders to find and apprehend you."

"Well, you've found me. Actually, I found you."

"And we have informed you that you are under arrest."

"You have. You've fulfilled your responsibility, and I'll even acknowledge your authority. But you don't have the power to take me into custody. Or am I missing something?"

Brodie said, "You have the power, Kyle, to come along voluntarily."

"That's not going to happen. But if it did . . . just curious . . . how would you get me out of the country?"

Brodie didn't want to mention Captain Collins at this point, so he replied, "We can work something out with the embassy. We'll get you inside, and the dips can negotiate an extradition."

"Okay. And once I'm in the embassy, I'm going to kill Worley."

"I don't think we can work that out, Kyle."

"Why not? He wants to kill me, so why can't I kill him?"

"Well . . . I suppose you could do that here. Or someplace else. But that's not really something you should do in the embassy."

"Then let's get him here."

"I think he's on the way. And not alone."

Mercer didn't respond. He picked up the sat phone from the table. "There's one number in this phone, and I'm guessing it's his."

"Good guess."

"Did he tell you he wants to kill me?"

"He didn't indicate that he knew you that well. But if that's true, it's better that we found you before Worley does. And better that you come with us."

"This is between Worley and me. Not you."

"I want you to tell us about that."

"Maybe if I call him, he'll tell you. But then he'll have to kill you. He kills people who know too much."

"Okay . . . I can believe that. In fact, Maggie and I will look into that when we leave here."

Mercer powered up the phone, and dialed the only number in the phone directory. He put it on speaker and placed the phone on the table.

Brodie heard the ring, then the pickup. "Where the hell are you?"

Mercer said, "Buenos días, Colonel."

There was a silence; then Worley asked, "Who is this?"

"Your worst fucking nightmare."

There was another silence, and Brodie thought Worley had fainted or something. Then he said, "Where are Mr. Brodie and Ms. Taylor?"

"Right here, singing like birds to get out of here alive."

"May I speak to them to see if they are alive?"

"Sure." He covered the mouthpiece and held up the phone toward Brodie and Taylor. "Just say 'Hello, asshole,' loud and clear for Worley's recording device." He uncovered the mouthpiece.

Brodie, without putting too much enthusiasm in his voice, called out, "Hello, asshole!"

Taylor called out, "Hello . . ." She glanced at Mercer. "Asshole!"

Mercer got back on the phone. "Satisfied?"

"All right . . ."

"I'm impressed with their tracking skills. CID knows how to find people. DIA and CIA not so much. In fact, you're all talk and no delivery. Just like in Afghanistan."

"I will find you."

"Not before I find you."

"You know where I am. United States Embassy, Caracas."

"That's where you hide. You're a ball-less wonder, Colonel. Same as in Afghanistan. You ever hear a shot fired over there? I did. Every fucking day."

"You had your job, Captain, and I had mine. And mine is now to find you. And I'm close."

"You were getting warm. Have you heard from Ted Haggerty recently? No? Well, I don't think you will until you meet in hell."

"Where is he?"

"I just told you."

There was silence on the line. Then Worley said, "You're a sick man."

"I know I'll be better when you're dead."

"That's not going to happen, Captain."

"If you have to die anyway, you should want to die in the line of duty with your phony reputation intact. That's better than me spilling my guts about what you did."

Worley, obviously thinking about the two witnesses who, though they were as good as dead, were not actually dead, replied, "I did nothing wrong, Captain. You did. And you will pay for that."

"I've already paid for my sins, Colonel. It's your turn. Sorry if I interrupted your day drinking." He hung up and turned the phone off, then glanced at his watch. "What do you think, Scott? Traced?"

"I don't know. Call him back and ask."

Mercer was tuned out again. He said, as if to himself, "Could kill him easily enough in Caracas . . . but I need to kidnap him and torture him to death. Slowly. Maybe a day for every month I spent in Taliban captivity . . ."

Obviously Captain Mercer and Colonel Worley had some issues, and two years in Taliban captivity wasn't enough time for Mercer to forget or for Worley to forgive.

Well, at least Brodie and Taylor knew who Ted was. He was Ted Haggerty, and now he was dead. And, as per Emilio, he was probably the gringo whose throat Mercer had cut in the prison hut. In a normal investigation, Brodie would certainly ask the suspect about that, but the less he and Taylor knew, the better their chances—which now stood at zero—of persuading Mercer to come home and face a simple charge of desertion.

Mercer stared off at the river. "I didn't torture Haggerty. He was happy to talk, so I gave him a quick release."

"Good," said Brodie. "I'm sure he's happy to be going home."

Mercer nodded. "He's gone home." He assured Brodie and Taylor, "I would give you the same quick release. I don't enjoy torture for its own sake. It's just for when people don't answer me truthfully." Mercer went dark again and stared into space.

Brodie didn't like it when Mercer was thinking and not talking. Brodie and Taylor could, to some extent, control the conversation—but if Mercer was thinking that he needed to know more about who knew the location of his camp, or if an operation was planned, then he might start asking questions that Brodie and Taylor wouldn't or couldn't answer. Then it would be fish and monkey time.

To get Mercer out of his dark thoughts, Brodie said, "I know why you're here—to kill Worley. But what is this camp all about?"

"It's about a lot of things."

"Right. Maggie and I have been racking our brains, and we can't figure out why you raised an army to whack Brendan Worley."

"Before you kill a man, you kill everything that means anything to him."

"Well . . . okay. So . . . ?"

"Worley was sent here because he has a good reputation for cleaning up the shit."

"He mentioned that to us." Brodie added, "Not to sound egotistical, but that's why I . . . and Maggie were sent here." Though Ms. Taylor had other qualifications.

Mercer looked at Brodie. "I'm sure you're good at what you do. Well . . . until recently."

"Right. So, back to Worley. He's here, obviously, to destabilize the regime."

"That's correct. And I'm here to destabilize him and his mission. To make him look bad. And to let him know I'm here to do that."

Brodie nodded. "Seems like an ambitious plan."

"It is. And it's working."

"But you understand that Colonel Worley's mission to destabilize the regime is in the best interest of your country."

"I have no country."

"Okay. But I don't see how you can . . . What are you doing? Helping the Chavistas?"

"That's what I'm doing."

"Do you sympathize with the Chavistas?"

"No. They're assholes. Gomez is an asshole. They're all corrupt, dishonorable, and stupid."

"Right. They're bad guys. So—"

"As they say in the Mideast, the enemy of my enemy—Worley—is my friend. So the Chavistas are my friends."

"I got that. But you should think of . . . if not your country, then . . . Luis."

"Who's Luis?"

"Luis is every poor bastard in Venezuela who's suffered under this regime."

"That's not my problem. That's Luis' problem. If people can't get rid of these assholes, they deserve the government they get."

"You're not helping the problem if you're helping the Chavistas."

"The problem is the United States, and arrogant people like Brendan Worley who go around the world trying to clean up shit that's none of their business. Shit that they make worse. Shit that gets American soldiers killed. And how do they clean up shit? With their own shit."

"Okay . . . geopolitics is not my strong point, but—"

"Shit that makes the Taliban look like a Civil Affairs team. And it didn't even work. It made things worse for the troops on the ground. If you're going to kill people, at least get something out of it."

"Right." Brodie was sure that Mercer was talking about Operation Flagstaff, but Mercer hadn't used the word, so neither did Brodie. That was for later. For now, Brodie asked, "I'm still not sure what you're actually doing here."

"I'm assassinating enemies of the Chavista regime, and making Worley look bad. Maybe Washington will recall him, like they did in Afghanistan. But they'll just send him someplace else to fuck up, because they're stupid, and Worley tells everyone he's smart. And instead of him paying for fucking up, he's rewarded with another assignment." He looked at Brodie. "In the real Army—the Army you and I served in—an officer with his track record would be relieved of his duties. But in the world Worley lives in—smoke and mirrors—the idiots think he's doing a good job."

"I'm sure he's up for a star."

"You can bet on it. But he won't live long enough to enjoy it."

"Well, I still think a court-martial might be a better way to end his career."

Mercer ignored that and said, "Not many people know this, but the U.S. is training a paramilitary force in Colombia to invade Venezuela."

Actually, Brodie had had two cabdrivers who knew that.

"This group is led by disaffected Venezuelan military officers, and funded by the U.S., of course. I'll be ready to take these people on when I recruit more men. In the meantime, Worley has recruited anti-regime politicians, journalists, church people, business leaders, and army officers to help shape the narrative and hide America's hand in this invasion if the invasion is successful in toppling the regime. My job is to kill these people, which I'm doing." He added, "Worley is having a shit fit."

"Right. But if you look at the bigger picture—"

"I like the small picture. And if Worley is recalled to the States, or reassigned to some other shithole, I'll follow him to the ends of the earth. I'm playing the long game, and enjoying it, and he knows this." He added, "He hasn't had a good night's sleep since he found out I was here."

Brodie was reluctantly impressed with Mercer's ambitious goals. If nothing else, they showed that he had retained some of the command discipline and tactical thinking that had been drilled into him. And that might be the only part of his mind that had retained any clarity.

Taylor, who had been listening closely, said, "If this is your life, and why you live it, I feel sorry for you."

He looked at her. "I'm enjoying my life."

"You enjoy this—?" She motioned at the dark jungle.

"I do. And when it comes out in the news someday that the famous deserter Kyle Mercer has raised an army in the Venezuelan jungle to assist the socialist regime, I'll be called the American Che Guevara." Even Mercer thought megalomania was funny, and he laughed. Then he got serious and said, "Politics are shit. Politicians are scum. Soldiers are real. I am a soldier. I have not been broken. Not by the Taliban, and not by people like Brendan Worley."

Brodie thought about that. Kyle Mercer was either suffering from the worst post-traumatic stress that Brodie had ever seen, or he'd found a new therapy for it.

Mercer continued, "And not by people like Ted Haggerty and his cronies who use and abuse soldiers." He added, "CIA officers deserve to have their throats cut."

Brodie glanced at Taylor, who might or might not agree with that.

Mercer concluded, "The law of the jungle is me."

Brodie thought it might be best to move on before Señor Kyle insisted on showing them his shrunken heads collection. He said, "Kyle, there's a question that's been bugging us—bugging everyone in the Army. And in the country. Why did you, a Delta Force captain, desert?"

"I didn't."

"Were you abducted?"

"No, I was trying to keep from being abducted."

"By whom?"

"By that asshole I was just talking to."

"Okay. So—"

"Enough." He slid Brodie's and Taylor's cell phones toward them. "Your codes."

Brodie replied, "There's no cell service here, Kyle."

"Your codes."

Brodie gave him his code, and Taylor did the same.

Mercer punched them in and looked through Brodie's phone, then did the same with Taylor's. "Lots of interesting texts and e-mails . . . I'll need time to look through all this."

"Take all the time you need," Brodie said. "We can do it together."

He looked at Taylor's phone. "Aerial shots of Kavak . . . the river . . . Still not sure how you pinpointed Camp Tombstone . . ." He looked up. "That's the name of my camp."

Brodie didn't think it was Camp Happy.

Mercer shut off both cell phones. "Don't have electricity here, as you see, but I can get new batteries if I need to." He continued, "We're electronically silent here, which makes it difficult for NSA or anyone to find me." He asked, "What brought you to Kavak?"

Brodie replied, "General Gomez."

"He's due here in a few days. I'll ask him."

Sounded to Brodie like a bluff—but if not, they had a problem. On the other hand, maybe they'd just bought a few days.

Mercer looked at Brodie. "Here's the big question. If you lie, you die." He asked, "Is there a military operation planned against this camp?"

Brodie replied, "I believe there is. And it will be influenced by Brendan Worley. And Brendan Worley takes no prisoners. He wants you dead, because dead men tell no tales. And maybe he wants me and Maggie dead, because maybe we heard things from you that he doesn't want us to know. So we're offering you a chance to come with us to Kavak. We have an aircraft there and a pilot who will take us to Bogotá, where you will be transferred to CONUS, where you will have an opportunity, in a judicial or non-judicial setting, to tell your side of the story." He added, "Your prior service record, which is outstanding, will be taken into account. Your two-year imprisonment by the enemy will also be taken into account. And whatever crimes you may have committed or may know about—including the crimes of other military personnel—will be evaluated for further investigation." He asked, "Am I making myself clear?"

Mercer had no response, but then stood and walked to the edge of the platform and looked at the river. "The Pemón have traversed these rivers and jungles for thousands of years. They form a network, a fabric of human Intel that is invisible to outsiders. I respect this history, and them as a people, and they respect me. And they know who is worthy of their loyalty."

Brodie didn't know if Mercer had heard a word he said, but then Mercer turned back to them. "There is no aircraft in Kavak. Your man, Captain Collins, was sent off—without his sat phone. He's probably back in Caracas by now."

Or dead. Brodie said, "There are other ways out of here."

"Not for me. And not for you."

Brodie was getting frustrated. "Kyle, get a fucking grip on yourself. Do you want to die here in a missile strike? Or in a firefight with your former Delta Force brothers? Because that's what's going to happen. Ms. Taylor and I are here to save you from being killed—silenced—by whoever it is that wants you and your story dead and buried. You want to get even with Worley for something? Do it in a civilized setting where the world can hear about it. The worst that could happen to you is getting the cell next to Worley."

"I am not going to prison. Not ever again."

"They serve bacon for breakfast, for God's sake." Brodie knew he wasn't supposed to promise anything, but given that he and Taylor were in a bad place, he said to Mercer, "If you give yourself up voluntarily, I'm pretty sure you can get off with a few years for desertion."

Mercer remained standing. "That's a few years too many. You should also know that I tortured and killed a CIA officer named Robert Crenshaw in Peshawar."

"We didn't hear that."

"You did. And I killed Haggerty. There's no going back."

"Okay . . . Then tell us why you killed those men."

He smiled. "If I tell you, I have to kill you."

"Well, then tell me why you didn't kill Al Simpson."

"He did nothing to me."

"Okay, Captain, as long as you're confessing, what did those civilians in Afghanistan do to you to make you kill them?"

Mercer stared at Brodie, then at Taylor.

Taylor said, "Operation Flagstaff."

Mercer stayed silent, then said, "I can still see the women trying to protect their children, the old men, the young boys and girls, taking full bursts of M4 fire, blood all over the place, and the screaming and crying that got on our nerves so much that we drowned it out with long bursts of fire until it stopped." He looked out at the river again, then at Brodie and Taylor. "I'll bet you've never seen that much blood."

Taylor made eye contact with him. "You need to tell other people about Flagstaff."

He shook his head. "That's not the way I want to be remembered."

"Kyle . . . that's not the way *I* want to be remembered."

He looked at her.

"I . . . do you know the village of Mirabad?"

He nodded. "But not one of my villages."

"It was one of mine." She said, "I helped gather Intel for . . . I'm not sure who . . . but one day my team went back to Mirabad, and everyone in it was dead."

Again, he nodded. "Civil Affairs. I always suspected they were part of Flagstaff."

"We didn't know."

"You knew. Or should have known." He added, "There were a lot of Mirabads."

Taylor didn't respond.

Mercer looked at Brodie. "You zap any ICs?"

"No."

"You're proud of your combat duty."

"I am."

"That makes all the difference. That's what you'll be remembered for."

"Maybe."

"Do you know how most of America remembers me? They remember me in that fucking Taliban video, kneeling in the fucking dirt like a whipped dog."

Brodie and Taylor exchanged glances.

Mercer continued, "Those fucking bearded bags of shit . . . they put me in front of a camera . . . me, Kyle Mercer, Delta Force . . . years of combat duty, never showed an ounce of fear . . . and that's what it came down to . . . kneeling in the dirt for the world to see . . . for my friends and family to see . . . my teammates . . ." He looked at Brodie and Taylor. "But did the world see the end of that story? Did anyone see me cutting off their fucking heads?"

"We saw it. The Army saw it."

"I want the world to see it."

"All right . . . Maybe you can present it at your court-martial."

Mercer seemed not to hear. "Two fucking years in that hellhole, starved, beaten, humiliated . . ." He looked at Taylor. "Sexually abused."

Taylor took a deep breath. "I'm sorry. Really."

Mercer remained standing, then looked at Emilio, who was looking at Señor Kyle in an odd way, obviously wondering what the hell was going on. Mercer shouted something at him, and he walked quickly down the ramp to the five other men who were still on the riverbank, ready to engage in a live-fire exercise using live targets. With the AK-47's cyclic rate of fire of six hundred rounds a minute, that would be fifteen hundred rounds coming at them in thirty seconds. So, best not to try anything. Actually, even if they were alone with Mercer, Brodie and Taylor weren't going anywhere. They had come a long way to hear this—the heart of this troubling case—and they were on the threshold of some answers.

Mercer had his back to them as he looked into the river, then noticed their boat. He said, "You had balls to come here alone."

Brodie replied, "Come back with us. That would show real balls."

Mercer ignored the offer and began speaking. "My team was on a night mission in a village outside Kabul, to grab a local Taliban commander, and it all went to shit. The locals had supposedly fingered this guy and wanted to get rid of him, but it was actually a trap, and I lost two KIA and five WIA. We got out with our dead and wounded, and I wanted payback for those fucking so-called ICs who set us up." He looked at Brodie. "That ever happen to you?"

"This is your story, Kyle, not mine."

He nodded. "Okay, so we don't do payback. We're not Nazis. Right? We do surgical removal of those responsible, except we never know who that is. So I'm back at the FOB to regroup, and my squadron commander, Major Powell, asks me to speak to a Colonel Worley, and to listen to what he has to say. So, okay, I meet this guy alone in a bunker and he's wearing civilian clothes, so he doesn't have to show his rank, his branch insignia, or his nametag. He seems like an arrogant prick, but he's cool as a cadaver on dry ice. And he says he's sorry for what happened, and he says we're not going to put up with this shit anymore. He says we are going to—get this—alter our posture, like instead of slouching, we're gonna stand up straight. We're gonna engage in a pacification program. He says Major Powell has agreed to this, whatever the hell this was, and that he'd like my team to lead off the program."

Mercer seemed to be trying to collect his thoughts, or maybe erase some of them. He went on, "So I say, okay, what's it about? But Worley doesn't say right off. He tells me that my team and some other teams from other squadrons are going to return to this village . . . can't even remember the name of it . . . and we're going to pacify the village so that no other American soldiers are killed there ever again . . ." Mercer nodded to himself. "So, I get what he's saying, and I get that he's picked other teams from other squadrons that had the same shit happen to them." He glanced at Brodie and Taylor. "He handpicked men who were pissed, and sick and tired of the fucking locals shoving it up our asses and getting away with it."

Brodie nodded. He'd heard similar stories from old Vietnam vets about the treacherous villagers, who were probably just terrified peasants trying to survive between two armies. In 'Nam, the troops usually just satisfied themselves with burning the village, killing the livestock, and sending the population to a government-controlled area. In Afghanistan—and Iraq—there was no formal program to deal with the problem. But apparently Colonel Worley—and probably the CIA—knew how to deal with it. They were going to pacify the hell out of those villages. All they needed to go that route were pissed-off warriors. Guys who'd lost friends. Officers who'd lost men. Like Captain Mercer.

"Pacification"—one of those creepy clinical words that the military brass loves to use to make bad things sound okay. And it did sound okay, unless you were on the receiving end of the pacification.

Mercer continued, "So I spoke to my team, we met up with three other teams on the helipad, and off we went. We never worked with these guys before, and we never saw them again, but when we got to the village, it was like we all knew what to do and how to do it. A lot of anger came out . . . understand? Maybe a lot of guys had thought about this—like, fuck the rules of engagement, fuck the Code of Conduct, fuck the Geneva Conventions, fuck the politicians, fuck everyone who's fucked us, and fuck everyone who's not us." Mercer looked into the deep jungle across the riverbank. "That's the way it's always been done. Since the dawn of time." He nodded to himself. "You don't need special training. When you're pissed, it comes easy."

Brodie and Taylor looked at each other, and Taylor nodded to Brodie—like, *Say something, soldier.*

Brodie said, "It comes easy. But it doesn't stay easy."

Mercer looked at him. "No. It gets harder. First time is easy. You're pissed. Second time, not so easy."

Brodie said, "Worley didn't do you any favors."

"We thought he did. Then . . . when I said something to him . . . like, we've had enough of this . . . he said something like, you went over the line, Captain, and there's no turning back. I understood that we were all in a new brotherhood. So we get orders to go to our fourth village . . . and some of my men say no. They were shutting down. They lost their pride. We weren't soldiers. We weren't Delta Force. We were killers. So I sat, phoned Worley and told him we're done. He says okay."

End of story. Not quite. Brodie knew not to interrupt a confession. Lots of criminals started to think of the interview room as the confession box— except in this case, the sinner could kill his confessor. So Brodie stayed silent.

But Taylor was ready to offer absolution and redemption. She said, "When I got to Mirabad, I was sickened by what I heard. Literally sick to my stomach. But . . . and I've never told this to a soul . . . I was also sick to death of how we were treated by the villagers . . . how they took advantage of us, how they lied, how they set us up for the Taliban . . . and, God forgive me, a thought flashed through my mind that they got what they deserved."

Mercer looked at her but said nothing, though he nodded.

Brodie, too, looked at her. Was this bullshit? Probably not. He'd had similar thoughts in Iraq. War is the dark angel on your shoulder that whispers bad things to you.

Mercer sat on the platform, cross-legged, and stared at the bamboo. He said, "Worley . . . the son of a bitch comes to my outpost by chopper, and says he needs a word with me. No surprise there. He tells me to calm down. He says my team needs some R&R and he'll take care of that. I tell him to shove his R&R up his ass. He reminds me that I'm speaking to a colonel, and he also reminds me that if I say a word to anyone about the pacification program, I'm going to jail for the rest of my life. He tells me to think about my men. They're going to jail too. I tell him he's going to fucking jail if I go to jail. He also tells me—and I'm not sure I believe this—that some of my men are okay with what we're doing, and not okay with me making a stink about it. He tells me to watch my dark corners and sleep with one eye open. Then he gets on the chopper and leaves."

Brodie nodded to himself. He could almost fill in the blanks and guess why Captain Mercer deserted his post.

Taylor said to him, "If it makes any difference to you, Captain, I was similarly threatened."

He looked at her sitting in the chair a few feet from him. "Did you keep quiet?"

"I did. And I'm sorry I did."

"Well . . . I was not going to keep quiet. Not after that son of a bitch threatened me. I was going to make a full report to the JAG office, to Major Powell, and also to the CID—" He looked at Brodie and Taylor, and the irony was obviously not lost on him. He continued, "I was ready to come clean and take my punishment, because I deserved it. And I was going to give testimony in exchange for immunity for my men . . ." He found something funny and said, "I had a Christ complex . . . willing to die for the sins of others—even my guys who were ready to betray me to Worley. Jesus . . . what was I thinking? I was thinking Worley was the devil—the tempter—and I fell for his shit. But he didn't fall for mine. The bastard knew I wasn't going to keep quiet, but he tells me I'm going home. End of tour. And I'm almost believing that, so I decide to keep my mouth shut until I get stateside . . ." He looked at Brodie and Taylor. "I had no experience dealing with a man like Brendan Worley. I was a warrior. He was a fucking snake. Still is."

That reminded Brodie of the fraught relationship between Maggie Taylor and Trent from the CIA. The difference, thought Brodie uncharitably, was that Maggie Taylor got laid, and Kyle Mercer got fucked.

Mercer stood with some difficulty. "The Taliban broke my ribs. And fractured my spine. So I get pain . . . and I think of Brendan Worley." He let them know, "I'm going to break every bone in his fucking body."

Brodie suggested, "Let it go at that."

"That's for starters."

Taylor pointed out the obvious. "He's still controlling you."

Mercer ignored the obvious and said, "He's going to pray for death, like I did."

Brodie changed the subject by asking, "Mind if we stand?"

Mercer looked at them, thought a moment, then said, "Do I have your word as officers that you won't try anything stupid?"

"You have our word," Brodie replied. "We won't even try anything smart."

Mercer looked at his men, who were about thirty feet away, and motioned to them that the prisoners were going to stand.

Brodie and Taylor stood, and Brodie hoped that the boys with the AKs didn't misconstrue the signal.

Mercer said, "I wasn't naïve . . . but I thought Worley was done lying . . . so I thought I was going home—where I could make things right. The next day, I get a call on the outpost's satellite phone. It's Major Powell, telling me that a helicopter is coming back at first light to take me to Bagram to meet with General Clark and discuss my concerns. He tells me he authorized my release from command, and I should pack all my stuff and prepare to fly to Washington if General Clark feels that my concerns need further consideration at a higher command level. Okay, so I say thank you, Major. And I promise him that I'll keep him out of any discussion, because he was out of this loop—these killer teams put together by Colonel Worley. Powell knew what was going on, but . . . someone higher than Worley was running the show. He thanks me and hangs up. Then a few minutes later, he calls back and he says . . . and I remember this . . . he says he doesn't know who is going to be on that helicopter, but that I should be careful. And maybe I should be concerned if any of my men get on that helicopter with me. Then he hangs up. And I'm standing there, in the middle of fucking nowhere, and a helicopter is coming for me at first light, and I don't know who to trust on my team. But whoever gets on that chopper with me is not someone I can trust. And I'm thinking that Worley could be on that chopper, and the pilot and crew could be Black Ops guys from the Agency who've seen people exit choppers at two thousand feet and think nothing of it. They were bringing you to Bagram for stress disorder, which is maybe why you jumped. Or why you tried to hijack the chopper, or some shit like that. Next thing everybody knows, you're out the door. Chopper swings around, makes a quick landing in Indian territory, and recovers the body. End of story. End of problem." He added, "Full military honors. Flag on the coffin. Taps at the grave. Mom was still alive, so she'd get the folded flag. Dad puts his arm around her. Everybody is sad, but . . . 'Why did he kill himself? He was a nice boy. Normal in every way. The war got to him. It killed him . . . it killed his mind . . .'" He looked at Brodie and Taylor. "So I'm standing there thinking that maybe Major Powell is overreacting to something . . . or maybe he's just saying be careful of what you say and who you say it to. Maybe it's me that's overreacting. I'm not paranoid, but I'm thinking of Brendan Worley. Is he going to let me talk to JAG or CID? Or General Clark? Is he ready to see Flagstaff go in the shit can, and him go to jail? I don't think so. So I'm in the commo bunker, and there's a radio there and the sat phone. But two guys are in the bunker—my guys, but I don't know if they're guys I can trust, or not trust. I can order them out of the commo bunker, but that's sort of a giveaway. So I'm basically stuck on an outpost in the middle of the night, and I don't know who to trust, and there's a chopper coming for me at first light. So I go in my bunker and sit on my cot with my M4 . . . and I decide that I'm not going to wait for shit to happen to me—I'm going to take charge of the situation. That's what I was trained to do. So at zero three hundred, I pack some stuff, including night goggles, and I slip over the wall and through the wire and minefield. There's a place we can do that in case we're being overrun. A way out that we can all do with our eyes closed. And ten minutes later, I'm on my way to Bagram—about a hundred miles through mountain terrain. About three days. Four if you travel mostly at night so the fucking T-bans don't see you. And I'm thinking about Worley coming in on that chopper at first light and finding out that I'm gone. And I pictured him shitting his pants."

Mercer went quiet, and Brodie figured he was picturing Worley shitting his pants. Aside from that, Brodie didn't recall any mention of a helicopter coming to the outpost on the morning of Captain Mercer's mysterious disappearance. Possibly there was no black helicopter coming to take Captain Mercer on a long horizontal and short vertical ride. Or the chopper had turned back when it got a report of Captain Mercer's absence from the outpost. And maybe the chopper ride to see General Clark was legit. No way of knowing any of that, but Brodie found himself hoping that Mercer had made the right decision for the right reason. Otherwise, those two years with the Taliban were not necessary. This is what's meant by the fog of war. The fog is in your brain—paranoia, rumors, stress, fear, fatigue, and a daily reminder of mortality.

Mercer said, "I almost made it. On the third night I ran into a Taliban camp . . . thirty miles east of Bagram. And that was the beginning of my two years of hell . . . and I thank Brendan Worley for that." He looked at Brodie and Taylor. "Still think I shouldn't kill him?"

Taylor said, "We're a society of law, Kyle. We do not take personal revenge. If you do, you become no better than the person who broke the law. You need to come home and make these allegations that you were going to make three years ago. You didn't want to kill Worley then, you wanted him to be held accountable for what he did. That would be worse for him than death. That would be public disgrace, loss of honor, and maybe imprisonment. That would be justice. It's no different now."

Mercer looked at her. "You didn't spend two years in a Taliban cell."

"No . . . I didn't, but if I did—"

"Don't even go there. What you're really saying is that you and Mr. Brodie would like to get out of here alive. And you're spinning the shit so it looks like gold, but it's still bullshit. Next you're going to tell me to let you go so you can tell my story."

Which was what Brodie was about to suggest, but that wasn't going to fly.

Taylor actually walked up to Mercer, and Brodie glanced at the firing squad, who looked tense. "Maggie . . ."

She stood more or less in his face. "You, Captain Mercer, made the first bad decision at your first meeting with Colonel Worley when you didn't tell him to go fuck himself. Your second bad decision was not reporting what he said to you. I know about that firsthand, and I understand not wanting to put your ass out there and get it chewed on. But everything that happened after your first meeting with Worley was a result of what you did or failed to do. And nobody made you pull the trigger in those villages. That was your decision, and you led your men into that hell. You violated every law and every code of civilized behavior." She looked up at Mercer, who was about six inches taller than her, but looked shorter now. "Does that sound like I'm trying to talk my way out of here?"

He stayed quiet for awhile, then said, "I was ready to take full responsibility for what I did."

"Knowing that the Army would go easy on you for following the orders of Colonel Worley. That's always the case in wartime. Just following orders."

Brodie was wishing she'd shut up before Mercer went over the edge and told Emilio to go get a fishnet. *Jesus, Maggie.*

But she wasn't done. She actually waved her finger at Mercer and said, "But are you now willing to go before a court of your peers and admit to torturing and murdering Robert Crenshaw? Or Ted Haggerty? Or whoever else you've killed before or since then? I don't think so."

Mercer seemed on the verge of either a meltdown or another homicide. Brodie wasn't sure he approved of this interrogation technique in this particular situation. What works in a jail cell doesn't always work in the field. Especially a place named Camp Tombstone. "Maggie—"

"I'm handling this, Scott."

Mercer said, "But not very well," taking the words out of Brodie's mouth.

Taylor said to Mercer, "Do you know that two men died looking for you?"

"I do. And I know their names. Do you?"

"If you give them to me, I'll say a prayer for them."

"I've already done that. Save your prayers for yourself and your partner."

"And I'll pray for you. But right now, Scott and I are getting in that boat. You can come with us, or you can stay here. Or you can order your men to shoot us. You've done that before."

Hold on, Maggie. That's not in the script. "Excuse me—"

"I've got this, Scott." She looked at Mercer. "We are not staying here to be tortured by you. I am not staying here to be raped by your men. I am getting on that boat, and you can do what the hell you want."

Mercer, who seemed to be regaining his composure along with his anger, glared at Taylor and said, "If you go toward that boat, my men will shred you to pieces."

Brodie thought it was time for him to exercise some command and control over his obviously distraught and pissed-off subordinate. He walked quickly to Taylor and took her arm.

She looked at him, and he could see she was someplace else. Clearly, Kyle Mercer's memories of death and betrayal had brought back some of her own. Brodie said in a low but firm voice, "You are relieved from duty."

"I'm getting myself out of here."

"You will obey my order and get yourself under control, soldier."

She took a deep breath and nodded.

Brodie glanced at Mercer, who seemed pleased that he didn't have to shoot the lady to show who was in charge here. But Mercer had summoned Emilio and his men, who were now on the platform, AKs at the ready, which Mercer must have found embarrassing considering the small problem with the lady. Mercer barked an order that caused the men to lower their rifles.

He walked over to Brodie and Taylor and said, "We are breaking camp. Leaving here. So if a missile strike or raid is planned on this camp, it will just hit another dry hole. Another Intel failure, which the Americans are getting used to. You two will come with me, as hostages, and as a further source of information—and a source of amusement."

Brodie wasn't looking forward to a trek through the jungle, and he wasn't sure Taylor was up to it. "Kyle, leave her here. Sink the boat. Whatever happens here, happens. But she needs to stay here."

"Chivalry, Mr. Brodie, is no longer required by the Army."

"I'll give you my word that I won't try to escape."

"You have a duty to escape and you are forbidden to give your word that you won't."

Taylor interjected, "We are not splitting up."

Mercer said, "There's your answer." He said something to Emilio, who motioned for them to put their hands on their heads.

Mercer said, "You'll wait in the stockade until we're ready to move."

"We need water."

"You'll have water on the march. Meanwhile, you'll enjoy your solitude in the stockade while we pack up and burn the camp." He seemed annoyed at having to do this, and annoyed that Brodie and Taylor's arrival—and maybe Ted Haggerty's arrival and sudden departure—made this necessary. So he said to them, to make them understand that he was not looking at this relocation as his defeat or as their victory: "I've scouted locations in this wilderness, and it's time to move anyway."

Brodie looked at him and they made eye contact. "You can run, Captain, but you can't hide from yourself."

Surprisingly, Mercer nodded in agreement. "But I can die like a soldier."

"But you won't die with honor. Only you can redeem yourself. And I really want you to do that."

"Thank you both for this talk. Sorry it didn't go well." He signaled to Emilio, who motioned them to follow.

Brodie and Taylor went with Emilio and the five men toward the stockade.

CHAPTER 45

Emilio, their appointed warden, ordered them into the stockade hut and watched as they snapped the padlocks on their shackles. Satisfied that his prisoners were secured, he stared at Maggie Taylor with a look that left no doubt about what he had in mind for later.

Brodie hoped that Señor Kyle had given Emilio instructions not to abuse the prisoners who were now his hostages. But Maggie hadn't helped the situation by telling Mercer that he had nobody to blame but himself for all that happened. Mercer knew that, of course, but he'd told himself a different story over the years, and he preferred his version. But, all things considered, Brodie was proud of Taylor for doing what had to be done, and he wished he'd done it himself.

Emilio said something to Taylor, and she replied. Then she asked for agua, and Emilio replied with a smile. He was not subtle.

Brodie noticed that Emilio's five men were not outside the door, so they must have gone off to help break camp. Or it was lunchtime. In any case, it looked like it would be just Emilio outside the door, guarding the two shackled prisoners—one of whom was probably going to get a beating, and the other was going to get raped. This was not good. So this was not going to happen.

Emilio glanced at his new watch, then said something to Taylor and left, closing the bamboo door behind him. Brodie had noted that there was no padlock on the door—which would have been redundant—so if Emilio was not posted at the door, Brodie and Taylor could theoretically drag or carry the log outside, and down to the river. No prison is escape-proof, and this one—which seemed more like a punishment hut than a prison—had been constructed to hold a single prisoner, which was why he and Taylor were sharing a set of leg irons attached to a weight that one person couldn't lift.

Well, this place had held CIA Officer Ted Haggerty, whose blood was still on the floor, but it wasn't going to hold Scott Brodie and Maggie Taylor.

The smell of cigarette smoke came into the hut, and Brodie looked at the bamboo door and saw movement through the open slats. Maybe Emilio.

Taylor was leaning back against the wall with her eyes closed. Brodie asked, "What did Emilio say to you?"

"The usual."

"Specifically."

"Scott, let me worry about—"

"I'm not looking for graphic descriptions—I'm looking for Intel."

"Okay . . . He said he was going to take me to the women's hut in about fifteen minutes for a shower and a good time in bed." She added, "And all the water I can drink. And some food."

"So we have fifteen minutes before he comes for you."

"I guess."

"That means he has the keys."

She nodded.

"Okay . . ." Emilio had the keys and he had a stiffy. And he was apparently alone. Sounded like all the qualifications Emilio needed to become a dead man.

Taylor said, "I know what you're thinking, Scott. I can't help you . . . I'm too weak."

"You're stronger than you know."

"I'll be stronger later . . . after I get some food and water."

"I don't want you to pay for that food and water. Or the shower."

She reminded him, "You said I should do what I have to do. I'm doing it."

"The situation has changed. We need to get out of here."

"You said nighttime was best."

"We don't have that long."

"Let me rest . . . I'll think about it."

"All right."

She put her hand on his arm. "Sorry I'm so out of shape . . ."

"You're in great shape."

"How are you doing?"

"I've got a few hours of gas left."

"I'll bring you some food and water."

He wasn't sure if Taylor could do that, or if she'd even be coming back. Time was running out faster than their options.

He changed the subject and said, "Well . . . we finally got the answers to everyone's questions."

"Worley already had those answers."

Brodie nodded. And so did Trent, and everyone else in the Intel establishment who had anything to do with Operation Flagstaff, including, apparently, the previous occupant of this cell. The only thing Worley and friends didn't know was the exact location of Camp Tombstone. But, assuming Haggerty had made some sort of report before he was captured, then Worley had a general idea of where Mercer's camp was, and it would take Worley about twelve hours to get recon drones on station—or less, if he could cut through the red tape. Then . . . either a Special Forces raid, which could take a week to put together, or a rain of Hellfire missiles, which could take days to get clearance for. Meanwhile, Maggie had fifteen minutes before getting raped, and Camp Tombstone was about to move.

Taylor had sent their last grid coordinates to Dombroski—who was now waiting for their sat phone call from Collins' aircraft. The question was, would Dombroski pass those coordinates on to Worley? Or would Worley call Dombroski for an update? Hard to know what these guys would do. They held the same rank in the same army, but that's where the similarities ended.

In any case, Kyle Mercer now believed that Camp Tombstone was on someone's radar and might soon become his graveyard. So he did what any good guerrilla commander would—you don't wait to see what's going to happen; you break camp and fade into the bush. And, if you're lucky enough to have hostages, you take them with you. So the good news was that Brodie's and Taylor's lives were now worth more than the bolívar. The bad news was that those lives were going to become a living hell. Just like Kyle Mercer's life had been for two years.

That was the small picture—a snapshot of him and Taylor. The bigger picture was no less disturbing. Long before Al Simpson happened to spot Kyle Mercer in a Caracas whorehouse, Brendan Worley and the Defense Intelligence Agency, and probably the CIA, knew that Kyle Mercer was in Venezuela for the purpose of killing Colonel Worley. And they hadn't shared that fact with the CID, whose job it was to apprehend Army personnel who'd committed or were about to commit a crime. There were other pieces of this disturbing picture that were now falling into place—the torture and murder of CIA Officer Robert Crenshaw, Operation Flagstaff, and now an interesting piece supplied by the fugitive himself: the helicopter ride to Bagram that, had it taken place, would have ended this case—one way or the other—before it began.

In cases like this, after you answer the question of *Why?* you need to ask the more legalistic questions of *Who knew what, and when did they know it?* Starting from the top: What did Army Chief of Staff Mendoza know? How about Provost Marshal General Hackett? And Colonel Dombroski? And then there was the chain of command in Afghanistan. Mercer's CO, Major Powell, knew enough to warn Captain Mercer about his suspicious helicopter ride. Apparently the people with the least information were Scott Brodie and Maggie Taylor—and she knew more than he did.

Brodie had no doubt that a lot of people were involved in Operation Flagstaff to one degree or another. Some people at the bottom, like Maggie Taylor, were just useful pawns. Some, like the guys on Mercer's team who carried out the pacifications, were just following illegal orders that they liked. People at the very top—the generals—were masters of willful ignorance, and they surrounded themselves with credible deniability. It was second-tier management—people like Colonel Worley—who were the movers and shakers of things like Flagstaff. In any army, the colonels who want to be generals are the hardest-working and most dedicated and devious staff officers. And if they happen to be Intel officers, like Worley, with connections to the CIA and other civilian or military agencies that are tasked with fighting the enemy in new and unconventional ways, then those guys are going to push the envelope, and when things go bad they have to cover their asses.

Meanwhile, no one had bothered to contact CID with the information that Captain Mercer might be in Caracas. But when Al Simpson did the right thing and reported his sighting to the Army, there was no choice but to make the search for Kyle Mercer official. And anyone who was tainted by Flagstaff could only hope that the CID failed in its mission so that

Brendan Worley and his friends in the Intel community could succeed in theirs—which was to find and silence Captain Mercer. Tangled webs indeed.

Taylor said, "Are you thinking about how to get out of here?"

"I know how to get out of here. I'm thinking about how we got here."

"I didn't mean to blame you."

"I blame me for not figuring all this out sooner."

"It's sort of moot, Scott. But you did think there was more to this than finding and apprehending a deserter."

"Right. And you made believe there wasn't."

"Sorry." She added, "Now that I know you better, I realize you're smarter than you look."

"You too."

She took his hand, leaned back, and closed her eyes.

Brodie returned to his thoughts. His instincts had been telling him from the beginning that there was more to this case, and that bringing Kyle Mercer before a court-martial was the worst possible outcome for a lot of people. And now he understood why.

So, what did that make Warrant Officers Scott Brodie and Maggie Taylor?

Unwanted characters in a long-running play where everyone else knew their parts. Or, to be less NYU and more CID, he and Taylor were a perfunctory legal response, sent on a mission that was presumed fated to fail. Sent for the sake of appearances.

Well, if that was the thinking in the Pentagon or in Langley, they should have sent someone else. Not to be egotistical.

But Dombroski, who Brodie truly believed had no knowledge of the bigger picture, had sent his best man. Again, not to be egotistical, but who else would you send to Caracas on the most high-profile case of the decade, if not the century? And if Brodie took all this information and put it in the right order, then Maggie Taylor being assigned as his partner a few months ago was not a random occurrence. If Trent and his pals were thinking long-range, they were concerned that CID would eventually get on this case. They might or might not have known where Kyle Mercer was at that point, but some inquiries would tell them that if CID got the Mercer case, then

CID would want to assign one of their few combat veterans—someone who could think like Kyle Mercer and who could talk his talk, man-to-man, if the time ever came. And this needed to be a top investigator, an exceptional detective, and a man who had a few snatch jobs under his belt, a fearless rogue who took chances but got the job done. And that would be . . . well, Chief Warrant Officer Brodie.

And somehow the CIA got their asset, Maggie Taylor, assigned to Warrant Officer Brodie before the CID even knew where Mercer was. Taylor might have been part of the process herself, asking to be partnered with Scott Brodie. And voilà—everything fell into place, and the CIA could count on having eyes and ears on the ground in the unlikely—but possible—event that the CID would eventually get a tip on Mercer's whereabouts, and that Scott Brodie would get the case. Or . . . maybe it was vice versa: The CIA had influenced the decision to put Brodie on the case because Brodie's partner, Maggie Taylor, was their man. Or, in this case, their lady. Trent's lady.

If even part of this was true, he had to admit that the Agency had some good thinkers onboard. Probably Trent, in this case.

He said to Taylor, "Did you ask to be partnered with me?"

"I did."

"Why?"

"Trent told me to do it."

"Right. If you're going to place a mole in an organization, you put the mole next to the fastest-rising star in that organization."

"I'd never even heard of you. And when I asked around . . . I got mixed reviews."

"Really?"

"Everything from brilliant and tough, to arrogant asshole."

"Some people are jealous."

"A female investigator did say you were charming, handsome, and always a gentleman."

"Who was that?"

"Not telling. But she also said you never showed unwanted attention toward female personnel. I liked that, so . . ."

Brodie knew that even if he looked like Stanley Dombroski, Taylor was under order from Trent to apply for the job. This manipulation of the CID by the CIA was disturbing. But that was the least of his problems today. Nevertheless, he asked, "Who was the lady?"

"No one you slept with."

"That narrows it down."

"I'm sure."

"Sorry about my unwanted attention last night."

"Not entirely unwanted. And not all on you."

"We'll wait until we have dinner at your place."

She nodded, then said, "A pigeon."

"For dinner?"

"No. How the hell can you mistake a heron for a pigeon?"

"I got it right on the second guess."

"You only get one guess, Scott."

"Mercer was on to us anyway."

They heard Emilio's voice outside, and it sounded like a one-way conversation, so maybe he was on a walkie. Brodie asked, "Ready to bust out of here?"

"I don't know . . ."

"You can do this. Ready?"

Brodie got himself into a crouch and worked his hands under the log, and Taylor did the same.

He said, "Think of this log as one of your Civil Affairs people with a sucking chest wound who needs to be lifted onto a medevac."

She nodded.

But don't think of what's going to happen to you if this doesn't work. "Okay, one, two, lift!"

They lifted the log, but Brodie found it heavier than last time, meaning he was weaker, and he could tell that Taylor was drawing on the last of her strength.

"Hold on." He walked the log around so his end was about three feet from the door. "Call for Emilio to come in."

"Scott . . . my knees are buckling . . ."

"You have to get this guy on the chopper, Maggie. He's bleeding out. Call Emilio."

She took a deep breath, but instead of calling she asked, "Are we going to kill him?"

"No, we're just going to crush his fucking skull. Call him."

"My arms . . ."

"Kneel. We'll get this on our shoulders. You can do it."

They both knelt and pushed up on the log until it rested on their right shoulders. "Okay . . . stand."

They both got themselves into a standing position, and Taylor said, "That's better . . ."

Emilio must have heard them talking and he shouted something through the door.

Taylor took a deep breath and said something that included the words "agua" and "baño."

Brodie saw Emilio through the narrow slats of bamboo as he approached the door. Brodie hoped for two things—that Emilio was alone, and that Emilio had the keys. One out of two would not be a win.

Brodie whispered, "When I say go, you step forward smartly, soldier, with a full thirty-six-inch stride."

"Okay . . ."

The door opened, and Emilio stepped inside and squinted in the dim light. "Qué?"

"Go."

Brodie lunged forward holding the log tightly on his shoulder, and the end of the log connected with Emilio's face, crushing his nose and jaw, which Brodie actually heard cracking.

Emilio fell back like he'd been hit in the face with a two-hundred-pound log. He was half in and half out of the door, and Brodie quickly scanned the small clearing in front of the hut. No one there, but he heard voices in the distance.

He glanced back at Taylor, who had sunk to her knees. "Okay, let it roll off."

She let it drop to the floor, and her end fell on one of Emilio's legs, causing him to let out a groan. Brodie's end came down on Emilio's chest. He rolled the log off and quickly went through Emilio's pocket, found the keys, and unlocked the padlock on his shackle, then handed the keys to Taylor.

While she unlocked her shackle, Brodie retrieved his Glock from Emilio's waistband and found the extra magazine in Emilio's pocket. He grabbed the chain with both hands and told Taylor to do the same, and together they dragged the log out of the doorway and into the hut; then Brodie grabbed Emilio by the ankles, pulled him inside, and closed the door.

Brodie gave Emilio a quick glance. He was still breathing and his face was a mass of blood, with one eye bulging out of his broken eye socket.

Taylor knelt beside Emilio and unstrapped Brodie's watch, telling the dying man, "You won't need this where you're going." She handed the watch to Brodie, then went through Emilio's pockets, finding Brodie's Swiss Army knife, which she kept, then a half bottle of water, which she drank from and passed to Brodie, who finished it. Taylor unclipped Emilio's walkie from his belt and clipped it on her T-shirt, then handed Emilio's sheathed KA-BAR knife to Brodie, who stuck it in his pocket. She gave Emilio a final pat-down and located a Zippo lighter, which she passed to Brodie. "You want his cigarettes?"

"Only if they're edible. Okay, let's get this log back where it was."

"Why?"

"To cover the scene of the crime."

Taylor nodded, and they each grabbed a chain and dragged the log to where it had been. Then they covered Emilio with armfuls of palm fronds, so if anyone poked their head in and didn't see Emilio in the dim light, they'd think someone had taken the prisoners somewhere else. Brodie looked at the mound of fronds, which was moving. "It would be better if he wasn't breathing." He looked at Taylor.

They made eye contact, and she shook her head. "We don't do that."

"All right . . . but—"

"We don't become them. We did what we had to do."

Taylor was showing great restraint. Brodie, on the other hand, wanted to cut Emilio's throat, but only to minimize the danger to themselves. He knew where he'd learned this stuff, but he didn't know when it had become part of him. Brodie's pacifist parents had forbade him even playing soldier. Goes to show you. It's baked into the Y chromosome.

Brodie heard someone speaking in Spanish, and he pulled his Glock and turned quickly toward the door.

Taylor said, "It's his walkie." She listened, then scanned the channels. "Just normal chatter."

"Okay. Keep monitoring." He moved to the closed door and listened. "Okay . . . let's go."

They exited the hut and closed the door. Brodie looked around the clearing to see if anyone had left an AK behind, but no such luck. He motioned Taylor to follow, and they began moving in single file down the narrow trail, with Brodie holding his Glock at his side.

Taylor came up behind him and whispered, "Where are we going?"

"Two choices. The jungle or the river." He stopped and they both crouched. Brodie said, "The jungle is all around us, and it's easy to get into but not so easy to get out of." He listened a moment, then said, "If we get a boat, we can go downriver to Kavak—if we think Kavak is safe. Or we can go upriver and get close to that jungle landing strip we saw." He let her know, "Kavak is a crapshoot. Finding that airstrip and calling Worley for a plane is a roll of the dice. Take your pick."

"Scott, hate to mention this, but we don't have a sat phone to make the call."

"Right. I forgot to mention—we can see if Mercer is still on that fishing platform with our sat phone."

"Are you joking or crazy?"

"Neither. Maybe both."

They remained crouched, listening to the sounds around them. The firing from the range had stopped, so Mercer must have called a halt to the training, and everyone was preparing to evacuate the camp. Or they were all going to lunch. Hard to figure out what was going on in Camp Tombstone. But if anyone was coming to relieve Emilio so that he could take a shower with the lady prisoner, that relief man would be coming up this path. Eventually someone would find Emilio, and Brodie wanted to be long gone by that time.

"Scott?"

"Could you make a trek through the jungle?"

"To where?"

He'd given this some thought and replied, "Brazil is less than a hundred miles to the border. A four- or five-day hike."

She thought about that. "I took a survival course at Bragg."

"How'd you do?"

"Like I do everything else. Just fine."

"You eat a snake?"

"I did."

"Good. But . . . the river is an easier way out of here if we had a boat. But not so easy to get the boat . . ." He looked at her. "I say we go for the whole enchilada. We go see if Mercer is still communing with nature on the fishing platform. If he is, we have him, the sat phone, and the boat. If he's not there, we still have the boat."

"If the boat's still there."

"Right . . . but there may be other boats. Mercer's boats on the mudflat. The river is the way out, Maggie. If nothing else, we can swim across and be on the other bank, away from these fucking lunatics." He asked, "Can you swim?"

"I can. And so can the crocs and the piranhas."

"We're down to only bad options."

She nodded and seemed to be considering those bad options.

Brodie was confident that they could survive four or five days in the jungle by living off the land. But the land could also live off them. He pictured himself in the warm embrace of a python. He recalled Collins' advice on that subject: Take the river. He also recalled his E&E takeaway—the escape part is easy compared to the evasion part. And taking the camp commander as a prisoner along the way was not part of the course.

Taylor suddenly stood. "Let's see if Mercer or the boat is still there."

He looked at her. "You sure?"

"What's the goal? Survival or completing the mission?"

"Both."

"Then let's do it."

"You understand that if we get captured, we're going to pay the price for killing Emilio?"

"Scott, I understand we're as good as dead here. Let's go."

"Okay." Brodie continued down the trail, moving quickly, but slow enough to take in his surroundings. He found himself growing fatigued, and the heat was becoming oppressive. He glanced back at Taylor a few times; she was keeping up, apparently reenergized and renewed.

They reached a cross trail, and Brodie whispered, "If we continue on, this will take us too close to the center of the camp—where we saw the ladies' dorm. We need to make our way down to the river. Once we get there, we might have a few other options."

She nodded, then put the walkie to her ear. "Nothing unusual. Wait . . . someone is trying to call Emilio . . ."

"He's sleeping. Let's go."

They moved quickly downslope toward the river, which would be a ten- or fifteen-minute walk. As they came to a bend in the path, someone rounded the bend coming toward them. Brodie dropped quickly into a kneeling firing stance and almost squeezed off a round, but then saw it was a Pemón woman with a wicker basket on her head of what looked like laundry.

Brodie lowered the gun and stood. The woman stopped, and they looked at each other. The woman noticed Taylor, who said, "Buenos días, señora."

The woman returned the greeting, and they all stood there. Well, what do you say after "Buenos días"? "Come here often?"

Taylor spoke to the woman, who replied, and Taylor said to Brodie, "Juanita wishes us a safe journey home."

"Right . . ." And the best way to ensure that would be to coldcock Juanita and lay her in the brush.

Juanita was keeping eye contact with Brodie so she didn't have to notice the gun again.

"Scott?"

"Okay . . ." He gave Juanita a smile and a salute and moved past her, with Taylor behind him. He said, "No good deed goes unpunished."

"Every good deed is recorded by the angels."

"I'll check on that when I get there."

They continued down the path and Brodie glimpsed the river ahead. As they got closer, he could also see the mudflat they'd seen from their boat— the mudflat where Carmen had disembarked when she and Mercer had come from Kavak. Brodie had his bearings now, and he quickened his pace toward the river—their jungle highway out of there. Or their path to glory, if Kyle Mercer was still on the fishing platform downriver.

Taylor was right behind him, monitoring the walkie and urging him to move faster.

As they neared the mudflat, he slowed down as he'd been trained to do when approaching a river, stream, road, clearing, or structure. He stopped, motioned Taylor down, and dropped to his knee. They both looked and listened; then Brodie stood and continued.

They reached the natural clearing around the mudflat and did an eye-recon. There didn't seem to be anyone in the area except a few howler monkeys in the trees who didn't react well to the intrusion of two other primates. Brodie wanted to tell them to shut the fuck up, but they probably only understood Spanish.

There were a lot of footprints in the mud, probably Pemón, but also boot prints. He moved cautiously toward the river, about thirty feet away, and noticed a large snake slithering into the water.

Taylor whispered, "Scott—over here."

He turned and saw Taylor pointing to a pair of boats—similar to their flat-sterned canoe—lying in a thick patch of vines. Both boats had oars in them and outboard motors. He nodded, then moved slowly across the mud to the riverbank. He looked both ways, then motioned for Taylor to join him.

She crossed the mud and looked where he was pointing.

About three hundred meters downriver was the fishing platform, also known as the observation post. A man was standing on the platform. It was Kyle Mercer. He seemed to be talking on a walkie—or maybe abusing Worley again on the sat phone. Hard to tell at that distance.

Taylor held her walkie to her ear and scanned the channels. "I hear him . . . he's asking . . . he wants everyone to report to the . . . salón . . . the dining hall. He will speak to them there." She kept listening, then clipped the walkie to her T-shirt.

Brodie said, "He's probably going to announce the move. The good news is that they'll all be in one place. The bad news is that Emilio is someplace else."

Taylor nodded, then glanced at the two motorized canoes. "We scuttle one and take the other."

"Right." Brodie walked to the canoes and checked out their fuel tanks, finding them both half-full—or half-empty if you weren't having a good day. He pulled the starter cord a few inches on one of the motors and cut it with the KA-BAR, throwing the starter handle into the brush. Taylor also cut off the bow line and wrapped it around her waist in case they needed extra rope for something—like hog-tying Kyle Mercer. Brodie said, "Okay . . . ready to launch?"

"Where are we going, Scott?"

"Upriver, downriver, or across the river and into the woods toward Brazil. Whatever way will put distance between us and Camp Tombstone."

"I thought we agreed to try to take Mercer." She reminded him, "The whole enchilada."

"Now that we're here and we have this boat, I'll settle for half an enchilada." He added, "We're almost out of here."

She didn't reply, and they both grabbed the bow line and dragged the boat the short distance across the mud to the river.

Taylor looked downriver and said, "He's still there, Scott." She reminded him, "We have a weapon, and we didn't see a weapon on him."

Brodie looked at the fishing platform and could make out the lone figure of Kyle Mercer, his back to them. Tempting, but . . . "Doesn't mean he doesn't have one. We need to wait here until he's gone."

"No. We need to go get him while he's there."

She was starting to sound like Scott Brodie, and he wasn't sure he liked that. "He could turn around any minute. He doesn't need his binoculars to see two gringos coming toward him in a boat."

"Those bastards captured us there, and we're going to capture him there."

Really? "I think upriver would be a good way to go."

"We don't know what's upriver except for that landing strip, and we don't have a sat phone to call Worley."

"Okay . . . so we'll wait for Mercer to go address the troops, then we drift downriver with the current, and when we've gotten clear of this place we motor up and head toward Kavak to check out the situation. If we don't like what we see, we keep going until we find something that looks like civilization."

"That's not what we agreed to do."

Brodie glanced back at the fishing platform.

Taylor said, "Fate, or whatever you believe in, has given us this one opportunity. He's there, and we're here. We'll never see him again."

Brodie thought about that. "Right." If Worley found Mercer, he'd make sure Kyle Mercer never made it back to the States. If another CID team found Mercer, Dombroski would buy the team beers in the O Club and not invite him or Taylor. If nobody found Kyle Mercer, he'd be free to continue his deranged mission to undermine American interests in Venezuela. Maybe more importantly, Kyle Mercer would continue to get away with murder.

On that subject, Taylor said, "Even if we can't capture him, we can kill him."

Now you're talking. That would be easy. Or easier.

"Scott?"

"Okay . . . anchors aweigh."

They pulled the boat into the river and pushed off on the oars until they caught the current and began drifting downstream. Taylor turned down the volume on the walkie.

They steered the boat with the two oars and the outboard rudder, keeping it close to the shoreline, but away from underwater obstacles. Brodie figured it would take about five minutes to reach the platform. Maybe less. If Mercer left the platform, they could conceivably beach the boat and follow him—depending on how crazy they felt at that moment. If he turned and saw them coming, Mercer had a few courses of action: run, get on his walkie, or pull a weapon if he had one. Then it would be a shoot-out, with Mercer holding the high ground while his sitting ducks drifted toward him. The only thing that could keep Mercer from hitting them was if he was laughing too hard.

Taylor leaned toward him and said, "We should go under the platform, secure the boat with a line, then come onto the shore, up the ramp, and tell him to surrender or die."

"Maybe I should pull my gun first."

"If you have to shoot him, shoot him."

"That makes a lot of noise. Okay, let's see how this goes."

They were within a hundred meters of the platform now and Brodie could still see Mercer, still holding his walkie to his ear. He also saw the boat they'd taken from Kavak, tied to the platform. If they killed or captured Mercer, they could put him in either boat and head upriver toward the jungle landing strip, call Worley on the sat phone—assuming Mercer still had it—and make the rendezvous with Worley's Otter. What could possibly go wrong with that plan?

They were within twenty meters of the platform now, and Brodie could see only the top of Mercer's head—then Mercer turned, and Brodie drew his Glock. But then Mercer's head disappeared, and Brodie guessed that he'd sat down.

They steered between two pilings and the boat was suddenly under the dock, where it hit bottom with a thump that Brodie thought was as loud as a landing craft hitting the beach. Not waiting for Taylor to find something to tie the line to, he scrambled out of the boat and made directly for the open space between the platform and the riverbank. He found himself slipping in the mud, then got his traction and came out on the shore, jumped on the ramp, and pulled his Glock and charged up to the platform. The element of surprise.

And there was Kyle Mercer, sitting in the same chair, his back to him. Unfortunately, there was another man at the table sitting in a chair facing Mercer, and also facing Brodie. *Surprise!* The man's eyes doubled in size, but he recovered from his shock and went for the gun in his shoulder holster.

Brodie fired at his center mass, and the man did a backflip, taking himself and the chair over the side of the platform with a splash. The sound of the gun blast echoed into the trees. Mercer didn't even turn his head as Brodie yelled, "Surrender or die."

Kyle Mercer, Delta Force, had another idea, and he grabbed the table with both hands, spun, and swung it at Brodie, who ducked and squeezed off a round that would have hit Mercer in the chest, except that Mercer had done an impressive back roll over the edge of the platform and into the river.

Taylor ran onto the platform and took in the situation quickly.

Brodie flipped his gun to her. "Cover!" He dived off the platform and began swimming toward Mercer, who was headed quickly downstream, doing a backstroke that was as impressive as his backflip.

Mercer's jungle boots were slowing him down, and he couldn't get them off and swim at the same time. Brodie kicked off his running shoes, and within a minute he was within arm's reach of Mercer.

Mercer sensed Brodie behind him and suddenly got upright, revealing a long knife in his right hand that gleamed in the sunlight. He brought the knife down toward Brodie's head, and Brodie did his own backflip in the water as he drew Emilio's KA-BAR and plunged it toward Mercer's submerged abdomen, but the current had pulled Mercer back about a foot out of reach.

As Brodie came up, he saw that Mercer was making toward the shore, and he followed.

Mercer found traction on the river bottom before Brodie did and he scrambled up the bank, but instead of running into the trees, he stood on the shore facing Brodie, who stopped about twenty feet from him in waist-high water.

Both men were breathing heavily, both holding their knives, and both keeping eye contact.

Brodie glanced back at the platform, but he didn't see Taylor. He took a deep breath and said, "The choice, Kyle, was surrender or die."

"I give you the same choice."

"Okay, I surrender. Come and get me."

"I don't have to. There'll be thirty armed men coming to get you in about five minutes. All I have to do is sit here."

More like ten or fifteen minutes from the camp. And possibly the sound of Brodie's two shots had not reached the camp, or if they had, no one in Camp Tombstone thought anything of it. But there could be some truth to Mercer's statement, so Brodie did what he did best—he taunted him. "You're the ball-less wonder, Kyle. Not Worley. Come on, asshole. You got a knife, I got a knife. No gun."

"I know that. If you had your gun, you'd have pulled it—because it's you who have no balls."

"I'm chasing you, Kyle, you're not chasing me." Brodie started walking through the water toward Mercer.

Mercer dropped into a crouch, his knife out in front of him. "I'm gonna put your head on a pike."

"I'm gonna put your dick over my fireplace."

Brodie didn't have time for a long knife fight if Mercer's men were on the way, so he had to make this a short knife fight. He pulled off his T-shirt and wrapped it around his left hand and forearm. He thought Mercer would do the same, but he didn't. Maybe he'd missed the knife-fight class. That would be good.

Brodie was in knee-deep water now, less than ten feet from Mercer. He again glanced at the platform; no sign of Taylor. The platform was about a hundred and fifty feet away, just at the edge of the Glock's effective range. Taylor might be lying prone on the deck, practicing fire discipline and noise discipline. Which was good. But if Brodie got any closer to Mercer, she'd have to be Annie Oakley to hit the right guy.

Mercer asked, "Having second thoughts?"

"I'm thinking you're stalling for time so your thugs can get here."

"Either way, Mr. Brodie, you're dead or you'll wish you were."

Brodie had no idea where Taylor was—maybe she'd found the sat phone and was calling Worley or Dombroski—or Trent. That wasn't a nice thought.

Mercer said, "I'm not coming to you. You come to me."

Brodie had to make a decision. If he closed in on Mercer, then Taylor—wherever she was—wouldn't have a clear shot. Mercer couldn't be sure his men were on their way, but there was nothing lost for him in prolonging the dick-wagging. So Brodie had to finish this. He stepped out of the river and onto the black, slimy bank, his knife thrust in front of him.

Mercer backed up until he came in contact with a wall of vegetation. He had no room to fall back in a knife fight, which was a disadvantage, but he was on higher ground, which was an advantage.

Brodie moved a little closer and he saw Mercer smiling, which was what you were supposed to do before a knife fight to mess with the other guy's head. Apparently Mercer had taken that class.

Brodie returned the smile and said, "Al Simpson told me you played a lot of Call of Duty when you were a kid. That's pretty lame, Kyle."

"Fuck you."

"Maybe your father can work that into your eulogy."

Brodie moved within knife thrust of Mercer and waited for him to make the first move, which, if it was the wrong move, would be his last.

Mercer stared at Brodie, then seemed to relax, which caused Brodie some concern. Had Mercer heard his men coming?

Then Mercer said, "Where's your gun?"

Mercer hadn't seen Brodie toss it to Taylor after Mercer back-flipped into the river. Brodie replied, "None of your fucking business."

"No, what I mean, Scott, is you're supposed to ask me—'Where's your gun, Kyle?'"

Oh.

Mercer switched the knife to his left hand, reached into the pouch pocket of his camo pants, and pulled out a big automatic that looked to Brodie like a Desert Eagle. Good gun.

Mercer said, "And now I have you where I want you." He added, "Smart guy."

Brodie couldn't think of a good response to that. "My bad" wouldn't begin to describe how stupid he felt. He hadn't seen a gun when he and Taylor were taken to Mercer, but it's the guns you don't see that can kill you. Shit happens.

Mercer tried to make him feel better. "Balls are good, and you have balls. But you forgot to bring your gun and your brains to this knife fight."

"I'm still wanting a knife fight, Kyle."

"Next time. Meanwhile, throw your knife at least ten feet away, put your hands on your head, drop to your knees, and wait for further instructions. Now."

Brodie hesitated long enough to get further instructions from Mercer. "I won't kill you. Promise. But I will put a round through your right knee. Then we wait here for my very pissed off jungle fighters."

Brodie threw his knife—Emilio's knife—to the side, put his hands on his head, and dropped to his knees.

Mercer asked, "Where did you get the knife?"

"I don't answer questions, Kyle. I ask them."

"Then why didn't you ask me where my gun was?"

"That was going to be my next question."

"Answer this, wise guy—how did you get out of the stockade?"

"Ask Emilio if he checked to see if my padlock was locked."

"All right. Where is your lady?"

"Emilio took her for a shower."

Mercer nodded, so apparently no one had yet checked on the stockade, or if they had, they hadn't noticed it was a crime scene—they thought Emilio had gone AWOL with the new meat. And that seemed to be what Mercer thought. Meanwhile . . . where the hell was she? AWOL?

Mercer said, "You left that nice lady for Emilio to have?"

"Chivalry is dead, asshole."

Mercer didn't seem to believe that Brodie had run off without his partner. But in case that was true, he said, "You'll soon be together again. You
and Ms. Taylor have a lot more information to give me. Full debriefing. And
we'll play a version of that Arabian Nights game—for every good story you
two give me, she'll sleep alone that night. When you run out of good info, or
if I find out your story is bullshit, she'll have company all night."

"You really are sick, Kyle. Worley was right."

"Worley is the reason I haven't been myself for awhile."

Brodie didn't respond, but he listened for the sound of men coming
through the bush, then glanced at the fishing platform to see if Mercer's men
showed up there. Maybe Taylor had somehow gotten caught by them. He
could see the boat they'd taken from Kavak, still tied to the platform. But he
couldn't see into the darkness under the platform. Was the other boat still
there? Had Taylor taken it and left him to water-wrestle with a well-trained
killer? Was it something he said?

"Did you hear me?"

"Right. Worley sucks. He needs to pay—"

"Let me worry about that. Okay, Scott, you don't look comfortable. Lie
face down in the mud, hands on the back of your head."

"I think you have to shoot me, Kyle."

"Okay." He seemed to be thinking about that. "Stand up so I can blow
your kneecap off."

"How about I stand up, turn around, and bend over so you can kiss my
ass?"

Mercer took a step closer to Brodie. "How about I put a round right between your legs, about an inch below your balls? Am I that good a shot?"

"I am," said Taylor, and fired a round between Mercer's legs, which
kicked up some mud as she shouted, "Drop it! Drop it or I put one in your
fucking head!"

Mercer was partially blocking Brodie's view, but he saw Taylor step out
of the trees in a two-hand firing stance. "Drop it!"

Mercer was doing the math—spin, aim, fire.

Brodie thought he was going to go for it, or at least fail to comply, but

Mercer knew that the CID lady meant business, as they say, and Mercer threatening to kill Brodie would not lead to a standoff—it would lead to a bullet in his head.

Brodie stood and encouraged him, "Drop it, Kyle. It's over."

Mercer let the gun fall from his hand.

Taylor went into cop mode. "Down! Down! Face down!"

Mercer dropped to his knees and lay face down in the mud.

Brodie quickly snatched Mercer's gun, backed off, and pointed the big Desert Eagle at him, saying to Taylor, "He's covered."

She stuck the Glock in the back of her waistband, then unwrapped the line that she'd taken from the boat and crouched beside Mercer, tying his hands behind his back. She remembered to say, "You're under arrest."

Brodie said, "Leave his legs free to travel."

Taylor stood and shouted to Mercer, "Roll and stand!"

Mercer rolled on his back and sat up. Taylor and Brodie arm-locked him and got him to his feet.

Brodie pulled on his wet T-shirt while Taylor frisked the prisoner, finding only the knife and a wet handkerchief.

Brodie asked Taylor, "You get the sat phone?"

Taylor patted her pocket. "It was lying on the deck."

"Okay. We're in business. Except we have to relocate. His men could be coming to see what the shooting is all about."

She nodded and glanced at the tree line, then down the shore at the fishing platform. She took the walkie off her T-shirt and scanned the channels.

Mercer spoke for the first time. "When they get here, I advise you both to put a bullet in your heads. That's what I should have done to save myself from two years of torture, starvation, and rape."

Brodie glanced at Taylor, who looked more angry than frightened. She said to Mercer, "Shut up unless I ask you a question."

She was in total cop mode, noted Brodie, but this wasn't a drug bust back in the States. This was a snatch job on Mercer's home turf. Time to move.

Taylor told Mercer to get back on his face, then motioned to Brodie, and they walked out of earshot of Mercer. She said, "Escape and evasion is your department."

"Okay, what do you hear on the walkie?"

"Hard to follow . . . a few guys are asking where is Señor Kyle. I guess they're waiting for him in the mess hall."

"What's for lunch?"

"Us. If they find we're missing." She added, "I heard someone ask about Emilio again. And about another guy, David, who may be the guy you shot."

"Right. David is floating past Kavak by now." Brodie also thought about the Pemón woman and hoped she didn't have lunch duty today.

"Scott?"

"Well . . . this bastard is not going to come along willingly. He's waiting for his posse to arrive, and he's an anvil around our necks."

Taylor glanced at Mercer, still lying face down. "What are you saying, Scott?"

"I'll do it."

"We can't do that. I won't let you do that."

"We discussed killing him."

"Only if he presented a danger to us. You know the rules."

"Maggie . . . we have three choices—try to take him with us, leave him here alive, or leave him here dead. The first choice could leave *us* here dead."

"I understand that. But he is our prisoner, and you have to forget what he's done and remember what was done to him. He served honorably until he didn't. We are not his judge, jury, and executioner."

"He would be ours if the situation was reversed."

"Doesn't matter what *he'd* do. It matters what *we* do."

"He cut Ted Haggerty's throat, for God's sake. And he tortured and killed Robert Crenshaw, and dismembered one of his guys who raped Carmen. And he's done a lot more that we don't know about." He reminded her, "Your friends in the CIA want him dead. Do Trent a favor, and do yourself a favor. Do Worley and everyone a favor—including Kyle Mercer."

"Are you stooping to the level of Trent and Worley?"

"Just for today."

"When you cross that line, Scott, you can never go back. Ask me about that."

"Okay . . . but I can't let him go, so . . . we'll take him with us."

"That's the only right thing."

"Tell me that when his posse is on our tail and he's dragging his ass and calling out to them."

"I know how to handle a prisoner."

"Good. Start with a swift kick to his nuts. You usually get compliance."

"I'm in charge of the prisoner. You're in charge of E&E. What do we do?"

"Okay . . . I'll go get the boat. You get him on his feet and into shallow water where he'll be easier to handle. Hold his head under if he drags his ass. Piranha only take little bites, but watch out for the crocs and snakes. We'll meet up, put him into the boat, and off we go upriver toward that airstrip." He added, "I'll call Worley from the boat. We should be in Bogotá, Panama, or Gitmo in time for cocktails."

Taylor didn't reply, and she walked back to Mercer.

———

Taylor pulled Mercer's knife from her pocket and cut a strip of cloth from his pant leg to use as a gag.

He said to her, "When my men get their hands on you, they'll make you dance naked every night before they each tell you what they want—a blow job, anal sex, or vaginal sex."

"Your men are not very nice, Captain."

"You'll pray for death, or maybe you'd enjoy it."

"What happened to Captain Mercer?"

"He died in Afghanistan."

She shoved his wet handkerchief in his mouth, then tied the gag tightly around his head. "Let's get up." She tried to help him up but he resisted, so she rolled him on his side and threw a roundhouse punch into his groin.

Mercer screamed in pain through his gag, but the sound didn't travel very far.

"Okay? Do we stand, or do we get another one?"

Mercer was more cooperative on the next try, and Taylor got him on his feet.

She took the end of the rope binding his hands and passed it between his legs, then led him toward the river and into the shallows, then upstream toward the fishing platform. She could see Brodie, who was more than halfway to the platform, alternating between wading in the water and swimming where it was deeper.

She glanced at the shoreline near the platform, scanning for Mercer's men, and she noticed that Mercer was doing the same thing. Eventually someone would come to look for him. This was going to be close.

———

Brodie reached the platform and quickly checked the fuel level of the boat they'd taken from Kavak. Half-full, same as the one they'd taken from the mudflat. He stood in the waist-high water, pulled his knife, and cut the starter cord, then went under the platform to the other boat and saw that Taylor had tied the bow line to a supporting stilt. He cut the line and dragged the boat off the river bottom and out into the current, where he scrambled aboard.

The boat drifted downstream. He didn't want to start the motor, so he paddled with an oar, canoe-style, like he'd done as a kid upstate, keeping the boat close to the riverbank but away from the shallow bottom.

He saw Taylor ahead, making her way toward him with Mercer in tow. The prisoner seemed to be compliant, but not moving at his best speed, so Taylor was yanking on the rope to adjust his balls and his attitude.

Brodie glanced back at the fishing platform, expecting to see the boys with the toys, just like earlier this morning, but there was no one there. Must be a good lunch.

Brodie suspected that Mercer's men were not used to showing initiative and that they were smoking and joking at lunch, faithfully following their last orders, which were to wait for Señor Kyle. Hopefully, they'd still be waiting when dinner was served. If not . . . he and Taylor had a problem. The next five or ten minutes were critical.

He and Taylor were about twenty feet apart, and Mercer, who Brodie noticed was gagged, didn't seem to want a canoe ride, so he stopped and played donkey. Taylor swung around and apparently kicked his legs from under him, and he fell face first into the water. With his arms tied behind his back, he wasn't getting up so easily, especially with Taylor holding his head.

She wasn't actually waterboarding him, but maybe she should let him up for air before he drowned. But she held him there, and Brodie could see Mercer's legs and heavy boots thrashing.

Brodie knew that Taylor could be tough on the job, taking no shit from the guys they'd arrested at Fort Campbell. But he was certain that Taylor was giving Kyle Mercer a little extra attention because of the attention he'd given her. Yet she didn't want to terminate Kyle Mercer with extreme prejudice, as her CIA former boyfriend would say. She had a soft spot, so maybe she should let the poor bastard breathe.

Just as Brodie was about to say something, she pulled Mercer up by his T-shirt.

Mercer looked half-drowned, because he was, but he also looked compliant.

Brodie steered the drifting boat closer to the riverbank where the water was only a few feet deep, and Taylor intersected with Mercer in tow. They wrangled him onboard, and Taylor completed the hog-tying as Brodie started the motor and turned the boat upstream. Good-bye, Camp Tombstone.

Brodie asked, "You okay?"

"I got bit by something, but the water was refreshing."

"I don't think Señor Kyle would agree."

"He was being stubborn."

"He should thank you for bringing him home alive."

"We're not actually home yet, Scott."

Brodie steered toward the opposite bank, away from the fishing platform, which was still ahead of them. He glanced at the platform. If they could get around the next bend in the river, they were safe from AK-47 fire. But if anyone from the camp spotted them going upriver, Mercer's men would surely follow the river on foot, and if the river made more bends that those guys knew about, it was possible for them to intercept the boat at some point. But if they knew that Señor Kyle was onboard, they probably wouldn't fire on the boat. Or . . . they'd decide that killing the gringos was better for them than trying to rescue Señor Kyle. Hard to get into the heads of men like those who had seen too much and done too much. For them, there was no line that they had to worry about crossing.

Brodie said to Taylor, "You took down a Delta Force guy."

She didn't reply.

Brodie looked at Mercer lying hog-tied across the narrow bench seats—just as he'd imagined him in his Mission: Accomplished fantasy. Now that it was reality, Brodie almost felt sorry for the poor bastard, who'd gone through hell—who'd been a soldier once, and had served his country.

Taylor seemed to know what Brodie was thinking and said, "You were right. He didn't betray his country. His country betrayed him."

Brodie nodded. That sounded like the last line in Captain Mercer's attorney's closing argument.

They passed the fishing platform and continued upstream to the mudflat, which looked as deserted as when they'd left it.

They came to a bend in the river and lost sight of the mudflat and the fishing platform.

Not home free, but a phone call away. He said, "Hope you still have that sat phone."

"High and dry." She pulled the phone out of her bra.

Brodie said, "This is a good time to call Worley."

"It's never a good time to call Worley, Scott, but it's a good time to arrange a flight out of here." She handed him the sat phone. "You do the honors."

He took the phone, but before he dialed, he said, "We did it, Maggie. Couldn't have done it without you."

"My next partner will appreciate me even more."

Brodie smiled and dialed Brendan Worley. He pictured the Otter landing on the jungle airstrip and taking them away to someplace where he could get a hot shower and a cold beer.

He glanced at Mercer again. Would Brendan Worley be happy to see Kyle Mercer alive and well? Probably not.

So maybe home was not a phone call away.

The phone rang, and continued to ring.

CHAPTER 46

Brodie shut off the sat phone. Worley would, of course, think it was Mercer calling from that number, and for some reason Colonel Worley didn't want to speak to his old partner in crime. He looked at Mercer lying face down across the seats, hands and legs hog-tied, gag in his mouth. The situation had changed since that last call.

Worley didn't know that. But Mercer did.

Taylor said, "Call Dombroski."

Brodie twisted the throttle and the boat picked up speed. "You always make the most important call first. The call that can get you home quickest."

"Dombroski can call Worley."

"Dombroski can talk a battery dead." He opened the gas tank and pulled out the dipstick. "Fuel's a problem too."

"What's the good news?"

"Haven't seen a croc in awhile."

"Do you think we can drink this water?"

"Ask Mercer. He drank a lot of it."

Taylor put her hand over the side, scooped up some water, and looked at it. "It has bugs and stuff in it." She dumped it. "Maybe it'll rain." She added, "This is a rain forest."

Brodie remembered the Iraqi desert. Now and then they'd get low on water, and water became everyone's obsession. It's the little things that you take for granted—like food, water, and ammunition—that become critical when they're gone. He said, "We'll drink it if we have to, and worry about it later. Meanwhile, keep an eye on the right bank. If Mercer's men discover that Senor Kyle is missing and they see that one of their boats on the mud-flat is gone and the other boats are disabled, they might be bright enough to figure out we're on the river with their boss."

"They'll probably think we went downstream, toward Kavak—not farther into the interior."

"Hope so. Also keep an eye out for Pemón in boats or Pemón on the riverbank with rifles—or blowguns, or whatever." He added, "We're not in Quantico anymore, Maggie."

She thanked him for his perceptive observation and added, "If the gas runs out, we'll have to paddle."

Brodie nodded and looked again at Mercer. He was like the trophy fish you caught—the two-hundred-pound prize that was too big for your small boat.

"Try Worley again," she suggested.

Brodie cut the engine and called Worley's number. This time the call was picked up, but no one answered. Brodie said, "It's me, Brendan. Don't hang up."

Silence. Then Worley said, "Are you . . . ?"

"We are free. Captain Mercer is not."

"Okay . . . are you saying—?"

"We busted out. Ms. Taylor and I are in a boat on a river called River. We have the fugitive with us, restrained and ready for pickup."

Worley didn't seem as excited as he should be, and asked, "How did you do that?"

It occurred to Brodie that Worley—who lived in a world of suspicion and deception—might believe that this call was being made under duress, like with a gun pointed to Brodie's head. If they'd established a code word, Brodie would have used it. Instead, he said, "The CID always gets their man, Colonel. What we need from you is your flying Otter."

"All right . . . Where are you?"

"Hold on." Brodie pulled up the phone's menu, retrieved the GPS coordinates, and read them to Worley. He added, "We did an aerial recon on the way in, and spotted a landing strip somewhere farther up the river—maybe a mile from the western bank."

"Okay . . . hold."

Brodie assumed Worley was at the embassy, not day drinking at the beach club, and he was now pulling up satellite imagery of the area.

Brodie looked at Taylor, who had moved from the bow and was sitting on the narrow bench next to Mercer's feet. She asked, "What's happening?"

"I'm booking a flight." He covered the mouthpiece and added, "Worley may not believe our good luck and may think Mercer is laying a trap for him."

"Great. What the hell else can go wrong?"

"Earthquake?"

She glanced at Mercer. "Maybe we can get him to say something."

"If Worley's not believing me, he's certainly not going to believe Kyle Mercer. But . . . why don't you punch him in the balls so Worley can hear him groaning?"

"Scott—"

"Hold on—"

Worley said, "All right, I see the airstrip. Probably made by drug runners. Hopefully not active. It's about seven miles from where you are, as the crow flies. But if you follow the river, I'll give you the coordinates for a place where you can come ashore and hike into the woods, about two miles to that airstrip."

"Okay. How long will it take the Otter to get to the airstrip?"

"About three hours from the time I get him wheels-up." He added, "The Otter doesn't actually have retractable wheels. That's just an inside joke." He paused. "That means you'll be waiting forever."

"That's really not that funny, Colonel."

"Just a joke. All right, how long do you think it will take you to reach the airstrip?"

Brodie did some math and replied, "It'll take us about an hour to go seven miles upriver, then . . . maybe two hours to trek two miles through the jungle to reach the airstrip with our prisoner in tow."

"Then this should work out for a rendezvous in about three hours, give or take."

"Right. I need the pilot's sat phone number. Now."

"He will have your number. He will call you."

"Didn't we have this conversation once?"

"I believe we did. The security considerations haven't changed since then."

Brodie didn't want to antagonize the man who was going to get them out of there, so he said, "All right. We'll wait for the pilot's call."

"If you think there's any danger for the pilot to land, or if you are under duress, use the code word . . . 'asshole.' Can you work that naturally into a phone conversation?"

"If I'm talking to you, no problem. Just kidding. You know that Taylor and I were under duress when we called you 'asshole.' Right?"

"I assumed you were. All right, I'm going to give you the coordinates of the point in the river where you need to cut into the jungle. You should use your—my—sat phone to check your location. Ready to copy?"

"Ready."

Worley read off the coordinates, and Brodie repeated the numbers to Taylor, who, he hoped, could commit them to memory.

Worley also gave him the coordinates of the airstrip, and again Brodie read them aloud.

Worley continued, "This is a six-seater Otter. One seat is the pilot's seat, three are for you, Ms. Taylor, and your prisoner. There will be one, maybe two armed security personnel onboard to provide airfield security, and to ensure that the prisoner poses no danger during flight." He added, "This is standard procedure."

"Okay . . . but Maggie and I are all the security we need. The prisoner is hog-tied."

"I'll advise our security people of that. It's not my decision." He added, "Your call sign is . . . let's say Lucky Duck."

"Better than Dead Duck."

"The pilot will be Otter One."

"Copy. Why don't you take a ride out here? You'd enjoy seeing Mercer trussed up like a pig."

"The Otter is coming from Aruba."

"He can make a quick landing at Francisco de Miranda and pick you up. Don't you want to be part of this?"

There was a silence on the phone; then Worley said, "The Venezuelan government has severely restricted the movements of all U.S. Embassy personnel. I'm always followed, and I wouldn't want to compromise this extraction by being followed to the airport."

"Okay. Just as long as you don't think Mercer has a gun to our heads and this is a trap."

"I don't think that. But I'd like to hear Ms. Taylor's voice."

"You wanna hear her punch Mercer in the nuts?"

"Just her voice, please."

Brodie handed the sat phone to Taylor. "He wants to hear your voice."

Taylor nodded and said into the phone, "It's Taylor, Colonel." She listened, then said, "Yes, he's restrained. And gagged." She listened, then moved up a few seats and held the phone to Mercer's ear. "Captain Mercer can hear you, Colonel."

Brodie wondered what Worley had to say to the man who, if you could believe Mercer, he had planned to drop out of a helicopter. Whatever Worley said, it upset Captain Mercer and he got agitated, trying to shout something into the phone that sounded liked, "Fuh U U fuhen . . ." They obviously had some issues.

Taylor took the phone away from Mercer's ear and said to Worley, "Captain Mercer was more articulate when we were his prisoners."

She handed the phone to Brodie, who said to Worley, "Captain Mercer has been read his rights and placed under arrest. He is our prisoner and we will return him to U.S. jurisdiction."

Worley stayed silent for a moment, then said, "You understand that the man has gone mad after two years of Taliban captivity."

"That would be a good legal defense for any alleged crimes committed since he escaped his captivity. But the charge as of now is desertion, and he wasn't crazy when he deserted." In fact, he would have been crazy to get on that black helicopter. But Brodie—and Taylor—had already said more than they should to Brendan Worley, who had a reputation for cleaning up the shit, covering his own ass, and possibly silencing witnesses. So, to make sure the Otter arrived, Brodie said, "I'm calling Colonel Dombroski now and filing an oral report."

"All right . . . and by the way, Colonel Dombroski led me to believe that you and Ms. Taylor were leaving the country as ordered."

"We are leaving the country, though not as ordered."

"How did you and Ms. Taylor get to where you are now?"

"Probably the same way Ted Haggerty got here." Brodie added, "Sorry about what happened to him."

Worley did not respond, probably thinking that Brodie and Taylor should have met the same fate. He did say, however, "I'm glad you don't work for me."

"That makes three of us. Four, if you count Captain Mercer."

Worley had no response to that and said, "I'll get on the Otter."

Brodie didn't think he meant that literally and asked, "Where are we being taken?"

"That is not information I possess. But you can assume Gitmo or Panama."

"As long as it's not Caracas."

"You're hot in Caracas, Mr. Brodie. SEBIN is looking for an American named Clark Bowman."

Brodie didn't know if that was true, or if Worley was trying to ruin his perfect day. Brodie asked, "Did you get those visas for Luis and his family?"

"I believe that was done."

"Let me know for sure when we speak again."

"I'll check." Worley put a friendly tone in his voice and said, "Congratulations on getting your man."

"Thank you. You've been most helpful."

"Thank you for returning the briefcase."

"Sorry we took your stuff, but we needed it."

"Do you have the Glocks? I need to account for all firearms."

This seemed to be a day when everyone was asking about who had a gun. Well, Brodie had Mercer's Desert Eagle, and Taylor had Worley's Glock. But Brodie thought it might be time to play Who Has the Gun? "Sorry, Brendan, we barely got out of there with our lives. In fact, I lost my boots. I'll get CID to reimburse."

"I'll charge it off to experience. Would you like your condom back?"

"Keep it. I have no use for it."

"Sorry to hear that."

"Not as sorry as I am. Well, I doubt we'll meet again, but it's been interesting working with you, Colonel."

"Let me call for the Otter. Call me when the extraction is complete."

"Will do. Adiós."

"And to you and Ms. Taylor."

Brodie shut off the phone to save battery and said to Taylor, "Colonel Worley is a worried man." He added, "I told him we had no weapons."

"You're more devious than he is." She asked, "Are we okay with this extraction?"

"We will be after I call Dombroski."

"Then call him."

"In a minute." He looked at Mercer, then said to Taylor, "If I was as devious as Worley, I would not have told him we had Mercer in custody, because if he wants Mercer dead, we could be collateral damage."

"I know that. But here's something to make you feel better. Worley knows from Mercer's sat phone call to him that we spoke to Mercer, and that Mercer was probably speaking freely to us, his prisoners. Therefore, whether or not we had Mercer in custody, we have Mercer's story. So whatever Worley is planning for Mercer, he would also be planning for us even if you and I were alone."

"That does make me feel better."

"Call Dombroski and get a life insurance policy issued."

"Okay." Brodie turned on the sat phone and called Dombroski's cell.

It rang, but there was no answer, which was unusual for Colonel Dombroski, who answered his phone even when he was on the table in his proctologist's office. Possibly the satellite connection hadn't gone through, or the sat phone number on Dombroski's screen looked like his ex-wife's attorney's number.

Brodie was concerned that Worley might be able to monitor the sat phone calls, so he left a short message for Dombroski that he classified as "Urgent," then upped it to "Most Urgent." "Critical," as Dombroski had once advised him, is only for when you're hiding in a closet because the husband came home. Meanwhile he had to leave the cell phone on for the callback.

"You should have called him first."

"That's like calling your insurance company when your house is on fire, then calling the fire department." He reminded her, "We needed to get that Otter airborne."

"I have some concerns about that extraction, Scott."

"Worley may be devious, but he's not reckless. He knows we're calling Dombroski."

"Nevertheless, an accident might happen at the airstrip."

"You can only cover up so many crimes. This is not one Worley can cover up."

"If he thinks his freedom depends on it, he'll find a way."

Which was true. But Brodie assured her, "Have I ever misjudged a situation?"

"Every day, Scott. Almost hourly."

"Okay. Have I ever gotten us into a situation that I can't get us out of?"

"We're about to find out."

They continued along the river, and Brodie sensed that the current was getting stronger, and the boat was not making good progress. They could pick up some speed if they chucked Mercer to the piranhas. Brodie had no idea how long it would take to make the trek from the river to the airstrip. Should be less than two hours, but the terrain could be impassable, and the prisoner could be dragging his ass, and Brodie had lost his shoes. How long would the Otter stay on station? Depended on his fuel reserve. And at some point, Brodie had to waste battery again by keeping the sat phone on to receive the pilot's call, because asshole Worley wouldn't give him the pilot's number. Brodie checked their fuel again. Low, but maybe not critical. Just urgent. And rowing against the current was not really an option in their condition. Which reminded him that he was dehydrated, hungry, and getting sunstroke.

He looked at Mercer, who wasn't moving much. "He okay?"

Taylor felt his cheek, then his pulse. "He may be overheating."

"Not so tough after all."

"Show a little compassion, Scott."

"Yeah, like he did." Brodie said, "He's playing possum so he doesn't have to make that trek through the jungle." He yelled at Mercer, "Won't work, Kyle. If you can't keep up, we leave you tied in the jungle for the panthers to eat."

Mercer remained motionless.

Taylor said, "I'm glad you didn't become a medic."

"I can spot a malingerer a mile away."

"We need to cool off. Head to shore."

Brodie checked his watch, then looked at the sat phone and got their coordinates. "We're still two miles from the point where we need to head inland. And almost an hour has gone by since we started. We need to push on."

Taylor nodded, then pulled off her boots and used them to scoop water from the river, which she poured over Mercer, then over Brodie's head, then herself. She kept at her task until everyone was cooled off, but the water in the boat's bottom didn't do much for its speed.

Brodie looked at Mercer again, and he seemed to be stirring. Taylor took her Swiss Army knife out, then pulled down Mercer's pants and cut off his boxer shorts, which she draped over his head, then pulled his pants back up over his bare ass.

Brodie inquired, "You learn that in survival training? Or someplace else?"

She didn't reply and pulled off her T-shirt and put it over her head, saying, "You should do the same."

"I'll keep my shorts and T-shirt where they belong."

They continued upriver, and Brodie checked the sat phone's grid co-ordinates and battery life. If the battery died, he wouldn't have the coordinates for beaching the boat or for finding the airstrip. Then they would die. As for the fuel, it would run out when it ran out. Truly they were up shit's creek.

Taylor suggested, "Try Dombroski again."

Also known as the Hail Mary call. "Okay." He dialed Dombroski again, but there was no answer, and Brodie left a longer message: "Mission accomplished, but I'm hiding in the closet and the husband is home." He glanced at Taylor, who must think he had heatstroke. "This call may be being monitored for damage control. Okay, we're on our way to a rendezvous for an air extraction. Call Colonel Worley for details. Or call me, ASAP. Battery is low. Taylor and I are fine, but don't feel much like dancing." He added, "Worley has assured us this extraction will be safe and successful. Please speak to him about his assurances." He also added, "Taylor has done an exceptional job. She should be officially commended." And no, I didn't sleep with her. "Call soonest."

Brodie left the phone on and said to Taylor, "Assurance, insurance. What do you think?"

"I think he understands. And I understand that you think our calls are being monitored in the embassy."

"I don't know their capabilities. But it's their sat phone."

"Do you think that Worley could block our calls to Dombroski?"

"I don't know if the embassy commo people could do that, but thanks for the thought."

"Try the message line."

"Good thought." Brodie called the command message line, punched in Dombroski's number, and left the same message. "Okay. See if that works. Hope he checks his messages."

Taylor nodded, then asked, "What was that about you hiding in the closet?"

"Secret code."

"For what?"

"Means it's a critical situation."

"Okay . . . I get it." She let him know, "The Army is still a boys' club."

"Always was, always will be."

She said to Brodie, "Thank you for commending me to Colonel Dombroski."

"I give credit where credit is due."

"How is that going to square with your report about my involvement with the Agency?"

"There will be no such report."

"Why?"

"Well . . . because you did a great job, and because there's nothing gained by adding another charge of malfeasance to this mess."

"Also you like me, and you'd like to sleep with me."

"That too."

"You're honest."

Actually, horny. Though Maggie Taylor wasn't looking her best today, even in her sports bra. "I like you very much."

"Same here." She got off that subject and said, "It's all going to come out anyway. Whatever investigation there is into Operation Flagstaff will reveal Trent's name, and eventually mine."

"I'm sure he'd cover for you."

"Maybe. If I sleep with him."

"Do what you have to do."

Before she could respond, the sat phone rang, and Brodie answered, "Brodie here."

"Where is here?" Colonel Dombroski's voice had never sounded so good.

"Here on a river near a village called Kavak—"

"Actually, I spoke to Colonel Worley, who gave me a quick briefing—before you did."

"Did you get my two calls on your cell?"

"You're sounding like my ex-wife."

"Those calls could have been blocked by Worley."

There was a silence; then Dombroski said, "So you got Mercer."

"I did. We did."

"Outstanding, Mr. Brodie. And Ms. Taylor. Is she there?"

"Right here. And Captain Mercer is restrained and on his way to the extraction point."

"Excellent. Did you read him his rights?"

"Ms. Taylor did."

"And I assume you didn't follow that up with an interrogation."

"The suspect spoke voluntarily without prompting."

"Okay. What did he say?"

"It's a very long story, Colonel, and I don't have enough battery or saliva left to tell you. But he did clear up the meaning of Flagstaff."

"What's the meaning?"

"It's the Afghan version of Phoenix."

There was another silence on the phone. Dombroski said, "Are you sure?"

"Got it from Mercer, who was part of it."

"Holy shit."

"And Colonel Brendan Worley was a big part of it."

"Holy shit."

"And he doesn't want Captain Mercer returned to U.S. soil to testify about Operation Flagstaff. But we can discuss that in a more secure transmission. Or in person."

"All right . . . So how in the hell did you snatch Mercer?"

Brodie realized that Worley had never told Dombroski about the call that Worley received from Kyle Mercer himself—the call made when Brodie and Taylor were the ones in custody. Which meant Worley had assumed that Brodie and Taylor would wind up dead, like Worley's friend Ted Haggerty. Logical assumption.

Brodie asked, "Didn't Worley tell you that Taylor and I had been captured by Mercer's men?"

"What?"

"And Mercer used our sat phone to call Worley, and Mercer put us on the line to speak to Worley."

"Are you . . . ?"

"Yes, very serious. And pissed."

Again a silence; then Dombroski said, "For another time." Then he remembered something. "I instructed you both not to risk looking for Mercer's camp."

"Right. We were just doing a river recon and somehow ran into—"

"And why did Ms. Taylor call the message line earlier, and not my cell?"

"Well . . . quite frankly, Colonel, we were disobeying your orders not to look for Mercer's camp, so I told Ms. Taylor to use the message line."

"I'm not sure how to respond to that, honestly."

"You could say, 'All's well that ends well.'"

"I would never say that." He asked, "Where is Mercer's girlfriend?"

"In Caracas. She got cold feet." But has a warm heart.

"All right. What is the condition of the prisoner?"

"Very unhappy."

"His physical condition."

"He'll live." Until Worley gets his hands on him. Brodie said, "We don't want Captain Mercer dying in transit."

"I understand what you're saying. And how are you and Ms. Taylor? Ready to dance?"

"Maybe a slow one. But we'll be okay."

"They rough you up at that camp?"

"No worse than those POW training camps."

"Did they . . . abuse Ms. Taylor?"

"They were planning to."

"Okay . . . What the hell is that camp all about?"

"It's about Kyle Mercer wanting payback for two years in Taliban hell. It's about Worley recruiting him into Flagstaff, then double-crossing him. It's about Mercer training a guerrilla force to undermine American interests in Venezuela."

"So Captain Mercer is also a traitor."

"Captain Mercer deserves his day in court."

"All right . . . So you gave me a grid coordinate when you left a message this morning. How close is that to the camp?"

"Close. Recon drones can find the camp a few miles southeast of those coordinates."

"Good. I'll pass that on."

"Mercer's last order to his men was to break camp and move. So whoever gets this assignment needs to move fast. And be advised that there are civilians in the camp. Indigenous workers and nurses who cure homesickness."

"I understand. Okay, how close are you to your rendezvous?"

"Maybe a half hour on the river, then two through the jungle."

"And you know where you're going?"

"We'll figure it out. Let me give you the lat long for this airstrip."

"Okay . . . but Worley has it."

"Which is why I'm giving it to you."

Dombroski didn't respond to that, but said, "Ready to copy."

Brodie recited the coordinates from memory, then said, "If the extraction is delayed or otherwise compromised, see if you can send a military aircraft for us."

"Understood."

Taylor said to Brodie, "Ask about Luis."

Brodie nodded and asked, "Did our driver Luis from Caracas call you?"

"He called me General. Your idea?"

"No, sir. Language problem. He's okay?"

"He and his family are in the hands of ICE. You and Ms. Taylor can vouch for him when you get here."

"Good. Okay, there's more to discuss, but my battery is low."

"How many times have I heard that?"

"This is not my sat phone."

"Call me from the airstrip."

"Will try."

"Or from the air, as you were supposed to do earlier."

"Will do."

"Excellent work. I will inform General Hackett."

"Someday, thanks to me and Ms. Taylor, you'll be sitting at his desk."

"Someday, thanks to you, Brodie, I'll be sitting at the desk next to yours."

"It would be my pleasure."

"Not mine. Godspeed."

Brodie shut off the phone.

Taylor said, "Did I understand that Worley never told Dombroski that we had been captured and were being held in Mercer's camp?"

"It may have slipped Colonel Worley's mind."

"He was going to leave us here to die. Or worse."

"I think what Worley was going to do was try to get a fix on Camp Tombstone and blow it and Mercer off the face of the earth."

"And us."

"High explosives solve problems." Brodie added, "If Dombroski knew we were in the camp—and maybe even if he didn't—he would have pushed for a Delta Force raid to capture Mercer alive. Which is why Worley never mentioned the phone call."

Taylor nodded, then said, "And now Worley is going to send a plane to rescue us and Mercer."

"Now that the secret is out with Dombroski, Worley has no choice."

"We do. We don't have to make that rendezvous."

"What do we do instead?"

"We . . . call Dombroski back, explain our concerns, and have CID effect the extraction."

"Here's what's wrong with that idea: Our time as healthy soldiers is running out. It could take Dombroski a full day to get a rescue operation in place. Worley now owns that airstrip, and I don't know where there's another. Do you? And finally, no one in the Pentagon is going to approve of switching the rescue operation from Defense Intelligence—and probably CIA—to CID. Time is of the essence right now, and time is running out." He added, "We're in a fucking jungle, surrounded by Indians, cougars, snakes, and crocs. We are at the bottom of the food chain. And for all we know, Mercer's men might be tracking us along the riverbank." He concluded, "I'd rather take my chances with the snake we know—Worley—than with the unknown. Besides, we'll be lucky if we even make the airstrip. But once we're there, we'll make a threat assessment."

Taylor stayed silent, then said, "I think we can survive in this jungle and explore other options."

"We'd have to eat Captain Mercer."

"All right . . . I'll let you make this decision."

"There's no decision to make." He said, "If it makes you feel better, I think Worley is in a worse situation than we are, and he's at the stage where he's hoping for the best, which would be us getting eaten by a croc. Meanwhile, he's putting out the word that Captain Mercer has gone apocalypse now." Brodie glanced at Mercer. "He would not make a credible witness against the well-respected Colonel Worley."

Taylor also looked at Mercer, and nodded.

"Colonel Worley's choice now is between completing what he had planned for Captain Mercer two years ago in Afghanistan, or taking him home to tell his wild story, and to explain Camp Tombstone to a very un-sympathetic Army."

Taylor looked at Brodie. "You underestimate the power of the truth."

"The first casualty of war is the truth."

"I never believed that until I went to war."

"Hard lessons there."

She nodded.

Brodie turned on the sat phone and looked at the coordinates. "We're almost there . . . maybe a few hundred meters, give or take." He slowed the boat to conserve fuel and veered toward the right bank.

Up ahead he could see a small break in the wall of jungle vegetation, and he steered toward it. "Could be a trailhead. Like an animal watering trail . . . maybe Pemón. Maybe both." Which would speed their progress into the jungle, but they'd be sharing the trail with Pemón, big cats, and crocs.

Taylor said, "My survival course instructor said avoid trails."

"So did mine. Sounds good in class until you see the jungle."

"Agreed."

Brodie thought he heard the engine sputtering, but it might have been his stomach growling.

He cut sharp right so that the bow of the boat would hit the muddy shore at a right angle. "Hold on."

Taylor pulled on her T-shirt, then put one hand on the gunnel and pressed the other on Mercer's chest.

Brodie kept the throttle fully open, and as he approached the shore, he heard the propeller getting fouled in underwater vegetation. The boat slowed, then hit the shore and came to a sudden stop with the bow a few feet on land.

Brodie cut the engine and he and Taylor jumped into knee-deep water. They pulled on the bowline and got the boat a few feet farther onto the mud. Taylor tied the line around a tree and sank to her knees. Clearly she was suffering from heat exhaustion and dehydration. Brodie didn't feel his best either and saw spots in front of his eyes. He wondered how Mercer was going to do with no incentive to make a two-hour trek to an aircraft that would take him to jail.

Taylor stood and nodded to show she was okay. Brodie motioned toward Mercer, and they moved back to the boat. They were supposed to practice noise discipline in situations like this—quiet movements and minimal talking—so Taylor motioned for him to come to her side of the boat. Together they tipped the narrow boat, dumping Mercer onto the mud.

Taylor whispered to Brodie, "We shouldn't leave the boat exposed."

Brodie looked around for a place to conceal the long boat, but the vegetation on both sides of the narrow trail was too thick. He whispered, "We'll capsize it and send it downriver."

"What if we need it again?"

"It's out of fuel and we're out of gas. This trail goes only one way."

She nodded, and they pulled the boat away from Mercer, then capsized it. Taylor cut the bow line and they pushed the boat into the river, walking it out until it got caught in the current.

Brodie watched it floating hull-up, downstream toward Mercer's camp, then Kavak. There's nothing like a capsized boat to signal that the passengers went overboard and are probably in the food chain. Also, for him and Taylor, getting rid of the boat was the equivalent of burning their bridges behind them.

But first, a cooling bath in the warm, muddy river. Brodie held his sat phone up and went under a few times while Taylor stood motionless in neck-deep water which they shared with the crocs, snakes, and piranha. There had to be a better way to make a living.

They waded back to shore, and Brodie now noticed the croc tail tracks in the mud.

Taylor retrieved Mercer's shorts, which had fallen in the mud, and wrapped them around his neck; then Brodie dragged him into the shallows to get him cooled down. Mercer lay in the water and stared up at Brodie, who stared back.

Taylor came over to them and they dragged Mercer back to shore. Brodie crouched beside Mercer and said, "Okay, Kyle, here's the deal. Listen closely. Maggie and I are going to hike up this trail for about two hours. Somewhere in that jungle is an airstrip. An Otter is coming in to take us to someplace nicer than this. You are welcome to come along—but only if you keep up with us. We are not missing that flight. If you don't want to come along, we leave you here, hog-tied, for the next croc that comes along. I shit you not. Very serious about that. And if you decide to come with us and you drag your ass, we're leaving you behind with your hands tied so howler monkeys can bite your balls. And you have no underwear. Right? As for the cougars and panthers, keep in mind that they are an endangered species, but not as endangered as you. And finally, the constrictor snakes. You ever see one of those wildlife shows where a constrictor slowly wraps itself around—"

"Scott. He gets it. We all get it." She crouched beside Mercer. "Will you come with us, or stay here? Nod or shake."

Mercer kept staring at them.

Brodie said, "I'm not trying to oversell this, Kyle, but your last—and only—chance to get back at Worley is to come with us. You have, literally, five seconds to decide. I'm running late." Brodie counted, "One . . . two . . . three . . . four . . . four and a half . . ."

Mercer nodded.

"Good choice, Captain."

Taylor drew her knife and cut the rope around Mercer's ankles, leaving him with his hands tied behind his back.

Brodie and Taylor lifted him to his feet, and Brodie said to Mercer, "I'm leaving the gag in, but if you step lively, I'll take it off when we find the airstrip. Understand?"

Mercer nodded.

"I'll let you keep your good jungle boots, and I'll hike in my socks. But that could change real quick if you drag your ass and we decide to leave you here. Understand?"

Again, Mercer nodded.

"Good. So we understand—no malingering, only compliance. Malingering, which is punishable by up to six months' imprisonment under the Uniform Code of Military Justice, is punishable here by death. Got it?"

Mercer nodded, but Brodie didn't see defeat in his eyes—he saw fire. Hate. Defiance. Brodie hoped Captain Mercer got at least life in prison, because if Kyle Mercer was ever freed, Scott Brodie and Maggie Taylor would join Brendan Worley on Mercer's must-kill list.

"Okay. I'll take point, Kyle middle, and Maggie brings up the rear." He turned toward the narrow trail, drew Mercer's Desert Eagle, and walked into the jungle. Next stop, a drug runner airstrip where an uncertain rendezvous with fate awaited them. Did it get any better than this? Yes, it did. But not today.

CHAPTER 47

The ground sloped uphill from the river, and the trail was so narrow it almost didn't exist. But it was better than cutting through the brush and vines, which could take hours. Brodie checked his watch. If this trail came close to the airstrip, they might be only a half hour late for their rendezvous.

He turned on the sat phone and got a beep, which was the battery's way of telling him it was dying. If people had a dying beep, he would be beeping. He looked at his present grid position and tried to correlate that with the grid of the airstrip, but he'd need another reading to establish his direction of march. He shut off the sat phone. He hoped it had enough juice left to give him grid coordinates along the way, and also enough life so he could leave it on to get the call from the Otter pilot. If there was an Otter.

The jungle was quieter than he'd thought it would be, but now and then he heard howler monkeys and the screech of birds. The humidity was over a hundred percent, if that was possible, and the air smelled of rotting vegetation and dank earth. He brushed his hand through webs with spiders the size of walnuts. Vietnam was probably like this. Iraq was no treat either, and he was sure Afghanistan sucked. The U.S. should declare war on Bermuda.

He glanced back at Mercer and Taylor. Mercer seemed to be living up to his end of a bad bargain, but Taylor was falling behind. Brodie was starting to feel the difference between walking with boots and walking in his socks. He wondered how the Pemón trekked barefoot over this rough terrain. Brodie knew, as every infantryman did, that it's not how strong your legs are, it's how strong your mind is. *Push on.* Think about cool pools and hot babes, they'd told him in infantry training. Ironically, it was Mercer who looked okay because he'd swallowed a lot of water. Brodie hoped Mercer didn't get the shits on the flight out.

It was still uphill, and Brodie put one foot in front of the other, which was the only way to move forward. He glanced back at Mercer and Taylor again, then slowed up so Taylor could close the gap. He was glad he'd kept Mercer gagged, because Brodie didn't want to hear the Delta Force officer telling them to get the lead out of their asses and step lively. Actually, Mercer, with his hands behind his back and his body hunched forward, chewing on his gag, looked almost professorial, like an absentminded dean at an English school, mumbling to himself as he walked across the quad. Brodie wondered what Kyle Mercer would look like in a courtroom, dressed in greens and a tie. He could beat the desertion rap, and even beat his Flagstaff involvement. And as for the murders of the two CIA officers on opposite sides of the earth, that wouldn't be easy to prove. If the trial officer and JAG threw enough at him, something might stick. But even if it did, Kyle Mercer, former hero and Taliban prisoner, might walk in a few years. Things that look crystal clear to the cops don't look so clear in a courtroom. Especially when the accused is wearing his crisp uniform with a few rows of service ribbons, which often influenced the court-martial board.

Brodie had a mental image of Kyle Mercer knocking on his door someday. Or Taylor's door—assuming they had different doors.

Brodie never thought twice about the men he'd put behind bars. They were mostly losers, malcontents, and stupid, and posed no post-confinement threat. Kyle Mercer, however, was another species, a smart killing machine with a big grudge.

So . . . maybe Worley was right, but for the wrong reasons. Maybe Captain Mercer needed to die—not just to shut him up, but also to make him pay for the crimes that could confuse the court—but not confuse anyone else involved in this case.

Brodie looked at the gun in his hand—Mercer's gun. If Brodie had been alone, or with some other guy who saw it as he saw it, Mercer would have been dead a second after he dropped his gun and raised his hands.

He glanced back at Maggie Taylor. She had a moral compass, even if the needle wandered a bit. He was a little pissed off at her now, but he was certain that in the days and years to come he'd thank her for keeping him from acting on his worst primitive instincts. Without women, there would be perpetual war and chaos. With them, there was only chaos.

Brodie raised his hand to signal a halt. He took a grid reading; the sat phone's beeping continued, and now the battery indicator was flashing empty. He turned off the phone and walked toward Taylor, who was kneeling. As he passed Mercer, he said, "Nod if you'd like to kill me."

Mercer nodded enthusiastically.

Brodie knelt beside Taylor. "How're you doing?"

"Legs are cramping."

First sign of severe dehydration. It goes downhill from there. "We'll keep an eye out for water. Can you get up?"

She struggled to her feet and almost fell over. He caught her and helped her sit.

"I'm fine . . ."

"You're not fine." He stood and looked around at the vegetation, then walked back to Mercer and asked, "What's safe to eat? What has water?" He untied the gag and pulled the handkerchief out of Mercer's mouth.

Mercer took a deep breath and said, "Asshole."

"Is that safe to eat? C'mon, Kyle. You live around here. We're all in this together. Be a good soldier."

Mercer took another breath and said, "Worley is going to kill me, and kill both of you."

"Let me worry about Colonel Worley. We don't want to die of heatstroke. What's to eat and drink here?"

Mercer hesitated, then replied, "Lots of things . . . manioc root . . . some fruit trees . . ." He looked around at the jungle growth that crowded the trail. "Easiest is the vines. The ends are moist and edible."

"Sort of like asparagus tips?"

Mercer had no reply, and Brodie told him to sit, then drew his KA-BAR and pushed into the brush. There were vines hanging from trees, and vines crawling through the brush and along the ground, so it wasn't difficult to find the succulent green ends and cut off about three dozen.

He got back on the trail and walked to Mercer. "You first." He shoved a vine in Mercer's mouth, and Mercer chewed it and swallowed.

"Seconds?"

Mercer nodded, and Brodie fed him a second vine.

Mercer said, "Untie me. I have to pee."

"Next you'll be asking me to hold your dick. Pee in your pants."

Brodie moved quickly to Taylor, and they shared the rest of the vine tips after wiping them off on their dirty T-shirts. Brodie said, "Jungle trail mix."

"Scott . . . please . . . you'd find a hanging funny."

"They can be." Brodie chewed. "They taste like kale or shit." He looked at her. "Let me know when you're ready."

She stood. "I'm ready now."

"Okay. We'll take it slow."

Brodie fed the last vine tip to Mercer, then re-gagged him. "Get up."

They had only about an hour to go, and they should be able to do that with bellies full of vine-ripened vines. Unless they were poisonous.

Brodie kept the pace slow but steady. This was definitely a game trail, though maybe used by the indigenous people. He wasn't concerned about running into a cougar or panther—they generally avoided people, and in any case he had a gun. Poisonous ground snakes could cause a fatal encounter, but most snakes also avoided people. The biggest threat to people was other people, and what he didn't want to run into were Pemón with rifles. The Pemón seemed friendly enough—despite César's larceny—but encounters in the wild brought out the worst in human beings.

Brodie made a quick check of his sat phone, and was now convinced that this trail either intersected with the airstrip or came close. This was a walk in the park. Canaima National Park, to be exact. Someday, when the socialists were kicked out, there'd be condos here.

He glanced back at Mercer and Taylor and they seemed to be doing okay, so he picked up his pace, but his stockinged feet were starting to feel raw.

After what seemed like forever, he looked at his watch and saw that another hour had passed. He checked his sat phone coordinates, glanced at the sun, and realized he was supposed to be at the end of his journey. But he didn't see an airstrip.

He stopped, and Taylor came up beside him. "Problem?"

"We're supposed to be at the airstrip. These sat coordinates can be off by twenty or thirty meters. But I think we're close."

Taylor reminded him, "Close only counts with horseshoes and hand grenades."

"Right."

Taylor looked around at the walls of vegetation, then looked up at a gnarled thirty-foot tree. "I'll shimmy up there."

"Okay. Watch out for snakes."

Taylor waded into a thicket of growth, reached the tree, and climbed up its knotted trunk until she got about ten feet above the lower growth.

Brodie watched her as she looked around; then she suddenly stopped and pointed.

Brodie gave her a thumbs-up, then looked at Mercer, who was expressionless, staring into his future.

Taylor climbed down, then dropped the last ten feet and moved quickly back to the trail. She got her bearings and pointed. "About fifty meters."

"Let's do it." He said to Mercer, "Follow."

Brodie and Taylor drew their knives and began cutting through twisted branches and vines, and within ten minutes they could see sunlight ahead where the airstrip slashed through the jungle.

Brodie looked overhead, scanning for an aircraft, but he didn't see or hear anything. He glanced back at Mercer, who seemed to be lagging behind, as though their goal was his penalty box.

Brodie broke out into a clear area partially overgrown with brush. The airstrip. Trees towered around the short runway, so only a plane that could make a steep drop in and a steep climb out could use this jungle strip. Worst airfield he'd ever seen. Made Kavak look like Dulles.

Taylor, though, seemed to like it, and she gave him a big hug. "We did it."

He looked at his watch. They were half an hour late, but that was well within the parameters for this rendezvous in the middle of nowhere. Probably the pilot was late too, if he'd gotten a late start or hit headwinds from Aruba. Brodie said, "We should be in Gitmo or Panama in time for cocktails."

"I'll settle for a beer."

"On me."

Brodie glanced at the sky again, then looked at the airstrip. You'd think drug runners could do better. But here it was—either their magic carpet ride out, or the genie had fucked them.

Mercer, looking more unhappy, if that were possible, walked onto the airstrip and looked around.

They had intersected the airstrip in what was almost the middle of the western side—sort of the fifty-yard line—and Brodie didn't know what end the pilot would want them on, so he told everyone to sit. There was no wind sock, and in fact there was no wind, but he'd hold up his own sock if he thought it would help the pilot choose which end of the runway to approach.

Mercer started making sounds, and would have pointed to his gag if his hands weren't tied behind his back.

Brodie looked at Taylor. "I really don't want to listen to his shit."

"You promised." She stood and moved beside Mercer and cut his gag, then pulled the handkerchief out of his mouth.

Mercer took a deep breath and said, "If you trust Brendan Worley, you're not as smart as you think you are."

Brodie said to Taylor, "I told you." He said to Mercer, "Shut the fuck up or I'll stuff my socks in your mouth."

Mercer had no reply.

They sat at the side of the airstrip. Brodie turned on his sat phone, which beeped as he listened for the pilot's call.

He thought about calling Dombroski, but calls took juice, and he also didn't want to be talking to Dombroski when the Otter pilot called. But Brodie did send a quick text: *Arrived airstrip waiting 4 Otter low bat.*

Taylor asked, "Are you prepared for . . . the unknowns of this extraction?"

Brodie assured her, "I'm always ready for anything, but prepared for nothing."

"That should be your personal motto."

"It is."

Mercer said, "It would be ironic if you got this far and were killed by friendly fire."

Brodie suggested, "Shut up."

"Untie me. Let me run. I'd rather die in the jungle than be killed here."

Neither Brodie nor Taylor responded.

Mercer said, "If I'm not with you, you have a much better chance of getting on that aircraft and getting out of here."

"Kyle," said Brodie, "you're getting yourself worked up. And you may have been in the same state of mind when you thought Colonel Worley was going to drop-kick you out of that helicopter. You don't even know if he was on that helicopter. The real irony is that you ran from something that you imagined, and ran into the hands of something real—the Taliban. And now you think history is going to repeat itself—but it's a false history."

"If I believed that, I would have killed myself in the Taliban camp. It was the thought of killing Worley that kept me alive."

"Right. When you're in Leavenworth, try God. Or maybe yoga."

"Untie me."

"I will. As soon as I get a pair of handcuffs."

Taylor leaned toward Brodie and whispered, "You don't believe his story?"

Brodie actually did, but he was not above tormenting a difficult prisoner, especially Kyle Mercer. He said to Taylor, "The only thing I care about now is that the boss has our backs."

She nodded, but said, "Desperate men do desperate things."

They waited in silence, sitting at the edge of the airstrip with the jungle at their backs. The only sound was the sat phone, whose beeping was getting on Brodie's nerves. He said to Taylor, "If the phone dies, we go out to the middle of the airstrip, and if we see the Otter, we wave like hell."

Taylor replied, "I'll wave my bra and T-shirt. He'll be on the ground in record time."

Brodie smiled. She was feeling better.

They listened for the sound of an aircraft, but the only things in the air making any noise were the birds.

The sat phone rang, and Brodie answered.

A voice said, "Lucky Duck, this is Otter One."

Brodie replied, "Lucky Duck here."

"All right, sir, I am about two minutes from your location. I will be coming in from the south and my rollout will take me to the north end of the landing strip where I will turn and meet you. Confirm that and confirm number of passengers."

Brodie looked at Mercer, who seemed resigned to his fate, or who was going to make a break at the last second. Or put his head in the propeller. Desperate men do desperate things.

"Sir?"

"Roger north end. Three passengers." Brodie asked, "Who's onboard?"

"A security detail."

He glanced at Taylor. "Water?"

"Yes, sir. Some snacks."

"Good. You want any vines?"

"Sir?"

"See you shortly."

"Two minutes."

In fact, Brodie could now hear the drone of the Otter's single engine, and within a minute they spotted the aircraft coming in low over the tree line.

"Okay," said Brodie, "let's go meet him." He tucked the Desert Eagle in his back waistband and headed toward the north end of the short landing strip. Taylor followed. Mercer did not.

Brodie doubled back and, without a word of reasoning or warning, delivered a powerful blow to Mercer's solar plexus and got the prisoner over his shoulder as Mercer doubled over.

Brodie carried Mercer toward the end of the airstrip, a few hundred yards away. He glanced back at the Otter, which was flying slowly in a steep vertical descent.

The Otter cleared the trees and seemed to drop onto the airstrip, bouncing and kicking up dirt and dust.

Brodie put on a burst of speed and caught up with Taylor just as the Otter rolled past them and continued on until it stopped just short of the trees at the end of the strip.

The pilot turned the Otter around and the prop idled down. Brodie, still moving fast with his two-hundred-pound tuna across his back, looked into the cockpit and saw the pilot's arm coming out from the side window. *Halt.*

Brodie dumped Mercer on the ground and said, "If you move an inch, I stomp your balls."

The Otter taxied slowly toward them.

Taylor, breathing hard, looked at Mercer on the ground. She said to him, "You're going home, soldier."

He shook his head.

She said to Brodie, "Is your gun where you need it?"

He tapped the small of his back. "Always."

Taylor shoved her Glock in her waistband and covered it with her T-shirt.

They looked at the Otter, which had come to a halt opposite where they were standing, about thirty feet away. The left-side passenger door opened and a man jumped down onto the airstrip. The man walked toward them, and Brodie could see he was wearing aviator glasses, a black polo shirt, khakis, and boots. It was Brendan Worley, wearing a holstered pistol. He waved to them, but they didn't return the greeting.

Worley stopped about ten feet away and looked at Mercer on the ground with his hands tied. "I'm surprised he came along peacefully."

Brodie replied, "I told him I had the name of a good lawyer."

Worley smiled.

Brodie said, "I thought you weren't taking this trip."

"You convinced me to come."

"Good. Now let's go."

Worley didn't reply, but walked to Mercer and crouched. "You don't look the same, Captain."

Mercer replied, of course, "Fuck you."

Worley looked at Brodie and Taylor. "Are you sure this is the famous and dangerous Captain Kyle Mercer?"

Brodie replied, "We can do the taunting onboard, Colonel. Let's get out of here."

Worley, apparently in no hurry, turned back to Mercer. "You know, when I saw your ragged ass on TV, I felt bad for you. No one deserves what happened to you, especially a soldier who has given so much of himself for his country. But then . . ." Worley paused and took off his aviators and got right in Mercer's face. "What you did in Peshawar, that was something else. Mr. Crenshaw was a patriot, a family man."

Mercer got himself into a sitting position and glared back at Worley. "I've killed a lot of family men, mostly on your orders. Killed their families too."

"Civilian pacification is an aspect of war as old as war itself, Captain. It's gotta get done from time to time. Like mowing the lawn."

"You're a sick fuck."

Well, thought Brodie, this was a hell of a reunion, and he had a bad feeling about how it was going to end. He reiterated, "Time to go."

Worley looked at Brodie. "I don't think he wants to go home, Mr. Bro-die." He stood and motioned toward the Otter, where two men were com-ing around the aircraft from the right-hand door. As they cleared the plane, Brodie could see that they were wearing boots, jeans, and camo shirts. They looked Hispanic, and they were both carrying AK-47s.

The men positioned themselves well behind the tail of the aircraft, so that if there was any gunfire, the Otter wouldn't be hit.

Brodie had the feeling that the two men were not there to provide secu-rity. He said to Worley, "What's happening, Brendan?"

"Well, what's happening, Scott, is you've got my first name wrong. It's not Brendan. It's Colonel."

"Yes, sir." He added, "You're still an asshole."

"And you're insubordinate." He looked at Taylor. "I had hoped you could pull the reins in on your partner. Save him from himself."

Taylor did not reply, but looked Worley in the eyes.

Worley told her, "Trent sends his regards."

"Trent can go to hell."

"I'll pass on your final words to him."

Brodie was keeping an eye on the two so-called security guys, a.k.a. hit men. They were about fifty feet away, within effective range of the Desert Eagle, but only if they remained stationary targets, which they would not. Also, they were armed with the six-hundred-round-a-minute Russian lawn mower. Should he be concerned? Probably.

Brodie said to Worley, "Is there any good reason we're standing here?"

Worley replied, "There's no reason either of you should be standing."

Well, they could keep standing there exchanging veiled threats and dou-ble entendres all afternoon, and Worley seemed to be enjoying himself. And maybe he had more he wanted to learn from Brodie and Taylor before he did what he was going to do.

Worley pulled his gun and aimed it at Brodie. "Sorry, Mr. Brodie, but this won't be a full flight."

Apparently there was nothing more that Brendan Worley wanted to hear from them.

Brodie's first thought was to cut the head off the snake, but it was too late for him to go for his gun, though he hoped Taylor did.

Then everything happened quickly, though it seemed like slow motion.

Mercer, still on the ground, kicked out his feet and knocked Worley off balance, allowing Brodie to pull his gun from the small of his back and fire three shots in quick succession at Worley, who seemed surprised to see the gun. Then Brodie dove to the ground behind Worley's still-moving body as a stream of red tracer rounds from one of the AKs sailed over his head.

Taylor was already on the ground returning fire as Brodie also pumped rounds downrange, using Worley's body for cover, then Worley's pistol when his ran out of ammunition.

The Otter pilot, who hadn't signed on for any of this, started moving his aircraft down the runway, and the two AK guys began running after it, leaving the gringos to work out their problems. One guy caught up to the Otter on the right side and disappeared into the plane. The second guy jumped into the open cabin door on the pilot's side as the Otter gained speed, and Brodie thought he'd seen the last of them, but then the guy braced himself in the open doorway and fired a long line of tracers. A few hit the dirt in front of them and the rest hit Kyle Mercer, whose body lurched with every hit, as Brodie was splashed with blood.

The Otter picked up speed and now—one passenger lighter—it lifted easily off the ground and sailed over the trees at the end of the runway.

Brodie got to one knee and looked at Taylor, still on the ground. "You okay?"

"Yeah . . ."

Brodie stood, went over and took her hand, and helped her up.

She started to say something, then noticed Mercer and hurried over to him. Taylor knelt beside Mercer and stared at his blood-soaked body.

Brodie stood to the side. Mercer had been hit about six times, but it was hard to tell with all that blood. He'd seen this before—no head or heart wounds, but lots of internal and external bleeding. He'd bleed out in about two minutes.

Brodie crouched beside him. "Can you hear me, Kyle?"

Mercer gave a small nod.

"Thank you for that. Brendan Worley is dead—or will soon be." He looked into Mercer's eyes. "You're going home, soldier. Your dad will see you again."

Mercer again nodded.

Brodie looked at Mercer's face, which was now white.

Taylor took his hand and said, "We leave no man behind. You'll be home soon, Captain."

Mercer's body rose in an arc, then fell, and it was over.

Brodie closed Mercer's eyelids and stood. He walked over to Worley, who was still alive, and said, "You're under arrest for . . . whatever."

Worley stared up at Brodie and shook his head as though he didn't agree that he was under arrest, or he was reprimanding Brodie for screwing up something that Worley had worked so hard to do.

Taylor looked at Worley. "You lost your way, Colonel. We all did."

Worley was taking long to die, so Brodie and Taylor walked away and stood in the hot sun on the abandoned airstrip. A noisy group of howler monkeys, who'd gone quiet during the shooting, started making odd noises, almost like howling laughter, thought Brodie. Best-laid plans, gone to shit right at the end. The great cosmic joke.

He said to Taylor, "Can we say mission accomplished?"

"Maybe. When we're airborne."

"Right. Okay, let's call Dombroski and get out of here."

Taylor nodded, something still on her mind. She looked over at Kyle Mercer's body. "People talk about leaving part of themselves behind in war but . . . when I got home from Landstuhl, that's not how I felt. I just felt like I'd been changed, and maybe not for the better, and maybe for no good reason."

Brodie thought about that. "War's a thing that happens to you, even if you volunteer. Because you don't really know what the hell you're signing up for. You didn't, I didn't. Kyle Mercer didn't."

"We are still responsible for what we do."

"We are."

Taylor looked back at Worley, who seemed to have stopped breathing. "Leave no man behind. Even him."

Brodie looked at the bloodstained bodies of Brendan Worley and Kyle Mercer lying in the grass next to the airstrip, and he thought back to the many somber ramp ceremonies he had been a part of at the military airfields around Baghdad, when the flag-draped coffins were escorted through a column of uniformed soldiers and loaded onto the C-130s to be taken to Dover. Brendan Worley and Kyle Mercer wouldn't get that kind of send-off when they headed home, but they'd get something. More importantly, they wouldn't get left here.

Taylor said, "This is another place that we can leave, but it will never leave us."

"We can handle the baggage."

"I'm thinking I belong back in Civil Affairs."

"I'm thinking I finally found a good partner."

"I will never again work with you or for you, Mr. Brodie." She added, "You're out of your goddamn mind."

"Sleep on it."

Taylor shook her head and smiled. "We'll see."

Brodie looked around. "Time to call home."

Taylor agreed. "Time to go home."

THE END

ACKNOWLEDGEMENTS

This book would not have been possible without the valuable insight and perspective of a number of Venezuelans, both expats and current residents, among them Nilhza Mas-y-Rubi, Angel Zambrano, Fabiana Zambrano, Ander Zurimendi, Paloma Azpúrua, and Catalina Goldstein.

We also wish to thank Alex's friend Taylor Krauss, who assisted with some of the Spanish translation.

Alex also wishes to thank his wife, Dagmar Weaver-Madsen, for her unwavering love and support, as well as her valuable feedback over the long process of writing this book, during which time we welcomed to the world our beautiful daughter Margot.

We also want to thank Bob Atiyeh, private pilot, who gave generously of his time and knowledge in the writing of the flying scenes in this book.

The authors are grateful for the opportunity to thank our editor, Marysue Rucci, for her keen editorial eye, and her tact and patience in dealing with this new father-son collaboration.

And finally, thanks and gratitude to Dianne Francis and Patricia Chichester, Nelson's super-assistants, who make miracles happen.

———

The following individuals have made generous contributions in charity auctions in return for having their names used as a character in this novel:

John F. Collins—NYU Winthrop Hospital/Mollie Biggane Melanoma Foundation and **Ted Haggerty**—Boys & Girls Club of Oyster Bay–East Norwich. I hope they enjoy their fictitious characters and that they continue their good work for worthy causes.